I0573909

Dark Awakening

CASCADE SAGA

By
M.A. Kastle

Dark Awakening/ M.A. Kastle. -- 1st ed.
Paperback: ISBN 978-1-7359534-0-3
Ebook: ISBN 978-1-7359534-1-0

My love always,

        Mr. K and the Minions

I'm losing.

A swift sweep followed by a hard kick landed on her thigh, unbalanced her, and forced her to retreat. Jordyn limped backward, risked a quick glance at the welt inching across her upper thigh, and watched it blend into the other scarlet and purple bruises. *That hurts.* Taking her fighting stance to test the damage, she gingerly put pressure on her right foot. A sting radiated around her leg where a dull ache weakened her knee and travelled down to her ankle. If he continued to target her thigh, she wasn't going to be able to stand much longer, let alone defend herself.

Lost the round.

The bruises would take time to heal and the pain would remain unless she shifted into her wolf form. That was a hard no. Jordyn wasn't shifting. She wasn't depending on her wolf. Cursing under her breath she reminded herself she wasn't without power. An ability not common to the average werewolf was the power to heal without shifting. She wasn't average and possessed the skill and had kept it a secret from everyone, including the master of combatants. If she healed and erased the bruises and eliminated the pain, it would take him seconds to tell the baron, and another second for the baron to summon her to his office. The questions would never end.

Leo, master of combatants, hesitated as if he was going to let her have her pained retreat and time to recover. Each of his kicks sent her reeling, and his punches left smeared bruises on her sides. At least he left her face alone. Jordyn's body drummed with pain; its effect on her mentally was taking its toll.

Because you're beaten and broken. Jordyn wanted to quit. If healing her wounds created questions, then quitting would bring on an hour long lecture.

Flat brown eyes gauged her like she was a deer staring at a set of headlights. Leo trained the pack's enforcers, soldiers, shadows, and slayers turning them into efficient fighting machines. Jordyn had been a soldier, had been trained to protect the pack, but it was a long time ago. Years ago, before she left the pack and then lost control of her life. She didn't think there was a shred of training left in her. Jordyn was embarrassing herself with her half-assed attempts to defend herself. Threads of his frustration with her lack of care and training reached out to her. One thing she was accomplishing was driving him crazy.

"Pay attention," Leo demanded as he sauntered in.

He landed another kick to her reddening thigh, punched her side, and skipped backward. He was mocking her. The hit sent a vibration burning into her muscle, making her entire leg tingle with numbness. Jordyn's knee grazed the vinyl when she caught her balance, stopping herself from dropping like a bag of sand. She shifted to her left foot, backed up, and tried to ignore the pain. Leo was toying with her, and when he smiled and hopped side to side, he pushed the knife further into the wound. This was pissing her off. Limping to the right, she put more distance between them, inhaled and exhaled. She had to ease the swelling and pain if she was going to continue.

"Defend yourself," Leo ordered.

Pay attention. Defend yourself. I couldn't defend myself when the witches kidnapped me, can't do it now. "I am," Jordyn mumbled.

"This training is meant to build your confidence and enhance your skills. You will take an active part." Leo stood in a relaxed stance, hands on his hips, and met Jordyn's haunted gaze.

She knew he wanted to explain to her it was simple training, an exercise to work her body and mind. He would tell her there was no losing. No winning. However, she was damaged goods and the teacher in him stopped him from yelling at her. Instead, he glared at her. She wanted to defend herself by telling him after everything she believed she lost, winning and losing was how she saw the world.

Rutger, losing.

Her family, lost.

The pack, losing.

Her future, losing.

She didn't have a win.

Like she didn't have a reply and didn't care when all Jordyn wanted to do was go home. "That's what the baron said."

"Then defend." Using his werewolf speed, he rushed in, landed a round of punches to her side and stomach, then jogged backwards.

Jordyn twisted, doubled over, and held her stomach while fighting to catch her breath. Leo's signature moves for this training session. Shoot in, cause injuries, and leave. He was going to beat her until she gave up. Placing her hands on her knees, she straightened, and accepted she was out of options. In the seconds he gave her, she whispered a string of focused words, comfort words and healed her injuries. Jordyn didn't have to verbally call her power, but with her mind divided, the words helped her concentrate.

Jordyn saw surprise streak across Leo's stern face as he searched for her wounds. *Yep, master of combatants, there it is.* Werewolves and therianthropes, basically all shapeshifters, could take a lot of damage, the body heals, meaning no one has had to worry about getting hurt. Their lives had assimilated to human's ways long before Jordyn was born and remained in a state of uninterrupted peace. Did humans think of them as non-humans? Yes. Did humans think they were dangerous? Yes. It didn't change the fact shapeshifters and humans ate at the same restaurants, shopped at the same stores, and drove the same cars.

This integrated living made her manifesting abilities, like healing without shifting, an oddity in the pack and the magic-born world. After being linked with the pack as their soothsayer, Jordyn's powers continued to mutate, increase, and mutate again. What the extent of them were and how to call them and manipulate them, she had no idea. *What else is new?* It didn't matter when she was living in a permanent state of detachment from life and feeling sorry for herself.

"Nice move. Good to know you can heal without shifting." Leo eyed her as he hopped back and forth on the balls of his feet.

Shit. "How am I supposed to gain self-confidence when you're beating me up?" Jordyn asked.

Without answering her and wearing a smile, Leo swept in and landed another kick followed by a series of punches.

The two thousand square foot Enforcer's office on Foxwood property, had been demolished, rebuilt to ten thousand, and included an updated communications room, a reception area capable of going into lockdown, and a second floor complete with dorm-style rooms, bathrooms, a full-size gourmet kitchen, and med room. One hundred feet below ground was a one thousand square foot room with cells, cages, and interrogation rooms. With the remodel the office was self-sufficient and could be manned twenty-four hours a day. The exigency to protect the baron and the pack came after a coven of witches, intending on killing Jo and using her power to raise a dead god, killed one of their own and mutilated others. The witches had cloaked their presence with a charm, making it impossible for the enforcers to use their werewolf senses to find them. It had left the pack vulnerable and defenseless.

That would never happen again.

Immediately after the incident at Butte Springs, Foxwood, the Baron's estate, the Summit, the pack's ceremonial grounds, and Rutger's house had been outfitted with ballistic glass, reinforced steel doors, cameras, palm vein scanners, motion sensors, and license plate readers. Each place had a military-grade security system linked directly to the communications center where an enforcer monitored the information. In the event an intruder activated the system cameras began recording to create a video and transcript, at the same time it was live streamed to communications and could be accessed by an enforcer from the laptops in their vehicles.

Rutger tapped the end of his pen on the desk as he stared at the computer screen and watched it shift between the gate to Foxwood, the parking lot, and the baron's front yard. He hoped it did his work for him ... it didn't. Rutger held the report, read it, put it down, and began reading it from the beginning and somewhere in the middle his mind drifted and he started over. He had been trying to read it for ten minutes and still had no idea what it was about. His attention splitting into a million different directions wasn't new. *I'm losing it.* Over four months he had been hiding out in his office reading reports, rereading reports, and working patrols to keep his mind from focusing on Jo. *The ghost I live with.*

If worrying about Jo wasn't pushing his stress level into high gear, the constant need to remember his months of probation to prove he wasn't going to lose himself to his beast and go Bestial taunted him. He felt the walls of Celestial, a magic-born specific hospital, closing in on him and the chill of the concrete floor on his skin when he collapsed after they gassed him. Rutger shook himself, forcing his thoughts back to the present. The report stared at him.

Growling with frustration, Rutger stood. He needed to walk and get out of his office. With his hand on the butt of his Glock 21, 45 caliber pistol, Rutger left his office and walked down the hallway, his boots heavy on the tile floor, and headed toward the gym. His home away from home. He paused when he heard Jo's voice, and then Leo's low rumble. They were in the gym where she had been training every day for two weeks, coming home battered and bruised, exhausted and silent. Continuing, he made a left, opened the door, and without turning a light on-he felt less intrusive sitting in the dark-he sat in one of four chairs.

A thick, black mat took half of the one thousand square feet, while weight machines, free weights, and cardio equipment like treadmills, spin bikes, and rowing machines took the opposite side. From the observation room, Rutger could see Jo and Leo, and if he wanted to hear them, he would turn on the speaker. One of three rooms, it was designed to allow enforcers, slayers, shadows, and soldiers to watch cadets, and the others training. Jo couldn't see him through the two-way mirror, and since she had blocked him from sensing her, as she did most times, he didn't fear her finding out he was watching. Rutger stood, leaned closer to the window, and flicked a switch. Jo's harsh breathing sounded through the speaker filling the room.

"I'm not *beating* you up. You're a soldier for the pack ... or have you forgotten? You have yet to fight, and I can't *help* you if you're not going to utilize the basics of self-defense," Leo explained. "You showed me you can heal without shifting, now use your werewolf strengths."

Leo pinned Jo with his brown glare. His flaxen hair holding highlights of strawberry sat at his neck, while stray strands clung to his sweat-damp cheeks. He had taken his familiar stance of frustration with his hands on his hips, his fingers grazing the waist of his shorts. His gray T-shirt, with the Cascade pack's crest on the back and Combatants Instructor on the front, was dark under the arms and down his spine from sweat. He wasn't breathing heavy like he should have been since he had been working with Jo for over an hour.

Jo used her power to heal herself, and in order to use her power she had to call her wolf. That hadn't happened in months. As if sensing him, she looked in the direction of the two-way mirror and the instinct to step back rocked him. Jo's eyes, swirling with her wolf and power let Rutger know she was thinking. Over thinking. The way she had been for months. It was hard to get through to her when she would rather sit in her head than talk to him. Fury burned his veins with her indifference as if she wasn't alive and didn't care about her life.

"It's not worth it," Jordyn mumbled. "This is not confidence building, it's an epic waste of time." Every day she got her ass handed to her. It was getting old. She could be at home worrying about her future with the Highguard, her failing relationship with Rutger, when he was going to mark her then scar her with silver, why he was never home, and why she didn't care. Jordyn cut her power and the feel of her wolf, and wanted to remind Leo a witch coven had taken her life. Figuratively and literally.

"Giving up? I never expected weakness from you, Soothsayer. You did defy death." Leo cocked his head to the left like he was unsure of what her response was going to be.

No one was supposed to know. The baron didn't want anyone to know the truth, especially her parents, and made up a story to tell the pack. *How did he find out?* Jordyn would ask him except she didn't think her voice would hold. Embarrassment crawled from her stomach and into her throat, and any energy she had to fight back died.

Unfair. Rutger watched the memory cross Jo's face, and for a second saw raw pain in her cocoa eyes. Not only wasn't anyone supposed to know the truth, but no one had spoken to Jo about the kidnapping, Butte Springs, being held prisoner, and then drugged. Rutger saw the witch cut her throat and felt her as she died, then watched the baron bring her back to life. No one knew she died, just she had been injured and *could* have died. *Defied death.* The baron, using the moon's power, pushed his magic into her lifeless body and into her wolf's spirit, pulled her wolf from her, and forced Jo to obey the moon and shapeshift. Feeling her heart stop when she died in his arms, Rutger lost control over his beast and had to be sedated.

They were both transported to Celestial for medical and psychological treatment. The pack, the klatch, and surrounding factions avoided the topic and continued as if it never happened. If someone dared to think about saying something, they apologized and walked away. No one challenged Jo. Except Leo. Rutger wanted to protect her, but knew Jo needed to embrace her pain, her nightmares, and use them to destroy her enemies. Because there would be others. The Highguard was demanding her presence at court, where the royals would confront her, test her, and question her connection to the Collective. She needed to be prepared. They might not fight her in hand-to-hand combat, but they would fight her emotionally. Being physically resilient would help her remain mentally strong and keep her from crumbling and falling into her pain. Then there was Shadow Lord and his threats hanging over Rutger's head.

"Fighting stance," Leo ordered.

A little harsh, Rutger thought. An instant of anger flared followed by the instinct to protect his mate. He heard her heartbeat and then it was gone. *Not real.* She was in front of him. His wolf swam through him with the memory. *Yeah, a little too harsh. Calm yourself, it's training.*

A whispered swish sounded from Jordyn's bare feet as she took her stance. The soft material of her black shorts feathered her thighs and showed signs of sweat like her blue tank top. She tucked loose strands of raven hair behind her ear, and standing in front of Leo, wanted to throat punch him. The comment about her death brought instant pain and shame.

When Flint and his flunkies came to kidnap her, Jordyn hadn't defended herself. *Didn't want the humans to know I had been lying to them for years. Howdy neighbor, you live next to a werewolf. Sorry, lycanthrope.* Jordyn knew she let Flint take her, and in doing so felt she put the pack in danger. An image of Rutger's wolf shadowing him sat in front of her. Jordyn didn't think she was weak. Not really. She was dealing with a lot of bullshit the only way she knew how. It made training an epic waste of time. Epic.

Leo started toward her, his dark brown eyes gleaming like chocolate diamonds glowing from within, and zeroed in on their target. His fluid motion and silent steps didn't give his away his advance. Jordyn tracked him, wishing she was somewhere else, and with her thoughts betraying her, the division slowed her reaction time.

Defend yourself.

At the last minute she turned, but not fast enough. His elbow connected with the side of her head, and she dropped to the mat. On her back, she prayed she remained conscious, gasped for air, and waited for the gym to stop spinning.

Rutger's palms flattened on the mirror and he growled a low animal sound. "Get up, Jo."

Leo stood over her, his brows drawn, anger rolling from him. "You are not concentrating, Soothsayer. Focus."

Stop calling me that. Jordyn covered her face in the bend of her elbow and swallowed the raising nausea. She wanted to give up and cry but feared if she started, she wouldn't stop. And she would be damned if she let Leo see her fall apart. Jordyn needed to get her shit together.

Rutger's wolf pushed on his instincts to protect her. *Damn, Jo, get up.* She lay on the mat, one arm over her stomach, one over her face, and blood seeping from a wound on her head. *You aren't dead, get up.* Focused on Jo, and trying to bury the urge to stop the training, Rutger ignored the whisper of the door opening and the feel of someone entering the room.

"Son," Healey greeted as he sat down, "join me."

Rutger tore his eyes from Jo to face him. "Baron," he greeted through clenched teeth.

"Sit. Down." Healey saw the edges of Rutger's wolf shadow him as his eyes bleed to a dull gold as if warning Healey. Rutger was living on the edge of losing himself to his beast, being locked in a cage and losing the life he created and losing his mate. So much loss.

Jordyn rolled to her side, got to her knees, and awkwardly made it to her feet. She gingerly checked the side of her head with her fingers, saw blood, too much blood, wiped it on her shorts, and healed the wound. Lightheaded, she returned to her fighting stance, determined to pretend to care.

Rutger watched Jo, and grudgingly obeyed. "To what do I owe this visit?"

"Jordyn. Leo reports, her training isn't going well. Did she heal her wound?" Healey asked. Jordyn's powers were increasing, her strength improving, but she was emotionally and mentally damaged.

"Yes. The training is going terrible. It's like she isn't there," Rutger answered. *Because she's a ghost.*

"Where is she? Where are her thoughts?" Healey watched Jordyn and saw her indecision and hesitation.

"I don't know. It could be anything," Rutger replied absently. Witches. The Highguard. Pick one.

"Anything? Like the two of you?" Healey knew the answer was yes. They weren't good. He feared their relationship was becoming a victim of both their pain. A repeat of three years earlier when Jordyn ran from Trinity and the pack to live by herself. At the time, Healey believed Rutger and Jordyn needed time to grow up and mature without the influence of the other. He wished it could be that simple now. Prime, the Highguard, and Shadow Lord cast fear over both of them.

"I'm not talking about our relationship." Rutger stared forward. Or lack thereof. Jo was back in her stance, a lazy version, while her entire being was not focused on Leo.

"That's fine. You can't deny fate bound the two of you together. You both have overcome the past and started a future. Don't let the witches, who are dead and buried, take what you have worked for. Build a relationship, it'll help the both of you to heal." Healey looked at the side of Rutger's face and the way the last couple of months of stress and worry had taken their toll. He hadn't shaved, his cheeks sank in to match his darken eye sockets, and his skin had lost its bronze of summer. Opposite of his beaten down look, his shoulders and arms were thick with muscle, and with each controlled inhale his wide chest stretched his black T-shirt. Anxiety might have robbed him of color and sleep, but Rutger spent hours in the gym. Staying away from home and Jordyn. "You have to resume a normal life. Take her on a date. Lock yourselves in your house and talk."

The damn witches. "A date? With the Highguard sitting over us like an ax about to fall?" *Normal, what the hell was that?*

"The Highguard isn't going to ride in, take her, and ride out. Jordyn is the soothsayer for the Cascade pack and the Highguard and Prime must abide by the canons. Right now, you need to concentrate on your relationship. Don't wait until it's too late." Healey stood, watched the pathetic sparing between Jordyn and Leo, and knew what he needed to do next. Jordyn needed help.

As silence stretched out between them, Leo rushed in, launched an assault of several punches, and ended with a quick leg sweep, sending Jo to the mat. Landing hard on her side, she groaned, got to her knees, and not letting her stand, Leo pushed her over with his foot.

"What the fuck?" Rutger stood, the chair skating backwards on the tile.

"Language, son." Healey expected the insult of having Leo shove her with his foot to enrage Jordyn. As soothsayer for the pack, she had status and authority, and outranked Leo. But there was nothing. No emotion. No response. He watched Jordyn gather herself and stand.

"If she isn't defending herself and fighting back, why does he continue? Why doesn't he send her home?" Rutger's voice deepened and a growl laced his words. He needed to protect her. He failed her when the witches targeted her and failed a second time when he couldn't control his wolf. The time he spent fighting himself in his cell ate his nerves.

"Easy, son. Leo is going to push her. She fears pain and lives to save herself from experiencing it. I reminded him she won't break, and if she does, she'll heal," Healey explained. He kept his own concerns over Jordyn to himself. She hadn't been the same since Belle Ridge. He hated himself. Butte Springs.

"Why the hell would you turn Leo loose on her?" Rutger faced the baron, his eyes bleeding gold.

"Language. She needs to face her pain and understand she'll live through it. Jordyn is trying to keep herself from what she experienced. She is alive. And I'm the baron, I can.

Rutger, you're not going out on patrols anymore. You're the Director of Enforcers, it's not your responsibility. Do you understand?"

No, he didn't understand. "I need two more bodies. There aren't enough people to patrol all the properties." An excuse at the ready. There were cameras canvasing the Cascade properties, he could check them all from his office or the communications room. But then he wouldn't have an excuse to drive into the mountains, shapeshift, and run. It calmed his wolf and kept his thoughts from torturing him with Jo's silence and her pending absence.

"Get two more. You're done, it's an order." Healey grabbed the door handle as Leo shot in and Jordyn sprawled out of his hold. "You can't ignore the problems you and Jordyn have, they won't disappear. You need to talk to her. Ask her out on a date. Once communication has been restored, everything else will be easier to handle. Be there for each other."

I've tried. "Yes, sir," Rutger replied absently. He could picture it ... *Hey, babe, because you hold the Collective of the pack and can read minds, the Highguard wants you for themselves, but wait, I'm going to mark you like some animal, do you want to go out on a date? Taco Tuesday?* Their lives were chaos.

Healey watched Jordyn, turned his attention to Rutger, and felt his authority as baron and alpha was worthless and made him powerless to help them. He opened the door and left the observation room, with Rutger standing at the window.

Jordyn took several steps back, her confidence teasing her, and watched Leo. He shot in, again; this time she wasn't quick enough, and he took her to the ground. She tried scrambling out of his hold, he took mount, his thighs squeezing her sides, at the same time he pinned her arms above her head. *Defenseless.*

A burst of anger flared, burned in her veins, and in a breath Jordyn's wolf swept through her, its strength empowering her. Instinctively, she jerked her arms from his hold, grabbed the front of Leo's T-shirt at the same time she bumped her hips up and in a swift motion, she tossed him over her. Jordyn let go, scrambled to her feet, as Leo rolled on the mat. He got his balance, faced her, and his eyes gleamed dark mocha with his wolf.

"I'm done," Jordyn hissed. Her body shook; her wolf wanted its freedom and pushed her to shift. How many weeks? Lost count. How many moons had she denied her wolf? Too damn many. "I am done." She turned, giving her instructor her back as if he wasn't a threat, and marched toward her duffle bag.

"No, you are not," Leo thundered. "You've made progress."

Stopping at the edge of the mat, Jordyn twisted to face Leo. "I'm. Done." Without waiting, she left the mat, and with shaking hands, grabbed her bag, and headed for the door. She was going home.

Rutger watched Jo's wolf embrace her in its power, like a silver veil tracing then molding to her silhouette and flowing over the contours of her body. Under the lights of the gym the mark on her bruised thigh glittered. With his heart thundering in his chest, he placed his palms on the two-way mirror. Using the strength of her wolf, Jo escaped Leo's hold, and in a blur stood. Jo called her wolf. Leo's order jerked Rutger back and after disregarding the combatant's trainer, she headed to her things. Rutger wasn't going to risk being caught, and not stalling, left the observation room and went straight to his office. If Jo found him checking on her, it would make matters worse. If that was possible.

Jordyn flung her duffle bag over her shoulder as she walked down the hall, the adrenalin and her wolf coursing through her veins begging her to give into them and making her jumpy. Like she needed an added glitch in her psyche. As she walked, Jordyn healed her superficial wounds, but knew there was going to be deeper bruising and her body was going to hurt for days. *Another conse-quence.* Focused on getting the hell out of the office building, she considered not stopping at Rutger's door. Jordyn paused and stared at the name plate Director of En-forcers, Rutger Kanin, damn she should say something to him. *Just got my ass kicked, almost lost control, see ya.* The distance between them hurt her heart and made her bones ache. But she didn't know how to climb out of the pit of despair she called home.

"Soothsayer."

Jordyn jumped, twisted, and laughed a low, sad sound. "Yes."

"My apologies. The baron would like to see you," Sousa reported. His eyes dark with worry glanced at the door and back to her while his rigid body stilled. He stood in the hall-way, the pale walls behind him and wearing jeans, boots, and a crisp white button-up shirt with Cascade's crest in sil-ver, black, and red thread on the left side. "I'll escort you."

"Perfect." Faking a smile, Jordyn trailed after the baron's personal sentinel.

They left the hall, went through the reception area, and out of the building. She didn't think Rutger would be angry, nor would he say anything to her when he found out why she hadn't stopped. Or he would add it to the list of her shortcomings and not come home for a week. Jordyn sighed. She was losing.

Outside fall gripped the mountains with an iron fist turning the leaves to burnt crimson, honeyed golds, and amber reminding her of bourbon and fire. And that reminded her of Rutger. *Stop.* The bright sun and cloudless cerulean sky feigned warmer temperatures and made you believe it wasn't October. Warmth from the sun couldn't stop the bite Jordyn felt from the wind's bitter chill as it swept over her heated skin, leaving a sting in its wake. Sousa turned enough to make sure she was following, then continued across the parking lot to the house.

"Soothsayer," Abigail, one of the baronesses' personal sentinels, greeted. She wore the same uniform and shoulder holster as Sousa, and opened the door for them.

In silence, Jordyn continued trailing behind Sousa through the entryway, past the dining room, formal greeting room, staircase, and to the baron's office.

"He's waiting for you," he said as he opened the door.

"Thanks," she mumbled. Jordyn entered the room and faced the desk. "Baron, you wanted to see me."

"Yes, Jordyn, please have a seat." Healey stood, waved to indicate the chair, and waited for her.

The baron stood behind his large, walnut desk, it's top holding a stack of papers, a computer, a phone, and folders. On the left side, despite the computer, was a leather-bound book he recorded the dates and names of people who had requested to see him. He left his pale steel blue button-up shirt open at the collar, revealing the edges of his tattoo. His black vest was also unbuttoned, and ended at the waist of his dark denim jeans. He combed his auburn hair back, then ran his fingers through it as if he wanted a casual look, but nothing-his hair, nor his unbuttoned shirt-could disguise the intensity of his burnt mahogany gaze riddled with gold flecks. Rutger's eyes held onto the gold like it wanted to beat back the onyx. It resembled twisted slivers. Jordyn had to shake herself to get rid of the image and sat down in a leather chair in front of the desk, then placed her duffle bag beside the leg. She felt like a kid sent to the principal's office.

Don't let this be about Leo.

"Leo tells me, you walked out of training," Healey started.

Damn. "I don't think it's having the desired outcome. I'm not committed to it." *Can I cancel my gym membership?*

"I know you're distracted. I was hoping training would give you the opportunity to focus your thoughts and re-lease some stress. Maybe help you regain your self-confidence." Healey sat forward, his shirt hugging his shoulders, and placing his elbows on his desk, his gaze narrowed on her.

Jordyn wanted to laugh, and cry, and wanted to go home. "I don't need anyone helping me with stress or my self-confidence. I know Leo has a job to do and I don't want to waste his time."

"He works for the pack. You're pack. You're not wasting his time." Jordyn sat across from him, her hands in her lap, her hair in a messy ponytail while rogue strands feathered her ears. Blood matted the side of her head and peppered her blue cotton tank top, and bruises marred her arms. To distract himself from their problems, Rutger had the enforcers, the gym, and Foxwood. Jordyn had nothing, no one. She lost weight, looked gaunt, refused to participate in pack runs, and was reluctant to leave her house. She became a shell of the person he knew. "Have you gone out and taken any pictures? I was driving back from the Summit, and saw the leaves have turned to fall colors. It's very beautiful," Healey said trying a different approach.

"No." She sat straighter. She hadn't touched her camera in months. She didn't know where it was.

"As alpha, it's my responsibility to make sure my pack is taken care of. You, as I have pointed out, are pack and have status. Your absence at the runs doesn't go unnoticed. You are their soothsayer, and your parents have called me asking why you aren't speaking to them. What's going on, Jordyn?" Healey asked.

Parents, lost.

Camera, lost.

Still no win.

What wasn't going on? Jordyn worked to deny her wolf by refusing to run, but couldn't stop her powers from increasing ... and they were increasing. As the soothsayer for the pack she heard the Collective, the pack's memories as if they were in the room with her, and felt their emotions when she saw their pasts. The chaos and noise were making her crazy. Jordyn had to strengthen her barriers to keep them out and it worked. Sometimes. Then there was healing herself without shapeshifting, not a big deal, and the ease of slipping into someone's mind and reading their thoughts. Controlling their thoughts. That was a big deal. She killed Flint, the leader of the witches, by telling him to shoot himself. Even with a detective as a witness, it put the pack in danger of being investigated. Jordyn grappled for an answer. She considered lying. Maybe telling the truth about her and Rutger's relationship.

Rutger, losing.

No. It would get back to Rutger and who knows how he would respond. *More silence.* She could leave and not answer at all. Jordyn wouldn't get two steps out of the office before Sousa either bullied her back into the office or physically moved her there. No one was going to let her leave the house until the baron dismissed her.

"The pressure from the Collective is getting stronger. It feels like my head is going to explode." Half-truth. Better than outright lying.

Healey watched her struggle with her thoughts and accepted she wasn't going to answer. When Jordyn lied, he wasn't surprised. "Are you seeing memories? Hearing voices?"

"Both. Mostly in my dreams when I can't control my mental blocks." Another half-truth.

Jordyn did see them in her dreams. There was a part she wasn't ready to admit to herself, let alone the baron ... her dreams turned into nightmares and included Flint. She was always in the cell with him, his coven, and the remains of the dead. One of her pack. Zachery's essence created pain and loss, and like an open wound, it bled and never healed. When she fought to wake up, Jordyn felt her heart stop in her chest and her lungs seize. Death sat inside of her like a physical thing trying to take over. Day after day, Jordyn tried convincing herself she dealt with what her therapist referred to as a traumatic experience, but lying to herself made the nightmare worse. She knew it made her sound weak and mentally unstable, and she hated it. What would the baron think? She knew the answer-he would feel sorry for Rutger.

"The Collective is getting to difficult for you to control. You're saying you need to learn how to encase its force until you learn how to manipulate it. I think I have someone who can help," Healey offered.

Her insides caved. She should have told the truth. If she refused the baron's help, he would know she lied to him. "Who?" Jordyn asked. She couldn't imagine who was going to help her.

"Lady Sloan. I received a call from her, and she gladly offered to teach you. Lord Erven and the Diablo pack have graciously opened their doors to you and Rutger." Healey sat back, anticipating Jordyn's reaction. It would serve as an honor and give Jordyn status to have Lady Sloan, the soothsayer for the Diablo pack, teach her how to control the Collective. The Diablo clansmen would serve as an example of how a soothsayer protected the Collective and employed its power when needed.

Jordyn felt like her mouth opened and her jaw dropped. "Teach me. You're kidding me?" Now she wanted to leave. She hadn't told anyone about Lady Sloan and wasn't sure how she was going to explain it to the baron. Or if she was ready.

"Are you surprised?" Healey asked. "The Diablo pack is one of the oldest in the world, and one of the most powerful. Lady Sloan holds their Collective and serves as one of the Twelve holding the Collective for the Highguard. Prime regards her with respect. She has a wealth of knowledge and has information to share with you."

An understatement. If it was appropriate to roll her eyes and huff at the baron she would have, but it wasn't so

Jordyn stood, walked behind the chair, and started pacing. If she stopped the voices in her head, and the emotions didn't intertwine themselves with her own, she might be able to conquer everything else. Her relationship. Her nightmares. The dead man and his torture haunting her. She was going to have to start somewhere. Maybe this was her chance to start healing.

Was facing Lady Sloan worth it? Was it going to give her a light at the end of the tunnel? Jordyn faced the baron; the worry in his mahogany eyes and the tension in his shoulders was enough to make her consider it. His intense stare wasn't demanding she tell him, it was pleading with her. He was tired of seeing a mess. She saw her failure when training and again with Rutger. He was scared for her. Jordyn felt ashamed and embarrassed. She needed to tell him the truth.

She cleared her throat, inhaled and exhaled, and said, "The Highguard's letter called me a scion, do you remember that?" Placing her hands on the back of the chair, the cool leather sank into her palms. *Calm down and don't rush.*

"Yes, you're Lord Langston's Pureblood daughter. Your grandmother was a Pureblood and soothsayer who had passed her magic onto you when you were born," Healey replied.

Mia, Jordyn's mother pushed Jordyn to leave Trinity in an attempt to extinguish her magic. It might have been successful if Rutger hadn't stopped Jordyn from leaving. When Mia's emotional manipulations ceased to effect Jordyn, she accused Jordyn of being dark like Ethan's mother. '*Soothsayers are inherently dark.*' Mia also blamed Healey for taking the Cascade pack into the dark ages. The woman didn't understand there was something happening in the world of the magic-born. Or knew and didn't want to admit it, like others in the pack.

"While it's true my grandmother was a soothsayer, and my father is powerful in his own right, this isn't about them. I am my mother's scion." Doubt held the baron's face.

"You're mother?" Healey scoffed at the idea. "Mia believes all of this is dark magic and ancient lies," he countered. "There is no one in her family with the talent, let alone the kind of magic needed to pass on to a child."

"Mia is not my mother." There it was. Out in the open.

"Jordyn, explain."

"You know I can read thoughts." She wasn't going to explain Lady Sloan ... yet.

"I know you manipulated Flint, you said you used his magic to do it. And I know you contacted Rutger and there's a level of telepathy with those in the pack. You're their soothsayer, and you're link with them will continue to strengthen over the years. It doesn't mean you can enter someone's mind and read their thoughts," Healey pointed out.

"Flint wasn't pack and I read his thoughts, altered them, controlled him, and made him believe what I said was true. I was his voice and he needed to obey. I don't have to have an outside power. I didn't need his magic. It's been me the entire time," Jordyn explained. She had months to learn the truth.

"All right, what am I thinking?" Healey challenged and sat back. If it was true and she could read minds it meant she used telepathy-a way to communicate from one person to another without human sensory or physical interaction. Skeptics called it pseudoscience; a belief mistakenly based on scientific methods. Like Jordyn's magic, it's from the past when magic-born weren't criminalized for acting on their instincts. It didn't change the part of him doubting her. He waited as Jordyn's eyes gleamed copper, making him expect to feel her wolf, her power, and the familiar hum when she touched his mind.

Without raising her power, Jordyn slid into the baron's mind. No barriers. She didn't have to try hard to hear him; while there was his stream of consciousness, he concentrated his thoughts on purpose. "You have to know if it's true." With her answer his eyes widened. *For my next trick.* "You fear Rutger and I are allowing our pain to destroy our relationship. You told him to ask me out on a date. I could have gone without knowing you told Leo, if I break, I'll heal."

Healey didn't sense her wolf's magic and didn't feel her use her power. "You don't need your wolf?"

"Yes and no. We are one, not two separate entities." Jordyn walked around the chair and sat down. Her wolf howled in her ears as if it was calling her a coward for having denied its need to run.

"What is Rutger thinking?" Healey asked.

"I don't feel comfortable hearing his thoughts without asking him," Jordyn tried. She did not want to be in Rutger's head. *Please don't make me.*

"Noted. What is Rutger thinking?" Healey demanded.

"I could tell you anything. He isn't here to correct me." Putting all her pleading in her eyes, she held his gaze.

"You won't lie, Jordyn."

True. Sad as it was. Jordyn was going to hate herself. She inhaled and thought about opening the bond between them to feel him. She had blocked him for months, reasoning she was protecting him from her weakness. If she opened the bond, he would feel her and her emotions like a tidal wave. That was a hard pass. She was going to ghost through Rutger's thoughts as quickly as possible.

Jordyn sent her senses in search of Rutger, easing through the threads of people around her. When she found his essence, she followed the curving twine, his feel a soft touch to her magic. Damn, she never listened to his thoughts, never planned to, and never wanted to, because she didn't want to know. There was too much hurt between them. Rutger hadn't expressed an emotion, good or bad, in months, and hadn't talked to her even in passing. His silence and refusal to engage in conversation was like he gave her approval to sink inside of herself. He didn't need her. Was she blaming him for her giving up on them? Yes. Jordyn created a numb world empty of people and feelings and trusted only herself. She feared listening to his thoughts when the possibility of learning he saw her as weak, broken, and he hated her for the pain she caused.

Found him. Jordyn eased toward Rutger at the same time she readied to hear what kept him on the defense and his anger as an intimate lover. She scarcely touched his thoughts when the words *protect, mine,* and *losing* slammed through their bond and into her. *Losing Jo.* No. No. Stop. Jordyn couldn't get out of the link and couldn't stop his emotions from swallowing her. She lowered her head, held her face in her hands, and struggled to shut him out.

"Jordyn, what is it?" Healey stood, started around the desk, and stopped when he stood in front of her. His hands were inches from her shoulders when he stopped himself from touching her. "Jordyn."

"As fated mates, we have a link to one another. Our wolves have a bond. It's more powerful than the link I have with you or the pack," Jordyn explained through a ragged breath. Suddenly there wasn't enough air and she couldn't think past his thoughts. "I tried to sense him. The link between us opened and I can't stop it."

"What is he thinking?" Healey pushed.

The air burned her lungs and bright white spots flickered in her eyes. "He was watching me from the observation room, wanted to protect me. Hates seeing me hurt. He thinks he's losing me. The silence between us is damaging him." *His fear makes keeping the beast restrained, harder. It's my fault.* Jordyn squeezed her head between her hands as his stream of thoughts plundered through her. "It's like he's inside my head."

"I'm sorry." Healey raised his power, his wolf circling them, and giving strength from the alpha to his kith. "Is this better?"

The baron's power helped her block Rutger for a second and gave her time to build her walls. She buried her power, felt it drain from her and the link, and she struggled to shut out the outside world. "Sure," she mumbled. The thunder from Rutger's emotions echoed off her skull; his pain screamed at her, and his loneliness stabbed her. Jordyn didn't risk opening her eyes for fear of seeing the room spin. She counted to fifty, seventy, one hundred, and the ache receded. Hesitantly straightening, she met the baron's gaze. Was that pity? Rutger's presence and closeness teased her. She wanted to feel him. And didn't want to feel him.

"You've proved your point," Healey admitted.

Goody for her. "Anything else?"

"Who is your mother?"

Why couldn't this wait?

"Jordyn, tell me," Healey demanded.

"Lady Sloan," Jordyn confessed through a breath.

Healey sensed no lies. She was telling him the truth. It would explain why the Highguard had taken an interest in the Cascade pack. Over a two month period, three alphas, around the Cascade territory, had been challenged, beaten, and a new alpha inaugurated. Rumor spread the Highguard was hand picking people and putting them in place. He didn't want to believe it, but now he had no choice. The Highguard surrounded the Cascade pack with their own.

"You need her. She is the only person who can help you to learn about your powers and teach you to control the Collective." Healey leaned against the desk his arms crossed over his chest, and noticed Jordyn hadn't tried to wash the blood out of her hair. As if she didn't care or notice it was there.

"Baron, this means the Highguard knows about me, has known. My entire life. They know what I've done, what I can do, and what I might be capable of doing. Both of my parents are powerful. How long before the Highguard orders I go to court and serve my time, like Lady Sloan? I don't want to go to Mountain Fortress. What will I be? Entertainment? Or another acquired power?" *What if I fail.*

I don't want to leave Rutger. The thought shocked her.

The Highguard's court, Mountain Fortress, situated somewhere in the Canadian mountains, was a massive estate in a harsh environment, fitting for the Highguard. Because of its remote location and weather humans rarely explored the estate, and when they did, they were shown an eccentric group of magic-born living in luxury and without society. There, the Highguard wrote laws, consulted faction leaders, worked to resolve disagreements between factions, and acted like they were royalty. The lords, ladies, masters, mistresses, dukes and duchesses, and earl and countesses, made up the Highguard's powerful court. At faction level were the barons and baronesses, alphas, their heirs, soothsayers, and elders of the pack who had adopted lord and lady titles.

The exhaustion and desperation in her voice struck him. "You've known this and have kept it to yourself?" Healey asked. "You've shouldered this alone?"

"Not alone. Rutger knows." *'Don't fucking lie to me, Jo,' he growled.* She hadn't. She told him the truth fearing if she lied, she was betraying him and pushing his already fragile control, she would lose him to his beast.

After Rutger found her at Belle Ridge, she corrected herself, Butte Springs and held her against his body, he begged her to stay with him. She couldn't risk the safety of the pack and chose to use the rest of her strength to break the charm that kept the enforcers from sensing the witches. Her heart stopped, her breath left her lungs, her world turned to darkness, and he lost control. His wolf turned beast and became the master. Over the months, she watched him struggle to restrain the primal beast and gain balance between the man and the wolf. It was her fault. She did it to him.

"Have you told your father?" Healey left the desk and sat in the seat beside her.

"No. I'm not saying anything to him or Mia, until I have no other choice. Our relationship isn't good ... there's stress because I'm a soothsayer, and I know Mia isn't my mother. It's the reason I haven't spoken to them," Jordyn answered with a shaky laugh. She wasn't sure she could look at either her dad or Mia and not start yelling at them. The way they had treated her as if she were some kind of monster infuriated her. With the secret out, she felt exposed. "I would like to keep this between us."

"What about Lady Sloan? She can help you," he countered. He wasn't going to promise to keep it a secret; the girl needed her parents, at the very least her father. There was no reason for her to handle it by herself.

"I know. Baron this needs to stay between us," Jordyn insisted. Damn she should have never told him.

"I'm willing to make a deal." He smiled, attempting to lighten the situation and ease some of her anxiety. The edges of her fear threaded in the air around Jordyn and he speculated the abuse and torture were the foundation of that fear.

"A deal? Fine," she replied with irritation in her voice. *This is going to cost me.*

"You promise to take the training seriously. You know, Leo won't break, and if he does, he'll heal."

Jordyn tried laughing. It sounded tight and fake. "All right, deal."

"And-" Healey began.

"There's more?" Jordyn mumbled.

"Be honest with Rutger about your feelings. You need each other. Promise me." Healey reached his hand out and held her shoulder. With his touch, she flinched. *Was Rutger scared to touch her*? he wondered.

"I guess, he is." Jordyn's head jerked up and she met his gaze. The look he gave her confirmed he hadn't said it out loud, and heat from embarrassment crawled up her throat to her face. "I didn't mean to."

"Not since you came home from Celestial?" Healey asked. He wasn't worried about her hearing his thoughts.

Talking about the lack of intimacy in her relationship with the baron, alpha, and almost father-in-law made her want to crawl in a hole. *Nothing like a cry for help.* "Basically. The letter from the Highguard, the trial, I made Flint commit suicide, and the witch's murder investigation, hasn't help matters."

With Flint's suicide the trial hadn't taken long. It was easy for the lawyers to paint Flint as a superpower and mastermind behind the coven. His loyal followers became victims of his insanity. The court system released several witches saying they had been coerced and helpless to deny Flint. Weeks later they went missing, one by one. The same detective who witnessed Flint's suicide was the first to question Rutger and bring homicide detectives to their house. They swarmed the place for weeks, searching for evidence to prove Rutger was responsible.

Rutger, consumed by revenge, tracked down every one of the released witches, and then he and Ansel tore them to pieces. Jordyn didn't know how or why the dead witches ended up on their property where Flint had been hiding. Rutger never would have put them there, but there they were. It didn't matter to her. Before Flint shot himself, he confessed he killed them for betraying him. All the wicked witches were dead.

"Wolves are pack animals, and they have mates to balance them. You're fated mates, Jordyn, you need to be with one another. It's like a spiritual connection, a sharing of your wolf essences that make you stronger. Taming the beast, you might say."

Taming the beast. She was sure he was trying to be funny, but it hit to close to home. *Taming Rutger.* She met his gaze. "Got it." She had to get out of there, the situation was crumbling in front of her, and she didn't need any more advice from the baron. Everyone looked on them with pity in their eyes. Rutger was never home and Jordyn was never not home. Feeling defeated and exposed, Jordyn stood, and the baron took his hand back.

"I'm giving you time, but you have to have help. You know as well as I do that person is Lady Sloan. You have the same power as your mother."

"I know. How long?" Jordyn asked. Her life had become one countdown after another.

"One week. We'll meet and you will tell me how you're doing." Healey studied her and kept his senses open to feel her reactions.

Not before Leo gave him a detailed report of her training. "I can do that." *Probably not.* Jordyn grabbed her duffle bag, and started out of the office.

CHAPTER THREE

Rutger grabbed the door handle, waited for a second, listened, and using his senses didn't feel anyone. Opening it, he checked the hallway for Jo. Nothing. He could have sworn he felt her, like she had brushed him as she walked by. He looked left then right as a chill of awareness crawled over him like it had nails and dug into his skin and his mind. Hoping it was Jo, he let himself feel for the link between them, knowing full well, he was risking feeling nothing except the cold void. Rutger looked in the direction of the gym and didn't hear her or Leo. The link stayed out of his reach but didn't hesitate to throw the nothing he hated at him.

Exhaling his anger, he thought, *There's no way she left without saying anything to me.* Rutger walked down the hall, passing several offices, the communications room, and walking through the reception area with people staring at him, left the Enforcer's building in search of her.

Her red SUV sat in its usual spot beside his truck and the sight brought a wave of relief that surprised him. He didn't want to miss her and believed she wouldn't leave without saying good-bye. Their relationship was suffering, and they had their differences, but Jo possessed a level of relationship etiquette. She wouldn't leave without saying something to him. Good or bad.

Rutger started across the parking lot, toward the house when Sousa opened the door and Jo emerged. She turned to talk to Abigail, giving him her back and allowing him to watch her. She hadn't put her sweatshirt on, despite October's chill, and wearing her onyx hair up and the racerback tank top, left traces of her tattoo and the flawless skin of her throat and shoulder exposed. It made his teeth ache and his wolf rise. *Mark her.*

Stop. With a second look, he saw her too thin frame, lack of color in her skin, and the way she seemed to cower. As if to prove his point, her brittle laugher drifted to him sounding more ghostly than pleasurable.

When was the last time she laughed? Really laughed? When was the last time they enjoyed each other's company? He didn't know. It felt like a lifetime ago.

The baron might have brought her back from the dead, but she refused to embrace life. It was like she was clinging to death and becoming a ghost. Rutger shook himself. He didn't want to believe the woman he loved and would fight and die for, was giving up on her life. Giving up on them. Jo slung her duffle bag over her shoulder, walked down the steps, and met his gaze. Rutger shutdown his thoughts, they caused more problems and watched her approach. *Come to me.*

His shoulder-length mahogany hair hung loose, framing familiar dark eyes while gold flakes swirled in their depths. His gaze narrowed, targeted her as if she was the only person at the house and there weren't sentinels watching them, it made her pause. Jordyn took in his body and the way his broad shoulders pulled his black, long sleeve shirt tight across his chest. The director shifted his stance, making his holster tight around his thigh and his boots scraped asphalt. He exuded strength, authority, and power and she loved it. The sight of him made her body warm all over like he was holding her against him, then it cut through her and she felt loss.

Jordyn yearned for the time when she could touch him and be with him. Then he tensed and his face changed to a neutral scowl. That's right, she looked weak. The gold flakes in his brilliant eyes faded and became sunken and frustrated when he looked at her. He wasn't pretty handsome, he was ruggedly handsome, with strong features, that told you he had the resolve to keep going. To pick up the pieces and fit them together the best he could. She couldn't do it, wasn't doing it. She left the pieces of her life drifting in the wind and hoped she never saw them again. The truth hurt. Director Kanin, Second to the Alpha needed a strong, independent woman to stand beside him, not the broken mess she had become.

"The baron wanted to talk to me," Jordyn explained as she stopped in front of him. She kept her distance, not wanting to crowd him, and not wanting to watch him walk away from her. She couldn't handle another round of rejection. And she didn't want the guilt of having taken a trip through his thoughts to show on her face.

"Was it about your training? Does he know you hate it?" Rutger asked. The baron telling Leo if she broke, she would heal, played in his thoughts. He was going to talk to them both and make it crystal clear it was not the case. No one hurt Jo when she had yet to heal. Squinting his eyes against the sun, Rutger attempted a smile to cover his concern. He failed. It seemed to be a theme.

"He convinced me to give it another try." Jordyn looked up at him. Her five feet, two inches was a stark difference to his six feet, four inches. His muscled build from days at the gym and self-assurance contrasted to her small frame and weakness. She worked out, the training demanding she improve her strength, which had given her sculpted muscles, but the differences were there. They were opposites. Strength versus weakness.

"The baron has a way of doing that." Civil conversation, nothing to it. He met her rich cocoa gaze streaked with copper and forced himself not to fall into their depths. His anxiety began easing, then he watched her eyes glance at her SUV. Like it would start by itself, the doors would open, and she could jump in and escape him.

"We've come to an agreement. I give it a week and if I still hate it, I can stop." Jordyn wasn't going to admit to having *quit.* It would make her sound weaker than she already was and her lie would sound worse.

Lying to me? Rutger clung to it, striving to feel more of her and was denied. He didn't understand why she was lying to him, and it added to the hurt festering inside him. He watched her stare at her car. "I've got things to do here. It should be a couple of hours, and then I'll be home."

Jordyn's gaze flicked from her SUV to Rutger. He wasn't going to spend the night at the office. "You don't have patrols tonight?"

"No, Ansel and Kellen are taking care of it." *Say something.* Rutger couldn't think of one thing to say. Not when he wanted to say a million things. Her eyes were on him and not on him. She wasn't there. His words and their meaning would be wasted.

"I'll see you later. I'm going home and taking a shower." Jordyn hadn't finished her sentence when she took a step to get around him. She stopped when he grabbed her upper arm, sending a spark of power between them, and held her. His hand on her, the feel of his rough palm, and warm fingers on her skin, caused her to inhale. Damn she missed him.

Rutger chased the power warming his skin as he looked at his hand on Jo's arm. He leisurely moved his gaze up and prayed his stare drilled through the haunting darkness he saw when he met her eyes. He desperately wanted to tell her he needed her. How was he going to when he didn't trust his voice and didn't trust himself not to screw it up? Her detachment destroyed whatever nerve he believed he possessed, and the chance to make her see him. Jo was keyed up and focused on getting the hell away from him. If he said anything wrong, it would make things worse.

His eyes were on his hand on her skin, his fingers completely circling her upper arm, and he mumbled, "Sorry." Letting go of her, he took a step back, making sure he was out of her way.

Jordyn hated the sound of the regret and pain in his voice ... it was going to make her fall apart, and there was no way she could look at him. She left him behind and continued to her SUV, opened the door, threw her bag across to the passenger seat, and got in. Sitting behind the steering wheel, she wanted to cry and scream. Instead, she started the engine, and backed out of her parking space. With the mile-long drive in front of her, she dove into her world which had become her prison.

Damn it. Rutger watched her and the distance growing between them morphing into a void. He should have said something, kissed her, made her talk to him, anything but nothing. He tried to remember the days before their lives fell apart and their relationship sat on the verge of destruction. The thought, if it wasn't so sad, almost made him laugh out loud. They didn't. After he hurt Jo and she left and let three years of silence sit between them, she returned for her sister's wedding and that's when Rutger decided he was finished pretending. He told her how he felt, and she threatened to leave.

Before she could run, Jo helped him and the Organized Paranormal Investigations, OPI, to confirm the people responsible for several murders and one of their own were witches. They reunited during a wedding and a murder investigation. Not normal. They were forced to talk, which destroyed the deadlock on their lives, and they spent the next twenty-four hours together. The baron made her the soothsayer for the pack, he reclaimed his place as Second to the Alpha, they had sex, great sex, and then without telling him, she left to confront her human boyfriend and got kidnapped. By the witches. Enter losing control of his wolf. Perfectly normal relationship. It was a fucking joke. Rutger growled as he stared at the empty drive.

"Rutger, do you have the report?" Healey asked. He approached his son, and when he was within arm's reach felt Rutger's desperation.

The baron's voice jerked him back to reality, and he shut down his thoughts and faced him. "Which one?" There was an entire stack sitting on his desk. Untouched.

"Butte Springs."

Right. "It's in my office. Did the sale go through?" Rutger needed to go back to pretending to work.

"It did. I had to create a conservation easement to permanently limit the land's uses, but it's ours. I'm waiting on a permit from the Forest Service to have it logged, I don't need a fire going through there. And another to tear down the dilapidated buildings, and get rid of all the trash. What I really want is the trees where the human remains had hung, gone," Healey explained. The sound of human bones clanging in the wind like warped bone chimes was not a sound he wanted to hear, ever.

"That's good news. It will be nice to get the area cleaned up. I'll get the file and have it brought over to you. I also have the week's call log, and incident reports," Rutger rambled on. He didn't know what he was saying.

"Mmmhm. Why don't you call it a day and head home?" Healey advised. The week's call logs; it was Wednesday not Friday.

Why would I go home, it had become a tomb to the ghost living there? "I have work," Rutger replied. Not lying. He needed to pretend to read reports, plus the acquisition of Belle Ridge-the area's real name, Butte Springs-meant he needed to get a diagram going for security and place an order for cameras and motion sensors.

"Jordyn is headed home, which means you need to go home. I could order you." Holding his son's gaze, Healey watched his thoughts haunt his eyes.

Jo is going to their house but her home is inside of her head, inside of her fear. "Is this you pulling rank?" Rutger thought about it, he also thought about the way she looked at him when he held her arm.

What did she see when she looked at him? A monster? A threat to her life? An uncontrolled, weak wolf who wasn't worth fighting for? They might live together but they weren't together, and hadn't been since Butte Springs. Maybe the baron was right, they needed to start with the simple elements of getting to know one another.

"Do I have to pull rank?" Healey asked.

"No, sir. I do have work. When it's completed, I'll go home." Rutger sounded like a teen version of himself.

"Good. I know she's distracted, but have patience and talk to her. Even if you're the only one talking, just talk." Healey watched Rutger's thoughts pass over his face, his eyes giving away the pain he was living with. "Son, this will pass." He grabbed Rutger's shoulder and squeezed. "I promise."

"If she survives her fear, I'll face losing her to the Highguard." The words rushed from him like a sad confession. Their life together was captured in an hourglass, and the sands of time were going too fast and in the wrong direction.

"I've talked to her. I explained I'm getting her help and calling Lady Sloan. Jordyn needs someone who understands her magic and what she's going through. She also needs a mother."

"She told you?" Rutger's hand went to the butt of his gun, his jealousy burning through him, she didn't talk to him. Jo hadn't said anything to him about the conversation she had with the baron. She was going to face her birth mother and her magic. She should have confided in him. Rutger shoved the rage down before he lost his mind.

A swift energy escaped Rutger flashing between them like a lightning bolt. "Yes. She used the Collective and Lady Sloan as excuses for her lack of interest in training. Jordyn wouldn't talk about you or your relationship." Healey paused, looked at the Enforcer's office, the garage, his land, considered his status as baron and alpha, the power he wielded, and felt the familiar pang of helplessness. "Finish your work and head home. Send the files when you have time, no rush." Healey turned to the porch and started toward the stairs. He could feel the apprehension rolling from Rutger like a storm getting ready to unleash its wrath.

Rutger watched Sousa open the door for the baron and they disappeared behind wood and wrought iron as Abigail and Nick took their positions. Nick was a new hire for sentinel, Rutger should have known. *The paperwork is probably on my desk,* he thought as he headed back to the office. In a second, his thoughts strayed to Jo and Lady Sloan. She could have said something to him about revealing who her mother was, in case the baron asked him. He didn't want to get caught lying. Why would she talk to him? Like he opened up to her about what was happening in his life? No. Rutger sat heavy in his chair and sitting back gazed at the latest report. He grunted at the sight of the Olivers' names. Damn he hated seeing them fall apart.

After their son, Zachery, was tortured and murdered by the witches, they hadn't been the same, and who could blame them? They lost their only son, only child to psychotic serial killers. The way the news portrayed the werewolves of Cascade and the trial, it made the mutilation and what they did with the boy's body parts cruel. Pictures of Rutger, Jo, and Zachery along with the witches and Flint, their leader, were everywhere. They couldn't escape it. It helped send Jo into hiding.

Over the months, it had become common place for the enforcers to respond to the couple's house several times a week. It involved taking domestic violence reports or finding Mr. Oliver drunk in the woods, which with a werewolf's metabolism took a lot of hard alcohol, or Mrs. Oliver locked in the bathroom threatening suicide. The entire pack was aware of their problems and watched out for the couple, intervening when they could, and keeping it within the pack. Human law enforcement wasn't an option and no one needed the hassle. Besides, the humans would take extreme measures to subdue Mr. or Mrs. Oliver, and if they were taken into custody, they would be put in cells lined with White 47, a synthetic silver. Rutger's top priority was protecting the pack from outsiders and keeping its reputation of strength intact. Cascade's kith and kin were not weak.

Rutger straightened, took a pen, and made a note to have Dr. Carrion, Jo's therapist, call them. If they forced him to handcuff them and drive them to Celestial himself, he would. He didn't want to see them hurt one another, get divorced, or held in the cells beneath the Enforcer's office. Rutger didn't want the damn witches to destroy another couple. *Like me.*

Should have made them suffer, Rutger thought as he scrawled his notes, and checked his initials on the report. Setting his pen down and sitting back, his thoughts went to the pain the witches inflicted and how it kept going like it was on a rail with no end in sight.

Chatter in the hall caught his attention. It quickly faded, and his mind returned to his relationship and its failures. He should call Jo and make sure she made it home safely and tell her he would be leaving the office earlier than anticipated. They needed to talk about the great divide between them. He refused to be a casualty of the witches ... serial killers. Holding his cell, hesitation dug in and he saw the distant look in her eyes as she stared at her car, and her escape. Jo was a runner. Always trying to escape. Was she going to escape him? The pack? She could try. The baron would never let the pack's soothsayer and keeper of all secrets go very far. If she didn't return on her own, the slayers would track her down and bring her back for punishment. As legatee, Second to the Alpha, he would have to serve as the witness to the types of punishments the slayers inflicted and report it to the baron. How was he going to save her?

Rutger touched the screen, knowing he could hit speed dial, but somehow going through the motions made his nerves calm down. It rang once, twice, three times and her voice told him to leave a message. He hung up. Rutger looked at the time. Twenty minutes to the house. Maybe fifteen in the shower. An extra fifteen to be safe, not paranoid. He tried again. Voicemail. She should be home. He tried again. Damn voicemail.

"Director," Mandy greeted as she entered the office.

He covered his worry laced with irritation with a scowl. Per normal. "What is it?" Rutger set his cell on the desk and leaned forward.

"There's a problem at the Summit. The baroness left to attend a meeting with a group of women and now is parked across the street unable to enter. There are protesters and they won't let her pass. Nor will they let the women inside, out," Mandy reported. She stood in the door wearing a black V-neck T-shirt with the pack's crest on the left and her name on the right, and black BDUs pants, boots, and her thigh holster and Glock 21, 45 caliber pistol. She wore her dark brown hair back in a braid, and her blue/violet eyes narrowed on him and held her anger.

The Summit Sanctuary, considered a wildlife preserve, covered twenty thousand acres, contained three ponds, while two rivers ran through the property, and the thick forest provided a secure place for running in their wolf forms. The open amphitheater setting was a safe environment to hold their meetings and celebrating traditions like the inclusion of new members. The sacred burial ground sat behind the meeting area, secluded in the woods and offered privacy for mourning or meditation.

Even before the witches, the Summit had been secured with fencing, was gated, and had a descent security system. Like every building and property, the Sanctuary transformed into a compound with its clipped concertina razor wire topped fencing, palm vein identification, number code, and cameras. A lot of cameras intended for curious trespassers, visiting leaders of other factions, but more specifically the Highguard. Protesters? Rutger never thought there would be protestors. What were they protesting?

"Protesters?" Rutger questioned. His attention focused on the women stuck inside and the baroness, waiting outside. The witches, the Olivers, Jo's voicemail, for the moment, forgotten.

"An anti-paranormal group. They call themselves Humans Against Paranormal Influence. HAPI for short," Mandy explained. The anger drained as she struggled to keep the smile off her face.

"HAPI? I want to laugh, I really do. Humans Against Paranormal Influence, what influence do we have?" he questioned. It wasn't a real question; he was talking to one of his own, who knew how much power in the human world and politics they didn't have. "How serious are they?"

"I couldn't stop from laughing. They clearly put a lot of effort into their name." Mandy grew serious. "No one has reported violence, so I'm going to report it as low. They're outside the gate and are walking back and forth with picket signs. The baroness said she talked to Claudia Ingalls and everyone inside is fine. However, they're scared of leaving."

"No one has tried to leave?" Rutger asked.

"Negative. They don't want to hurt one of them. The protesters are human. They aren't." There was a growl lacing Mandy's words. The injustice of being trapped and unable to defend themselves because of someone else's hate blazed with fury. "The baroness requested you."

"All right, I'll go. I need Kellen and Luke as backup. If I run into problems, I'll call the sheriff's department," Rutger explained as he stood.

"Affirmative. I'll contact them and have them met you at the Summit, and I'll call the baroness and tell her you're en route."

"Copy. If Kellen and Luke beat me there, advise them there is zero contact. If the protesters block the entrance, they are not to engage or try to pass," Rutger ordered. "We don't need charges from a human martyr or a damn lawsuit against us for hurting their feelings."

He didn't need his name or the pack in the newspapers, on the news, social media, or anywhere else again. His face had been splashed on every news outlet and on every social media platform, after the witches disappeared and the homicide unit considered him a suspect. *Rutger Kanin, eldest son to Baron Kanin of the Cascade Clan, is being investigated for the murders of...*

No one cares. Growling low in his chest with the memory, Rutger grabbed his coat, pulled it on, grabbed his cell phone, and considered calling Jo, then shoved it into the inside pocket of his coat. He left his office trailing after Mandy down the hall to the communications room.

"I want you to start recording from the street and the camera at the gate," Rutger ordered.

"Already did, sir, as soon as I got the call." Mandy sat down in the chair and faced three monitors showing video in real time, a fifty-five inch screen mounted on the wall, and another monitor chirping with transcripts from the enforcer's reports.

On the wall-mounted screen, Rutger watched a mix of males and females parading back and forth in front of the gate, carrying signs. He counted ten protestors and could make out the words on one of the signs. Printed in block letters that slanted down to fit the entire word, to the edge of the poster board, stating 'humans first'.

"Any idea how long they've been there?"

"Negative, sir. Kellen is en route," Mandy reported.

"Have you noticed if there is a leader?"

"Negative. Luke is en route."

"Got it." Rutger left communications, headed through reception, and out to the parking lot.

"I heard from your mother. What is the threat level?" Healey asked, falling in step.

"Low. They haven't trespassed, they haven't tried to contact anyone, and there hasn't been violence. The women are staying back so they don't insight a reaction. Kellen, Luke, and I are going to check it out," Rutger responded. He got in his truck and started the engine. "If they advance and there is a threat, I'm calling the sheriff's department. Mandy is having the situation recorded for evidence."

"This is one time I'm glad Jordyn isn't participating in the women's events. It would have damaged the progress she has made," Healey said.

Rutger met the baron's stern gaze. "Agreed." Sitting in his truck, the diesel engine purred, and he was thankful she escaped to their house.

"Keep me updated." Healey stepped back letting Rutger close his door, backup and drive out of Foxwood.

CHAPTER FOUR

Jordyn sat in her car, staring at the walnut garage door with wrought iron framing the windows, and listening to her cell phone ring. *Stop calling,* she wanted to yell. The shrill ring, which she needed to change, was pulling her from her thoughts and disrupting the numbness she was actively embracing. She didn't want to feel. She didn't want to think. Her thoughts bullied through and she sat there thinking about what she was going to do about the baron, Lady Sloan, and Rutger. Time was running out, and as much as she wanted to, she couldn't hide forever.

Picking up the phone, she turned the sound off, and tossed it to her bag. Every time he called, it contradicted the times he refused to touch her, and when he spoke to her it was as if he was trying to talk an invisible being. It chipped at her confidence. She squeezed her eyes closed, fighting back hot tears, pressed the palm of her hand against her forehead, and inhaled. Maybe the baron was right and she needed help with self-confidence.

"I'm losing," Jordyn mumbled.

Jordyn-0.

Flint-1.

She turned the key, the engine went silent, she grabbed her duffle from the passenger seat, and got out of the SUV. The sky, a pale gray, with thick clouds shielding the sun, felt cold, distant, and there was a crisp chill drifting on the wind. In the house there was a hot shower and a sweatshirt with her name on them. She stood at the door, which mirrored the garage doors-all bulletproof glass, steal-and pressed her palm on the pad. A violet UV light blinked, a subtle reminder of the Highguard and her pending departure, and she entered the number code. The date of their anniversary. Each number was like typing out *you're losing.*

The pad turned from violet to green, the locking machination clicked, and the door opened. She crossed the entrance, and without closing and locking it, let it close on its own. Jordyn breathed a sigh of relief with the empty house, no one talking, no one to judge her, and went straight to the fireplace. She dropped her bag on a chair, took the stoker, and began pushing chunks of charred wood around. Flames flickered and died, red embers glowed and dimmed. Jordyn added wood, and when it caught, flames crawled up and over the sides, between split pieces, and hissed as it consumed the rough bark. Sinking to her knees, she felt comfort from the gentle heat, and watched the flames dance. Rutger. The baron. Lady Sloan. The Highguard. Jordyn didn't know how to deal with them while drowning in her nightmares. *It's safer in my nightmares than living in reality.* Unable to stop herself from sinking into her prison constructed from tragedy, she let her thoughts take the path of least resistance. And the worst consequences.

Her mind ceased being hers and filled with men and women's voices as they barked orders while others replied with rushed words Jordyn didn't understand. She didn't know where she was, how she got there, or why she was there at all. Time slowed down, and somewhere along the way she lost herself. Crawling in the muck of her mind, she tried to escape the haze and pain to reach for what had happened.

The night air teased her as the slithering chanting of the witches created fear she felt in her bones. Jordyn had been hanging from a tree and Flint was going to kill her. Needed to kill the soothsayer. With her next breath, Rutger clutched her to his body, his eyes blazed gold with his wolf, his strength and grief pouring from him and into her, through her. Like her body had been a sieve, she couldn't hold onto him.

Let go. The whisper promised to take the pain away.

Rutger's roar thundered over her, its vibration shaking her core, as its raw pain sent chills down her spine. Her heart felt like it was going to explode when it stopped and she watched Rutger fade and black's veil shrouded her. *I died. I left him and his wolf turned on him and became a beast. Bestial.* Rutger's life in the Scared Writ of the pack would state he had gone Bestial. The weakest of the pack.

Maybe she should end it and they should go their separate ways? Their relationship was killing them both. Rutger deserved more, he deserved someone who would love him unconditionally. She wasn't capable of loving him when she was too weak to fight her own battles. Jordyn could hear the accusations and judgements coming from the pack about her failure. She should have tried harder. She should think about someone else besides herself. Selfish. Rutger works hard and she pushes him out of her life while holding him hostage. She didn't have a real job, who was she to lock herself in the house and play the victim? Her heart ached, her body hurt, and the pain was eating her.

Her memories blurred, twisted, and turning into scarlet and gold flames they reached up the chimney. "How do I fix this," Jordyn asked the fire.

"Fix what?"

Jordyn stood and whirled around to face the open door. The turmoil of her life froze in place with the sound of his voice. *No.* "Louis?"

"Lost in thought, Jordyn? Or is it Jo, now?" Louis charged, his condescending tone targeting her. He walked to the living room, stopping at the edge of the slate and wood flooring, his hands in his pockets, like he belonged. His dirty blond hair, perfectly styled, its pretentiousness matching his white button-up shirt, and dark blue slacks. "Were you crying? How odd for someone who is clearly living the dream." He waved his arms at the house.

Jordyn wasn't going to wipe the tears from her cheeks and give him the satisfaction. As her wounds opened the need for a sweatshirt-anything to cover her tank top-drove through her. It was a habit to cover herself believing it was a protective barrier.

"How did you get in?" Jordyn asked.

"Expensive security systems keep people out *only* when the door is closed and locked, Jordyn. Nice place," Louis' narrowed azure gaze searched the room, and eyeing the framed sunset photograph sitting on the mantel, his lips thinned. "A slight step up from the hovel you were living in."

A slight step up? The four thousand square foot log home with a deck and views of the lake made Louis' place look like a hovel. Sitting on the mantle was her black-framed photograph of Sunset Reflected. It had been in several magazines and commercials and had given her respect and recognition amongst her peers. Jordyn caught the shadows from the boats anchored near the shoreline, breaking the colors of golds and pinks reflected on the water while Rutger waited for her. Wearing worn jeans, slung low on his hips, his bare feet buried in a mix of smooth pebbles, and sand, the water turned the cuffs dark. The photo helped her land the partnership at the gallery, where she worked for three years in Butterfly Valley. Where she dated Louis. At one time it represented her career, now it represented the time she spent in Butterfly Valley had been a lie. She didn't care. With one comment, Louis disrespected her independence. She paid for the house. *I liked the hovel.* Jordyn hadn't depended on the pack, her parents, or anyone. *Not like now.* Shoving the feeling of helplessness down she concentrated on Louis.

"See you've added your personal touch to the place," Louis mocked.

That hurt. She didn't own anything in the house except her clothing and camera, and she had no idea where her camera was. It was Rutger's house. While Jordyn recuperated at Celestial, the baron ordered movers go to her *hovel* where they packed everything into boxes and wrapped furniture in plastic, then they hauled it to Trinity and stored it in the pack's private storage building. From the sheets and blankets, she put on her bed, to pictures she had hung on the walls, she hadn't seen her stuff in four months. Jordyn was sure they packed all the food in the cupboards. She had pasta sitting in a storage unit. How sad.

"And you've kept up with the house keeping." He laughed. "Not that it matters when there's nothing of yours here. You moved in and lost your identity." Louis checked the stairs, stared at the tossed running shoes, T-shirts, abandoned socks, and backing up, stared at the bar and back to her. He wore a smirk when he said, "A bar? Rutger Kanin must be a real renaissance man. Does he toss a few drinks back then howl at the moon? Do you throw caution to the wind, let the lycan loose, and join him?"

Jordyn ignored the statement about Rutger, who the hell was Louis to say anything? As she saw her house-the mess, the dust, and lack of care through new eyes-embarrassment burned through her. Jordyn let herself swim in pity and acting like a cancer was infecting everything around her. Everything that wasn't hers.

"Louis, why are you here?" Jordyn asked.

"I'm here to take you home, babe." He paused, as if he didn't believe what he said.

When Louis found out Jordyn lied to him and gone to Trinity and stayed with Rutger, he called her a dog in heat. For lying to him about being a werewolf, and then her betrayal, she deserved the hate he threw her way. Fine, he was pissed off at her, it was over. They were over. There was nothing between them except lies and bad feelings. Louis didn't see shapeshifters as equals, let alone lycans-he saw them as a second class population who didn't deserve rights. So why did he want to take her anywhere?

"Why don't I believe you?" Where was her phone? *In my bag, shit.* She should have paid better attention to the speech Rutger gave her about the security system.

"Please, Jordyn, I'm trying to help you. Look at what you've become. This house is disgusting, and you, look at you, you're a shell of the woman I once knew." Louis looked behind him as a man approached them. "I want you to meet Doctor Peter Holmes. We met at the university. He is the founder of Humans Against Paranormal Influence."

Louis can't be serious, HAPI, she wanted to laugh.

"He has been working with shapeshifters for years and understands what happened to you," Louis explained, as he waved the doctor closer.

What happened to me? Flint. Soothsayer. Rutger.

"This is true. Jordyn Langston, daughter to Ethan and Mia Langston, Pureblood lycans, and elders in the Cascade clan." Dr. Holmes let his knowledge sit between them as if he was proving his superiority. It explained what Louis saw in him. "Louis explained your life in Butterfly Valley had been fulfilling. You had a career, and a genuine relationship. When you returned to Trinity, they brainwashed you and you were forced to stay here." He lifted his arms, bringing attention to the house. "Louis has asked me to help you?"

Nothing he said impressed her, especially when Mia wasn't her mother. Dr. Holmes' high-pitched voice grated on her nerves, his beady eyes reminded her of a rat, and his demeaner was wrong. Deceitful. Jordyn's instincts screamed she needed to get away from him, them, and she took a step backward as fear slid down her spine. A warning crawled over her. If she didn't go with them willingly, they were going to take her against her will. Kidnapped. Again.

"You can have your life back." Stepping forward, Louis held his hand out. "You have nothing here. You don't have the gallery. Your independence. By the look of your house you don't have your pride. I guess it would be hard to remain independent when you've given your freedom to the Wolf Enforcer. I'm here to help." Louis raised his hand, keeping his eyes on her. "I can give you your independence."

"Listen to him, Jordyn. You could have it all back. Your career," Dr. Holmes added.

"It's like you've given up on life. Have you stopped living, babe?" Louis asked, softly. "Come with me."

I have stopped living. "You don't know what you're talking about." She had to get away from them. Jordyn watched both men, their slight movements, while her senses picked up the wave of emotions coming from them. The situation reminded her of Flint and the morning he took her from her hovel.

"I don't? By order of the baron. All hail the baron. Since you've given your life up, do you wait for the Wolf Enforcer to come home and then follow his orders?" Louis laughed. "Maybe fix the Wolf Enforcer dinner. If you cook like you clean, I pity the man. What am I saying, man?" he seethed the words, barely stopping himself from screaming. He shuddered, got himself uncontrol, straightened and stared at her.

"You were brainwashed. They brainwashed you. Tricked you into giving up your independence and making you believe you had to stay here with the Wolf Enforcer. Because they made you a soothsayer? You would have to be brainwashed to believe the lies they're telling you. It's all myths, Jordyn, it isn't real. None of it is. The lies were created to make non-humans feel special, to feel better about themselves." His eyes glazed over, his pupils eating azure. "Witches. Are you listening to me? Witches, kidnapped you and poisoned you with herbs. What kind of person believes that?" He turned in a circle, checking the house, and when he faced her, he set his furious gaze on her, and visibly shook himself. "You let the Wolf Enforcer touch you. God Jordyn really."

Wolf enforcer.

Fear wrapped around her. It wasn't from Louis or Dr. Holmes … no, Jordyn was confident even with the memory of Flint and the shitty day she had at training, she could escape him and his lackey. The terror she had been clinging to, and allowing to rule her life, roared with Flint's words. His voice echoed in her head, and she suddenly smelled lavender. It crawled over her skin like cold oil.

"You look terrified. Are you scared of the Wolf Enforcer? Is he the reason you were on your knees crying? Does he hurt you to make you stay? Is that blood in your hair? Did he hit you? Does he abuse you? Is this what you want in your life? You can tell me. Please, Jordyn, let me save you from this and that monster." Louis took a step forward.

Raising her hand to her head, Jordyn felt the crust of dried blood and matted hair and forgot Leo landed a solid hit. She was failing the training and only wanted to get the hell out of the gym and go home. He continued stabbing her with questions, forcing her to face what she really wanted. Her pride, what was left, was destroyed by the victim living inside of her and she let it rule her. Damn the constant feeling of losing and failure were going to kill her. Jordyn wasn't going to answer his questions when he was trying to take her apart piece by piece and her answers would make her look weaker.

"You loved me, Jordyn." Louis held his hand out to her, his fingers curling and beckoning her to go to him. "You could love me again."

No. Not only no, but hell no. Jordyn's face wore her disgust as she looked at the men with clear eyes. She couldn't deny the fear when it reminded her she was broken and the shards of her life were scattered around her feet. Like someone had taken a hammer to her and turned her into a million pieces she didn't know how to stick back together.

But his accusations, the invasion of her home ... damn her territory infuriated her, and burned the walls she was hiding behind. Grasping the anger boiling in her middle for the first time in months, Jordyn wanted to know what the hell had she been doing with her life? She saw Rutger when she left Foxwood, his body crumbling under the misery they were living with. That she was creating. What did she want? Jordyn wanted to listen to music, drink wine, run, and laugh. She wanted to be with Rutger. She wanted to be free of the chains tethering her to her pain.

"I do want my life back," Jordyn mumbled, as if realizing it for the first time. "I want my life." Saying it gave her power, and she wanted it like she wanted nothing before. Ever.

"That's it. You can have your life," Louis assured, his eyes bright with victory like he had won her over. "Leave with me."

It took Louis, or him forcing her to defend her life in Trinity, to jolt her from the suffering she was creating. With the cluster of fear and pain swept to the side, she needed to focus and think of something to get them out of the house.

"How are you going to help me?" Jordyn asked, her voice soft, submissive.

"That's my Jordyn. You leave with us right now, and I'll protect you," Louis promised. He took a step forward with his victory, the toes of his shoes on the edge of the area rug.

Lying to me. His evil hovered around him proving Louis' intentions had nothing to do with protecting her. Jordyn slipped into his mind, while trying to keep him talking so she could figure out why they were there. "How can you protect me from the pack, Louis? Where would we go? They would search for me. Hunt me down."

"Dr. Holmes has a facility where you can hide. There he will clear your head of their brainwashing, destroying their hold on you." Louis took another step toward her. "You will be free."

"Once the brainwashing has been cleansed, we will purify you. The baron and the Wolf Enforcer won't have any influence over you. You covet your freedom, and this is your chance to take it back," Dr. Holmes promised.

"After the purification process, you will get your tattoos removed. There will be nothing marking you like an animal. It will end their violence, rituals, and animalistic ways," Louis continued trying to convince her.

Purification. They are crazy. "I would be free of them. Freedom." The damn security system needed to be voice activated. Her cell phone-mini know-it-all computer-needed to know she was in trouble and call Rutger. Hell, all the enforcers.

"Yes. Rutger Kanin, Director of Enforcers, and the Cascade clan will be a memory." Dr. Holmes took a step forward to stand beside Louis. "You could rekindle your relationship with Louis. The two of you will be happy together. A human love, not a forced union with an animal. A dog."

"You won't be controlled by a tyrant and made a female submissive. I heard before the animal lost his mind, he yelled *mine* when referring to you. Do you want to be owned like a pet?" Louis let his remark hang between them. "By coming with me, you will have the right to choose what *you* want to do."

Own me. Jordyn felt Rutger hug her to his chest, his arms wrapped around her, and then heard his rough roar as she sank into darkness. *He didn't lose his mind. He lost his mate.* He released his sorrow the only way he knew how. As if she was back at Celestial, his voice caressed her, erasing the pain of Butte Springs from her. Mine. Fated mates. Jordyn closed her eyes as the thought sent a twist of warmth and sadness through her. She was going to lose him.

"Listen to him, Jordyn, you will become a different person. You will be treated with respect, like a human," Dr. Holmes assured.

She was sick of listening to them and wanted them to shut up. Jordyn forced herself not to cringe as she waded into Louis' thoughts and into his anger, fear, and the hate saturating his memories. She felt their sharp edges like they were physical things when they cut through her mind. Overriding his emotions was his hate. Concentrated. Focused. She was the reason. He despised her.

"You're lying. Why are you here, Louis, when you hate me?" Jordyn asked, coolly. Their gazes locked, and she saw his fake affection shatter under the force of his raw disgust.

Louis' eyes darkened with his fury, his hands clinched into fists, and he let hate etch his face. "You lied to me, you little bitch." He laughed a high squealing sound. "*Bitch.* The Wolf Enforcer's bitch. No pun intended." Louis grabbed her wrists, yanked her closer, her face close to his chest, and lowering pressed his nose to her cheek. "People. Humans mocked me because of you. Who would fuck a lycan?" he grated through clenched teeth, his lips touching hers. "You should have told me you like to be beaten, Jordyn, I would have given you what you wanted. In spades."

Louis was there to hurt her. It should have pegged her panic button and sent her into the depths of her despair.

Something broke loose inside her. Jordyn calmed, her wolf infused her with strength, and her power saturated her. She survived Flint, barely, but she survived. *Damn straight, I survived.* With his grip on her tightening, she pushed him. He stumbled back, sending him off balance, and Jordyn jerked her wrists from his grip. Her eyes blazed liquid copper from her human face and she laughed at their fear.

"Don't touch me," Jordyn growled. "Get the hell out of my house."

"I wanted to do this the easy way. Pity, I really thought you would take the bait since Louis told me you hate being a lycan," Dr. Holmes said from beside her. "I'm not here for an infected lycan or a sad excuse of one. I'm here for the Pureblood who doesn't have one drop of human blood in her body. I'm here for the Cascade clan's soothsayer."

Oh shit. Jordyn wanted to focus on them but couldn't think past the fire encasing her wrists. She rubbed one after the other, attempting to get rid of a flaring pain as she exited Louis' head and slipped into Dr. Holmes'. Jordyn waded through Louis' thoughts and memories and the layers of emotions to easily find the truth. In Dr. Holmes', she trudged through the levels of chaos, deceit, and manipulations, their intensity catching her off guard. Dr. Holmes used the university to recruit followers and indoctrinate them with his beliefs. And by feeding into Louis' hate for her, Louis let him use the Paranormal History class as his personal hunting grounds for shapeshifters and the magic-born. Screams thundered, pain ate them, screeching echoed off the warehouse's metal walls. Inhaling, Jordyn struggled to keep her reactions under control when she saw him dressed in scrubs and looming over a body, his hands glistening scarlet. He was experimenting on them.

Great educational system. Spreading hate and enabling a mad man.

"You're coming with me, lycan." Louis broke through her trance.

"No. I am not." Jordyn held Louis' gaze. "Rutger will be here." Of course he will. *No, he won't.* She stopped talking to him. Remember you ignored his calls all morning? Jordyn was on her own, perfect.

The scene reminded her of the way Patriot Angels, the group responsible for infecting humans, experimenting on them, and kidnapping the magic-born, worked. Jordyn couldn't let them leave without learning the location of the warehouse. She went deeper, searching and filtering through information, at the same time both men approached her.

Run. Jordyn's wolf howled in her ears, her instincts blared a warning, at the same time her body demanded she go for the door, escape, and get help. If she ran, she wouldn't learn the location of the facility. She wouldn't be able to stop Dr. Holmes from destroying other's lives. *When he's done torturing them, if they live, they'll turn into me.*

"No, he won't. Your Wolf Enforcer is busy." He used the term again. Louis' gaze narrowed on her, his face twisting with his triumph.

"Tick-tock, Pureblood." Dr. Holmes lips drew back in a smile revealing yellow/brown tinted teeth like he smoked a pack of cigarettes a day.

"I'm not going anywhere with you," Jordyn growled as her eyes gleamed copper. There was a flash of fear, and it was her turn to smirk with victory. Yeah, she was going to kick Louis' ass.

"This isn't my first time, Pureblood," Dr. Holmes mocked.

Jordyn wore bracelets of fire around her wrists, and every time she rubbed them it made the pain worse. Forget about it, she found the information she needed and jerked herself out of his mind. Before Jordyn understood the muffling sound, a sting spread down the back of her arm and into her wrist where the fire was spreading. *It burns, from his touch.* She looked at her wrists as if flames circled them and her flesh was scorched and peeling from her arms.

Louis' guttural laugh had her clumsily raising her head. The room was spinning around her, the sunlight disappearing and letting darkness crowd the edges of her mind. *Damn, this is going to hurt.*

CHAPTER FIVE

Rutger slowly rolled down the street, saw the baroness'
silver luxury SUV parked across from the Summit, while
parked behind her were her personal sentinels, Sadie and
Abigail. They all watched the protesters marching back and
forth, swinging their signs in front of the gate. Kellen pulled
to the side of the road, parked in front of the baroness
while Luke parked on the same side as the Summit. With
the protestors noticing their presence, Luke backed up to
keep a safe distance from the group.

This wasn't a time for talking when the humans weren't
going to listen to a *lycan*. Rutger needed to get around the
protesters, inside the Summit, and check on the women of
his pack. They would see Rutger as threat. A non-human. A
lycan. A werewolf. Rutger didn't need to scare them with
his wolf. He hoped the magnitude of his full size truck,
heavy steel grille guard, and diesel engine would be
enough to intimidate them. He pulled into the turning lane,
made a left, drove another seventy-five yards, and stopped
when a man with shaggy hair, half zipped sweatshirt, and
torn jeans stepped in front of him. The protestor didn't
look like a threat. In fact, Rutger evaluated them and none
of them, male or female, looked threatening. They were
college students whose parents didn't know where they

were. *Little Bobby Joe is playing hooky from school and you're paying for it.*

Being human gave them power and leverage, and if Bobby Joe got hurt, it would create problems for the pack. The group was ten feet in front of him and standing their ground, judged him, their eyes wide, and waited. They weren't making a move to confront him ... in fact they didn't move. All right. Rutger honked his horn, once, twice, and two kids darted to the left.

That's right kiddos, move along.

The first two were followed by four more. *Making progress.* He revved his engine, its rumble sending two more running. He eyed the last two, inched closer, and they retreated. They stood on either side of him with their signs resting on the ground. Pulling up to the gate, he lowered his window, quickly hit a switch for the security pad, and pressed his palm on the marked area, then entered the number code. The gate rattled open at the same time the protesters began yelling obscenities.

Cowards. Figures they resort to name calling.

Rutger drove through the entrance, waited for the gate to close, confirmed no one followed, and continued to the parking lot. Several women stood around Claudia's car, while other women joined Claudia and they all watched as he parked and got out.

"Director," Claudia greeted. "Thanks for coming to the party."

"When did it start?" Rutger asked.

At the gate, the group started yelling, their voices drifting, making it impossible to understand what they were saying.

"About an hour ago. We were waiting for the baroness, when they showed," Claudia explained. "We didn't want a fight so we stayed back."

"Smart move." Rutger counted the women present.

"Every so often, and once in a while I get it right," Claudia replied with a smile.

"I need everyone over here." He waited while they circled around him. "There are thirty of you?" he asked. He was surprised there were only thirty of them when the gathering was important to the entire pack. He was also thankful there were only thirty. Keep it business.

"Affirmative." Claudia watched him look at the group, his eyes skirting over them and not looking at them.

"Rutger," Kory greeted as she moved to the front of the circle.

He gave an auto response and nodded his head as he tried to decide how he was going to get them through the gate without a protester putting themselves in danger. Thirty. At least there weren't that many cars. "All right-" He stopped. Rutger listened; there were sirens and they weren't far. "Did one of you call the law?" Rutger demanded.

"No," they replied at once.

"Claudia?"

"Negative, sir," she quickly answered.

At least no one went against his order. "Did you see anyone else? A car? A van?" Besides the baroness and the sentinels, he didn't see anyone else.

"No. We were sitting inside the Conclave," Kory answered over Claudia.

"Director, Deputy Harley is requesting entrance," Kellen reported over the radio.

Rutger clicked the mic and responded, "I'll let her in." Anger flared as he marched to his truck, opened the door, got in, and brought up the security screen for the Summit. He punched the number code, his personal pin number, and the gate jerked into motion.

The patrol car rolled through the entrance, down the two-lane road, and slowly toward them. Deputy Harley sat behind the wheel of the white SUV with its black hood and top and Paradise County seal glittering on its side. Her blonde hair was back and braided, and she wore her signature scowl etched on her face.

This will be fun, Rutger thought.

Deputy Harley didn't take the enforcers seriously, law enforcement in general didn't, let alone his position as director. As a state-regulated private security company, the Cascade pack's enforcer agency possessed the authority to patrol its lands. Applicants received tactical training, completed a physical fitness boot camp, fulfilled patrolling hours, and passed a criminal justice class, in addition to a paranormal history class before becoming an enforcer. Rutger had received more training, possessed more certificates, and was held to a higher standard than Deputy Harley, but she had gone through an academy and carried a badge. The sheriff's department saw the enforcers as non-humans who wanted to be tacticool. Nothing more than mall cops. Of course, the homicide investigation into the murdered witches hadn't helped him. Deputy Harley's lack of tolerance for Rutger quickly spread to the entire pack.

"Deputy Harley," Rutger greeted and waited.

"Director Kanin," Deputy Harley replied. Her hand rested on the butt of her Beretta 9mm holstered at her waist, her other hand held a small notebook.

That's new. She never addressed him as director; it would be respecting his position as a mall cop. "How can I help you?" he asked casually.

"One of the protesters reported you tried to run them down with your truck and then intimidated the others," she explained. Deputy Harley took a pen from her breast pocket, flipped through the pages, found one, and her ice blue gaze met Rutger.

"Negative, I did not try to run them down." *Intimidated, yes.*

"Do you have proof?" Deputy Harley asked.

"Affirmative. I can have the video sent to you," Rutger replied.

She sighed as if the call was a waste of her time. "I figured you did. I'll sit at the gate while everyone leaves. How many cars?" Deputy Harley asked. She replaced her notebook in the side pocket of her trousers, her pen in the pocket of her shirt, and met the gazes of the women present.

"Twenty-five cars. Thirty women," Claudia replied.

"Thank you. How's it going, Claudia?"

"Same shit different day. How's your day, Jessica?" Claudia asked.

"Same. Are you ready to leave?" Deputy Harley asked. A couple nodded their response, others said yes. They quickly dispersed and got into their vehicles. Looking at Rutger she said, "All right. Give me a minute. Are you going to open the gate?"

"Affirmative." Rutger watched her to go her patrol vehicle and when she started to turn around, he turned to Claudia. "Jessica?"

"I have my connects, Director." Claudia smiled, her hazel eyes swirling in forest green with slivers of a deeper emerald, and she walked to her car.

Of course she did, and no doubt the baron knew about every one of them. With a Pureblood werewolf father and Fae mother belonging to the family of fairies, it made Claudia a Illuminate-half werewolf and half magic-born. Her bloodline and magic gave her the ability to sense the extent of someone's power and their root magic. She often worked for the baron when magic-born from other factions visited Trinity or Foxwood.

The baron, taking advantage of Jo and Claudia's friendship, had Claudia spy on Jo when she returned after being gone for three years. Her boyfriend, Jason, one of the sentinels for the baron, was ordered to be Jo's shadow. Shadows were specially trained soldiers and enforcers-their objective was to get close to a specific target, watch the target and report back to the baron. The pair had proven their loyalty and their power to the baron, and he rewarded them.

"Rutger, you look worn out," Kory started as she approached him. She flipped her blond hair over her shoulder, and stopping in front of him, placed her hands on his chest. "Seeing you reminds me of how much I miss you. And... how good we were."

Rutger grabbed Kory's wrists, held them tightly, and removed her hands from his chest. He wanted to recoil from her touch, her closeness, like she violated him. "We were never good."

In a huff Kory jerked her hands from his hold, and stepped back. "Do you know why we're here? Because the pack is falling apart, divides are happening, and it's because of her. She is killing the pack. She is killing you. You look beaten. I'm not the only one who sees your demise and knows the once great Director of Enforcers is going down in a weakened heap of what use to be a powerful wolf. How long before others see the Second to the Alpha as weak? When the pack is divided how many will challenge the baron? The baron will lose you again and the pack will pay, again."

The Highguard won't let it happen. They need the baron to take care of the soothsayer. "Get in your car," Rutger ordered, ignoring her.

"I loved you, could love you again. She. Does. Not. I bet, she has never told you she loves you. She would have to love someone besides herself." Kory's voice began rising with her words, jealously lacing them, its static zapping the air between them.

'Jo was living in a nightmare,' he wanted to say in defense, but couldn't. Kory's words stabbed him in the heart and was a sword to his already wounded confidence. There was nothing he could say when they hadn't said they loved each other. There hadn't been time, and now there was silence. "Get in your car, Kory. Now."

"Director Kanin gave you an order. Get in your car," Claudia demanded. Several feet might separate them, but Rutger knew Claudia thought of it as her way of giving Kory a fighting chance. Her face said she wanted Kory to push her.

"Or what?" Kory spun around to face Claudia, her hands on her hips, her body tensing.

"I'll kick your ass. That's what." Claudia's eyes blazed emerald with her wolf, her power increasing and surrounding her. The Fae blood adding an electric edge. "You've been warned."

Kory's shoulders straightened for a second, like she might take the challenge and fight back, then her eyes went to the ground. A second ticked when she risked a look at Claudia from under her lashes. "Low class mutt," Kory mumbled. She gave Rutger a glare-intending on killing him with it-and strutted to her car.

"Sticks and stones." Claudia watched Kory making sure she got in her car, left the parking lot, and started toward the gate. When the cars were lined up behind Deputy Harley, she looked at Rutger. "Tell me you didn't entertain the thought."

He could see in her eyes; she thought he was broken and beaten and Kory was right. "I won't dignify that with a response." Rutger inhaled, struggled to understand the pain in his chest, and exhaled. "I don't need help from you. I had it handled." Yea, confusion and hurt held him like a vice.

"Making sure."

It was out there for the pack to judge, talk about, and add their twist to Rutger and Jo's lives. Fated mates. The baroness did her best to give the appropriate excuses for Jo's absence and for Rutger; she even tried to explain what fated mates meant. Rutger knew Claudia hadn't seen Jo in weeks but she had heard the rumors Jo was having a hard time dealing with having been kidnapped. Then when Jo thought she was safe, Flint came back. No one knew how to treat her so no one talked to her. Jo saw them staring at her with pity and uncertainty in their eyes.

Rutger took a step, hated seeing the pity in Claudia's stare, waited for her to join him and they walked to her car. "You can't threaten a pack member. Unless it's a formal challenge."

Claudia stopped at the driver's side door, faced Rutger, and smiled as if nothing had happened. "Come on. I really want to kick her ass, been provoking her for weeks. Don't ruin my fun." Claudia opened her car door and got inside. "Director."

As Rutger walked to his truck he shook his head, got in, and started the engine. He bet the baron was going to let Claudia do whatever she wanted if she continued to report to him. At the entrance, Deputy Harley waited, the women lined up behind her, and he went through the procedures to open the gate. Behind Claudia and bringing up the rear, he drove out of the Summit. Once through, Deputy Harley pulled her patrol car to the side of the road, and getting out, addressed the protesters. The baroness and her sentinels took lead with the women following while Kellen and Luke waited.

Rutger grabbed the radio. "We'll met back at Foxwood. I have to get a copy of the video to the sheriff's department."

"Affirmative." Luke drove off.

"Affirmative." Kellen drove off.

When they were on their way, he checked on Deputy Harley, found her with her pen and notebook, and talking to Bobby Joe. He didn't understand why they would protest in front of the Summit? How did they know there would be someone there? The Summit was usually empty. Had someone in the pack given them information? No. He wouldn't believe that ... yet. Was HAPI spying on them? Probably. It made the most sense.

When Rutger was in his office he would write the report, make a point to ask Deputy Harley if one of them told her why they were there, and replay the information to the baron. Rutger left the parking lot, waited for the gate to close, and headed back to Foxwood. Absently, he rubbed his chest where Kory laid her hands on him, and applying pressure felt the sting sink through his skin, bones, muscles, and flare inside of him. It burned like someone doused him with gasoline and lit it. Rutger cringed from the pain and the feeling Kory somehow assaulted him. His wolf howled in his ears, his heartbeat fought against his sternum, and instinctively he knew Jo would make it stop. He needed to see her. It almost made him turn around, but then he saw her eyes and the way she saw straight through him like he wasn't there. The office and his job needed him more than she did. Hell, his reports needed him more and he ignored them.

"Director."

Rutger jumped with Mandy's voice. Back to reality, he replied, "Go ahead." He was happy he sounded like the director-firm and not conflicted.

"There's been an alert at your house. The front camera read an unknown license plate and I can't get Jordyn on the phone," Mandy reported. "Could be nothing, but until I get the license plate back, and face recognition has an ID, I don't want to take the chance."

Neither do I. Damn you, Jo. "Understood. Send the alert to my console and notify me when the plate comes back. I'm en route." It should have gone to his cell automatically. He would have to check the system.

"Copy." Mandy was gone.

Rutger slowed, jerked his truck to the side of the two-lane road, and waited for traffic to pass. "Hurry the hell up." When the road cleared, he made a fast U turn and headed in the direction of his house.

It could be nothing. Right. Because people drove to his house all the time to visit a woman who doesn't have friends and never leaves. Rutger couldn't stop the kidnapping, Butte Springs, their past, her disconnect from life from eating him alive. Like acid to his skin it was going to destroy him while giving him visions of the past.

Jo.

His instincts invaded his dread and gave him possibilities he didn't want to think about. Rutger saw her kneeling in mud, the rain making her makeup run down her cheeks, and the tip of the gun barrel pressed to the side of her head.

No. Nothing is wrong, Rutger told himself. First the protesters, an actual anti-paranormal group named HAPI, and now there was an unknown car at his house. Were the two related? *Can't be possible. Don't let it be possible.* He touched the screen of his console and tapped Jo's cell phone number from the list. It rang once, twice, three times and he got her voicemail. Growling, he squeezed the steering wheel.

"Why do you have a fucking phone, if you never answer the damn thing?"

"Be advised the owner of the vehicle is Louis Myers out of Butterfly Valley, California."

Rutger didn't hear anything else Mandy reported after hearing Louis' name. A low growl vibrated his chest with instant fury. "Affirmative."

Jo's ex-boyfriend, a human who blamed Rutger for Jo's kidnapping, and had been trying to see her for months, making every excuse to meet with her. What the hell did Louis want? *Explains why Jo isn't answering her phone.* But why would she ignore his calls?

Because she's talking to her ex-boyfriend, the one who isn't planning on marking her and who doesn't have a day-to-day fight with his beast.

She has never told you she loves you.

Rage erupted. There were a million reasons why, and they had Rutger nearly crushing the steering wheel and turning his knuckles white. His wolf pulsed inside him, over him, and he felt himself losing control. Inhale. Exhale. Inhale. Exhale. *Control. Don't let the beast win.*

"FYI, when the alert came in, it triggered the system and automatically began recording. Sir, there is a second man present. Face recognition identifies him as Doctor Peter Holmes, founder of the anti-paranormal group HAPI. There's the leader of the protesters, sir. His file has been red flagged based on his affiliations with Patriot Angels," Mandy reported. "Do you want me to send an enforcer as backup?"

Fuck. "Affirmative. Aydian and Ansel," Rutger replied. He hesitated, having second thoughts about Aydian facing Dr. Holmes. There was a chance the doctor's presence might affect Aydian's performance and Rutger didn't want Aydian to escalate the situation.

"Sir?" Mandy's voice cracked.

"ASAP, priority one," Rutger responded. He needed Aydian.

Rutger gave Enforcer Kia Sato the job of conducting Aydian Collins' background investigation when he requested inclusion into the Cascade pack. When she gave him the completed file, Rutger reviewed the information, learning Aydian's past included an Army career and years with the organization Patriot Angels. Which sent a red flag and meant an immediate termination of the request.

Over four hundred years ago, when the Crimson years, the bloody battle between humans and non-humans came to an end, the non-humans were hunted down. Those lucky enough to escape went into hiding and became known as the Cloaked. The captured were sent to different states where they were forced to live in encampments. Five years turned into twenty, then into sixty, and during those years the encampments grew from hundreds to thousands. Their lives nearly forgotten allowed another thirty years to pass and the encampments grew into small cities, and home to tens of thousands. The increase in population, demand for supplies, and need for personnel caused a financial strain on the government. The cost and manpower required to operate the facilities became overwhelming at the same time several new generations of humans, learning about the Crimson years as a part of history, saw the encampments as antiquated. However, it didn't mean non-humans, magic-born, were equal to humans. The United States government created United Force; an agency specifically designed to deal with non-humans. UF implemented laws, sanctions, and restrictions to their rights and believing the non-humans were under control released them and abandoned the encampments.

Non-humans weren't satisfied with their limited freedom, so they created Resolution through Sedulity and fought the UF and the United States to gain back their rights. Their equal rights. After years of court battles and politically-driven agendas, non-humans were granted their equal rights and allowed to live in the open. Feeling they lost control over non-humans, the UF created Patriot Angels, an organization whose public purpose was to produce a cure for the therianthropy and lycanthropy viruses.

Protected by their quest for a cure the researchers experimented on the non-humans to find their weaknesses. Using media for their advertising, UF became nothing more than a propaganda machine to keep a divide between humans and non-humans.

Rutger turned off the highway, his tires squealing around the corner and onto Rock Cradle road. Further investigation uncovered Aydian's military background, the reason for his medical discharge, and explained his connection to PA. A right onto Collins Way, and Rutger pushed the truck to go faster as his thoughts circled Jo and the reason Louis was at their house. Did she let him in? And if so, why hadn't she answered Mandy's call?

Damn it, Jo. He tapped her number displayed on the screen of his console and the first ring filled the cab of the truck, like the second, third, and fourth, then her voice told him to leave a message. He hit the steering wheel with his fist.

To occupy his mind and keep from going crazy, Rutger's thoughts went Aydian. As part of an elite Army team, designed to eliminate non-human threats, the Black Wolves were sent to find and contain what they had named-despite them being mountain lions and not lions-the *Muah Pride*. The therians had turned savage, believed to be Bestial, and attacked a small mountain town in the Sierra Nevadas. After killing and eating the residents, they moved onto the next town. The Black Wolves followed the trail of bodies or what was left of the victims in two MRAPs. The team received a distress call and promptly responded and just as promptly the therians trapped the human team. The report stated it had taken two days for the therians to kill, eat, and torture the team. Humans against a pride of Bestial, cannibal therians. Damn fools.

The Army sent another elite team and a rescue team to find Black Wolf. The team succeeded in killing the therians and burned the bodies while the rescue team found Sergeant Aydian Collins. He was in an MRAP, clutching his empty rifle to his chest, was beat and bleeding, missing chunks of flesh and barely alive, and mumbling about cats. After a soldier pulled him from the vehicle and a medic had given him a light sedative, fluids, and protein, Sergeant Collins was coherent enough to explain in detail the events that had taken place. To secure the contaminated area, the soldiers called in air support and bombed two towns incinerating everything. Anyone, human or non-human seen trying to escape was gunned down.

Despite being bitten by a Bestial therian, Sergeant Collins hadn't been infected with the therianthrope virus. As a human, he spent six months in a hospital healing from his wounds and another six in a metal health facility. They classified him disabled, having diagnosed him with PTSD, chronic anger, emotional detachment, survivor guilt, and a fixation on cats. The facility documented him as unfit for duty, medically retired him, and added the report to the Citizen Base. Sergeant Collins-with an accomplished career in the Army-became Aydian Collins, damaged human, and was discharged.

Understanding he hadn't been infected and believing he might help their research, Patriot Angels intercepted him at the medical facility and took Aydian into custody. The report stated with Aydian's mental health problems he was a danger to himself and to society. PA promised they would give him a safe environment to adjust to civilian life, and after counselling he would be free to leave the institute. He was there for three days when they began injecting Aydian with the lycanthrope virus, eventually infecting him and making him a *Wight*. A half human, half shapeshifter. Wight meant a specified kind of magic-born, and was regarded as unfortunate, or a creature, due to having been infected or having a human parent. The shapeshifter population regarded the Wights as a weaker species. The strongest and most powerful being Purebloods, the second being Illuminates-half magic-born, half shapeshifter.

Aydian spent the next three years being experimented on until the government disbanded the organization. The *patients*, who hadn't been outside the walls of the Patriot Angels' facility in years were released. Aydian and his demons were living on the streets when an enforcer found him, detained him because he was a rogue-locked him up. Rutger interrogated Aydian, and the man requested inclusion. The pack took him in, gave him a place to live, and a job. His crystal blue eyes held a hard edge, he kept his sandy blond hair cut in a military style, and he had sculpted a muscled body from hours at the gym. Adding to his PTSD and chronic anger, he lacked a conscience, empathy, and viewed a situation with a cold edge. If Dr. Holmes had an active role with the remnants of PA, Rutger was personally going to make sure law enforcement found out and shut it down.

At Mill Creek road and he drove until he saw Ansel waiting in his sliver truck, the Cascade pack's crest on the doors, and Aydian in the passenger seat. Rutger nodded as he passed them, and watched Ansel pull in behind him. Entering his driveway, Louis' sedan came into view, and he couldn't stop wondering why he was there with a doctor. Months ago, when the human confronted Jo, he had called her a dog in heat, and turned his back on her because she was a werewolf. What the hell did he want? Rutger growled, the human parked his sedan behind Jo's SUV, trapping her.

Rutger stopped beside the sedan, killed the engine, and got out. Ansel parked behind Rutger and both enforcers exited the vehicle. Aydian didn't wait for orders, he automatically headed to the back of the house to cover the doors, while Ansel scanned the area with his senses. Rutger should have been inspecting the area for others, confirming whether or not Dr. Holmes had brought backup, but he wasn't. With the cocktail of anxiety and rage coursing through him, he marched in the direction of the house and the open door. The sight made his heart pound and his imagination go wild. Did Jo let them in? No. He couldn't believe that.

Leaves and pine needles drifted from the swaying tree limbs, as a rush of wind sounding like a river, sang through the tree tops. Drifting on the wind was the sound of waves crashing on the shore and dragging rocks in its clutches. Rutger heard nature but didn't hear people. Humans.

"The humans in the house are the only ones here," Ansel reported.

"Affirmative." Rutger didn't attempt to try and sense Jo; she hadn't let him feel her for months, it left the link between them a cold void. He focused on the house and the heartbeats inside.

Near the stairs, Rutger stopped as power flared in the link, its force unbalancing him and making the earth spin. *Jo.* He doubted she wanted him to feel her when she closed herself off but there she was. Her wolf rushed from her, slamming into him while her heartbeat thundered inside his head. Something was wrong. He had to get into the house. Another hesitant step. The earth spun, and he stopped.

"What is it?" Ansel asked. He placed his hand on the butt of his gun at the same time his eyes bled a deep bronze with his wolf.

"Inside. Need inside," Rutger mumbled through a growl. Jo's presence weakened, releasing Rutger from its claws. He didn't bother with the stairs. He leaped to the porch, and in two steps was through the open door. The details revealed themselves as the scene unfolded in slow motion. Jo hadn't changed out of her tank top and shorts, her hair was up, blood matted one side, and she wore her running shoes. She hated shoes.

If there was any doubt why Louis and Dr. Holmes were in his house, it vanished. They planned for the protestors to be at the Summit to distract Rutger and keep him there. Her absence from their link toyed with his mind and, seeing her in Louis' arms pushed slivers of resentment forward. Rutger knew she let them in their house. The betrayal was like a quick bite from a knife.

CHAPTER SIX

Louis met Rutger's glare with his own, wrapped his arm around Jo, bringing her closer to his body, and took an awkward step. Looking at him, he knew she wasn't seeing him and didn't know he was there. As if she was giving up, Jo's eyes closed, her knees buckled, and she sank to the floor. His mind raced trying to get past his resentment and assumptions to see the truth.

Rutger clamped his raging emotions and tried to look at the scene as the enforcer he was. Clarity graced him with its presence and he made his plan; first, he would deal with the humans, second, he would question Jo. No. Whatever clarity there was fractured when staring at him from a side table, behind the men, was a discarded syringe. Damn them. They drugged her. They were trying to kidnap her. His mind reeled from the thought. They were trying to take her from him. Dr. Holmes, founder of HAPI, with connections to Patriot Angels, was trying to kidnap his mate. *Mine*.

Jordyn struggled to keep her eyes open as she sagged in Louis' arms, her face smashed against his side, his scent invading her nose, and an inferno sweeping around her body. The sharpness of his fury mixed with his human weakness acted like toxic concoction and made nausea roll in her stomach. She strained to fight against the darkness crowding her mind, the haze the drugs created, and the pain eating her. Without her senses she felt blind. She wasn't going to make it and Rutger wasn't going to find her. Grasping onto the dark depression she had been living with, Jordyn gave up; her legs crumpled from under her and she sank lower. They were going to take her away from her home, Rutger, and her pack. It broke her heart. When Rutger came home he would find their messy house empty and believe she ran from him.

She would be damned if she looked any weaker in front of Louis. She hated him. The hate and anger didn't stop the tears from slipping down her cheeks from her loss. Regret clawed at her, and joining the drugs they began drowning her and she didn't stop them.

Jordyn drifted. Louis tugged on her smashing her face against his hip. He couldn't hold her up. She wanted to laugh, but it would end in tears. She wished she would go to sleep and never wake up. Her chest tightened like steel bands wrapped around her. The pressure increased, forcing tears from her eyes, and a moan from her lips, and when she thought her ribs were going to break from Louis' hold, Rutger's wolf charged through their link. The force hit her like a blast; his urgency flooding her as his thoughts pummeled her mind. *Mate. Protect. Mine.* Relief coursed through her and eased the worst of her panic.

He was there. He came for her.

Giving up wasn't an option. Jordyn dug her nails into Louis' arm, and using him as leverage tried to stand. The drugs threaded in her muscles, her strength failed, she dropped closer to the floor. She needed to see Rutger to make sure he was real and it wasn't a sad dream she created. Using the last of her energy to beat back the haze, Jordyn opened her eyes to meet his gold gaze and a face cut from stone.

He was furious.

She wanted to say she was sorry and beg for his forgiveness. She was sorry for running home and not talking to him when they were at Foxwood. Damn, she was sorry for not talking to him at all. She was sorry for leaving the door open, and for Louis. Dear god, Louis. What a mistake. With a dark copper gaze drowning in drugs, Jordyn held Rutger's stare, and whispered, "Wolf."

"Don't come any closer, Wolf Enforcer, and we won't hurt her," Dr. Holmes warned. His attention concentrated on Rutger, Wolf Enforcer, his gold eyes, his massive size, the black on black uniform, and gun holstered at his thigh. Slowly, as if trying not to alarm Rutger, his eyes moved to Ansel.

Wolf. The word cut through him making Rutger's wolf howl. *Stay with me babe*, he pleaded. As if mocking him, Jo's body went limp and she sagged in Louis' arms. *Keep it together.* "Give her to me," he ordered with a growl tangling his words. "Ansel, have dispatch call the sheriff's department and tell them Louis Myers and Dr. Holmes have trespassed and attempted to kidnap Jordyn. And I need Dr. Hyde."

"Copy." Ansel saw where the doctor's eyes had gone, and rested his hand on the butt of his gun as a warning, then tapped the side button on his radio. Dr. Holmes' confidence liquefied into fear, its weakness pouring from him.

Clearing his throat, Dr. Holmes gathered himself, and straightened his shoulders. "Rutger Kanin, Second to the Alpha of the Cascade clan, Jordyn Langston denounced you as her mate and has agreed to leave with us. She has chosen Louis Myers as her mate, eliminating your claim to her." Risking taking his eyes off Rutger, he looked at Louis. "We have to get out of here. Now."

Denounced? What the hell was he talking about? Rutger ignored his babbling, since he wasn't holding Jo, and wanted to tell them both he could sense lies. "Stop, Louis," Rutger ordered. His voice thundered in the room, making Louis flinch. *Cowards.*

"She told me, she loves me, Wolf Enforcer," Louis taunted, and took a step toward the French doors with Jo hanging from his arms. "She wants her life back."

Jo probably does. The flames scorching his chest seared across his torso to his back where the blaze met and crawled up his neck. *Lies. All lies.* It didn't stop the hurt and rage from flooding the void the breakdown in their relationship had created. Rutger's uncontrolled emotions charred the restraints he had on his beast. It stormed inside of him, feeding his hate, and Rutger wanted to kill them. He longed to see their blood spill and smell it on the air like metal rain.

Control. "You're not leaving with what's mine." Rutger took another step.

"*Yours*? Like she's a possession of some kind," Louis squealed. Fighting with Jo's body, her arms hung at her sides, and her knees nearly touched the floor. "Your pet."

"Mate," Rutger growled. He took several steps, his boots hitting the slate flooring, his hand on his gun. "Let her go."

Dr. Holmes eyes narrowed on the gun and he took a step back. "You can't shoot us. You would put your clan at risk ... again. How would it look if you were the suspect in another murder investigation? Try assault with a deadly weapon, and if you shoot me and I live, I will sue you and your clan, destroying everything. You can't stop us from taking the Pureblood."

"Yes, how would the baron react?" Louis sneered. "You belong in a cage!"

Louis' yelling pushed on his wolf and his patience. "You've trespassed on my territory and are holding my mate. Let go of her." His eyes had gone fully gold, holding a predatory weight, and his taut muscles turned his entire body into a piece of rebar. With a death grip on his control, he was doing everything he could to stop from shifting and attacking them.

"Law enforcement is en route. Dr. Hyde is en route. Enforcers are en route," Ansel reported.

Their house was about to be swarmed by his enforcers. His pack. "Give. Me. My. Mate."

"Soldiers are en route," Ansel continued. "Armed with rifles, they'll take their positions. Veto on less lethal."

"What's happening?" Louis asked. His bloodshot eyes darted to Rutger, Ansel, over to Dr. Holmes as his confidence drained from him.

"They're going to seize the house." He looked at Louis. "We're about to be overrun with lycans. Let the Pureblood go. We can't fight them, and I'm not getting between a possessed Wolf Enforcer and his mate. She isn't worth our lives. We have to get out of here before the cops arrive," Dr. Holmes urged.

He watched Rutger, saw his insanity in his gold wolf eyes, while Ansel's eyes bled to bronze. Rutger's focus narrowed, his senses sharpened, and he saw the hair stand up on the doctor's arms as his fear told Rutger he understood he had become their prey. "Give her to me."

"Jordyn is coming with us. You said she was coming with us," Louis insisted. "You said."

"Look at him," Dr. Holmes demanded as he pointed at Rutger. "Look at the lycan. I promise this isn't over, but the cops and their backup are on the way."

Awkwardly shifting Jo from his left arm to his right, Louis faced Rutger. "You can't stop me."

While Louis struggled to drag Jo, Dr. Holmes went to the French doors and opened the right side. Where he was going to go when there were at least thirty steps, and he would have to circle around the house to get to the car, Rutger didn't know. He watched Dr. Holmes stop, hesitate, and take a step backward as Aydian crossed the threshold ... his icy azar eyes in the shape of his wolf, and the barrel of his gun even with Dr. Holmes' face.

"Wrong way," Aydian growled, and bared his canines. "Take two steps back and go to your knees."

"No. I'm leaving." Dr. Holmes spun around and faced Rutger. "I'm leaving."

Aydian touched the barrel of the gun to the back of Dr. Holmes' head. "Go to your knees."

"You'll pay for this," Dr. Holmes protested as he knelt on the floor. "I'll press charges."

Rutger wanted to shake his head and throat punch the doctor, but that would make things worse. Instead, he ordered, "Ansel, cover Louis." Louis wasn't armed, wasn't a threat, but ordering Ansel to cover him, spiked Louis' fear making Rutger's wolf howl in victory.

"No. No. You're going to stay away from me, or I'll kill her," Louis threatened.

"You won't." His wolf crept over him, like a slow storm slithering over a mountain range, and he let the faint features of his wolf shape his face. The fire raging inside his chest spread down his spine and inched towards his hips. Need Jo. "Louis, if you don't take your hands off my mate, I will break every bone in your body. Slowly," Rutger threatened. His deep voice carrying a growl.

Despite the conflict and splintering control, he felt inside, his words were steady. Rutger stalked to Louis, and when he was within arm's reach, he towered over the shorter man. His muscled arms were twice the size of the professor's, his wide chest stronger, and Louis cringed from Rutger's closeness.

Leaning back, Louis tried putting distance between them while continuing to hold Jo. Had Rutger not been in pain, desperate to touch Jo, and make sure she was all right, he would have provoked him and enjoyed intimidating the human. Disappointingly, he didn't have the time; his body demanded Jo, and he needed to get her to safety. Rutger scooped her into his arms, as if she weighed nothing, and heard a gasp from Louis and Dr. Holmes. With Jo in his arms, he tightened his hold, squeezing her to his chest. The fire eased, his wolf backed down, and the link between them opened and a calm reached for him. *She knows I'm holding her.* Rutger held her tighter, her face by his neck, listened to her heartbeat, and felt her warmth.

"Director, Dr. Hyde is here," Ansel advised as he watched him. "The enforcers are here."

Rutger's shoulders hunched while the corded muscles of his arms showed through his long-sleeved shirt.

He didn't move. Couldn't move. Rutger stood there with Jo clasped to his chest, her warmth seeping into him, and her power flowing through them. Rutger didn't know how things were going to be when she woke up, didn't care. He would worry about it if and when they went back to the way they were, passing ghosts living in their tomb. Would this push Jo to finally break her silence and talk to him? Rutger clung to hope's cruel spirit.

Dr. Hyde rushed through the open door and paused with the sight of him holding Jo. She inhaled, masked the emotions passing over her face, calmed her nerves, and gently ordered, "Rutger, take Jordyn to your room and I'll check on her."

Rutger listened to the firm and calm order as she used their names and not their titles in her best doctor voice. Meeting her worried gaze, he saw Dr. Hyde had left Celestial in a rush. She wore a hoodie over her scrub top, a pair of pink scrub bottoms, and running shoes. He wasn't sure if she exuded assurance and authority. He tried talking, failed, and growled.

"Please take her upstairs," Dr. Hyde repeated.

Safely cradling Jo in his arms, and without a word-fearing he lost his voice-Rutger left Ansel, the doctor, and Louis. Obeying Dr. Hyde, he walked from the living room to the stairs where he stopped. The door hung open, letting a chilled breeze and the wail of sirens invade the house. The deputies were closing in on them. The enforcers had taken their positions. The soldiers were taking their positions in the tree houses, which were sniper points. He desperately needed to be alone with Jo.

With regret of what their lives had become, Rutger stepped to the first stair, and without Dr. Hyde, without anyone, he continued up the steps. He didn't notice the setting sun, the hues staining the October sky, or its reflection on the lake. It seemed the simplest of enjoyments he held onto were being stripped from him one by one.

I'll lose my mind if this continues.

"I hate lycans," Louis mumbled.

Stupid human, Rutger thought as he continued down the hall. He felt Louis' control on his anger, fear, and jealously turning to ash. He wouldn't act on his aggression …

no, he was at his core a coward. The doctor's presence gave Louis enough courage to make it inside the house while he left it to the doctor to drug Jo. The wave of emotions coming from Louis felt like they were trailing after him. No doubt the human hunted Jo down for revenge. To make sure she suffered the same embarrassment, pain, and disdain he thought he had. Maybe to avenge himself for the years she lied to him. To see her protected by Rutger and the entire pack crushed any confidence he would succeed.

"You are not very smart, are you?" Ansel asked. He met the gaze of the human and saw an echo in their depths. "You are surrounded by lycans." Ansel felt like he needed to explain the obvious to the human.

Mr. Myers cocked his head, his eyes wild with insanity. "Lycans," he whispered.

Ansel read his body language, sensed the frenzied emotions shooting from him like they were bullets, and knew Mr. Myers was losing his mind.

Sirens blared in the distance, their red and blue glow casting their colors on the woods. With human law enforcement approaching, Dr. Holmes stood making Aydian take a step back.

"We're human and human law enforcement is here. It'll be our word against yours." His narrow face and small eyes wore his arrogance and confidence.

Typical. "Dr. Holmes, we're aware you orchestrated the protest at the Summit, you're the founder behind the hate group HAPI, and we know about your history with Patriot Angels. Because of the threat level, you have been added to our watch list. As far as law enforcement is concerned, you were found in a Cascade pack member's house and after drugging the residence, attempted to kidnap her." Ansel watched the doctor's confidence falter.

Aydian stepped forward with his blue eyes gleaming like cobalt stones from his face. There was no emotion, just stillness and his sharpened human features. "Patriot Angels."

"Aydian, backdown," Ansel ordered. He should have kept that to himself. "We have his background information. Don't do anything here."

"Here?" Dr. Holmes asked with a grin. "Not anywhere."

"Keep telling yourself that," Aydian mocked.

Ansel saw a flash of rage blaze a path across Aydian's face the power of it adding weight to his glare. He wondered what Aydian was thinking about, was it PA's facility, being infected, experimented on for years, or how he was going to kill the doctor. Ansel bet it was a combination with emphasis on the last. Like a blast from a cold wind, Ansel felt Aydian's fury whip around him. Definitely thinking about killing the doctor.

Dr. Hyde cleared her throat, breaking through the standoff, then lightly touched Ansel's sleeve sending a shiver down his spine. He had to keep it together. She leaned closer and said, "I didn't touch the syringe to check its contents, but I smelled it. He gave the mistress a sedative, common in human hospitals. It's the dosage, I'm worried about."

"Mistress?" Mr. Myers questioned and grunted.

"Who gave Mistress the sedative?" Dr. Hyde asked.

"He did," Mr. Myers answered quickly and pointed. Failure and hopelessness creasing his pinched face.

Dr. Holmes cast Mr. Myers a look of disgust. "He lies."

"What was the dosage?" Dr. Hyde asked ignoring his denial.

"I don't know," Dr. Holmes scoffed as he dismissed her.

"Tell her," Ansel ordered. He pulled the gun a quarter from its holster and took a step forward. "Do I need to repeat myself?"

Dr. Holmes considered him, for a heartbeat, knew he wasn't going to get anywhere, and turned his egotism to Dr. Hyde. "You're a doctor, figure it out," he huffed. She took a step closer to him, her eyes in the shape of her wolf's. He stepped back, and stammered, "Enough for deep sedation. I wasn't counting on her being so thin."

Dr. Hyde smiled at him. "Wasn't that easy?"

"Get away from me," Dr. Holmes demanded.

"Dr. Hyde, when law enforcement arrives, you can explain it to them," Ansel advised. Neither man moved, they kept Mr. Myers and Dr. Holmes between them.

With Dr. Holmes' connection to Patriot Angels, no one needed to explain how quickly a werewolf's metabolism would burn through the drugs. Depending on the dosage, Jordyn's body would process it in a matter of hours. If she was struggling with the sedative, Dr. Hyde had a medicine to counteract the effects. However, if she was alert enough to shapeshift, shifting would purge the drugs from her system in seconds. Either way, nothing Dr. Holmes gave Jordyn would hurt her. Dr. Holmes hadn't intended on hurting her ... no, he wanted to take her somewhere else. They got there just in time. Who knows what Dr. Holmes would have done to her if he had succeeded?

"I'm going to check on the mistress," Dr. Hyde told Ansel.

"Copy." Ansel nodded but kept his gaze on Dr. Holmes.

Red, blue, and white twisted on the walls of the entrance while the sirens blasted into the house for several irritating minutes and cut off. A second later, an enforcer entered the house.

"Deputy Elm is here and requesting to speak with the director," Kellen reported.

"Where is he?" Ansel asked. He knew the deputy was being detained outside by enforcers and watched by the soldiers in the tree houses. For the benefit of Dr. Holmes and Mr. Myers, he wanted Kellen to explain when they were on pack territory enforcers were in charge.

"Waiting to be granted entrance. We have eyes on the visitors," he replied.

Ansel met the scared stares of Mr. Myers and Dr. Holmes. "Escort him in."

"Yes, sir."

"I'll get the director," Dr. Hyde offered.

"Are you a clan or a militant group?" Dr. Holmes questioned.

"Is there a difference?" Mr. Myers asked with disgust.

"Both." Ansel turned to Dr. Hyde meeting crystal blue eyes tinted with honey. He didn't know how he would react if Dr. Holmes had gone after her. "Copy."

"Where is Miss Langston?" Deputy Elm asked. His tawny brown eyes holding a level of sadness as he looked around the house. The same reaction everyone had.

"Deputy Elm, I'm Dr. Hyde from Celestial." She pulled her hospital badge from her pocket and showed the deputy. If he scanned it, a report of her position at the hospital, contact information, and genetics would be displayed on a screen. It would tell him she was Priority Alpha, member of the Cascade pack, and a *Wight*, half human, half shapeshifter. "Dr. Holmes gave her a sedative, rendering her unconscious. I'm confident the drugs are harmless but I'm going to evaluate her condition. Director Kanin took

Miss Langston to her room," Dr. Hyde explained. "After I see her, I can give you my statement."

"I would appreciate it," Deputy Elm replied. "You'll need to add the information to my report."

"Of Course. I'll tell Director Kanin you need to see him." Dr. Hyde gave the deputy a small smile, nodded to Ansel, saw the other enforcers at the door, and headed to the stairs.

Ansel watched Dr. Hyde as she crossed the loft, then Deputy Elm as he scanned the room, his glare landing on Mr. Myers and Dr. Holmes. No doubt, he was taking in the Cascade pack's enforcers and the others taking their positions as if they were a military unit.

Holding Ansel's gaze, he took the mic pinned at his shoulder. "Elm 16, requesting two units."

"Copy, Elm 16. Units en route."

CHAPTER SEVEN

Rutger unlaced Jo's running shoes one at a time, and taking them off, dropped them to the floor. Working on auto, he grabbed the thick comforter from the end of the bed and covered her to her waist. When she didn't react, he turned his attention to the dying fire and black coals. His thoughts, worries, and fears twisted inside of his head, making him crazy. Did she let them in? And if she had, why? Did she want to see him? Did she need to talk to him?

Yes, because I'm never here.

Rutger didn't know. He grabbed a piece of wood and fed the fire, then watched as its crimson and straw flames climbed over the bark. Outside, the ruby and golds of the evening sun glowed through the windows and French doors. He rubbed his chest, the fire increased, and he thought about going out on the deck, jumping off, and leaving.

He sensed Dr. Hyde at the door before she raised her hand and knocked three times.

"Come in."

The door slowly opened with a whisper, her footsteps sounded on the wood flooring, then she stopped and inhaled. Rutger knew what it was and cringed from embarrassment and failing as a strong mate. Dust covered every exposed surface while on the nightstand beside the bed were several water glasses, a couple of stacked plates, and to the left the closet door stood open, its contents leaking out. Shirts and pants clung to the arm of a chair where they had been thrown, their cuffs touching the wood flooring and abandoned socks. Plates of half eaten fruit and sandwiches were stacked on top of one another and littered a tabletop. When Jo retreated inside her head, she completely shut down and stopped taking care of herself, the house, her life. Rutger couldn't take watching her life drain from her, like a slow suicide, and left her alone.

"Has she said anything?" Dr. Hyde asked. The doctor was clearly struggling to concentrate on Jo's condition as she looked at the filth and chaos of the room.

"No. She is still unconscious. Jo hasn't moved," Rutger answered and turned from the fireplace. He heard the exhaustion in his voice. *I'm losing it.*

Dr. Hyde sat down beside Jo, held her thin wrist, sighed, then placed her fingers to the underside to listen to her heartbeat. "It's a common sedative. I would give her something to counteract the effects, but I think she needs the sleep."

He agreed. Dr. Hyde looked up at him, and he saw the pity and horror in her eyes that he saw in everyone's. His dark eyes looked hollow, his shoulders caved in, his wolf sat beneath the surface, and he felt his features sharpening.

"This, whatever is going on, is not healthy. The both of you need to talk to Dr. Carrion. And you need sleep, Director, doctor's order."

Dr. Carrion, Jo's therapist. He didn't think so. *Sleep.* Rutger closes his eyes and the images of Jo hanging upside down from a tree or her kneeling in the mud with a gun to her head tortured him. Even asleep, Rutger felt the emptiness in their bond. He didn't need the pain. He was better awake. "I'll work on it." Drawing his eyebrows Rutger stared at Jo and his heart ached.

"There's dried blood on the side of her head. What happened?" Dr. Hyde leaned over and searched beneath the matted hair, then looked at him.

Was she accusing him? "She trained today with Leo. He hit her," Rutger explained like he was defending himself. If she breaks, she'll heal. *No, she won't.*

"It's healed. I had to make sure." Dr. Hyde inhaled and exhaled. "Deputy Elm is downstairs. After you talk to him, everyone is leaving and you're staying home. I'll call the baron and make it a formal order, Director," Dr. Hyde threatened as she stood and stepped out of Rutger's way.

"You would." Rutger leaned down, his hands beside Jo, his weight sinking into the comforter, and stared at her black lashes against her pale cheeks. Her face held a softness, like peace, he hadn't seen in months. Was it possible for his touch to affect her? Jo calmed when he held her. *Wolf.* He kissed her lips, tasted her spice, and his wolf's grip eased and the fire searing his chest and insides receded. When he stood and faced Dr. Hyde, she was staring at him with a calculating blue gaze. "What?"

"You kissed her and her heart beat in response. The baron was telling the truth when he announced you as fated mates?" Dr. Hyde stared, her gaze switching between them.

Fated. Yes, they were. They shared their emotions through a link. Jo had shared her power, and they shared the magic that made them werewolves. "Yes." He didn't know if he was going to say more, the hierarchy of the pack had changed. The way they treated their acquaintances had changed. He didn't have anything to lose, and if Dr. Hyde believed it was possible, the others would believe. "Kory touched me today." He wanted to change his shirt because she touched it and wash his hands because he held her wrists.

"How?"

"She put her hands on my chest," Rutger confessed.

"I'm going to kick her ass," Dr. Hyde grated. "Sorry, Director."

He grunted at her apology. "You'll have to stand in line." He looked at Jo. "Her touch hurt. Like I was in the center of an inferno. Touching Jo made the pain end, she quenched the fire." Rutger knew he was talking like a Neanderthal, unable to describe what happened. Clearly. He faced Dr. Hyde. She understood his answer, and he saw the wonder in her usually confident eyes.

"It means things are changing?" Dr. Hyde asked.

The rumors about transitions among the magic-born spread like wildfire and made everyone question the future. What did it mean? How were their lives going to change? Human against magic-born. Magic-born against magic-born. The majority of the pack accepted the change and would follow the baron's lead. The others stated they liked their humanized existences, their luxury cars, careers, and houses. The changes were based on speculation, myths, and legends. Nothing solid. No proof. The baroness scheduled the meeting at the Summit to create a team to help sway the doubters in the pack. Dr. Hyde didn't wait for him to answer, he didn't have to.

She gave him a shielded gaze and walked over to Jo, met his questioning eyes, and placed her palm on Jo's chest. "No change." She waited longer. "Touch her." Dr. Hyde removed her hand and stared at him.

"Dr. Hyde," Rutger growled. The tension tightening his shoulders pulled his muscles taut enough to cause pain.

When things were calm and magic wasn't trying to change the world, the differences between strength and power of the alpha's family and the pack wavered on non-existent. No one challenged the baron because he was seen more as a mayor of a city than the alpha keeping a pack of a thousand organized and the klatch nearing eight hundred magic-born civilized. The baron and the director were men doing their jobs, but right then he reminded Dr. Hyde of her place. She was a member of the pack.

Her shoulders caved slightly with his authority, his sharp tone, and the scowl he wore. Then she straightened and met his glare. "Don't growl at me. You want the pack to believe we're changing and there's an unknown threat coming, right. That we have to be prepared to face obstacles which might take away what we've worked to have ... our normal lives without being persecuted? It's not a secret, there's a divide happening within the pack. Those who believe in the baron and believe what he is saying is true and stand behind him, without question. Then there are those who don't, and won't stand behind him. The divide will weaken the pack and put the baron's position at risk as well as all of our lives. All magic-born associated with Cascade. Rutger, the doubters don't want to believe and they're using Jordyn, her absence, and the threat of the Highguard to sway others. If there isn't proof, they'll recommend the baron be removed and have vote of no confidence. Now touch her."

Rutger hesitated. He looked at Jo while Dr. Hyde's words sank in and the truth sat in front of him. Kory had threatened him with the divide, saying it was Jo's fault. They couldn't put the pack in danger. He stepped around

Dr. Hyde, then gingerly, like he would hurt Jo, he held her hand.

"There was a slight change. She knows it's you. Touch her like a mate would. A lover," Dr. Hyde demanded. She watched him with analyzing eyes, her thoughts racing behind the crystal blue.

After Jo was released from Celestial, Rutger didn't touch her for fear, he would lose control and hurt her. Mark her against her will. He hadn't touched her in the preceding months, and once Jo understood he wouldn't, she cut him out of her life and lived in her head. When she closed herself off from him and became a ghost in his life, he willingly embraced the numbness created by their separation. Despite the pain and the void.

Rutger drew a slow breath, his heart dropping to his knees, and dreaded what he was going to feel. Jo was going to react to him, he knew this, but was unsure if she would accept him when she woke up. Rutger wanted to feel Jo's passion, desire, and need, and he wanted it to flow between them unrestrained. He needed her to call his wolf.

"Do it." Dr. Hyde inched closer.

Rutger sat on the side of the bed, his weight bringing Jo closer to his hip, her body touching him. He twisted and reaching for her, held her throat. His thumb feathered her lips, while the tension of her muscles danced against his fingers. He tightened his hold, lowered his thumb to the underneath of her jaw, and squeezed. The link lit up with their wolves and Rutger let his power find Jo.

"Her heartbeat is pounding. And it matches yours," Dr. Hyde mumbled.

"I know." *I can feel it.* Closing his eyes, Rutger held onto the connection he feared of losing.

"Director, they want you downstairs," Ansel reported as he entered the room. Rutger's large frame was over Jordyn and he was holding her throat. "Sorry, I didn't mean to interrupt."

"I'm on my way," Rutger replied automatically. He didn't want to let her go.

He had to face the deputies, the baron, and the questions coming from every direction about what happened. What did happen? Why did she let them in? He didn't have the answers and didn't know what he was going to say. He needed to see the video. To prove Jo let them in. To prove somehow, they disabled the alarm. Rutger wasn't sure what he wanted to know. One second ticked, another, and another, when he gently released Jo, and stood. A tinge of despair threaded around her, its urgency begging Rutger to stay, and slowly faded. He would be back and he wouldn't leave.

"Deputy Elm called for backup and a transport for Mr. Myers and Dr. Holmes. He is waiting to question you," Ansel explained. "I told him we had surveillance cameras and video for him."

"Noted." Rutger paused. "I want to see the video before we hand it over."

"Affirmative. Do you want me to have it sent to you here?" Ansel asked.

"Negative. Tomorrow, I'll go to the office. What happened here and the protestors at the Summit are connected. Deputy Harley is going to need video from the Summit," Rutger answered. He hesitated, turned enough to see Jo hadn't woken or moved, and giving Dr. Hyde and Ansel a shadowed stare, headed to the bedroom door.

"Director, she's going to be all right. Take care of your business, then come back. She needs to know you're here,"

Dr. Hyde advised. As if she were speaking to a child, her voice became the calm, assuring sound of a doctor.

He didn't need to be handled as if he was going to break. Without facing Dr. Hyde or Ansel, Rutger replied, "I will." He left the room, made his way down the hall, his gait showing the damage from stress and lack of sleep, and the depth of his exhaustion. Behind him, Dr. Hyde whispered her argument to Ansel about his departure. *Good luck, Ansel.*

"I told him he needed to stay here with the mistress. It's important he's here. Jordyn needs him close to her if she is to get stronger," Dr. Hyde stressed.

"No one orders Director Kanin around." Ansel thought about what he said. "Except his mate."

"Right. Speaking of which, she doesn't need us in her room." Dr. Hyde checked on the mistress one last time, listening to her breathing, her heartbeat, and started out of the room.

Ansel followed, stopped, closed the door, and waited for Dr. Hyde to lead the way. He wished he was able to talk to her, freely. Together, they walked down the hall. It opened to the downstairs, living room, and faced a bank of windows with sweeping views of the lake. Like they were capable of stealing the brightness from the sunset's amber and rose smearing the cerulean sky, Deputy Elm and Deputy Bodie recited the Miranda warnings. Each stood behind one of the men while they placed Mr. Myers and Dr. Holmes in handcuffs.

How did human law enforcement workout for you, doctor? Flanked by Aydian, Luke, and Kellen, Rutger stood back, his shoulders bunching from strain under his shirt as

he watched the deputies, his gold gaze targeting Mr. Myers.

Ansel couldn't imagine the amount of self-control it was taking Rutger to keep his wolf from emerging after wit-nessing a human hold his unconsciousness mate. Then standby while the humans walked out of Rutger's house. His territory. At the least, the humans should have been beaten for trespassing on pack territory and harming one of their own. Beaten and left for dead. Ansel stopped at the stairs and observed Rutger. He feared his friend and pack brother was slowly decomposing from the pain they en-dured and the emotional scars left like untreated lesions. When would it end?

"Dr. Hyde, is Jordyn going to be all right?" Ansel asked as he stared. "I don't mean physically. I mean, is this going to damage her further?"

This wasn't a conversation between the pack's doctor and the captain of their enforcers, it changed when he feared Dr. Hyde was his mate. After what they had been through, he wouldn't put her life in danger. He straight-ened and changed his demeanor. This was between pack mates who were concerned about their kin. A silent strength gave into his concern as Ansel's eyes softened with his worry. If Jordyn suffered the same way she had at Butte Springs, Rutger would slip further into himself, allow-ing the beast to control more of him. If he lost control and submitted to the beast and became fully *Bestial,* the magic powering the symbiotic relationship between man and wolf would become corrupted, and like poison saturate his body, warping his mind and destroying the balance they shared. The shadow of his wolf would encase him and the shift would sweep over him and turn him into a half man, half wolf humanoid. The beast's primal instincts would drive him mad.

Saving Rutger from being caged and observed had become Ansel's responsibility. Rutger was Second to the Alpha, Director of Enforcers, and fated mate to their soothsayer. It was well known he had been ordered by Prime to mark his mate and it made him a danger to Jordyn. With his need to mark her and driven by primal instincts and blood lust, there was a chance he would force himself on Jordyn, take her throat and kill her. Her death would touch him through their link, and driving him harder he would move on and kill whoever tried to stop him. Rutger the man would be gone, he would lose himself, Jordyn, his place as director, and his kith. The baron wouldn't risk the lives of his kith and kin, the klatch, the magic-born, or the innocent humans of Trinity; he would imprison Rutger for the rest of his life. Once Bestial and caged, Rutger's life would be measured in hours not days.

"I know you're worried about Rutger and his reaction to what happened to Jordyn. While I don't know what actually happened, I don't believe she will regress. I hate saying this, despite their intention of kidnapping her, giving her a sedative was the best thing they could have done. She needed sleep and now she is sleeping. Jordyn is stronger than we give her credit for. In fact, Rutger's wolf was hovering over him, twisting his human features, when Jordyn calmed him down. The shadow of his wolf faded and he gained control. That's why I need him here."

"How?" Ansel questioned. "She's unconscious." He wanted to believe what Dr. Hyde was saying, but couldn't let hope and its painful disappointment consume him.

Dr. Hyde looked down at the living room as the deputies escorted the handcuffed Mr. Myers and Dr. Holmes out of the house. "I know the Highguard with the court, and lords and ladies, keep the old ways, and think they're superior to us. Maybe having a soothsayer and a fated pair, is like having a part of ancient times in the pack and something in common with the Highguard. But I have never believed it, and did not believe it when the baron announced Jordyn as the soothsayer, let alone their relationship had been fated." Dr. Hyde hesitated, doubting how to proceed and regretting having admitted to an enforcer, she doubted the baron even if it was Ansel.

"Ignoring my doubt and trusting my alpha, I've done some research to prove the possibility to myself. True fated mates have a bond, like a link to one another's essences. They can *feel* the other. Imagine you don't have to use your werewolf senses ... instead, you reach for the link and feel your mate's essence."

Ansel didn't want to feel anything. He lived in a permanent state of stress from watching Rutger withdraw and Jordyn cut herself from the pack. The fear of losing his kin sat in his stomach like a heavy knot. He didn't know if he wanted to hear what Dr. Hyde was going to say. Maybe if he understood what the hell was happening, he could help them. "Explain."

"They call it *moira*, the word is Greek, meaning destiny, share, and fate, and obviously has a relationship with Greek mythology. We would know the myth as the Fates, they were white-robed manifestations of destiny. I explained this to you to emphasize how old this is. Greek mythology, according to my resources, is over two thousand years old. Two thousand years," she mumbled the last part. Dr. Hyde inhaled and exhaled.

When did magic die and when did the world humanize? Ansel watched the deputies, enforcers, and Rutger. Magic didn't die, it had gone underground like the Cloaked, the magic-born living in hiding. It was waiting. Had been waiting, he corrected, it wasn't waiting any longer. It was making its presence known little by little and through people he considered kin. Rutger. Jordyn. Himself. Dr. Hyde.

"Jordyn knew the difference between when I touched her and when Rutger touched her. It wasn't a reflex reaction and I know Rutger felt their link and they shared something because she calmed him. I'm telling you as a medical doctor, I have doubted it, but as a werewolf, I felt their power and their wolves. I believe them. I believe the baron. Now I don't know if I'm jealous of them or if I pity them."

Ansel held Dr. Hyde's crystal blue eyes and saw her worry. "Pity. It's a curse." Dr. Hyde hadn't given him anything that would help Rutger. She made it worse. Ansel stepped around her and headed downstairs.

CHAPTER EIGHT

A scream pierced Rutger's sleep as if someone was stabbing him with ice picks and the hurt in the cry rang in his ears. He jolted awake, sat up, the blanket falling to his lap, and his bare feet hit the floor. He strained to see through the night-darkened room, and barely saw her shadow as she sank into the bed. He had been asleep for twenty-five minutes. Five minutes longer than the last time.

Across from him the fire had dimmed, the glowing red coals the room's only light. He tossed the blanket to the arm of the chair, stood, and padded over to the bed where Jo was lying on her side and gripping the comforter in both fists. Her face may have been hidden by a pillow, but he knew tears were streaming from her closed eyes. Her soft cries made his heart ache as her chest heaved with her breathes. Jo hadn't woken and hadn't said a word, even when he tried to shake her from the nightmare. Not one word. Her fitful sleep ended in screams, then she collapsed to the bed and cried. The sharp edge and soft sound of her whimpers broke him down until he wanted to run from the room.

Glancing at his watch, he saw it was closing in on five o'clock in the morning. "Ten hours, Jo. You've been having a nightmare for ten hours."

In response, Jo cried.

Rutger gently removed the pillow from covering her face, placed it against the headboard, and sitting on the bed with his back on the pillow, pulled Jo to his lap. He sank his strength into their link, as she curled into him, and letting go of the comforter, clutched his T-shirt. Her face rested in the center of his chest, her tears staining the pale gray cotton.

"Jo, babe. Please wake up," Rutger pleaded.

Jo cried.

Rutger held her shuddering body, praying she would wake up or stop crying, he didn't care which. He thought he was exhausted before, but the near kidnapping, and toll Jo's nightmare was taking from his body, he could feel himself deteriorating. With gentle sweeps, his hand caressed up and down her back, along her thigh, and up her spine, hoping it calmed her down. If the nightmare didn't end, he was going to call Dr. Hyde. The drugs should have worn off and she should have woken up. Trapped in the nightmare, he doubted Jo knew he was there, and the longer it continued the harder it would be for her to wake up.

"Babe, please," Rutger whispered.

Jo mumbled words in response, nothing he could understand, tugged at his shirt for a couple seconds, and letting go of him, relaxed into him. She stopped crying. Exhaling, Rutger held her and waited. When he was sure Jo was sleeping, he eased her back to the bed and covered her with the blanket. With exhaustion pulling on him, Rutger leaned heavy against the pillow and headboard, his muscles begging to release the tension gripping them, and drifted off. Quickly images of Jo, Louis, and Dr. Holmes colored his dream.

"Who would fuck a lycan?" Louis' voice echoed off her skull. His scent sank into her nose and incinerated her brain while the fire from his touch spread up her arms.

"Purification." Dr. Holmes' glared at her over his mask peppered with blood and his scarlet-stained gloves.

No. No. They weren't going to take her and torture her, she wouldn't survive. Claws dug into her arms, sides, and thighs making her scream from the pain. While she cried, they jerked her out of the nightmare, and she felt her skin tear as their wings and scales from their thick bodies grazed her insides. They wrapped around her wolf, tightened their hold, and squeezed. Their long necks curved up and over her, and eyes like obsidian stones stared at her from several large, scaled heads. Her wolf howled from the pain, and Jordyn was sure she was going to suffocate in their grasp. With her struggle to escape their claws, they dug deeper, and a searing sting laced her insides. *Please.* She would beg, plead, do anything to get away from the dragons and free her wolf. The pressure increased. Jordyn's desperation was going to force her to use her wolf and magic. She hated to do it, feeling like she was betraying herself. Her wolf, magic, power, they were the reason her life had been turned into chaos. Sad chaos. The dragons roared inside of her head, dug their claws in, and continued to squeeze.

She couldn't fight the dragons as they tore her sides, pulled her arms in opposite directions, while their claws slashed her thighs. Her screams drowning under the pain and their roars. Left with nothing, Jordyn raised her magic, building its force, and when she thought she would ex- plode, she released a blast. The dragon's claws retracted, her body jerked, and suspended for a breath, they let her free fall. Falling and falling, she closed her eyes and stopped. She remained still, her eyes closed, her limbs limp, her heart racing, her power coursing through her like an electrical current, and her wolf close to her. Warmth swamped her and she held onto the strength of her magic.

Why did she feel like she failed? Because she was ignoring her relationship, Dr. Holmes drugged her, and Louis' scent was on her. As her failures mounted, Rutger's essence weaved through her. *Wolf?* It wasn't real. His mahogany eyes bled gold, their shape changing from human to wolf. *Wolf.* He came for her. Jordyn saw Rutger's blurred outline, heard his deep voice, tried to stay conscious, and failed.

Despite drowning in darkness, she felt his arms on her, like metal bands, as he clutched her to his chest, trying to get her as close to him as possible. Jordyn breathed deep, inhaling his rich scent unique to him, sensed his wolf, and releasing her grip on the wall she put between them, his power rushed over her. Jordyn blocked him out and cut herself off from his strength, and it was killing her. She had been lost at sea and bobbing helplessly in every direction but the right one. Toward Flint. Toward uncontrolled fear. It had changed, the lost had been found and she wasn't going to lose Rutger.

Jordyn crawled out of the swamp of sleep, and nearly awake, rolled to her side and tucked her arm under her head. Cozy and having Rutger's scent on her, she felt the warmth from sunlight on the side of her face. The swamp tried tugging her back into the deep to bury her in the sludge at its bottom. She struggled; enough slivers of her memories riddled her thoughts and images of the day flooded her eyes. Jordyn shot up, sitting straight, and expected to see Louis and Dr. Holmes standing in front of her. Sunlight blazed through the windows of her bedroom, and she realized she was in bed, it was morning, and she was alone. He left her by herself after an attempted kidnapping. Her heart sank. Couldn't wait to get away from the victim she had become. She stopped, refusing to feel sorry for herself, and focused on the fact he saved her from becoming an experiment. At least he saved her from Louis. After the way she treated him, she deserved to be left alone.

Jordyn looked around her room and saw the mess through clear eyes the same way she had when Louis criticized her. She cringed, then looked at the window. The sun held the sky telling her it was morning. The next day. What happened to Louis and Dr. Holmes? Rutger and his enforcers happened. Jordyn couldn't remember the details and what happened after Rutger arrived. While she forced the information from her fogged encased brain, she absently rubbed her wrists. Realizing what she was doing, she expected fire to erupt. Louis' touch hurt her. Burned her. Rutger held her, eased the pain, and made it a memory. She held her hands out, turned them over to check her entire wrists and wouldn't have been surprised to see scars from burns. There was nothing. *Right.*

"Calm down. Think," Jordyn whispered. Dr. Holmes drugged her. Louis threatened her. Pushing through the haze, she felt Rutger before she saw him. He looked on her with gold wolf eyes, and then he disappeared. "Because the asshole drugged me." *Like the others.*

The others. Shit, she knew where Dr. Holmes' facility was and where he kept his captives. Jordyn had to tell someone. Now.

Kicking the comforter off, she looked down at her clothing and flinched when she saw she had slept in her gym gear. Her hair was up, at least part of it, as was the dried blood from training. She was a mess. Frist thing, she needed to take a shower and change before explaining, to human law enforcement, a professor and a doctor from the university were kidnapping shapeshifters and the magicborn and experimenting on them.

How did you get the information?

I read his mind, of course. With the past couple of months and my mental health history, if they lock me up for being crazy, I won't be surprised.

Jordyn needed to be smart about the information she gave the sheriff's department. The homicide detective had doubted Flint committed suicide, suspecting she and Rutger had something to do with it. If Jordyn exposed her secret, they would know for sure she was responsible and reopen the investigation. If they found out she lied, they would dig deeper and suspect Rutger of lying. Punishment for hunting and killing the witches would be swift and end with their public arrests, trials, and then their death sentences. Jordyn shrugged. At least the Highguard wouldn't be a problem. *Stop.*

She swung her legs off the bed, waited for the threads of nausea, but like the fire on her wrists there was none. She would swear she felt better than she had in months and she felt her energy returning.

It's sleep. She slept through the night, without waking nightmares. With Louis' invasion she cast off the shackles of fear and guilt. It was sad, she would have to thank him for challenging her, forcing her to change her life, and for the sleep. After that, she was going to make sure he didn't hurt anyone else ever again. Jordyn grinned with her thoughts, the pull on her face seeming foreign, and she cursed.

Nearly four months wasted because she felt sorry for herself, and who did she hurt? Rutger. Its force rushed over her with the confession. His heartache, helplessness, sorrow, and pain of watching her decline day after day, and believing he lost her, sat thick inside of her. He faced losing his mate for a second time. Jordyn strode over to the overstuffed chair by the fireplace and lifted the blanket from the arm, and brought it to her face. Rutger. She felt his closeness throughout the night as he slept across from her.

While holding the blanket to her face, Jordyn looked in the direction of the door. Where did Rutger go? The office. He was always at the office. Part of her wanted him to be home with her and part of her was thankful he wasn't. She had reservations about facing him. There were things she needed to sort out before confronting her mate. *Where do I start with him?*

Think about it later. To confirm he wasn't home, she sent her senses out to search. No one. She was alone. Her thoughts headed toward the dark side and she stopped herself. She had a plan and this was her opportunity.

In search of her cell, Jordyn headed out of her room and barefoot, practically broke into a run down the stairs to her gym bag. She rifled around a hoodie, pair of socks, flip flops, and an extra hair band, and finally found her cell phone. To cover herself, she needed to make some calls and set up the background for the information she was going to hand over when she called the sheriff's department. Then she was going to have to actually call the sheriff's department.

Three calls, fifteen minutes, and several 'I can't believe what happened to you' later, Jordyn had the information she needed and a foundation for having started her inquires. Proud of herself, she sat back on the couch, watched the fire, and struggled to not over think what she was doing. She was covering herself, Rutger, and the pack, to save innocent magic-born.

"Get it over with." Her finger hovered over the keypad; her fear was working on her, and she thought about waiting. No. Jordyn called the sheriff's department.

After explaining who she was and why she was calling, the receptionist directed her to the deputy in charge of the case, Deputy Elm. He was thankful she was all right, expressed his gratitude she was ready to talk to him, then gave her time to explain. He asked if she could meet with him in person, at the station, making a formal statement and answer some questions about Louis. Jordyn, with her heart pounding and her pulse in her ears, readily agreed.

The third task. Jordyn would deal with that when she returned from the station. She studied the screen of her cell as if the notifications were going to answer her questions then take the day before and toss it anywhere but near her. Maybe it would explain why people had a thing with kidnapping her. They saw her as weak. *Damn.* The missed calls, voicemails, and messages from Rutger and Mandy mocked her. Jordyn tossed the cell to the cushion, took her coffee cup from the table, and drank deep. *I'm not going to back down.*

When the last drop of roasted liquid slipped down her throat, Jordyn couldn't stall any longer. She left the couch, entered the kitchen, and placed her mug in the sink where six other mugs, a variety of plates, and a pot sat in cold dirty water. She needed to get her life back on track. She turned, putting the sink and dishes behind her, and made her way to the stairs. As she headed up to her room, her mind raced with what she had to do.

Jordyn walked through her room, hated seeing the mess, and took her clothes off. She tossed the bundle in the overflowing basket in the bathroom and turned the handle in the shower. A cascade fell from the showerhead, the hot water instantly creating a haze of stream. She turned it hotter, wanting Louis' scent and touch seared from her skin.

They hadn't taken her. They hadn't hurt her. Remembering what it felt like when anger sparked the dying fire inside her, she grasped it with determination. It was time to make sure they didn't do it to anyone else.

"Face your fucking fears," Jordyn growled as she stepped under the spray.

Rutger set the pen down and looked at his cell phone. No calls. No messages. When were they going to have the video feed ready? He needed to get it to Deputy Elm. Although the deputy believed everything Rutger told him, and Louis confessed his part, the video evidence wouldn't leave it up to human versus lycan. He hoped it would also prolong their jail time.

Selfishly, Rutger wanted to know what the hell happened. Did Jo let them in? Into *their* house. Not that he had been home much. Did she need someone to talk to? Did she want to talk to Louis? He was going to lose his mind if he saw Jo respond to Louis only to have him betray her and drug her. He could hear Louis promising her anything she wanted. Like a safe environment free from the pack, safe from the Highguard, and a mate too weak to control his wolf.

Luke leaned in the door. "Director, the video is ready. The baron is waiting for you in the communications room."

Rutger stopped himself from jumping. "Thank you. I'll be there in a minute," he replied. He didn't want to view the video with an audience. What were they going to see? How were they going to judge him? He left Jo alone after an attempted kidnapping.

"Tabby told me to give this to you." Luke set a stack of envelopes on the corner of the desk.

Tabby worked at the front of the office serving as the receptionist and gate keeper. If someone scheduled an appointment with Rutger, the baron, or one of the enforcers she notified the person, admitted the visitor, and completed the proper paperwork. Tabby also received the mail and dispersed it among the offices and the baron.

Rutger looked at the stack; he didn't need additional papers on his desk. "Thanks."

When Luke left the office, he closed the door behind him and his footsteps sounded down the hall. He didn't care what was in the stack, he hadn't read through the reports and mail already littering his desk. He groaned as he picked the letters up anyway, absently flipped through the envelopes, and hoped it killed a couple of minutes. His heart stopped in his chest when he stared at a crisp white envelope with scarlet writing. He held his breath, his lungs seized, and every muscle froze. He had been given a similar letter before. When Shadow Lord explained he found the bodies of the witches Rutger murdered and placed them at the tree where Flint planned on killing Jo. Shadow Lord used it to blackmail Rutger. If this was his demands, Rutger didn't know what he was going to do.

Exhaling a rough breath, he shoved the unopened letter in a drawer. He had a video to watch, and grabbing his cell stared at the blank screen, save for the background picture of Jo. Would she call him when she woke up? Not if she was going back to being a ghost in his life. Would she think he abandoned her after an attempted kidnapping? He left after he locked every door and window and checked them three times to make sure, and checked the control panel in the bedroom, entryway, living room, and kitchen. All lights blinked green. He hated leaving, convincing himself he was going home right after he watched the video.

That depended on what he saw.

I left out of fear. Fear of Jo not needing me. Coward. He shoved the cell in his shirt pocket.

Rutger headed to the communications room with Louis and Jo on his mind. When her nightmares consumed her sleep, he rushed to her, crawled onto the bed, and pulled her to his chest, and held her. She needed him then, at her weakest when she was unconscious and unable to tell him to leave her alone or walk away from him. Her tears slid down her cheeks, while her entire body trembled with the effects of the nightmare, making his chest ache. Rutger knew whatever was causing the amount of fear she was experiencing it was also killing the remaining shreds of the old Jo. He was going to lose the woman he loved. He hadn't told her he loved her. The chance had been taken from him. Stolen.

"Rutger," Healey greeted. "How was your night? Is Jordyn all right?"

Rough. "Baron," he greeted. "As good as can be expected." *He didn't know how she was.* Rutger stood at the back of the room, behind the baron, Ansel, and Luke, noticing his team, Kellen, Aydian, Kia, and Quinn were absent. At least they weren't there to witness his demise.

Lying. Healey gave him a narrowed gaze and faced Mandy. "Mandy, play the video."

"Sir." Mandy started typing and the wall-mounted screen blinked, then a clear picture of the front of Rutger's house filled the screen. "This is after Mr. Myers parked his car, you can see Dr. Holmes is just existing the vehicle."

Louis stood staring at the open door, a smile curving his lips as he waited for Dr. Holmes. Flanking the stairs, two logs, each vertical stood from the ground and stopped at the roof of the porch. Dead flowers in different colored pots sat on the left side of the steps, pine needles covered the sidewalk and the first stair. Rutger hadn't notice how unkept his house looked. He would have to be home to see it.

"Looks like Jordyn never closed the door. I have her deactivating the code eleven minutes earlier. It was never reactivated," Mandy explained.

Jo didn't let them in. What had her distracted, she couldn't close the damn door? Jo confessed Lady Sloan was her mother. She hated training. The Baron convinced her to continue training. *Me,* Rutger thought. He shifted as nervous energy flowed through him. He didn't want to watch.

"When the license plate came back to Mr. Myers, I checked the list, found him, then started emergency protocol. It immediately engaged the interior system. From here there will be audio," Mandy advised.

No one was having a repeat of law enforcement doubting them, the way they had when Flint forced Jo from her home.

When Rutger stared forward and remained silent, Healey replied, "Understood."

The picture cleared, and they watched Louis enter the house, stop, and watch Jo. She was kneeling in front of the fire, watching the flames, and he could hear her whispers over her crying. With the scene and the weak sobbing, the communications room went quiet. A dead silence. A feather could have landed on the tile and it would have sounded like an explosion. No one moved when Rutger took a step forward. He felt invaded and exposed. They were watching Jo. Louis was watching Jo cry.

"Fix what?" Louis asked.

Jo stood and spun around, shock on her face, her tears glittering in the sunlight. "Louis?"

"Lost in thought, Jordyn? Or is it Jo, now?" Louis charged, his condescending tone belittling her. He walked through their house and stopped at the edge of the living room, looking relaxed, at home, when he asked, "Why are you crying."

Louis said something else, but it was lost in the fury the simple question sparked and the rush of blood flooding Rutger's ears. He should have been there. He needed to break the vow of silence they lived with and tell her how he felt. *I can't go on without her.*

In defiance, Jo didn't wipe the tears from her cheeks. She visibly gathered herself and asked how he got in. Rutger couldn't believe the relief he felt knowing she hadn't let him in. Louis mocked the security system then called Jo's rental in Butterfly Valley a hovel, while he leisurely judged their home.

Louis' calm exterior slipped when he saw the photo-graph on the fireplace mantel. Quickly recovering, his attention was on the stairs. "And you've kept up with the house keeping. You have nothing here." Without waiting for Jo to respond, he backed up to look at the bar. "A bar? Rutger Kanin must be a real renaissance man. Does he toss a few back then howl at the moon? Do you throw caution to the wind, let the lycan loose and join him?"

"I don't see a problem with tossing a few back and howling at the moon," Luke commented.

Healey's dark gold glare narrowed, brows drawn in si-lent warning as he looked at Luke and back to the monitor.

Rutger looked at his house. It was his house. Jo's things were in a storage unit and neither one of them talked about getting them out. It was like she was living out of a suitcase, never making the house her home. Did she think of it as her home? Or his house? Or her prison?

"Louis, why are you here?" Jo asked point blank.

Jo's steady voice matched the look in her eyes. She was thinking. About the security system? Louis' presence in their home? It wasn't her home?

Louis stared at her as if for the first time, while trying to decide what to tell her. "I'm here to take you home, babe" he answered.

Babe? Rutger's body thrummed with rage.

"Seriously, he thinks she'll believe him after he just criti-cized her," Mandy stood from her chair and met the authority of the baron. "Sorry," she mumbled and sat down.

Jo looked behind her at the gym bag sitting in the chair. She must have left her cell in her bag. No wonder she hadn't answered Mandy's calls or his.

"I want you to meet Doctor Peter Holmes. We met at the university. He is the founder of Humans Against Paranormal Influence. He has been working with shapeshifters for years and understands what happened to you," Louis explained.

"Sir, Dr. Holmes has association with Patriot Angels," Mandy added.

"We need to get more information about HAPI, the doctor's relationship with PA, and if they have people trying to renew the agency. Then we have to advise all other factions as well as the magic-born in the area," Healey ordered. "When we have all the facts, we'll advise further."

"Yes, sir." Mandy began typing.

It was like they were watching a horror movie, and soon someone was going to say, 'don't go in there'. Rutger's attention remained on Jo, her reactions, and the look of disbelief etching her features. No, she didn't believe him and was less impressed when the doctor told her he knew who her parents were.

"When you returned to Trinity, they brainwashed you and forced you to stay here," Dr. Holmes explained.

"You can have your life back." Louis stepped closer to Jo with his hand out. "You have nothing here. You don't have the gallery. A job. By the look of your house you don't have your pride. I guess it would be hard to keep when you've given your independence to the Wolf Enforcer."

Rutger couldn't stop the growl rumbling in his chest, every muscle in his body tightened into steel beams, and his hands clenched into fists. The man was breaking Jo down one word at a time and trying to take his mate.

Healey turned enough to see Rutger. "Calm down, son. Jordyn is at home, safe and sound."

"Affirmative." *Yes, she is.*

"It's like you've given up on life. Have you stopped living, Jordyn?" Louis asked, softly. "Come with me."

Jo stared at Louis, then agreed with him. Rutger wasn't going to let her go but couldn't compete with the ghost haunting her. Louis continued his verbal assault adding the baron, himself, the witches, having been kidnaped, and the dirty house. When the human paused, Rutger thought it might be over, then he nailed his gaze on her, trying to intimidate her.

"You let the Wolf Enforcer touch you, God Jordyn, really."

Jo froze, her eyes shifting to the ground as if he had slapped her. When she raised her head, her eyes held their familiar haunting stare.

"You look terrified. Are you scared of the Wolf Enforcer? Is he the reason you were on her knees crying? Does he hurt you to make you stay? Is that blood in your hair? Did he hit you? Does he abuse you? Is this what you want? You can tell me. Please, Jordyn, let me save you from this and that monster." Louis held his hand out to her, his fingers curling and beckoning her to go to him. "You loved me, Jordyn. You could love me again."

Rutger watched Jo touch her hair as if she didn't remember being struck and didn't know the blood was there. She healed and hadn't paid attention to the wound or the blood, her mind elsewhere, like escaping him. The tension lashed out when his enforcers turned enough to look at him with doubt and accusations in their carefully guarded glares. Did they think he hit her? That he would hurt her? Seeing her hurt was killing him. Did they think someone else had and he didn't do anything about it? The same way he failed to save her from the witches? He would never hurt her. No one was ever going to hurt her.

"She trained with Leo," Rutger stated.

"Leo was on orders to challenge Jordyn," Healey explained, his authority eliminating any questions. "My orders."

There was a collective inhale, and one by one their attention returned to the screen. Rutger held his breath while Jo remained silent and staring at Louis. Was she considering his offer? Her tears were his fault. She feared him because he was too damn weak to control his wolf and he might hurt her worse than Flint ever had. And when she needed someone to depend on, he was too damn weak to comfort her. He left her alone after the human tormented her. *I'm the real threat to her.*

"I do want my life back," Jo mumbled. She straightened with her decision. "I want my life."

Rutger's heart stopped beating.

"Babe, that's it. I can give it to you," Louis assured. "Leave with me."

Mine. "The hell he will," Rutger growled. He caught himself as everyone turned to watch him.

"How are you going to help me?" Jo asked.

Everyone in the room heard her soft voice as if she was submitting to him. The entire fucking room. Rutger became an embarrassment to the pack. *Enough.* Rutger needed to get the hell out of there before he exploded and totally lost control. His enforcers and the baron were watching Jo choose a human over him, for the second time. While she made the easy decision to choose Louis, he wouldn't be able to touch another woman. The humiliation was going to eat him. There was no way in hell he was going to watch his mate turn to another man and leave with him.

"Pause this," Healey demanded. The scene stopped with Jordyn gazing at them with haunted eyes and a determined look on her face. She was deciding something, that he knew. Healey stared for another second at the image and the scene reminded him of the pictures on her camera. Turning from her frozen face, he faced Rutger and ordered, "Director Kanin, park yourself." His low voice making the others lower their heads to their alpha.

Rutger didn't turn around; his hand squeezed the door knob. "I have to leave."

"It wasn't a request, Director. It was an order." Healey watched his son's shoulders tense, his corded muscles like taut ropes under his shirt as pain and grief radiated around him.

Rutger faced the baron prepared to argue then stopped when power saturated in anger and raw authority flowed through the room.

"Park. It." Healey held Rutger's wild gaze dark with his wolf. He knew her fear wasn't from the Wolf Enforcer, it was Flint. The witch called Rutger the Wolf Enforcer. Healey prayed whatever Jordyn was doing, she would say something to prove she wasn't going to go with Mr. Myers. When Rutger ended the standoff and grudgingly took his place, Healey turned back to the monitor and said, "Mandy."

"Dr. Holmes has a facility where you can hide. There he will clear your head of their brainwashing, destroying their hold on you." Louis took another step toward her. "You will be free."

"Once the brainwashing has been cleansed, we will purify you," Dr. Holmes explained.

"Freedom." Jo met Dr. Holmes' gaze.

"After the purification process, you will get your tattoos removed. There will be nothing marking you like an animal. It will end their rituals and their animalistic traditions." Louis continued.

"Freedom," Jordyn mumbled again.

Rutger's guilt reared. He lied about Shadow Lord, kept the letter from him a secret, and was going to mark her like an animal. Animalistic traditions.

Weak. Liar. Violent. Why wouldn't she run?

CHAPTER NINE

"Yes. Rutger Kanin and the Cascade clan will be a memory." Dr. Holmes joined Louis and they crowded around her. "You could rekindle your relationship with Louis. The two of you will be happy together. A human love and not a forced union with an animal. A dog."

"You wouldn't be controlled by a tyrant and made a female submissive. I heard before the animal lost his mind, he yelled mine when referring to you. Do you want to be owned like a pet?" Louis asked. His smugness condemning Jo.

"I'm not a submissive," Mandy argued.

"They're using human taboos to manipulate her," Ansel growled. "They're corrupting our ways."

Rutger remained silent. They were bullying her and she was letting them. Did she believe them and that's why she wasn't defending herself? *No response is a response*, his mind screamed. Time stretched out, seconds ticking by, as Jo's silence invaded his strength. What was she thinking?

"You're lying. Why are you here, Louis? You hate me." Jo glared at Louis with copper wolf eyes.

Jo didn't get angry let alone pissed off. She shut down and retreated inside herself.

Louis inhaled, exhaled, and lost control. "You lied to me you little bitch." He laughed. "Bitch. The Wolf Enforcer's bitch. No pun intended." Louis grabbed her wrists and yanked her closer until they're faces were a breath apart and rubbed his face over hers. "People. Humans, Jordyn, mocked me because of you. Who would fuck a lycan?" Louis sneered into her face as he pressed his nose into her cheek. "You should have told me you like to be beaten, Jordyn, I would have given you what you wanted. In spades."

What the fuck? Rutger stepped forward unable to see Jo's face and waited for her to flinch, to cower from his words and escape into her head. To resemble the ghost, he was living with.

Jo leaned her head back, looked up at Louis, meeting his angry glare, and pushed him. Unbalanced, Louis stumbled backwards, and Jo jerked her wrists free. After she put distance between them, she laughed. "Get the hell out of my house."

"Welcome back Mistress," Mandy whispered and twisted to check on Rutger. He gave her a blank look, his emotions locked down.

"I'm not here for an infected lycan. I'm here for the Pureblood who doesn't have one drop of human blood in her body. I'm here for the Cascade clan's soothsayer," Dr. Holmes said.

"His threat level just increased. Mandy, his background takes priority," Healey ordered. "I want to know if there are non-human missing person cases. Then if he's had any mental health issues."

"Yes, sir," Mandy replied.

"She can make it out of the house. Hell, she just proved, she could take them, why the hell is she still there?" Luke asked. "Why isn't she calling us?" He looked at Rutger as if he had the answer.

Rutger didn't answer. He couldn't. Jo fought back. He watched their interaction, Jo's eyes, her body language, and the way she rubbed her wrists where the human held her. It happened to her the same way it happened to him. Rutger cast his doubts aside. She wasn't going to leave with Louis. She was staying with him.

"Jo called them out on their lies. Louis said there was a facility where she could hide, it must have been true," Rutger pointed out. His entire body uncoiling.

"You're correct, son. Jordyn is reading their minds, trying to figure out where they were planning on taking her," Healey added.

"She can do that?" Ansel asked.

"Yes. Expertly. And with ease." Healey looked at the monitor.

"After everything she has been through, she's risking her life to read their minds?" Mandy asked.

"Rutger will be here," Jo promised.

Risking her life. "She knew, I would be there," Rutger replied.

"Your Wolf Enforcer is busy," Louis countered.

"Tick-tock, Pureblood." Dr. Holmes reached into his pocket, pulled the syringe free, and held it.

"I'm not going anywhere with you," Jordyn growled as her eyes gleamed copper. She watched Louis, a grin curving her lips. She couldn't stop from rubbing her wrists and staring at her hands or from turning them over and studying them.

"This isn't my first time, Pureblood." Dr. Holmes stuck her with the needle, burying it deep in her arm.

Jo turned slightly. When she stopped, her gaze shifted back to her hands. Several seconds passed, her eyes bled into their natural cocoa brown. She looked at Louis with fear etched on her face and back to her hands.

"Something happened. What is she doing?" Mandy asked.

"Why is she looking at her hands?" Ansel asked.

Jo needed his touch as much as he needed hers. "Louis touched her. Held her. Her skin feels like it's on fire. She is trying to figure out why or looking for the reason," Rutger answered.

"How do you know that?" Healey questioned.

"Kory touched me. Where her hands were on my chest felt like I had been seared with a blow torch." Rutger met the baron's gaze. "When I held Jo, it ended."

"I'm going to kick her ass," Mandy grumbled.

"I've seen enough. It's proof they intended on kidnapping her and harming her. And the doctor has a fascination with the magic-born. It will serve as physical evidence," Healey confirmed.

Mandy stopped the recording, the screen going blank, a forced quiet sitting thick in the tension.

"The protesters at the Summit were a distraction." Luke's growl broke the silence and he started pacing. "I bet nothing comes back on them and the sheriff's department doesn't do anything. They were nothing but kids."

"Yes. I'm going to assume they had no idea why they were sent there." *Damn.* Louis berated her and he left her alone. Rutger needed to call Jo. Everything he saw gave him the impression she changed, somehow.

"I'll call Deputy Elm and tell him the video is ready and I'll email it," Mandy offered.

"No, I will. I need to know if Dr. Holmes or Louis said anything about the facility," Rutger explained. He hoped after the witches kidnapped and murdered four werewolves, it would push human law enforcement to take initiative and investigate paranormal crimes. "Dr. Holmes said it wasn't his first time, with proof, they can't refute, they'll have to investigate the possibility."

"Do you think the mistress knows where they are?" Ansel asked. "She looked pretty confident."

"Yes. I'll talk to her about making a statement," Rutger replied. Living under fear's hold, Jo retreated from life and became a recluse. He didn't know if she would go to the station and talk to Deputy Elm when she hadn't talked to anyone. Even her family.

"Careful, Rutger. They'll ask how she found out, and she can't expose she can read minds. It will bring more attention to her and will bring attention to Flint's suicide. The homicide detective questioned us about that," Healey warned.

"Understood." Rutger faced Mandy. "Have the video from the Summit uploaded to my computer. I'll email them at the same time."

"Yes, sir." Mandy started typing.

"After you talk to Deputy Elm, update me, then go home." Healey stood beside Rutger, placed his hand on Rutger's shoulder, and squeezed. "You need to talk to Jordyn about this ... and the two of you." Healey let go and walked out of the communications room.

Rutger followed, leaving communications, and walked the hallway, and entered his office. Behind his desk, he sat back in his chair and tried to digest everything he witnessed. Jo faced Louis, Dr. Holmes, and while they threatened her, she fought to get information. "Rutger will be here," she said, and believed it.

They hadn't talked, hadn't resolved anything, but maybe there was a chance they could start. Jo opened herself to their bond because she needed him. He closed his eyes, reached for the link, and tried sensing her. Nothing. Denied. Jo blocked him, proving it was all his imagination and he was wrong. Rutger straightened, brought his computer to life, and checked for the video file. When it was completely uploaded, he hit play. Fast forwarding through the beginning, he paused the feed when Louis grabbed Jo's wrists and held her close to his chest. Rutger's fury swept through him, his jealously riddling his thoughts. It made him feel alive at the same time it taunted the void from Jo's absence. Rutger shuddered, closed the video window, and quickly dialed Deputy Elm and waited. If he heard another greeting for voicemail, he was going to go insane.

"Deputy Elm, Director Kanin." At least he answered his phone.

"Hello, Director, do you have the video?"

"Affirmative. I have the video from the Summit as well. I'll email both to you shortly," Rutger replied. He hesitated to tell him about Jo, and the possibility there was more evidence. "Is the video with Mr. Myers necessary?"

"Yes and no. We have Mr. Myers' confession, but anything showing physical proof of their actions is always good to have. Can't trust defense attorneys." Deputy Elm laughed.

He didn't have to tell Rutger that. "If I can ask, what kind of charges will Mr. Myers and Dr. Holmes face?"

"Mr. Myers and Dr. Holmes are being charged with trespassing, attempted kidnapping, and battery with the unlawful attempt to commit a violent injury to a person. The battery is for drugging Miss Langston. Of course, if the allegations Miss Langston accused them of can be proven, they'll face other charges. Due to the magnitude of the allegations and the crimes Miss Langston spoke to us about taking place in Butterfly Valley, the Cottonwood County sheriff's department will assist the Organized Paranormal Investigations."

Rutger sat back and stared at the wall. "Miss Langston was at the station?"

"Yes, she came in this morning. After what she has been through, I was surprised, as was everyone in the station. Miss Langston is a determined woman."

God only knows how they stared at her. "I think so. How long will Mr. Myers and Dr. Holmes be held?" Rutger asked absently.

"The District Attorney is currently filing charges to keep them in jail for several months. This is where the video will be helpful. When I booked them into county jail, I requested they be held without bail. My reports states Mr. Myers was out for revenge, and is a threat to Miss Langston's life, and will try it again. Dr. Holmes was attempting to capture a Pureblood lycan, like a trophy to do who knows what with, and is a threat to her life. If the judge watches the video it might sway him to agree to no bail. They will be held until their hearing." Deputy Elm laughed a gruff sound. "I didn't answer your question. Six to eight months, after that, it's up to the court system."

Six months. If they were shapeshifters, they would be given life in prison. "Thank you for telling me."

"You're welcome. Is there anything else?" Deputy Elm asked. There were several voices in the background, radio chatter, and a man trying to get Deputy Elm's attention.

"No. Thank you, Deputy Elm." There was a click, Deputy Elm hanging up-and Rutger set his phone on the desk.

Without letting his imagination get the better of him, he picked it up and called Jo. One. Two. Three. Voicemail. Damn. She could be busy. He had no idea Jo would go to the sheriff's station and talk to Deputy Elm by herself. His first priority should have been to be there when she woke up. If she needed him, the phone worked both ways. She did call Deputy Elm. Jo went without him like she didn't need him. Or because he left, she didn't want him anywhere near her.

Rutger opened the drawer, took the envelope, and stared at his name in scarlet calligraphy. *What does Shadow Lord want?*

The drive into Trinity, taking all the backroads, listening to music, and enjoying the scenery felt natural. When she parked in the Paradise County sheriff's station parking lot, reality hit her in the gut. Jordyn was going to see the men and women who had watched her dying in Rutger's arms, and then shapeshift when the baron called her wolf. They all witnessed Dr. Hyde and the medics from Celestial put her limp body in a cage and cart her off like a wild animal.

"Who would fuck a lycan?" Hot embarrassment scalded her neck and face. Exposed and subjected to her faults, she rubbed her arms where Flint had cut her with a knife, while the gripping feeling of being a victim roared to life. Sitting in her SUV, she considered leaving, driving as fast as possible back home where she could close the door and shut out the world.

And return to the none existent life she was currently courting. *No thank you.* The image of Dr. Holmes' blood-stained hands reminded her it wasn't about her. It was about the magic-born and her responsibility to them. More so since she was the fated mate to the Second to the Alpha and was the soothsayer for her pack. If she didn't work to protect others, it would bring her shame as well as the pack.

She could do it. Having talked herself into getting out of the SUV, she entered the station. Once through the metal detector and multiple deputies, she finally made it to the reception area. She got a few glances until they recognized her, then they were all out stares. Her stomach clinched, her pulse raced, and their gazes crawled over her as she stood at the counter waiting to talk to a deputy.

Jordyn refused to back down. They were stares, nothing else. Relief flooded her when Deputy Harley greeted her, like she wasn't a spectacle, and took her to Deputy Elm. The longer she talked to them, explaining everything, and giving them the information about the warehouse, the better she felt. Deputy Elm assured her they would investigate, and with video proof coming from Director Kanin, they would have the undisputed evidence they needed.

Louis-0.

Jordyn-1.

Once she escaped the office and was outside, she felt relieved of the weight and empowered. She won a round. Jordyn had gone home and faced the mess of her house and the grief she had been living with. She changed out of her jeans and blouse and wore cotton lounge pants and a T-shirt to clean house. They were menial tasks like laundry ... her lounge pants and sweatshirt making her cringe as she tossed them into the washer. There was dusting and vacuuming, basic house cleaning no one was doing. She was stuck inside her head, and Rutger was at the office making sure the distance between them remained solid.

With the house back in shape, and her mind racing, she entered the bar. Because she was a renaissance woman, she poured a glass of wine ... the first in weeks. She sipped the silky liquid, knowing what she had to do next. It was time to face the creator of her fears.

Flint.

Holding her glass, Jordyn stood on the deck staring at the woods to the west side of the house with indecision holding her like a vice. The memory of Flint hiding and then taking her to his sacrificial tree to finish what he started, played in front of her. *I killed him*, she reminded herself, *and the woods are empty. The woods are mine.* Jordyn took a sip, unable to deny the call of the forest, its demands drumming in her head and pushing her wolf. Jordyn felt the shift and the freedom from running as if she were in the midst of the forest.

No. She could smell the sharp edge of blood and the threads of fear. It had awakened the dark entity of her death, turning her cold. *I'm not going out there. Isn't going to happen. Maybe next week.*

Letting fear win, she turned her back and faced the living room. No, she rounded to the woods. Tall pine trees, their limbs reaching out to the oak and cedar trees, thronged to the edge of the lake where water lapped at rocks. October's chilled breeze caressed her cheeks, sending a shiver over her skin.

"Flint ripped my territory from me," Jordyn said aloud.

That was the brutal truth. The fear he instilled in her was eating everything around her-Rutger, the pack, her relationship with her parents, and her sister. They hadn't spoken in weeks, if not months. A tremor of trepidation slithered down her spine, recreating the pressure of failure from her training and the conversation with the baron. She was destroying her life and becoming a shell of herself and eventually Rutger would get tired of watching her slow suicide and cut her loose to spare himself the pain. She deserved whatever resentment he held for her. Then where would she go, Foxwood? If she didn't watch him withdraw inside himself and deteriorate first.

It was time to take her life back.

Don't think. Jordyn set the glass on the table, kicked off her running shoes, tugged her T-shirt over her head, placed it on the back of a chair, then her bra and lastly, she shoved her underwear and pants down her legs, and escaped her socks. *Don't think.* Stepping out of her discarded clothing, she absently tossed her hair band to the table, but it missed and fell to the deck. A breeze caressed her bare body catching her hair and making the ends drift. In a concentrated trance, she walked to the first step and waited for the woods to acknowledge her.

Magic rose up through the layers of earth, and saturating the air around her it summoned her wolf. Images of dragons resembling the ones from her dream filled her head as Jordyn let her territory stroke her body and empower her magic. She loved its feel. Jordyn knew there would be a day when magic would be a constant in the world, like oxygen. Those who doubted the baron would have to accept it was real. The humans would have to admit to its presence.

What would be the cost? She wasn't sure and didn't know how long it would take for magic to take charge.

A gust of wind whipped her hair around her face and snaring the countless tree limbs, made them sing, like a serenade created for her. Closing her eyes, Jordyn eased into her power, its simmering ember increasing to scarlet flames, and holding on to the blaze, she leaped. In midair her body shapeshifted, and clearing the stairs, her front paws landed gently on the ground, then her back paws. Her power flowed freely through her; she felt it in her muscles and every nerve ending and it was delicious. The strength silenced the voices of the pack and loosened the shackles binding her to her fear. With her senses unleashed, other's powers teased her, beckoned her, needing her to find them and understand the changes.

Not yet. She would face them when she was capable and not teetering on the edge of falling apart.

Run faster.

Jordyn navigated the woods, jumping and weaving around logs, brush, and rocks. She slowed when she approached the tree, scarred with an upside down cross, the ground around it no longer stained red from blood. There were no hands, legs, feet, heads, of the witch's half buried in the rain-soaked dirt and glittering pine needles. The area was free of their tortured emotions.

Face your fears. Jordyn stared at the tree while the day played through her thoughts, the images changing from Rutger to Flint, to the detectives. If she had been in human form, her breathes would have come in heavy inhales.

She hesitantly approached the tree, ready to feel Flint's evil slither over her as it had on that rainy day. When nothing happened, her nerves uncoiled, and she believed he was gone. It was time to move forward. *Pull its evil from your body,* she demanded. In the months it spent embedding itself inside her, it clung to her. Jordyn felt the cold void of her death, and absorbing it into herself, found peace with her choice. She didn't choose death over life … no, she sacrificed her life for the safety of the pack. For Rutger. He would have done the same thing. Still, her mind nagged, acknowledging it and coming to terms with her actions didn't erase the forfeit for denying death and being brought back to life. It changed her and made her different. She felt the disparity when her power flowed through her and she shifted.

Jordyn shook her head trying to understand what was happening. Raw power. *No.* A rush of electric charges cascaded through her veins and muscles, gripping her wolf's body in manic fluxes, the force dropped her to the ground. *Not ready.* Jordyn's mind exploded with visions of dragons, acting as watchmen, while scarlet ribbons of power weaved around her, merging with Flint and his chants. As it streamed through her mind, Flint's evil presence fought to withstand the strength of her ancestors. He failed. Her ancestors tore Flint's evil from her core ... allowing Jordyn to accept him and his torture as a memory. Fighting harder, she recognized the pain as the past, not her present. The threads began to unravel, and slipping from her mind, its filaments slid down her body to her legs and through her paws to the ground where she buried them. In her territory.

She knew them, the dragons from her dream, and like before they guided her toward her power and to seek comfort with her wolf. Jordyn possessed the power to heal physical wounds and accept the scars. *I understand.* As if they heard her, and recognized they were no longer needed, shadows veiled them, their ancient power drawing back, its presence weakening with her liberation from her nightmares. The tension created by her fear let go, her muscles felt flexible, her body yielding, and she lifted her face to the sky and howled a hollow sound riddled with her pain, and the life she nearly lost. The strongest ache eased, and finally dying, Jordyn lowered her head. She beat Flint and his coven. He wasn't coming back and his touch faded with his ghost.

Her victory fed her foundation of confidence and a piece of the old Jordyn emerged. She stood, turned her back to the symbol of her fear, and leisurely headed back to the house, her steps carefree. *Not,* she mused. Jordyn ran as fast as she could with her senses open to feel the forest. Pushing to increase her speed, she elongated her body with each leap, the air on her fur like a secret caress. Magic wrapped around her, the woods carried her, and the earth opened for her, this was her territory.

CHAPTER TEN

"Dammit, Jo answer your phone." Rutger ended the call without leaving a message and set his phone on the desk. The letter from Shadow Lord, four words of terror, loomed over him while the attempted kidnapping and leaving Jo alone, ate at him. He read and reread the four words over and over, and each time fear seized his spine. *'You can't protect her.'* The hell he can't.

Rutger called Jo. No answer. He had no idea where she was or what she was doing. His worry increased and was actively consuming him. The security system worked when Louis had driven to the house, and so far, there hadn't been an alert. Why wasn't she answering his calls? *Because she doesn't need you. Because Shadow Lord has her.* He checked his cell for a message, a call, an alert, anything. A nervous energy grated down his spine and curled itself around his hips, forcing him to move. Rutger stood, the chair rolled backwards, and he left his office.

In the communication room, Mandy, an active enforcer, sat at the desk monitoring the radio and security cameras. "Any alerts concerning the properties?"

"Negative, sir. Peace and quiet. Except the Olivers, Kia is headed there to talk to Mrs. Oliver," Mandy reported.

"Noted. Make sure you keep track of her, I don't want Kia without backup." He didn't think the Olivers were capable of hurting anyone, still he wasn't going to take a chance if they saw Kia as a threat. Rutger stopped beside Mandy and looked at the screen. *Don't be paranoid.* If he checked on Jo, he's going to look like a nut case. Director of Enforcers was losing his mind. *Been there, did that. Fuck it.*

"I need you to check camera two at my place, I think there's a glitch."

"Yes, sir." Mandy typed her order into the keyboard, bringing up a grid, and entered the code name for his house, Director of Enforcers, and indicated camera two.

The front of his house came up on the fifty-five inch screen on the wall. Jo's SUV sat parked in front of the garage where it always was. The yard and stairs were clear, the front door closed. Rutger took his cell and called her again. Voicemail. *Dammit.* His worry was churning inside of him.

"Good. Check the cameras to the east and west," Rutger ordered.

"Is there a problem?" Ansel asked. Wearing his version of the Enforcer's uniform of black T-shirt, denim jacket, jeans, thigh holster, and boots, he stood with his hand on the butt of his Glock 21, 45 caliber pistol.

"Checking the cameras, could swear there was a glitch," Rutger replied and waited for cameras three and four to appear on the screen.

"Glitch?" Ansel asked, brows drawn. He felt the lie and wondered why Rutger didn't request to check the perimeter of his house. Everyone would understand after humans, one of them a doctor, attempted to kidnap his mate. Then he felt static anxiety coming from Rutger and understood he thought something was wrong.

"Affirmative." Rutger's one word answer had both Ansel and Mandy looking at him. Ignoring them, he watched the side of his house sitting in the late afternoon sun, its glow teasing warmth when October's cool bite was settling in and embracing the chill off the lake. "Camera five." The screen switched, and Rutger went silent when he saw her half-filled glass of wine sitting on the patio table, her T-shirt on a chair with her bra, and her hair band abandoned on the deck. At the bottom of the screen, he could make out the edge of the French door. It was open. *Not possible.* He hated what he was about to do, but he had to know. "Activate the interior camera, LR." The entire living room, the doors, and the deck would be visible.

"When I activate the interior camera, it shifts to emergency mode and will automatically initiate audio to record the entire session," Mandy warned.

"Duly noted." Rutger's patience was colliding with his fear.

"Yes, sir. LR activated."

The screen changed from the deck to the empty living room. Part of him was relieved he wasn't seeing another tragedy unfolding in his house, and he was glad Jo wasn't there doing something. Like what? Sitting on the couch and crying. Staring into the fire and crying. Cursing him. Packing her bags. Being kidnapped by Shadow Lord. Leaving with Shadow Lord because Rutger couldn't protect her.

Wolf, her voice whispered.

It was a perfect view of his living room-his clean living room-nothing was out of place. The oversized chair, couch, lamps, fireplace, doors, and deck. The fire was going as if she had recently stoked it, and cast a glow over the room. Where was she? After Louis and Dr. Holmes easily entered the house, why the hell would she leave the door open? And her clothes and wine outside? He searched the scene, trying to see if anything was out of place, if there had been a struggle. If someone made it inside and forced her outside. If she left a clue. Nothing. He called her again and heard her cell ringing. She didn't have her phone. *Where the hell are you?*

"You think something is wrong?" Ansel asked.

"I do. I think it's not like her," Rutger replied. *I think.* What was like her?

Before going to the sheriff's station, she hadn't left the house, except to go to Foxwood, and the baron pulled rank and ordered her to go. She never went into Trinity. Scared Jo, the one who flinched when his cell rang or when he raised his voice, wouldn't leave the door open.

Right. She left it open yesterday. He couldn't stop his fear. He turned to Ansel, and saw Kellen, and Quinn staring at him.

"Ansel, stay here with Mandy, you're in charge. Mandy, keep watching. If something happens, call law enforcement. Kellen and Quinn, you're with me."

"Director, wait. I think I saw a something coming from the west side of the house." Mandy switched views. Empty. "I swear I saw something."

"Camera five." *Let it be Jo.*

She hadn't touched her camera in weeks, but she might have taken it and gone for a walk. *Sure.* Jo stripped, left her clothing on a chair, and went for a walk stark naked, what the hell was he thinking. He saw her staring at the fire and crying and this was the person who was going to jump into the life she had before facing her death. Rutger anxiously waited and watched. A wolf loped up the stairs, stopping at the rail like it was leisurely looking at the lake, then turned to the house. It raised its head, its nose in the air, sniffed, and took steps toward the open door.

"I want a split screen with camera five and LR," Rutger ordered. His voice holding an edge of excitement and desire at seeing her in wolf form.

Her dark chocolate coat with tawny red feathering her sides was unmistakable. Like her liquid copper eyes. They gleamed in the setting sun's golden hue. Jo. She had been running. After investigating the entire deck, she approached the open door, and taking three steps, shifted mid-stride. Without stopping, Jo entered the house in human form.

"Holy shit," Quinn whispered.

"Damn," Mandy mumbled. "Just. Damn."

"She didn't stop walking," Ansel added. "She didn't pause."

Mine. Naked with sweat glistening on her skin it highlighted her curves and muscles. People feared the weight she lost and Dr. Hyde was always saying she needed to make sure to eat properly, but Rutger didn't see her like that. He saw Jo, the woman he loved, the woman who would always be beautiful to him. She strode to the couch where she picked up a T-shirt. His T-shirt. Holding it, she faced the deck, giving them her back and a view of the tattoos inked in her flesh-her family's crest and the runes Louis threatened to take from her. She continued to door, then paused to pull the shirt over her head. His T-shirt ended at her thighs while the Cascade pack crest covered her back and his name sat above her right breast. Drawing her hand along the ridge of her neck, she freed her hair from the collar. Onyx sat against her back, over the crest, the ends of her hair stopping at her waist. When did her hair get so long? He didn't know. Hadn't noticed. A chime sounded, getting her attention, and she went to the table where her cell phone sat.

"Shit. Shit. Shit," Jo mumbled.

They all watched her concentrate on what she was doing as her fingers moved over the screen. A couple of seconds ticked by and Rutger's phone rang. He looked at it, saw her name, and hit decline. The three enforcers looked at him, wearing the question, why he didn't answer the call. He stared at the screen, at Jo, and one by one they turned. Again, he ignored them. He couldn't talk to Jo while every emotion he was capable of feeling was controlling him ... god only knows what he would sound like. Confused, hurt, a man without his woman. No. A wolf without his mate. He would add embarrassment to the list of weaknesses his enforcers were no doubt keeping track of. No, he didn't need to make matters worse.

Rutger continued watching her. She changed screens, typed out a message, and waited.

Sorry, I missed you. Are you busy? appeared. Cell phone in hand, she walked out to the deck, set her cell down, and picked up the glass of wine. Spying on her instead of watching a recorded video sent a perverse thrill through him and was quickly becoming the ultimate level of eavesdropping and his favorite thing. He loved the natural way she held herself, without inhibitions and worry. He watched her take a sip when her phone chimed with a message. He hadn't responded, so who was messaging her? Jo read it, laughed a light sound, shook her head, set the phone down, and turned back to the lake and the setting sun.

Someone made her laugh, and it wasn't him. Rutger's worry had him considering stopping the recording, for fear she was going to prove she was leaving him. It was clear Jo wasn't in trouble, and he didn't want anyone else watching her, they had already seen more than they should. At least they were his team, his enforcers and he could trust them. By nature, werewolves weren't embarrassed by nudity the way humans were. Being naked was part of who they were and a part of their lives when they shapeshifted.

Rutger opened his mouth to give the order to stop the recording when she held the edge of the curved bowl to her bottom lip, rotated the stem between her fingers, and the rim rolled along the curve. The sensual movement, and knowing the rich spice of cinnamon was lacing her mouth, nearly caused Rutger to suck in a breath. With a confidence she lacked in the past, as if on a mission, she walked to the railing. Jo stayed there for several seconds, her face in the crescent of sun, its rose and golds playing on her skin.

She was thinking. Jo took another sip, her hesitation tensing her shoulders, like she was contemplating a decision. *What is it Jo? Am I going to lose you?*

As if in answer, she raised her glass in a toast. "I'm free."

From me. A sword stabbed through Rutger's heart as she drank from the glass, toasted the lake, turned, and picked up her hair band. She gathered her clothes, and with her arm full she retrieved her cell, and went into the house. At the oversized chair beside the fireplace, she dropped the pile of clothing and her cell. Jo kept her wine as she closed the door, locked it, then checked the panel to see all the green lights blinking.

"Locked." Jo pointed at the panel like she was going to give it a lecture, then laughed.

Rutger shook his head at her like he was there with her when he recognized the fathoms in her copper and coal gaze. She made a decision and wasn't going to backdown.

He stopped watching her to analyze the scene. She un-dressed outside, went running, and immersed herself in her power. *Mine.* He tracked her, and wearing his T-shirt and a grin of victory, she headed to the stairs and out of sight. He witnessed Jo's awakening. Was he going to stay asleep in the dark or stand by her side?

"Deactivate LR, and delete the footage," Rutger ordered. He was lucky his voice sounded normal and wasn't carrying his sudden lust, indecision, and need.

"Yes, sir." Mandy quickly highlighted the section and hit delete.

"The baron doesn't shift like that," Quinn mused.

"No one does," Mandy added.

"That's why it's been deleted," Rutger stated. "And no one talks about what they saw."

"It explains the Highguard's interest." Kellen met Rutger's gaze colored with his wolf. "The soothsayer is powerful. I can't believe some doubt her."

"Because they don't know," Mandy said as she tapped keys. "If they saw her it would change their minds."

He didn't need to be reminded of the Highguard and their real interest in Jo or the divide in the pack. "I repeat, no one talks about this," Rutger managed to say without letting his fury loose. "She isn't a thing. The soothsayer, Jo, is my mate."

"I bet your house is saturated with her power," Ansel ventured. When Dr. Hyde said she wasn't sure how she felt about fated mates, it made his decision to keep the truth to himself easier. Then witnessing the pain in Rutger's eyes and the sorrow he wore like a second skin, Ansel considered it a curse. But right then, after watching her and Rutger's reaction, he was forced to admit he was a little jealous. Fated mates and a powerful soothsayer. He wondered what it would be like to have a mate with equal power and feel her energy in the air and on his skin.

"Our home." Rutger's wolf howled a haunting sound, its echo reverberating inside his chest. When everyone turned to look at him, questions in their narrowed gazes, he snuffed it. He wanted to bathe in her power's silk. God, how he missed its feel. "I'm heading home." With his thoughts in chaos, he left the communications room, and walked to the reception area where Ansel caught up with him and they walked outside.

"I'll lock up your office."

"Right. Thanks," Rutger absently mumbled. He opened the truck's door and got in. "Say it."

"Brother, she isn't the same. Jordyn is giving you the opportunity to change things." Ansel watched him for a response, as his thoughts went to Dr. Hyde and his lies. "The woman in the video embraced her wolf and the power of the soothsayer. She needs her mate."

"I know. Damn, I know." Rutger stared forward, his hands gripping the steering wheel, his fear boiling and his guilt toying with him. "I left her today. And when she didn't answer her phone, and I knew something bad had happened. Had she not been there, I would have ordered the enforcers to cover my property and search for her. She has been feeding this fear, and accepting it in place of living. It's like a damn cancer. Its poison is in our veins like our blood. And I didn't try to help her. I had no idea how to help her." *It's fucking crippling.* In front of him the building's mass blocked the valley behind it. Along the mountain ridge, the peaks were eating the sun and draping the valley in a cloak of golds, scarlets, and violets.

"I believe Jordyn has broken free of fear's restraints. It's time you did the same thing. Go home and talk to her." Ansel clapped Rutger on the shoulder.

"I am." Rutger waited for Ansel to move out the way and closed his door.

Pressing the push start, the diesel engine rumble to life at the same time the laptop lit up, its screen listing alerts and messages. Rutger disregarded them all, backed up, and turning, drove the one-mile drive. When he was through the wrought iron gates of Foxwood, he pulled to the side and parked.

Taking his cell phone, he sent, **On my way home.** He waited, praying she would reply. A series of beeps sounded-he needed to change the irritating alert-and read her message.

Waiting for you.

Rutger's anxiety from fear and guilt drained from him. It was quickly replaced with a new edgy nervousness. What if she changed and she didn't need him? What if his silence and absence were testament to his weakness? Without answers to his questions, he set his phone in the center console and headed home to see his mate.

When she saw Rutger tried calling her, not once but several times, her insides caved in and worry turned to stress. It was stupid to miss his calls after not answering any of his calls the day before when Louis had tried kidnapping her. She immediately called him back, only to hear his voice tell her to leave a message. Thankfully, he messaged her to tell her he was on his way home.

He isn't ignoring me.

Jordyn's heart did a flip and landed hard inside of her chest. She hurried, figuring she had twenty-five minutes max ... maybe more like fifteen minutes before he came home. She leaned closer to mirror; the brush swept through her lashes, thickening them with black mascara. Putting the brush in the bottle, she placed it on the bathroom counter, and surveyed her appearance. Her straight coal hair held a sheen; her eyes lined with black, and black and smoky chocolate eyeshadow, brought out the flecks of copper. She wore her usual choice in clothing, and not the baggy sweatshirt and matching pants she had been hibernating in. And there was an upbeat country tune, something about ghosts and trucks, playing in the background that she absently hummed along with.

From outside the bathroom, she heard her cell chime. Jordyn left the mirror and passing her bed, walked to the dresser. Blocking her background picture, a sunset over the lake, was another message from Claudia, and it made Jordyn smile. They were going to get together, and it was about damn time. She reread Rutger's message, finding the time, and headed back to the bathroom.

"Jo, you're looking like yourself. Don't fuck it up."

While Rutger drove, his thoughts chased his need to mark her, which would hurt her. *Animalistic ritual.* He would watch her recoil from his touch, and he wasn't strong enough to watch her eyes fill with the hurt and dread he inflicted. Despite Jo getting better and leaving her fear in the past, if he hurt her it would deepen the divide between them. Then there was Shadow Lord's letter and the four fucking words haunting him. *You can't protect her.* From what? Shadow Lord or himself?

Rutger parked his truck beside her SUV, killed the engine, the laptop beeping and telling him it was shutting down, the music from the stereo fading, and he stared at his house.

Our home.

Honey hues of the evening sun highlighted the two logs flanking the stairs, its light unable to reach the dark walnut double doors decorated with wrought iron accents. He had them enforced with steel, replacing the doors with oval windows in their centers. The windows were security breaches in his eyes. At the back of the house and his bedroom, the new sets of French doors were made from steel and ballistic glass like the windows throughout the house. He admitted with all the steel, ballistic glass, palm vein identification, codes, and UV lights he had turned the house into a prison. Her prison. He left every day and spent time living a life. *Sort of.* Not locked behind a security system with nothing but time on his hands.

After grabbing his coat from the passenger seat, and his phone from the console, Rutger got out of the truck, and locked the door. Walking to the porch, he didn't know what he was going to find inside. He bowed his head, inhaled, and pressing the handle found it locked. *Good girl.*

Relieved when it didn't budge, he placed his palm on the sensor, a violet UV light blinked once, twice, scanned his palm, beeped, and he entered the number code. Every one of the twenty-four floodlights served two purposes. When on the LED setting, they lit up his house and the surrounding area fifty feet out. With a flip of a switch or activated from his cell, or the console in his truck, the LEDs changed to UV lights. Shadow Lord was a vampire, night walker, and there was no way he was coming near Jo. Rutger hit the last number of the code, their anniversary, and his insides caved as an anxious energy tangled with the hunger to have her. *Don't spook her.* The sound of the lock disengaging clicked and the heavy steel door opened with a whisper. He closed it, the lock engaged, and the lights on the control panel blinked green.

He paused in the entryway when he heard country music playing from a speaker on the side table, her cell phone bright with the artist. Music. Rutger immediately checked the French doors, making sure they were closed, the pad on the wall blinking green, confirming the doors were locked and the alarm engaged. The security system was state of the art but he wasn't going to rely solely on it, and used his senses to search. With his instincts on edge, his lust from spying on Jo burning in his veins it made searching difficult. He tried ignoring its influence, struggling to kill it on the drive, hoping for clarity. It didn't work. He inhaled, caught her wolf, its wild spice alive like the fire, and the tannins from her wine lying low in the mix. Wrapping around him, the combination stroked his desire.

Dammit, stop. He needed control.

Jo kept the fire going but hadn't turned on the lights letting the flames dance against the walls and cloak the room in flickering ruby, amber, and bronze. He could imagine her kneeling by the hearth and staring at the swaying flames as they highlighted her onyx and copper gaze. Not the scene of her knelt before it and crying. His conscience screamed he should have stayed home and not abandoned her. Louis and Dr. Holmes tried to take her from him, he left. Guilt played with him, and stabbing his desire with its sharp point tried to derail him. It tried but failed. He was too far gone. Rutger witnessed her strength when she ran and then shifted in mid-stride and knew she had been better off by herself.

A low growl of impatience rumbled from him as he walked to the border of the slate and wood flooring. He stood at the edge of the living room, staring at nothing and feeling like an intruder in his own home. Ansel could have handled the video and getting it to Deputy Elm, but Rutger needed to watch it to confirm she hadn't let the humans in and she was prepared to defend herself. Even as he looked at her abandoned clothing on the chair where she'd dropped them, he felt like leaving.

Rutger couldn't believe, she'd undressed outside and ran. Like a wolf. Like Jo. The memory of her standing in the sunlight, slowly undressing, and tossing her clothes in his direction, and tempting him to join her teased him with memories of a better time. At her beckoning, he would strip out of his clothes and they would shapeshift and run along the shoreline, and when they returned, they would shift and swim with their wolves burning in their veins. All alone and caught up in the intoxicating power of their wolves, they would have sex. It wasn't romantic and it wasn't making love, it was straight sex. The kind that drove them wild, like if they didn't have one another the world would come crashing down and they would burn to ash. Those days felt like a million years in the past.

Shaking himself from his memories, he was unable to stop the image from feeding his lust. The reflex to escape lessened with the promise she was on the road to recovery. There was hope he was going to have those days back.

Was he? With the beast close to the surface and the pressure to lash out always present he had his doubts. Weak. Uncontrolled. Bestial. And his beast demanding he mark his mate threw his thoughts in chaos and he couldn't think straight.

Rutger's senses told him, Jo wasn't in the living room, or their bedroom, where she usually was deep inside her head and far from him. He ended his search for her. As he unbuckled his belt, he walked over to the coat rack where he unclasped his thigh holster and hung it over a railroad nail. He stared into the dark bar as tension tightened through his shoulders, gripped his neck, and dug its claws into his spine. What was he going to say to her?

Hey babe ... No, he was not calling her babe, not after the human had. *Hey Jo, watched you shapeshift with a power no one has witnessed and then watched you pull my T-shirt on. You make me crazy.*

Wasn't happening when it might scare her. He scrubbed his face with his hand, refusing to add to her worry. He could repeat it all day when the truth was, he was keeping the glimpse into her life a secret. He wanted to be able to watch her whenever and for hours. He loved her way without inhibitions and the freedom of her movements.

He hung his coat next to his gun belt and continued to stare into the bar. Like the renaissance man he was, he considered pouring a bourbon. Rutger slowly turned around when a vivacity he compared to a smooth summer breeze drifted over him and called his wolf. Jo stood staring at him, wine glass in hand, gold and ruby from flames caressing one side of her face, embracing her passion, and the shadow's veil on the other. As if its darkness was guarding her magic. Her raven hair covered her shoulders, her makeup accentuating the almond curve of her eyes, and drawing out the copper. She wore a black fitted cotton shirt, not the oversized sweatshirt, and a pair of tight lounge pants that hugged her toned legs. Damn she was gorgeous and with power to match. He needed her.

"I thought I felt you." Jordyn hadn't used her senses and maintained a strong block wall in their bond. She didn't want to feel him, sense him, mostly she didn't want him feeling the deep sadness and fear consuming her. When he entered the house, a shiver cascaded down her spine and her soothsayer's power allowed his essence to find her. *I'm healing my wounds.* He took a step backwards, and she watched Rutger, wondering if he was going to turn and run from the house.

"Felt me?" Rutger mumbled. Like she wanted to sense him. He hadn't tried sensing her, rather he felt her absence, and he didn't feel her through their link. He had given up, hating the rejection, when she continually blocked him. "Where were you?" Questioning her, not a great start.

"Cleaning out the studio. I've been thinking about going to the storage unit and getting my stuff," Jordyn answered easily. His hesitation imbedded in nervous energy rolled from him. *Don't let him go.* "Are you going to stay?"

Shouldn't have left her. "Do you want me to? Stay."

"Yes." Keep it together. His intensity, strong features highlighted by the fire's light drew her in, and his wolf's power gleaming in his gold eyes made her pause. The ends of his dark brown hair grazed the collar of his shirt, gave way to his broad shoulders, and added weight to his presence. *Yes, I want you to stay. Need you to stay.*

"Then I'm staying. I was going to pour a bourbon." *Sure he was.* Rutger remained frozen where he stood. She had been in her studio and she wanted him to stay. *Don't fuck this up.*

Jordyn risked leaving him standing by the coat rack, prayed he didn't rush the door and bolt, and went to the living room where she set her wine glass on the table. She didn't drop it … Good. With a deep breath, she returned to find he hadn't moved. His gold and mahogany eyes, darker from the shadows, held her, his shoulders tensed under his long-sleeved shirt hugging his chest, and his stance mirroring his hesitation.

"Come here." Damn if there wasn't a tremble in her voice making her sound small.

"Jo." He took another step back, his nerves working overtime, his imagination creating scenes going horribly wrong. He wanted to touch her. Needed to touch her. But Jo looked driven and fragile at the same time. Her straight shoulders rose with her inhale and held her determination. *Mine.*

Jordyn closed the distance between them, took his hand, and a spark of power hit the two of them. "Come here." She lightly pulled, testing if he would follow, and when he did, she led him to the living room. When they stood in front of the couch, she stopped. "Sit down."

Rutger held her hand as he obeyed, her fingers slipping from his hold, and regretted letting go. *Come to me.* "Jo."

"Wait." She watched him for a breath and left.

Rutger stared at the fire trying to think of something to say, slid his palms, damp with sweat, down his BDU pants, and tried to breathe normally.

"Here." She handed him a glass. The amber liquid gleaming in the firelight.

"Thank you," he whispered as he looked down at the tawny liquor.

Not backing down. Jordyn sat on the edge of the coffee table in front of Rutger, and reaching out to touch him, saw her trembling hands, drew back, and took her glass instead.

She didn't want to feel him and his power if he was going to send her packing.

"I have been trying to acknowledge the past but instead have let Flint control me. What happened, changed me. I'm not the same person and will never be the same person. What I'm trying to say is, I don't know if you want this." She paused, fear telling her she was going to lose him, and make a fool of herself at the same time.

"This?" Rutger asked. His thoughts collided, and turning to splinters he felt lost and unsure of himself. He needed to say something. He needed to stop her.

Don't beg. "Me. I know … no, I don't know." She looked past him to the kitchen as frustration took bites of her. She wasn't explaining herself the way she envisioned. *Clumsy much.* "I don't know what it's been like to live with me. And then Louis coming here. I know I didn't protect myself like I should have. I had a reason, but it wasn't because I was scared. I promise, I wasn't going to go with him. I wasn't giving up on us."

Jordyn took a drink of her wine-*where was the damned alcohol?*-and set the glass down and stood. She walked around the table to pace in front of the fire, the light coming and going with each of her steps. "Louis invaded my territory, my house, and it made me furious. I realized, the last few months, I have been focused on what Flint took from me and ignored what I have. I don't want to be the broken mess I have been." Jordyn stopped and faced Rutger, his eyes glowing gold in the firelight, the shadows from the flames teasing his wolf features while it touched his clenched jaw, his chest, and legs. He held his glass with a death grip, and she imagined it shattering like their relationship. "Am I too late?"

Jo looked at her hands, rubbed her wrists where Louis had held her, like she was reliving the pain, and looked up at him. *Straight to the point.* "Jo, I want you. Do you want me?" His words broken in weakness and from drowning in his fear of rejection.

Jordyn froze when she heard the hurt and uncertainty in his voice. But she couldn't stop relief from sweeping through her. *Not too late.* Her knees weakened with the overload of emotions, making it hard to stay standing. "I want you. I want our life."

Tears slid down her cheeks leaving glittering trails in their wake, the sight and feel of her opening herself to him, ran him through. Rutger set his glass on the table before he dropped it, and stood. Denying the impulse to keep space between them, he closed the distance. He raised his hand, waited for her to flinch from his touch, and when she didn't, he gently wiped her tears away. "I hate to see you cry."

"Wolf, these are tears of happiness. I have you," Jordyn whispered.

Holding her hands, he walked backwards to the couch. His legs met the edge, and he sat down, gazing up at her, his body trembling, his heartbeat in his ears as he waited. *Come to me,* he pleaded. Jo hesitantly stepped toward him, and stopped. He watched her thoughts cross her face in the flames, her wolf playing in her eyes, and there was a spark of passion. *For me?* God, he hoped so. He gently tugged on her hands, and she took the last step and strad-dled him. After resting her hands at the back of his neck, she played with the ends of his hair. He bowed his head, caving to her light touches, and growled. Dread shouted his mistake, and he jerked his head up, expecting to see distain in her eyes and horror on her face.

"Sorry."

"Sorry? For what?" Jordyn asked. She searched his face, trying to guess where his apology came from. Her wolf howled in her ears with the sound of his deep growl of appreciation, its raw edge begging her to touch him.

Be honest. "You flinch when I raise my hand, my voice, or the phone rings. Are you scared of me? Do you think I'm weak and have failed you? I lost control and gave into the beast. It sits close to the surface, and I'm afraid of losing myself and hurting you." Rutger was fumbling around words, trying to say everything at once. He inhaled, attempting to catch his breath as he searched her face, her eyes, and waited.

"It's not you. It was the baggage I was carrying around. You faced losing your mate, that doesn't make you weak," Jordyn assured as she ran her fingers through his thick hair. Her voice a throaty mix of desire and wolf. "You can't hurt me."

"You don't know that. There are times I'm grasping at control and watching it slip from my hands. I won't risk hurting you and losing you," Rutger confessed. He saw the pain in her eyes and didn't want her haunted gaze on him.

"We are stronger together than we are apart." *Fated.* "I'm not scared of you, never have been." Jordyn had a confession of her own. "I have to tell you something."

"What?" Rutger quickly asked. Not weak. *Isn't scared of me.*

"I didn't choose death over life. I didn't want to die. I need you to know that. It was the only way to stop them." She fought to come to terms with sinking into the depth of her soul and abandoning life. The witches had to be stopped, she kept telling herself. It didn't change the weight from making the decision, and dying had taken its toll. Opening a wound, she didn't think was going to heal, its ache haunted her. The grim reaper watched her day and night. Rutger feared losing to the beast and she feared losing to death.

Placing his palm over her heart, Rutger's eyes slid closed as the memory of her heart stopping had his beast surging from his chest. *It isn't real.* He opened them to stare at his hand, its size covering most of her chest as his long fingers held her shoulder. In his ears, her heartbeat came alive, dismantling his memory, and he possessed its sound. *Mine.* Rutger looked up. "From now on we talk."

"Agreed." Jordyn felt like they had a victory. "Open communication."

Rutger wanted to stay how they were for hours, her fingers in his hair, her weight on him, all night, and all the next day. After weeks and months without her, touching her calmed his fear, and eased the pressure from the beast. Control slipped over him, giving him a clarity he hadn't possessed in weeks, and he made the toughest decision. Right then, he had questions that needed answers. Rutger gripped her wrists, and lowering them he placed her hands on his chest, covering the areas where Kory touched him. He covered hers with his own, their combined heat breaking through the cotton of his shirt and sinking into his flesh. With his hands covering hers and holding them, he met her gaze.

"When Louis arrived, you were crying. What kind of tears were those?"

Deputy Elm told her Rutger was going to give him a video, and of course, she knew he would watch it, but she didn't think she was going to be questioned. Jordyn didn't look away … no, she held his stare. "Desperation. Flint was winning and I was losing. I didn't know how to fix it."

Rutger left her alone to deal with her pain. "Until Louis?" The words were edged with jealousy and a growl. He hated the human.

"Louis invaded my territory and threatened to take me away from you." She didn't care about Dr. Holmes and his plans to dissect her. Jordyn made sure both men would be investigated and Dr. Holmes experiments stopped. *Next question*. By the look of concentration on his face, Rutger had several.

"You went to the sheriff's station today." *And didn't tell me.*

You left me alone. Jordyn exhaled and narrowed her gaze. "I did. Louis was here for revenge, but Dr. Holmes was here because he wanted to capture a Pureblood. The great Cascade pack's soothsayer. He experiments on magic-born and uses the Paranormal History class as his hunting ground. I had to tell Deputy Elm."

"Did he ask how you knew about Dr. Holmes?"

"Yes, he did. I told him that Louis admitted there was a facility, and gave him subtle hints to its location. To make sure my lies were convincing, I made calls to a few magic-born friends in Butterfly Valley about Dr. Holmes. They confirmed he's a whack job, and is known for recruiting humans for the hate group Humans Against Paranormal Influence. They meet at his lab where he does his *rehabilitations*. I gathered information and turned it over to the authorities, Director," Jordyn explained. She covered her bases.

My girl. "You said you weren't scared. Why?" Rutger splayed his hands, stretching his fingers, and wrapped them around her wrists and squeezed.

His rough palms grazed her skin. Jordyn inhaled, as Rutger's power thickened between them, and she fisted her hands. "They weren't a threat. I could have kicked their asses, walked out the front door, and they wouldn't have stopped me. At least Louis wouldn't have, he's scared of me. I needed more information from Dr. Holmes and took the risk. I have a state of the art security system and figured if my plan went to hell, I know a guy. He's the Director of Enforcers." *You watched it.*

"You put yourself in danger." Rutger's face became stone, his fury sharpening his features. *You risked your life again.*

"You would have done the same thing," Jordyn countered. "The information is going to save other magic-born and maybe from anyone thinking it's all right to kidnap me or hurt one of us. I went to human law enforcement, made a report, and will cooperate with them. My involvement will add to the relationship and the protection of the Cascade pack. The pack, klatch, and the magic-born will see we aren't afraid to protect our own."

On point. "Why was the door open?" Rutger moved his hips, Jo's legs spread wider, and she slid forward.

"I didn't close it." Jordyn couldn't stop from smiling and was barely able to stop herself from laughing, knowing it was the worst thing to do. She almost got herself kidnapped. Then she filed a report with the sheriff's department, making this a serious conversation, and Rutger needed to ask his questions. His therapy. She should be taking it seriously, but she had been taking everything seri-ously. All she wanted to do was feel like her old self.

"Next time close the damn door and answer your damn phone," Rutger ordered. He kept a straight face, despite her smile trying to destroy his resolve.

"Yes, Director." Jordyn spread her legs, rolled her hips, and felt Rutger hard beneath her. "Anything else?"

Sucking in a breath, Rutger forced himself to remain still and not respond to her. Her strength and power seeped from her like water bubbling up from drought-hardened ground and promising a flood. With the change in her, he needed to know what happened. "Where did you go to-day?"

Jordyn stopped teasing him, and answered, "The sher-iff's station."

"No, when you ran?"

Rutger held her narrowed gaze, her wolf in its copper depths, and then it darkened. *Damn.* If she shut down, he wouldn't forgive himself. "Where did you go?"

"How do you know I ran? Are you spying on me with the damn security system? The helpless victim," Jordyn accused, and scooted backwards and off him. Her instant anger fed her heated desire, the need to touch him, and it frustrated her. Yea, it may have saved her life, but seriously, spying on her. The victim. Too weak to take care of herself. *Your dependence on the Wolf Enforcer is embarrassing.* The mighty soothsayer and werewolf unable to escape humans. Jordyn looked around the house, the walls, the ceiling, where were the damn cameras?

"Wait." Before she sidestepped the table, and was out of his reach, Rutger grabbed her arms and pulled her back. "Wait." Their gazes locked, wolf on wolf, hers holding a challenge. When she stopped resisting and was straddling him once more, he looked over at the chair. *Not a lie.*

Fury burned through her when she followed his gaze and saw the pile of clothing. The anger and feel of invasion drained from her, leaving an awkwardness behind. *Should have taken care of those.* Meeting his gaze, she admitted, "The tree."

Close. He didn't have to admit his panic attack because she wasn't locked in the house. "Why did you go there?" Rutger let go of her arms, trailing his fingers down her sides to her waist where he held her hips. Her anxiety and the tension gripping her muscles eased under his touch. His body ached with fresh pain, and he wanted to nudge her to get her to roll her hips.

"I buried Flint." Jordyn wanted it to be hers and hers alone. Her win.

Flint-0.

Jordyn-1.

Game over.

If he needed to know she would tell him. She wasn't going to tell him about the dragons and her ability to call the power of her ancestors. Or how they had invaded her dreams to bring her back from her free fall into her selfishness. Not until she understood what they meant.

"Buried him. You did this after you went to the sheriff's station. How do you feel?" Rutger asked.

I won the game. "Well, Doctor... or is it Director of Enforcers interrogating his suspect? I feel like I'm tired of talking about it. It's over and done with." Sarcasm dripped from her words as she removed his hands so she could put her hands on her hips. *Stop questioning me.*

Rutger watched the challenge return to her eyes and wanted to drown in the copper and onyx swirling in her heated gaze. *Focus.* There was another topic they were ignoring, and they needed to face it. "I know it's questioning, I'm sorry. I am trying to talk to you, like your mate. Husband. I don't have much practice in this area."

Bowing her head, Jordyn closed her eyes. It wasn't going to be perfect in an instant. She started the process by getting Flint out of her head, but there were emotions she had been denying raging with renewed energy. "I'm sorry." She looked at him. *My husband.* He was making sure she was all right and it was a normal thing to do. Normal. Were they going to have that?

"One more thing." Rutger placed his hands over hers.

"One. Why do I *not* believe you?"

Her smile sent relief through him. "Maybe two." Rutger laughed, surprised at his own amusement, and her soft giggle while she sat on his thighs. This was not the time. He was going to wait. Their entire conversation was laden with stress, hurt, unhealed wounds, and he wasn't going to push her. His fears of her leaving were his fears alone. And there was no way he was going to be responsible for shattering the gleam in her gaze. "I'm not going to work tomorrow. We'll do something together, anything you want."

Do not question his motives. What you're thinking, victim, weak, he needs to babysit you-are lies. The conversation with the baron filtered through her thoughts. "Like a date?"

"Yes."

"Are you taking the baron's advice?" She tilted her head to the right, and gave him a grin.

"Maybe. Maybe you shouldn't worry about it and think about where we're going to go." Rutger leaned back. Jo shifted, positing herself on him, her eyes softening and lingering on his lips. He was sure she wasn't looking at his lips. "You're thinking."

"You told me to." *I'm thinking about what we aren't talking about.*

She knew Rutger wanted to mark her, driven to do it like a primal need, and he had been ordered to by the Highguard. Would they talk about it before he did it? His lips parted with an inhale, and her eyes moved to his mus-cled chest. She watched the rise and fall of his breathes, as if for the first time, and wanted to touch him, needed to touch him. Like she would starve without him. Her mind was spinning with her thoughts each going in different di-rections. Sure, she could get past the noise in her head, the constant drumming of mistrust, and concentrate on Rutger. She slowly reached out and placed her palms flat on his chest. His muscles tensing under her touch, his thighs flex-ing under her, and he gripped her hips.

"Wolf."

"*Mea*," Rutger growled.

"What is that?" Jordyn whispered. She thought she should know. The information was there somewhere in the mess of her head. Wasn't it Latin? And why did she in-stantly think *fatum?*

"Latin for mine. You are mine, Jo, always will be." He wasn't going to risk marking her and sending her back to embrace her fear. He would mark her with a name he owned, and only he would say to her. Basking in the fact she wanted him, her need tangling with her power and sur-rounding him had his wolf rising. *Slow down*. Let her feel her way.

Fatum, Latin for fate. They went together. *Mea* and *fa-tum*. His possession of her, and his restraint toward her made her hesitation decline a little. Jordyn ran her fingers down his shirt to his waist where she freed it from his pants. Lifting it exposed tanned skin over toned muscles. Rutger leaned forward, his face by her neck, where he in-haled, sending a shiver over her skin, and she tugged it over his head and tossed it to the floor. He leaned back, his arms at his sides and the fire's light catching the knotwork style tattoo that started at his right shoulder. It covered the muscle in black, and curving under his collar bone reached the center of his chest where its edges met the Kanin family's crest of a wolf's head. The right side depicted a wolf with a gold eye-Rutger's wolf and that of his family's-while the left side was a wolf's skull. In the skull's empty eye socket were two interlocked silver rings signifying their commitment to one another. One-Flesh.

Her gaze dropped to the dark line of hair, turned auburn in the flame's colors. With a finger, she followed the soft streak, causing the muscles of his stomach to flex, and stopped at the waist of his pants. Jordyn flattened her palms on his stomach, and inching them up his chest, each muscle constricted, further and over his shoulders he tensed with his fight for control. Linking her hands behind his corded neck, she left barely there kisses on his collarbone. His taste sat on her lips, wolf and male, the woods and strength, and she slowly moved to his neck, and giving her room he tilted his head. Her desire simmered as she nuzzled him, drawing him in, she rolled her hips, while her hands caressed his neck, shoulders, chest, and sides.

Needing to see him, she leaned back, their gazes met and she knew her eyes gleamed with her wolf. She could feel the change as her power increased. Before she let go of her restraint and slipped and the voices of the pack came roaring back, she needed to stop. It had been too damn long.

"Mea, don't block me. Not anymore. I don't want your absence," Rutger pleaded through a growl. "I have to feel you."

Nearly breathless, from simply being able to touch him freely, she whispered, "Let me ease into it."

"Mea, anything."

Jo's touches left heated tracks across his flesh, criss-crossing over him, burning his control, and had him begging for more. She stroked every nerve ending, giving him pure pleasure. Rutger gripped her hips, and gently rolled his to meet her. Her warmth sank into him, her power, like a drug, swirled in the air, casting a veil over them. Rutger couldn't ignore her fear and hesitation threading through their bond, reminding him what was at risk. His mate was a soothsayer and the trauma must have weakened her ability to control the pack's Collective. Why hadn't he considered that? Because he's a selfish bastard. The baron told him she used the pack as an excuse to quit training with Leo. If she was struggling with the Collective, he wondered what the baron said to get her to change her mind.

"Wolf." Jordyn's lips grazed his neck, her hair fell forward, feathering his shoulders and chest with the sweet spice of her wolf. "You're thinking."

"About you," Rutger responded with a shudder. Jo straightened, her gaze locked on him, and she took the bottom of her shirt and pulled it off. Holding his gaze, she slowly unhooked her bra, let one side slide down her arm, waited for a breath and let the other side fall. "I missed you." His words husky, rough, needy with sex, and his breathing grew harder when she dropped her bra to her shirt.

"As I you, Wolf."

Rutger gazed at Jo, the way her breasts rose and fell with her breaths and the softness of her skin highlighted by the fire. With the intensity and fervor of her copper eyes on him, there was no equal. When she looked at him, he knew he was the only person in the world and he would do anything to keep her attention. Rutger sat straighter, wrapped his arms around her, and hugged her to his aching body. *Need her closer.* Skin on skin. Warmth touching warmth. Magic intertwining with magic. *Slow.* Forcing himself to let her go, he unwrapped his arms, and put space between them.

"Tell me what you want." A rumble escaped him sounding rough.

Jordyn paused. When she played this out in her head, she had a plan and thought she knew what she wanted. With Rutger watching her, his heated desire warming his eyes from within, she didn't know. His control and compassion left her confused. Unsure. Like fear. *Don't lose focus.* Before she betrayed herself, she whispered, "I want you to touch me."

Jo's soft confession sounded louder than a gunshot, and entering him like silver, it coursed in his veins. Taking her by the hips, he brought her closer to him until her breasts were pressed against his flesh. "Like this?" Jo nodded and Rutger gently moved his hands inside the waist of her lounge pants, under the thin line of her G-sting, and stopped when his hands covered her backside. Urging her toward him, Jo's weight stroked him through his BDU pants, her heat sinking into him, creating a growl in his chest. Rutger's lips feathered her neck under her ear, to her jaw, and he took her mouth in a desperate kiss.

"Wolf," Jordyn murmured. Her lips moving against his as she rolled her hips.

Pressing her into him, he brought her closer and whispered, "*Mea.*"

Jordyn leaned back, trying to create space, except his hands held her and she felt the calluses scoring his palms on her skin. Keeping her eyes on him through her lashes, she kissed the linked silver rings, tattooed above his heart. Lower she licked his nipple. He gasped, and she smiled as his spice, wolf, and the wild woods living within him laced the tip of her tongue. She licked him again and swallowed, spreading his spice and drowning in Rutger. Holding his gold gaze, she pressed herself on his hardness, and intertwined her fingers at his neck.

"Mea," Rutger growled. His hips met her, and holding her, ground against her.

"Wolf."

"Need you. Now," Rutger demanded.

Without waiting for her to reply, he removed his hands from her waist, letting her scoot back, the separation bringing cool air to his thighs and he missed her touch.

Jordyn stood, her legs weak with anticipation, and hoped she didn't embarrass herself by sinking to the floor. She slid her pants down her legs, did the same with her pink G-string, and stepped out of them. Jordyn looked at the pile of clothing and felt a sliver of regret as she thought about the oversized sweatshirt and loose pants she had been camping in. Those days were over. With a satisfied grin curving her lips, she watched Rutger struggle.

Too damn long. Months. They felt like years. She excited him, made his body melt under her touch as she pushed his wolf, making his hands shake. Rutger bent and hastily began untying his boots, promising to buy a pair without laces, and tugged his socks off. Once free, he stood and started unbuckling his belt, his fingers struggling to release it from itself. With his concentration focused on getting out of his BDU pants-why was he having problems? -he sucked in a breath and stopped. Completely naked, Jo grabbed his hands, and taking them, placed them on her hips. The backs of her fingers grazed his stomach, making his abs tighten, as she unfastened the tactical nylon belt. Making a whispered sound as she pulled it free from the loops, Jo looked up at him and dropped it. She gave him a hooded gaze and unbuttoned the top button and the zipper slid down. Rutger gasped as she worked his pants down his thighs with his boxers, lowering at the same time. He looked at her to see her staring up at him with gleaming eyes lined in black. He thought the silence of the last couple of months was going to kill him, not even close. Watching Jo undress him was going to be the end of him.

With her body drumming with passion and heat spreading to her arms and legs, Jordyn forced herself to cling to her shredding control. Her hands slid up his muscled calves to his thighs and further to his hips.

Rutger's entire body trembled; his was going to crash to the floor. His muscles tensed, and his attention focused on Jo. "*Mea*," he whispered.

Jo's heated copper gaze, looked up at him, making him want to take her and toss her to the couch. *Control.* As he took an unbalanced step backward, his legs met fabric, and he sank down, bringing her with him. Jo remained standing, gazing, and when he thought he was going to melt under her stare, she placed one knee on the cushion. Rutger shifted his hips, understanding her intent, his body needing to touch her. Be inside of her.

Leaning in with her weight on her right knee, Jordyn's left knee sank into the cushion beside Rutger's thigh. She took her time lowering herself on him, feeling each sensual inch as she fed him inside of her. She missed him. His feel. The way he filled her.

Rutger growled when she rolled her hips, a gravely moan leaving his parted lips. "You feel like silk."

Jordyn's fingers sank into the cushion behind Rutger, she rolled her hips, their skin slick with sweat, and their heavy breathing. Deep inside of her the pressure was building. Her body grabbed it and tightened around it as her power increased, and the walls she had in place to protect Rutger from her emotions began crumbling. If she let go of one, the other was going to plow through her.

The fatal feel of her trying to block him inched into his senses. "Come to me, *Mea*." Rutger's voice mirrored his touches to her breasts, thighs, and back, desperate, like he would never touch her enough. "Let me feel all of you."

I don't deserve our bond, his doubt screamed. *Weak*. Rutger growled. No, he didn't. Who was he to demand she open herself to him? No one. He had a purpose, and it was to protect what was his. Taunted and tormented he knew he wouldn't. Damn, he couldn't. Not a man who had been helpless to save her and then almost lost his life to the beast. As her mate it was his responsibility to defend and guard her, not cause her more pain.

Jo breathed a soft moan as the ends of her hair feathered his chest and she leaned down, their lips barley touching with their rhythm. Losing himself in her husky moans, her skin on his, the scent of her arousal in the air, and his growing desire, his fingers dug into her hips. Rutger could prove to her he was strong enough and was worthy by giving her what she needed. He would protect her, give his life if he needed.

Jordyn heard him and ignored him. She fought to bury the sharpest edge of her power. Responding to her denial, his wolf rose to surround them, like a protective barrier between them and the world. He didn't try to seek her through their bond. Like a soft touch, his wolf's essence beckoned her wolf, its feel carrying his promise of security.

Her wolf's instincts and needs to be with its mate overruled her, telling her there was no threat and Jordyn's fear eased.

The walls holding her power and blocking their bond crashed to ruble. Fire flared up and through her, opening the bond and releasing a flood of emotions. She expected them to cut through her, them, twisting her mind, and when they didn't, she let the wave ride itself out and it was gone. Controlled. Jordyn's pleasure freely swept through her, and inhaling their combined scents, she matched Rutger's thrusts. The fire spread to him, and she heard him growl from the intensity. She could feel him, sense him, and have him without being consumed by the Collective and the pain she had been harboring. She straightened and leaned back, her hands on his thighs, as Rutger gripped her hips and ground her against him.

"Mea," Rutger moaned. "I feel you."

Jordyn met his hard gaze as her body thrummed from the mounting pleasure and the edge of her release. She didn't reply, she couldn't form words. Leaning down she answered him by licking his bottom lip. He wrapped his arms around her pressing her to him, kissed her, and teased her with his tongue.

Jo's body clenched around him, her hips rocking on him. Breaking from her, Rutger's lips, curved and with a husky voice he whispered, "You're coming for *me*."

My wolf. Jordyn's smile faded, she flattened her palms on his chest, met his gold gaze, then gripped the cushion. Breathless moans escaped her as pleasure erupted and saturated her body in heated pulses.

Rutger seized his control and held it tight, telling himself he was going to make it last as long as possible. He wanted Jo on top of him, him inside of her, and their power and wolves weaving around them. Ecstasy as he had never known. Jo's moans filled his ears, her thrusts quickened, and her nails pierced his skin. Working like a trigger, his hunger drank her in, and building, his lust shattered his concentration. Rutger couldn't stop the low growl rumbling in his chest and escaping him.

Mark her. The primal urge twisted with his desire, making his teeth ache and his wolf forced its way through his control. No. No. He was not going to destroy the moment by taking her throat. Rutger focused on Jo's body, her moans, and her hands gripping his shoulders. Keeping his mouth from the tender skin of her neck and shoulder, he pushed backward into the couch. The strongest need drowned under his roar as ecstasy rushed through his veins, dousing his body in pleasure and making him shudder with his release.

Jordyn's lips curved as she lazily rolled her hips, her skin warm and her body trembling. She leaned forward to rest her forehead on Rutger's chest, and listened to their heartbeats. She felt his struggle with his wolf, and his control over his beast. Amid letting pleasure sweep her into bliss, she was sure if he marked her, she would have let him. Now she was thankful he didn't. They needed to talk without months of silence sitting between them, the pressure of the past weighing down on them and clouding their minds. They needed time. As if there was such a thing as extra time.

Rutger's hands gently feathered Jo's back, up, down, following her spine, his fingers grazing her quivering muscles. When she didn't look at him, worry threaded through his words. "Mea. Jo."

Jordyn couldn't look at him, not yet. She didn't want him to see the goofy grin she knew she was wearing and the satisfaction she felt. *Should have had sex months ago.*

"Mea, please." Rutger bowed his head, his lips by her ear, kissed her, then nudged her.

Jordyn sat up, met his gaze and the grin curved her lips. "Wolf."

"Are you all right?"

"What do you think?" She straightened and stretched her arms above her head.

Holding her hips, he urged her back then forward. "I like what I see. I especially like it when you're naked and I'm naked and we're together."

They stared at each other for several seconds with the fire popping behind her. The charred pieces of wood caved into each other causing weak flames to reach for the chimney. A slow melody drifted its lyrics of flowers and sunsets floating on top. He hadn't noticed the music.

"I don't want to leave you but the fire needs wood."

As hot as her skin felt, Jordyn didn't think there was a chance the cold was going to bother her. His eyes gleamed as if he knew what she was thinking, and leaning to him, she kissed his lips. "Fine." She rose, left his lap, and when he stood, she grabbed the throw, sat down, and drew it up to her chest. Jordyn watched him, his words in her ears, and the feel of his body against hers. In languid movements, his muscles flexed, his shoulders seeming broader, straighter, as if a part of him had returned.

Scarlet embers drifted, turned black, and fell to the blaze and crawled over the added pieces of wood. Rutger watched the flames as his clarity and strength felt secure. *Like I'm whole.* Not tormented by loss. There was only one more thing they had to face and the worst would be over. He had to mark her. His wolf demanded it. Turning, he faced Jo, she was sitting with her glass in hand and watching him.

"Lay with me for a minute?" he asked as he approached her.

She warmed with his words. "Yes." Jordyn set her glass on the table and standing, waited for Rutger to lie down on the couch. After pulling the throw over them, she cuddled next to him, her back against his chest, her head resting on the bend of his elbow, and watched the flames. The thick tension they had been living with ceased, replaced with a comfortable silence. Together, they listened to the music and watched the colors of the flames play in the room.

"Wolf," Jordyn whispered, and stared at the fire.

"Mea." Rutger's hand found her hip and holding the curve pulled her closer and held her tight.

"I want to say thank you."

"My pleasure," he growled in her ear.

Arrogant wolf. Jordyn heard the grin in his words and smiled. "That too. But I meant-" She stopped, closed her eyes, and inwardly sighing, hated herself for not letting the moment last longer.

"Look at me." Rutger backed deeper into the couch, giving Jo room to turn and face him. "We didn't have a chance to be together before and this relationship is new to the both of us. I need you to know, I wouldn't do anything to betray your trust."

Jordyn stopped herself from flinching from the haunted look in his eyes. She did it to him. Like he saw her closing herself off from him. "The Highguard. We have to answer to them."

"We aren't going to think about the Highguard. We are going to work on us. Mate, I worry I'll hurt you and you'll barricade yourself inside your head and I'll never reach you. I can't lose you. I never want to feel the emptiness again." He kissed her forehead, lingered for second thinking about his honesty, and how she was going to react. She didn't turn from him, didn't back down from him. Her fearlessness gave him the courage to continue. "When you're ready, I am going to mark you. I promise, not until you ask me to," Rutger assured. As he stared at her, doubt reared its head. If he buried his beast, would he be able to keep his promise? It was proving to be impossible? He tried repeatedly and failed.

Jordyn felt his wolf rising and wrapped in the frantic edge of his beast, hadn't been afraid. If he asked her, she would admit its feel was intense, like Rutger, demanding, powerful, and she liked it, needed its force. He was her mate, an alpha, and was supposed to be strong. She gazed at him, relaxed beside him, and read the worry in the lines fanning out from his eyes.

"I felt your struggle," she admitted softly. Jordyn drew her fingertip over the linked silver rings tattooed on his chest.

"You did?" *And you weren't scared?* Rutger was surviving on strict control over every aspect of his life for fear he would push Jo too far. But if she wasn't scared of him.

We are bonded. Jo made an agreeing sound and nuzzled into him, her body a perfect fit to his. He didn't ask her to explain. Draping his arm over her side, he wondered what else she felt and what she was thinking about. Rutger listened to Jo's heartbeat-it had become a need-her light breathing, and when her muscles felt as if they unwound, he drifted into an easy sleep.

A shrill ring of a cell phone blasted the silence, jerking Rutger awake and almost sending Jordyn to the floor. "Not mine," she mumbled still half asleep and clinging to him. She lazily sat up and scooting to the side, giving Rutger room to dislodge himself from the back of the couch and the cushions.

Rutger rummaged through his abandoned boots, socks, and boxers, pausing when he found her white lace bra, picked it up with one finger and dangled it in front of her. "I like this." He let it drop and fumbled for his pants. The ringing blared as the screen lit up his pocket and turning his pants over he pulled it free. The number and picture, the two of them standing outside of Foxwood after Tanner's wedding, told him it was his father, the baron. *Damn.* He considered ignoring the call, except he wasn't going to the office in the morning, and if the baron was calling this late, he had a reason.

Rutger cleared his throat, trying to sound as if he hadn't been asleep, and said in greeting, "Baron." He turned and gave Jo a bored look.

When Rutger's shoulders caved and he acted like the phone call pained him, Jordyn smiled and giggled. Taking the throw, she brought it to her chest leaving Rutger naked, his firm back and hips in front of her, and sitting on the edge of the couch. The baron's gruff voice, booming with his authority, carried, and she half-heartily listened to their conversation. Jordyn reached for her glass, and with wine in hand sat back, and went over their evening. They had come to an agreement about the Highguard's demands, when he was going to mark her, and they confessed their fears. Where did it leave them? Jordyn didn't know. She sipped her wine and heard the word *date*. Wow. Shaking her head, she couldn't believe that's where they were. Fated mates, dating.

It could be a romantic night in the woods, Jordyn thought, because she had no desire to go out in public.

"Yes, baron," Rutger replied and nodded his head like the baron could see him, and repeated, "Yes, baron." He held his tumbler of bourbon and sipped the amber liquid, while nodding. "Yes, baron, goodnight." He tossed his phone to the table causing it to skid a couple of inches.

"What's happening in your world?" Jordyn asked.

My world. "Ansel reported I wasn't going to be at the office tomorrow, and the baron figured it was because something happened between us. We've been invited over for an interrogation ... I mean, dinner tomorrow night." Rutger leaned back, his shoulders low on the cushion, the plain of his abs flexed, the muscles in his thighs tight, and tension running through him.

Jordyn watched him take another drink of his bourbon, his eyes staring at nothing. *Interrogation is right.* "Maybe it won't be. We'll go, visit, have dinner, and leave."

"Remember, I can sense lies," he countered and turned his head to look at her. The throw dipped, clinging to the curve of her breasts, and just covering her thighs. When her lips parted, he saw the inside of her bottom lip was dark from her wine. He tasted the spice tangled in alcohol as if he had taken a sip.

"It won't be if we don't let it. Anyway, let him ask his questions, it can't hurt. Between the baron and baroness, it might convince them we've taken the first step in repairing our relationship. They'll stop questioning us, and more importantly they'll stop worrying." Between her and Rutger, neither looked their best. Sadly, they looked tired, stressed out, and scarred.

Rutger's lips curved in a wicked grin. "It was a great first step."

Jordyn scooted forward, set her empty glass on the table, and leaned back on the cushions. "Wolf," she whispered.

Rutger heard her grin in the word and sitting straighter, finished his bourbon, set the glass next to Jo's and faced her. She turned to her side, the throw up by her shoulders, and was staring at him. "Mea."

"I'm exhausted. Take me to bed." Jordyn yawned, her body giving into the secure feel of Rutger, and the nonexistence stress.

Rutger stood, his muscles flexing with his movement, gathered Jo in his arms, and holding her against him, walked to the stairs and headed to their bedroom.

Up early, and not having to go to the office, Rutger stood at the bedroom window, hands on his hips, his fingers grazing the waist of his shorts. With a peaceful silence in the room, he watched the golden halo of the sun crest the mountaintop, making the ridge glow before fully rising and casting its cool yellow on the lake and house. There was no pain, no empty void sitting between them and eating him from the inside. He was happy. Satisfied.

Jo slept, without nightmares, soundly behind him, her essence drifting freely in their bond like a warm wind. As hers caressed him, he knew his felt weighted, like it carried his beast within it, and it stalked not drifted. He remained at the window, watching a world he ignored for months and listening to Jo's heartbeat. He found concentrating on its rhythm made the pain of having lost her weaken while the mere beat soothed his beast. Before he woke her up just to see her eyes open and the gleam in their copper and onyx depths, he left the bedroom.

Rutger grabbed both glasses from the night before, rinsed them out, and set them in the sink. Next, he fixed coffee, and waiting for it to finish, he stood with his palms flat on the concrete counter marveling at the night they shared. From her admission she wasn't scared of him or his struggle with his beast, to her touching him and responding to him with eagerness and moans gave him confidence. Were they going to have the life they wanted? Were they going to have each other?

God, he hoped so.

Jordyn rolled to her side, the thick, cotton comforter soft on her bare shoulder and side, and her thoughts about the night surfacing as sleep descended. Cuddling deeper in the flannel sheets, she enjoyed the content feeling of having the night pass without a nightmare, a panic attack, and her staring at the ceiling for hours with tears burning her eyes. She slept through the night, content, naked, and beside Rutger and his warm naked body.

"Wolf," she mumbled. Inhaling, she drew in his wolf's scent, exhaled, and reached across the bed to touch cold sheets. Gone. Sitting up she searched the room and found herself alone.

"Nice way to wake up." She couldn't hide her disappointment or the hurt in her rapidly beating heart from the months of being left alone. Jordyn instinctively protected her dark emotions by encompassing them.

After the night they shared and the promise to keep communications open between them, Rutger wouldn't leave her alone. *Right.* And they promised each other they were going to work on their relationship. Her mind chased the trail promising to hurt the most and it reminded her, he left her alone after an attempted kidnapping. By Louis.

Stop. Jordyn focused, sent her senses out, and meet his essence sitting in their bond and his wolf reached for her. Relief flooded in with his presence at the same time it chased fear from her. Damn, she let her fear get the best of her and it rattled her with an intensity she wanted to deny.

"He didn't leave," she told herself. "Get a grip." Shoving the feeling down, Jordyn tossed the covers. She padded across the room, entered the bathroom, and without turning a light on, gazed in the mirror at her reflection. Despite the moment of panic, her eyes didn't show it and weren't dark and haunted. The normal. Normal since becoming a soothsayer. Staring back at her was onyx swirling in copper. She liked seeing it, and a spark of power shot through her. *Getting better.*

Jordyn brushed her teeth, put her raven hair in a messy bun, and on the way out, grabbed Rutger's T-shirt from the counter and pulled it over her head.

Rutger's head jerked up, gold rolled over his eyes reflecting his wolf, and he searched the loft and double doors of the bedroom. Her heartbeat pounded franticly, her sadness swept through the bond as if it might engulf him, and in an instant, it was gone. Cut off. Her absence like a knife to the heart. He begged her not to give him the void and there it was filling the link between them. Rutger checked the security panel, all green and blinking, then sent his senses out to check for trespassers. Nothing besides the usual run of wildlife, squirrels, chipmunks, a mountain lion, and deer. No humans. Unless they were cloaking themselves.

"Shit," he mumbled as he darted from the kitchen through the living room and to the stairs.

Witches. Was it possible there were others and they had come back for revenge? Rutger took the stairs three at a time, his wolf emerging and a growl building in his chest as he ran down the hall and burst through the doors.

"Jo, where are you?" he demanded as he rushed inside. She wasn't in bed. Hadn't gone outside. The windows and balcony doors were all closed, the windows locked, alarms blinking. He barely stopped himself from inspecting the bathroom when he heard her voice.

"Right here." With wide eyes Jordyn sat straighter and twisted to check the windows and French doors to the second story deck. Did she miss something? An attack? Was someone outside? She didn't know it was possible when the once rustic, two-story log home had been transformed into a fortress with the all-knowing security system.

It meant witches. They were able to cloak their presence with magic. *Not from me*, Jordyn thought. Using her senses, she searched for magic, a power source, spells, their essences, and found nothing, except Rutger. He didn't move, his bare chest rising and falling with his heavy breathes. He continued to stare at her with his wolf's burnt gold eyes like she wasn't real. Jordyn slowly stood, and turning couldn't stop from rechecking the room and the control panel. All lights blinking away telling her she was locked inside. All right, she was spooked.

"Is someone here?" she asked.

Jo was sitting in the chair in front of the fire, the throw over her lap, and wearing his T-shirt. Clearly reacting to his fear and tracking his movements, she checked the French doors and deck, windows, and the panel. He was lost for words when she stood, the throw falling to the carpet, exposing her legs and bare feet. Jo checked the doors again, and when she faced him, the haunted look she discarded the night before returned. His mind was a tangle of uncertainty and a rage he was unsure how to control. "What happened?" His question more bark than words.

"What are you talking about?" Jordyn asked hesitantly. A hazy veil in the shape of his wolf hovered over him, its frayed edges touching his shoulders. He was losing control. What the hell pushed him? Jordyn turned to check the deck, only to make sure there was no one there. "There's no one outside. I would have sensed them," she tried assuring him. His muscles tensed and turned to cords under his skin, then his body shuddered as if he was fighting himself. With his hands in tight fists and the beast hovering over him, Jordyn refused to flinch. Because she wasn't scared of him. For a split second, she thought she should be, then asked herself why.

I felt you cut me off. "You blocked me, Jo. Don't fucking block me." Rutger regretted the growl, dreading she would recoil from his anger, but was unable to stop himself. His eyes darted over the room, the windows, and landed on Jo.

This isn't about witches. "Block you?" Jordyn mumbled with her brows drawn in confusion. What the hell was he talking about and why was he angry? Jordyn watched his eyes flicker between mahogany and gold, and he clenched his jaw. *Oh hell.* It was habit to guard her weakness by closing herself off. Jordyn needed to fix her mistake. Her wolf rose, its power caressing her skin, and she held onto it as she opened the bond between them. Uncontrolled, his fury mixed with insecurity poured from him and roiled around him. Jordyn needed to calm him down. In a low voice she said, "Wolf, I can explain."

Wolf. Rutger scarcely heard her over the rush of his pulse in his ears and the howling of his wolf. His anger and desperate need to feel her overpowered him and he was having a hard time locating reality. When her strength embraced him, her calm traveled the bond, and finding him, soothed his beast. Even with pieces of lucidity telling him she was all right, no one was in danger, and her essence flowed in their link, he wasn't budging and ignored her. "Explain?"

"Come sit and I will." Jordyn gave him heavy eyes, held her hand out, palm up, and waited. He seemed to consider her, thinking about what she needed to tell him, and she feared he was going to ignore her. When she felt a calmness replace his wolf's agitation, she relaxed.

Jo looked wounded, her hand out for him like she had done something wrong. *What have you done?* Rutger tilted his head, trying to figure out what happened, and took an uneasy step, another, and unclenching his fists, placed his hand on Jo's. "Tell me." Jo raised his hand and kissed the inside of his wrist. She let go of him and turning him, motioned him to sit down. *Come to me*, Rutger thought as he sat in the chair.

Jordyn needed to be near him, touching him, when she explained herself. Sitting on his lap, her legs draped over the arm of the chair, she met his gaze. "I woke up and you were gone. I was scared you left. Like seeing the empty room easily destroyed the progress we made last night. I want to be normal, but there's this fear and it's hard to fight."

Nothing. Nothing happened. He left her yesterday, and the day before that, and the day before that ... Damn, he didn't have a great track record. *Can't blame her.* Rutger's rage filtered through him turned into nothing and the tension gripping him released him. He rested his forehead on her arm. "You were sleeping and I didn't want to wake you, so I went downstairs and made coffee and breakfast." He raised his head and met her gaze. "I understand. But when you blocked me, it meant something bad was happening."

"It would be nice if there was an easy fix." Jordyn hoped by burying Flint the rest would fall into place. The battle was continuing and she didn't know how to make it end and adding to her unease were the feelings raging out of control. Feelings. No. Awareness. Her senses were telling her a hundred things and she didn't understand.

"You didn't act on your fear, besides blocking me." His lips curved with an attempt at a grin, a subtle warning saying don't do that to him again, and he wouldn't go full on beast. "You stopped the feeling and reacted to the facts. You felt me here, in the house, I didn't leave you. It's a step," Rutger tried assuring her.

"You raced up here not knowing what you were going to find. I hate that." *A weak mess.* Jordyn leaned into him, his warm skin against her, his arms wrapped around her, and he kissed her head.

"I was worried. Not over you, you're good." The sight of her shapeshifting mid-stride played in front of him. If she fought with the same power, she would easily beat the enemy. "I was worried because you're popular with others. I didn't want to see someone here trying to take you from me." Rutger held Jo to his chest, her touch reassuring him she was there.

Jordyn bowed her head and wanted to laugh but at the same time she wanted to cry. "No one is going to take me. Not again. Not ever."

"I believe you. It's going to take us time to beat the conditioned fear and create our normal." Rutger nudged her, Jo straightened, and he took her chin in his fingers and turned her head. When she faced him, the onyx swirling in her eyes made him pause. "We've had our excitement for the morning. What do you want to do today?"

Nothing. "I don't know. Can we start with coffee and food?"

"Absolutely." Jo eased off his lap to walk over to the bench at the end of the bed where her lounge pants were. Rutger watched her, making sure she wasn't over thinking the morning. Even if he was guilty of doing the same damn thing. "It'll be ready when you are." He stood, his body feeling like it had been in a vice, and went to the door. "I made bacon, eggs, and there's croissants."

Jordyn absently nodded as she shoved her foot into a leg of her pants, her thoughts going to how she was going to extract the fear from everything she did so she could think clearly. They survived the incident, as best they knew how, and she considered it a win. No one was hurt. No one shutdown. They talked about it and were back on good terms.

"I'll see you downstairs, then." Rutger knew the silent, 'I'm thinking' expression etched on her face and knew she wasn't listening to him. He had to let her work through her thoughts, even if it pained him.

A pounding started at the front of her head as she straightened her pants, sat down in the chair, and pulled on socks. Pinching the bridge of her nose, Jordyn squeezed her eyes shut with her racing thoughts. She needed to kick the fear loose. And witches. With Rutger's worry over her she thought the witches had retuned. But she knew they weren't there. She would have sensed them the same way she sensed Rutger and other magic-born. She had to believe her senses and have confidence in her abilities. With her hands on her knees, she exhaled. She was able to sense power, not the person, which meant she could sense anyone.

"Anyone. Anytime. If I get rid of the bullshit cluttering my mind." Jordyn looked at the empty room, exhaled, inhaled, and stood.

With views of the lake, Rutger placed the plate of sliced strawberries, then the bacon and eggs on the table beside the croissants and went to the counter to grab their cups of coffee. He studied breakfast, hoping Jo would eat, and hoping she might tell him what consumed her thoughts so quickly. There were varied reasons for it, anything from the fear she lived with, the witches, or other intruders. Like Shadow Lord. Only he hadn't told her about him and this morning convinced him he wasn't going to. And what did she mean when she said she would have felt them? Was she still dealing with having been inside Flint's head? Guilt headed him off, telling him it was his fury. He scared her when he burst into the room ready for a fight and accusing her of what he didn't know. While it might be part of it, it wasn't the reason. It had to be her powers. Like shifting in mid-stride.

Were they changing?

If they were, what was happening to her?

Rutger's phone chimed, jerking him back to reality, and he groaned. Leaving the kitchen, he entered the living room, and finding it on the table where he left it the night before, picked it up. He assumed it was the baron reminding him of their dinner plans, so when he saw the screen lit up with an alert, his heart stopped. For the second time. Rutger couldn't check the message quick enough. Swiping across the screen, he read the notice. It was the sensor and license plate reader at front of his driveway. It would take

Mandy, after she saw the alert, a couple of minutes to run the plate and send him the information. Rutger looked at his bedroom doors, then the front door. He had a few minutes before his guest arrived.

To save Jo from being surprised by their visitor, Rutger quickly typed out a message telling her someone was coming and if she came downstairs, she needed to get dressed. Like not wearing his T-shirt. He sent the warning, and a second later a soft chime sounded and he knew she received the message. It wasn't an enforcer, Ansel, or one of his family, the alert would have given him their information because it was on file. An unknown was heading toward his house and his mate, and he wasn't taking any chances. Rutger took his Glock 21, 45 caliber pistol from its holster, and with weapon in hand opened the front door and watched a dark blue crossover ease down the driveway then park behind his truck.

Rutger leaned against a log flanking the stairs, an open door behind him, shirtless, his clan's tattoo covering most of his chest, an elaborate black band around his left bicep that bulged with muscle, was shoeless, wearing basketball shorts, and brandishing a weapon. His shoulder-length hair looked combed through with his fingers, more out of nervous habit than grooming, and his five o'clock shadow looked like it was going on a forty-eight hour rally.

"You look like hell," Detective Watt greeted. He grabbed his tablet, closed the car door, and faced the Director of Enforcers. "If your appearance is any indication of how well things are going, I'm going to believe the rumors. Neither of you are doing well."

Rutger helped Detective Watt with the Organized Paranormal Investigations, providing information and answering questions about non-humans. As a liaison between the pack and human law enforcement, Rutger assisted the OPI when the witches began their killing spree. The last time Rutger saw the detective, he found him at Butte Springs with a bullet wound, bleeding out, and sitting behind the wheel of his SUV, that had crashed into a tree. What the hell did he want?

"Why are you here?" Rutger asked ignoring the detective. He tightened his grip on his gun, not bothering to hide it.

Detective Watt glanced at the weapon. "Cottonwood County along with the Paradise County sheriff's department have handed Miss Langston's case over to the OPI. I'm the lead investigator," he replied. "I need to talk to her."

"She gave her statement to Deputy Elm and I emailed him the video. You can't refute physical evidence," Rutger argued.

"Affirmative, I have the report and the video, and no, I can't. No one is. I still need to talk to her," Detective Watt insisted. "It won't take long. I wouldn't want to interrupt your stellar quality of life."

Rutger didn't want him in the house or anywhere near Jo, after the morning they had. Becoming a suspect in the murder investigation of missing witches quickly destroyed law enforcements confidence in him and put him on their watch list. If there was so much as a missing person a deputy or detective contacted Rutger. If he denied the detective's request, it would make him look guilty and he didn't need the trouble. He did, however, need law enforcement on his side. He had no choice.

"Fine," Rutger mumbled in an annoyed tone. Without inviting the detective in, he turned around and walked into the house leaving Detective Watt waiting by his crossover.

Standing in the entryway, Rutger turned to see the detective stare at the palm vein reader, keypad, and flood lights lining the porch. "She left the door open." That was going to be his question. How did the humans get into house if there was a security system?

"I watched the video. The system is impressive. I noticed you were waiting for me, armed. Did you use your senses, or is there more?"

"There are sensors at the entrance of the driveway, a license plate reader, and facial recognition. I should have your information in a minute," Rutger explained.

"All of this after Mr. Platt trespassed?" Detective Watt entered the massive log house taking in the few photographs displayed, the rustic décor, the huge beams in the vaulted ceiling, and the wall of windows with views of the lake and mountains. Lycans loved nature. Jordyn Langston had been a successful landscape photographer whose work was displayed in a gallery before Mr. Platt kidnapped her. He figured there would have been several of her pieces on display not two. He noticed most the furnishings were masculine, borderline forgotten, and there wasn't a feminine presence.

"Nice place," Detective Watt said.

Rutger ignored him. "I'll get Jo."

"No need." Jordyn left the stairs and walking across the living room side stepped the detective to stand beside Rutger. She handed him a T-shirt and she asked, "What's going on?"

Detective Watt talked with Miss Langston at a murderer scene, but nothing prepared him for her picture when they were trying to figure out where Mr. Platt could have taken her. He considered her beautiful with her onyx hair, dark cocoa eyes lined with black, and her confidence, what he suspected came from her Pureblood genes. She intrigued him, and the image stunned him and made him pause. It was the first time he thought he could see a lycan as a woman. That was then. The woman standing before him looked gaunt in her oversized hoodie and loose cotton pants. Worse, her eyes of onyx and copper looked haunted. Kidnapping and torture would break anyone. He hated seeing what it did to her.

"Miss Langston, I'm Detective Watt with the Organized Paranormal Investigations, you might remember me from the case involving the witches. I'll be the person responsible for the investigation into the allegations against Mr. Myers and Dr. Holmes. I need to ask you a couple of questions," he explained.

Jordyn remembered him. "Would you like to sit down?" Because she needed to sit down. Keep it together.

"Thank you." Detective Watt noticed Rutger had set his gun on the table to pull the T-shirt over his head. He would keep an eye on it. He sat across from Miss Langston and watched the way her movements looked weak and indecisive. He prayed she was going to be able to help him. "After Dr. Holmes' arrest, the anti-paranormal group HAPI, went silent. I've talked to several people who know about it but I can't find members, or anyone with a connection to the group. No one is talking. In your statement, you said Mr. Myers told you about a facility?"

Hopefully HAPI went to hell. "Yes. Dr. Holmes said they *rehabilitate* shapeshifters there," Jordyn answered with emphasis on rehabilitate. Thankfully, her voice held and she didn't sound like she felt. Like a victim.

"Do you know where the facility is?" Detective Watt asked.

Yes. "No. I made some calls, trying to find out, but got nowhere." Lying to a detective, nice. At least humans couldn't sense lies.

"I've talked to the people you mentioned to Deputy Elm. However, I think you do know. And I need its location," Detective Watt demanded, as his eyes narrowed on her.

"I said, I don't know," Jordyn repeated. *Keep it together.*

"Was that your question, Detective Watt? She said she doesn't know." If Jo answered the question honestly, it was going to put them both under suspicion. He was ready to toss the detective out of the house. "Are you finished?"

Ignoring Rutger, Detective Watt concentrated his attention on Miss Langston. He was bullying a victim. A lycan. Her shoulders visibly tensed under his stare and the sight almost made him change his tactics. Almost. "I know what you can do, like getting into someone's head, I was there. I know Mr. Platt used his ability as a non-human, classified witch, and your ability as a soothsayer to establish a connection to you. I'm not an unbelieving human. I believe in the powers non-humans or the magic-born have. So, I know you learned the location of the facility. Tell me and I'll leave." Detective Watt leaned forward a sliver, keeping his attention split between Miss Langston, Rutger, and his gun.

"What do you mean, you know and were there?" Jordyn asked. Her gaze shifting to Rutger and back to the detective. Threatened, the hoodie didn't help from feeling as if her skin was being stripped from her and leaving her exposed to the world.

"In an attempt to locate you and the witches, we were looking through the pictures on your camera. Halfway through, you contacted Rutger and showed him where you were being held. I watched him," he explained. "I'm not accusing you, as you have been cleared of any wrong doing, but I know Mr. Platt did not have the intestinal fortitude to take his own life."

Not accusing me, but reminding me. The faint scent of lavender and Wolf's bane drifted. She wanted to wave it away, but stopped herself. Jordyn couldn't stop from twisting her hands and worry from infecting her. "Who else knows?"

"No one. I want to show you something." Detective Watt swiped his finger over the screen of his tablet and her voice sounded followed by Louis', then it stopped. Satisfied, he handed it to Miss Langston.

Jordyn took it and the screen showed Louis gripping her wrists and holding her close to his face. "I was there," she stated flatly and handed it back him. Jordyn stopped herself from flinching, but wasn't able to stop from rubbing her wrists where Louis had held her.

Damn him. "You've crossed the line," Rutger warned. He had pieces of the old Jo, there was no way he was losing her.

Detective Watt watched the video a hundred times, trying to memorize her every move, the way she reacted to the men, her facial features, and the different changes in her voice. He watched the way she let them ramble on about how they could save her when she had zero intention of going with them. His obsession with the female lycan, photographer, woman, Pureblood, didn't stop with the video. He did a thorough background investigation on her, including getting her medical records, then handed the information and video to the OPI's criminal profiler unit. After they analyzed Miss Langston, they gave him a complete work up on her. It wasn't bad but it wasn't good. If he needed to, he would play everything he had.

Rutger watched Detective Watt observe Jo like she was a curiosity as her nerves got the best of her. She twisted her hands, once, twice, then her wrists the same way she had in the video and Rutger knew the detective had watched the video more than once. It meant, he also watched her pause, as if she was thinking about something, besides being kidnapped. Like she was trying to concentrate.

Jordyn jumped when Rutger's phone rang, filling the room with its shrill sound. "Sorry."

Jo flinched, he wanted to roar. "Kanin," Rutger answered. They stopped talking, their attention going to him. Rutger stared at Detective Watt. "Yes, that's him and he is here. It's all right, Mandy, tell Ansel I'll talk to him later this evening. Going to be at Foxwood for dinner. Affirmative, bye." Rutger set his phone on the table and met Detective Watt's uneasy gaze. "Your information. Took longer because your car is registered to the state."

How the hell was Rutger getting information? Did he really want to know? No. Detective Watt met Miss Langston's dark stare. "You didn't give the deputies the location of the facility because the video would be used as evidence and prove no one told you. Your admission would have created questions, like how did you get the information? You fear it will expose your ability to read minds, which will lead to questions about Mr. Platt's suicide. If he didn't commit suicide, then there would be doubt he didn't kill his followers. Because you're non-humans, there's no statute of limitations on the crimes filed against you, meaning the investigations would be reopened. The both of you, the main focus on Rutger, would be investigated, again. You lied in your statement, to Deputy Elm, and could be charged with obstruction of justice and perjury."

Detective Watt trapped her. "Your point?" Jordyn asked. Great, she was going to be charged with Flint's murder and Rutger was facing being charged with the murders of the witches. If she could kill Flint again and again, she would.

"This picture shows Mr. Myers holding you close to him." Detective Watt turned the tablet screen to them. "As you can see, no one can see his face and no one can hear him. While he was holding you, he could have told you the location," Detective Watt explained.

Right. "They'll believe I just happened to remember that little detail?" Jordyn asked. "And what happens when Louis denies he told me? They'll see me as a lycan trying to trap a human."

Detective Watt sat back, his tablet in his hand, he looked at the picture and back to her. "I will say I came here, we watched the video, and it triggered the memory. You're the victim of an attempted kidnapping, they drugged you, and your suffering is well documented. You gave me a vague location, and I investigated. No different than Butte Springs. Anyway, I've talked to Mr. Myers, and he is struggling to keep track of what day it is, let alone what he did or did not say while he was here."

Louis, once a respected professor, was in jail for attempted kidnapping, being part of a hate group, and was losing his mind in jail. And what was she doing? "By my suffering you're referring to my mental health."

"Statements from Dr. Carrion and your medical records at Celestial hospital confirm you've been diagnosed with post-traumatic stress disorder. You have displayed avoidance of social situations, have severe emotional distress, overwhelming guilt over not protecting yourself, and have had a hard time moving past the kidnapping and Butte

Springs. No one is going to question you if you forgot a detail when you faced another attempt on your life," Detective Watt assured.

"How did you get her records?" Rutger asked. He was going to talk to the baron about the employees at Celestial.

Detective Watt smiled. Rutger didn't know he had been at Celestial. "Don't blame your people, I had a warrant. Miss Langston is the focus of a criminal case, and to prove Mr. Myers and Dr. Holmes are a threat to her, physically and mentally, it was necessary."

No, it wasn't. She hated hearing her weaknesses and she doubted the human. "I don't believe you. What is to stop you from exposing me after I tell you?" Jordyn held his gaze.

"We'll make a deal. You tell me the location and work as a paranormal consultant, and I'll keep my mouth shut," Detective Watt proposed.

"You've stooped to a new low, supplying the lies," Rutger accused, a growl running through his voice. "Blackmail."

Detective Watt heard the accusation delivered by growl and dismissed it. He witnessed Rutger losing control over his wolf and knew this was different, he was angry and needed to protect his girlfriend. "I will use every resource available, including Miss Langston. You wanted paranormal crimes investigated and treated equal to human crimes … well, here I am."

"I was thinking you would be law abiding," Rutger countered.

"No. I'm getting the job done. Miss Langston?"

Damn him, Jordyn didn't have a choice. "Paranormal consultant?"

"If I need information about witches, shapeshifters, and the magic-born, basically the entire non-human community, or if I have a question about myths and legends, I call you."

"If I'm not here?" The Highguard hadn't contacted her yet, but it was a matter of time. Jordyn wasn't going to risk being exposed when it was out of her control.

"We'll cross that bridge when it happens. Miss Langston, do we have a deal?" Detective Watt insisted, his impatient tone adding pressure.

If she had access to cases the OPI was investigating she could protect the magic-born. She would be able to see the changes happening throughout the area and not just Trinity and Paradise County. Changes. Did she believe the magic-born world was going through a transition? She did, she felt it when the magic rose up from the earth and the woods called her.

"I can't say no," Jordyn grudgingly replied.

"Excellent. Where is the facility?" Detective Watt sat forward.

Jordyn inhaled and exhaled. *Signing my death warrant.* "It's near the industrial area south of Butterfly Valley. There's an airport a couple of miles off the main road, it's there in an airplane hangar." Jordyn had time to think about what she saw and compare it to what she knew about the place. She drove past the industrial area when she travelled between Butterfly Valley and Trinity. Or when she was sneaking pictures, like the ones Detective Watt and Rutger saw on her camera. Those days felt like a lifetime in the past and floated through her thoughts to tease her.

Incredible. Miss Langston possessed the power to read minds and convince someone to kill themselves. He didn't lose sleep over Mr. Platt's death. He and his followers murdered several non-humans, making it the worst crime committed by serial killers in decades. And Mr. Platt tried to kill him and his OPI team. It didn't make her any less dangerous. It was better to have the petite woman sitting in front of him, looking defenseless and wounded, on his side. Trying to act unfazed, he casually stood and said, "I have what I came for."

"Why isn't Cottonwood County doing the investigation?" Rutger asked.

"They don't want to be associated with an investigation into the university, or Dr. Holmes and Mr. Myers. That isn't to say both counties won't assist. It's politics," he explained. "Again, thank you, Miss Langston."

"I would say it was nice to see you, but ..." Rutger stood, walked to the door, and opened it.

Detective Watt held Miss Langston's gaze, drawn to the onyx and copper and the power she was capable of harnessing. He could spend years in her eyes and never understand the woman in front of him. "I'll be touch." Detective Watt left the living room and stopped at Rutger's tense mass. "I never had the chance to say thank you, for saving my life. I would have died on that mountain. Thank you, Rutger Kanin."

"If I had known you would come back and threaten my mate and blackmail her, I would have left you for dead," Rutger countered in a gruff voice. His eyes held a combination of truth, he would have left him for dead, and humor.

Mate. Detective Watt needed to remember *what* he was dealing with and would have to treat them accordingly. He said through a laugh, "I'm sure you would have." He would take what he could get. Detective Watt left the angry lycan behind him and continued to his crossover.

Rutger watched him back up, turn around, and head away from the house. Closing the door, he locked it, checked the blinking green lights, then took his gun from the table and placed it in the holster. He walked to the living room, his mind feeding him images of seeing Jo in the fetal position crying, Jo with her face in her hands crying, Jo falling apart and fading into the ghost he had been living with. Jo stealing their link from him and taking her warmth and passion with her. Rutger prepared himself as he entered the room. The empty room. Jo wasn't there. Damn. Had she run to their bedroom to hide from the world that kept coming after her?

Rutger stopped the questions and listened. No, she hadn't run. He made his way to the kitchen and found her sitting on a stool at the bar-height table picking at a croissant.

"How are you?" he asked as he handed her a cup of coffee. He needed to act as normal as possible.

"Is it too early to start drinking?" *Like whiskey.* Jordyn met his eyes and saw worry etch itself on his face. *I'm sorry. I'm not falling apart. I'm not even worried.* Was the calm feeling real? Was she going to fall apart? It was her routine.

"I can call the baron and cancel dinner," Rutger offered without answering her question. "If your upset and don't want to leave the house."

No, really, is it too early to drink? She could self-medicate to deal with her mental health problems. With her luck, someone would add it to her records. Her medical records might as well as described her as unfit for society. Thank you for trying to play life, you've failed. While that might be true, Jordyn faced the detective, his threat, and hadn't backed down. Her worry centered around the pack. She had to protect them.

"You can't cancel. I have to explain the deal I've made with Detective Watt to the baron and you have to talk to Ansel. We have lives. Anyway, we need to go and prove we're not crumbling under our self-made pity. It's sad, me leaving the house is proof I'm not losing my mind." She stuck a chunk of flaky, buttery goodness in her mouth and chased it with coffee. Each bite of croissant, the strawberries, bacon, and her coffee, tasted like it was the first time. She was starving for food and life.

Rutger regarded her like an experiment he was trying to understand. Every time he thought he figured out what she was feeling, how she was dealing with it, and what triggered her fear, it changed. How was he going to protect her if he didn't know how? She took a slice of strawberry, popped the entire thing in her mouth, then took another one. "Detective Watt's visit didn't upset you?"

"No, I accused Dr. Holmes of experimenting on shapeshifters and the magic-born, a visit from the OPI was bound to happen. Let's face it, if I wanted him to forget about my ability, I would have told him to." *Uh-oh.* What the hell was she saying? Jordyn met Rutger's surprised stare and smiled. "It's true. I know I let fear get the best of me and have been living with Flint's ghost, but there's more. Since I stopped focusing on him there have been these feelings. Like the change that's happening to all magic-born. It's not clear, but I can feel something."

Rutger reached for a piece of bacon. "It's been a day and a half, and you're sure you're all right? This isn't too fast?"

"I'm fine. I've denied my wolf for too long and the instinct of the soothsayer." Jordyn grabbed another croissant. When was the last time she ate and enjoyed food? She didn't know. "And being your mate. You can't continue to carry the weight of us on your own."

Come to me, Mea. "I will for as long as I have to. And would do it again," Rutger promised. *Not going to let any-one hurt you.* "We have the day to ourselves, what does my mate want to do?"

Jordyn finished the croissant, drank her coffee, and grabbed a couple slices of strawberries. What to do? "Run."

"What?" Rutger's heartrate sped up, his wolf rose with the prospect of running with Jo.

"Run. Us. Along the shore." Jordyn turned in her seat to face Rutger. He wore his answer on his face, the grin looked good and matched the excitement in his eyes. "My wolf says yes."

"Yes." Rutger dropped his T-shirt on the table.

"I have something to show you," Jordyn said as she hopped off the stool.

While she made her way to the living room, she tugged the hoodie over her head, revealing she hadn't put a bra on. Setting it on the back of the couch, she started on her pants and then socks.

Rutger waited by the French doors, watched Jo undress, and didn't want to leave the house. "What is it?"

Free of her clothing, Jordyn stood straight and met Rutger's stare. She felt his weighted gaze on her, the night before, and the feel of him rushing through her and re-turned the favor by admiring his board shoulders tapering down to his narrow waist, and muscled legs. Her eyes glided up to the line of dark hair and further to his eyes. "You'll know when you see it."

Rutger wondered if the surprise was the tree where Flint had planned to kill her. Where she achieved her revenge.

Having been freshly reminded of it by Detective Watt, he worried if they went there it would feed her fear. *'I buried Flint.'* Maybe not. "The suspense is killing me," he managed, his voice giving away his uncertainty. He watched her saunter over to him, brazen with her nudity as she had been when he secretly watched her. Despite his worries, his body warmed as his desire for her grabbed him and held him in a heated fist.

"Good." Jordyn noticed the doubt in his eyes and the half ass attempt to cover his fear. He had no idea what she was going to do and how it was healing her. Detective Watt's visit could have derailed her, sending her to the darkness and self-pity. Back to her medical diagnosis. She cast it off, opening the door, and stepped out to the deck to have the early morning sun's warmth touch her skin. A breeze threaded through the warmth carrying the chill from the lake. The air held the smell of fresh water, and the varied scents from the trees.

The woods called her as they always did and she paused, letting the magic veil her in its power. Turning, she said, "The woods call, Wolf." Jordyn smiled, near giddy knowing what she was about to reveal, and the level of power it took to accomplish it. They were stronger together than apart. Jordyn could feel her power flowing through every part of her and saturating her body. She watched Rutger's eyes blaze gold with his wolf, then she gave him her back. Walking to the first step, she twisting from the waist up, and met his gaze. "Catch me." She waited a heartbeat, his eyes widened, a blast of excitement hit her through their link, and laughing, she leaped.

"No." Panic hit Rutger like a hammer. He reached for her, his hands swiping empty air where she had been. Jo lost her mind. Rutger stood at the top step, helpless as he watched Jo try to clear more than thirty steps. "Jo."

Rutger stood motionless, his mouth open, his arms hanging at his sides as he watched her body transform like she was made from liquid, smoke, and mist into her wolf. With her transformation, a wave of magic rolled over him, making his heart pound. He felt her magic and the raw power she generated. Jo landed softly on her front paws, then her back, and turned to target him with copper eyes. *Mine.*

Exhilaration surged in her veins, its energy feeding her power and flowing through her, over her, and into her territory. It was easier than the first time, as if her wolf and power drove her transformation. Not a transformation. She didn't have to call her wolf when its spirit was always shaping her. Jordyn faced the stairs to see Rutger standing at the top step in wolf form. Black ran from his muzzle to his ears, faded out to dark walnut, and blended with charcoal down his sides and belly.

My wolf. He stood proud, his strength capturing him, his gold eyes tracking her. With the bond between them open, and more powerful then when they were in their human forms, she easily linked with Rutger. *"Well?"*

In wolf form, they were their animal counterparts leaving no verbal communication between them. They relied on the natural order of wolves, body language, and sounds. Yes, he was surprised, twofold. Jo's question sounded in his head as if it was his own. He met her gleaming copper eyes. *"Surprised doesn't express what I am."*

"Good. It's time to run, Wolf." Jordyn took off towards the woods.

Rutger watched her shapeshift and thought he knew what kind of power she was capable of using. No, it was like wielding a flame from a torch. But watching her leap from the stair and shift in the air, to land safety on the ground, he underestimated her. He finally understood Jo's body was never in one form. She lived in the ether. The space between both forms and with the company of the Collective. What kind of damage was she doing to herself when she didn't shift and run under the full moon? It was no wonder she suffered. And it was no wonder why running and facing Flint had been a victory. He fought losing control over his wolf turned beast, fearing the ether, fearing the loss of control and the loss of himself. He would be damned if he was going to be drugged and locked up in a cage under the Enforcer's office building. How many times had the baron threatened him if he didn't get his shit together? Too many. Jo embraced it and had the force to control her wolf, the Collective, and the traits of the soothsayer.

His mate.

Rutger heard Jo's thoughts, tempting him. He howled, and chased after her, his wolf tracking her by her magic, the thrill of the chase urging him to run faster. Over fallen trees, rocks, brush, and saplings, Rutger caught up with her. A sharp right and her dark form headed deeper into the woods. He followed, chasing his mate, while the freedom of running changed his mood, the fight with his wolf, and eased the anxiety clinging to him.

Living like a time bomb.

Jordyn slowed, craned her head, and searched for Rutger. She didn't find him behind her. His essence was close, but it was the feeling of being stalked, altering her instincts. She became his prey. There was no denying the heated thrill it sent through her. Jordyn ran faster, dodging limbs, trees, and bushes as Rutger's feel continued closing in.

Rutger's instincts targeted her, tracked her, and getting close enough to her to touch her, she ducked under a low limb forcing him to go around the tree. Getting out of sight, he ran parallel to her, and when she slowed, he made his move and cut in front of her. Jo skidded to a stop, her claws digging into the dirt, causing small rocks and pine needles to spray the ground, and her body expanded with her hard breathes.

"Got you." Rutger stepped closer, his head above Jo's. In wolf form he was foot taller than she. His six-foot-four-inch human form and his weight transferred to his wolf form, making Jo's petite size noticeable. Where he thundered through the woods, she was agile and lithe for a werewolf. A Pureblood. With their bodies touching, he rubbed the side of his head against hers and she leaned into him.

Jordyn edged forward, lowered her head, and raising it rubbed the underneath of Rutger's throat. He growled a low sound of appreciation then moved his bulk to cover her as if shielding her. When he eased back, she faced him.

"Do you think you won?"

He cocked his head as she sprinted off. Nearing the lake, she slowed, then stopped, and waited for him. Jordyn didn't notice the chilled water touching her paws, the sand sinking under her weight, or the small pebbles being taken out by waves. The moments with Rutger faded as threads of her fear, holding onto invasion, corrupted her thoughts and forced her to focus on her surroundings. *No one is there*, she told herself. Jordyn searched, pushing her senses through the forest and pursuing magic. *Empty*. Save for ... Rutger. She heard him before she saw him, his movements in the woods taking her attention. When he stalked out from a thicket of trees, his gold gaze pinned her under the weight of a predator.

Take your mate, his wolf demanded. *Mark her. Mine*. He made a promise and wasn't going to risk losing her confidence. Denying his instincts, he didn't know how much longer he was going to be able to control himself.

"I felt you searching. No one is here, Mea. I won't let anyone get close to you."

Jordyn lowered her head, her nose close to the water while waves lapped at her legs, and she instantly regretted letting her fear twist her thoughts. But they had gotten close to her. *Stop*. She met Rutger's gold gaze. *"I needed to check."*

Rutger nodded his head, knowing she will always check He needed to change the subject. *"I like talking to you this way."*

"Me too." Jordyn looked down the shoreline toward the house.

Rutger walked over to her, his paws twice the size of hers, and nudged her with his head. *"Come."* Turning from the direction of the house, he started along the shore. Jo followed, choosing to walk higher and out of the water but close enough with their gait, their fur touched. Each of her brushes sent a throng of emotions through him, promising they were going to have the life they wanted. He couldn't help but inwardly shudder as the fight to control the growing urge to mark her raged on.

Golds swept through ruby highlighting the cerulean sky above them, its mirror image reflecting on the lake's glass surface. They strolled along the shoreline in silence, each deep in their thoughts and content with being with one another. Jordyn could walk beside Rutger, the lake at their side and the mountains around them forever, but knew they needed to get back. Foxwood waited.

She stopped. *"We need to get back."*

Regretfully, Rutger stopped. He didn't want to. He longed to stay with Jo by the shore, the woods, and hold onto to the sense of peace for as long as he could. *"I know,"* he responded, and turning caught the sun on the lake and faced her. Seeing her in wolf form would never get tiring. *"I would love to stay out here."*

"Yes."

They stared at each other, like they were afraid if they left the shore, they would never see it again, and their lives would be altered forever. The darkness in their eyes echoed their mutual need for peace, each other's assurance, and a foundation for them to stand on. It didn't change the energy burning in Jordyn. She wasn't going to end the stroll by slowly walking back to the house with her head down and tail tucked between her legs. No. She was going to challenge her mate. Jordyn raised her head as if she was scenting something, her eyes swirled with onyx, and she looked across the lake to the other side.

"What?" Rutger asked. He matched her, his muzzle to the sky and inhaled. He didn't smell anything. He didn't sense anything. *"Jo."*

When Rutger turned his body to the water and was facing away from her, she took off. Amused, Jordyn wished she could laugh as she raced toward the house. Behind her, Rutger howled, his claws digging into the soft dirt, and she heard his hard run pounding the ground. Her heart rate spiked, she ran faster, and faster, adrenaline pulsing in her veins and her muscles elongating with her stride. They didn't have to run far when their leisurely pace took them within sight of the house. Jordyn saw the dock, she was close to home, at the same time Rutger's rough exhales sounded like he was right behind her. Faster. She needed to go faster.

Why? To beat him to the house and win. And if he caught her? What would he do?

Jordyn held back letting his essence close in on her when his wolf drowning in aggression and desire seared the link. The force stopped any thought of being caught ... it pushed her to run, to get to safety. Fast.

Rutger saw her stretch her body as she bounded over a fallen log, and landing, her speed took her further from him. Not if he could help it. *Mine.* He needed her. He didn't want her leaving him. Jo slowed down and he thought she was going to wait for him. *Mine. Mark her.* A growl rumbled in his chest and his wolf howled in his ears when she took off once more. She was playing a game, but his wolf surged with its primal need to chase its prey, to have her, and mark her. He saw it in front of him. Her ravaged skin, her whimpers burning his ears while her blood coated his lips, its spice coating his mouth, its warmth on his skin. He could taste it like he could taste her on the air.

His mind split in two. He would be damned if he was going to turn a run with his mate into a hunt. Against his instincts, which caused a fight between animal and man, and fire to streak across his mind, he slowed to a jog. He watched her approach the stairs and when she started up to the deck and he lost sight of her, his wolf backed down, and he relaxed. Rutger approached the steps at an easy jog, stopped, gathered the splinters of his control, and shapeshifted. He waited another couple of minutes, letting the breeze feather his sweat-soaked skin, and the drumming from shifting to fade. Gradually, he took them one at a time and letting seconds pass, he shoved the beast to its cell and looked like a normal man. What had become his normal.

Rutger entered the house, naked, beads of sweat peppering his torso, legs, and arms, his inhales deep, and his exhales caving his chest. The wolf tattoo shifted with him, looking as if it had a life of its own. The thick, black band around his bicep acted like it might give up the fight, break in two, and fall to the ground. Jordyn met his mahogany eyes laced with gold, as tension tightened across his shoulders.

"I'm sorry. I didn't mean to push you." Jordyn held a tumbler of bourbon, and lifting it offered it him. "A peace offering."

"It's not your fault." Jo stood before him naked, her eyes holding her wolf, her skin a soft bronze, and her power eddied around them. Taking the glass, he sipped the smooth liquid waiting for its warm vanilla and caramel notes to touch his stomach and the alcohol to touch him anywhere. "I felt your excitement and your power. It's been so long and the closeness and the running ... Mea, you drive my wolf."

"I wanted to prove to you I'm all right. We're in this together." She raised her wine glass and they toasted. "Is there anything I can do?"

We are? He sipped, his mind racing with her words, and lowered the glass. "Go get cleaned up so we can have dinner with the baron and baroness."

"If you're sure." Jordyn hesitated. When his lust and fury hit her, she feared for him. His fight wouldn't end until he marked her. The pressure behind the need would continue to build, making his grasp on his beast weaken. She was fooling herself if she thought he was going to be able to deny it for much longer.

"I'm sure. I'm going to enjoy my drink, and when you're finished, I'll get cleaned up." Jo hesitated, watched him for a second, her concern blatant in her eyes, and turning walked to the stairs. Was that what she saw when people looked at her? Pity. Like they were waiting for her fall apart and crash to the ground in pieces? No wonder she didn't want to leave the house.

When Jo crossed the loft and entered their bedroom, he waited to hear water from the shower. A minute later, a bluesy song drifted from the room, its rhythm finding him, and another minute he caught the vanilla scent of her body wash. Rutger sat down, set the tumbler on his knee, and listened. Leaning back, he closed his eyes and let his muscles relax one by one. The vision he saw of Jo lying beneath him, bloody, and crying, sent chills over his heated skin. *Bestial.* The pressure was getting worse. His idea of what was going to happen when he finally marked her was going to drive him insane. The images were turning into living nightmares, giving him her screams and pain. He was living with two forces, his beast and the instinct, and the chaos of them was going to tear him apart. As long as he didn't hurt Jo, he didn't care.

After setting the empty tumbler on the table, he stood, and headed to the stairs. Rutger stopped, went back to the living room, pulled his shorts on, and headed to the garage. Through the kitchen, down the hall, he paused at the open door leading to Jo's studio. Her camera, laptop, and notebooks sat on the simple, rustic desk. She had been working. The sight warmed him, calmed him-she was his, and she wasn't leaving. Continuing to the garage, he opened the door, hit the button, and waited while metal clanged and groaned as it slid open.

The concrete floor ate the honey hues laced with violet and rose peeking into the cold space. The smells of dust, dried grass, and motor oil stood their ground for as long as they could before the breeze carried them off. Rutger walked down the stairs, and into the three-car garage. At one point, he had started cleaning the right side. He moved boxes, yard equipment, gear from work, and crap he should have thrown away months ago but hadn't. It felt like everything stopped and refused to start. Today they made the first hard shove against the barricade and made a dent. Ignoring unfinished work, he walked to the left side where his Jeep was parked.

Ten minutes later, and covered in dust, there was plenty of room for Jo's SUV. Rutger went back inside, listened to her singing along with a song, grinned like a fool, and grabbed the keys. After parking her car in the garage, he backed his Jeep out. They would take the Jeep to Foxwood, not his truck. Tonight, he wasn't playing Director of Enforcers ... no, he was Jo's mate. He stopped with his thoughts. They were One-Flesh, fated mates, the pull between them too strong for either them to deny. Yet they hadn't said they loved each other.

Kory's words stabbed him, his heart wanted to burst and bleed out, but he stopped it. He had asked her to marry him and Jo said yes. She said yes. Then left. After three years of silence they had been thrust into a relationship. Did she love him? Or feel bound to him? Did he love her? Yes, madly. Why hadn't he told her? Because he didn't want her to stare at him with 'I'm sorry' in her eyes if she didn't feel the same way.

With his thoughts running rampant in his head, he walked into house, up the stairs, and listened to another song and Jo's sultry voice as she sang along.

In jeans, running shoes, and a comfortable pale pink top, Jordyn pulled a coat on and walked to the front door. Rutger waited for her, his chest filling out his soft, gray T-shirt, and his black, red, and gray flannel shirt. Its hem ended slightly past his waist, his jeans hugged his hips and thighs and ended with his worn boots. He had combed through his thick hair with his fingers, the ends just below his ears holding a tinge of water from the shower. His appearance teased an expensive, refined look while staying true to his rugged life. They stood staring at each other, letting her openly gaze at him. He resembled the old Rutger and damn if he didn't look good with longer hair.

"Ready?" Jordyn asked before she hung up her coat.

"No," Rutger answered his voice breaking with the word. "Would prefer to stay in."

"Me too, Wolf. If we cancel, they'll think something is wrong and either send enforcers to check on us or come here in person. I don't want them here." She looked up at him, her face open, natural, and smiled. "We need the house to be our house. Our home."

She was giving him what he thought he had lost. "I agree." Rutger opened the door, waited for Jo to pass, and closed it behind him. He checked the alarm system, saw it blinking, tested the door, it didn't budge, and walked down the stairs. Jo stood back from the Jeep and looked at him.

"The Jeep?" Jordyn asked. She hadn't ridden in it for years. Three years to be exact.

Approaching her, he answered, "Thought we would be more comfortable than in my work truck."

"Brings back memories," Jordyn mused. Stepping up to the passenger side, she thought back to all the summers they had ridden through the mountains with the top and doors off to feel the sun on their faces. So long ago. With October's chill, Rutger fitted it with a soft top and the doors. "When was the last time you drove it?" Jordyn faced Rutger as he walked to the driver's side and instantly regretted the question. She opened the door, caught the smell of leather, dust, and age, and had to hop in due to the lift kit and tires.

"Two years. Once I became director, I didn't have a need to drive it," Rutger answered honestly. *It reminded of you*, he wanted to say, *and couldn't take the pain*. He sat behind the steering wheel, Jo beside him, the way it should be, and wanted to go back and start from the beginning.

I'm sorry. The same time he relinquished his position as Second to the Alpha to become the Director of Enforcers, because she left him. The punishments for stepping down and taking a lower position in the pack had been severe. They started with his parents. As if Rutger had abandoned his birth right, the baron treated him like he wasn't family, but a pack member, a submissive, and demanded Rutger refer to them by their titles. The baron restricted his visitation to Foxwood to the Enforcer's office, and ordered he not be allowed entrance to the house without an invitation from the baron. The baroness couldn't invite him over without consent from the baron. It hadn't ended there, the Highguard took his birth right, making his brother Second to the Alpha, and titled Rutger a coward in the writ of the pack. Rutger lost everything while she had a hovel and Louis. Jordyn sank into the seat as the years and months weighed down on her. What a mistake. She was a mess and she had done this to him.

She noticed his voice was nearly monotone like he was trying to keep his emotions from oozing all over his words. Can't say sorry enough. "This is a great idea. I've missed it."

"Me too." Rutger stared at her for breath, his mind going to the last time they were together in the Jeep. It would have been when he asked her to marry him. Damn.

Cool yellow sunlight peeked through tree limbs and leaves, casting shadows that danced in the breeze. Rutger sat on a log, his legs stretched out in front of him, the heels of his boots in the dirt, and watched her.

"Jo, are you listening? Do you know what I think we should do?" A growl ran through his words.

"No." Jordyn knelt by a purple flower she didn't know the name to, zoomed in to catch the sun on its petals, and snapped two shots. One more, another purple flower, and she stood. Facing him, his eyes gleamed gold, his short dark hair sat at his neck, his T-shirt hugged his chest and arms. There was nothing like being in the mountains and the woods with Rutger.

"No, you aren't listening to me, or no, you don't know what we should do?"

"Both." She smiled, put her camera in its case, and closed the distance between them.

"Funny girl. Come here." Rutger held his hand out. "Please, baby."

Jordyn swung the camera bag from her shoulder, set it on the ground, and with Rutger's help, straddled him. He held her hips and kissed her. "You have my attention."

"That's all it takes?" Rutger teased.

"For now. You were going to tell me what we should do?"

"Aww, but this right here is distracting," he said as his right hand cupped her breast.

"Then stop." Jordyn leaned into him and nuzzled his neck.

"I like the distraction, but I'll stop." Rutger straightened. "The thing we should do is life changing. Life altering. Quite possibly earth shattering."

It was Jordyn's turn to sit straighter, her senses searching Rutger when his eyes bled from gold to a brunt gold, holding his emotions and his thoughts. Not earth shattering. They would be forever.

Rutger smiled, inhaled, and exhaled. "I love you."

"The earth shattered." Her body drummed with excitement.

His hand held her neck while his fingers caressed her skin. "Jo."

She was going to explode if he didn't ask her. "Rutger."

He grinned. "I want you to marry me. Please, baby, say you'll marry me?"

I said yes, Rutger, it hasn't changed. Jordyn held his stare, his eyes bleeding to his signature burnt gold, and the urge to tell him everything she was feeling and she loved him roiled inside her. If she opened that door, the one to her feelings, she wouldn't be able to stop from spilling her guts all over the place. If she started talking, she wasn't going to be able to stop and they wouldn't make it to Foxwood.

"It hasn't changed," she said trying to think of something to say. It sounded stupid.

I love you, Mea, marry me. The strength behind the words surprised him, and he cleared his throat. *Must tell her.* They needed to see the baron and baroness, take care of business, and then he would tell her he loved her. "Ready?"

"Yep."

The drive to Foxwood felt like hours as tensions ran high between them. Jordyn blamed it on the Jeep, the memory of his marriage proposal, and heading to Foxwood. The marriage proposal was meaningless when they were One-Flesh in the eyes of the pack and the Highguard. The Highguard would never allow Rutger and Jordyn to have a human type wedding. They had become something from the dark ages and would obey the canons and traditions of the past as their present.

Jordyn couldn't stop jealousy over her sister's wedding from snaking into her. Images from the day-like Rutger in a tux, standing strong beside her, and the reception where everyone celebrated the union-fed her jealousy. She turned enough to see Rutger, his profile, and his hands gripping the steering wheel. If she let this moment destroy what they accomplished and let it sit between them, what memory would add to it? What else was going to cause a divide between them? They were going to fall into the same ravine of silence and sadness they had been living in, and it had to stop. She looked at the scenery passing them in a blur and wanted a distraction not silence. Jordyn wanted Rutger to know she was with him because she loved him, not because they were fated. *I could tell him I love him.* Perfect. If he responded to her with his cold front, she would be crushed.

Rutger sat beside her, eyes on the road, hand clenching the wheel, and Jordyn felt him like a storm preparing landfall and promising destruction. To break the silence and ease the strain between them, she turned the radio on. Being in the Jeep might have taken them to their past and reminded them of the pain, but it wasn't going to steal what they shared. It was time to move forward and create a future. Jordyn needed to change the mood. Her mood. Rutger's mood.

When an advertisement for tires ended and a new song played-she didn't know, but it didn't matter-she pretended to have a microphone and sang along. He gave her a sideways glance and looked back to the road. *Tough crowd.* A fast-paced pop song started, she leaned closer to him, her head by his shoulder, and gazing up at him fumbled with the words.

"I know what you're doing," Rutger said. Jo gave him an innocent stare and struggled with the song. "You don't even know the words." He laughed, giving into her attempt at humor and easing the mood. Letting go of the past, Rutger couldn't stop from smiling at her. Jo's eyes were bright with her enjoyment and her mouth curved in a smile.

"No, I don't. Never heard it before. I don't even know what it is," she admitted and sat straighter. She hadn't listened to any kind of music for months, and whatever the radio was playing wasn't her taste.

"It's not the bluesy mix you were listening to earlier." Rutger cast her another glance. "While you were taking a shower."

"Far from. As I recall, Wolf, you like the blues," Jordyn mused, leaning closer to him.

"True." His easy grin catching him off guard. The battles were waiting for them, hiding in their future like unseen landmines. Shoving the thoughts down, he wasn't going to let anything dampen the easy going mood between them. It felt like old times. The good times when they were just them. Rutger and Jo and nothing else. The older model Jeep didn't have a digital stereo, rather it had a push button for FM and AM and a dial to change the station. Jo sat back in her seat, humming to the new tune, and looking out the passenger window at the passing mountains. With her distracted, he slowly turned the dial causing static to sound.

"Hey, hey," Jordyn protested.

Rutger pretended to swat her hands away as he turned the dial. *I know you're there.* Nearly out of options-damn, he didn't want to go back to the pop songs-he gave the dial a half turn. The dark rhythm rumbled in the Jeep, the sultry voice promising love, and satisfied, he sat back.

"Nicely done." Jordyn rested her head on the seat and closed her eyes. Rutger's hand squeezed her shoulder and moved up to her neck, and turning into his hand, met his gaze. "This is nice."

"I think so," Rutger whispered, his voice lost in the moment he was convinced would never happen.

When Rutger slowed down, Jordyn sat straight, fixed her coat, and watched the gates to Foxwood automatically open with their approach. "They were expecting us if the gate opened by itself."

"Yes. An enforcer watches the gate at all times," Rutger replied. It was probably Mandy pulling another shift. "There are motion sensors and sensors in the road at the entrance that alert communications. A hundred yards back the license plate reader took a picture of the plate and ran it through communications. They knew we were headed here long before made it to the gate."

"What does it report since it's us?" Jordyn understood there had been changes, she didn't think they were that extreme. Her house wasn't the only prison.

"It'll display kindred, and our names," Rutger replied. *Along with a code for each of us and the time of arrival.* He wasn't going to bore her with the details.

"You've been busy," Jordyn mumbled. Had she turned the pack into paranoid victims like herself?

The gate rattled then ran smoothly along the rail to close behind them. "All property owned by Cascade has been outfitted with the security system. There are cameras everywhere. Even along the drive," Rutger said with pride. He leaned down, craned his head, and looked up at the fake trees he had installed with cameras. You had to know they were there, they blended into the pine and oak trees. Behind the tree lining the road there were others, tree houses. Sniper points.

"I didn't know." Jordyn noticed the difference for the first time. She did this to them.

Seconds later, they were parked in front of the house. "We're here."

"Yes, we are. I don't think my talent for singing is going to help us," Jordyn mumbled.

"I don't know. You could challenge the baron and baroness to a lip sync battle. I would pay to see that," Rutger replied. He felt like he had been ordered back home after a runway attempt. Kinda he had. "Are you going to be all right? I mean, you haven't been social."

I know. "If I said it wasn't tempting to turn around, go home, and hide, I would be lying." She turned in her seat to face him and saw worry in his eyes. She didn't want to see it and was tired of seeing him worried for her. "I'm not going to ruin what we've started. We are stronger, and therefore, I'm stronger," she insisted. Jordyn smiled and she believed it reached her eyes.

"We are." *I love you.* Rutger leaned to her, took her chin in his fingers, and gently kissed her lips. Lingering, he rubbed his cheek against hers, and breathed in her scent.

The passenger door opened, a wall of chilled air swept in, Jordyn jumped, and she heard Rutger growl. She rested her forehead on his and whispered, "Here we go." Jordyn met Rutger's narrowed eyes, his apprehension blatant and causing her pause. *Get a grip.* She turned in the seat to see Abigail holding the door open.

"My apologies," Abigail muttered, her eyes on the ground. "I didn't mean to interrupt, Soothsayer."

It's Jordyn. "No worries," Jordyn assured, as she got out of the Jeep. "How are you?"

"Good, thank you."

Rutger walked around the front of the Jeep, meeting Jordyn, and together they followed Abigail to the front door. Sousa held the heavy wood door with frosted glass in its center and wrought iron decorations depicting wolf heads and the moon open.

"Sousa," Rutger greeted.

"Sir. They will greet you in the formal greeting room," he said like he was giving a report.

"Thank you." Odd they were going to be greeted, not welcomed to the house for dinner.

Abigail took her place on the right side, while Sousa waited for them to pass then closed the door behind them.

The formal greeting room, used for greeting the elders of the pack, taking council with pack members, or entraining dignitaries, was decorated with rich cherry wood and walnut antique tables, chenille couches, leather wingback chairs, and several bookcases, all holding an extensive collection of modern works and others over hundreds of years old. Paintings of mountains, rivers, sunsets, and sunrises reflected Paradise County, Trinity, Foxwood, and the Nearctic Valley.

With his hand at the small of her back, Rutger guided Jo down the hall, under the arched entrance, and into the room. He turned left, and opened the door to the closet, took Jo's coat and hung it on a hanger. Rutger debated hanging up his flannel shirt but decided he was going to keep it on. If something upset Jo and she needed comfort, she used like it was a barricade around her, he was going to give it to her.

A fire burned in the massive open fireplace, framed in gray stone and topped with a dark walnut mantel. On the tables were lamps giving the room a cozy feel without drenching it in unwanted harsh light. Rutger checked the chairs, couches, and bookcases where the baroness was known to spend time. They were alone. He could search the house with his senses and find out where they were, but why? The baron would have been alerted as soon as the sensors detected them. Everyone at Foxwood knew they were there.

Jordyn released the breath she had been holding, when faced with seeing the baron and baroness, and walked to the fire to stand in front and enjoy the warmth.

"You're nervous. Is it about being here?" Rutger asked. Standing behind her, he placed his hands on her hips.

She leaned against him, feeling his warmth, the muscles in his chest, and his wolf. "No. It's being confronted. I don't want to explain myself or why I've refused to leave the house." *Interrogation.*

"I won't let them. Jo, I'm here to protect you. To stand beside you," Rutger promised. Lowering his head, he kissed her neck, and nuzzled his face in her hair.

When she saw them standing in front of the fire, Laurel stopped at the entrance and watched Rutger with Jordyn. Rutger was wearing plain clothes, not his uniform. His choice of flannel over a T-shirt and jeans made him resemble the man she once knew. *My son.* Before his world became hell on earth. And Jordyn, wrapped in his arms, was the woman he had fallen in love with. She stepped back, turned, and with her back to the wall, leaned against it for support. Laurel covered her mouth with the back of her hand as tears welled in her eyes. They were a fated couple made One-Flesh, and after tragedy, had risen from heartbreak.

Over the day and afternoon, Laurel worried about what she was going to say to them. Her intention was to sit them down and have a heartfelt talk. She wanted to know how she could help and if they thought they could be helped. But now, she didn't have to, they were healing one another. The feeling of helplessness and worry she lived with for months eased, the weight lifting from her heart and freeing her. Laurel felt her tears building from the sudden release of stress and she felt as if she would sleep for a week. She would do anything to support her son and now her daughter. Especially Jordyn, she needed solid support in place of the absence of her mother and family.

"Wife, what are you doing?" Healey whispered. He stood in front of her, gazing into the room, and back at her.

Laurel put her finger to her lips to stop Healey from talking. She grabbed his arm, and they walked down the hall and into the kitchen where they would have less of a chance from being overheard. Laurel wiped tears from her eyes with a tissue then met Healey's questioning gaze. "You're going to say I should be a stronger baroness and mate to the alpha. He is my son and what I am is an overemotional mom. I saw them."

Communications notified Healey with a text message Rutger was at Foxwood, then he sensed the both of them and their wavering anxiety. He expected the apprehension and was pleased when fear wasn't an issue. A welcomed change from the day before. "And?" Healey waited for her to continue, and when she didn't, he said, "They're strong. The kitchen is filled with the smells of roast, fresh bread, and butter, my favorites. We're going to have dinner with them and not hide from them. Let's go visit with our son and his wife."

"You're always calm. The stable and unemotional baron," Laurel jested, giving him narrowed eyes.

"No. I hide it better. Come." Healey extended his arm, waving Laurel to take the lead. He followed, watching intently as his wife straightened her shoulders, became the unwavering mother, and covered the fact she had been crying.

Jordyn stood with her back to the fire, Rutger in front of her blocking her right side, his hand on her hip. They were talking softly, their bodies brushing each other's.

"Rutger, Jordyn," Laurel greeted.

Rutger faced the baroness and baron. "Baron. Baroness," Rutger replied.

"I'm your mother," Laurel corrected. "This isn't business."

"Good evening, mother." Rutger hugged his mother and stepped back.

"That's more like it," Laurel said with a smile.

Jordyn saw the interaction between Rutger and the baroness, and it stung her heart. What did she have? Mia, who hated her and what she was, and Lady Sloan, an absentee mom who still thought her secret was safe. The baroness approached, and Jordyn plastered a smile on her face. "Baroness."

"Please, there are no formalities between us. Call me Laurel. This is supposed to be a relaxing evening, not business. I want you to be comfortable."

Jordyn smiled her response. There would be business because she made a deal with Detective Watt and it effected the safety of the pack.

Laurel hugged Jordyn, held her for a second, and backed away. "Are you all right?" Laurel asked. Power veiled Jordyn, its presence acting like a barrier.

"Yes, fine. Why?" Jordyn didn't like what she saw in the baroness' eyes. Pity. Worry. A challenge?

"I believe it's your power, Jordyn, its palpable. Are you projecting it?" Healey spoke before Laurel had the chance.

"Before the conversation turns into a pack meeting, Jordyn, would you like a glass of wine?" Laurel asked.

Jordyn met Laurel's gaze, saw it change, her demeanor returning to relaxed. "Please, thank you," she answered. Jordyn turned her attention back to the baron. "I'm not." Jordyn drew in as much as she dared but knew she couldn't hide it absolute when it helped her control the Collective. "Better?" she asked. Looking at Rutger, she wanted to ask what he felt when he was around her.

"I didn't mean for you to hide it. You're among your own. I was curious," Healey answered. The strength of her power eased, but its force was circling her. He felt she reached a new level, as if she was becoming stronger. "Is the pressure from the Collective continuing to be a problem?"

"It's not as bad as it was," Jordyn replied. *I'm taking care of one thing at a time.* All the fractures. She needed her power to fix them, not spend energy on hiding.

"Here you are," Laurel said as she handed Jordyn a glass. "Your favorite."

"Thank you." They had been there for five minutes maybe, and the visit already turned uncomfortable. Should have tucked tail and ran home. Nervous and uneasy, Jordyn was lost with what to do. Sit. Stand. Stare at the baron and wait for his questions about the changes happening. *Don't ask me.*

"Let the girl sit down and enjoy her wine, Healey. Remember, we're here to relax and visit," Laurel chided. "Jordyn, have a seat. Rutger, you too."

Relieved, Jordyn didn't hesitate and chose the corner of the couch furthest from the three of them.

"Unfortunately, we do have business to take care of. Detective Watt, I helped him with the case involving the witches, and we transported him after he was shot." Rutger waited for recognition to register on the baron's face. "He came by the house today."

"He's the one with the OPI?" Healey asked.

"Affirmative."

"How is he involved? Wait, does this have anything to do with Mr. Myers and Dr. Holmes?" Healey asked.

"Yes. It's a paranormal crime, and they're from Butterfly Valley. Because of the sensitivity of Louis and Dr. Holmes' affiliation with the university, Cottonwood County will assist the OPI," Jordyn answered. She took a sip, her eyes on Rutger over the rim. Having him in sight made her nerves less edgy.

"Bourbon?" Healey touched Rutger's arm, getting his attention, and lifted his brows.

"Yes." Rutger walked to the couch and sat down beside Jo, resting his hand on her thigh. "You don't have to be the one to explain, I can."

"I will. I'm the reason it's happening," she insisted. Just like she was the reason behind their house and Foxwood becoming prisons. Jordyn gave him a tight smile.

"What are you talking about? They came here to Trinity, why is Butterfly Valley involved," Laurel asked. "Your part of the investigation, excluding the trial, is over. Does Detective Watt doubt you?"

"No. He believes me," Jordyn answered quickly. "The attack was in Trinity, Paradise County. The facility, headquarters for HAPI, Louis spoke about is in Butterfly Valley. The OPI isn't hindered by jurisdiction issues."

"You read his mind," Healey stated as he faced them. He wasn't going to create an awkward situation by telling her, he watched the video, and saw what they had done to her. Walking over to Rutger, he handed him the tumbler and sat on the arm of Laurel's chair.

"Yes. Both of them. You know from the video, Dr. Holmes was after a Pureblood, and besides collecting shapeshifters and other magic-born, he is kidnapping them to *rehabilitate* them. I saw images of his experiments and the location of the facility. I tried to tell Deputy Elm, covering myself by explaining I had talked to friends in Butterfly Valley and that's how I knew. But Detective Watt witnessed what I could do firsthand when I contacted Rutger and showed him where Flint was holding me," Jordyn explained.

She wasn't going to sink into the familiar fear she embraced for months. Inhaling and exhaling, she continued. "Any gap in information, he figured I knew." Rambling much.

"He asked you where it was and you answered." Healey moved from Laurel's chair and sat in another beside her. He watched Jordyn's reaction, the way she fought her fear, and sipped his scotch.

"I wasn't going to, but he basically-"

"Blackmailed her," Rutger interrupted. "Us. He kindly reminded us, we were cleared of any wrong doing in the deaths of Flint and the witches." Indebted to Shadow Lord and Detective Watt, a damned place to be in. He met the baron's gaze, and they shared the truths and the lies.

Healey understood Rutger's worry, at the same time he tried to understand what the detective wanted from Jordyn. "I'm assuming he wants something?" His voice held a low rumble of irritation. What was Detective Watt going to take from them? Both Jordyn and Rutger were close to each other, open, and the haunted look in their eyes appeared to be fading.

"I'm to work as a paranormal consultant when he needs help. I'm not completely against it … I mean, I'll have access to their files. And with the change gaining momentum, I'll be able to keep watch. My only worry is the Highguard. If they demand my presence, and Detective Watt calls, I could be exposed. It would put the pack at risk."

"Detective Watt may be human, but he isn't stupid. He won't risk exposing you and allow his lies to unravel. He would become an accessory to murder. And if he did, he would lose his job and favor with the Cascade pack. He needs us as much as we need him," Healey assured. "You said the change is gaining momentum."

Jordyn lowered her glass, her nerves pulsing with anxiety. How much was she willing to reveal. "Yes. I can feel it. Magic is increasing, and powers of the magic-born are shifting." Absently, she looked to the window and the hues of twilight, her power rising, her instincts searching and giving her information. *Don't expose yourself.*

"I was going to ask if you were changing with it but I don't have to, do I?" Healey asked. "Empowering you." His eyes skated to Rutger, who was watching Jordyn with fascination and apprehension.

Jordyn rubbed her thigh, feeling the raised mark, the friction creating a physical sensation. "Yes. To what extent I don't know."

"It's important we talk to Lady Sloan," Healey insisted.

"Yes." Jordyn took her glass and sipped her wine.

"Excuse me, sir, Ansel is here to talk to the director," Sousa reported. He had taken his coat off leaving his polo shirt and holster to frame his board shoulders.

Healey stared at Jordyn for another second before turning to see his guard. "Show him in." To Jordyn he said, "We'll continue this."

Saved. For the moment. "Yes, Baron," Jordyn responded.

"Healey. At this moment, I'm your father-in-law, not an authority. Please, relax. Laurel." Healey gave his wife a look expressing the need to take care of Jordyn. The Highguard won't waste time once they know Jordyn's powers were expanding. It explained what he felt but didn't explain why he thought she was holding back. Maybe hiding what she was becoming. After being kidnapped because she was a soothsayer, did she feel she had to guard herself? *Yes.*

"Sir." Ansel waited at the entrance to the room, his hand on the butt of his gun, his black long-sleeved shirt tucked into dark jeans.

Jordyn watched Sousa leave and caught Ansel, Captain Wolt's stare as he fixed his narrowed gaze on her. Her insides caved and played on her nerves that felt like tight guitar strings. *He watched the video. It was in his stare.* He watched Louis try to convince her to leave Rutger, her pack-*Who would fuck a lycan?*-and when Louis' touch burned through her skin. Let's not forget when Dr. Holmes shoved a needle in her. No doubt, he was at the house as Rutger's backup. Did he see her unconscious body? Jordyn's mind threw his scent at her. He had been in her room. Who else knew? Damn, Jordyn wished she could crawl under the couch and hide.

"We'll have this meeting in my office. You ladies enjoy your wine." Healey took his tumbler, stood, and made his way out of the room.

"Are you going to be all right?" Rutger asked, his hand squeezing Jo's thigh. Her heartrate spiked and her unease threaded through their bond. But she didn't block him out. *Please don't block me.*

"I have wine." Jordyn raised the half empty glass in mock toast, and looking at him from under her lashes, smiled.

"Mea," he whispered and shook his head. Where the hell did her strength come from? He stood, gave Jo one last look with gold eyes, and followed the baron.

"Mea?" Laurel asked when the men were out of the room.

"It's Latin for mine." Jordyn drank her wine.

"Marking you without marking you. I don't mean to pry …" Laurel let her remark hang between them in the silence of the room.

Jordyn saw the questions in her eyes and how it affected the pack. "We've discussed it. It involves our future and the pack, so there's no saying no," she explained. "We've come to an agreement."

"Good. I'm glad you have open communication." Laurel smiled, although she knew Jordyn was struggling and knew she couldn't do anything to help.

"I might be the one prying, but has the Baron ever wanted to mark you?" Jordyn asked.

Jordyn should leave it alone. The coming change hadn't started when Jordyn headed to Trinity to go to her sister's wedding … no, it had to have been brewing for days, months, could have been years. When she lived in Butterfly Valley, it might have fed her instinct to be in her territory. To feel the magic of the land, her land. If that was true and it was sending impulses of power, it could have been the driving force behind Flint's actions. Jordyn hadn't thought of that. What other crazed group, faction of the magic-born was going to come out of the wood work seeking a power source? *The Highguard.* Only no one would stop them when they were the ultimate authority and backed by Prime.

Laurel gazed at her wine, turning the bowl of the glass in her palm. "No." She met Jordyn's stare, the feeling they were demanding something from the two of them, they themselves weren't prepared to go through played in her worry. "I think he wanted to have the instinct, believing it would prove he was the powerful alpha the pack needed. Healey didn't, and with the growth of Trinity, and living freely among humans, he wouldn't risk making us outcasts.

I don't know what the change means or why it chose you and Rutger, but I'm not alone when I say, what you and Rutger share is a privilege."

A shared curse. Not wanting to risk being asked about their relationship, she stopped talking. Jordyn was trying to deal with the repercussions from being a soothsayer, and learn about her increasing powers, and felt like if she failed, she would take Rutger down with her. It made her self-conscience about everything she did. In an attempt to understand herself and the change, Jordyn was going to find out when the differences began happening, then find others the change had chosen. Tonight, however, she was free to pretend those problems didn't exist and it wouldn't do her any good to ruin the evening her in-laws planned. In-laws? It felt like a lie.

Laurel noticed Jordyn's eyes darken with her silence and wanted to know what she was thinking about and which of her worries were consuming her. "I understand, Rutger took the day off?"

"Yes. It was nice to relax at home, together," Jordyn replied.

"Back to normal?"

Normal. Jordyn wasn't sure she knew what that was. Wasn't normal relative? "As much as we can be."

Jordyn's power drifted around her as if building a protective wall, its fringes feeling like flames, no one would dare cross fearing they would be burned to ash. Laurel needed to extinguish the stress. "Wine?"

She looked at the baroness as if she had asked a different question, then at her glass, and seeing she finished it, she realized she had lost herself in her thoughts. Jordyn needed to pay attention and not let her mind drift. Yes, she wanted more wine, but even with a werewolf's metabolism, she didn't need to push the boundaries. Except for the wine she had yesterday, she hadn't had alcohol in months.

"Yes." Who was she kidding?

CHAPTER FIFTEEN

Healey closed the door behind him, making his office sound proof, so Jordyn wouldn't over hear their conversation. He fully understood if she wanted to know, all she had to was read his thoughts. It was unsettling and fascinating at the same time.

"Have a seat, Rutger, Ansel."

"Sir, I have the usual reports, nothing important," Ansel began. "Checking in with Rutger."

"I was going to let it go, but after what Jordyn said this evening, I want to know why I wasn't told about the video," Healey questioned, ignoring Ansel.

"Which one? You approved both, and I emailed them to Deputy Elm," Rutger countered. No way it was the one from yesterday.

"Yes, the Summit and the attempted kidnapping. I'm talking about the one where Jordyn is alone. Who ordered she should be recorded?"

Where did he start? "I did. Like an idiot, I left her home alone." He stopped, scrubbed his hand over his face, calmed himself, and continued. "I talked to Deputy Elm about the kidnapping video and he told me Jo had gone to the station and made a report. She didn't tell me, why would she. When I found out what she had done, I tried calling her, several times. There was no answer. I was worried something happened," Rutger confessed. "I knew something was wrong. I had Mandy check the cameras, and once she activated the interior, it began recording."

"You didn't tell me," Healey accused. His calm character of father and father-in-law while in the greeting room stopped, and he became the alpha and baron.

"There was nothing to tell. I saw she was safe and had the recording deleted." Rutger sat forward, his elbows on his knees, his face in his hands. "How did you see it?"

"Everything is sent to my computer in real time. You deleted it from communications, however it still creates an event, and stamps it with a date. You should have a copy on your computer," Healey explained. If Rutger ever looked at his computer. "You say, nothing? Son, I watched it. She shifted while in mid-stride, without pausing as she walked into the house. Her power is increasing so much so she can no longer hide it. As alpha, my sensitivity level is high in order to recognize challenges, strong werewolves, and other alphas, but your mother noticed. Not only noticed it, but it affected her. Jordyn is actively using her power and it isn't about keeping the Collective under control. She is becoming more than a vessel for the Collective. Her power is continually feeding her information, she is becoming her own power. An entity."

"You made her a soothsayer," Rutger accused.

"Jordyn was born to be a soothsayer. She wouldn't have survived long, if I hadn't," Healey stated.

Ansel inhaled a controlled breath. "She is becoming what the myths and legends have told us for centuries. Only we thought they were stories of old told by even older crazier magic-born. No one believed them."

Rutger knew the baron was right. They had run through the woods the way they had three years earlier and he wanted to believe they were defying their present. God, he knew it. Was Rutger in denial about her? Yes. If he faced the truth, he would have to accept her life was at risk, and it would weaken his control.

"I need to get her help." Healey couldn't risk waiting any longer, he needed to call Lady Sloan. He saw the indecision in Rutger's eyes. "If you have something to say, Rutger, you need to tell me."

The baron was right, Jo needed help, he didn't want her power to tear her apart. There were no other options, he had to tell the truth. "What she did in the video is nothing. I told her we could do anything she wanted, and she said she wanted to run. I was excited since she hasn't shifted, ran, or has had anything to do with her wolf. Then she said there was something she wanted to show me." He hesitated. Was he betraying her by telling her secrets?

"Rutger, what happened?" Healey pressed.

No. He was protecting her. "In human form, she leaped from the top stair of the deck and shifted in the air to land as a wolf. It's more than thirty feet. She took off running, and the woods embraced her, I felt it. I didn't have to track her by her scent, I tracked her by her power. I followed its trail. Once she freed herself from Flint's grip, she has been free to indulge in her magic. And her magic has been free to empower her." Rutger's voice held his pride for his mate and her evident power at the same time he knew it held a tremor of fear for her future. "Imagine if there was nothing holding her back."

"Imagine if someone used her," Ansel mumbled. The woman he saw as kith, a friend, and the mate to his pack brother was becoming a living myth. His enforcer side wanted to warn them Jordyn was becoming a weapon. He would have to make sure she was well guarded.

"She isn't an inanimate object. Jo wouldn't hurt anyone," Rutger said in defense.

Healey saw her rub her leg where the mark of the dragon scared her skin. "I'm worried Prime won't be able to protect her if Shadow Lord insists on her presence at court," Healey began. "She wears the mark of the dragon, which is twofold, Ethan and Lady Sloan."

When Jordyn told him Lady Sloan was her real mother, Healey researched Sloan's past. As a descendant of one of the purest packs, Dacia, their soothsayer, and one of twelve for the Highguard, her power was untainted by a weaker line. Her magic originated from her ancestors in the purest form. Ethan, Jordyn's father, and Pureblood from his line, carried the legacies of the soothsayer of his mother, another Pureblood. Before dying, Ethan's mother used her power to transmigration her magic into Jordyn. Jordyn had been a baby. Ethan rejected his magic and raised his daughter to be believe magic wasn't part of her. No one was going to stop ancient powers from being resurrected.

"Did I miss something? What does Lady Sloan have to do with Jordyn?" Ansel asked. He drew his hand through his thick hair, rubbed his neck, and slid his palm down his jeans. He had been in some edgy situations when he was part of the covey, then as a rogue, and as an enforcer. He faced danger when he hunted the covey and when he helped Rutger hunt the witches, but none of that compared to the nervous energy in the office. Ansel wanted to get out of there.

Rutger faced his second in command, Captain of the Enforcers, and his trusted friend. "Lady Sloan is Jordyn's birth mother."

"Oh damn." The last people Ansel thought had skeletons in their closet was the distinguished Langston family.

His thoughts raced toward the covey, his lies, the danger he put Dr. Hyde and another enforcer in, and the mistrust he created. He wasn't sure why he was in the meeting if they were talking about their secrets. "I shouldn't be here."

"Negative." Healey knew where Ansel's doubt came from and wasn't going to let it overshadow his position in the pack. "I want you to understand the situation and the kind of security required and why," Healey answered. "I need you. This is for Jordyn and Rutger."

"I can take care of myself," Rutger protested. Yes, he felt as if he failed Jo, but he no longer was a broken man and victim to his beast. Jo needed the security.

"I like what I see before me. Son, your beast's fury has calmed and your wolf has taken back its dominance. If something happens to Jordyn, your bond would unravel the control you have gained. I won't risk you or Jordyn," Healey explained. "It won't happen tonight, but I need to sit down with Jordyn and talk to her about the moon runs she has missed. Do you think she'll attend the next? Or do I have to order her?"

"You won't have to. She'll be there," Rutger answered. He wasn't actually sure. There were four days before the full moon and he hoped it gave him time to talk to her. He did know, she wouldn't let the pack down by missing another run.

"Good. It'll be a testament to the entire pack." Healey sat back in his chair, his hands clasped in front of him, and looked at Rutger. He had to do everything in his power to keep them safe. "We need to keep what Jordyn is capable of a secret until things settle down."

"Agreed. Dr. Hyde mentioned there was a division. Those who believe the change is real and those who think you're creating it," Rutger stated. "This will become a security risk. For the pack and for Jo."

Healey's heart felt heavy. His son was returning. The Director of Enforcers and Second to the Alpha was getting stronger and his mind was becoming clearer. They were healing. "There is, and I'm aware. We won't concentrate on the change effecting the magic-born, as it will be overwhelming, and I need to take council with the elders of the pack. My first priority is to explain, for now, the change within the pack. Did you know Jordyn's powers were increasing?" Healey asked.

"No. I wasn't there to notice and she didn't want me to know. I went home after watching her, and despite what I saw, I expected the same ghost I had been living with. Jo hasn't used her senses, power, has denied her wolf, and has been blocking me from feeling her. She cut me completely out her life, so when she met me at the door, I was surprised. Jo felt different, stronger, her wolf enveloped her. Her eyes were liquid copper swirling in onyx." Rutger inhaled with the memory and the feel of her on his skin. "She didn't answer her phone because she had gone running. I found out where and why." *Ghost.* Rutger watched his mate drift towards oblivion and was nearly sucked into the void with her.

"What did she do?" Healey asked, his gaze narrowing.

"Jo said she buried Flint." Rutger explained everything to the baron the same way Jo had explained it to him. Conveniently leaving out how he interrogated her and lied about knowing she went running.

"You said she was a ghost, what pushed her to change?" Healey asked. Jordyn was taking care of herself without help from the pack, without her alpha, and her mate. She was internally processing her life, and with the tools availa-ble to her, healing herself.

"Louis." The name tasted sour. "He invaded her territory and threatened our life. I never thought I would say this, but Louis did me a favor by going after Jo." *Sad confession.* Rutger raised his glass to his lips and sipped, the amber liq-uid warming his tongue before it slid down his throat. Jo's essence threaded around him, her power finding him and caressing him. He fought the urge to close his eyes and get lost in its pull. Another sip, then he lowered the glass, and sat back. He wanted to leave Foxwood and take her home.

"Jordyn's need to protect will save others as much as it saved herself." Healey leaned forward, his elbows on the desktop. "What does her power feel like when she isn't try-ing to hide it?"

With Jo's essence embracing him through their link, Rutger was taken back by the question. It felt intimate, pri-vate, Jo's feel belonging solely to him. He needed to tell the truth; there were going to be others and the baron needed to understand what the hell was happening.

"I don't sense her the same way I do Ansel, or you. My wolf recognizes your essences and knows you are shapeshifters, and more specifically werewolves and kith and kin. You as my father and alpha and understands your authority, and it knows Ansel is strong and a brother. My wolf recognizes her as my mate, a part of me, and her power is like silk to my skin. Her strength doesn't challenge me, it's there for me to drink. It makes me stronger. We complete each other." *We're stronger together than apart.* "It feels infinite." Rutger's eyes bled gold, his expression hardening with his admission.

"I'm here to protect you and help you. Nothing about her will leave this office. You have my word, Rutger," Healey assured.

"I understand." Rutger lifted his glass and over the rim saw the baron's doubt. "I do." And he sipped.

"You said it's there for you to drink, have you? Is it possible?" Healey asked. What had they shared?

How far was too far?

"Son, if we're going to keep her safe and be there to help her understand her powers, you need to tell me," Healey urged. Not wanting to challenge Rutger, he kept his tone neutral and without the authority of the alpha.

Rutger took a drink of his bourbon, set the glass on the desk, and sat back. He did not want to explain what they had shared. What Jo shared with him. Keep it to himself or protect Jo. The baron was right, he needed to protect Jo and he needed help.

"I'll leave if you want me to," Ansel offered. He didn't know why they were trusting him with their intimate lives. He placed his hand on Rutger's shoulder. "After what happened to the both of you, this has to be hard."

"Don't leave. This is important and the baron is right." Rutger appreciated Ansel's offer but had to push his hesitation aside. "It was after you announced us as One-Flesh." He paused and tried to pick his words. "We were making love when Jo breathed her power into me. It was hot energy, and when it hit my insides it filled every void and wrapped around my wolf. Jo marked my wolf. And now my wolf craves the energy and the need to be part of her. Like I need-" Rutger stopped, feeling as if he said to much and hadn't explained a damned thing.

"Like you need to mark her. It's natural, Rutger, don't be ashamed. Before we assimilated to the human's way of living, shapeshifters marked their mates. The few with the instinct were said to be powerful. You have been chosen for a reason," Healey explained.

"Doesn't make me feel any better. What if I hurt her? Jo will revert back the ghost she has been and block me out because I'm responsible. I won't survive inside of the void, its emptiness will destroy me. I won't make it," Rutger said, the last part in a whisper. He wouldn't. It wasn't living, it was existing.

"I don't believe Jordyn will regress. Marking her may strengthen her. The Highguard observes the old ways … recognizing you have marked her will give her status among them all. She is capable of sharing her power with you and she marked you and will always be able to find you," Healey responded. "What other effects do you think there are from her power?"

"Today when we ran, we talked to each other like you and I are talking now. There's no static or brain fuzz, the wolf's thoughts are my own. It's as if our human minds and the wolves' have merged. They aren't two separate beings. There's no human. No animal," Rutger continued. To have something to do, he took his glass and holding it in both hands turned it in his palms.

"It wasn't a feeling, as Laurel explained?" Healey asked.

"No. We spoke to one another. We had a conversation." Rutger took a sip as tension threaded through his shoulders and up his neck. He wanted the meeting to end and desperately needed to leave Foxwood and take Jo home.

"I wonder if she can talk to any one of us. And if we could learn how to talk to one another while in wolf form." Jordyn read his mind with ease and listened to his thoughts but he hadn't felt her. Because she didn't want him to?

Healey had heard tales about shapeshifters being able to talk to one another and doubted its authenticity. He wasn't able to communicate with Laurel, his mate and wife, and he was an alpha.

As in every culture there are stories passed down from generation to generation-the core remains the same while other details may be exaggerated or understated. The last is what happened to the tales about shapeshifters. Their physical abilities and magic gifts were downplayed and turned into stories one told around a campfire. The strength in its truth grew weak in the telling and reimagining of the past. Healey believed the past, filled with denial and the rejection of magic, was the reason they were facing its resurgence. With that in mind, it motivated him to do reexamine the stories, myths, and legends.

In one tale, taking place over a century ago, shapeshifters were able to speak to one another and they had more than one form-the animal form and another, a combination of human and animal, the image resembling what he knew as Bestial. The shapeshifter stood on hind legs, over eight feet tall, its muscled arms thicker than its human counterpart, its hands were claws, and its wide chest made it look like a creature from a myth. Healey doubted it told of a second form rather it was a warning to scare magic-born, shapeshifters, and humans about the dangers of going Bestial. He was thinking about changing his mind. What if it was all true?

"I don't know," Rutger replied absently. He finished his bourbon, lowered the glass and stared at the bottom. "Are we done here?"

Healey wasn't going to push Rutger when he needed to do more research and he needed to contact Lady Sloan. "I would like to give the women a couple more minutes without us. Son, I am proud of the progress you've made. I feared losing you."

"I feared losing myself." To remind him he wasn't completely healed, the beast sat under his skin as if waiting for Rutger to give in and let it have its fury.

Jordyn relaxed, the tension in her shoulders easing to a dull ache, as she sipped her wine, and sat in a comfortable silence with the baroness. She couldn't stop thinking about what the baron and Rutger might be talking about. It had to be her. Jumping from the deck and talking to Rutger while in animal form had been freeing, but now, she saw it as a threat. If the baron wanted to know what was happening between them, Rutger wasn't going to lie. Her powers wouldn't be a secret. The crazies would never stop coming after her.

"Jordyn," Laurel tried. She was watching Jordyn when her stare rolled in onyx and copper, the twists nearly swallowing her entire eyes, and her power threaded through the air like an electric current. "Jordyn."

"What?" Jordyn met the questioning gaze of the baroness. "Sorry, lost in thought."

"I noticed. Are you all right? Do I need to get Rutger?" Laurel felt the energy in the room fade, Jordyn's eyes bleed to their natural cocoa streaked with onyx. She hadn't paid attention to the difference in Jordyn's face, her eyes, she was harder, cold. If Jordyn looked at you and wanted to scare you, she would pin you down with a steely gaze devoid of emotion. The witches stole her innocence and burned the door to her hate and freed its evil.

"No," Jordyn replied. "Please, no." She didn't need Rutger. Standing, to burn anxiety, she walked to the fire, her back to the baroness, the heat on her face.

"Baroness, Lord and Lady Langston are requesting admittance," Sousa reported.

Jordyn turned, faced Sousa and Abigail, then looked at the baroness. "Did you tell them I was going to be here?" She couldn't control the instant anger from making her words sound sharp.

Like a shot of flames Jordyn's eyes blazed copper. "No, I wouldn't do that to you. However, I can't deny them, I have to accept them. You're their daughter and they have status in the pack, refusing them would make them look weak. You know about the unrest among the clansmen and *we* can't add fuel to the fire. Mia is part of those who don't believe the baron. Do you understand? *We* have an obligation to them and it comes first," Laurel stated as she stood.

No. "Yes, Baroness." Jordyn drank her wine emptying the glass. She felt trapped and wanted to go home.

"Listen to me, Jordyn, you are the soothsayer for the pack, are One-Flesh with my son, the Second to the Alpha. I'm your mother-in-law, you will refer to me as Laurel. You will remind Lord and Lady Langston of the status you hold within the pack, not only as their soothsayer but as the mate to the second. You are part of the baron's kith." Laurel waited for a response as she dreaded Jordyn was going to shut down. She felt divided and deliberated whether she should call Rutger. "Jordyn."

"I understand. Would you like a refill?" Jordyn asked. She painted her face with the best neutral look she could muster.

Jordyn let the mother-in-law thing go unnoticed. Her current mood and feeling trapped reminded her, they weren't married. The Jeep reminded them they had been engaged and they withdrew into silence. They hadn't said they loved each other. Announced as One-Flesh didn't mean anything if they didn't love each other. Was that why Rutger compromised and said he wouldn't mark her? He was having second thoughts and didn't love her. As a fated mate he had no choice but to be with her. Was their relationship based on obeying fate and not on how they felt? Jordyn hung her head and closed her eyes. She didn't know. Now she had to face her father. *Keep it together*.

"Yes please." Jordyn's shoulders straightened, it would have to be enough, and Laurel met the gazes of the sentinels. "You may escort them in."

"Baroness," Abigail replied and left, Sousa behind her. Their footsteps silent as they headed down the hall.

Jordyn stood at the walnut bar, poured wine into their glasses, while her nerves tried pushing her into a panic attack. Her doubts about Rutger weren't helping her. *This is too soon*.

"Daughter," Ethan greeted as he entered the room. His dark brown eyes narrowing and taking her in.

"Dad," Jordyn replied. She handed the baroness her glass and approached her father.

Ethan hugged her, clamping her to his body, his arms tight around her. Jordyn wrapped one arm around him and held the glass of red wine away from his pale blue sweater.

"I'm sorry," Ethan mumbled as he let go. "I've missed you."

"Soothsayer," Mia greeted coldly.

Jordyn wanted to roll her eyes. "Mia."

"How did you know she was here?" Laurel asked. "Have a seat."

"After what happened with Louis, I needed to see Jordyn. We went to their house and when they weren't there, I figured they would be here," Ethan answered. "We aren't intruding." He couldn't be intruding when he wanted to see his own daughter.

"Of course not. Is there anything I could get you?" Laurel asked. Her suspicion eased. It was natural for a father to want to see his daughter, especially after an attempted kidnapping.

"Wine, please," Mia requested.

"Scotch. Where is Healey and Rutger?" Ethan asked.

"Pack business," Jordyn replied. *Talking about me.* Her voice held, as did her shoulders, and she thought she was going to survive. "Captain Wolt is giving them a report. I'll get the drinks," Jordyn offered.

"No, sit," Laurel gently said as she reached for her cell phone.

Jordyn met her stare and understood where this was going. "Of course, Laurel." She smiled and sat down in a winged back chair by the fire.

Laurel wanted to laugh when she saw surprise race across Mia's face. The games they play. She finished typing out a message and waited for Sadie. "How have you been?"

"The usual," Ethan answered first. "How have you been, Jordyn?"

"I'm good, Dad. No need to worry." Jordyn sipped her wine.

"That's not what *we've* heard," Mia questioned. "And we've only heard through the rumor mill because no one speaks to us about our daughter. You don't think it's important to tell your parents Louis found you and tried to kidnap you? Or the enforcers and soldiers were deployed to your house? Not to mention, your frail mental health, this couldn't have helped you."

Frail mental health. Detective Watt's words came back. Jordyn saw Laurel and stopped her from coming to her rescue. "There's nothing Louis can do to hurt me." Should have kicked his ass. That's the kind of therapy she needed. Jordyn's thoughts of revenge came to a stop, her smile died, and her eyes bleed completely copper, when her instincts screamed. She set her glass on the side table and stood.

"What is it?" Laurel asked.

"Someone is here." Jordyn replied. She stilled, waiting to understand where it was coming from.

"There was no one here except us," Ethan said.

"I can't sense anyone. If someone was here Abigail, Sousa, or Troy would have reported them," Laurel tried to assure her.

"It's wrong. Where's Sadie?" Jordyn asked. The magic crawled over her, its fingers touching her skin through her clothing. Whoever it was possessed a lot of power and they were making sure Jordyn knew they were there.

"The soothsayer's instincts are better than the baroness' and ours? I don't see the baron running in here, or his enforcers," Mia challenged. "It could be stress and your mental health. You couldn't defend yourself against two humans, and you want us to believe your instincts are stronger than ours."

By the way, Mia, I didn't let two humans do anything to me. Jordyn shook her head and looked at her wine. Mia was right. What the hell was she thinking? It could be stress, her parents unnerved her. What did Dr. Carrion say about PTSD and her emotional responses? Was stress corrupting her instincts and power? As if challenging the questions an old, other worldly force slithered into the room and over her. No. She wasn't going to let Mia's doubt infect her. If Jordyn was wrong, it was better than not doing anything.

"I'm going to go check." Jordyn set her glass on the table and stood.

"You didn't hear what I said, Soothsayer. If there is a threat, where is the baron?" Mia asked. "He isn't here."

If I could kick them out of my house. "It's not your place, Jordyn," Laurel warned. "The security system at the gate would have notified Healey, the enforcers, and the soldiers if there was a problem. And, I have sentinels for a reason."

"It is my place. You can't sense magic and I can." Jordyn started for the entrance with her instincts blaring a warning and her wolf gliding under her skin.

"Leave her be. Maybe she'll find Sadie," Mia scoffed. "Would like to have a glass of wine while I watch the entertainment."

"You could get it yourself." Ethan met Mia's stare. He listened to his wife's scorn as he watched his daughter stop under the archway.

He could feel her power as if she was building a wall around herself with its force. It wove through the air, its ribbons carrying its energy as it twisted and turned and searched. Ethan wished he could take Jordyn away from them and hide her from the world, the Highguard, and her mother. While Jordyn was more powerful than she had been, her body was thinner, lacking muscle, and showed stress had been eating her alive.

What was the baron doing about it? What was Rutger doing to help her? Not a damn thing. They were waiting for her to give her life to the pack.

With the feel of their doubt behind her, Jordyn looked to the left; the dim hall sat empty and silent, no evidence of the meeting between Rutger, the baron, and Captain Wolt. She looked to the right, saw the double doors, and the porch lights like shards of white slipped around the wrought iron carving of the Cascade pack's crest. She didn't see the sentinels, they were missing. Jordyn waited, hoping they were on either side of the doors. When no one moved, she used her senses, and felt nothing. Damn. What the hell was going on?

"Your sentinels are missing," Jordyn reported, without turning around.

"I'm getting Healey." Laurel stood.

Jordyn faced the baroness. "No. Let me check first. Just to be sure." Have the baron, Rutger, and Captain Wolt witness her failure and insanity. Or she allowed stress to further damage her mental health. No, thank you.

"Don't want to make a fool of yourself?" Mia asked.

"Mia, enough. You will not speak to the pack's soothsayer or the Second to the Alpha's mate with disrespect," Laurel warned. "Jordyn, do what you have to do."

Jordyn nodded her response. Maybe she should get Rutger. He would understand where the sentinels, enforcers, and soldiers would think she was crazy. "I'm going to get Rutger. Captain Wolt is with him and they can alert the enforcers," Jordyn explained. Here's hoping she didn't sound insane.

"We'll wait here," Laurel replied.

Jordyn hesitated, meeting her dad's sad eyes and wanting to tell him she wasn't losing her mind, and she was all right. She didn't know how to assure him, didn't know what to say to convince him. She was staring at him when shadows crossed the shards of light, causing ripples on the wall and marble flooring. *Thank god.* It had to be the sentinels. "I think your sentinels are outside."

"Jordyn, come here. Now," Laurel whispered. Glowing yellow eyes blazed, its gray body emerged from the dark hall. As it raised a clawed hand, its black nails lengthened, and melted together into a spear. "Please, Jordyn."

"Someone is outside," Jordyn assured.

In slow motion, the baroness stood, her eyes wide, and she dropped her glass. It shattered on the area rug, sending shards flying as burgundy pooled and soaked into the material.

Jordyn didn't understand and started toward the baroness when death crawled over her like thick, slim on her skin, making her shiver from the sensation. She had to be losing her mind, and acting crazy was scaring the baroness. Forgetting about Rutger, she planned on checking in with the sentinels-*to give myself some peace*-she took a step when her breath caught. A quick bite latched onto her, fire spread out from her chest, followed by cold as if someone stuck a piece of ice inside of her. Jordyn watched the baroness' lips move around silent words and her eyes filled with terror.

She didn't look at her chest, she couldn't. She raised her hand, and with trembling fingers felt the tip of a spike. How? Jordyn looked down while shock gripped her body, and saw a bloody tip resembling a black talon sticking through her skin and her pink shirt. It took seconds for the wound to bleed scarlet saturating the material. Jordyn felt blood's warmth on her skin and sliding down it stopped at the waist of her jeans. She tried stepping away from it, whatever it was, and the talon twisted in her chest and ground against bone. Jordyn stopped, her pulse rushed in her ears as fear and pain like a fire engulfed her body. It twisted the spike tearing skin, hitting bone, and blood poured from around it. A low whimper, she couldn't get enough air to cry-left her with blood peppering her lips. Another twist, Jordyn groaned a guttural sound, then it pulled back, ripping free of her chest cavity and back. She crashed to her knees, felt something give under her weight, and blood poured from the wound.

"Jordyn," Ethan yelled and stood. He stopped when the rage and death flowed from the creature and into the room. Its large muzzle opened, exposing rows of sharp-ened teeth as four more creatures flanked the first. "Easy." Ethan raised his hands and slowly sat down, not wanting to provoke them.

"Rutger. Please, Rutger," Jordyn whined. She stared at the marble floor as blood dripped from her mouth, then sat back on her calves. "Help me."

He couldn't hear her. Jordyn pushed panic down to a low roar and tried to think. How long was it going to take Rutger to find her? Her mind raced, she needed to stop the bleeding. With shaking hands, she feebly bunched her shirt and shoved the gathered material into the hole. Wincing as the frayed skin ripped into the fleshy part of her breasts and then down her sternum. Jordyn fought through the pain to concentrate on stopping the bleeding. Blood cov-ered her fingers, was running down her back, her front, soaking the waist of her jeans and creating a pool on the marble flooring. She couldn't stop the bleeding.

She was going to bled to death. She was going to die as her family watched. The chance to fix her relationship with Rutger would be lost. She would lose her family. Her dad. Her sister. Jordyn's vision blurred, she swayed, struggled to remain upright, and sweat beaded along her hairline. Shock. Blood loss. Hurt seized her heart in its steel grip when she thought about the people she failed because of her selfishness.

Please Rutger. What was this going to do to him? She leaned to the right, put her hand out, and slipping in blood, she hit the floor with her shoulder. Jordyn gulped for air around the rising nausea bubbling in her stomach when long fingers with black nails circled her throat and cut the air off. Holding her, it lifted her off the marble and turned her around until they were face-to-face. With her back to the living room, she couldn't see the occupants and their terrified gazes. She didn't know what they were doing but heard their cries and demands. Jordyn wanted to tell the baroness to call the baron, Rutger, or Captain Wolt ... anyone. She needed help before she bled to death.

"Put her down," Ethan ordered, a panicked edge cutting through his words.

It tilted its angular head, its pointed ears laid back on its hairless skull, and shrieking it slammed her against the hallway wall. Jordyn tried crying out, it strangled the sound in her throat.

It was dead. It carried death. She was wrong. Its huge yellow eyes glittered with cold menace as they reflected the fear in her copper gaze. It wasn't a vampire. She didn't know what it was. *"Wolf, help me."*

CHAPTER SIXTEEN

"Wolf, help me." Rutger bowed his head as fear and pain blasted into him. "Jo."

"What?" Healey stood and walked around his desk. "What's happening?"

"Pain. She's been attacked," Rutger answered. He left his chair and stumbled around the baron.

"Are you sure?" Healey asked. No one could have gotten into the house. Holding Rutger by the upper arm, he tried keeping him upright. "You thought something bad had happened when you initiated security. She went running. Could this be the same?" he asked with caution.

The baron's accusation made Rutger pause. "No, I didn't know what she was doing then. The pain is in our link, I feel it." Rutger's eyes glowed gold with his wolf as he hit his chest, above his heart, with his fist. "Right here." He stumbled as he stepped out of the baron's grip. "She called me. Her voice filled my head." Rutger gained his balance, stepped back from the baron, and marched out of the office.

"Alert the enforcers," Healey ordered. "I don't know how anyone could have gotten past security or my sentinels."

"Sir," Ansel replied. He took his cell phone from his pocket, pressed the quick dial for the emergency line, and when he heard it ring, he waited. One second. Two seconds. Three beeps sounded and the call ended. He tried again and got the same result. Communications had been cut off.

Rutger stumbled out of the office, steadied his gait, and running down the hall, his heart seized. Skidding to a stop, he froze in front of a creature with muscles cording its body. It held Jo in its clutches, its gray sinuous arm was extended, ending in long, slim fingers with nails. Standing naked, it didn't have physical features, it was a blank canvas, not giving away if it was male or female. With its height, it towered over Jo, holding her about twenty inches above the floor. Rutger guessed it was over seven feet tall.

"This is not happening." *He should have his gun.*

Blood splashed the walls and floor, turning the white and charcoal veined marble into a grotesque gleaming stage. Thick, thin, and wet scarlet splashed up and down, scarring the soft pearl walls. Rutger inhaled for calm and drew in a metallic scent, fresh blood, spice, and werewolf. The combination teased his wolf and called his beast. Challenged his beast. His wolf recognized Jo's blood, and it sent his wolf into rage as its howl deafened him.

Bringing Jo toward its muzzle, the creature growled, the wall behind her stained, the long lines inching their way down. It held her for a painstaking breath, then it shoved her to the wall, pinning her, the movement making every corded muscle in its body undulate. As it held her, Rutger watched blood seep from a hole in her shirt. It stabbed her through her chest. Her once pink shirt was now scarlet. The thin cotton, which hung on her shoulders, was translucent and he could see her bra while more blood darkened her jeans, and a pool glittered beneath her.

"Jo," Rutger whispered. He couldn't lose her. "Jo, can you hear me."

She whimpered and a tinge of energy traced the link giving Rutger her weakness. His wolf erupted, fraying Rutger's restraint and begging him to let go and turn into the beast. *Don't lose control.* Loss of control means losing Jo. Rutger gained a semblance of dominance over his wolf and sent his strength through the link. He couldn't stop the witches from taking her, but he could save her from whatever the hell the thing was.

The creature shrieked, the ear-piercing pitch making Jordyn's skull feel like it was splitting into a million pieces. Her muscles turned liquid from blood loss, her heart slowly giving up as she hung from the creatures clawed hand. Black dots danced between its yellow eyes, blurring the thing's face. She wasn't going to make it.

Rutger had to do something. The feeling of her heartbeat stopping as he held her sank into his skin. "Mea, heal yourself. You have to heal yourself."

Too weak. Jordyn's mind buzzed like a thousand bees were borrowing their way into her brain matter. Gray shadows inched around her, taking the curves and angles of the hallway. She recognized the feeling and fought to stay awake. To stay alive.

"I can't get through to the office. Aydian called using his cell phone and reported they're under siege by more creatures. They have everyone locked inside. There are two cars parked out front. The system didn't register either of them," Ansel reported.

"We don't know who did this?" Healey growled.

"Negative."

Healey caught sight of Laurel as she approached the entry, her eyes wide with fear, and wringing her hands. "No farther." When she nodded, he turned his attention to

Rutger. His back strained against his flannel shirt, his shoulders bunched with tension, his legs resembled steel beams as he forced himself to remain where he was. Healey saw the hazy outline of Rutger's wolf shadow his frame, felt his power surging from him, and feared Rutger was going to turn Bestial.

"Ansel, get a tranquilizer," Healey ordered. If Rutger started to crumble under the pressure, Healey would sedate him before it went too far.

"He won't turn," Ansel countered. *Don't you fucking turn, Rutger.*

Healey faced Ansel, his eyes burnt gold of his wolf, and his features sharpening. "Now."

The baron's sharp power sliced through Ansel, and turning, he headed back to the office.

Rutger was barley aware of the baron giving orders, his full attention zeroed on Jo's weakening heartbeat. "Mea, heal your wounds. Your heartbeat. Please," Rutger pleaded. He took a step forward.

Jordyn felt his wolf, his power, and wanted to be in his warm arms. Warmth. Her arms were cold and going numb all the way to her fingers and she couldn't feel anything from the waist down. *It's shock. I'm bleeding to death. "Mea, heal your wounds."* His voice drifted through her and faded. She was going to lose him.

The creature tightened its grip. Jo coughed at the same time she raised her hands, her thin fingers feebly clawing at the twisting muscles holding her. While she struggled, it turned its head, its muzzle lifting its lips, and targeted Rutger with its yellow eyes. As they stared at each other Jo's scarlet-stained lips parted and turned blue. The tangled colors creating an indigo tint that spread out from her lips and into her cheeks. Jo opened her eyes, the corner of her left eye filled with red from blood vessels bursting. Rutger grudgingly took two steps backward, and the creature eased his hold and brought her closer to its maw. Its yellow glare challenged Rutger as its muzzle touched her cheek. Mocking him, it slammed her back to the wall, her head hitting with a sharp crack.

"I'm going to kill you," Rutger promised. He didn't know if it understood him and didn't care. Taking another step back, his fury exploded and he roared, its raw emotion thundered in the hallway.

No. No. No. Jordyn wouldn't watch Rutger lose his life to the beast. Not again. She wouldn't watch as he turned Bestial. She had to save herself. The creature drew her closer, Jordyn knew it was going to slam her into the wall again. Its thick lips lifted as its ashen tongue flicked and the forked tip feathered her ear. Her stomach clenched, pressure built, and she knew she was going to throw up.

It was driving Rutger's anger, making him crazy. Jordyn heard Rutger growl as the creature shoved her backwards, her head bouncing off the wall. A rainbow of dots played in front of her, blurring the creature while her blood-soaked shirt stuck to her like a second skin working to squeeze her chest. She was having a hard time breathing, staying conscious, and thinking clearly.

"Mea, please," Rutger growled.

She could do it. "Heal," Jordyn whispered.

The creature squeezed her neck, taking her breath, and black flecks bounced in her peripheral vision. *Stay awake.* Focusing her energy and bringing her wolf to the surface, the hot fire radiating from her chest and back flared then eased, and she felt her skin react with a warm caress. A soft vibration tingled inside her chest as the wound began mending from the inside out. Closing her eyes, she focused on powering the healing and ignoring the creature.

When Jo's eyes closed and her head rested on the wall behind her, Rutger's body shook, the beast shadowed him and his human features faded. He was going to lose control, and when he did, he was going to kill the fucking creature.

Behind Jo and the creature, the double doors of the house swung open and three more creatures entered the foyer, their nails clicking on marble. A second later the hall light came on, revealing a seven-foot man wearing a hooded robe. The deep hood hid his face, covered his entire body, and swished against the flooring as he approached the creature and Jo. He stopped when inches separated them, the hem of the robe turning dark as it soaked up Jo's blood.

"Get away from her," Rutger ordered through a growl. Thickening and growing tangible, the beast's shadow took more of him. Rutger wasn't going to stop it when the feel of power strengthened him. Like he was in control. The way he used to feel. He let it grow stronger, then stopped and held onto the beast.

Healey watched his son and gauging the deterioration tried to decide whether or not to use the tranquilizer. "I am Baron Kanin. You are trespassing on Cascade territory," Healey warned. If the hooded man decided Jordyn was to die, they were powerless to stop him. No one was going to risk Jordyn's life by attacking the man, the creature, or the creatures standing guard for fear of provoking them. Healey wanted to join Rutger and roar his frustration knowing Jordyn would bleed to death if they didn't help her. "She's dying!" Healey yelled.

They watched the cloaked figure ignore them. Rutger held his breath as the stranger raised a pale hand and drew the back of his long fingers down Jo's blood-stained cheek. The intimate touch struck him, the hit fading when she didn't react, didn't respond to the touch. Her eyes remained closed, her face slack, her head resting on the wall, her jaw on the area between the creature's thumb and first finger. He was going to lose her.

Rutger roared, his T-shirt and flannel shirt tightening around his arms and chest, his jeans constricting his legs. "Tell it to let her go. She'll die."

A gentle wind, as if someone waved her thoughts to the side to make room for their own, cleared the way for the scene to play in her head. Jordyn felt his authority and the confidence slip over her, then his arrogance as he easily disregarded Rutger and the baron's orders and demands. She sensed, he was keeping his focus on the wolf, the Second to the Alpha, mate to Soothsayer, and Director of Enforcers for fear he would lose himself to the beast.

"Predictable." She heard the word inside her head, a delay as if he was thinking, then an English translation. It confused her; she didn't speak another language.

When his fingers brushed her chilled skin, Jordyn wanted to jerk her head from him, then she saw herself and the summer bronze of her skin dying under a bloodless pale hue. His power reached out, its ribbons entering her mind as he searched her, the soothsayer, and scion. An exhale escaped Jordyn's blue-tinged lips, and he realized she wasn't unconscious or dying as they thought ... no, she was fighting to heal her wounds. But not before almost bleeding out.

"Shouldn't have waited, oλiyo Soothsayer."

What the hell did he know? Jordyn hadn't intended on being stabbed by a creature.

Her mind screamed as he opened himself and felt her power swirling inside her and her wolf's fury burning and waiting to fight. He didn't sense fear, and smiling, his thin lips curved, his sharp teeth gleaming from behind the cream-colored hood. The creature turned its hand, her head rolled to the left, her eyes opening, and she stared at him with a copper gaze. Azar eyes gleamed for a second, bleed violet ringed with bright white, and she knew she was seeing things. His attention as he watched the swirling copper with onyx flakes eddy around her pupils possessed her. Sensing her raw power, he leaned in, his eyes flickered between violet and azar, to roll over to his natural being, his body abandoning the human façade, and leaving a sliver between their lips.

"Soothsayer," he whispered in English.

Jordyn, dazed and weak, saw opal lips and stared into violet eyes and fell into their fathoms. Magic rose up, and tangling with her own, she drank it in and a spark ignited. "Prime."

Rutger heard Jo's weak voice and the beast eased back. "What did she say?" He couldn't sense the cloaked stranger, couldn't sense what he was, or his power. As if the invader wasn't there. Dead space.

"I don't know," Healey replied with frustration.

Jordyn wanted to tell Rutger not to worry as she struggled to meet his gold gaze. Prime raised his hand, and with his fingertips gently closed her eyes, blocking Rutger from her. It felt like he ripped Rutger and the security he promised from her. Again, she heard Prime's thoughts and was seeing the world through him. He closed his eyes for a heartbeat when the slightest vibration skated over him as Soothsayer began drinking from him.

"Ροφώ," his whisper drifted, his accent curling around the word.

When he entered the house and searched her, he felt the underlying darkness and recognized the familiar essence roiling in her fractured magic. The truth was revealing itself and bringing the past to the present. He called his magic, threads from his death, and wove them into Soothsayer, enabling her to watch through his eyes and listen to his thoughts. He expected resistance and fear, not the thirst for strength he encountered. To protect her from drowning in his power, he shielded the intensity of his magic. Guarding the truth, he didn't reveal his magic was dangerous to her and the possibility of the smallest amount might drive her insane and kill her. It was a necessary risk. His travels, searches for keepers of the past, and days and nights spent with tomes were proving successful.

Prime bypassed their security systems, held the enforcers and soldiers prisoner in their own office, entered the house unnoticed, and wounded their soothsayer. If there had been any other way to demonstrate their inadequacies and show them she wasn't safe, he would have done so. He needed to protect her. Prime stepped back as she continued siphoning his power, to help her heal her wounds, and kept her heartbeat in his head. Soothsayer didn't understand she was taking a piece of him into herself. Taking the first step of possessing and then marking her as his. When his essence merged with her power, if she survived the infusion, Prime would make himself her protector. His power, like a signature, would be a warning to those seeking her.

While Jordyn's body absorbed Prime's magic, it sank into the fibers of her being and carried her out of the haze of pain, but not out of his thoughts. He took his gaze off Soothsayer, eyed the baron, his second, and another wolf in the hall. They looked upon her as if she was a victim and was going to die in front of them. Would there be a day she proved she could take care of herself? Not if she continued this way. The weight of Prime's thoughts bullied through hers, taking her attention. He showed Soothsayer his true form, wanting her to see him for who he was and not the humanoid the Highguard insisted he pretended to be.

His need to reveal himself rocked her as a rush of magic swept over him, masking his black skin. His flesh turned a shade darker than alabaster with a tinge of olive, his eyes bleed to a common blue, like azar, and his hair a honey hue. He looked from the Mediterranean, from his hidden island in the Aegean Sea, and not a descendant of the ancient Greek Ceuthonymus, daemon of the underworld. She fought the onslaught of memories not wanting them in her head. Jordyn had enough problems with her memories, she didn't need anyone else's.

The slightest wave of magic spread out in the hall and touched Rutger's skin with thousands of soft vibrations. The three of them watched the man shrug the robe from his shoulders causing the cream-colored fabric to fall freely and pool around his black shoes. His amethyst button-up shirt molded to his shoulders and chest and highlighted the azar of his eyes. His tailored black dress pants drew the eye to his narrow waist and long, lean legs, and radiated distinction. An onyx clasp held his soft gold hair back, the length following his spine to his waist. Rutger took his gaze from Jo to the man standing before them. With his wolf howling a warning, he recognized authority and power, and the man possessed both.

Prime, while the absolute ruler over magic-born, was a demon and descendant of the underworld, and part of the hidden magic-born known as the Cloaked. He chose to live secluded from society on his island off of Greece, having his staff and members of the Highguard as his only contacts. Shapeshifters and some magic-born, like witches, lived in the open with humans as their humanoid appearance allowed them more freedom and less attention.

"Prime?" Ansel asked with awe. The hair on the back of his neck rose, his wolf growled, and his instincts raced with a warning.

"What is the meaning of this?" Healey demanded.

"Evening, Baron," Prime greeted.

"Tell the thing to let her go," Rutger ordered and took a step.

"No. If your soothsayer is to live, she will free herself." Prime listened to her heartbeat and heard it strengthening. "Director, stand down."

To warn Rutger, the creature squeezed its clawed hand. Jo moaned, blood seeped from her chest, and red from her soaked shirt dropped to the creature's gray feet and black nails. Rutger stepped back. A memory put him at Butte Springs and he heard himself begging Jo to shapeshift to heal herself. She hadn't. She died. In his arms. He feared she was going to hang there, and while Prime talked, she would die. Jo failed to defend herself against one of their own and two humans, how was she going to defend herself against the creature and Prime? His worry had his wolf drowning into the beast and he felt the shadow's weight on his body.

"Your Second is weak and uncontrolled, I hold you responsible, Baron. Where is your ascendency?" Prime goaded.

"You came here, invaded my territory, had your Numina attack *my* soothsayer, my daughter-in-law, to question my authority?" Healey demanded. He walked to Rutger's side and stopped.

"Would it matter if I had, Baron?" Prime asked.

The magic-born answered to the Highguard, but the absolute power came from Prime. Healey wouldn't, couldn't argue. "No, Prime."

His eyes skirted over the baron, the director, and landed on Soothsayer. "There have been reports the soothsayer is failing. She hasn't attended moon runs, I assumed those were mandatory, and if she didn't shapeshift it was a threat to her wellbeing. Further, she hasn't had contact with the pack nor has she embraced the Collective or her powers. Without the Collective she will lose her place in the magic, like being lost at sea. The magic inside her will tear her apart, and she will lose her mind. The fact this hasn't happened yet is testament to her strength and will to control her wolf. However, it goes unchecked. I don't have the time or the patience to wait for her to recover and leave the dark place she's in, or for you to act like her alpha and force her. The Highguard has contentions about the Cascade pack's ability to function."

"The soothsayer isn't human. You are not human. And yet you deny magic. You rely on security systems to protect you, which I proved are inadequate when I *invaded* your territory. You rely on Celestial and physicians to heal you when you're capable of regeneration. You are immortal shapeshifters, *vrykolaka*, powerful enough to merit the title of baron, and to keep a territory, but you live as humans.

Aidiastikos," he cursed. "It's an insult to your kind, the Highguard, and all magic-born."

Fury escaped Rutger in a rush, and in defeat his beast gave into the wolf. Prime was right, he was weak and un-controlled, and the baron let him stew in his own failing. *Should be caged.* His skin chilled with the thought of losing Jo and spending eternity, or until the baron gave the death order, in a silver lined prison. But if it saved Jo, he would walk into the bowels of the Enforcer's office where a cage was waiting for him.

She isn't the soothsayer. Jo is my mate. "She is dying," Rutger pleaded as he watched her. "Jo. Is. Dying."

Prime heard the tremble in the Second's voice, fated mates, and glanced at Soothsayer as color crept up her throat and into her cheeks. *It's a wonder she found her powers at all.* She sank into the Numen's clutch with a weak moan and her eyes remained closed. Her passion, will to live, and loyalty to her pack was in there somewhere, he had to find the right provocation. *Come to the surface, Soothsayer.*

"After what I have witnessed, your Second's weakness is a danger to your status, Baron, and a danger to Sooth-sayer's life. Due to the threat, I renounce the Scared Writ of One-Flesh between Rutger Kanin and Jordyn Langston. Di-rector of Enforcers, Second, to the Alpha Healey Kanin, Baron of the Cascade territory, you are unworthy to be the mate of Soothsayer Jordan Langston, scion of Lady Sloan, Soothsayer to the Diablo pack, and one of the Twelve serv-ing the Highguard. I strongly suggest you imprison the beast. Immediately."

"Prime-" Healey started. Prime was going to take Rutger from them at the same time he exposed the truth in front of Lord and Lady Langston.

"No, he's right," Rutger interrupted. He couldn't keep her safe, wasn't able to save her from himself, and couldn't keep from losing control over his beast. *I'm going to lose my mate.* His wolf howled in his ears. *You can't protect her,* mocked him.

"No. No," Jordyn whispered. Her lips parted around the weak words and she wasn't sure if she had said them out loud. The exhaustion from blood loss and pain ate at her, and she couldn't keep her eyes open no matter how hard she fought.

"Your dispute is noted," Prime responded with a quick glance at her.

Rutger watched her eyes open and copper blaze. "Mea."

Jordyn kept the link between them open wanting Rutger to sense her and understand she wasn't dying but was trying to heal her wounds. *I need time.* She didn't want him to lose himself to the beast. Guess she denied him too many times for him seek the truth in their link. Jordyn sent her essence, that's all she had, into the link and felt him respond with his own. Despite his effort to conceal his emotions, she felt his grief and fear. No one was going to take Rutger from her.

"Release me," Jordyn mumbled past the grip on her neck. The creature's fingers tightened, threatening to crush her trachea, and spots danced at the edges of her vision. Damn thing was going to make her work harder.

"Soothsayer, save your strength, you're going to need it," Prime warned.

Jordyn slipped into its mind, if the mass of confusion, like a continual explosion filling its skull could be called a mind. Latching onto the strongest thread, the strain made her squeeze her eyes closed and the energy she built up dissolved with her effort. It fought against her, seeking Prime's presence, and forced her to unravel the connection. So much pain and exhaustion made it hard to concentrate. She clung to the thread as she invaded its thoughts and repeated the order. One second. Two. Three. *Come on.* Four. It loosened its grip and began to gently lower her.

"Hold her," Prime ordered.

Jordyn smiled-the movement of her mouth felt foreign-and met its yellow gaze. "Put me down. Slowly." Her feet touched, flattened, and when her weight was on her legs, she scooted down the wall and stopped when she sat on her claves. Jordyn held onto the creature, making it crouch in front her. "Give me a minute."

"Mea," Rutger whispered. He was positive he was going to lose her. The blood. The hole in her chest. The creature slamming her into the wall. He heard her head hit and crack when it bounced off. The Numen knelt in front of her, waiting like a dog for her to give him a command. He wasn't sure what he was witnessing.

"I'm all right." Jordyn wasn't going to risk looking at him. If she saw him with his beast's outline hovering over him, it would send her over the edge. She needed to be strong. Jordyn stood with the help of the Numen and faced Prime. She looked up at him as his eyes wavered between violet and azar. "I said no. Rutger is my mate."

"After taking control of my Numen, you are challenging my edict?" The azar blinked out and violet ringed with white blazed in warning.

"Yes. I. Am." Jordyn inhaled, didn't know what the hell she was doing, and exhaled. While healed, the hole in her chest hurt like hell and she was surviving on fumes. Healing and holding the Numen's mind was draining her.

"Jo, don't do this," Rutger pleaded. "We both know it's the truth. It was a matter of time."

She wanted to sink back to the floor when every muscle in her body screamed. She fought it and looking at Rutger, met his gold gaze, and saw the fringe of the beast. Prime ordered his Numen to stab her in the back, he threatened Rutger, and their relationship, which they had started working on. He used Jordyn to watch Rutger lose control. Yes, she was going to do this.

Jordyn searched for the proper canon, and thinking she remembered the correct one, she held Rutger's gaze as she announced, "I, Soothsayer for the Cascade pack, mate to the second, scion of Lady Sloan, Pureblood daughter of Lord Langston, challenge Prime." Her voice rumbled with a growl and carried her anger.

"Dear god," Laurel mumbled. Her eyes wide and going from the blood splattering the walls of her home, to Healey, Jordyn, Rutger, and stopped at Prime. They all stood in the arched entrance to watch the scene unfold, the line between the room and hallway divided by blood and creatures.

"Daughter, please," Ethan begged. Jordyn called herself Lady Sloan's scion. She knew the truth. His secrets and the past he worked to hide was coming back with a vengeance and targeted Jordyn. "You cannot challenge Prime."

"He'll kill you, Soothsayer." Mia stood beside Ethan, her face wearing a mask of indifference.

"You manipulated her," Healey accused. His entire body sang with tension, its claws wrapping around his muscles.

It had been easy. Mistake after mistake, when was it going to end? Jordyn shook the lingering thoughts loose and waited for Prime to respond.

"What do you want?" Healey demanded.

"Manipulate is a strong word." Prime took in the pale pink scar from the two-inch hole, her crimson-soaked shirt, gaunt body, and the fire in her eyes. *Yes, I manipulated her.* She healed her wounds, took possession of his Numen, and challenged him. "I want Soothsayer to prove her worth. If she triumphs, the second will be spared and the Scared Writ of One-Flesh will be recognized as if I hadn't said anything at all. If she doesn't and she fails, she will become my *katoxí*, possession, and will reside at Mountain Fortress as part of the Highguard. Second will remain with you in a cage. Baron, you will write an open invitation and send it to your pack, those of the klatch, and the factions. The challenge will take place during the moon run. There they will hear how their soothsayer defied my authority, and afterwards they will witness the repercussions of her actions. I am Prime." He met a copper glare. "Until then, Soothsayer."

Jordyn nodded her head in response, scared if she opened her mouth, she would say something she shouldn't. The Highguard's court, Mountain Fortress, where magic-born acted like royalty, would drive her crazy.

"Release him," Prime ordered.

"Say please," Jordyn shot back. Behind her she heard gasps of disbelief. Screw them. Screw him. She had a hole in her chest, was having a hard time standing, and he played her. Prime could order her to do anything he damn well pleased. Just like he came into their territory unannounced with his gang of creatures without the fear of the consequences.

"Please." Prime smiled, his opal lips reflecting a rainbow of colors as they pulled back to reveal two rows of sharp teeth.

Prime was changing how she saw him and she didn't know if it was real. He wore a human appearance, human skin, but Jordyn would never forget his silver/blue hair, black skin as if coal painted him, and his violet eyes ringed with white bright enough to blind someone. She wouldn't forget the dark, faintly sweet taste of the death lacing his power as she drank it in. Jordyn wanted to believe it was possible because she had been dying, but the truth-she held death's essence inside her-couldn't be ignored.

"All yours." The sight of him and the hum of his power as it touched Jordyn's skin unnerved her.

The Numen's muzzle lowered to rest on his bony chest; clear slime slid from its mouth to land on its gray skin and mixed with her drying blood. A heartbeat later, its head jerked up, its yellow eyes gleamed, and it growled. If it decided to turn its claw into a spear and attack her, she was going to be pissed. It was possible Jordyn would die after having burned through her energy and the strength it took to heal. Would Prime's power save her? She didn't know. The first time she leaves the house, she challenges Prime, the authority over all magic-born and used his power to heal herself.

"Settle down." It took a step backward to stand beside Prime. *Good boy. Thing. Numen.*

"Thank you," Prime said through his smile, his eyes narrowing on her. He didn't wait for the others to acknowledge him and turned toward the open double doors. Behind him, the Numina mirrored his movements, and in unison trailed after their master like soldiers.

Silence sat thick as they waited for Prime and his followers to exist the house and disappear into the night. No one made a sound. Outside, car doors opened and closed, engines started, then their tires drove over asphalt, and Prime and his horde were gone. Motionless seconds ticked off the clock as silence laced with tension weaved between them. Breaking the forced quiet was the sentinels; Sousa, Abigail, Sadie, Troy, along with Aydian, Quinn, Kai, and Luca from the enforcer's office, then Sawyer, Alexia, Charles, and Raine from the soldiers racing into the house, their boots and running shoes, sounding like a stampede was approaching.

As one they skidded to a stop at the mouth of the hallway, their nostrils flaring from the scent of blood, their eyes blazing with their wolves as they studied the scene. Jordyn stood out in the front, the weight of their stares on her as they all searched her. Her face was peppered with scarlet, her shirt ripped, blood-soaked, and torn exposing her chest while the ends of her hair were in sticky clumps. Crimson stained the walls with thin slashes and her body print and the floor glittered with her blood. The hall resembled a horror movie. With Prime gone, she didn't have to pretend to be as strong as he thought she was. Jordyn let go of the will power she had been holding onto, and swaying, she hit the wall with her back and slid down. Her shoes slipped in the puddle of blood causing her to land on her butt.

"Mea." Rutger rushed to her side, and kneeling on one knee, his jeans drank the blood off the marble.

"I don't feel good," Jordyn mumbled as she looked at the possession in Rutger's gold gaze. Her arms were at her sides, her legs straight out in front of her. She had zero dignity. *Here I am, the victim. Will there be a video we can watch with popcorn?*

"You shouldn't. I'll get you out of here," Rutger assured.

Aydian stepped forward, his stone glare unfazed by what he saw. "The creatures pinned us down in the office. We couldn't get out. What the hell were those things?"

"Prime's *Numina*," Healey replied. "Horde of the Styx. Jordyn do you know what you've done?"

She closed her eyes. Yea, she knew, sorta. Later, when she wasn't covered in her own blood, there wasn't a scar from having a hole in her chest, and she could complete a thought, she might regret what she had done. Maybe. "He orchestrated a conflict."

"Do you need medical? I'll call Dr. Hyde," Ansel asked. For the first time, he wasn't sure what to do next.

Rutger tried answering but Jordyn interrupted. "No. No, doctors." She wouldn't be using Celestial anytime in the near future, if she could help it. Prime was right. She needed to strengthen her power and use her magic.

"Jordyn, don't let Prime influence you," Healey advised. "I saw the hole in your chest and the blood." He stood behind Rutger, his hands on his hips and his authority sitting in his narrowed gaze. "If you need medical, we'll make the call."

"I'm not letting anything he said influence me. Most of the damage is healed and once I shift, it'll be gone. Can I get cleaned up?" Jordyn asked. She hated smelling like raw and drying blood.

It had been almost two days since the cavalry showed up to save her from Louis and his drugs, she didn't need anyone else knowing Prime's creature stabbed her in the back. While she didn't lie, it wasn't the entire truth. Prime didn't have any influence on her, but his power did. The little she managed to leach from him was like a spark to her wolf and her magic.

"You're sure you're healed?" Healey asked.

"Yes, sir." Jordyn scooted up the wall, tried standing by herself, slipped, and landed hard. Everyone watching took a step forward, then back. The silence stretched out as Jordyn lowered her head, held the sides with her hands, and inhaled and exhaled.

"Let me help you," Rutger took Jo in his arms and stood, as if she weighed nothing. She rested her head against his chest and her muscles went limp. "I'm taking her to my room."

"After Jordyn is cleaned up, I want to see the both of you. There are things we need to clear up," Healey told Rutger.

"Yes, sir." Rutger left the blood-stained hall, the group watching them as if they were circus performers and headed to the stairs. Behind him the baron's voice, thickened with anger, thundered.

"I want two shadows deployed. I want to know where Prime is and what he is doing at all times," Healey ordered. There were four days until the moon run and if he was going to guess, he figured Prime was headed to one of his newly inaugurated alphas. "And get the Purifiers here. I

want the hallway sterilized before Jordyn comes downstairs."

"Yes, sir," the enforcers and soldiers answered in unison.

Rutger scrubbed his face with his hand and smelled
blood. Dark streaks stained his flannel shirt, T-shirt, both
hands, his hair, forehead, and cheeks. It had been an ugly
hour. Prime played with Jo's life for an hour.

"How are you doing?" he asked. He leaned against the
granite counter, not sure what to say or do.

"I'm sorry," Jordyn apologized. She looked up at him
and her heart stopped at the sight of her blood staining his
face and clothing, and the fatigue sitting in his eyes. It
drove into her like a stake. *I'm killing him.* "I was in shock. It
made me slow and I nearly died. I saw you and the beast
and didn't want to do that to you again."

"You're alive. And healed. And I'm fine." Rutger looked
at the empty shower and back to Jo and her copper eyes. "I
wanted to let go. I did, and I held into it. It's the first time I
started to feel like my old self, but I had more power," Rutger confessed. His beast hovered over him, waiting to
break free of his grasp and have its freedom. Rutger hadn't
lost control.

"I felt you." Jordyn yawned as she dropped her half-
dried shirt on the counter and stared at the reddish pink
circle, the ragged skin inching toward her breasts, and
knotted scar in the center of her chest. She was lucky it
hadn't hit her spine, shoulder blade, sternum, or a rib. It
sliced through without damaging bone. *He planned it that
way.* "It stabbed me in the back," Jordyn grated through an
exhale. Her pale skin streaked and stained looked worse

under the light. "Through the back in front of everyone. The thing can turn its claws into spears."

"You seem different. Distant." Rutger put his flannel shirt on the counter, then pulled his T-shirt over his head and tossed it to his abandoned flannel shirt. Still wearing his jeans and boots, he went to the large, walk-in shower and leaning in turned the nozzle to hot.

Jordyn felt herself pulling back the moment she saw the terror in her dad's eyes when the talon/spear was sticking out from her chest. "This is my life. You're at risk. The baron and baroness are at risk. My dad is at risk. I have to be stronger than the hot mess I've been. And I can't continue to be shocked every time I get hurt. There's a theme here." Jordyn tried to ease the tension with a light-hearted joke. She smiled, but the look on Rutger's face said it fell flat.

"You didn't mention Mia." Rutger returned to his place at the counter.

"No. She isn't going to run towards danger to save me," Jordyn responded. "Especially after hearing me call Lady Sloan my mother. Even Prime referred to me as Lady Sloan's scion. No one is keeping it a secret." Maybe Jordyn would learn the truth of what happened between her dad and Lady Sloan.

"True. Jo, you didn't block me from feeling you when the creature attacked. You called me. I heard you. When I saw you, I didn't sense fear. You weren't scared," he started. "If you can heal your wounds without shifting, who says the rest of us can't learn?" He inhaled and exhaled. "I'm not weak. I'm not going to lose myself to the beast. So don't use it as an excuse to distance yourself from me. If we are going to have a life and deal with Prime and the Highguard, then we do this together." Rutger took a boot and set it aside followed by the second, and in a fluid motion, placed his jeans and boxers on the counter beside his shirts. Steam glazed the mirror, its misty cloud rising to the ceiling where it clung to the pale paint.

"What are you doing?" Jordyn asked. Rutger, completely naked, closed the distance between them, and the sight of him sent a heated ember through her and pushed stress aside. The muscles in his shoulders flowed under his skin, his chest, taught from hours in the gym accentuated his waist and hips. They weren't married. They hadn't said they loved one another. Did it matter? *Not at the moment.*

Kneeling on one knee, he unbuttoned her jeans and the zipper slid down. "What does it look like?"

"You're undressing me. Look at me," Jordyn ordered and took his face in her hands. When they stared at each other, she said, "I'm covered in blood." As if to make her point, she let go of him and showed him her hands stained in crimson, the darkest red sitting under fingernails.

"You said this is your life and there's a theme here. It's not going to be the last time you'll be covered in blood." Rutger guided her wet jeans down her legs, and looking at her his eyes rolled gold, and he hooked her underwear in his fingers and worked them down to her ankles. "Step out," Rutger whispered against her stomach.

Jordyn's abs clenched when his warm words feathered her chilled skin. She stepped to the side, leaving her clothing, took another step backward, and swayed. Rutger remained on one knee, his gold eyes burning as he stared at her. "I can do this."

Rutger stood. "I'm aware. You're weak from blood loss and you used a lot of energy to heal." Taking her by her waist he pulled her to him and lifted her. Jo's legs circled his waist and she locked her ankles at his back. "Right this second you need me, and after we shower, I'll get you some food."

Jordyn heard him, yes, she needed him. She rested her head on his shoulder, in the curve of his neck, and nuzzled him. He smelled of spice, male, wolf, and ...

"Are you listening?"

"And wine," she whispered, her lips moving against his skin.

Rutger pressed her to his chest, skin on skin, smiled, and walked into the hot spray. The water spilled over them, turned crimson, and swirling the drain, it drank it down.

Jordyn left the stairs to meet a wall made from the vapors and stringent scents of bleach, disinfectant, and whatever else the Purifiers used to clean the hallway. Any evidence there had been an attack was gone as if it never happened. Erased. She wished she could do the same thing to her body and mind. Rutger's hand sat at the small of her back, and he gently urged her to walk when she stood and stared at the wall where the creature pinned her. Leaving the hall, Jordyn entered the greeting room and into a mass of anxiety at the same time a hush snuffed the chatter and all eyes were on her. Or them. It had taken them an hour to clean the blood from her skin, hair, and from under her nails.

Rutger wore his jeans, a clean T-shirt, but carried his flannel and dirty shirt. She had thrown her shirt in the trash and entertained the thought she could get the blood out of her jeans, bra, and underwear. From the same drawer he found the T-shirt, he grabbed a second one, with the pack's crest on the back, and a pair of sweats and handed them to Jordyn.

As she walked, she adjusted her borrowed shirt and held the waist of the sweatpants. She cinched the draw string as tight as she could to keep them from falling down while the cuffs pooled at her bare feet. Rutger stood six feet four inches, weighed at least two hundred forty pounds, and that didn't take in the size of his muscled arms, chest, and thighs. His clothing swamped her. Due to blood stains, she wasn't wearing a bra or underwear, and her hair, wet from the shower, was held back by a hair band she found in a bathroom drawer. She was looking a little ragged and lost.

"Jordyn, I can get you some clothes," Laurel offered.

"No. Loose is good." *Less pressure against my skin.* Jordyn gave a reassuring smile as she made her way across the room to the chair closest to the fire.

"Here," Rutger urged. He waited while Jo sat down and shifted her oversized shirt and pants then settled back. Taking a throw from the couch, Rutger handed it to her. "I'm going to get you something to eat."

Laurel cleared her throat. "Son, I'll help you. Does anyone else want anything?" She stood, her nerves and anxiety clashing with the need to be strong.

Jordyn met her dad's gaze and watched him search her while anguish gripped his face. She wished he hadn't been there to witness what happened. For some reason, she felt she needed to shield him from what her life was becoming. Guilt reared its head with the pain she was spreading to the people in her life. Her family.

"Wine," Mia replied. She flattened a wrinkle from her pale grey slacks and leisurely met Laurel's gaze.

"Of course." Laurel's patience teased snapping. Before she yelled at Mia, she grabbed Rutger's arm and lead him out of the room.

"How are you feeling, Jordyn?" Healey asked. He sat forward, his gaze on her and his instincts searching her.

If they weren't all staring at her like she was a freak on display and she hadn't been stabbed through the back by Prime's Numen, Jordyn would have rolled her eyes. "I'm good." She nervously tugged the blanket closer and tighter around her like it was a level of safety. She knew it wasn't and wouldn't go back to thinking it was. She buried Flint and freed herself from the constraints she created and moved on. Prime's attack proved she was getting stronger.

"I need you to tell me what happened?" Healey requested.

"I think she should rest first. She was attacked," Ethan insisted.

"Dad, I'm good. Could I get a glass of wine?" Jordyn asked. If she saw herself, she would see pleading and the toll the night was taking on her in her dark eyes and on her body. It must have been real because they held her gaze for five seconds to long. She had no idea what happened to the glass she had before the night went to hell and wasn't about to search for it. The blanket and chair were too comfortable and she was tired. It made her think of the baroness' wine. Jordyn searched the rug and floor and found nothing. Not one shard of glass or a drop of deep garnet stained the carpet.

"A trade then," Healey replied casually and stood.

"For the baron to serve you is above your station, Soothsayer," Mia said in objection. Her cold blue eyes nailed Jordyn like spikes of ice had been shot from them.

"I'm in my home with my kin. If I chose to get Jordyn, my daughter-in-law, a glass of wine, I will. Plus, we made a deal, wine for information," Healey explained. His voice wasn't the easy going 'I'm in my house with my kin and can do as I please', it was the stern tone of an alpha warning a lower member.

When Jordyn saw Mia's face contorting with her disbelief of having been chastised by the baron, she wanted to laugh. She didn't. Jordyn may have come to terms with being stabbed in the back, but there were threads of anxiety trying to tie her in a knot. If she started laughing, she wasn't going to stop and the laughter would only turn into hysterical tears.

"One glass of wine." Healey handed her the glass. "Let's hope no one interrupts this. Now, what happened."

Jordyn held the wine glass in her palm and stared at the plum liquid as it caught the flames from the fire. *My favorite.* The one with the bear on the label. She couldn't remember the name of the winery but thought it had a Z in it. And why was she thinking about it? It was better than thinking about Prime and the challenge. "We were sitting here when I felt a presence. Magic. It felt wrong. Not like one of us or the pack. I left the room to check the hall when the magic intensified and I could tell it carried death."

"Like Prime, his creatures are Greek and initially were from the underworld, it explains the death. There they carried the title of Horde of Styx, after the river Styx. When Ilario became Prime, he was counselled and advised by the Highguard to discard the Greek mythology persona as it might intimidate the weaker magic-born as they assimilated into a human life. Prime's purpose is to be there as an authority emanating confidence for the whole, equally, not to scare them into hiding or cause discord with the humans. He renamed his horde Numina, which is Latin. The slight shift from Greek to Latin allowed him to keep his ancient history."

The underworld. "I thought it was a vampire. I didn't know Prime's history or about the Numen," Jordyn responded.

"No one reads about his history and past life when, like his real name, they've been buried under centuries. With the shifts in humanizing the magic-born, no one will admit he's from the underworld. Humans consider mythology and anything associated with it as pagan religions. It's his decision to live as part of the Cloaked, as you saw, he doesn't have to. He creates a magic façade to appear human. You didn't sense anything else?" Healey watched Laurel and Rutger enter, both carrying trays of food.

"No. Magic and death. I saw the sentinels weren't at the door, told Laurel, and was headed to your office when it stabbed in me in the back," Jordyn explained. She reported everything, leaving out how death called to her, sipping Prime's power to heal the stab wound quicker, and it didn't make her cringe.

"What happened when it stabbed you?" Healey pushed.

"It pulled its spear from my chest, and I fell to my knees then hit the floor. That's when I called Rutger. It picked me up and slammed me into the wall and waited." Jordyn took a drink of her wine. This was her life. "It waited for you to find me."

"Did Prime say anything to you?" Healey asked.

"No, he didn't." He was in my head. "He made a point to show me his real face. The face of Ilario," Jordyn answered. It had to mean something besides she was in deep shit. Because she was sure it wasn't a good thing.

"You sensed his true self, death, and saw him." Healey didn't know what it meant. "How did you heal?" He was having a hard time hiding his irritation over the threat Prime posed to his pack. He invaded his territory, and made an advance on his soothsayer.

"I just did," Jordyn firmly stated. She met the baron's gaze and realized the conversation ceased being a conversation between father-in-law and daughter-in-law but baron and soothsayer. Accusations sat in his question and in his eyes. Was his change of attitude about the challenge? No. The baron wanted to know if she had taken from Prime. How did he know she could? She wasn't going to admit it. If she did it would be an insult against the baron. Like Prime tried stealing pack property.

"Jordyn, this is serious. He has ancient magic from the underworld. And there's a reason no one has been able to take the throne and title from him." Healey couldn't express the seriousness of the situation. He needed to know if Prime tricked Jordyn into taking his power. What would the repercussions be if she had? Healey didn't know.

The room sat in a forced quiet while the baron stared at her. She would bet money Mia was enjoying the baron's accusations. Would she go back and change it? Not if it meant keeping Rutger from losing control. "I called my magic and I healed. I didn't want to die, and it took every ounce of energy I had to keep my heart beating. If there was something pushing me it was Rutger. I never want what happened at Butte Springs to happen again. I won't lose him."

"Mea," Rutger whispered.

"While I can use another's power, the truth remains, you don't know what I'm capable of. I don't know. Prime came here because he thinks he does. He has Lady Sloan. The challenge is proof he is testing his theories." Jordyn lifted her glass and drank her wine. Her mind chased the trail ... Prime thought he knew something about her. Was it about her powers or her ancestry?

"The challenge is a farce," Ethan added, his nervous energy getting the better of him. He didn't need anyone talking about Sloan. "He tricked Jordyn by threatening Rutger. He knows what they've been through."

"It is a farce. He is testing me, Rutger, the baron, the pack. If he knows what I've been doing, he knows there is a divide in the pack. If I fail, it'll serve as proof the baron is weak and those opposed to him will suddenly be in the right. Prime will have the leverage he needs to convince the Highguard to agree with him, whatever that is," Jordyn stopped when everyone stared at her.

"The soothsayer thinks. Why don't you petition Prime and become the baroness? You certainly think you are as powerful as the baron," Mia mocked. She stood, gave the room her back as she walked to the bar and the wine.

Jordyn shook her head having to accept the woman was impossible. Damn, she didn't feel good and the exhaustion eating her wasn't helping. She was pinching the bridge of her nose when Rutger nudged her arm and handed her a large mug. Setting the glass down, she took the warm mug.

"It's a protein drink. Hot chocolate," Rutger explained. Jo smiled at him, sending a wave of warmth through him. She was alive.

"You're right. He targeted you. He forced you to make a choice while he evaluated your powers. He learned you can control minds, read them, and heal without shifting. He also knows you can sense magic. I don't think he understood you sensed him, and his death. And you exposed a weakness when you challenged him over Rutger. I don't understand the accusations you haven't embraced the Collective or your powers," Healey started. "For you to utilize these traits, you would have had to accept your powers."

"Not exactly. These *traits* are innate, I have them from my father and Lady Sloan. I think he's right. I haven't embraced the Collective. I know it's there, I can feel the pack, hear their whispers and sometimes I see the past, but it's not controlled. It's like the Collective is roaming free in my head. And the power, it's there and it builds and builds, and when it can't be contained, it seeps through and I use what has leaked out. The deeper power is out of reach," Jordyn explained. Dragons filled her head and she could feel their scales scraping the inside of her skull. *Stop*.

"Mea, you jumped from the deck and shifted before landing. You're saying you didn't use your full strength?" Rutger asked. *You shifted in mid-stride and walked into our house*.

Jordyn froze. Rutger confirmed they talked about her during the meeting and no doubt the video of Louis and Dr. Holmes. She met the gazes of the baron, the baroness, Ethan, Mia, and lastly Rutger who was kneeling in front of her. "That's right," Jordyn finally replied looking at Rutger. "You told the baron."

"I did." Rutger placed his hands on her thighs. "Prime said if you didn't accept the Collective the magic would kill you."

"No, he said I would go insane." Jordyn held Rutger's gaze as his eyes rolled gold. "There's a difference."

"Not much. You have to have help," Rutger countered.

"Sir, guests have arrived," Abigail reported. "They're waiting. I wasn't sure if Mistress was ready to see visitors."

"Who are they?" Healey asked. "Why weren't we alerted?"

"I'm checking now." Rutger stood, walked to the fireplace, and called communications.

"Lord Ervin and Lady Sloan," Abigail answered.

The night keeps getting better and better. Groaning, Jordyn sank into the chair, not wanting to see anyone, let alone Lady Sloan and the baggage coming with her.

"The soothsayer is worried about herself, how unusual," Mia chirped.

"You are not my mother, Mia. Lady Sloan is waiting because she is my mother and your lies have crashed and burned. This is going to be entertaining," Jordyn mocked.

"Daughter, please, how did you find out?" Ethan asked. He stood, took three steps toward his daughter, then stopped. "Never mind, I'm sorry."

"At least the charade is over," Mia mumbled.

Jordyn saw fear in his dark gaze and couldn't stop regret and pain from weighing on her. Why did she feel guilty for finding out they lied to her? "After coming back, being made the soothsayer, and being with Rutger, it was a matter of time before I found out. It just happened to be sooner than you wanted," she replied.

"Without fully invading their minds, Jordyn, what are they thinking?" Healey asked.

"Pay close attention," Jordyn ordered as she set the mug beside the wine glass. "This is how I found out. With their status in the Highguard they don't like waiting. However, Lord Ervin expected to wait or be denied entrance. Lady Sloan will wait for as long as it takes. Prime was successful in delaying their travel, making Lady Sloan uneasy, and that's when she understood his reasons. She senses I'm alive but doesn't know my condition." Jordyn held the sides of her head in her hands, lowered her chin to her chest, and fought the pain. The pressure was building forcing her to keep her blocks in place. "She is trying to get in my head as we speak."

Mia stood, and gripping the wine glass, walked to the other side of the room as if to get away from Jordyn. "I told you she was dark. Evil. The soothsayer reads minds. She can invade any one of us and take whatever she wants. Look what she did to the Numen."

"Mia, do you have something to hide?" Healey asked. Mia's eyes widened then narrowed, and she acted like she was going to argue, but stopped. *The woman can hold her tongue.* "Jordyn is the soothsayer for the pack. With or without her ability to read other's minds, she would be able to read the pack's thoughts. That is the way of the soothsayer. She isn't dark, she is doing what is expected of her."

"Lord Ervin and Lady Sloan," Abigail announced. Her wolf eyes glittered like chocolate diamonds in a human face as she met Jordyn's gaze.

Healey stood, and approaching the arched entrance he greeted his guests. "Welcome to the Cascade territory and Foxwood, Lord Ervin and Lady Sloan."

"Baron," Lord Ervin replied.

"I got here as quickly as I could," Lady Sloan said as she rushed into the room and closed the distance to Jordyn. "What did Prime do to you?"

Where did she begin.

Rutger watched Lady Sloan measure Jo's thin body and pale skin, looking worse with the white, oversized T-shirt and the thick, beige blanket covering her. A band held her wet, raven-colored hair back from her face while copper flakes, a feature from the Dacia ancestry, weaved through her onyx eyes. Lady Sloan searched for a reason, a wound, blood, anything to explain why Jo was wearing his clothes and wasn't suitably dressed.

"You mean after he trespassed on Cascade territory, locked the sentinels, enforcers, and soldiers in the office, and had his horde keep guard?" Jordyn asked in return. She saw the surprise on Lady Sloan's face, not used to being questioned, and continued. "One of his horde stabbed me in the back. By that I mean, it punctured through my back and out the front of my chest. Blood everywhere. Very gruesome."

CHAPTER EIGHTEEN

"Dear god," Lady Sloan breathed. By the look of disgust on her face, there was no doubt Lady Sloan had witnessed Prime's Numen and its claws turned spears in action. "You're healed."

"Yes." Jordyn chose her wine over the protein drink, took the glass from the table, and sipped.

"How did you heal yourself?" Lady Sloan asked with accusations in her eyes.

Prime allowed me to use him. "I can heal without shifting. So I did."

Lady Sloan paused, her gaze on Jordyn as if she was talking to a stranger. "You look exhausted. As the soothsayer for the pack, you have the Collective. It's a give and take. Your responsibilities to the pack require you to hold the essences of their wolves, their magic, their pasts, and memories. In return they serve as a power source," she explained. "You didn't have to use your own energy."

If I knew how. The Collective was out of her reach. There and not there. "Is this motherly advice?" Jordyn sounded like an upset spoiled brat because she hadn't gotten her way and they were being mean to her. She inhaled, set her glass on the side table, making it ting, exhaled, then tugged the blanket free from around her. Nervous energy drove her to stand and she walked over to the fire. "I'm fine on my own." She wasn't fine on her own. Jordyn turned her words into a cold accusation like she was challenging Lady Sloan to defend her choices.

"Now you know what I've had to deal with," Mia commented.

Lady Sloan ignored Mia. "You are not fine. I don't need to sense you to know you are fractured and your power is erratic and uncontrolled. You didn't use the Collective to heal yourself because you don't know how. It puts the nexus between you and your alpha at risk. Like the Highguard, I doubt your enshrinement."

"Jordyn is enshrined," Healey argued.

"If that's true, then it would have created a symbol, a rune of possession, your ancestry, and proof of the soothsayer's power." Lady Sloan's doubtful gaze shifted between Jordyn and the baron.

"She does," Healey answered before Jordyn could. The four of them-Rutger, Lady Sloan, Healey, Ethan, and Lord Ervin-surrounded Jordyn while Laurel and Mia watched. Healey watched Jordyn's eyes take everyone in and then stay on Rutger.

"It's from my family," Ethan assured Sloan and met her cynical gaze. "It is. It was my great, great grandfather's crest. He was the single person to own it."

"The dragon? Ethan, how you have forgotten." Sloan faced Jordyn.

"She's dark. Why do you think this is happening to her? To us. She cursed us," Mia accused from her place across the room.

"I'm supposed to take the word from one who doesn't believe? And I'm supposed to believe you, Mia? I think not." Turning from Mia, she glared at Ethan. "It is true the dragon endowed your great, great grandfather and your ancestors from Bulgaria have retained its magic and the Pureblood linage. However, the dragon bestowed its magic through the high priests to the Dacia pack whose territory is the Carpathian Mountains. Jordyn, may I see the mark?" Lady Sloan asked.

Dragons. Jordyn's worry hit a new level with Lady Sloan's explanation. What if she wore a mark from her dad and Lady Sloan? If she did, it explained Prime's interest.

"Stop it. Stop," Mia demanded, her voice rising. "Dragons. Bulgaria. The Carpathian Mountains. Seriously? Neither of you have ever been there. Ethan, you're an investment banker and live in Northern California. You drive a luxury car for god's sake. With the exception of the moon runs, when was the last time you ran in wolf form?" She glared at Ethan. "The places you are speaking of are immaterial today. We aren't the past. We aren't savages and we don't practice magic. We are people. I'm not sure, Sloan, if you noticed, but you drove here in a car that probably costs more than some homes. It was not by a horse-drawn carriage and you never traversed a gorge."

Did she witness a crack in Mia's concrete confidence? While Jordyn watched Mia's melt down, she sensed fear as the woman tried to grasp the tattered fabric of her humanized life. A change was coming and whether those like Mia wanted to admit it or not, it was going to happen.

They lost everything because of the Crimson years and were forced to adapt or be slaughtered. How were they supposed to go back to way they had been? "Mia." Ethan used a voice meant to calm down children as he approached her. "This is real. We need to accept it and plan accordingly."

She flattened her palms on Ethan's chest and met his gaze. "If we accept what is happening, how long before the humans take notice and come after us? There were protestors at the Summit."

"They were there to occupy Rutger while Louis tried convincing me to go back to Butterfly Valley." *By convincing, I mean drugged and kidnapped.* "They won't be back," Jordyn tried assuring her.

Mia turned from Ethan and faced Jordyn. "How can you be so sure?"

I made this deal. "Law enforcement is aware of the protestors and the anti-paranormal group." Jordyn wasn't going to explain Detective Watt and the information he knew.

"Human law enforcement. You preach there are changes happening and they will take us back to the dark ages, and then invite humans into our lives. It puts us in greater danger," Mia argued.

"It's a risk we have to take," Jordyn replied quickly. There was a fifty-fifty chance Detective Watt would screw them over, but the pack needed law enforcement. Of course, betraying the pack wasn't ideal for the detective.

"You make the decisions now? And Baron, how do you feel about this?" Mia goaded.

"The anti-paranormal group is a threat to others as much as it is to us, making law enforcement a necessary evil. As baron of a territory, it's my responsibility to protect its population. At the same time, I'm not going to ignore the council of my soothsayer. The pack will not ignore her either. There is a reason she is here," Healey explained. He didn't focus on Mia alone, he meant for everyone in the room to understand where he stood. "With that said, it's time for Jordyn to show Sloan her mark."

The baron would seek her council? It was a commitment she wasn't sure she was prepared to make, and if she did, what if she failed? Jordyn saw herself curled up in the fetal position and hiding in a corner. No, she challenged Prime. She wasn't a helpless victim. And Rutger. They hadn't made a commitment to one another ... rather they just kept going forward, day after day, as a happy couple.

Silence wrapped around her, taking her from her thoughts to everyone in the room. Jordyn watched them watch her and absently touched her thigh. At first the mark had been raised and touching it created a tingling sensation. When she wore jeans, the constant contact made the sensation shimmy down her leg to her foot. It had been pale pink standing out, as if someone had carved it into her skin and it scarred. That was months ago. Over the weeks it changed color to match her natural skin tone and became smooth. Except when her wolf swam freely inside her, it warmed and shimmered silver. The pack's color.

I'm in deep and it's getting deeper.

"Jordyn, please," Lady Sloan requested.

"I will. If you tell me why?" Jordyn replied. Was she ready to know why her mother left her?

"Why?" Lady Sloan asked.

"Yes. Why? Why the lies?" Jordyn pinned her copper gaze tinted with fury on the woman. Acting out, good one.

Lady Sloan gave her a patient smile. "I promise I will give you an explanation. One thing at a time. Your mark."

Jordyn thought about it, reeled her anger in, and calmed down. Giving them her back, she tugged the T-shirt to mid-thigh, keeping herself covered while with her right hand she worked the waist of the sweatpants down her legs. When she was sure the mark was exposed and nothing else was, she turned and gave the audience the view they requested. "There."

"You aren't wearing underclothes?" Lady Sloan asked.

"No. They're drenched in blood. The mark," Jordyn pointed out. She wanted to pull her pants up.

Lady Sloan inhaled and stepped backward. An X two inches in height by two inches wide with a box slightly smaller than the X in its center marked her thigh. It sat flat and matched her skin tone. "Marca drangonului, mark of the dragon. A Balaur. It is true, you wear the mark of the dragon. Bring your wolf." Obeying Lady Sloan's order, Jordyn's wolf weaved through her. "It glows sliver for the Cascade pack. You are enshrined and the scion of two pure bloodlines from two dynasties. You cannot continue in the fractured state you're in. I have to help you."

"No, it's not a Balaur," Ethan argued. "She isn't one of them."

Jordyn jerked the sweatpants back up legs, cinched the drawstring, her gaze going to her dad and Lady Sloan. She didn't know what they were talking about.

"You live in denial and it put Jordyn in the situation she is in. She should have been trained years ago. It is a Balaur," Lady Sloan insisted.

"Someone want to explain it to *me*?" Jordyn asked before the argument continued. At least it wasn't a random symbol and Balaur was better than referring to it as that thing on her thigh. *Right?*

"Explain this," Rutger demanded.

"Balaur is a winged, golden dragon from Romanian lore." Lady Sloan stared at Jordyn. "He was worshiped as a god."

"Is it bad? I mean, it's named after something from lore, it doesn't mean anything else, right? It isn't real." Jordyn didn't know how old lore had anything to do with her. As she searched Lady Sloan's face for a clue, she didn't like what she saw. Her eyes bled to the velvet copper of her wolf, exactly like Jordyn's only Jordyn's were sharper. Colder. Whatever Lady Sloan planned on saying it wasn't going to be good.

"There's the possibility you have the blessing of the ancients."

The dragons.

"It might be proof you are the child of two Pureblood dynasties, which you are, and when the baron enshrined you it brought forth the old magic. Or it's an emblem of power, or protection, it could be anything. I don't know what it means specifically to you," Lady Sloan explained. "It hasn't been seen in centuries."

"What does it matter?" Mia asked, her voice a pitch higher.

"Centuries? I recognized it as my family's. It doesn't have to be yours, Sloan. And it doesn't mean she's a Balaur," Ethan pointed out. His jealousy and resentment were getting the better of him.

Sadly, Mia was right. It didn't really matter when there was a challenge in the future, and if she lost, she was headed to Mountain Fortress and Rutger's future was in a cage. Jordyn wanted to believe her dad, but couldn't. "Dad said I wasn't one of them. One of what?" Jordyn pushed.

"Yes, Sloan, tell your daughter what you've done to her." Mia's ice blue eyes blazed white for a breath. "She'll want to know what it's like living in servitude to the crown."

Lady Sloan's patience was visibly thinning as she fought two battles-the one Jordyn was waging and the one with

Mia. "If you continue this, you'll make Jordyn resistant to fully accepting the Collective."

"No one can take Jordyn from the pack," Healey interrupted Sloan. "She has been enshrined, carries the Collective, and Prime knows she and Rutger are fated mates and have been made One-Flesh. Despite the threat of a challenge, it doesn't change what is binding. It would be ripping part of ourselves from us."

"Tell me," Jordyn demanded. Rutger stood next to her, rested his hand on her shoulder, and squeezed.

"There is very little written text, but what there is tells us most of the legend has been passed down from generation to generation through verbal stories. It's believed the first shapeshifters were given the ability to shift by the gods. There was no therianthrope or lycanthrope viruses. When the first shift took place, the animal spirit inside them determined what they would be. The gods gifted them, making them Purebloods. They served one purpose, to be warriors for their villages, towns, territories. They were protectors of all. After their transformation into their chosen animal, they spread out, creating their territories. Our ancestors created their own territory and served as Pureblood werewolf warriors. Warriors, Jordyn, however there's no text describing what the animal form looked like. Either it was kept secret to protect the shapeshifter or they guarded their territory in wolf form."

Two forms? Wolf form. Warrior form could be the same as Bestial form. It hit Jordyn like a hammer. It wasn't true. She turned enough to look at Rutger. Lady Sloan teased her, and everyone in the room, with the possibility of two forms. It wasn't worth the risk. "Our ancestors' animal spirits were wolves?"

"Yes. Of the purest linage."

"What does that have to do with dragons?" Jordyn's heartbeat pounded as the image of the dragons sat in her head.

"Rogue werewolves began infecting humans with the lycanthrope virus. The infected turned feral and attacked humans while others died trying to shapeshift. Fearing the werewolves, their ever increasing reach, and the virus, humans hunted them. Their actions turned humans against all shapeshifters and no longer were they the warriors preparing to defend their clansmen. They were evil men turned evil monsters and hunting villages. Their gods renounced them and abandoned them."

"They worshiped gods, multiple?" Jordyn didn't know if she believed anything Lady Sloan was saying.

"Yes. The pack saw their world crumble before them and blamed the Wights, the infected humans, for their gods abandoning them. Determined to remain strong, they set out to purify the bloodlines and stop the spreading virus. The Purebloods eradicated the Wights, then fled to the Carpathian Mountains where the high priests of Dacian gave them sanctuary. The priests introduced them to Balaur, the dragon. Their worship and faithful service empowered Balaur, and in return for their devotion he gifted the strongest with an element. One essence of either water, earth, fire, or wind. The wolves blessed by Balaur wore a symbol proving their power and their right to stand beside the high priests," Lady Sloan finished explaining. She exhaled, as if expelling the emotion from the story and met Jordyn's gaze. Jordyn saw Lady Sloan's worry in her eyes.

"And?" Jordyn didn't really want to know the point of the history lesson. She doubted it ... it sounded like a fairy tale turned horror story.

"Like I said, it could be an emblem of power, or protection, or a sign from your ancestors. If you're asking what I think, my instincts are telling me, daughter, you wear the mark of Balaur. You must prove your power."

Oh hell no. "No. Prove it to you? No. I thought I was some kind of abomination. I hid what I was, and every time I was forced to use it, it nearly killed me." Jordyn's anger lashed out in the room, making everyone take a collective inhale.

It was true. Rutger saw her using her camera bag as a pillow and sleeping in his truck, exhausted after being forced to use her magic.

"Prime knows my history, the ways of my ancestors, the power and magic of my linage. You haven't exactly kept your gifts a secret. He is here to test you and find out if you're powerful. You can't be seen as weak," Lady Sloan insisted.

"I wouldn't want to embarrass your legacy, Lady Sloan." Jordyn's voice went flat as if she pulled all emotion from it. An ancient power travelled through time to stamp her with a Balaur, and her estranged mother was telling her what Prime was planning. Not cool.

"You need to put aside your anger and focus. Yes, we should have told you, I'm sorry. As much as I want to change the past, I can't. I'm here now and I can heal your fractures," Lady Sloan assured.

"And if I refuse?" Jordyn remained in front of the fire, its heat on her back warming her chilled skin, was she ever going to get warm? Rutger standing beside her giving her his comfort and strength. It didn't stop Prime's threat of insanity from spinning around her thoughts and her anger toward Lady Sloan from poisoning her. She couldn't get rid of the feeling she had been left on her own. Abandoned. It was there, though, the need for help. She might be pissed off, she wasn't stupid.

"The Collective's voices and essences will surge forward to tear your mind apart, making you insane at the same time the power you possess will paralyze your wolf. You won't heal. You won't be able to shapeshift to save herself. You'll die," Lady Sloan clarified. "During my time as part of the Twelve, I have witnessed insanity in more than one soothsayer and witnessed their slow deaths as their magic ate their bodies. If you're thinking you can control it, you're wrong. If left unattended, which Prime will never allow, you will deteriorate and force those around you to make a decision. When your time came, your mate, who allowed you to fail, will be responsible for carrying out the death order. There will be a death order and Rutger will execute you. Are you prepared to make Rutger helpless to save you as he watches your magic eat you alive and then turn into your executioner, just to spite me?"

Jordyn looked up at him; his gold gaze held hers and her heart froze like it became a chunk of ice. She was sure she could feel frost creeping over the inside of her chest. Rutger. After feeling his fear when the Numen pinned her to the wall and seeing his wolf shadow him and the fragile control he clung to, she wouldn't risk hurting him. Losing him.

"I would never hurt you," Rutger growled. "I won't lose you." He saw the conflict in Jo's eyes as the copper melted into onyx. He had never seen her eyes turn completely black.

"Then you would both die," Lady Sloan stated.

Lady Sloan's gaze targeted Jordyn, and for the first time she saw raw power. Their depths seemingly endless. "I'm not going to refuse your help and force Rutger to kill me."

"Careful, Soothsayer, you let her help you and you'll be in her debt," Mia warned. "Mother or not, the Highguard's prices are steep."

"No, Jordyn is my daughter. I would never enact Highguard canon, making her beholden to them," Lady Sloan turned her attention to Jordyn. "I wouldn't trap you."

Mia laughed, letting her blatant doubt play in its sound. "Not so. In the eyes of the Highguard, the soothsayer is my daughter. I raised her. Her father and I raised her," Mia argued. She took several steps forward. "If you allow Lady Sloan to help you, she will want something in return. That's the way the Highguard works. You don't get something for nothing."

"I'm not arguing with you, Mia. Jordyn, the Highguard does demand compensation, but this isn't about the Highguard. This is about your life, your future, and your family. You are part of me and my ancestors."

"She is my daughter, from my linage, Sloan," Ethan countered.

"Listen to her, young soothsayer, Sloan speaks the truth. Your eyes have gone completely black as you struggle for control. How long do you think you can continue?" Lord Ervin asked. His voice stern, soft, and calm.

Black. Damn. Thought I was doing pretty good. The baron mentioned her power when they arrived and she forced it down. Tried to at least. Was she living with a constant struggle and it became a normal part of her life? Jordyn didn't know. She felt torn between choosing Lady

Sloan over her dad and didn't know if either of them was telling her the truth. "You can stop trying to scare me."

"Jordyn, please," Ethan interrupted. "I have my issues with Sloan, but I don't want to see you hurt. Not anymore. Not again." *My daughter nearly died, tonight, in front of me. I can't take the pain of losing her.* "The betrayal and lies are my fault. I took you from Sloan thinking if you were raised without the influence of magic you wouldn't know your powers. They would die out and you would live a natural life. We were uncertain with the changing times, living in the open, and assimilating to the human's ways. We gave up pieces of ourselves, like magic, our past, and our traditions, and while we gave up what made us shapeshifters, we did it so we didn't offend the humans. All very politically correct. Living in denial created a false confidence that clouded my vision as you changed. I refused to acknowledge the truth."

Her anger faded with the fear and regret in his darkened eyes. She had to save herself. "Dad, I don't blame you. I don't blame either of you. Lady Sloan, what do I have to do?"

"Open yourself to me." Jordyn's eyes widened and she took a step backward. "I won't pursue your secrets. I will seek the fractures and mend them. I give you my word."

"As a soothsayer, Lady with the Highguard and your pack, or my mother?" Jordyn didn't trust her.

"All the above."

She expected Lady Sloan to say mother and follow it up with a speech about how sorry she was and now was the time to trust her. She didn't. It made Jordyn feel slightly better. It also reminded her this wasn't about her, it was about Rutger and their relationship, and the pack. She didn't have a choice. "Fine."

"You're doing the right thing," Lord Ervin assured.

That remained to be seen. Jordyn gave Rutger a worried look and faced Lady Sloan. "Let's do this."

"Picture the magic inside of you like webbing with its center right here, the verve." Lady Sloan hesitantly reached out while watching Jordyn's eyes flicker between onyx and copper. When Jordyn didn't shy away, Lady Sloan placed her palm flat on Jordyn's chest, pushing on the raised scar from her injury and her chilled skin. "The magic courses inside of you, touching every part of you it constantly energizes itself. You have felt its strength, yes?" Jordyn's gaze held Lady Sloan's and she nodded a response. "If you deny the power, it begins to build then it becomes corrupted and there lies the danger."

A soothing vibration sank into her and spread out from Lady Sloan's hand. It extended deeper, and Jordyn would swear Lady Sloan had reached through her skin and was touching her insides. "What are you doing?" Jordyn couldn't stop her power from blazing with scarlet, silver, and onyx, her life source and magic intertwined with the Cascade pack, and her mate.

"Sensing the links of your magic. Every time you accept a facet, like reading minds, it creates a link to the other. They become one and strengthen your magic. You've achieved many facets, like manipulating people's thoughts."

"How can you know that?" *And what else can you sense?*

"You're my daughter. Our magic is the same. If it wasn't, I wouldn't be able to sense your root verve." Lady Sloan closed her eyes as their combined power increased.

"What is she doing?" Rutger asked.

"The verve is the foundation of her magic. We are all magic-born. Your verve gives you your wolf and is the foundation of your magic. Like your father, you are an alpha, and when the time comes your verve will mutate to suit your needs," Lord Ervin explained. "We are all advancing and integrating to our environments. As alpha you will have a soothsayer of your own."

Not a chance. Rutger wasn't going to do to anyone what the baron had done to Jo. "What will she do to heal Jo?"

"Jordyn wasn't trained. Her instincts guided her, but without proper training it's like gluing shards of glass together without knowing where they belong. If they don't fit together it creates fissures. Sloan's magic will mend those. It will balance her verve and allow the Collective to take its place as an extension of her," Lord Ervin replied as he watched.

"Dragons," Lady Sloan mumbled. "They're everywhere in her thoughts."

Their lithe bodies covered in shimmering scales matched the colors of Jordyn's magic. Every one of them weaved around the threads of her power as if protecting her.

"Mine," Jordyn growled. No one was going to take them from her. *Marca drangonulu. Balaur.* It was true. Lady Sloan's words slammed into her and their meaning became crystal clear. "I need them."

CHAPTER NINETEEN

"What does it mean?" Rutger asked. Seeing Jo suspended in her thoughts and growling about dragons had him wanting whatever was happening to stop. Jo's onyx eyes closed while her lips continued curving around silent words.

"What Sloan described is true. The mark is from Balaur. Or it could mean Jordyn's magic created them to protect her, although I don't know how. I don't have an answer. We'll have to wait and see," Lord Ervin mumbled with awe in his voice.

Rutger watched everyone stare at Lady Sloan and Jo. No one knew what was happening, and Lord Ervin was too caught up in the moment to answer his questions. "Mea," Rutger whispered. He felt talons digging into him as helplessness mocked him.

Lady Sloan focused her power and the webs of magic burned bright. The fractured edges blurred as their fibers twisted and stretched, knitting together to heal. From their perches, the dragons watched with their emerald eyes. If she was foolish enough to entertain the idea, she wasn't what Lady Sloan explained, this changed her mind. Jordyn and the dragons were one. She was part of the Balaur. A completeness wrapped around her as Jordyn sensed her magic gaining its full strength and the fractures riddling her sealed closed. She expected to feel Lady Sloan to pull back from her and leave, but she didn't. Instead, Lady Sloan hesitated, her thoughts betraying her when a glittering ebony jewel caught her attention and its presence enticed her.

Jordyn struggled to listen as Lady Sloan compared the jewel, just out of her reach, to the dragons. Damn it, she was going to betray her. Jordyn locked her thoughts behind a barricade as Lady Sloan reached out to the forbidden, and going further, deeper, caused alarm. The dragons spread out at the same time Lady Sloan's vision darkened as if someone cut the lights, closed the door, and locked her in a cell.

"Back off," Jordyn warned. She pushed at Lady Sloan's presence, trying to cut her connection. She didn't budge the woman. *"Get. Out."*

Lady Sloan heard Jordyn's warning, and fighting to stay held tight. "Let me see," she said aloud.

"No. You gave your word."

"I need to understand."

They were Jordyn's secrets. *And if they destroy me*? The battles she fought would have been for nothing. She felt the difference with the fractures healed and the difference in her magic.

"No one dominates death. Death dominates them," the dragon whispered. *"You live under its tyranny."*

"Then why continue?" Jordyn felt empty and tired.

"Failure is not acceptable." A hiss laced his rough words. *"You have a purpose."*

"Means nothing."

"Means everything, Mistress of Balaur."

Was she imagining the conversation? Had she finally lost her mind like they kept saying she would? Jordyn felt Lady Sloan's power increasing as it hammered against the wall of protection she'd built around her thoughts. If she was insane, there was nothing left to lose. *"What do I do?"*

"She wants you to reveal your secrets. Give them to her." One voice became more than a dozen and echoed.

"No. They're mine," Jordyn argued.

"They will fester inside of you and kill you quicker than the death infecting you," they warned in unison.

Damn it. Jordyn felt the truth in her bones and it left her with little choice. She wasn't going to ignore the dragons, but why did she have to expose her weaknesses to Lady Sloan? In seconds, the Highguard and her family would know what happened in Butte Springs. The humiliation and pain were hers alone. Not theirs. While Lady Sloan continued to bombard the barricade, she repeated her demand to see what Jordyn was hiding.

Lavender and Wolf's bane drifted in the stagnant air, their threads tying around Jordyn to take her back to her cell. Like a thick blanket, the haze suffocated her. The isolation and helplessness tangled with the agony and restlessness of the tortured wolves Flint murdered. Their remains wired to a cross and set in front of her to mock her. She hadn't been able to save them, let alone herself.

"You won't like what you see," Jordyn warned.

"Show me," Lady Sloan demanded.

Rutger didn't know what was happening. The conversation Lady Sloan was having appeared one sided, and what the hell did she want to see? He guessed Jordyn was using telepathy the same way she had with him. A blast of power hit the room, its force blowing over and around them. Rutger froze when Jordyn opened her black eyes, the ink swallowing her pupil as it ate the white. "Mea."

"Jordyn is defending herself. Lady Sloan's power is saturating the room. She is supposed to help Jordyn, not fight her." Healey met Lord Ervin's worried gaze and saw questions in their depths. This was a bad idea.

Jordyn could fight her for eternity while suspended in her consciousness. Fighting to protect her family and her pack from her sins.

"Soothsayer," Lady Sloan started. Her lips parted with her words, yet nothing but whispers escaped. "Balaur, let me see."

Lady Sloan breathed the name and the room fell into silence, no one spoke, and no one moved. Then tears streaked down Lady Sloan's cheeks, leaving glittering lines in their wake. Rutger searched their link, automatically assuming Jo would block him from feeling her as was her way. She didn't. The energy of her chaotic emotions crashed into him, making him stagger backwards. Rutger righted himself, met their gazes, and ignoring them turned his attention to Jo. What the hell was happening to her?

Jordyn heard Flint's voice as she held the barricade for a breath longer, then released her grasp. "*I warned you.*" Butte Springs came alive as everything she had been holding back for months flowed from her like water from a dam. Above Butte Springs, Jordyn sat on limb among the bone chimes and watched Lady Sloan from her perch.

The world shifted from vapors of Jordyn's memories to Butte Springs, and suddenly Lady Sloan was standing in the woods, a chilled breeze on her skin, and the full moon casting silver splinters through tree limbs. In the distance, a rhythmic chanting carrying magic drifted toward her and touched her skin as if evil had grown claws. The chanting, its pulsing intoning pulled Lady Sloan, and she headed in the direction of the lights and the crowd. As she ran the soft ground gave way, leaves crunched under her steps, and the breeze caught her hair as it made chimes play a dull tune above her. Anxiety and an excited energy gripped the air and charged it as if it were electricity. When she emerged from the wood line, bolts hit her like millions of needles.

Pain.

Humiliation.

Loss.

Death.

Lady Sloan didn't go any further, her fear of the unknown and their emotions freezing her where she stood.

"You wanted to see." Jordyn pushed her, and guiding her, she reluctantly walked from the wood line to the edge of the crowd.

Their bodies swayed, their chanting becoming erratic, and growing louder echoed in the trees. Lady Sloan breathed deep as the rich iron of spilled blood hung in the energized air. Searching the crowd, she shifted her gaze from the mass of people to the front where they were staring. A strangled cry left her when she saw Jordyn's body purging blood from her arms and neck, the thick scarlet splashing the altar.

"No."

"Yes." Jordyn cringed when the knife cut into her skin. The feel of weakness flooded her as her blood drained from her. She reminded herself it wasn't real and she conquered Flint.

The urgency swept Lady Sloan into its arms, taking her deeper into the scene, and she watched her reality fall to pieces. Lady Sloan tried walking and couldn't; her feet wouldn't obey her demands. Sensing her need to rescue

Jordyn, the crowd closed in, making a tighter circle and blocking her from the altar.

"Jordyn." Lady Sloan fought to move, to take one step, anything to get through the mass of people.

"I'm here."

Silence rode over the chanting, snuffing the voices, and the air became static while Jordyn's heartbeat drummed in the night. One. Two. Three beats. A man's laugh echoed and died when his mumbled words cut into Jordyn's body, making it jerk as he drove his spell into her. Six. Seven. Eight beats.

"Fight him, Jordyn."

Ten. Lady Sloan waited. Jordyn's magic weaved like a spider's web around her to save her. It expanded and captured the spell, twisted it, and while it freed her it ended their concealment. Lady Sloan breathed deep, her anxiety coursing through her, as she waited to hear Jordyn's heartbeat. Nothing.

"Please, one more time," Lady Sloan begged. Nothing.

Jordyn's eyes opened and an empty darkness held her blank stare. Lady Sloan pushed through the crowd, grabbing their clothes, and shoving them to the side. Franticly waiting for a heartbeat, she felt the seconds ticking into silence, giving her a black void.

Nothing. Dead. Her daughter was dead. He killed her. With the truth in front of her, she let out an anguished scream, her wolf howling in her ears at the loss of a child. She needed to get away from them, the woods, the pain. Lady Sloan jerked her hand back as the heartache and force of breaking the connection caused her to tumble backward and she landed hard on her back.

Jordyn's body ached with old pain as she drifted from the tree, Butte Springs, and Lady Sloan's hold. With the power cut, Jordyn fell to her knees, and a wave of relief washed over her easing the nightmares. For a second, she felt *normal.* The peace didn't last long when death came back with a vengeance, driving deeper inside of her, it rooted itself. Hard pain spread out from her middle to her arms and legs, forcing her to fight to stay upright.

"Jo." Her pain drove through him carrying her last heartbeat. Her stillness sat against his skin while the emptiness sat in his head. He hated the way it felt. Cold. Alone. The emotions forced him back to the past and sharp denial infected his wolf and fed his beast. It wasn't real. She was alive. Rutger concentrated on Jo and her strong heartbeat. He was in the greeting room, watching her swaying, and envisioned her falling backward into the fire. Unable to move, the baron swept in and caught her before she fell. He lifted her, and cradling her in his arms, stood.

Listen to her heartbeat. She's alive. Control. "Mine," Rutger growled.

"Easy, son. Come get her." Healey's voice stayed steady and calm. "Hold her."

Rutger stalked to the baron, as if he was hunting, and when he was close, he took Jo in his arms and clutched her to him. "Mine. Mine," he whispered.

Through half closed eyes gleaming copper Jordyn met Rutger's gaze. "Wolf."

"You should have let her go," Lady Sloan whispered. Tears spilled from her eyes, ruining her immaculate makeup and dragging black down her cheeks. Her hands were pressed against her chest like she could stop the pain and grief from spreading. "You should have let her go. I know the dragons."

Lord Ervin knelt behind her, letting her lean her trembling body against him. "Are you all right? What happened?"

"Never. I'm not losing my soothsayer or my son. It had to be done," Healey growled the words through clenched teeth. "You had no right. You said you would leave her secrets alone."

"Sloan, what happened?" Lord Ervin asked. "What dragons? What secrets?"

"You don't know what you've done because of your selfishness." Lady Sloan turned to Lord Ervin. "Death."

"You don't know what you're talking about," Healey accused.

"I do," she argued. Turning she met Lord Ervin's worried gaze. "Help me up."

"What *are you* talking about?" Ethan demanded. "What the hell are you two talking about? What dragons?"

"What do you know about Butte Springs?" Lady Sloan asked in return. She took a tissue and wiped tears and makeup from her cheeks, then smoothed her slacks and straightened her blouse. With help from Lord Ervin she walked to a nearby chair.

Ethan stared at Jordyn as he forced himself to relive the day a group of enforcers and soldiers found her. "It was some kind of sacrifice. The witch had injured Jordyn and she was forced to shift," he finally answered. "In her wolf form they caged her and took her to Celestial." Where she stayed for a month.

"No, Jordyn didn't shift. Healey forced her wolf from her."

"She was too weak to shift on her own. It doesn't mean anything, he's her alpha," Ethan challenged. Pain and shock corrupting his words. "She was hurt."

Lady Sloan took several deep breaths as she struggled to calm herself. "Jordyn was dead. She died in those mountains."

"Not possible," Ethan argued. "She's here and alive."

"Because Healey ordered her to obey the moon's call and forced her wolf. The animal obeyed. I watched her blood leave her body and I felt her use her dying magic to purge the witch's spell from her body and break the hold on the coven. She burned through her strength and died. Ask Rutger, he was holding her."

"Rutger?" Ethan asked hesitatingly.

"Her heart stopped and she died in my arms," Rutger answered. It was over. Hiding what happened to Jo was over. He squeezed Jo closer to him, his arms like metal bands around her.

"She healed tonight. Why didn't she heal then?" Ethan asked.

"For four days, Flint used Wolf's bane to paralyze her. She was starving, dehydrated, and hurt." Rutger held Lord Ethan's gaze then met Lady Sloan's angry glare. "She was paralyzed."

"Besides the torture they inflicted on her. Her humiliation of having been stripped, locked in a cell with the dead, and panic coiled around her core knowing she was going to die." Lady Sloan targeted the baron. "Death and Jordyn are one. It has fused with her wolf and feeds off her magic. Jordyn knows it's there and can manipulate it. At first, I tried to break through the barricade around her thoughts, and she blocked me, then she let me in. It's how I saw what happened to her."

"I warned you, Lady Sloan. You didn't stop, you called me Balaur," Jordyn accused. She tried to crawl out of

Rutger's lap, but he didn't budge and she remained in his arms.

"Not possible," Ethan argued. "No one can do that. People die and are brought back. It doesn't make her different. It makes her a survivor."

"You forget what our daughter is and the power she has." Lady Sloan looked at Rutger as he sat on the floor with Jo in his lap, her head against his chest, her clothing pooling around her. "Death opened the door for the dragons, her ancestors, and she embraced them, giving them life. Balaur has given her his blessing."

"You say it like it's a bad thing," Jordyn mumbled, exhaustion lacing her words. The dragons, her ancestors, completed her. Jordyn thought about staying in Rutger's strong arms where she was warm, comforted, and safe but knew she couldn't. She needed to face Lady Sloan and everyone else. She met his stare, grudgingly crawled from his-lap, he let her-and she sat on the floor beside him and close to the fire. Their legs were touching. "I warned you. You could have left me alone, but you didn't. You had to know. You fought me to know."

"Why did you let me in? You could have kept me fighting for as long as you wanted."

"I was existing under death's tyranny. That isn't living," Jordyn replied.

Lady Sloan paused as if she was thinking about what Jordyn said. "I won't apologize for the invasion. If you are to complete your transition to soothsayer, I have to understand what happened to you."

"You're going to help me when you think I should have died?" Jordyn asked. The idea Lady Sloan would have let her die hurt more than she wanted to admit. "If it was up to you, I wouldn't be here right now."

"You're my daughter and I'm responsible for leaving you alone to deal with your powers. Your memories were overwhelming. I'm sorry for the way I acted, but it doesn't change what is happening to you. Jordyn, I can try and help you manage its effects and influence." Lady Sloan's emotions built around her and Jordyn watched her fight tears as she squeezed the bridge of her nose. "Does Prime know?"

Its influence. Jordyn had been living with the guilt from her decision for months before cutting it out like it was a cancer. Death was there and would remain. *I can't change that.* Lady Sloan's question made her pause because she was going to lie. Jordyn sensed magic and then death, and when he revealed himself and she used, a slight amount of his power, she hadn't rejected it. It felt... natural. *He knew.*

"It was chaos, I thought I was dying, I'm not sure." Jordyn saw Lady Sloan's doubt. Or was it her lie toying with her. "I don't know."

"What did he say?" Lady Sloan asked.

Before Jordyn could answer, Healey interrupted. He needed to clarify several things, which meant he needed to start at the beginning. "May I, Jordyn?"

"Please." She sat back and listened as the baron explained the letter delivered by Prime's legates, stating Jordyn was a scion, ordering Rutger to mark her, and the reservations about her enshrinement. He conveniently left out Flint killing himself, the witch's bodies, Rutger's involvement, and the homicide investigation. Lady Sloan nodded, urging him to continue, and when he repeated what Prime said about Jordyn's power and his threat to cage Rutger, Jordyn felt guilt.

"Do you want to tell her or shall I?" Healey asked.

"There's more?" Lady Sloan questioned with exhaustion threading in her voice.

"I challenged Prime." If she hadn't been staring at Lady Sloan, Jordyn would have missed the flash of shock creasing her face. "It's set for the night of the moon run. Prime will address the pack, klatch, and whatever factions decide to attend."

"Baron, you have governed the Cascade pack and the magic-born with unmatched leadership and have maintained a cordial relationship with the Highguard and Prime. Cascade is considered one of the elite packs in the US, and in direct competition with others from around the world. Having said that, by defying his orders, you have shot the opportunity for leniency to hell. You've caused more trouble than most of the entire magic-born populace together. Jordyn, a challenge? No one challenges Prime, he will kill you," Lady Sloan explained.

"That's what I said," Mia added.

Thanks for the support. "What was I supposed to do? Oh great Prime, please cage my mate and take me away from my pack? No. If what you said is true and he knows about your legacy and what it means to my abilities, he isn't going to kill me." *I'm dead.* "If I lose, I lose Rutger. Prime understands for fated mates, separation is worse than death. Which was why he pushed the subject." Jordyn wanted to scream.

Rutger wrapped his arm around Jo and pulled her closer. "No one will take me from you. He won't kill you."

Jordyn turned into him and met his gaze.

"How sweet," Mia scoffed. "You don't know what Prime has planned."

Jordyn lowered her head as Rutger's hand held the nape of her neck, and relishing his feel she closed her eyes, and tried to calm down. *She wanted the night to end.* "I'll do what I have to."

"You'll be risking your life. Again," Lady Sloan pointed out. "He'll push you to find out the strength of your powers and its weakness. Your weaknesses, like Rutger, your pack, and your kin. Then he'll find the darkness inside of you. He's from the underworld and surrounds himself with those like himself. You're like him."

Jordyn wasn't anything like him. She slipped from Rutger's hold, and standing put her hands on her hips, the thick waistband under her palms, and her anger seething. "I have been pushed. And pushed. If he wanted to kill me, he would have tonight. He would have let me bleed out." *Everyone has fucked with me.* "I doubt Prime wants anything from me except to test me. I'm *your* scion." Jordyn's anger lashed out at the room.

"I would like to believe you." She inhaled and exhaled. "I have watched him punish his wards and felt the intense excitement he gets from it. As Prime he has to show no mercy. As a demon he feeds off pain."

"Prime left here without punishing her. We'll learn what he's after at the moon run," Healey stated.

Rutger rested his hands on Jo's shoulders and felt tension tightening her muscles under his palms. He needed to get Jo home. "We're leaving."

"Son, wait. The moon run is in four days." Turning his attention to Jordyn, he said, "It's imperative you start working with Sloan. It will help you survive the challenge."

Survive. In one piece? "I will. I've had enough for one night. I'll come back tomorrow." Jordyn looked at Rutger giving him 'we need to leave' look.

"Tomorrow then," Healey responded.

"I'll be here," Lady Sloan promised.

Ethan stepped in front of her, stopping her. "Daughter, I don't know how you've been dealing with this by yourself." Dark circles shaded the skin under her eyes, her pale skin, thin frame, and with her clothing swallowing her it made her look weak and defenseless. This was the woman who was going to face Prime. He faced losing his daughter in a matter of days.

"It's all right. It's the way things are." Jordyn hugged her dad. His arms wrapped around her, and she felt his power on her skin like a comfortable safety net. She didn't want to cut their ties or push her father away, but she didn't want him to get mixed up with whatever her life was turning into.

"Jo, we have to go," Rutger urged. He felt sorry for Lord Ethan and the pain and fear he must be dealing with but it was more important to get Jo home.

Jordyn backed up, met their gazes, saw doubt and dread, and couldn't do anything to stop it, and walked out of the room.

CHAPTER TWENTY

At sunrise, Jordyn had sat at the kitchen table drinking coffee and staring out the window at the sweeps of amber feathering the edges of lilac painting the early maya sky. Climbing higher, the sun's strokes of color highlighted the snow dusted mountain peaks. Her hopes for a sunny day died when the wind gusted and tossed gold, scarlet, and caramel-stained leaves to the lake. As if the wind was guiding them clouds began building over the mountains and swept in, taking the sun, its heat, and delivering a chilled fall day.

Jordyn didn't like it.

The gate raddled its way along the metal guide opening them to a narrow stretch of asphalt. Rutger drove through, stopped, and checked the rearview mirror to watch it make its trip back across to gently close. How Prime entered Foxwood without using the palm vein reader and code for the gate, he wasn't sure, and didn't know what had stopped them from getting an alert when Lord Ervin and Lady Sloan arrived. Then there was the face recognition camera and license plate reader neither of his cars triggered. He would have to discuss it with the baron and do an investigation.

Rutger continued down the two-lane road bordered by tall cedar trees, oak trees, and wild brambles. He caught sunlight reflecting off one of the fake trees armed with a camera, and the tree house further back. He was going to check the video feed. If there was any. Above them, the broken gray clouds of the October sky teased sunshine and matched the mood inside the cab-gloomy. Thicker clouds were gathering at the mountains and promised there was a snow storm coming. Silence filled the minutes when the log-home-inspired mansion of Foxwood and the matching architecture of the enforcer's office and garage came into view.

Rutger parked in his designated space in front of the Enforcer's office and killed the engine, ending the beeps and notifications. The truck sat silent save for their breathing. He checked the parking lot, the area between the office and the house, and the front of the house. Sousa and Sadie stood their posts on either side of the double doors. Lord Ervin's sporty luxury car sat out front where it had been the night before. With no one else outside, he looked at Jo. She stared out obviously, not at the front of the office, her eyes glassy with her thoughts.

"We can go home," Rutger offered. He sat half turned to face Jo. Through her hoodie he saw her shoulders sank enough he knew she was uncomfortable. She woke up early, showered, had done her makeup and hair as if on auto, and then joined him for breakfast where she drank coffee and played with a piece of bacon. "You don't have to do this."

Damn she wished that was true. When they left Foxwood, they had driven home in silence, the tension between them palpable. Her thoughts never leaving Lady Sloan, Balaur, Prime, her powers, the challenge, and what it meant for her future. Their future. Now, instead of training with Leo to improve her ability to fight, she would be training with Lady Sloan to understand her powers. And it would be training. Mentally. Physically. Emotionally. And she would have to accept what she was instead of trying to convince everyone she already had.

"Jo, do you want to go home?" Rutger asked the side of her face. She jumped head first into her head and wasn't coming out. The night before, as they lay in bed, he wrapped his arms around her, his body molded to hers, and fought the urge to ask her if she was all right. He didn't, and she didn't say anything, leaving them laying in silence. Finally, when her breathing slowed and her muscles relaxed, he allowed himself to drift off. He didn't think she slept well. "Jo."

"Yes." She inhaled. "No. I have to do this," Jordyn replied and met his worried gaze.

In a black, long-sleeved shirt with his title, name, and the Cascade pack's crest on the left and a larger crest on the back, Rutger dressed for work. He tucked the shirt into black BDU trousers and wore his webbed belt riddled with tactical gear and thigh holster. He looked like the Director of Enforcers and was ready for his day. Contrary to the Jeep that held a musty smell from being stored and the mixed scents of the two of them, his truck smelled of gun oil, gear, and the earthy smell of dirt, while a thread of spice and wolf lingered to tease her nose.

"I appreciate the offer," Jordyn mumbled.

"You're welcome. I think." Jo stopped paying attention to him. Rutger hadn't gotten through to her all morning and wasn't going to be given the chance to try. "Here comes Sadie." Jo looked at him, her eyes holding a dazed sheen, then followed his gaze.

The sentinel wore black dress slacks, a gray, button-up shirt, the colors of the pack, with Cascade's crest on the left pocket, and a shoulder holster with a Glock 19 in 9 mm, pistol. Their usual uniform of jeans and polos weren't good enough while Lord Ervin and Lady Sloan were staying at Foxwood.

"Great." Jordyn turned to Rutger, giving Sadie her back, and waited for the sentinel to cross the driveway. The night had been filled with fits of sleep, leaving her plenty of time to think about the Numen and what she had looked like pinned to the wall and bleeding all over the place. It was worse than Dr. Holmes stabbing her with his syringe. Jordyn was going to have to face the horror and pity in their eyes as they looked at a victim.

"It's not what you think." Rutger's rough voice carried his worry.

Jordyn wasn't in the mood for a pep talk. "What?"

"You've survived attempts on your life." He held her dark cocoa gaze. "They don't see a victim. They see your strength and their soothsayer and mistress. You are One-Flesh with the Second to the Alpha," he tried assuring her. "They see their pack mate."

"Do they?" she challenged. "I know what I see. And what I see is their pity." And fear. They don't understand what was happening to her. They did know she brought Prime and his Numina to Trinity and to the baron's house. She would see more than their pity at the moon run. She would see their accusations for bringing their world to an end.

"They don't pity you. If anything, they fear for you." Ruger knew arguing with her was a battle he would never win. Jo made up her mind. It made him hate Prime, Lady Sloan, and Lord Ervin for destroying the progress she made.

They spent one day together, living their lives, and enjoying themselves. One afternoon, it hadn't been a full damn day. Rutger watched her and felt her shut him out as she shutdown. Noticing Ansel at the office door-no doubt wanting to discuss the night before and the security breaches-Rutger tried one last time. "Jo. You can't worry about what they think, when you're unsure. Once you understand your powers, you'll feel more confident."

Jordyn doubted that.

Rutger shook his head and rolled Jo's window down. "Sadie."

"Good morning. Mistress, Lady Sloan is waiting in the greeting room," Sadie started. "Director, the baron is expecting you in his office."

"Thank you," Rutger replied. She stepped back from the truck and he hit the button to roll up the window. "Jo, are you going to be all right?"

"Don't ask me that again. Ever," Jordyn replied without looking at him. She didn't know if she was all right. Hell, she didn't know how she was going to be after training with Lady Sloan.

Sadie didn't leave after delivering the message; instead, she waited for them. Jordyn wanted to scream. She opened her door, got out of the truck, slammed it closed, and without waiting for Rutger headed in the direction of the house. With her blatant show of anger Sadie stepped back. *Good.* She didn't need an armed escort to walk across the freaking parking lot to the house.

Rutger's low growl of frustration rumbled in his chest. He got out of the truck, nodded to Ansel, and caught up with Jo. Sadie hung back, and when Rutger walked with Jo, she took her place behind them. Rutger sensed several other guards around the house, and taking a quick glance saw two standing guard on the second story balcony.

"Director, Mistress," Abigail greeted. Beside her, Troy opened the door and held it for them.

"Good morning," Rutger replied.

They entered the foyer continued to the first entrance- the left leading to the formal dining room and the right leading to the formal greeting room. He could hear women's voices coming from the greeting room, recognizing one of them as the baroness.

He hated leaving Jo. "I don't have to meet with the baron right away if you want me to stay with you."

"Go. I'll be fine," Jordyn replied absently.

You're not fine. "All right." Rutger leaned in and gently kissed Jo's lips and met her gaze. When he straightened, he let his fingertips trail over her hip and continued down the hall towards the baron's office.

Jordyn watched the muscles in Rutger's board shoulders and back flow under his shirt as he walked. Damn, she shouldn't have been a complete bitch in the truck, or last night, but Prime and Lady Sloan consumed her thoughts. Easy excuses. She spent her time between being angry and plunging head first into feeling sorry for herself. She could pretend to accept this was her life but she didn't. Every time she felt as if she overcame an obstacle there was a new one thrown in her path. And it was bigger, had talons, and was more dangerous. It was a matter of time before someone, an innocent, was caught in the crossfire and it would be her fault. The pack would blame her.

She absently rubbed the heal of her hand on the raised scar as she checked the front door where Abigail and Troy stood and stared. Jordyn was positive they would tackle her if she tried to run. There was no turning back when the moon run and Prime's challenge was in three days. Three damn days. Having thought about it all night, Jordyn came to the conclusion Prime had given her simple tests-healing, sensing his power, and control over his own-to see how she reacted and if they lined up with Lady Sloan's powers. It left her with questions about the challenge and if she was going to live through whatever Prime planned. All of it would be witnessed by the pack. The magic-born, not formally part of the pack known as the Klatch, and the other factions. More the merrier, said no one ever.

Lady Sloan's cultured voice glided from the room, and by the sound they were having an easy conversation. *That's about to come to an end.* Jordyn couldn't delay the meeting any longer, and entered the room. She saw the baroness and Lady Sloan sitting in wingback chairs, dainty coffee cups sat on the table between them, and the rich scent of fresh-pressed coffee drifted in the room. Jordyn wasn't a pressed coffee person-no, when she woke up, she wanted it now. Through large windows she could see the morning sun trying to break through scattered clouds to brighten the room. A fire crackled and popped its sparks climbing up the chimney. It was comfortable, warm, and inviting. She didn't feel like she belonged.

"Good morning, Jordyn," Laurel greeted. She wondered what Jordyn's appearance would be after the attack and was pleasantly surprised she had done her hair and makeup, and dressed in a hoodie, jeans, and running shoes. Despite the anxiety rolling from her, Jordyn looked well.

"Baroness," Jordyn replied and stopped. Did she sit down? Did she wait to be told? Did she stand there like an idiot? Sure.

"She refers to you as baroness?" Lady Sloan inquired. "I assumed with her status as mistress, your daughter-in-law, and soothsayer she would be granted exclusion from pack etiquette. Jordyn has earned the privilege to refer to you by your given name."

"No matter how many times I tell her, she always refers to me baroness," Laurel replied easily. Under the circumstances, it didn't surprise Laurel, Jordyn stuck to the decorum of the pack. The girl remained standing and waiting to be told she could sit down. Laurel met Sloan's gaze and didn't see humor or understanding; rather she saw she had offended Sloan. It appeared to her as a member of the Highguard, Laurel disrespected her scion and daughter. "My apologies, Sloan. Jordyn has the freedom to call me Laurel. In fact, to reinforce her status within the pack, her authority, and her relationship with Rutger, I insist. As does Healey."

"Is this true?" Lady Sloan questioned Jordyn. She crossed her legs, smoothed the wrinkle-free fabric of her cream-colored slacks, and met Jordyn's gaze.

If she could roll her eyes she would have. "Yes, Lady Sloan, Laurel insists, as does Healey. I'm nervous and I didn't think to greet her as Laurel."

"I see. Why are you standing?" Lady Sloan gave Laurel a slow, sideways glance, then returned her stare to Jordyn.

"I don't know." *I want to go home.*

Laurel watched Jordyn and could see a sleepless night along with stress were battling for their place on her shoulders. Confronting her real mother, the lies her parents told, being attacked, and challenging Prime's demand in order to stay with Rutger would steal one's sleep.

"After Prime's surprise visit, I'm sure Jordyn is dealing with some anxiety." Laurel explained to Lady Sloan. "Jordyn, sit. Would you like a cup of coffee?"

"Prime is here to test Jordyn's abilities. If stress cripples her to where she can't make a simple decision, he has already proven his point. Her abilities are irrelevant. She will lose the challenge and Rutger will be imprisoned. As One of the Twelve and spending time at court, I know Prime and he will use her weaknesses to manipulate the Cascade pack," Lady Sloan warned.

Jordyn stared out the window, not focusing on the enforcers and soldiers in front of the office or the parked cars and trucks. Her mind repeated every word Lady Sloan said and the warning. Several months ago, her problems had been where was she going to take her next picture, how would she have it displayed at the gallery, and what kind of takeout was she going to order. She also thought she knew her family. One minute a regular person, the next she was thrown into a new world. Not thrown, dragged, kicking and screaming. Jordyn wasn't equipped to deal with being a soothsayer, her birth mother, or Prime. The pack depended on her, Rutger depended on her, and yes, stress was crippling her. Worst of all, the more she thought about the past and what she lost the more its loss ate at her.

"Jordyn?" Laurel looked at Sloan to see her staring at Jordyn. "Jordyn?"

"Yes, coffee," she replied absently. Jordyn yanked herself back to the present, chose a wingback chair across from Laurel, and sat down. The weight of Lady Sloan's eyes and the pending lecture hit her like a thousand needles to her skin.

"After speaking to Ethan last night, I understand how difficult this must be. You were led to believe what was happening to you was wrong, and to protect yourself, you denied your magic. I can't imagine the day to day struggle and the strength you used in order to keep it a secret."

Lady Sloan stopped, letting what she said sit between them like a dramatic pause.

Jordyn waited as Lady Sloan took her cup from the table and sipped her coffee.

"Normally, children are tested, and if they show signs of abnormal magic levels, the magic is identified and the children are trained in their specific fields. No one gave you the luxury. But you can have it now, Jordyn. You don't have to hide what you are and the extent of your magic. And besides, you can't fight what you have become."

Jordyn wasn't hiding. Not really. Well, maybe. "And you're going to help me?"

The Baroness handed her a mug, not a dainty cup and saucer like she and Lady Sloan were using. Pausing for a moment, as if undecided, like she should say something, the baroness took her seat.

In twisted threads of steam, dark chocolate mixed with sweet smoke rose up and drifted. Jordyn inhaled and stilled as she turned the mug and saw the landscape picture wrapped around the porcelain. That's why the baroness hesitated. Jordyn was looking at one of her photographs. Hues of gold and scarlet reflected on the water as waves lapped at the shoreline, sweeping small stones back and forth with its current. In the background, a large pine tree had fallen, its limbs stretching out in the water, creating ripples around its submerged branches. The world shifted for a moment, sending her back to the lake. She was kneeling with one knee in the water while Rutger's shadow approached as he waded into the waves. She stopped the memory as the comfortable feel set in and teased her with the past. Jordyn had taken the picture four years earlier after a lazy day with Rutger and made him the mug because he didn't have any at his house. She planned to have more made, each one with a different picture of the area.

"Three years ago, Rutger came here smelling more of bourbon than coffee and demanded to see Healey. They were in the office for hours before Rutger emerged, his shoulders slumped, his face wearing pain, and in silence, left. It was the day he rescinded his title as Second to the Alpha. It would take another year and several challenges resulting in bloodshed and broken bones before he took the position as Director of Enforcers. The next time I saw him, he referred to me as baroness, was withdrawn, and there was an emptiness inside of him," Laurel explained. "He left the coffee cup on Healey's desk."

Guilt after what she had been through, nice. "Why are you telling me this?" Jordyn asked, and took a sip.

"Over those three years when you visited Coal Valley, and hid behind the gates, you acted like a submissive and were withdrawn. Like Rutger. I'm explaining this to you because when he saw you at the Timber House, he changed. You changed. The energy between you buzzed and your wolves recognized the other. As fated mates, you need each other. You have to be strong for one another," Laurel explained. She hoped her message challenged Jordyn's fear.

"Is this true, Jordyn?" Lady Sloan asked.

"What part? I left my mate and pack, and when I visited, I hid at my parent's house. Rutger stepped down from being Second because I left? I left because he cheated on me? We made each other miserable? Pick one." *We're still making each other miserable.* Jordyn could go on and on. Like a knife, guilt cut through her with dredging up the past. *We have never said we love each other.* "The pressure to be the perfect couple nearly destroyed us. Now we don't have to worry about it because we have royally fucked up."

"You haven't, Jordyn," Laurel tried. "God, you two are together doing the best you can and you're alive."

"You aren't the couple you were then and you are definitely not the woman you were three years ago. Be thankful. It's time you faced who you are today." Lady Sloan let a minute of silence pass before continuing. "Have you used your powers?"

"No." Jordyn looked down at the dark liquid, praying it would save her. From herself? "I've spent my life denying who I am, what I am, and then when it's all right for me to be this person, I put the pack at risk. My pack isn't afraid of the Highguard or Prime, because they haven't been part of their world. Now they are. Prime and the Highguard are both in Trinity. Prime and his Numen invaded the baron's estate. You're here. If I hadn't come back, this never would have happened."

"Jordyn you can't live in the past. Anyway, if you hadn't returned and your magic destroyed your control Healey would have sent the slayers to quell a soothsayer who had gone rogue. That's saying nothing about your relationship with Rutger as fated mates. Every action has a reaction and a purpose," Lady Sloan explained.

It sounded like a lecture. Jordyn knew Lady Sloan was right but wasn't about to admit it. She couldn't think about not living with Rutger even if they were dysfunctional. At the moment.

"Powers are building. We are changing. You feel this and are aware. It doesn't matter how the pack feels. When it comes time to standup and fight for them you will be on the front line, and because Prime and the Highguard value you they will help you. They are your allies. You can sense magic, and you sense it increasing, you'll know when it becomes a threat to your pack. Left alone, would they survive?"

"I don't know?" she answered honestly.

"No. There will always be believers and doubters, it happens everywhere with everyone. You're here as a believer and the pack's connection to Prime and the Highguard, and you serve as proof the baron is telling the truth."

"I hadn't thought of it like that," Jordyn mumbled.

"Daughter, it's time to embrace your magic and receive the pack's Collective." Lady Sloan set her cup on the side table as she called her wolf. "Are you ready?"

Jordyn set her mug down, inhaled, and answered, "Yes."

"Do you feel my power?"

Electricity hummed in the air sending pin pricks over Jordyn's skin. "Yes."

"Call your wolf and let it flow through you." Lady Sloan placed her palms flat on the top of her thighs and closed her eyes. "I need to know the nexus between you and Healey is true. Tell me something only Laurel and Healey would know."

Jordyn felt her reaching out the same way she had the night before. With her wolf encompassing her, Jordyn closed her eyes and called her magic. She spent energy blocking the Collective and their whispers for fear of losing herself in a nightmare. Being forced to break through the wall between her thoughts, her magic, and finding one out of thousands sent an ache across her skull. With a crack in the barrier, whispers flooded her ears. Jordyn held her head and inhaled and exhaled.

"Concentrate, Jordyn," Lady Sloan urged.

Like I'm not. Jordyn searched through the mess for the baron and his memories. A thread of fear and grief drove through her, making her catch her breath, and before it weaved back into the memories, she grabbed ahold of it. "When Gavin was born, he was sickly and weak, they feared for his life. He survived, but when he shapeshifted for the first time, he nearly died. He wasn't strong enough to control the wolf and it tried to tear him apart. The baron saved him by pulling his wolf from him and he stayed in wolf form for four days. As alpha and baron, the Kanin children should have been able to easily shapeshift, proving the strength of the family. It was the reason they kept Gavin's weakness a secret from the pack."

"How do you know this?" Laurel asked as her face paled. Gavin bleed from his eyes and ears, his deformed arms and legs twitching while his body convulsed as the wolf continued to ravage him. Her son had been minutes away from dying right in front of her.

"I saw it. I feel the fear and grief of the moment," Jordyn answered and shuddered. "It lives inside of me." Her eyes remained closed and her breathing heavy while she fought to keep from crying.

Laurel looked at Sloan who was staring at her. "It had been easy for Rutger, obviously because he's a strong werewolf and the future alpha of Cascade. Tanner has always been strong with a natural ability to lead. Unlike his brothers, Gavin understands he will never be an alpha or a leader."

"Yet you put the pack at risk by allowing him to take the place of Second when Rutger stepped down," Lady Sloan questioned.

"Healey knew it was temporary. He planned on making Jordyn the soothsayer, and knew if Jordyn stayed in Trinity, she and Rutger would get back together. My concern is, what are you going to do?" Laurel asked with fear in her voice. Sloan could tell Prime and Gavin's place as third would be stripped from him and he would be shamed as weak. They would lose everything they worked for.

Ignoring her question, Lady Sloan said, "I want you to understand the magnitude of a soothsayer and understand the responsibilities you have given to Jordyn. You made the decision to hand her the mantel of the pack. She is the pack. They won't do anything without her knowledge. She will feel their pain, happiness, grief, and will know their secrets. This was a minuscule portion of the information she possesses. More so, if a clansman dies, she will feel their death and grieve for them. It will feel as if the pain is trying to tear her apart and there is nothing she can do to ease it."

Jordyn stared at Lady Sloan, realizing she had experienced that pain more than once.

"I understand." Laurel wanted to go back to that day, stop Healey, and change everything. "You didn't answer my question."

"Do you understand what she is? What you've given her?"

"Yes." Laurel held Sloan's stare.

"The information is a means to an end and nothing more. Your secrets will remain yours. A word of warning, if one feels Jordyn might expose confidential information this person might try to stop her from doing so."

Attacks and deaths. Just what she needed to know.

"She will be protected," Laurel promised.

"Or there will be consequences," Lady Sloan threatened. "The nexus is strong. It's time for Jordyn to accept the Collective."

"She hasn't accepted them yet?" Laurel asked.

"No. Jordyn, can you hear me?"

"Yes."

"Use your magic to call the Collective," Lady Sloan directed.

Jordyn tried manipulating her magic and forcing it around the voices like she was corralling them into a tight circle. With every attempt they fought her. Getting bolder, the whispers and tones turned into screams and she gave up. She couldn't control them. They were going to rip her brain to shreds. Jordyn's head lowered as sweat dripped from her forehead and cheeks from fighting the mass of chaos. She applied pressure on both sides of her skull and squeezed harder and harder. The screaming joined the drumming of her pulse and both intensified, causing her entire body to shudder. Prime's warning blared through them all. She was going to go insane. Jordyn was going to lose.

Jordyn-0.

Collective-1.

"What happened that day? The day Healey enshrined Jordyn?" Lady Sloan demanded.

Laurel sat frozen, staring at Jordyn. Her elbows were on her thighs, her head bent, her hands clasping each side and she squeezed as if she was trying to crush her skull. Harsh murmurs left her lips as tears dropped to her jeans. How much pain was she going to have to endure?

"Laurel. What did Healey do?" Lady Sloan repeated her demand. She pushed her urgency into her voice to get through to Laurel. "I have to know if I am to help her."

Laurel hesitated. Was she betraying her husband? She didn't know. Jordyn sank into the chair and she saw the day repeating itself. Laurel started explaining everything she saw from her place on the deck, the words tumbling from her as if a faucet had been turned on. She detailed the amount of power both of them were projecting, the way Healey held the back of Jordyn's neck, Jordyn's hands on his chest, and their faces a sliver away from one another. "Minutes later, Jordyn relived one of Healey's memories. She clawed at her face and throat. Rutger stopped her and pulled her back to reality."

"He had no business," Lady Sloan mumbled. "He poured raw energy into her and gave her a lifetime of pain and nightmares. Your inexperience is going to be the death of her." Lady Sloan nearly yelled.

"I didn't know. You have to talk to Healey," Laurel pleaded. "Please."

"No." Lady Sloan left her chair to kneel in front of Jordyn, then placed her hands on Jordyn's knees. "Don't control the magic. Let it guide you to the Collective. You are fighting them. They are an extension of you like your magic, your wolf. Like the death inside of you. Embrace them and hold them."

Through the screams, a familiar voice weaved into the noise and she recognized it as Lady Sloan. She must be failing if Lady Sloan was back in her head. Jordyn didn't wait, she grasped onto the words and clung to them like they were a life preserver and would keep her from drowning. With a firm hold, Jordyn heard the words *'Instincts. Guide you.'* At the same time every reflex ordered her to fight harder. Her wolf wasn't flowing through her as if made from water, it was trying to claw its way up and out of the

Collective's storm. *Instincts.* Little by little, Jordyn eased her influence while her wolf withdrew. When she was clear and the Collective sat inside free of restraint it stopped the worst of its assault and the pain waned.

"Jordyn, stay with the Collective. Concentrate on their essences and open yourself to them, then merge with them. They need you," Lady Sloan advised.

Jordyn lowered her hands to her lap, the creases across her face from pain smoothed and her power threaded in the air sending soft vibrations. With her eyes closed, she slowly nodded in response. She saw the Collective as a white flame going from her hips to her chest, its heat licking at her wolf and teasing the impulse to protect herself from its burn. Lady Sloan told her to merge with it. Sure thing. What did she have to lose besides her mind? Nothing. Jordyn inhaled a deep breath, reached out with one hand, and watched her fingers flicker in the warm, translucent edges. Before she changed her mind and slunk back like a coward, Jordyn walked into the firestorm. Bright white built up around her and enveloping her, blinded her. She was going to lose if she stayed there. Her wolf howled in her ears in warning as a million hands grabbed her and pulled her into the eye of the storm.

"Jordyn. Jordyn." Lady Sloan squeezed her knees, making her knuckles turn white.

"What's happening?" Laurel asked. Jordyn remained unfazed and unreachable.

"I lost her. I can't sense her. I can't feel Jordyn's wolf, her power, or read her thoughts. There's nothing." Lady Sloan mumbled. "She's somewhere else. Gone."

Jordyn held her breath as their heated hands and fingers gripped her body while they passed her from one to the other. This was happening in her head. *It isn't real.* Her breath caught when the flames climbed higher and she felt the Collective's lives draw back and they started leaching their emotions from her. One at a time, as if they were taking pieces of her, she felt sadness, happiness, anger, fear, and love drain away. They continued to siphon their past, making Jordyn weaker and weaker.

Was this her opportunity to leave the Collective? Jordyn didn't have an answer. If it was, she wasn't going to fight them. The mass exodus gained strength and to help them along, she called her magic.

CHAPTER TWENTY-ONE

"The shadows tracked Prime to Willow Creek and to Alpha Milo Bryer's estate. It sits fifteen miles outside of Granite Peak, and another ten from the main road in the thickest part of the woods. It's a perfect place for Prime to preserve a level of anonymity. I suspected the Highguard had something to do with the Granite Peak clowder when after thirty years and zero problems, Robert was challenged and then removed. This confirms it," Healey explained.

"What does Prime want with bobcats? By nature, they're solitary and suspicious, and refuse to take orders. I can't imagine the clowder accepting a new alpha. Or the new alpha learning the ways of an old clowder," Rutger replied. It was all he could do to pay attention when Jordyn hadn't spoken to him all morning and was stuck with Lady Sloan and the baroness.

"The Highguard put Alpha Milo in place. The clowder isn't going to disobey. Over the last couple of months, three alphas have been replaced, Robert makes four. The replacements make a circle around Trinity. I fear they're watching Jordyn, and watching how Cascade proceeds. If Jordyn fails any suspicions or doubts about us may increase exponentially." Healey sat back and drank his coffee. "If word spreads that Prime bypassed our security and attacked our soothsayer, it will make us look weak. I need you to tighten security here, at your house, and I want more patrols."

Our soothsayer. You mean my mate. "Yes, sir." Rutger took his mug from the desk and stared at the dark liquid. His nerves running tension across his shoulders, up his neck, and over his skull where a headache was building.

"You have something on your mind, son?" Healey asked.

"Thinking about security. I'll have a meeting with the enforcers and have Torin brief his soldiers. With the moon run in three days, and the klatch, and an unknown amount of factions planning on attending, we'll do patrols in unmarked vehicles so we don't attract attention. There are going to be questions, no need to escalate doubts about our strength by looking like we're scrambling out of fear." Without drinking his coffee, Rutger leaned forward and set his mug on the desk.

"You have security covered. What is really on your mind?" It was Healey's turn to abandon his cup to the desk.

I need to tell Jo I love her. "Everything is on my mind. The challenge. Jo. Shadow Lord. I haven't told her what the letter said," Rutger confessed. He carried the lie, its poison infecting his nightmares, and felt like a weight around his neck. "And this." He tugged the folded envelope from a side pocket and tossed it to the desk as if it might bite him.

"I understand your worries. First thing is first, the moon run and the challenge. The outcome will determine Prime's next move. Shadow Lord is the least of your problems. And, son, don't feel guilty about not telling her. Jordyn has enough to worry about. Don't you agree?" Healey asked. He carefully started unfolding the envelop, met Rutger's gaze for a second, then freed the thick page and began reading. With his brows drawn in he read, "You can protect her. We'll protect her. You didn't answer me, don't you agree, the less she has to worry about the better?"

"Yes. I don't like lying to her. If she knew-"

"It would be a problem added to her list," Healey interrupted. "She challenged Prime and will endure whatever he has planned. If she fails, she will be judged, and it will be harsh. Any questions, accusations, or opposition from the pack will be justified."

Before Rutger responded a presence-as if someone entered the room-made him turn in his seat and look behind him. The dark wood door remained closed and there was no one there. The office was empty. It felt the same when he thought Jo had walked by his office without saying anything to him. As if a presence brushed him.

"What is it?" Healey asked as he looked at Rutger.

"I thought someone was at the door." There was no way his senses were wrong. He earned his place as director for a reason. His wolf flowed through him at the same time it howled in his ears. Rutger searched the link to Jo and didn't sense her. While it wasn't a surprise, the rejection stung. Damn, if they had more time, they could build a foundation for their relationship. His wolf howled from feeling the void and louder with a warning.

"Son, if there is something happening, explain it to me," Healey demanded.

"I don't know what it is." Rutger checked the door. Nothing. There was no one outside either. The women were in the greeting room, the sentinels by the doors. "I guess it's nothing." Rutger faced the baron and found him slumped in his chair, his chin resting on his chest, his arms hung over the sides, and his legs were sprawled out in front of him. "Dad," the word rushed from him.

Rutger stood, the chair scooting back from the force, and he raced around the desk. Using his senses, he checked the baron's heartbeat, its weakness matching his pale skin slick with sweat. What could have happened in seconds? Rutger had no idea. "Dad?" He touched the baron's forehead with the back of his fingers and met cold and clammy skin. As an immortal, the baron was resistant to viruses, cancers, sicknesses, and wasn't going to have a heart attack or stroke. In his life, Rutger never saw his dad in a vulnerable condition. The baron never showed weakness, it was one of the things Rutger admired and hated about the man.

The baron remained silent while Rutger did a quick check of the room. Nothing. He checked his cell for an alert. Nothing. The house was fortified inside and out, including the grounds, and there were more than two dozen enforcers and soldiers present. It made a physical attack impossible, and if it had been chemical it would have affected Rutger and the others would have noticed. It left him blaming magic. After the display of power, getting past Rutger's security, and proving Foxwood wasn't as fortified as Rutger thought, it left one person. Prime. He could bring the baron to his knees.

"Dad, can you hear me?" *Please hear me*. Rutger's panic surged through him, and with his wolf shadowing him, he grabbed the baron. "Dad, wake up."

Healey opened his eyes a sliver-they were dark gold, struggled to focus, and he whispered, "Jordyn."

"Is this normal?" Laurel asked. She stood beside Jordyn, trying to keep her from sliding out of the chair.

"No. I don't know what this is and I don't know why she's getting weaker." Lady Sloan closed her eyes. "I'm going to enter the labyrinth of Jordyn's magic." Seconds ticked and turned into minutes. "She is destroying the Collective and purging them from her body."

"That's not possible." Laurel didn't know if it was possible or not, wasn't completely sure what it meant to be a soothsayer, and had no idea how the connection between Jordyn and Healey worked. Or how she held the Collective or what the Collective was as far as a physical entity. The past and lives of the dead and the present were beyond Laurel's comprehension. Her instincts told her Jordyn was doing something wrong. And impossible.

"She's using Healey's magic." Lady Sloan couldn't hide the uneasiness in her voice. "Eventually she will destroy the nexus."

"She is bound to him, she wears the Balaur to prove it. I thought it was irreversible. How can she destroy their connection?" Laurel watched as Jordyn's body went limp.

Lady Sloan met her worried gaze, her copper eyes dim with worry, and explained, "Jordyn is the nexus, she will destroy herself, therefore eliminating their connection."

Laurel watched Jordyn's skin grow pale while her eyes moved under her lids. *She's killing herself.* "What will she do to Healey?" She had to stop her panic from controlling her, and she needed to stop thinking Jordyn was dying when Rutger was down the hall. No doubt they would sense trouble and investigate.

"Something happened to the baron." Rutger rushed into the room carrying him. He headed toward the antique couch where he gently placed him and stood.

"Healey," Laurel whispered. Sloan hadn't answered her question. With her attention split between checking on

Healey and staying beside Jordyn, Laurel felt torn. "What happened?

"I don't know. One minute he was fine, the next he was like this." Rutger saw Jordyn slumped in the chair. Not possible. "What the hell is happening?"

"Jordyn is drawing Healey's power and using it to separate herself from the Collective. Right?" Laurel was looking at Sloan and the anxiety creasing her usually controlled features. Sloan, a powerful soothsayer with her pack and the Highguard, was facing the emotions of being a mother and watching her child suffer.

"Essentially." Lady Sloan stood and taking slow steps backwards sat in a chair. "I don't know why she's doing this? Being a soothsayer is an honorable station. She has power and status."

"Jo never wanted power or status. She wanted freedom," Rutger mumbled the last words. Her freedom had been stripped from her. "Her life has been a nightmare." Rutger wanted to roar his frustration. He left the baron's side and went to the baroness. "Go to your husband."

"Thank you, son." Laurel gave Jordyn one last look and made her way to her husband. "What will happen to Healey if she continues this?"

"He will weaken until Jordyn completely purges the Collective and destroys nexus," Lady Sloan answered. She wasn't going to explain to Rutger what *might* happen to Jordyn. The situation *might* change.

Rutger grabbed a thick throw from the couch and straightened it out in front of the fire. When he finished, he went to Jo, gathered her limp body in his arms, as he had done the night before, and gently set her on the blanket. His worry and anger battling for his attention, each demanding him to feed one of them. He shifted his gun, knelt beside her, placed his hand on her stomach, and watched her. "Let me guess, Jo will purge the Collective and because they're part of her and her power, she'll die in the process." If he could go back, he would end her damn silence and fight for her.

"What is happening?" Lord Ervin asked as he entered the room.

Rutger didn't need another person in the room with them.

"Jordyn is purging the Collective," Lady Sloan answered. She turned to Rutger and he watched her face hold onto her regrets. "Yes, Rutger. I'm sorry."

"Does she know she's killing herself?" Rutger asked, his voice flat and unemotional. Leaning down, he feathered her cheek with his fingers. If she understood what she was doing, she might save herself.

Lord Ervin watched him as he held Lady Sloan's shoulders. "No. Understand, Jordyn isn't unconscious, she is in the ether and she is awake. She believes she will absolve herself of the responsibilities of a soothsayer. She can't. It's part of her magic. It's why she is alive. Jordyn will use her strength and power until the Collective is eradicated. When its depleted, her magic will have been exhausted, her body will fail, and she will sleep." Lady Sloan closed her eyes, shuddered, and opened them in defeat. "Laurel said you broke through to her before. You need to do it now."

"I can't. If what you say is true, she's out of my reach. I can't feel her." Rutger couldn't do anything but watch as her life drained from her. *Mea.* He saw her standing at the railing of their deck, her skin glistening in the setting sun's golden hue. They survived the last couple of months and he thought he was getting her back. It was a lie. His mate was drifting away from him. He looked at the baron lying on the couch and the baroness sitting beside his unmoving body. If the baron died, Rutger was next in line and he had no desire to take his place much less comfort a grieving baroness. "Explain again what is happening to the baron."

"She is draining his strength. Jordyn is the nexus between them and once she dies her death will destroy the connection and he will be free. The shock will leave him weakened but his strength will return," Lady Sloan explained.

"What happens to the Collective?" Laurel asked.

"They will remain in the ether. The Cascade pack will lose their history." Lady Sloan met Rutger's haunted eyes. "You have to reach her."

He ignored her. "You're saying the baron is safe? Right?" Rutger needed to eliminate one worry.

"Yes, he is safe. Jordyn is not, you need to try. You are fated mates. Use the link between you."

Jo is never safe. Would he always face her death? Rutger wanted to laugh, growl, and roar. If he could reach her, he would. "If she can heal herself without shifting and we're immortal, why is she dying?"

"When you invoke your magic, you call your wolf and shapeshift. A soothsayer can summon their magic without shifting. With the Collective, it feeds their power, meaning the stronger they are, the more powerful they are and the easier it is to summon their magic. She is using her power against her magic to purge the Collective. She is attacking herself and the very thing making her what she is. Once it's exhausted, Jordyn will have nothing," Lady Sloan explained. "Please try."

Rutger's voice and feel invaded the link as he tried to stop her. Jordyn ignored him, pushing forward, and promised when it was over, she would explain she did it for them. The Collective followed her demands and continued to ebb from her consciousness. She felt like she was purifying her body while liquidating their presence, spirits, and substance. As their feel faded, their elimination left echoes of their lifetimes and riddled her with voids. She hated the cold emptiness and hated feeling them die. No ... diminish. As if they had never been alive. They were being reduced to phantoms. Is that what she wanted? Was she going to toss her pack and their essence to ether? Yes. A pang of guilt drummed and she shoved it down. She wanted to be free of the responsibility and Prime. Jordyn was doing this for her future.

Blue/white light swirled into flames and climbed higher, creating a wall between her and life outside of herself. Jordyn stopped the purge, her breath stuck in her lungs, and her heartbeat pounding. The flames weren't hot or cold; instead, they radiated energy, as if she could reach inside them and touch someone. Blue/white bowed, bended, and churned. Watching their edges flow backward, they parted and a boy appeared. Not a boy, a young man.

He approached her with his thick, brown hair sitting at his ears, his well worn T-shirt molded to his body, and his jeans matched his scuffed boots. He never turned twenty and wouldn't. When she left Trinity for Butterfly Valley, he would have been in his teens and attending high school. She had been engaged to Rutger, working on her photography and closing in on thirty-two. Jordyn hadn't known him when he was alive, and didn't need to know him. She knew his essence and his wolf. He was her kith.

Zachery Oliver stood in front of her.

After Flint and his witches murdered him, they hollowed out his body, then wired his ribs to a collage with the rest of their victim's body parts. What they didn't add to Flint's *Advent Calendar* they served to her on a plate for her to eat. She spent days feeling his death and essence of his stolen life. They left his hollow body at Foxwood with a poem penned by Flint to taunt the pack with her death and prove they were superior. They could go anywhere they wanted, unseen. She didn't know what Zachery wanted, why he was there, or how he got there.

"What are you doing, Soothsayer?" he asked. His voice was smooth, giving away his youth.

He knew her. *"Nothing."*

His eyes blazed with her lie. *"Don't make me leave."*

This is not happening. *"I have to."*

"No, you don't. You're going to kill me a second time." His big, brown eyes bled to cinnamon of his wolf and held a glimmer of life.

"You're already dead," Jordyn pointed out. His remains sat in front of her while his death hung in the air, and the pain, he endured at their hands radiated. She couldn't stop her tears or hide the tremble in her voice.

"I'm alive here." Zachery smiled, exposing a set of perfect teeth and dimples, making him three years younger. *"You've given me this."*

A spark of happiness stabbed her, its infectious energy making her smile. No. No. *"Please stop."*

He looked at the flames and back at her. *"I miss my parents."* He paused, swallowed his sorrow, and covered his grief with a sly grin. *"I kissed Vette, she liked me. We were seeing each other. Her laugh was like music."*

Jordyn needed to end the conversation and get out of there. A jolt of excitement hit her with the force of a lightning bolt then faded. *"I understand, you had a life."*

"No. You. Don't." Zachery's deep voice thundered between them as his mood darkened and panic and fear reached out. Pain scarred his innocent features and tears slipped from his eyes to slide down his cheeks. *"They murdered me. He murdered you. I lost my family. You became a host."*

A host to death. "I know. *I know they took you,*" Jordyn breathed. She wiped tears from her cheeks while heartache ate at her bones and she watched Flint and his witches torture Zachery. *"I saw you. I'm sorry."*

"I became yours, Soothsayer. Let me stay. Let us stay," Zachery pleaded. *"Without you there will be nothing left of us. We'll be lost."* He looked at the flames again, his thoughts passing over his face, and they reached higher and higher, their colors changing to bright blue and deep garnet and twisted with his emotions. He cocked his head like he was listening to someone, then met her gaze. *"We have chosen you."*

They chose her. Jordyn considered herself a coward, she didn't deserve their respect. *"No one chose me."*

"The Collective chose you."

"If they did why are you here? Why not someone else from the Collective?" Jordyn asked. Good, questioning the dead. *Can I speak to a manager?*

"It's easy for you to recognize me. And I'm not afraid of the dragons," Zachery answered. Smiling, he winked.

"You can see them?" Jordyn inhaled, attempting to control the tears and her surprise. She couldn't believe this was happening. It was in her head. She waited too long and lost

Rutger and her mind. Prime was right. She had gone insane.

"Yes. We are part of you. They empower your magic and guard you. They're a testament to your strength. They would not have chosen a weaker being."

Zachery looked older and sounded older as if someone was speaking through him. Jordyn sensed the other like she sensed the Collective in the flames.

"When you accept us, we will merge and you'll become our soothsayer. Our lives will become the history of the pack. The Collective doesn't want to wane," Zachery explained.

"Jo." Rutger wiped tears from her cheeks, then grazed her bottom lip with his thumb. "Mea, what's happening? Wake up tell and me." Silence held the room, making Rutger's pleas louder and more desperate. Each time he asked her to wake up, everyone waited for her to open her eyes. She didn't. "Can Prime help her?"

"No. This is between Jordyn and the Collective," Lady Sloan answered with grief threading her voice. She left the chair and sat beside Rutger. Placing her hand on his shoulder, he turned to meet her gaze. "Try harder, we'll lose her."

The Collective, trailed by their emotions, floated in and out of the flames like kites, and around Jordyn as if they were watching and waiting for her to make a decision. She was waiting for her to make a decision. If she decided to keep the Collective, she would face Prime's challenges and again be in the crosshairs of whomever wanted to rid the world of the Cascade pack's soothsayer. And Rutger. If she gave the Collective up, she would end the threats and he wouldn't have to control his wolf. The danger of going

Bestial would no longer be a problem. There would be no more threats against them.

Jordyn hit a new level of selfishness.

"You have to hurry. Time is running out." Zachery watched her like she was prey and was considering fleeing.

A tremor shook her core and weakness slithered through her. It teased at fatigue making her feel like she needed to rest. It was false. She knew the feeling. *"You weren't going to warn me?"*

"I'm begging you to stay, isn't that enough. Either you want us or you don't."

"Zachery."

"Soothsayer." His voice echoed off the walls of flames at the same time his body waivered like heat off asphalt.

Their time had come to an end. *"I am sorry."* Jordyn held his cinnamon stare.

"Our time is up, her heartbeat is slowing," Lady Sloan whispered. "She's going to sleep."

"She didn't know," Rutger growled. He didn't need Lady Sloan announcing Jo's heart was failing when he heard it himself. Taking Jo's chilled body in his arms, he held her to his chest.

He hadn't been able to reach her, which told him she wanted him to let her go. There would be no more fighting when Jo's heart finally stopped and she had taken her last breath. Rutger breathed in her scent, memorizing it, knowing he was next. He'd had enough of the fights, the silence, and the attacks. Neither one of them was strong enough to deal with the pack, Prime, and the Collective. He didn't have the courage to be honest with her let alone fight Shadow Lord. Burying his face in her hair, he clutched Jo as her heart struggled to keep her alive.

CHAPTER TWENTY-TWO

"Son, listen to me. You waited for her and she came back. You've been holding onto her, and now you're going to let her go? Just like that?" Laurel was standing, her hands on her hips. "Rutger you're stronger than that."

Rutger lifted his face from Jo. "Maybe I'm not. You don't know what we've been dealing with." He wasn't angry, he wasn't sad, he was confused, helpless, and prayed numbness swallowed him.

"I don't, really? I survived the encampments. The death of our own. The persecution. The torture." Tears slipped down her cheeks as she held Rutger's dark eyes. She was going to lose him. She was going to lose them both.

Rutger met the baroness' gaze and saw the years and time in the encampments in their vexed depths. He never saw her pain, never saw her give up, and never heard her complain. What he said made him sound like a coward and proved his selfishness. "Baroness-"

"I'm your mother. Mom. I'm mom," Laurel insisted. "The baroness is a figure for the pack, not my family."

Zachery's eyes blazed cinnamon, red and brown twisting, his body solidified and he stood straight. When the flames died, shadowed figures appeared, their energy charging the void as their essences reached out to her.

Jordyn drew them in as she called her power and promised, *"You are mine. All of you."*

"Yes, Soothsayer." Zachery bowed his head. *"Always."*

The dragons roared, her wolf howled, her magic raged.
She was the soothsayer for the Cascade pack, she held their
essences, their pasts, and would protect them with her life.

"Wife," Healey mumbled as he shifted and sat straight.
"What are you going on about?"

Laurel twisted around. "Husband. Are you all right?"

"Yes. What is going on?" Healey rubbed his eyes, the
back of his neck, then ran his fingers through his hair. He
felt like he got hit by a truck.

One breath. Two. Three. Jordyn waited for the pain to
lessen before she risked moving. While she waited, she
searched for the divide and felt none. They were merged.
There weren't splinters damaging her magic, the Collective,
or her wolf. Death weaved through her, its veins stitched
into her magic and pulsing with her power. Just as it had
given her the ability to keep the dragons, it gave her the
ability to talk to Zachery. She had become a host and
wouldn't change things. Jordyn knew instinctively she
would need death's power in the future. Right then she
wasn't going to think about it. The merging mended her
from the inside out, making the combination of wolf, Collective, power, and magic one. The pressure from the
Collective was gone and replaced by their presence. A sure
and confident force.

Jordyn remained inside herself when Rutger's fear and
anguish sank into her. It called her, pleaded for her to rise.
He thought he was losing her. His wolf's essence traveled
the link between them and his howl of raw pain echoed.
She never wanted to feel Rutger's sorrow or hear his wolf's
pain. Turning into his solid chest, his strong arms held her,

and with her cheek against his shirt, she opened her eyes to meet Rutger's worried gaze. "Wolf."

"Mea," he whispered. His eyes rolled gold and he leaned in and kissed her.

"I'm never leaving," she whispered against his lips.

Jo's eyes blazed copper with her wolf while her warm lips lingered on his and he wanted to take her home. "What happened?" Rutger searched her face, taking in the peaceful look and the self-reliance in her eyes.

"I understand my purpose."

"Could you come to an understanding without almost dying?" Their lips touched and he felt her smile.

"I'll definitely work on it." Jordyn kissed him, then sat up. "I'm sorry."

"I'm glad you made it through whatever it was." Hugging her to him, he held her for several seconds then released her. They dodged a bullet.

Jordyn stood and straightened her clothing, then looked at Rutger as he sat cross-legged on the floor wearing all his gear. He stared at her with gold and mahogany eyes with his wolf's essence drifting around him. *I love you.* "Thank you."

Rutger stood, shifted his thigh holster, belt, and straightened his shirt. *It's because I love you, Jo.* "That's me, your knight in shining armor."

"Jordyn explain to me what is going on," Healey demanded.

She turned from Rutger to see the baron, baroness, Lady Sloan, and Lord Ervin all staring. At the entrance, Sousa and Sadie were flanked by Abigail and Troy who stood with a blank looks on their faces and their hands on their guns. She wished she could shoot her problems and blast them into nothing. Outside, she felt the presence of enforcers and soldiers, they had responded to the power and magic being used as she merged with the Collective. Jordyn felt them. Whatever happened in the future their lives were her responsibility, and if one of them died she would feel their death. She needed to protect her pack.

"My apologies, Baron," Jordyn began.

"We're all alive. Just explain what you did." Exhaustion tugged on his muscles and weakness threaded through his power. She nearly drained him.

"Lady Sloan told me to merge with the Collective. While I concentrated on them, I found I could remove them. I saw the chance to free myself of the them, the responsibility, and Prime. There was a chance for a normal life." Jordyn looked at Rutger. "This and whatever is coming is dangerous for the both of us. I thought I could stop you from living in fear of going Bestial or of me dying."

"Mea-" Rutger started.

"It was tempting. I didn't know I was killing myself," Jordyn said, interrupting him. Facing the baron, she continued. "I learned the process siphons your power until the Collective is completely removed. At the same time, I'm using my power and destroying my magic, and when there's nothing left, I die. With my death, the Collective is lost to the ether. No one would ever know them and the history of Cascade."

"What made you stop?" Lady Sloan asked. "You were close to destroying the nexus with Healey and purging the Collective."

I was close to dying. "The Collective used Zachery to talk to me. He explained they chose me and wanted to stay with me." She sounded like a crazy person.

"Zachery. Who is this person?" Lord Ervin asked, his eyes shadowed with his doubt.

"Zachery Oliver, is pack. The witches murdered him," Jordyn answered.

"You talked to this dead person?" Lady Sloan asked. Jordyn saw she wanted to doubt her. Just as everyone one of them wanted to doubt the power of Balaur. "By saying the Collective chose you, it means the entire pack chose you. You don't think it could have been your imagination? Maybe convincing yourself to accept it."

"I was hoping it was. Nothing would have been better than to have Zachery an image from my imagination and result of my need to accept being a soothsayer. He was real. He told me things I didn't know, like Vette. He saw her before the witches kidnapped him and he kissed her. He thinks her laugh sounds like music. I couldn't send him to the ether. They chose me and they gave themselves to me." Jordyn turned from Lady Sloan to Rutger. "I need to see Mr. and Mrs. Oliver. I have to talk to them."

"After what happened, do you think it's a good idea? They haven't been doing well," Rutger warned. He didn't need them attacking Jo and then have a domestic disturbance at Foxwood. "You were unconscious a second ago." Minutes ago, he was ready to let her go and follow her. He was prepared to end it all.

"And I need their files," Jordyn added, ignoring his warning.

"If you really talked to him and it wasn't your imagination, did he tell you if you purged the Collective you would have died?" Lady Sloan continued.

Jordyn searched through the emotions coming from Lady Sloan and found jealousy at the root. Not doubt. "No, he didn't. He watched as I drained my power and I watched him fade." The feeling of loss had her narrowing her glare on Lady Sloan.

"The merging is successful?"

"Yes."

"The Collective is intertwined with the death you harbor." Lady Sloan eyed her as if she was a direct descendant of evil. "I'm not going to call it dark magic. I believe you're need to protect your pack will keep you from succumbing to death's demands. I fear you'll find it tempting to use."

Dark magic. "It's there and will always be there. I won't use it if I don't have a reason." Jordyn needed to fully understand what she was dealing with, what the dragons meant, her past, and the full history of her Balaur. She couldn't trust her father or Lady Sloan for the information, no, Jordyn would have to ask someone else. Prime. He wouldn't be bias and maybe would tell her the truth instead of giving her his opinion.

"Be careful, vampires escape death's grip ... however not before trapping their souls. The life of their mortal selves sits inside of them the same way our wolf spirits sit inside us. It waits for true death to stop their hearts, then it rips their souls from them. They die twice. You can read minds, manipulate a person's actions, sense magic, and are able to speak to the dead," Lady Sloan stated.

"I can talk to the Collective, my kith and kin, because I'm their soothsayer. I can't talk to a corpse." Jordyn's heart raced, she could feel a victim's death, understood how it happened, and the void they left behind, long before Flint murdered her. He had nothing to do with her magic gifts. Dark magic. *Means nothing.* She already had a one-on-one with Prime and didn't want to get any closer to him. Asking him questions about her past was a bad idea. He would learn her weaknesses and her strengths. She was back to square one and having to find someone to help her.

Rutger stopped from physically shuddering when a chill raced down his spine. His mind zeroed in on Shadow Lord and his interest in Jo and her gifts. Lady Sloan voiced his fear and gave it weight. He met the heavy gaze of the baron, and the two of them stared at each other. They were going to have to tell Jo the truth.

"Yesterday your power radiated from you letting any magic-born in the area feel it. It's gone. You've concealed it inside you. The merging is final, the nexus with your alpha is true, and you wear the crest of Balaur from your ancestors. You are enshrined within the pack." Lady Sloan stood, and squeezing her hands, walked around the back of the chair and faced Jordyn. "If Prime wanted to permanently move you to Mountain Fortress to serve at court, he can't. You are bound to the pack."

Was she saved? "I have that going for me," Jordyn mumbled. No, she didn't think putting check marks in the boxes was going to keep Prime from doing whatever he was planning. She turned her attention to Rutger. "I need to talk to the Olivers."

"Jo, are you positive?" Rutger held her upper arms while his lies drifted through his thoughts.

The darkness in his eyes caught her attention. "Yes. Please bring them here," Jordyn insisted. If she hadn't been staring at him, she would have missed the shadow passing over his features. Was he hiding something? Yes, his pain from watching her almost die. Jordyn forgot about it and made a list of things she needed to do. Before she started the quest to find out what was happening to her, she had to take care of her pack. The Olivers deserved closure.

Sensing the urgency, Rutger took his cell phone from the side pocket of his pants and called the office. "Mandy, I need to talk to Ansel." Silence stretched out between them when Ansel answered the phone. "Take backup, go to the Olivers, detain them, and bring them to Foxwood. We'll be waiting in the formal greeting room. Ansel, by any means necessary." Rutger ended the call and replaced his cell. "I hope you know what you're doing."

"They're here," Rutger reported. He stood at the window, his back to Jo, and was watching the soldiers and enforcers.

The gray SUV baring Cascade's crest on its side slowed and stopped in the front of the house. With concise movements Ansel exited from the driver's side at the same time Luke withdrew from the passenger side. Going to the back passenger door, Luke opened it, and Mrs. Oliver stepped out of the vehicle. Her hair was up in a loose bun, she wore loose, pink lounge pants, slippers that were once white, and a gray sweatshirt. It was after noon and she hadn't showered. She stared at Luke like she was going to ask him a question, then looked at the house with haunted eyes. Mr. Oliver, mumbling and making jerking motions with his hands, walked around the back and joined Mrs. Oliver. He wasn't much better. His hair was uncombed, his flannel shirt hung on thin shoulders, his jeans were stained, and his boots wore scuffs and mud.

"They have had a hard time," Rutger warned, his low voice expressing his regret.

"I know." Jordyn finished reading the Olivers' incident reports and closed the file. "Hopefully this works."

"What are you going to do?" Healey asked.

"I'm not telling you. You can't interrupt me. You have to let me do this," Jordyn insisted.

"Just promise me, I won't find myself unconscious, drained of strength, and having been carried to another room." Healey had no idea what she was going to do, but if it meant she was going to fully accept her place then it had to be done.

Jordyn held the baron's mahogany eyes, the reds deepening the color. "I promise."

"Mr. and Mrs. Oliver," Sousa announced.

The couple entered the room with hesitation weaving between them. Their eyes darted over the area and then over the three of them.

"Welcome," Healey greeted. "Please make yourself comfortable and have a seat." He waved his hand toward the couch. "Coffee?"

"No, thank you. What is this about?" Mr. Oliver demanded. "We were threatened."

"We're sorry, Baron," Mrs. Oliver mumbled.

"It's all right," Healey assured as he looked at Jordyn.

"Mr. and Mrs. Oliver, my name is-"

"We know you," Mrs. Oliver interrupted. "What do you want?"

"To help you." Their anger seethed from them, entangled in their grief, and finding its target, it slid into her flesh as if they were stabbing her.

"Take us home," Mr. Oliver demanded.

"You c-can't h-help anyone," Mrs. Oliver stammered, her anger making her words shaky.

Jordyn was going to have to change tactics. She took the file and spread the papers out on the table. "I'm sorry, is being here, in your alpha's beautiful home, stopping you from doing something? Let me see, drinking all day? Locking yourself in your bathroom and threatening to kill yourself? Wandering around the woods crying? Screaming obscenities at your neighbors? Fighting the enforcers when they're trying save you from dealing with human law enforcement? Maybe feeling sorry for yourself while life passes you by? Maybe you would like to go home to cause a scene … I mean you are behind at this point. Is it a challenge now, how many incident reports can you have filed on you?" Jordyn pointed at the reports. "I think you've got time to listen to me."

"How dare you," Mr. Oliver growled as he took a step forward.

Sousa, Abigail, Luke, and Ansel all took a step toward them. Rutger held his hand up stopping them.

"Do you think your guards scare me?" Mr. Oliver sneered.

"I don't care if they scare you. You should be scared of me. Now go to the couch and sit down," Jordyn ordered. She raised her power, held her wolf, and infused a touch of death in its feel. Since she possessed it, she would use it. Her magic weaved in the room, its cold claw holding the Olivers, and promised them pain. She didn't have to raise a hand to hurt them.

Mr. Oliver looked behind him at the enforcers and sentinels, then at Rutger and the baron. He walked to the couch, refusing to sit. "You have no right to say anything to us. You've spent the last months holed up in your house. How are you any different?"

Jordyn waved Mrs. Oliver, who stood frozen, to the couch and waited for them to sit. "Sit down, it's not a request." She waited, and when they grudgingly followed her order and sat, she continued. "I'm not. I'm just as pathetic."

Jordyn sat down, wanting her regret in her voice and needing them to understand she was being sincere.

"You're the reason our son is dead," Mr. Oliver accused.

"Mr. Oliver-" Rutger started.

"I take responsibility," Jordyn spoke over Rutger. "I've made my peace with him."

"How convenient," Mr. Oliver seethed. "It was hard for us to have a child, and when we did, he's murdered. You have no idea what it feels like to lose a child."

"You're right, I don't."

"Why are we here?" Mrs. Oliver asked. Her anger drained from her, embarrassment took its place, and heating her cheeks, she looked at the reports and shifted her eyes down to stare at the carpet.

"Mrs. Oliver, look at me, please." A curl of brown hair hung loose as she raised her head and sad, pale brown eyes focused on Jordyn. "Thank you. I had them bring you here because I'm going to give you a present."

"I can't believe this," Mr. Oliver scoffed, crossing his arms over his chest.

At least Mrs. Oliver was listening. "Before I give you this gift, you have to promise to go to Celestial and join their GriefCare group. You can also talk to Dr. Carrion, who will help you with your grief, privately without the group environment. You'll get the help you need to move forward."

"No." Mr. Oliver glared at her.

"You will promise and you will get your shit together. If you don't, I will take it back. If you force me to take it back, I will make you regret it and it will be painful. Like cutting a limb from your body. Do you understand?"

They exchanged looks, looked at the baron, who stood like an unmoving sentinel, and when he didn't say anything, they met her gaze. "What is it?" Mrs. Oliver asked.

"I'm not telling you what it is." They both stared at her. All right. "You have to promise."

"I have nothing else," Mrs. Oliver quickly replied.

"Promise."

"I promise." She looked at her husband. "We have nothing to lose."

"Promise," Mr. Oliver growled.

"Say, *I* promise," Jordyn ordered.

"*I* promise."

"Everyone present serves as a witness. If you don't go to Celestial and seek counseling you will have broken the promise. If the enforcers respond to a call to your house, you will have broken the promise. When I find out the promise has been broken, the enforcers will apprehend you and bring you here. I will take back my present and make sure you leave in pain. By that I mean, you will cry, wail, and live with your regrets until you're finally put out of your misery. Do you understand?"

They looked at other as Jordyn's threat filtered through their despair. "Yes," they replied together.

"Excellent. Please close your eyes," Jordyn instructed.

They gave each other a shielded gaze, their fear and hesitation darkening their eyes, then faced Jordyn and closed them. She waited several seconds, staring at them, waiting to see if they would disobey. They didn't, and she called her wolf. She felt her eyes change from dark cocoa to copper and then onyx. Her magic flowed through her, and she beckoned the Collective. Reaching into the mass, she searched for Zachery and his emotions. When she found him, his calm presence touched her as if he was sitting beside her.

Zachery's essence opened itself to her, allowing her to explore his emotions, and when she found what she needed Jordyn captured part of him. She held it in her hand, greedy and not wanting to lose it, not wanting to lose a piece of Zachery. A part of her Collective. Zachery's presence brushed her, leaving a trial of warmth. Jordyn thanked him, and Zachery weaved back into the mass and disappeared to leave her alone.

She inhaled, attempting to recover from the loss, increased her power, and focusing it an invisible hand pulled the emotion from her. It hung between her and the Olivers, its energy glittering in the room as if lit up from within. A slice of their son's life. The absence created an ache within her, its pain spreading, and she fought the instinct to take it back.

Give them peace.

"I can smell him. I can feel him," Mrs. Oliver whispered and opened her eyes.

"Me too. I can," Mr. Oliver mumbled. He opened bloodshot eyes that were wet with tears.

"Look at me." Jordyn's heart ached and her chest felt tight as she held their gazes. "If you break your promise, I'll take him back. I will make the both of you nothing more than empty shells."

"I understand. I promise. How did you do that?" Mr. Oliver asked. Red streaked his eyes, his chest heaved, and he twisted his hands.

"I'm your soothsayer and you are my kith," Jordyn responded.

"Thank you." Mrs. Oliver wiped tears from her cheeks with the sleeve of her sweatshirt.

Needing to end the meeting and get them out of the house, Jordyn stood. "The enforcers will take you home. I hope to see you both at the moon run."

"You will. We've heard Prime will be there. I want you to know, you have our confidence," Mr. Oliver vowed. He flattened his palm over his heart.

"It means a lot, thank you. Take care of yourselves," Jordyn replied. By giving her their confidence, they pledged their loyalty to her. She watched them follow Ansel and Luke out of the greeting room and down the hall.

Rutger walked over to Jo, placed his hands on her shoulders, bent down to her ear, and whispered, "You gave them their son."

She wished she could have given them their son. Inhaling to recover from the loss, Jordyn gathered herself. "He loved his family. I gave them that emotion. A little piece of him." Walking to the window, she watched them get into the SUV, and felt the missing slice of Zachery like she had cut herself and left the open wound bleeding and unhealed. Whether or not it was worth it remained to be seen. Either way, she would have to get used to the feeling. Her mind drifted to the moon run, Prime, and what she was going to have to survive. Was she going to have to fight? If so, who? Was she going to have to read his mind? Would his Numina be there? There were to many questions without answers.

"The sacrifice you've made, might be a temporary fix. The Olivers' actions have been consistent. There's a good chance they will continue to let their grief rule over them. If they do, and they break their promises, are you prepared to follow through with the punishment?" Healey asked. He stood across from Jordyn, his brunt gold eyes gauging her, their weight landing on her.

"Yes, Baron. If they break their promises, I will take back what is mine," Jordyn answered. She didn't recognize her own voice, the possession it held, and the menace behind it. Part of her was scared of what it meant while another part embraced the strength.

"You have become the soothsayer the pack needs. At the moon run, the pack will give you their confidence as you stand in front of Prime." Healey couldn't keep the respect he had for her out of his voice. "Then the klatch will give you their confidence and you will serve the Cascade territory."

If she failed there was a chance the pack wouldn't give her their confidence. She would be taken to Mountain Fortress, stripped of her territory, and Rutger would be caged. "Thank you, Baron."

"I'm not sure if you have concluded your business, but there is something we need to discuss," Laurel said as she entered the room. "It's important."

CHAPTER TWENTY-THREE

Concluded business. Jordyn did finish business. The baron allowed her talk freely, no one second guessed her, no one interrupted or tried to stop her. He let her have control. When her job and the gallery had been taken from her, it felt as if her purpose had been ripped from her. She had nothing. This changed things. Jordyn's head swam with the idea she had a reason for getting up in the morning.

"I suggest we talk in your office," Laurel advised.

"All of us?" Healey asked.

"All of us," Laurel replied. Behind her Sloan and Ervin stood at the entrance of the room.

Healey walked out and stopped in the hall. "I want you and Abigail outside of the office, and I want Sadie and Troy at the front door."

"Yes, sir," Sousa replied. He opened the door and re-layed the instructions to Troy and Sadie.

Healey waited for Sousa and Abigail, then started toward his office. Behind him Laurel, Rutger, Jordyn, Sloan, and Ervin followed in silence.

Jordyn's attention was on the itching feeling she was missing a part of herself and the instinct to fix it, and the moon run. She took even breaths-in, out, in, out-and slowly her heart hurt less and the ache from unshed tears eased. As they walked, she assumed the meeting was about Gavin and she had exposed a family secret. It had been a moment between husband and wife, father and mother, and a secret between baron and baroness. It was a weakness for the alpha.

Healey opened the door and held it as everyone entered. Sousa and Abigail took their places on either side as Healey closed the door behind him. Rutger crossed the room and remained standing, his hand on the butt of his gun, his shoulders square, his strength wrapped around him. Jordyn took the seat closest to Rutger, while Lady Sloan and Lord Ervin sat together and baroness sat beside Jordyn. Healey took his seat behind his desk, placed his elbows on the top, and met their gazes. Books with cracked covers, broken spines, smelling of dust and age took up the right side while papers with his hard handwriting were spread out on the left.

"What is this about?" Healey asked. His eyes drifted over them, paused on Jordyn, then stopped at his wife.

"Jordyn-" Laurel started.

Jordyn wanted to roll her eyes and scream until her throat burned.

"Wait," Rutger interrupted. "I can't believe after what happened there's more."

"I know what this is about and it is serious." Jordyn turned in her seat and looked up to see Rutger. "The baron has to know."

"If you're all right with it." Rutger wasn't all right with it. He didn't know what *it* was.

"Sloan needed to confirm the nexus between you and Jordyn was true. She asked Jordyn to tell her something from your past that effected both of us." Laurel paused, not believing they were having this discussion. They had kept it a secret for thirty years and forgot about it. It was irrelevant at this point.

"Are you going to tell me what it is?" Healey asked. His wife hesitated, her worry sat in her usually soft eyes, and she wore tension as if it was a heavy coat. "Laurel."

"Gavin. She explained Gavin's birth and first shift."

While the baroness recited word for word what Jordyn said, she held the baron's gaze. It was his alpha glare meant to make you confess even if you didn't do anything wrong. There was anger in his dark eyes and the muscles in jaw strained when he clenched his teeth. The baron's anger was palpable as it twisted around him. *I'm in trouble.*

"Why?" Healey asked.

"Why, she explained that specific memory? Or why did I ask her for proof of the nexus?" Lady Sloan asked in return, taking a moment of attention from Jordyn.

"Frist, why did you need proof? And second, why that specific memory," Healey demanded. He didn't take his eyes off Jordyn.

"For Jordyn to hold the Collective without them destroying her, she needs a true nexus with her alpha. Which she proved. The memory obviously holds high emotion for the both of you and projected itself over the others. She didn't go through your lifetime and chose one, in her state she couldn't have," Lady Sloan explained. "This is what a soothsayer is and the force inside of her. An advisor would have warned you, but you didn't think you needed help."

"You can't seriously be mad at Jo," Rutger stated. He approached the desk while a gold sheen colored his eyes.

"I'm not angry with Jordyn, son, settle down. I am wondering what Lady Sloan will do with the information," Healey replied. He tore his stare from Jordyn and placed its weight on Sloan.

"As I explained to Laurel and Jordyn, the information serves as proof, nothing more. I am bound by the canons of the Highguard and the Diablo pack, assuring what is said to me is privileged information. Also, I'm not here in a professional compacity. Jordyn is my daughter, and as such, I'm here to make sure she isn't harmed. If I were here as a representative with the Highguard, I would have warned you what type of information, sensitive, could be revealed," Lady Sloan clarified.

"I wanted to talk about this for two reasons," Laurel started. "The first being you needed to know what had been said. Personally, I don't see why it matters anymore. The second is Jordyn's safety. She needs sentinels. The past holds many secrets and there are those who will feel threatened."

Jordyn stood. "No. No sentinels. I already live in a prison and don't need guards added. There are a dozen security measures to keep people out and ready to tell an office full of enforcers who is at my house, if they're lucky enough to make it inside," she protested. Her mind went over every alarm, every sensor, and the spot lights on the house as she tried to create her argument against the sentinels. She stalled when she remembered the UV lights, and it touched on the conversation she had with Lady Sloan. Vampires and the price of immortality is living with their souls trapped inside of them and dying twice. A chill slid down her spine.

"Unless you leave the door open," Rutger said, teasing her.

"You're a funny man." Jordyn met his gaze and forgot about the UV lights when the humor glittering in his mahogany eyes forced a smile from her. Shaking her head, Jordyn knew it was losing battle to argue with the baron and baroness. She had the feeling Rutger had jump ship and joined them.

"The baron and baroness have a valid point, about the sentinels. You don't have to have real information, the threat alone will scare people," Rutger added. "Your safety will be compromised."

Yep, the Director of Enforcers jumped to their side. By the smug expression on his face he knew he was going to get his way. "If I don't say anything to anyone, no one will know," Jordyn tried. *I'm losing.*

"If the Olivers were able to keep what you did a secret, their change in behavior will be testament something happened. Word will spread, and every time someone retells it, they'll embellish the story. Your argument isn't good enough, Jordyn, not when your life is at risk. Tomorrow you will pick two soldiers and they will become your sentinels. After that, they will accompany you. Everywhere. I will advise Torin," Healey confirmed.

Jordyn-0.

Them-1.

"I don't want sentinels," Jordyn mumbled. Losing the fight, she sat down in defeat.

"Daughter, as the soothsayer for the pack you should have sentinels. It reflects your importance, authority, and status in the pack," Lady Sloan added.

"Well, thanks, Mom." Jordyn gave her a sideways glance, met eyes matching her own, wondered how she never noticed it, and looked back at the baron. "Who from the soldiers would want to guard me? They won't like babysitting the soothsayer. Especially when some of them saw what Prime did. And today."

Healey raised his eyebrows over Jordyn's sarcastic response and dismissal of Sloan. "It's no different than my security. It's a job they're supposed to do. If it makes you feel better, I'll have Torin *ask* if there is anyone who would like to volunteer to babysit the soothsayer." Healey gave Jordyn a soft smile.

"Thank you, Baron."

"Now, about the memory. I trust you Jordyn. If I didn't, I wouldn't risk the safety of the pack by making you their soothsayer. I don't fear the knowledge you have. However, remembering the pain of nearly losing a son caught me off guard. I agree with Laurel, it has no merit today. Gavin isn't the weak child he once was, but I understand he'll never be as strong as Rutger or Tanner, there aren't many that are. I don't see him as a weakness in the pack just as I don't see the weakness in others as threats. I had to fight and kill to become alpha, and killed again to remain alpha. I had to use force, negotiation skills, and had to be cunning to prove I was strong enough to become Baron of the Cascade territory. At the time, having a frail son was a reflection of my own strength and ability. No more."

"Noted, Healey, and I agree. As I explained, I can't share the information," Lady Sloan assured. "I didn't become soothsayer for the Diablo pack and One of the Twelve of the Highguard by using my ability to expose people and betray them. I hope this show of trust eases your worry."

"It does, Sloan, and I appreciate your consideration," Healey replied.

"And I hope Jordyn trusts me." Lady Sloan met Jordyn's narrowed gaze.

"I trust you won't betray my pack," Jordyn answered.

"I'll accept that for now," Lady Sloan responded.

She stared at Jordyn, letting her emotions of almost losing her and facing the baron sit in her eyes. Jordyn didn't know what to say.

"Then the meeting is over. Rutger you were going to talk to Ansel about security and the moon run?" Healey asked.

"Yes, sir." Rutger placed his hand on Jo's shoulder and squeezed.

Jordyn stood, her focus on getting away from Lady Sloan, Lord Ervin, and the baron and baroness to have a moment of peace. A quiet minute to mourn the loss of Zachery and to internally accept she was the pack's soothsayer. The moon run was ahead of her and she needed to talk to Rutger.

"Jordyn, please stay. I need to talk to you," Healey requested.

That's sad. "Sir." She grudgingly sat down. Looking up at Rutger, she gave him 'help me' eyes.

"I'll be at the office. When you're finished here, come get me." Rutger bent down and kissed her. "Come get me."

"I will." Jordyn gave him a slight smile, wishing she could leave with him, and watched his back until he turned to the hall.

"Coffee and something to eat is in order." Laurel followed Sloan and Ervin out of the office, closing the door behind her.

When the door clicked, signifying it was closed, Healey stood, then walked around his desk to lean against its edge. "I understand this is overwhelming and you would like nothing more than to escape. I wanted to tell you how pleased I am to see you haven't become withdrawn from us and Rutger."

She ignored Rutger all morning. "I keep telling myself this is my life and I have to accept it," Jordyn replied.

"It will take time." Healey crossed his arms over his chest and let several seconds pass between them. "I know facing the Olivers couldn't have been easy. You expressed compassion for them and showed them your strength. They don't see the woman, Jordyn, they see you as their soothsayer."

"They deserved some sort of relief from their grief." Strength. She felt like a fraud. And their soothsayer. She wanted to be Jordyn. Plain Jordyn.

"You can help people who want to help themselves. Understand while you helped the Olivers, you can't give away pieces of yourself. The pain is in your eyes and I can sense you're hurt."

"I won't do it again. I can't," Jordyn replied.

"To change the subject, how is your relationship with Sloan?" Healey asked.

"My opinion of Mia is based on a teen's point of view and the way she treated me when I came back. It's not right or wrong but she raised me. I'm not going to disregard Lady Sloan as my mother, but I'm not going to start calling her mom any time soon," Jordyn answered honestly. "I appreciate her help and will continue to learn from her."

"It's a start, and I'm glad you decided to continue to work with her. I don't want you to hold yourself back. Explore your powers and what you can do with them. Prime will expect you to be the same as you were yesterday. Scared. Driven by emotion. He won't expect you to have grown stronger." Healey held a hand up, stopping Jordyn from interrupting him. "He made you an emotional mess when he attacked you, and then backed you into a corner when he threatened Rutger. You were easily manipulated and you reacted exactly how he knew you would," Healey stated as he pushed away from the desk to sit in the chair beside Jordyn. "It didn't take courage to challenge him when you didn't understand the repercussions. It is going to take courage to face his Numina, his plans for the challenge, and then the pack and the klatch."

"Putting the Collective in place has taken the pressure off. I'll be able to concentrate on Prime." She looked at her hands as she twisted her fingers, turning her skin pale from the pressure. Jordyn exposed her ability to absorb another's power when she took from Prime. She proved she could heal herself without shifting. She proved she could control his Numina's minds. She proved she could sense him and his Numina from a distance. She handed him the answers to every question he had. *Manipulated.* Prime knew her weaknesses.

"Concentrating won't give you the courage. You need to have confidence in your magic."

"He has the power and the authority to kill me. Why would he orchestrate the challenge when he all he has to do is create doubt and make a fool out me in front of the pack, klatch, and the other factions? They will see I'm weak and not worthy of the trouble I've brought them. They'll vote a confidence motion. Shame will be brought to my family, your family, and now Lady Sloan, sending waves of discord all the way to the Highguard. Because the pack doesn't want to believe in the old ways, they could vote a confidence motion toward you. The Kanin family would be removed from the Cascade pack and a Highguard puppet would replace you."

If she was right, would the elders of the pack fight for the baron and his family when they were responsible for abolishing the encampments, building Trinity, and creating the life every one of them enjoyed? Jordyn didn't know. She didn't know the extent of the divide because she had been hiding from the world and neglecting her responsibilities. She did know she was going to be held responsible if they lost the baron and Trinity.

"I expected an argument from you, maybe defending yourself, not a list of political repercussions. I like you've taken myself, the pack, and your family's future into consideration. It shows you have put them first and yourself second and are a leader. While what you said is true, I doubt it's Prime's motive. He wants to see you and your power. He understands and sees the same thing I did when you were a child. There's a power source inside of you, fueling your magic, and I'm not talking about being a soothsayer. You heard Sloan, you wear the crest of the Balaur, proof of your ancestor's Pureblood linage. Your power has gotten stronger despite you. You have no idea what you're capable of or if it means it's possible for the entire pack to benefit from it. Rutger said you spoke to him while you were both in wolf form. I've read tales about the ancients being able to speak to one another. The challenge is a must. And you *must* win."

Jordyn took in the books, papers, scrolls, and the combined ages of them all. Information hundreds if not thousands of years old sat in front of her. It all became clear. As if someone created a montage from the last couple of months and played it for her. Jordyn saw herself at the tree and talking to the dragons, walking into the house and shifting, healing herself, talking to Rutger in wolf form, listening to the chaos in Louis' head. There she was telling the baron what he was thinking.

"You're going to use me as an experiment?" Jordyn asked. "You want me to face Prime and risk losing to find out if I'm the key to the myths in those books? If being a scion of ancients makes me different. You want the pack to be more powerful. You want the myths to be true."

"Yes." Healey's eyes rolled gold as if his wolf had risen with the hope the myths were true. "For hundreds of years the magic-born have assimilated into the human's ways. We humanized ourselves, giving up our traditions, beliefs, and criminalizing our ancestors because of their way of life. We don't use magic out of fear of being ostracized, tortured by White 47, shackled with Cobalt, or thrown into silver-lined prisons. And those who don't fit into human society's perimeters remain with the Cloaked."

The baron's stern glare showed her his passion at the same time it told her their talk was over and his order was final. Jordyn had her job. Make his beloved myths real. She was going to win the challenge and then spend her time trying to resurrect the past, break the barriers holding them back, open the doors to the Cloaked, and somewhere along the way she would call the ancestors living inside of her and use them.

"What about Rutger? You threaten him with going Bestial and imprisoning him. There are myths about shapeshifters having two forms, Lady Sloan touched the subject as well. The animal and the beast." It was her turn to glare at the baron with copper swirling in her eyes.

"I have them." He pointed to the stack of books. "The early writings tell of both forms and their appearance. The later writings threaten death when the beast has taken over. I believe it is the beginning of our humanization. With your help, there's a chance he won't lose himself to the beast. He will survive. It's a risk I'm willing to take to make us stronger," Healey replied. "Rutger is powerful enough if it happens, he will prove his strength and will be the first to experience both forms. No one, the Highguard or Prime, can dispute the power of the Cascade pack. The threat of a confidence motion will be moot."

Fucking, no way. "How are you going to do this?" She didn't want to know.

"I'll pull his wolf from him. He is an alpha and his wolf will react as if I challenged him. He will fight it and his wolf will fight him," Healey explained.

"You want me to watch him lose himself and then control his beast." Jordyn would have his life in her hands. If he went Bestial and there was no turning him back, she would lose him to a cage. How long would the baron give her to try to save him? A day? A week? When word spread her mate and Second to the Alpha had gone Bestial the Highguard would question the baron. It would be her failure. She was back to losing the pack's confidence and the Highguard's. No pressure. "I won't risk his life."

"I'm not saying it's going to happen today or tomorrow, but it will happen. It isn't up to you, Jordyn." Healey walked back to his chair. "I think we're done here."

Jordyn couldn't move from the shock of learning the baron was going to make Rutger a sacrifice. Sacrifice them both. She stared at the stack of books like they planned the betrayal and trapped her. Several seconds ticked across her thoughts when she placed her hands on the arm rests of the chair and stood. Her knees felt weak and exhaustion pulled on her muscles. She didn't need this. He could have waited until after the challenge to tell her his crazy plan.

"Jordyn, I think it's imperative we keep this between us. Like I said, it's not going to happen today." His shoulders pulled his button-up shirt tight, making the collar open and exposing the black points of his tattoo. Alpha. Pureblood. Baron. "Do you understand?"

No. No, I don't. "Yes, sir." Jordyn stood on weak legs and giving the baron one last glare, turned and left the office. He put a secret between them. Like a poison it was going to course in her veins and slowly kill her until the day Rutger faced his beast. She needed to tell Rutger she loved him, and they needed to make their relationship stronger before their lives went straight to hell.

Rutger sat at his desk, his elbows on the top, his mind replaying Jo's near death, and the conversation with the baron. No one talked about Gavin's weakness because it didn't matter, and hadn't for years. They would be there for him as they would be there for anyone in the pack and the klatch. Gavin didn't feel the same way and would compare himself to Tanner or others, saying he wasn't strong enough to hold a position in the pack. Gavin's weakness made him resentful, spiteful, and he carried a chip on his shoulder the size of California. The weight of it added to his fury.

When Rutger withdrew his birthright as Second to the Alpha and took the position as Director of Enforcers, Gavin cursed at him for a good hour. He accused Rutger of being able to hold any position he wanted and by giving up he became a coward. He raged on about the baron forcing Rutger to accept his place as Second and push Gavin out. Rutger, hurt and wounded by Jo's absence, argued he didn't care, he wanted space and time away from the baron. It seemed pointless now that Rutger held Second, continued as the director, and made One-Flesh with the soothsayer of the pack. Somewhere their lives, Rutger and Jo's, were fading under titles and challenges. Thankfully Gavin was with Tanner and his wife, Bailey, the three of them acting as ambassadors for the pack. It was up to them to negotiate contracts with the extended factions to secure their confidences. He wasn't around to relive the pain from his childhood.

"Rutger, are you listening?" Ansel asked for the tenth time.

"Yes." He easily ignored the reports, files, and messages waiting for him to read. One day. He was out of the office for one day. "Did you run a full diagnostic check on the equipment?"

"Affirmative. I've checked and rechecked the license plate reader, palm vein scanner, cameras, the gate, the computers, every sensor, and they are all functioning properly," Ansel explained. "I had the techs check the monitors, the face recognition software, the list goes on. There's nothing. I have no idea how Prime drove through the gates and made it to the house without us knowing."

"And Lord Ervin and Lady Sloan. Prime is magic, he could have disrupted the equipment." It was possible. Maybe. "If he created a charge, it would be enough to knock them out."

"If there was a disruption there would have been a disconnect, and if there was a disconnect there would have been an alarm. The entire enforcer's office would have been blaring," Ansel argued with frustration. "You would have been able to hear it at your house."

Rutger mumbled a response, took a file, opened it, skimmed over the report, not noticing names or events. He gave up, and closing it set it back on the pile. "He is power-ful and magic."

"You said that. Still, there should have been an alarm." Ansel watched him shuffle papers and pick up a pen. "There's the off-chance moonbeams blasted through the wiring and fried the system."

"Could be. Did you check the system?" Rutger asked absently.

"You aren't listening."

"I am. You were explaining something about the sys-tem," Rutger said in defense.

"I said ... Never mind. What's on your mind?"

"These reports."

"You're lying. Remember, I'm a werewolf, the captain of the enforcers, and your only friend."

Rutger inhaled and exhaled like he could expel his stress. "Where do I start. This morning Jo tried to purge the Collective." Rutger tossed his pen to the desk and sat back. He had no idea what the reports were reporting.

"And?"

"She almost died."

"She needs to stop doing that." Sitting back, Ansel watched stress plant itself on Rutger's face. What he was witnessing solidified his reasons for not wanting a fated mate.

"No shit. It's over, she has the Collective and is stronger than before. You saw what happened when she faced the Olivers." He wanted to see Jo walk through his door so they could go home.

"Stronger. I can't believe it's possible. I'm not surprised Prime is interested in her. I thought watching her shift in mid-stride was impressive, but watching her heal without shifting was next level. And everyone saw her. She is becoming a thing. People are going to start talking."

Dr. Hyde utilized a combination of alternative and conventional medical treatments. Werewolves healed when they shapeshifted, and if they were unable to shift, they healed but it was slower. If they couldn't shift, Dr. Hyde would give them something that would speed up the process. Jordyn hadn't healed a flesh wound... no, in minutes she healed a hole through her back and chest. The blood loss alone should have made her too weak to heal.

Rutger paused, not knowing if he should share his thoughts of the baron's beliefs. *It's Ansel,* he told himself, and he had to tell someone because he was going to lose his mind. What if Bestial wasn't a threat, but a second form, like Lady Sloan lead on? Trying to further convince himself it was all right to tell Ansel, Rutger assured himself they had worked through the lies associated with the Unseelie court case, they had been friends for years and he trusted Ansel with his life.

"What if the baron isn't delusional by sending us to the dark ages but bringing the old ways *back* to us. All those stories about shapeshifter's abilities. Healing. Talking to one another in wolf form. What if they're true? What if we lost the ability because we conformed?"

Ansel thought the same thing as Rutger but wasn't going to say it out loud and give it life. There were going to be believers and non-believers. "We are all magic. I know this. It didn't mean I believed soothsayers were real, and here in Trinity, and Jordyn. Then to have fated mates, I thought it was impossible. My mind has been changed because I witnessed it. I know where you're going with this. Does it mean you aren't at risk for going Bestial? I don't know. You could try shifting into a second form and possibly lose your human self. If you failed, you would be spending the rest of your life, which wouldn't be long, in a silver cage in our dungeon," Ansel warned. The baron would never risk the Second to the Alpha and his son's life. Ansel's thoughts went to Dr. Hyde, his connection to her, and their conversation about Rutger and Jordyn and fated mates. Would there be others? Was there a second form? "Are you willing to risk your life?"

"No. When the wolf turns into the beast its power becomes an addiction. I want it. I want to lose control. There is a fight for dominance between man and animal. It's maddening." Damn, he wished it were true. Rutger could feel his wolf and the power it promised. There was nothing good from thinking about a second form.

"Did you fear losing control last night?" Ansel asked. The baron had been prepared to tranquilize him.

"Yes and no. If Jo had been seriously hurt and was dying, I would have lost it, but she wasn't. I can't believe I said that. I was scared. The thing made a hole in her chest," Rutger replied. Her blood made a puddle on the floor.

"How did you know she wasn't going to die?" Ansel suspected Jordyn told him through their bond. His mind went to Dr. Hyde. If he told her the truth, would they share a union no one else had? And pain. No one needed that.

"After I calmed down, I kept my senses on her heartbeat and heard it strengthening. She used our link to assure me," Rutger answered. He picked the pen up, looked at the stack of reports, and dropped it. Where the hell was Jo?

"How about you leave the reports. There's nothing there. No one wants to meet with the baron, no one has disputes, and the pack and klatch are behaving. We took the Olivers home and they haven't made a peep. All that was for me to tell you to go rescue your mate from the house and go home. We'll go over security for the moon run later." Ansel stood. "I'll have teams taking shifts throughout the day and night until Prime leaves. If we can't stop Prime with the security system, then we'll use manpower. If you need one of us, Mandy and Quinn will be monitoring communications."

"Good. The baron is supposed to talk to Torin about having two soldiers serve as Jo's sentinels. I want their backgrounds files. All of them," Rutger ordered. "Have them sent to my house. I'll look over them tonight. Jo is going to have to choose tomorrow."

"Understood. I'll send Aydian and he'll stay at your place," Ansel advised.

"Affirmative." Rutger stood, pushed his chair back, and walked around his desk when the phone rang. Half turning to look at it, he debated not answering. Someone called his office line, not reception or communications. Rutger reached over and grabbed the handset. "Director Kanin."

Ansel recognized the deep voice and the way every word sounded like it was being pushed through gravel. Torin, the head of the soldiers.

Rutger hung up the phone and faced Ansel. "I don't need the background files. Tracy and Charles have requested to serve as Jo's sentinels. We'll have a meeting tomorrow morning."

"Interesting. I understand Charles, he was there at Butte Springs and has an understanding of her. Tracy, I'm not sure about," Ansel said, making his doubt known.

"Me neither. We'll find out tomorrow." Rutger checked his desk, hated seeing it looking like he had abandoned his work, and turned to the door.

"Director, there's someone on the property," Mandy reported over the intercom.

Rutger headed out of the office and to the communications room. "Did you get them on video?"

"Affirmative. But you're not going to like it," Mandy replied.

The gate appeared on the screen … nothing, then a blur leaped over it and disappeared.

"What the hell is it?" Ansel asked.

"I don't know," Mandy answered.

"Activate the alarm," Rutger ordered. A second later, the wail of the alarm blared over Foxwood.

"Did the cameras get anything?" Ansel asked.

Mandy hit a button. The blur raced down the drive toward the house. "I can slow the footage and check it."

Rutger didn't care. "Jo." He growled and ran out of the communications room and down the hall.

CHAPTER TWENTY-FOUR

Jordyn stalled in the hall, leaned against the wall, and tried processing what the baron was going to make them do. At the double doors, Sousa and Abigail watched her like she was either an explosion waiting to kill everyone or a lost dog. She felt like a lost dog. The sentinels were watching her, and both Lady Sloan and the baroness knew she was standing in the hall. Jordyn would get some air, see Rutger, then she would go back and talk to Lady Sloan.

Pushing off from the wall, she straightened, poised like the soothsayer she was, and headed to the doors. "Abigail, Sousa."

"Mistress," Sousa responded, and opened the door.

Jordyn walked down the massive stone steps to the driveway and to meet October's chilled breeze as it caressed her cheeks, moved her hair from her neck, and smelled of burning wood and leaves. Mmmm, this was what she needed. She inhaled, relaxed, and for a breath let the moment take her from her thoughts of the challenge, Lady Sloan, and the baron's plan to sacrifice Rutger. With a calm moment, she made her plans to tell Rutger she loved him, and then she would find a way to protect him from his beast.

They were going to survive this.

As if mocking her optimism, a siren screamed a high-pitched warning from several speakers. Enforcers and soldiers stopped what they were doing and raced to their posts, others jumped into their vehicles, and several rushed from the office. They skirted her, not going near her as she raced across the yard and straight for Rutger.

She spun in a circle, lost her footing and skidded on the loose gravel. Nearly falling, she gained her balance, and covered the fire searing her right arm. Jordyn checked to see scarlet seep from between her fingers and land on the ground. Her heart pounded inside of her chest as the attacker sliced her upper left arm, then her right arm and across her fingers. Like a red-hot poker had slid over her it left a fire in its wake, pain engulfing her. Jordyn wanted to yell at the enforcers and soldiers she was being attacked and he was trying to cut her to ribbons.

The sun reflected off the blades as the attacker, a dark blur, circled her and attacked her left side. Circle. Slice. Circle. Slice. Jordyn's thighs bled, her arms bled, her sides bled. All the cuts burned, their flames scorching her skin and reaching into her insides. Jordyn shuddered from the pain and her knees felt weak. It wasn't silver. It was worse. The blades were White 47, the synthetic version of silver. Every slice bit into her and fire erupted. Jordyn twisted, took several steps. Another slice … she needed help. Jordyn faced the office and tried running toward Rutger.

Rutger pushed the door open and started across the asphalt toward the house. He stopped when he saw Jo, her clothes soaked from blood, and staggering as she twisted and the blur easily made rings around her.

"Get medical. I want a team to check the perimeter for others, and remember you're werewolves use your senses, catalog the scents, track them, find them, bring them here.

The others, take your positions," Ansel ordered. "I want four with me."

Rutger barley registered Ansel giving orders as he marched towards Jo. She was cowering and shielding her face with her bleeding hands and forearms. Shredded material from the sleeves of her hoodie drifted in the wind, while crisscrossing her forearms were thin cuts, each one bleeding and peppering the lot crimson.

"Jo, can you hear me?"

Jordyn dared to lower her hands from her face to meet Rutger's gold gaze. *Help me.* A quick bite nipped her cheek, blood welled and slid down to her hoodie and soaked the fabric. She had to focus and get the hell away from the thing. Bracing herself for another attack, she took small steps. It shoved her back, slashed her neck and pain burned a trail to her chest. Jordyn tried to heal her wounds; her power flared, and died. She wasn't healing.

"We can't get a lock on whatever it is, and even if we did, we risk hitting Jordyn," Ansel reported. Behind him Kellen, Luke, Aydian, and Kia stood waiting and watching.

"We aren't fast enough to catch him," Kellen added.

Rutger growled. "He's making a joke of us." He felt the link between them open and felt her pain, frustration, and confusion. She wasn't scared. She was bleeding from multiple wounds and wasn't scared. That alone worried him.

Another bite from White 47 sank into her neck, and warm blood coated her shoulder, chest, and soaking the cotton made the material heavy. Nausea gripped her, spun in her stomach, and her head ached as if she'd been hit with a hammer. She had to stop this.

"Stop," Jordyn demanded. Barely a whisper. She needed her voice.

A second ticked. Nothing. Jordyn lowered her hands and opened her eyes. He stood in front of her, his chest rising with his deep inhales. He wore his flaxen hair back and tied, his black-on-black clothing molded to his lithe frame. His sun yellow gaze held his fight and told her he was magic-born. Fae. She wasn't sure what kind, but knew his essence wasn't shifter or a witch. Behind him, Rutger and four enforcers waited. She felt the baron's presence along with the sentinels and the baroness, Lady Sloan and Lord Ervin. Everyone was there. Watching.

Why weren't they helping her? Maybe they were waiting for her to defend herself. Jordyn's mind threw training at her and the failure that had been. She held onto him and begged for someone to shoot him. *Help me.*

His face contorted with his struggle, the tendons in his neck straining. Baying, he broke her hold and shot toward her. In a wild curve, his hand gripped the knife above his head. Time slowed down, the seconds suspending her, and the dragons shot out from their depths. This is who she was. She needed to fight. Jordyn called her wolf, and magic erupted from within her and spread out over her. For a split-second he hesitated and surprise gripped his features. If she hadn't been watching, she would have missed it and missed the thrill it sent through her. Jordyn felt her eyes bleed onyx as magic and power continued surging.

"Stop," Jordyn ordered, her voice thick.

He stopped.

Rutger took a step toward her, and Jordyn raised her power forcing him back, forcing them all back. They would stay there. She didn't need them to save her again. Pulling more power, her magic created a barrier, like a wind funnel, around them. This was about her. Jordyn wove her power over his mind, making sure he didn't move. Cool air sank into the cuts on her cheeks, legs, arms, and sides, her hoodie nothing but strips of material stuck to her as blood poured from wounds. Her shoes scraped asphalt and gravel with each pained step. As she ambled toward her attacker, she left a trail of scarlet behind her.

"Cut the alarm," Rutger ordered. Silence swept through them weaving tension into the air with Jo's magic and her whispers.

"No one attacks me," Jordyn whispered. "No one invades my territory." Every stress, feeling of frustration, anger, and grief coiled inside her like a tightly wound spring and fed off her pain. She saw Louis, Dr. Holmes, the faces of the witches, Flint, Prime's true form, and heard everyone giving her orders. They stared at her as they mocked her weakness and tried to hurt her over and over again. She doubted herself and it almost destroyed her. "Not this time," Jordyn seethed.

When she stood in front of him, she drew her fisted hand back and with all of her strength punched him in the face. Cartilage crunched and thick, dark blood poured from his broken nose. He dropped the short knives, their blades glittering in the stark sun, covered his face, and stumbling backwards he tripped over his feet and fell to the ground. Adrenalin surged through her, combining with the sight of his blood and incinerated the hold on the coil. Her restraint shattered. With curses curving her lips Jordyn began kicking the downed man, her breathes coming in strained gasps.

"Oh hell," Ansel mumbled. He took a step back with Kia and Kellen, while Aydian took a step forward.

Oh hell, was right. Jo's fury lashed out, its ends snapping in the air as it created a blockade between them, its force keeping everyone from getting close to her. Rutger clung to the link and kept her heartbeat in his head. Scarlet stained her cheeks and saturated her hoodie and jeans, the slick gore gleamed in the sunshine. Every wound bled freely, and each one was turning black. Rutger glanced at the knives lying on the ground; White 47. It was a matter of time before she wouldn't be able to stand. With silver poisoning her bloodstream, Jo wasn't going to be able to heal the wounds, she needed medical.

"Are you going to stop her?" Kia asked.

"Not yet," Rutger replied. His eyes stayed on Jo and his heartbeat pounded with each kick she landed. "No one interferes." He met the baron's glare across the lot and nodded.

"You have to stop this," Laurel pleaded.

"It's silver poisoning. I demand you stop this," Sloan ordered. "You can smell her skin rotting."

The sharp scent of White 47 on flesh drifted on the waves of poisoned blood. Healey didn't reply; he watched Jordyn lose herself as she took her aggression out on her attacker. This is what he wanted to see and feel as her anger turned the air static while her magic surrounded her like a wall of barbed wire.

Sloan took a step and was stopped when two sentinels blocked her from going any further. "I'm with the Highguard. I demand you stop this, Baron."

"Negative, Lady Sloan," Healey warned. "As you said, you're not here in a professional capacity."

"Do you know what you're doing? What you're doing to her?" Lady Sloan met Rutger's steel gaze.

"I know exactly what I'm doing. She needs this." Healey watched Rutger for signs of his beast at the same time he monitored Jordyn's heartbeat.

Jordyn heard voices ... they sounded far away and tangled and drowned under her rapid pulse in her ears and the veil of red she was looking through. She drove her foot into his side, heard bones breaking, and a giggle escaped her. In the frenzy of pain and punishment she felt her strength and energy draining from her as silver poisoning ate her flesh. She didn't care.

"Were you going to kill me?" Jordyn yelled. Her eyes blazed black as her wolf saturated her insides.

"Yes!" he yelled. His lips pulled back from white teeth, he opened his mouth and screamed, "Evil."

The Fae rolled to his side, brought his knees to his chest, and covered his head with his arms. He groaned from the pain and cursed as he tried getting to his knees. Jo kicked his arm out from under him, breaking it, then connected another hit to the side of his head, and Rutger heard bones break. Were they Jo's? Or the attacker's? Jo drew her hand back. The broken bones in her fingers sagged, then straightened.

Damn. Healed. He inhaled and exhaled as her violence escalated, making it frightening and exhilarating at the same time. Watching her beat the attacker hurt Rutger's heart. He wasn't going to let her kill him. She didn't need blood on her hands, and they needed to find out who the hell he was and what he was doing.

Jordyn pounced on him to straddle him, her knees grinding into the pavement, the toes of her running shoes slipping on gravel while she continued to land punches to his face and the sides of his head. He twisted under her, fighting to free himself, and tried to shove her off him. She dove into his mind, found his magic, paralyzed it, and sensing his true self, identified him as an elf. His name screamed into her head and her lips moved around Arvid. As quickly as his essence emerged, his hate welled up from his depths, its cold edge touching her. So much hate. For her and those like her. He was on a mission to destroy them all.

If that's the game, you want to play.

She reared her fist back and landed another hit. The next hit sent pain into her hand and wrist. With her anger fueling her, she scarcely noticed her broken fingers and shattered knuckles. Dark garnet mixed with scarlet smeared his swollen face and stained his flaxen hair. Her onyx gaze glared at the sun yellow eyes staring at her like small points encased in bloated flesh. Blood the color of grape jam brimmed from the cuts her hits caused and bled freely. She slowly, deliberately, raised her hand in front of him, healed the broken bones enough she could make a fist, saw his shock, smiled at him, and hit him.

"I'm going to fucking kill you." Jordyn saw it happening, could feel his heart stopping and his body going limp beneath her. She would feel him die. She would hear the last time his heart beat.

"Do it, Soothsayer, finish what you started." The words spilled from between his split lips, making him spit blood.

Rutger heard Jo's promise and it was time to stop her. He closed in on Jo and felt her magic and wolf keeping a wall around her to protect her from their interference. When he was a couple of feet from her, it opened, letting him in, and the bites of fury was replaced by a familiar heat like a phantom hand caressed his skin. She let him in and knew he was there.

"Mea, can you hear me?"

Jordyn pulled her hand back, made a fist with bloodied, crooked fingers, and growled. One more hit. One. More. Hit.

"Finish it," he groaned. His left arm laid to his side while his right arm laid limp above his head, his hand pointed the wrong direction, and grape color streaking his yellow eyes.

Jordyn wanted to finish him. Needed to finish him. Her mind raced with what she learned from him and what the repercussions of her actions would be. If she killed him, she would make him a martyr for his cause. She would make him immortal to his people. She wasn't going aid him in his quest to strengthen the wills of the other assassins.

"Mea, please. You can't kill him," Rutger said softly. She didn't follow through. She held her fist back, her arm shook, her chest heaved with her breaths, and her eyes remained on the beaten man. He called his wolf, and easing his control it sharpened, grew more powerful, and gave him the taste of power he craved. He needed its force to send in their link and break through Jo's bloodlust. Rutger focused on the energy of their link and sent his power into the thread and whispered, "Come to me."

Rutger's familiar low roar threaded through his words and flickered inside of her head. His wolf's presence flowed over her, soothing her, and she couldn't stop herself from turning her head to see him. "Wolf." The silhouette of his beast hovered over him sharpening his wolf's features. Her beautiful beast. He would be used as a sacrifice.

"Yes, Mea, come to me." He held his hand out to her.

Jordyn faced the elf one last time, thought about hitting him, and backed down before she gave in and completely lost herself. Pushing off him, she stood on weak legs, the motion causing nausea to churn in her stomach, dizziness slushed in her head, and she stopped herself from gagging. The fury was gone, the adrenalin rush drained from her, and the target of her wrath beaten. Pain swallowed her in an instant while the cuts began oozing black blood and ribbons of dead skin fell from her. Turning to see Rutger, she knew she looked insane.

"It's White 47. It's eating me alive. I'm too weak to heal myself," Jordyn mumbled.

God, please stop talking. Her right cheek hung lose where a cut started at the corner of her mouth and went deep into the flesh. The cut in her left cheek dug in the center and ended at her ear; he could see her back teeth. A sheen of black and scarlet fell with her words as the two sides of flesh pulled independently. She was lucky she had a face at all.

"I know, Mea, medical is coming," he assured her.

Jordyn didn't think she was going to make it until medical arrived. Lifting her hand to reach for Rutger, she saw her bent, twisted fingers and bloody knuckles. Hot embarrassment heated her ravaged cheeks, making her acutely aware of the damage, and she lowered the gnarled appendages. Jordyn looked down and gazed at her hands, turning both over and seeing her misshapen fingers, cuts, and bruises. She did this to herself and she shuddered with the thought. What was she becoming? Jordyn didn't know. She pushed the question aside as her body felt alien, numb, and she didn't understand the numbness settling in her sides and legs. *Maybe shock*. Looking up at Rutger, she wanted an answer, and his reaction. Please don't be dying.

Horror held Jo's eyes when she saw the damage to her hands and then the worry when she met his gaze. Keeping his face passive, he wasn't going to allow her to see his disgust and fear. "You're going to be all right."

"He's Fae. Elf. His name is Arvid," she whispered around the sagging skin. Jordyn tasted silver-poisoned blood on her lips, its tang carrying rot made her stomach clench. Lifting her arm, she was going to wipe the blood off with the sleeve of her hoodie. She didn't have one; they had been cut to shreds. Bastard. "If they keep attacking me, I'm going to run out of clothes."

If it continues you might die. "You'll get new ones," Rutger replied. *Please stop talking.* The intense urge to grab her, tell her he loved her, wrap his arms around her, and hug her to his body to keep her safe overwhelmed him. He desperately needed to touch her and know she was alive, and he needed to keep her from adapting to the attacks, the death, and the pain. She deserved to keep some of her innocence. Most of all, he wanted to feel her against his body and her heartbeat against his skin.

He stopped himself.

Rutger was witnessing Jo's strength. She remained standing, covered in cuts and blood after an attack, and suffering from silver poisoning. The pack, Lady Sloan and Lord Ervin, the baron and baroness were witnessing her strength. Soldiers and enforcers saw her raw power and the violence she embraced. They saw their soothsayer and the mate to the Second to the Alpha. She would stand on her own for as long as she could.

"New ones." Bummer. Jordyn liked the old ones. Rutger blurred, came into focus, and blurred. She was going to pass out. *Stay awake.* If she stayed awake, she didn't think she was going to remain standing, the numbness was crawling up her legs and inching toward her waist. She needed to tell Rutger about Arvid, the others, and their plan to eliminate the *Potents,* what he believed to be the magic-born affected by the *Emanation*. Magic's invasion into the world. *It's coming for us,* her mind screamed.

A car engine roared in the distance, her senses told her it was Dr. Hyde, and medical was nearly there. She was alive. Jordyn beat the Fae and survived. "Dr. Hyde is coming." She didn't know if she said it out loud or not. Rutger blinked out for a second then came back. She was going to pass out. *Stay awake.* Her legs felt as if someone had cut them from her body and she was waiting to fall. Jordyn held Rutger's gaze as he slid from her view and she saw the sky-a storm was coming-and then black.

Rutger caught Jo before she hit the ground and held her in his arms. "I'm taking her to the med room."

"We'll take care of him," Ansel stated.

"She said he was Fae, elf, his name is Arvid," Rutger started.

"I heard her, I have people taking care of it," Ansel assured.

"Make sure to tell Dr. Hyde. Lock him in a Fae cell, and restrain him with Cobalt 27," Rutger ordered. If the elf decided he was going to use magic to escape, if he was able to walk, the synthetic Cobalt 27 would suppress his powers.

"Sir." Ansel met Kia's gaze and ordered, "I need a gurney."

"Yes, sir."

Rutger took a quick glance at the baron closing the distance, his gold eyes holding his authority and controlled fury. Following orders, the enforcers left Rutger and Ansel.

In the midst of the fight, Healey saw his son's beast lingering over him and part of him wanted Rutger to lose control. He hadn't. And now its fading outline resembled Rutger's human form. "Son, she fought with injuries, silver is in her system, and she forced her bones to heal repeatedly. Exhaustion and blood loss might be too extensive for the med room. It won't be enough," Healey advised. "I'm warning you she may have to be transported to Celestial."

"I understand." Unleashing his wolf was a risk, and meant everyone saw him. He needed the wolf's strength and force to battle Jo's power enough he could reach her.

Rutger hugged Jo to him, gently without pushing against her wounds, and carried her through the staring group. He needed to get to the med room.

An enforcer opened the office door for him and once inside the rooms blurred. He could have taken the exterior entrance and elevator making the trip shorter except the energy, anxiety, and adrenalin pumping in his veins forced him to walk to burn some of it off. He pushed through the double doors of the medical facility and entered the room that resembled a trauma center. Rutger crossed to the first bed and gently lowered Jo to the mattress.

CHAPTER TWENTY-FIVE

"I'm here," Dr. Hyde announced. "I have Dr. Warren and an ER nurse attending the man. With me, is Dr. Baines."

Rutger watched Dr. Hyde rush into the room with the other doctor trailing behind her. She sucked in a breath when she saw Jo's wounds, then hit a switch on the wall, instantly shrouding Jo in bright white light. Details of her lacerations, blood, dying skin, torn clothing, and dirt stood out and somehow looked worse. Rutger nodded to the man wearing dark blue scrubs, running shoes, and a badge clipped to his pocket. His blond hair highlighted by red was cut short, and his light green eyes were narrowed on Rutger. They had been working at Celestial when Mandy called them.

"Dr. Clio Hyde, authority code One Heka, Dr. William Baines assisting. I'm reporting an attack on Mistress Jordyn Langston." Mechanisms sounded as the order disengaged the locks on the cabinets at the same time the surveillance system began recording. "I understand the perpetrator used two White 47 blades. Is that right?" Dr. Hyde took a pair of black gloves out of the box beside the bed and pulled them on.

Mistress Langston. He needed to marry her and have her hold his name. "Affirmative." Rutger stared at Jo, the blood, slices on her cheeks and neck, and the black skin.

His arms hung at his sides, his heart pounded in his chest like it was trying to escape, and his wolf howled in his ears. He needed to tell her he loved her. "Why is she still bleeding?"

"White 47 is destroying her platelet count. With the blood loss and silver, how long has she been unconscious?" Dr. Hyde's facial features betrayed her like her eyes as they gleamed blue.

"Minutes." Rutger didn't know what to do.

"Excellent." Dr. Hyde rolled a cart to the side of the bed, then an IV stand. Moving with swift and efficient actions, she cleaned the bend in Jo's arm, inserted a catheter, its wings conforming to her contours, and locked it to a longer piece of tubbing. "I'm starting a line of BioThropy." Dr. Hyde hung a clear bag with pink-tinged liquid from a steel hook. "I saw the amount of blood in the parking lot and hoped it wasn't the mistress'." Dr. Hyde checked the contents and met Rutger's gaze. "It's a synthetic blood made specifically for shapeshifters. It'll give her red blood cells and hemoglobin at the same time it increases the platelet count to help her fight the silver."

"I understand," Rutger mumbled.

"Dr. Baines, I'll clean up the lacerations next to her mouth and steri-strip the wounds closed. I'm counting on her healing herself once the BioThropy has reduced the silver's progression. Help me with her clothing," Dr. Hyde ordered.

She handed Rutger a pair of gloves, and a pair of surgical scissors. He paused, pulled the gloves on, then worked on what was left of Jo's hoodie. Dr. Hyde took a scalpel and began cutting dead skin from Jo's cheek, dropping the fragments into a stainless steel bowl. Once the black skin was completely removed, she placed the scalpel down, and began cleaning the lacerations.

"She broke her hands and tried to heal them. They don't look good," Rutger added. He cut the side of Jo's hoodie revealing more black skin and an oozing wound.

"Noted." Dr. Hyde placed four steri-strips across the wound on Jo's left cheek and repeated the process to the wound on her right cheek. She shook her head at the sight and turned her attention to Dr. Baines. "Start on her jeans."

"Ma'am." He took Jo's shoes off, placed them to the side, then with a pair of scissors, started at the cuff and cut up the left side of her jeans. The blood-soaked denim stuck to her skin, forcing him to gently tug the material.

"Tell me Mistress kicked the guy's ass," Dr. Hyde said. Stepping in front of Rutger, making him step back, she took the scissors from him. She cut up the opposite side of the hoodie and dropped the wet fabric to the floor.

"You haven't seen him?" Rutger asked.

"No. I ordered Dr. Warren to attend whoever Captain Wolt had on the gurney, then saw the parking lot. The baron ordered us here." Dr. Hyde dropped a clump of crimson-stained cotton.

"Jo was going to kill him but something stopped her. I thought it might have been me, then she said he was an elf, and his name was Arvid. She read his mind and must have found something important," Rutger replied. His attention fixed on Dr. Hyde and Dr. Baines and Jo's nearly naked body.

Dr. Hyde stopped and looked at Rutger. "Seriously."

"Yes. Is there anything I can do?" Rutger asked. He held his hands up, the black gloves glistening with fresh blood. He hated feeling helpless and his impatience and nerves were going to tear him apart.

"Was the attack against the pack as a whole? And they attacked Mistress because she was outside and an easy target?" Dr. Hyde asked trying to make small talk.

"I don't know," Rutger admitted. He would find out since the elf was going to be in a cell.

"The skin around the lacerations is rotting and sticking to the material," Dr. Baines reported. His face contorted in a grimace as he held a piece of denim and showed Dr. Hyde the black skin. "Do you want me to start anesthesia?"

"No," Rutger answered. "No, anesthesia." If Jo was in pain, he would feel her. He didn't. And she didn't need anything else hindering her ability to heal.

With his order, Dr. Hyde looked at Rutger. "As long as she isn't fighting us, I believe she will heal quicker without it. Keep going."

"Ma'am." Dr. Baines dropped the material and started on the right side. The sound of scissors cutting through the thick material and their breathing were the only noises. Each cut revealed more skin, more blood, and more cuts. He worked to keep from tearing the damaged skin. "Her right side matches her left side. Three lacerations on her upper thigh, two at mid-thigh, for a total of ten."

"Noted. One laceration from the corner of her mouth into her left cheek. One laceration from the center of her right cheek to her ear. Two on the left side of her neck, and two on the right side. I have four more on her upper arms and a dozen more, which look like defense wounds, like she was protecting herself, on her forearms, hands, and fingers. I don't like the way these lacerations look. They're different from the others."

Dr. Hyde stopped to examine the wounds on Jo's neck and upper arms. With her hoodie and T-shirt completely removed, Jo looked gaunt, thin, and her ashen skin gave her ghostly appearance. Rutger sensed Dr. Hyde's apprehension and knew she was thinking the attack was going to set Jo back emotionally and physically. A werewolf needed its pack for emotional support and needed to consume large amounts of protein to keep up with their metabolism. Jo shutdown her emotions, didn't surround herself with her pack, hadn't been eating properly, and it showed.

"Laceration on the right side of her abdomen below her ribs and one on the left side, same placement. They are superficial and aren't showing strong signs of White 47 poisoning," Dr. Hyde stated.

"It's true." Dr. Baines griped the scissors in his right hand and took a step back while his mumbled words were intangible.

"Yes. You need to get back to work," Dr. Hyde ordered.

He was staring at the side of Jo's leg, his face a shade paler than it had been. Rutger and Dr. Hyde watched Dr. Baines' professional veneer crumble. Rutger should have questioned Dr. Hyde about him, but hadn't wanted to waste time. He clearly should have. It was a rash decision and a security breach.

"The mark is pulsing between her natural skin tone and silver." Dr. Baines took a step and pointed. "She's a soothsayer. It's real."

Rutger's senses hadn't picked up a shapeshifter, not that he was paying attention when he was focused on Jo and her suffering, but now they tingled with a familiar feel and it crawled over him. The sensation brought back raging emotions and a torrent of images. "You brought a witch to Foxwood and the Enforcer's office. To my mate. To the pack's soothsayer," he accused, his gold glare on Dr. Hyde. "I talked about her abilities and the pack."

In the med room and their close proximity his accusations, carried by a growl, thundered between them. He glared at Dr. Hyde, with the promise in his stare, if the man made a wrong move or started chanting, he was dead.

Dr. Hyde swallowed hard with his harsh reminder of her place. "Yes. He's part of the Lapis Lazuli, part of the klatch under Cascade rule, and has passed all background checks to work at Celestial. I did my part to ensure the safety of the pack, so don't give me your death glare, Rutger, I'm on your side."

To Rutger's left, Dr. Baines took another step back from Jo while attempting to put space between them. *Good luck.* "I'm warning you, Dr. Hyde," Rutger growled.

"Your threats won't do any good, *sir.* I'm in charge of this med room and anyone in it, that means you. It's my responsibility to keep Jordyn alive, and since I never know what the hell has happened to her or by whom, I needed someone with a vast knowledge of shapeshifters, their history, the magic-born and their history. He's good at what he does." Dr. Hyde stood her ground. "I have my senses, instincts, and training, and what I don't have, he does. Calm down, step back, and let us do our work. If you can't do that, get out of my med room."

Rutger didn't pay attention to the lack of titles, an implemented rule after they tightened security and took on a more formal approach to their operations. It gave the impression they were a military unit not a pack. Some hated it, and some liked the change. Part of him missed the friendly conversations and relaxed setting. With Jo becoming a powerful soothsayer, the need for military discipline was imperative as a show of force. His anger drained from him with the truth in Dr. Hyde's words. His eyes bleed to mahogany, and his shoulders lost some of the tension tightening his muscles. "One wrong move," he promised.

"Director." Dr. Hyde turned to Dr. Baines. "Look at these, the ones on her neck, and upper arms, they're different from the others. Darker. There's liquid pooling under the skin. I'm guessing poison." Dr. Hyde put her fingers on either side of the top laceration on Jo's right arm, and pushing, they watched green/yellow puss ooze out.

Dr. Baines didn't move, didn't look at Jo, he watched Rutger. *You should fear me, witch.* "Dr. Baines, I believe Dr. Hyde asked you to look at Mistress' wounds." Rutger tried to keep the growl out of his words and his hate of witches from his eyes.

"Yes, Director," Dr. Baines replied. With hesitation, he stepped closer and paused as he waited for Dr. Hyde to give him room. He examined the lacerations, their color, and the fluid. Leaning down, he inhaled, exhaled, and after several seconds, straightened. "You're right. What happened during the attack?"

"He attacked her and Mistress tried defending herself," Rutger answered.

"He didn't have any other weapons?"

"Negative."

"You said he was an elf?" Dr. Baines asked.

"Affirmative. You think the knives were poisoned?" Rutger looked at Dr. Hyde.

"Affirmative. It's the only way he would have gotten the poison into her skin. Who has the knives?" Dr. Hyde asked.

Rutger grabbed the radio mic hooked to his BDU blouse. "Bring the knives to the med room." Static sounded for a second and cut off.

"Affirmative, Director."

Jordyn sank deeper within herself as the numbness crawled over her body, leaving deadness behind. Even as the haze swallowed her, she knew her heart was slowing and it was getting harder to breathe. It was a matter of time before her heart and lungs stopped and once her lungs seized, she would suffocate. She was going to lose the battle with silver. She survived witches, Prime, his Numina, only to be murdered by an elf. It figures.

Maybe it was better this way. Rutger would be free to live his life. *Rutger.* Thinking about him made the pain worse, her heart ache, and her chest tight like metal bands were squeezing her. It wouldn't end with Rutger. Without her, the baron and baroness would be free of Prime and the Highguard. The pack would return to normal life. She laughed a sad sound, until magic flooded the world and changed their lives. Her thoughts slowed as pain tugged on her arms and legs to drag her deeper into the depths of numbness. Rutger. She couldn't stop worrying about him. She wished she could see him, his eyes gleaming gold with possession, his body embracing pure masculinity, and his wolf enveloping him.

Her heart beat and stopped.

Another weak beat and it stopped. She reached for her power, searching for her magic and the energy of the Collective. A void met her. One weak beat. Two. Her heart stilled. It was over. The dread starting in the center of her chest told her, her lungs were failing.

Jordyn let go of the struggle, because it caused more pain, and let weakness carry her towards the death she denied. It would hold her this time and leech her wolf of power and its strength and she would fade away. She would leave Rutger on his own, her pack without their soothsayer, and the Collective, she promised to hold would drift to the ether. She saw Zachery's face and felt the sliver of absence. Sadness welled inside of her, snuffing the need to fight, and she felt herself crumbling, as if her skin was falling from her and her veins, muscles, and tendons were next.

"He's an elf. What's your best guess?" Dr. Hyde asked Dr. Baines.

"We've all assimilated into the human world and yet have kept traditions. Elves have retained their past and use foliage for everything from poisons to antidotes, and teas to holistic healing. If he's from the Seelie court of the Shasta-Trinity forest he would have used something local. They take pride in their ability to garden, harvest, and use their plants," Dr. Baines explained.

"This was an assassination attempt," Rutger pointed out. "He wouldn't use something that would lead us back to the court. We're werewolves, all we have to do is identify a scent and follow it."

"Right." Dr. Baines touched the laceration and found it was warm. "Did she collapse?"

Rutger saw Jo standing in front of him, her eyes a pale comparison of themselves, black skin falling from her cheeks, and blood staining her skin and hoodie. "Her knees buckled before she passed out."

"What is her heartrate?" Dr. Baines asked.

Dr. Hyde held Jo's wrist, closed her eyes, and the seconds ticked by as silence rapidly swept in, eating the room and feeding the tension. "Twenty-eight per minute," she responded. "And slowing. A werewolf's normal heartrate should be above two hundred when resting. Her heart is going to stop."

Dr. Baines checked Jo's eyes, and rechecked the wounds. Taking a tongue depressor, he ran the tip up one foot, then the other, and with no response, he drew it along the inside of her thigh. Rutger growled when Dr. Baines leaned in then ran the tip over her left thigh. "My apologies, Director. There was no response. Even unconscious she should have responded," he said to Dr. Hyde.

"Is that true?" Rutger asked.

"Affirmative. There should have been a reflex response," Dr. Hyde answered.

"The soothsayer-" Rutger glared at him. "My apologies, Mistress isn't responding because she's paralyzed." Dr. Baines hadn't finished his sentence when Dr. Hyde hit a button and a panel slid down, revealing controls and an oxygen mask.

"What's happening?" Rutger asked.

"I believe it's a concentrated amount of Deadly Nightshade. It might have been laced with something like an accelerant to ensure it worked on a werewolf. It paralyzed her and is moving to her heart and lungs. We can keep her lungs functioning but it will stop her heart," Dr. Baines answered. "Do you have an anticholinesterase?"

"How do you know?" There were millions of poisons. Rutger didn't trust the witch and trusted his diagnosis less.

"No, it's not standard. Since the magic-born have antidotes and shapeshifters aren't affected by poisons, I don't have it here or at Celestial. We could contact a human facility." Dr. Hyde adjusted the mask, checked the gauges, and started the oxygen.

"I have travelled extensively studying plants," Dr. Baines started.

"So, you've said. Do you have a bachelor's degree in botany?" Dr. Hyde asked.

"Yes," Dr. Baines answered, as he held Dr. Hyde's gaze.

"You mean you've studied poisonous plants," Rutger accused. "Why do you need to know about or have poisons?" Rutger was going to look into the edict the Esme signed when the baron gave them the authority to govern themselves and see if they had violated the agreement.

"I study plant science and biology. Compared to shapeshifters, witches are basically human. We don't have heightened strength, enhanced senses, and we don't turn into three hundred-pound animals with teeth and claws. It's our defense," Dr. Baines quickly explained.

Rutger watched the doctor consider him with questions and uncertainty in his eyes. *Yes, doctor, I was investigated for the deaths of several witches.* "How do I know your coven isn't growing Deadly Nightshade or a dozen other plants? You could be supplying the elves with any poison they want," Rutger said continuing his interrogation.

"You don't. There are probably a hundred poisonous plants on this property alone, but you're a werewolf and like Dr. Hyde pointed out, it isn't a threat to you." Dr. Baines gathered himself and calmed down.

"Where do we get the antidote?" Rutger demanded.

"Butte Springs put doubt into everyone's minds about the moral values of witches, and my coven has been dealing with the aftermath. We've lost the public's trust. Since then, the coven has been careful not to attract unnecessary attention and are working to better our reputation. I know what this is and I know someone who can help. It's a natural remedy and will help Mistress heal." Dr. Baines waited, and when Rutger's hard, gold glare met his, Rutger saw him cringe. "Helping you will help us. Unless you want humans involved."

"Who exactly will be helping?" Rutger asked.

"The Esme."

"Director, the Esme is the leader of the Lapis Lazuli coven, her name is Rosslyn, and she has helped the pack in the past. Butte Springs to be exact," Dr. Hyde explained. Her voice changing when she said Butte Springs. Like Rutger, no one wanted to say it and give the place power and weight.

He knew who she was, what he didn't know was if she was going to help them. The Lapis Lazuli coven had gone silent after Butte Springs and just recently were back in the public, and in contact with the baron. They hadn't gone near the pack. "The coven has kept their distance from the pack, how do you know she'll help?" Rutger's voice sounded inhuman and laced with his anger.

Dr. Baines hesitated then answered, "She is my mom."

CHAPTER TWENTY-SIX

"Let me get this straight ... you not only brought a witch to Foxwood, but the damn Esme's son. Fuck, Dr. Hyde, if he had been injured, it would have put the baron and the pack in conflict with the coven. From now on, if anyone is to come here, I want an enforcer to do a full background investigation and the files on my desk and they will sign non-disclosure contacts, release forms, and whatever else I can think of or they won't be permitted on Foxwood property. Do you understand me?" Rutger demanded.

"Yes, Director."

Dr. Hyde's blue eyes with hints of brown gleamed with her wolf as she held his glare. He shouldn't have treated her like she was incompetent, especially in front of Dr. Baines, but she needed to understand the security risks. As a Wight, Dr. Hyde felt she wasn't equal to the Illuminates or the Purebloods, and fixating on the differences drove her to push herself harder.

"Now, may Dr. Baines call his mom?"

Claws dug into her shoulders, sides, and legs and holding her they took her higher and higher and further from death. The dragons. Their roars echoed against her skull, their power pouring from them and sinking into her from their claws. In an instant they released her and she hung suspended, her body weightless, and completely numb. Like slow waves, energy rolled over her, under, and against her sides, teasing her with life. Was she going to ignore it or use it to heal herself? She wanted Rutger and whatever future they could carve out of the changing world. She needed Rutger. Her anchor.

Forcing the crushing sadness from her mind, Jordyn replaced it with images of the woods, her territory, and the pack. The Collective let out a shared breath carrying their emotions, and the force behind it vibrated her core. She wanted to keep her promise and save them from the ether. She had to save herself first. How was she going to when she couldn't defend herself? Jordyn slipped, and the sadness moved closer to her.

"Your responsibilities to the pack require you to hold the essences of their wolves, their pasts, and memories. In return they serve as a power source," Lady Sloan explained.

Jordyn let go of her control, allowing her soothsayer's instincts to call the Collective. She remained suspended inside of herself, the dragons keeping watch from a distance, and her heart fighting to keep her alive. A presence ascended from within magic, and bringing hundreds, then thousands to her, their whispers gained strength. They were her wolves, Cascade, and the ancients from who's lineage she came from.

Was she supposed to ask? Demand them to help her? Maybe explain she needed to use them in order to live? Could she talk when suspended inside of herself and dying? Jordyn didn't have answers and didn't know what to do. Lost was becoming a theme in her life. *Was a theme,* she corrected.

"You may speak with us?" a man said.

Jordyn blinked as if the voice snapped her out of a dream and she saw a figure across from her. She wasn't in her head or her body or wherever she had been. They were at the conclave, in Summit Sanctuary with a full moon above him, casting its silver light on his face. His features looked old-not in age but from a different time-rugged, harsh from a life of struggle, and his eyes gleamed with silver flakes drifting through the sea of brilliant blue. His long, black hair ended at his waist, its ends feathering his cotton pullover shirt.

"Who are you?"

"The eldest." When he saw the blank look on her face, he continued. *"Soothsayer, you should know your alpha from years past."*

Jordyn had to burn energy to think, and felt pain remind her she didn't have a lot of time. Her memories were jumbled, hazy, and distant, and putting the effort into dissecting them was dragging her down. Pushing harder, she fought the fatigue, expanded her search deeper into the past, deeper into the Collective. Her muscles burned like she was physically making the trek back in time and she wanted to give up.

Where are you? Jordyn's legs were going to give out, her mind was caving in on itself, when she found him.

"Christian, a Pureblood. You're from here, the US. Trinity, but not one of the Cascade."

"Your Cascade, no. Mine was of a different time. I am buried here."

Jordyn relaxed, stopped the search, and let his life swirl around her. She expected to find he was from a different country, like her ancestors, and with hundreds of years of dysfunction, like her family.

"Soothsayer." He inclined his head and loose strands of black hair fell.

"Can you help me?" Jordyn asked. Time was slipping from her.

"Yes. Reach for me," he said softly. His eyes bleed silver as his wolf, a perfect copy, shadowed his body like a pale veil.

Two forms. Jordyn memorized him, praying she remembered every detail if she lived. Reaching for him, she clasped his out stretched hand, his warm fingers gripped her as old power surged through her, aiming for her struggling heart.

"Feel your Collective, Soothsayer."

The Summit, Christian, and the moon shattered when the line struck her heart like a lightning bolt, sending white hot pain through her chest.

A blast of magic exploded in the room at the same time Jo's back arched off the bed, her eyes opened wide, focusing on nothing, every muscle tensing like rebar. Rutger watched her as she stayed there for three seconds, four, five, when she finally collapsed. The machine monitoring her heartbeat screamed with alarm and went blank.

"What the hell was that?" Rutger asked. His senses focused on Jo's heartbeat. It was there, stronger but struggling.

"A flare of magic. She might be trying to heal herself," Dr. Baines answered.

"Maybe. This is unprecedented." Dr. Hyde looked at the questions in the Rutger's eyes and knew neither of them had answers.

A flare of magic. Jo tried to purge the Collective. Could she sense the poison, and feeling her life ending purge her magic and send the Collective to the ether? God, he hoped not. Even as blood seeped from her wounds, he didn't believe she was going to die. She healed herself. Rutger saw her strength as she stood at the railing of the deck having put her fears behind her. After getting her back, he wasn't to lose her.

"If she felt the Collective was in danger, could she purge her magic?" Rutger asked. He hated it, but he had to know and he needed to ask someone.

"Why would she?" Dr. Baines asked in return. He looked like he had never heard of the idea.

"To protect them. To send them back to the ether," Rutger answered. "So they don't die with her."

"If it's possible and her instincts demand she protect them, maybe. At this point I believe anything is possible." Dr. Hyde's eyes grew dark as she stared at Jo. "Rutger, I'm not going to let Jordyn die. May Dr. Baines call his mom?"

Rutger didn't trust the witch and his faith in Dr. Hyde was fading quick. The sound of Jo's heartbeat reminded him of Butte Springs. Shaking the dread loose, he focused on putting his emotions aside. He needed to treat this with the same competency he did the other cases. In minutes someone would deliver the knives, Dr. Hyde would test the residue to confirm Dr. Baines' statement or prove him wrong. What he didn't know was how long the testing would take. Damn. Did he doubt the doctor because he needed to protect Jo or because he hated witches? He couldn't let his hate of witches cloud his decision and put Jo in greater danger.

His actions played out in his head. He saw himself making the call to a human hospital and requesting an antidote for Deadly Nightshade and then explaining what happened and the attack. They might believe him and they might not. If they did, by law the staff was required to inform the sheriff's department of the attack, and because it's a paranormal crime, they would hand the case over to the OPI, Organized Paranormal Investigations. It would get the attention of the homicide detective who had investigated Rutger, and bring Detective Watt back to their front door. The Cascade pack would be back on law enforcement's radar and back in the media and Rutger's past would be dredged up. Jo would be a victim of another violent attack, making the entire paranormal population suspects in the eyes of humans. It was an easy answer and he hated it.

Dr. Baines was either going to help Jo or he was going to end up in the same cell as the elf. "Call your mom," Rutger ordered. An undercurrent of a growl laced his words and his eyes gleamed gold.

A high-pitched buzzing filled her ears, an ache drummed in her head, and her body felt like someone had tossed her in a garbage disposal, let it run, then yanked her out. And she did not want to know what her hands looked like.

Images floated before her ... some she remembered, others she wasn't sure if they were real or part of dream. Jordyn opened her eyes to a dark room, the only light a dim glow from the setting sun filtering through beige blinds. Like a spider was staring down at its next meal, black globes glittered from the ceiling. Jordyn closed her eyes, counted to ten, and opening them saw dark, recessed lights.

Good. Next, where am I? Panic surged for a painful heartbeat before she recognized the smells and sounds. She relaxed when she understood she was in the Enforcer's office, and more specifically, by the equipment around her, the med room. *At least it's not Celestial.* She inhaled and felt the sheet pull on the gown she was wearing. Bra, no. Underwear, yes. Thank god she wasn't naked. Still, someone had to have taken her clothes off to treat her wounds and then to put the gown on. Most likely it was Dr. Hyde. Rutger wouldn't let anyone else near her.

"There you are," Rutger whispered. Seeing her eyes open sent his heart into chaos. He stood from his chair and sat on the edge of the bed.

Dr. Hyde and Dr. Baines carefully cleaned blood from Jo's face, neck, arms, and her sides and legs after Jo closed the wounds. Despite their effort, streaks of crimson stained her hairline and down behind her ears. Dark flakes from dried blood dusted the shoulders of her light blue gown. A gray line started at the corner of her mouth and ended in the middle of her left cheek while another line started in the center of her right cheek and ended at her ear. The lines on her neck looked like someone drew them with a marker. He shielded his worry with a soft smile as he pulled the throw to her chest and smoothed the side.

"Dr. Hyde is here. Do you need anything?" Rutger asked.

Gold slivers twisted in his mahogany eyes as if they had a life of their own and his hair was ruffled like he pushed his fingers through it in hast and frustration. He ditched his gear and the top to his uniform. Hugging his chest was a black, long-sleeved shirt with the pack's crest and his name. Looking at him gave her a sense of security, confidence, and put her at ease.

"Mea, do you need Dr. Hyde?" he repeated. She gazed up at him with copper swirling in her eyes and the sight released the metal bands around his chest. Rutger didn't know what she was thinking and didn't care, she was awake.

"No, please, no," Jordyn mumbled. She didn't want to see anyone. She would have said so except talking tugged on the corners of her mouth and cheeks. Faint images of Arvid's attack accompanied by a stinging pain reminded her of what happened. "My hands. How are they?" She saw her broken fingers and bloody knuckles.

"As soon as Dr. Hyde stopped the progression of the silver and you were given the antidote, you healed the shallow lacerations and your hands," Rutger explained, as he picked up her right hand. He wasn't going to tell Jo the Esme had been reluctant to help, fearing the Seelie court would think the coven was picking sides. "Are you in pain? Does anything hurt?"

"Antidote?" Drugged, stabbed, and poisoned, it had been shitty couple of days. The sentinels suddenly looked like a great idea. She wasn't sure if she was sad or happy that the drugs explained the dreams and visions of the Collective.

"Jo, he coated the blades with Deadly Nightshade and another toxin. We have the blades in evidence and they'll be tested for confirmation. I believe he was trying to kill you. He didn't know the extent of your powers and didn't know you could read his mind." Rutger watched for her response and signs she was hurting.

The poison explained why she lost feeling in her legs. "He was here to kill me," Jordyn confirmed. "I need to talk to you about Arvid."

"I've started an investigation." Rutger hesitated, he didn't want to push her. "I figured you read his mind, when you didn't kill him."

"I wanted to. He's prepared to die for his cause and doing so would have made him a martyr. His death would have given him immortality and reaffirmed the motives behind the attack and their belief system." Talking hurt. Everything hurt. "My head is killing me."

"Do you want me to call Dr. Hyde." Rutger couldn't imagine the pain she was in.

"No. How long have I been out?" Jordyn asked.

"About eight hours. It's evening."

"All day," she mumbled. Hating having lost an entire day, Jordyn closed her eyes, and called her magic. A warmth swept through her, joining the strength of her wolf, its force easing the pain and knitting the broken pieces of her.

Power, soft as silk, wrapped around him, leaving him with his eyes closed and sinking into its feel. "Are you strong enough to use your magic?"

"Yes," Jordyn whispered. As long as her heart beat and she had the Collective's energy to feed her magic she was able to use its force. Christian's artic blue eyes drew her in and held her as her magic healed her body. The Collective, her pack, her wolf, and magic made her whole.

Beckoned by Jo's increased power, Rutger's wolf rose up to shadow him. Doubt and fear churned in his gut as he felt Jo using her senses to gauge him. *I'm not losing control*, he wanted to assure her.

Jordyn felt Rutger letting go and debated stopping the healing to focus her magic on him and his wolf. In unison with Rutger's beast, the conversation with the baron weighed down on her, bringing guilt. He would sacrifice his son. Her mate. The man she loved. Jordyn needed to protect him, but how was she going to when she couldn't protect herself? The damn elf tried slicing her to ribbons at Foxwood where security was supposed to stop the best of the best. Jordyn shut down her thoughts. Relaxing her muscles, her magic swept over her like a wave at the same time she sensed Rutger. In search of his emotions, she felt his confidence, his control, and she concentrated on her wounds.

Rutger's senses told him Dr. Hyde and Dr. Baines had retuned. They must have felt Jo's magic when she gathered her power to heal her wounds. Entering through the double doors, a whisper sounded, the doors closed, and they stopped. Rutger would ignore them as long as they stayed where they were and didn't interrupt Jo.

He knew he judged Dr. Baines unfairly. There were wounds not yet healed, and seeing the doctor was like tearing them open. Rutger's respect increased when two enforcers followed by two soldiers escorted the Esme, his mother, to the med room. She had given Dr. Baines a shielded glare-it showed her anger with him for having asked her to help, and for being at Foxwood. Dr. Baines risked angering his mom, and the Esme of his coven to help them. When Rutger spoke with the baron he was going to tell him about Dr. Baines.

Rosslyn, the Esme, explained after the antidote had been administered it would take fifteen minutes for Jo to respond, but if what Dr. Baines told her about Jo's abilities, she should respond in minutes. Rutger wanted to protest, they didn't have fifteen minutes, and he couldn't stand there any longer doing nothing. Rosslyn handed the green-tinted liquid to Dr. Hyde, saying it needed to be administered by a pack member. She also suggested using less, as Jo had started to heal. He thought back to the blast of magic, her heartbeat strengthening, and his heart ached all over again.

After Dr. Hyde administered the antidote, the enforcers and soldiers escorted the Esme out of the med room, the office, and to her car. Rutger, Dr. Hyde, and Dr. Baines waited and watched. Two agonizing minutes and ten seconds, because Rutger was keeping time, ticked by when Jo starting showing signs of healing. First, she shed the dead skin, returning it to its natural olive with a dusting of bronze. After she healed the sliver damage, the lacerations began knitting together. No one said anything when tears streamed from the corners of her eyes and her fingers crunched and curled. Time passed, Rutger didn't think his anxiety could get any worse, and the need to help her crawled over him like it had claws.

The second hour drifted into the past and Rutger feared her fingers would remain gnarled. He didn't want Dr. Hyde breaking them and setting them. Jo continued to silently cry through the process, making everyone wish they could do something for her. It had taken over six hours for her to heal both hands and the minor lacerations. When it was over, purple and yellow bruises marred her face, sides, legs and black and gray lines, like spider webs, darkened her skin.

From the moment she was attacked to them watching her heal had taken eight hours. He sat on the edge of the bed, with Dr. Hyde and Dr. Baines, as the gray lines on Jo's neck faded, and her lips curling around silent words as her skin wove together to erase the deep lacerations scarring her cheeks. Rutger raised her right hand and held it in both of his. As if pulled from inside of him, his wolf shadowed over him and their power continued to weave and inter-twine.

Jordyn's wolf eased back at the same time she pulled her magic back inside of her. Healing left her body feeling like she was wrapped in the thickest, warmest blanket and she wanted to stay in her cocoon. She did not want to face reality. Squeezing Rutger's hand, she opened her eyes and meet his gaze. She lived through another attack with the Collective's help.

"Wolf."

"Mea," Rutger whispered. He raised their clasped hands to his lips and kissed Jo's perfect fingers.

"The doctor is in," Dr. Hyde announced as she ap-proached the bed. Wearing a white top with a pastel floral print, black scrub cargo pants, and running shoes, she stopped beside the bed.

Jordyn felt the residual magic feather her skin as it slowly faded. Rutger let go of her hand, she straightened, and sat up. "Dr. Hyde."

"Mistress, good to see you're healed. This is Dr. Baines, he is my assistant and helped today," Dr. Hyde explained.

"Thank you, Dr. Baines. I understand there was an anti-dote." Jordyn pushed the pillow against the bed frame, leaned back, and grabbed the thick throw she recognized from her house. She didn't know who Rutger had sent to retrieve it but was thankful they had.

"Do your hands hurt?" Dr. Hyde asked. "It took a while for you to heal them."

Dr. Hyde watched as she straightened her fingers then clinched them into fists. "They're sore." Jordyn touched the corner of her mouth and felt smooth skin. A lifetime of be-lieving she was incapable of healing except when shifting was going to take some getting used to. It did give her the confidence to face Prime. Maybe he wouldn't kick her ass right away.

"The lacerations look good. You know if people find out they can heal, I'll be out of a job," Dr. Hyde teased. "Yes, the antidote. A natural treatment for Deadly Nightshade, it allowed you to heal yourself, and there won't be any lingering effects. The original prescribed amount changed as you began healing. There was an increase in magic, like a blast. Do you remember it?"

Christian. The Collective. "No," she replied. No reason to make herself a bigger freak in front of the pack than she already was. Jordyn looked at Rutger, and changing the subject said, "He ruined my favorite jeans."

Dr. Baines stifled a laugh, coughing into his hand, as everyone turned to look at him. "Sorry, Mistress."

Rutger glared at him, understanding the magnitude of the situation. Jo nearly lost her life, and she was complaining about her jeans.

Jordyn was watching Rutger stare at Dr. Baines when a familiar magic slithered over her senses. "Explain to me why you needed the help of a witch," Jordyn growled. His type of magic flowed through him like the blood in his veins and she caught his connection to plants and the faintest scent of lavender. She hated lavender. Hated it. "The antidote. Am I indebted to the coven?"

Dr. Baines' eyes widened as he stepped back. "No. No."

"Jo, listen, Dr. Baines figured out what kind of poison the elf used and the Esme freely gave you the antidote," Rutger began explaining.

"You're lying to me," Jordyn accused. She nailed her gaze on Rutger to watch his eyes gleam gold.

"She had reservations about the Seelie court and the pack. They have kept their distance for this exact reason. I wouldn't put us in debt to anyone." He lived with Shadow Lord's threat over his head, he didn't need another one.

Paranoid and didn't trust anyone. Is that who she was? It wasn't what she wanted to be. Dr. Baines fought to remain standing in front of her as her magic twisted around them. Targeting the witch, it found him and pressed down on him like she was going to crush him.

"Your life and safety are important to the Lapis Lazuli and the Esme. We would never threaten the relationship between the coven and the Cascade pack. As a sign of good will, the Esme gave willingly," Dr. Baines assured though clenched teeth.

Jordyn thought about what he said then using her senses sought his lie. There was none. He was telling her the truth. She cut her power like a switch, the room returned to normal, and she freed Dr. Baines from her touch. Her instant anger draining from her. "You understand my distrust?"

"Yes, Mistress." Dr. Baines exhaled and caught his breath.

"I have taken full responsibility for bringing him here," Dr. Hyde confessed. "My apologies."

"No, Dr. Hyde, I'm sorry. Old wounds. I wish I would have been warned. Feeling a little vulnerable." Jordyn smiled at the doctors and saw Dr. Baines hadn't quite recovered. It made her happy because she wanted to look like she was a badass soothsayer who had beaten an elf within an inch of his life but knew she failed. Sitting in a hospital bed wearing a gown with her favorite blanky, and god only knew what she looked like, made the attempt hysterical at best.

"Jordyn," Healey greeted. Behind him, Tracy and Charles took their positions on each side of the doors. He stopped beside Dr. Hyde and the side of the bed. Jordyn's raven hair was tangled, the curled ends sitting on her shoulders, and her pale skin looked worse next to the blue gown and white sheets. He would take it over watching her bleeding in the parking lot. "How's the patient?"

His hair was perfectly combed back, his rust-colored, button-up shirt open at the collar, letting the black ink of his tattoo peek out, like it had been that morning. He tucked the shirt into dark indigo jeans and wore a pair of brown loafers. With the baron's confident voice and calm demeanor no one would have guessed an elf trespassed and attacked her.

"The patient is healed. Because she spent hours mending broken bones, lacerations, and the bruising. Now she needs rest and needs to eat," Dr. Hyde advised. "I'll bring in a meal replacement drink, if you're up to drinking something?"

She was starving. "Sounds good," Jordyn answered.

Healey nodded at the doctor and turned his attention to Rutger. "I had the enforcers leave you alone while Jordyn was being treated. With her up, you need to get caught up on what's happening. They found three others and detained them."

"Yes, sir," Rutger replied. Straight back to business.

"Jordyn, I would like you to meet Tracy and Charles." With their names they both took a step forward, each dressed in button-up shirts, tactical pants, and shoulder holsters. They wore a modified version of the sentinel's uniform, conforming to the security duties surrounding Jordyn.

"I know who they are," Jordyn mumbled, and halfheartedly smiled. She had the sinking feeling they were her sentinels.

"They are your sentinels. They will go everywhere with you, understood?" Healey wasn't asking, he was telling her. "Once you're comfortable with their presence, you'll be given four others." It was time for him to implement his next plan.

"Yes, Baron," Jordyn replied. She gave the stone faces another slight smile and felt like an idiot. Sentinels. She had guards. Babysitters.

"Good. Also, do you think you can give a statement?" Healey questioned.

"Baron, she needs to rest," Dr. Hyde argued.

"Yes." Jordyn smiled at Dr. Hyde who shook her head.

"Good. I want you to watch the questioning," Healey continued.

"Is that code for reading their minds?" Jordyn asked. She would read their minds and expose their plans.

"Yes. I explained to Chancellor Roarke we have begun our investigation and will show him the evidence tomorrow. My guess is, he won't risk the publicity and will deny human law enforcement's involvement. If that happens, I'll demand to have the right to decide punishment," Healey explained.

"Prime expects to have a challenge with Jo, he won't like learning someone tried to kill her." It meant the chancellor and the elf didn't know. "What did the notification say about the moon run?" Rutger asked.

"The moon run has been cancelled due Prime scheduling a visit, and it states his request to address the pack, the klatch, and any visiting factions. While the pack and klatch were ordered to attend, an invitation has been sent to the masses. Due the numbers, we'll need to make adjustments to the Summit and increase security," Healey stated. "Are you thinking the elf didn't know Prime was in town?"

"Affirmative. The chancellor wouldn't order an attack when punishment might come straight from Prime." Rutger lost his one suspect. "We'll need to have a meeting to address the Summit and the visiting factions. This is turning into a nightmare."

"An invitation to the masses," Jordyn whispered. What was she going to have to do?

"I'm sorry, Mea," Rutger offered.

"Prime is requesting an audience and is making a production out of the challenge. He has something to prove," Healey said.

"To prove to the pack, I'm not worth their trust," Jordyn responded.

"I doubt it. There has to be another motive, what it is I have no idea," Rutger replied.

"You challenged Prime?" Dr. Baines asked.

"Yes," Jordyn answered.

Rutger gave him his death glare. "You won't tell anyone, will you, Dr. Baines?"

"No, sir." He stepped back and behind Dr. Hyde, his height making him several inches taller than her.

"Rutger, we have to question the others." Healey turned to Dr. Hyde. "Take Dr. Baines and go to my office, there is a lawyer waiting for you with paperwork."

"Yes, Baron," Dr. Hyde replied.

"Jordyn." Healey turned his stare to her.

"I need clothes and a shower." She wasn't going any-where the way she looked. They were going to stare at her, but it didn't mean she couldn't be presentable while they stared. She felt dried blood pull on her skin when she moved and the weight of matted hair on the back of her head. If they brought the throw, they had to have brought her things. Jordyn gave Rutger a hopeful look.

"I have clothes." Rutger leaned over, took her face in his hands, and kissed her forehead. "Thought you might like a new pair of jeans."

I love you. "Perfect."

"All right, get cleaned up and meet us in Rutger's of-fice," Healey ordered.

"Yes, sir," Jordyn replied. She waited as everyone watched her. "I'm half naked."

Healey's worry eased, letting his anger over the elves trespassing and the attack take more of his energy. He forced a laugh, gave Jordyn a smile, and turning walked out of the room. The doors closed behind him, and Tracy and Charles returned to their posts.

"Dr. Clio Hyde has discharged Mistress Jordyn Langston. Shutdown order One Heka," Dr. Hyde announced. Locks engaged, a computer beeped, and the cameras turned off. Within the hour, the transcripts from the day would be sit-ting on the baron's desk and a recording would be sent to his computer. "Please drink the meal replacement. You have to take in nutrients."

"I will. I swear," Jordyn assured.

Lingering, Dr. Hyde stared at Jordyn. "Don't get into trouble. Dr. Baines, you have paperwork to sign."

Jordyn nodded, then watched them leave and when the doors closed, her eyes skated over to her sentinels and she met Rutger's gold gaze leaden with thought. "What?"

"If this sets you back, don't block me. Don't give me the silent treatment. Talk to me. Let me help you." The words left his mouth and their weight cleared his mind. He knew exactly what he had to do.

"It's not going to, I promise. I'm all right. You might regret telling me to talk to you," Jordyn joked. "I could keep you up at night."

"I look forward to the possibility." Splinters of stress dislodged themselves from his nerves with her promise. He sensed her truth, its weight carrying in the link, and it felt good. "I'll see you in my office."

"Yes, Director." Jordyn almost saluted to see the look on Rutger's face. She didn't. Behind him the sentinels were watching them. Right then she didn't know how to act around them and their presence was going to take some getting used to.

Rutger walked around the bed, and when he stood on the other side, he faced her, and bowed his head. "Soothsayer." Jo laughed a light sound; it was like music to his ears. He didn't want to leave her or her laugh. Giving Jo his back, he made his way to the double doors where he paused, then turned enough he see her, again. Exhaustion pulled on her and her thoughts wanted to corrupt the life in her eyes. Wearing the oversized gown, her hair a mess, and dried blood crusting the sides of her face and neck, it didn't change how beautiful he thought she was. She was alive and was going to be all right. His eyes rolled gold, and when she gave him copper in return, he turned to the doors and the gazes of Tracy and Charles, and walked out of the med room.

CHAPTER TWENTY-SEVEN

Jordyn listened as the doors closed with a soft swish. She was alone. As alone as she was ever going to be. She sighed and her shoulders sank as Rutger's words sat inside her head and she held onto them. She wasn't going to let the elf's attack drag her back to hell where she would lose Rutger and her future. Jordyn needed to protect him from the baron and tell him she loved him, her truth putting a stop to the doubt between them. Raising her hands, she turned them over, amazed at the flawless skin as the sounds of breaking bones played louder than her thoughts. She fisted both hands, then straightened her fingers, and a light soreness wrapped around her joints. *Damn elf.*

Dropping her hands to her lap, she stared at the bag from a department store and a pink and gray stripped overnight bag. A shower sounded like heaven, and afterwards when she felt like herself, she was getting something to eat. *That's right, a completely normal thought.* Okay. She shoved the throw and sheet down her legs, expecting to see a rainbow of bruises, and was surprised when like her hands, her skin was unmarked.

Jordyn hung her feet off the side of the mattress and checked her thighs. She did it. She healed. At what expense? Dr. Baines, a witch and employee for the pack. A threat inside their numbers and his relationship with the

Esme a liability. *Not a normal thought.* Changing modes, she concentrated on the baron and Rutger waiting for her so she could hide behind a two-way mirror and read minds. *Not normal.*

"Tracy," Jordyn said as she slid off the bed to the cold tile.

"Ma'am." Tracy stepped forward.

"I need a shower and a room to get dressed in." Jordyn took her time, testing her legs and the strength of her muscles.

"Mistress, the female dorm has rooms and full bathrooms," Tracy explained.

"Will you show me?" Jordyn heard about the med room, the common area with a kitchen, and the dorms, but hadn't been to the newly constructed second floor. She had been too busy hiding at home. Jordyn opened the department store bag and was happy to see a pair of jeans and a shirt. She hated wearing new clothes, preferring the comfort of her well worn favorites. Then again, after the morning she had she needed the clothes. Checking the overnight bag, she saw her underclothes, socks, a hoodie, and toiletries. She had everything she needed.

"Yes, Mistress," Tracy replied. "Do you need assistance?"

Tracy was five years older than Jordyn, putting her in her forties. Her body was toned from cardio and training with her husband, Torin, the commander of the soldiers. She usually wore the soldier's uniform, not the sentinel's uniform of slacks, button-up shirt with the pack's crest on the left side, and shoulder holster. She did keep her running shoes versus boots. Jordyn didn't know why she volunteered for sentinel duty but there she was and her voice had taken on a parental tone. Jordyn assumed after collapsing in front of an audience, Rutger scooped her bleeding body off the ground and carried her to the med room. It was enough, Jordyn wasn't about to have a sentinel act like caregiver and escort her to the dorm room.

"No, just point me in the right direction, thank you." Jordyn slung the overnight bag over her shoulder, clutched the department store bag with her left arm, and held the back of the gown closed with her right. "They made these gowns to remind you, you don't have any dignity."

Charles laughed, an honest male sound, and smiling his blue eyes lit up. There was another person she didn't know why he volunteered. Maybe she had become an attraction and they wanted to see what tragedy happened next.

"Before we leave this room, I need to say something. As you probably have heard or witnessed, I've been drugged by humans, nearly kidnapped, stabbed through the back by Prime's Numina, and today cut up and poisoned by an elf. Being anywhere near me is going to put your life in danger." Whatever was changing the magic-born was going to make her a tempting target. How was she supposed to keep the pack safe, Rutger safe, and threats from hurting those she loved? How was she supposed to work with the OPI and have sentinels? "Don't feel obligated, and if you change your mind and want to step down, I understand and the baron will understand. You would be free of the responsibility." Jordyn shifted the bag with her right hand and felt a breeze on the back of her thighs. Zero dignity.

"I understand having sentinels is a first for you. When there's time, I will explain our duties and we'll set boundaries," Tracy explained.

"Mistress, if we had been there it might not have happened," Charles replied. "I will protect you. We will protect you."

Jordyn met his crystal blue gaze framed by thick black lashes and an image of Christian flashed in her mind. She paused, shoved it aside, and reminded herself she needed to focus on the present. Charles waited for her in silence as she gathered herself, and had no doubt, he would risk his life to save hers and those of the pack. His truth burned across the room and hit her in the chest, its magic rippling over her skin. Like a weak electrical shock, it didn't hurt, it caught her off guard. She inhaled, exhaled, and waited a second to see what else was going to happen as it slowly faded. *That was new.*

Straightening, she said, "Lead the way. Half-naked soothsayer walking." The double doors with the Cascade's crest and the Rod of Aesculapius on each side stood in front of her. In Greek mythology the serpent-entwined rod belonged to the god Asclepius, a deity linked to healing and medicine. The medical room served as an extension of Celestial and with Dr. Hyde in charge of staff and equipment, the symbol reflected the relationship. At least, she hadn't been taken to Celestial.

The corner of Charles' mouth curved in small smile as he opened the left side and held the door. Jordyn walked by him, clutching the back of the gown, and her bags. Blood stained her legs, arms, neck, and clumps of black hair sat on her shoulders. She got the feeling, even with Tracy's confidence, neither of her newly appointed sentinels understood exactly what they signed up for. Charles may have witnessed the attack because he had been in the enforcer's office, which meant he watched her take her aggression out on the elf. And she knew he had been at Butte Springs. Was there anyway she was going to stop being a victim? Nope.

"Mistress," Charles said.

Ahead of her, Tracy stopped and turned at the same time she did. "What is it?" Jordyn asked. The stone look on his face and steely gaze added weight to his straight shoulders. He had something to say to her. Maybe he was going to take her offer, quit his babysitting job, and go back to being a soldier.

"I want you to know, as your sentinel I have sworn my life to protect you. But I understand my real job is to provide interference to give you time to fight the enemy." Charles' voice lowered letting his wolf weave through his words. Frowning, he narrowed his gaze. "My apologies if I have over stepped my bounds. I wanted to be up front with you."

Give her time to fight the enemy ... she wasn't excepting that. Pressure built inside her. He thought she was powerful enough to fight for them. 'The pack chose you.'

"Mistress." Charles took a step back and waited.

Jordyn didn't know what to say. "You saw the elf?"

"Yes, ma'am. I was at Butte Springs, I found the cell he kept you in," Charles added.

Jordyn saw the cell, then it blurred and she saw Charles and respect. Not pity. She wasn't a victim. "You didn't cross any boundaries. I appreciate what you said. I will do my best to be the soothsayer you and the entire pack needs." There, she did it. She hoped she was able to keep her word.

Rutger sat behind his desk playing with a pen and occasionally tapping its top on a stack of papers. His mind replayed the attack, the fight, spending hours beside Jo as she healed herself, and their conversation. If she cut him off from her life, he was going to lose what was left of his mind, leaving himself vulnerable to the beast. The questions started to build and toppling, he didn't know if he was going to crawl out from under them.

What else were they going to have to endure? What did Prime have planned for her? How bad was it going to hurt her? Rutger didn't have answers. He didn't have a way to find answers. It was like life threw everything in the air and the pieces were crashing down and out of his reach.

"Do you hate the pen?" Healey asked.

Tap. Tap. Tap.

"What?" Rutger hit the end on the desk, sending the push button and tube flying across the top to land on the tile floor. He inhaled and exhaled. Looking up from the remains, the baron's gaze darkened to burnt gold for a heartbeat, then slowly drained to their natural brown. "What?"

"I understand the stress you're under, and I don't want to add to it," Healey started. There was one of two ways the discussion was going to go ... bad or good. He figured it was going to be the first.

Pushing his fingers through his hair, he wondered how much more he was supposed to take. He wanted the day to end. "Just tell me."

When pin pricks of anxiety left Rutger, Healey knew he wasn't ready to hear the seclusion he and Jordyn coveted was going to be taken away. Healey switched topics and explained, "The shadows lost Prime. It's reported his Numina remain at the Granite Peak clowder's estate."

"How did they lose him?" Rutger asked absently. He lifted the pen and its guts fell free to land on a stack of unread reports. Scooping them up, he dumped the pieces into the trash.

"It wasn't necessary for them to risk exposure, and the pack face reprimand from Prime. They also reported the clowder have gathered their soldiers. It could mean they heard about the attack and believing we aren't the sole targets are adding extra protection. Or it could be Prime's presence and the night of the address," Healey explained.

"How could the clowder have heard about the attack?" It happened that morning and the pack wasn't talking. Rutger knew there were a dozen ways the clowder could have found out, like Dr. Hyde being called away from Celestial. His mind was in chaos and unable to focus, he didn't try to figure it out.

"I talked to Chancellor Roarke and told him I've detained four of his people. He doesn't want the details exposed and the secret means the Seelie population doesn't know, and they're making assumptions. Rumors are spreading. We need Jordyn to tell us why they attacked, if they have planned another one, and if they're following the chancellor's orders."

"If the elf's plan had been successful, he would have left the same way he came, and we wouldn't know his identity. We would have been forced to call human law enforcement, and they would have to determine it a homicide. Then their detectives would start an investigation. That would have tied my hands, and while they worked their investigation, as best they could, I would question the klatch, hoping someone knew something. The klatch won't say a word, not after Butte Springs, and not when there is a divide in the pack, and they would see our interrogation as unfounded accusations and an infringement on their region. You would appear to be using your authority to challenge the factions and look like you've lost control of the pack and desperation was driving you. It would make you look weak and incapable of keeping Trinity. While this shit show was happening, I would have to bury my mate." Rutger hated saying those words. "I don't believe the chancellor had anything to do with it. The Seelie court doesn't have a history of confronting the pack. In fact, it's the exact opposite.

"I want to agree with you. Before I make a decision, I want to hear what Jordyn uncovers." Healey watched Rutger play with a new pen. "Are you going to be able to concentrate on this? If you can't, I understand, Ansel will take your place," Healey suggested.

"No. I'm doing this." Rutger sat back in his chair, rolled his neck, felt the tension digging in, and stared forward. "She broke her hands, healed them, and broke them again. Jo was upset her clothes were ruined, not about having been attacked. Poisoned. How? What does she have to do to live a normal life?"

"It's over, Rutger. Normal as we know it is over. The elves know it. The witches know it. Prime knows it. There has been a shift in regimes, and I believe the Highguard is behind the exchange. The Highguard and Prime are stacking factions, why when no one would defy their orders, I don't know. Then there's Jordyn, and she is exhibiting magic shapeshifters aren't supposed to possess."

Rutger considered the baron and what he said. "If the chancellor gave the order to attack Jo, what are we going to do?" He didn't want human law enforcement involved.

"What you said is factual. I won't put the pack at risk or force the klatch to pick sides and then face retaliation from the Seelie court by abusing my authority as baron, and I won't have the factions in my territory thinking I reacted irrationally. I'm handing the evidence and the responsibility over to Prime. He's here, he can have the pleasure of hearing the evidence, the elf's testimony, the chancellor trying to save one his own, and make a decision and determine a reprimand. I will obviously demand a punishment to fit the crime."

"Arvid should be put to death," Rutger growled. He wanted to be the executioner. Wild and unhindered in his wolf form to rip into the elf's flesh. Rutger imagined the scene and a hunger deep inside him ached.

"Agreed. While we have the elves detained, security needs to be on alert. I don't know when Prime will address the situation or how long it will take him to come to a ruling. In the meantime, we know talk will spread about Jordyn, making her the center of attention, potentially giving anyone with a grudge a reason to attack her. It's imperative the sentinels remain with her, and the both of you stay alert. If you think your property has been compromised, or there is danger, I want you both back here."

"Protected and strength in numbers," Rutger mumbled. They were going to lose another part of their lives.

"Affirmative." Healey twisted in his chair enough he saw the clock on the wall. Ten. The day flew into the past and the night slowed to a crawl.

Rutger glared at the door. It opened a sliver, letting murmured conversations, some coming from the communications room, filter into the office. His frustration burned when the person responsible hadn't knocked or announce themselves. He nearly ordered the person to close the damn door-where was Tabby to stop anyone from interrupting them-when his anger quickly cooled and his heart stopped in his chest. The familiar scents of vanilla and spice drifted into the room, followed by Jo's laughter. He should have used his senses or reached her through their link.

Healey watched the lines fanning out from Rutger's darkened glare fade, and his cheeks and mouth relaxed enough he wasn't snarling. It had to be done. Without Rutger's knowledge, Healey contacted a real estate agent and using the pack's lawyers purchased the land surrounding Rutger's house. His architects were currently designing two houses with med rooms, armories, and the capability of accommodating enforcers and soldiers. He was going to have soldiers and slayers near Rutger and Jordyn twenty-four hours a day whether they liked it or not. In different locations, Healey purchased four other homes and was actively having them transformed into safe houses. He didn't know how their lives were going to change, or what dangers they were going to face, but he wouldn't be ill-equipped. The safety of the pack and the klatch were his responsibilities.

Jordyn had gone through the door in the gym, avoiding the reception area, and attempting to avoid seeing anyone when she ran onto Mandy in the hall. She listened to the enforcer struggling to make small talk and watched as Mandy's gaze flicked from Tracy, Charles, and back to her. It was obviously painstaking but there was nothing Jordyn could do to do ease the tension. And there was tension ... it sat in the air like a blanket of fog. If she stopped and considered what they might be thinking as she made her way to Rutger's office, with her sentinels in tow, she would have screamed.

To her side Charles stepped forward, took the door from her, and held it open while Tracy took her place on the left side. The baron's sentinels, Sousa and Troy, stood their posts near the entrance of the communications room and across from Rutger's office. Four sentinels in a building with more than a dozen enforcers and soldiers, not normal.

"Late for a meeting," Jordyn said as she hitched her thumb at the open door.

"Sorry to keep you," Mandy replied.

When Mandy disappeared into the communications room, at a near run, Jordyn shook her head and entered the office. "Baron." Behind her, Charles closed the door, silencing the noise.

"Jordyn, how do you feel?" Healey asked.

"Good. Getting out of the gown and into clothes helped." Jordyn felt Rutger's eyes on her like they were boring into her head and trying to read her thoughts. She sat down in the chair and met his gold gaze. "Really, I'm good. I don't think they are."

"They'll get over it," Healey said.

Jordyn wore her raven hair straight, its ends at the center of her back. Black lined her eyes, emphasizing her long lashes, and framing her cocoa eyes, and soft pink tinted her lips. A gray, zip up hoodie covered a wine-colored T-shirt, and her jeans ended in running shoes peppered with blood. Her clothes, while fitting her, left room to spare.

"How was your shower?" Rutger asked. "I haven't checked the facilities out."

"Great. Had a sentinel standing guard at the bathroom door and one outside. Nice and relaxing," Jordyn tried to ease the tension.

"They're for your safety, Soothsayer," Healey reminded her. "Rutger said you read the elf's mind. What did you find out?"

"His name is Arvid, he's part of a group, I didn't get the name. He referred to the change as the *Emanation*, and those affected, like me, as *Potents*. They believe if they cleanse the world of Potents it will stop the Emanation from happening," Jordyn explained.

"Did you find out what they think the Emanation is?" Healey asked.

"No. I can only assume it has something to do with the increase in magic."

"If it is, they can't stop it, no one person is responsible for the shift in magic," Rutger offered.

"We'll have to investigate the group. Are the elves in the interrogation room?" Healey asked.

"Affirmative. We can head there now," Rutger replied. "Jo, are you going to be all right with this? Facing them?"

Jordyn stood wanting to get it over with. "Yes."

CHAPTER TWENTY-EIGHT

Three men sat at a table, their arms stretched out in front of them, their wrists and forearms shackled with Cobalt 27 to the steel top. The Cobalt at their ankles glittered dark blue under the bright LED lights lighting the room.

The word cobalt originated from the German word kobold meaning goblin or elf, and used as a weapon against the Fae. Scientists believe it effected the Fae because it wasn't found as a free element in nature but found in mineral ores. What the difference between the two was or why it suppressed Fae powers, Rutger didn't know and didn't care. It worked to restrain their magic or kill them, that's all that mattered.

Besides elves, the name Fae included pixies, brownies, goblins, nymphs, sylphs, and a dozen other magic-born. The groups who's features resemble human forms lived in the open as freely as shapeshifters and witches. There were two groups of elves, the Seelie court and the Unseelie court, and both were ruled by a chancellor. They lived by strict rules and avoided contact with other magic-born and humans as much as possible. Chancellor Roarke ruled them, while being part of the klatch and under the baron's authority. The relationship between the Cascade pack and the Seelie court was cordial if not casual friendly. They were allowed to live secluded and deep within the Shasta-Trinity National Forest, because of their culture and belief system.

Jordyn sat in one of six chairs, facing the large window. They wore the same clothing as the attacker, black on black like they were trying to be ninjas. *They failed.* Jordyn sensed their magic and their attempts to conceal them-selves. *Failed.*

"Are you ready, Jordyn," Healey asked.

"Yes."

Rutger met her stare as he pushed a button and a panel slid back, revealing another control panel. He hit the inter-com. "Begin the questioning."

"Affirmative," Ansel replied. "I am Captain Wolt with the Cascade pack's enforcers. Be advised, this questioning is being recorded as evidence. Are you prepared to give a statement?"

An elf with brown hair searched the mirror, his hazel eyes darting from one side to the other. "No."

"No," the second responded.

"No," the third responded.

Rutger's anger came in a heated wave and he wanted to roar and tear the elves limb from limb and beat their corpses with the bloody stumps.

"Arvid is in stable condition after having his arms and nose broken, his jaw dislocated, and his ribs broken. He also has a concussion and he won't be seeing out of his left eye anytime soon. A doctor has treated his injuries and stopped the internal bleeding." Their eyes widened with their surprise but no one said anything. "Chancellor Roarke has been notified of the offences and has been given evi-dence."

"You've got nothing," the brown-haired elf mumbled.

"We'll see," Ansel replied. They weren't going to talk. "Director."

Rutger would have loved to tell Ansel to transport the trio to the secluded black house, where he had taken the witches, nothing more than a prison with a variety of devices designed for torture. There they would start a real interrogation. He met the baron's gaze and asked, "Do you want to proceed in questioning them?"

"One more, doesn't matter what it is. I need to check off a box to prove I did my due diligence," Healey answered. "Jordyn, it's your turn."

"Proceed, single action," Rutger ordered through the intercom.

"We have Arvid's name, and we know you call those with advancing magic Potents. Silence isn't doing you any favors. The three of you were waiting, Arvid's the one facing trespassing and attempted murder charges. Your confession will help you when you face the chancellor and the baron," Ansel assured. Keeping his tone stern, he tried threading an easy 'come on, tell me' into it.

"Attempted. The soothsayer lives?" the second asked.

"Affirmative. Who do you think gave him the beating?" Ansel countered.

Jordyn cringed when she heard the captain, then looked at him when she caught the pride in his voice. Maybe there was more than Charles who didn't think she was a twisted form of entertainment and the cancer that was about to bring down the pack. *Maybe.*

"Do you need a pen?" Ansel asked.

"No," they answered in unison.

"They admitted they knew Arvid's intent was to kill her. They expected to hear she died," Rutger said with a growl clinging to his words. He was consumed by the attack, furious, tired, and wanted to take Jo home.

"Jordyn-" Healey stopped when she stared forward, her eyes gleamed copper for a second before onyx filled them.

"They refer to each other using old Scandinavian names. Arvid, Randy. Agnar, Bruce. Benedik, Rich. Erling, Dean. They call themselves Krijgers, it's Dutch meaning warriors," Jordyn explained. "As I said, they believe by eliminating the Potents they'll keep the Emanation from happening. They absolutely believe they're fighting for the good of the world. The Krijgers have members across the nation and from around the world. This is happening everywhere," Jordyn explained. She drew back from Bruce's mind and sat back in the chair. "The assassinations were supposed to start with me. They think killing the Cascade's soothsayer would prove their power. With their failure, maybe it will send a message to the others."

"Prime's presence will send a clearer message," Healey said.

"The fake names explain why our search on Arvid came back with nothing," Rutger started as he watched Jo. At least it wasn't their contacts and equipment failing them. "They're keeping it old-world Fae. Which I don't understand if they're planning on killing the Potents."

"Why do you say that?" Jordyn rubbed her temples. Diving into their minds created an ache and it started streaking through her forehead. The shower made her feel normal but the affect was wearing off.

"If they're risking everything to protect *normal*, why call themselves ... what did you say?" Rutger asked.

"Krijgers. It's Dutch." Jordyn met his mahogany eyes and watched gold float around his iris. She could see exhaustion weighing on him, his worry gripping his face, and his frustration sharpened his jaw. The day sucked.

"Right. Why not use something American? Neutral. They're against the old world and old ways." Rutger looked at the three men, clearly brainwashed, remain with their silence and shackled to the table. "Did you get anything else?"

"Those untouched are called *Standards*. Bruce, the first one on the left, will follow Randy to death if need be. The others, not so much. They're not happy hearing I didn't die and their leader, the strongest among them, was beat up and apprehended. The leaders of Krijgers aren't going to be pleased with them. The second guy is thinking about the others who doubt the Emanation. They're confident they'll be turned over to human law enforcement, where they'll be given a chance to defend themselves. Other than that, nothing of importance," Jordyn answered. They didn't like knowing she survived. "They fear me."

"They should," Healey stated. He placed his hand on hers. "They're in for a surprise when they realize this is being kept from human law enforcement."

Jordyn looked at the baron's hand, his ageless skin, his strength, and soft tan remaining from summer's sun as fall continued to sweep in. "I don't want the pack and the klatch to fear me. They will. And this will continue, only it will come from within." Jordyn half knew it was exhaustion and the headache gripping her skull making her sound dark and pitiful. And paranoid.

"We will take measures to ensure your safety," Healey assured. "I think you've been through enough. We have the information to add to the report. It should prove their intent to Chancellor Roarke and prove we have a bigger problem."

"Does this mean I can go home?" Jordyn asked. She wanted to crawl in bed for a week.

"Yes. Rutger, take your mate home," Healey ordered.

"Are you asleep?" Rutger asked.

They had been driving in silence for ten minutes; Jordyn spent the time slunk in the seat and staring up at the night sky. "No."

"Are you good?" He wasn't going to ask if she was all right. He turned off the highway onto a dark, two-lane road and started out of the city.

"I am. I'm tired, hungry, and I'm sure there is a jackhammer in my head," she answered. Jordyn sat up, lowered the window a couple of inches, and inhaled night's fresh air. The med room smelled of sterilizer, decaying skin, and blood while the lower level of the office where the cells were smelled like concrete, recycled air, and the musk of too many people. Jordyn had caught the scent of Arvid/Randy, and the smell of his blood made her feel better.

"Do you want me to call Dr. Hyde?" Rutger asked.

"No, it's late. What horrors would she think of if she saw your number? Don't do that to her. I'm good, I just need to sleep." Jordyn was looking at the side of Rutger's face and saw a hint of a smile when awareness skated over her. Twisting in her seat, Jordyn searched the side of the road and the woods. "I didn't know someone lived there," she said, pointing. Warm light glowed from the once empty, two-story log home, its chimney puffed with plumes of smoke.

"Me either. We've been preoccupied," Rutger answered.

"Stop."

"What?" Rutger took his foot off the pedal.

"Stop."

With Jo's hard tone, Rutger slammed on the brakes, causing the truck to skid to a stop. In the rearview mirror the headlights of the sentinel's car closed in and stopped right behind him. "What's going on?" He sent his senses out and searched for elves, Prime, the creatures, witches, anyone.

Jordyn didn't answer. She opened the door, hopped out of the truck, and started in the direction of the house.

"Shit." He put the truck in reverse, waited for the sentinels to give him room, and started backing up. The motion closing the passenger door. At the entrance, he turned the wheel and backed into the driveway. Killing the engine, he got out and met up with Jo as she knocked on the door.

"It's almost midnight. What is this about?" he ordered.

"You'll see," Jordyn replied. She knocked harder. One second. Two seconds. Three. She could hear their heartbeats and feel their wolves. "I know you're in there."

"Jo, Mea, you've had a long day and it's getting longer. Maybe exhaustion is playing with your senses," Rutger tried. He cringed when she knocked harder. "Jordyn, really."

With her full name she faced him. "Don't doubt me. Never doubt me." She held his gaze as she threatened, "Do you want me to read your minds?"

"Director?" Tracy asked.

Jordyn stepped out from behind Rutger to face Tracy. "You are *my* sentinel and I'm the soothsayer. You don't ask the director questions. Is that understood?" She met Charles questioning look, and felt like she had hit the highest level of a crazy, paranoid freak. Giving them her back she said, "You asked for it."

Everyone froze as the door slowly opened. "I call cheater move," Claudia said as she stood in the doorway.

"Again, I'm the soothsayer. Did you think I wouldn't notice you?" Jordyn asked. "You know I can feel you, right? I hold your life inside my head."

"Yeah, and it creeps me out," Claudia mumbled.

The door opened wider, and Jason stood behind Claudia. "Rutger, Jordyn. We thought it might take a couple more days, especially after today."

"The baron did this?" Rutger asked. What else was the baron doing?

"You could have told me," Jordyn accused.

"Yes, the baron did this. We were on strict orders not to or I would have been the first person to spill my guts," Claudia insisted.

"You aren't supposed to divulge privileged information," Tracy lectured. She stood behind Rutger at the bottom step with her hands on her hips and a scowl on her face.

Jordyn inhaled, knew frustration and exhaustion were playing with her emotions, and slowly turned around to face the sentinel. She was going to have to prove her authority if she wanted her sentinels to stop questioning her. Yes, walking up to a door and knocking when it was close to midnight was odd, but she was odd. Jordyn felt the dragons of her ancestors rising with her power ... it teased a memory, or a dream, she couldn't tell, and met Tracy's hard gaze with an onyx glare. "Do I need to remind you of who and what I am?"

"The baron's order-" Tracy started.

"If pertinent information has been revealed, creating a threat to the pack, I will personally speak with the baron."

Jordyn's words felt like steel and sounded hard. Too hard for her having said them. She hated the callus person she was becoming and hated the look in Rutger's eyes.

"Jordyn, come in the house," Jason started. "We don't need a anyone driving by and stopping."

"You will refer to her as mistress," Tracy ordered.

Her stare weakened under Jordyn's. *About time.* "No, he won't. I have to have some semblance of a normal life. At one time I was a nobody, a nobody no one cared about and they were my friends," Jordyn explained. "I had a life."

Grabbing Jo's upper arm, Rutger turned her from the sentinel and towards him. Her onyx eyes held an edge of hardness he hadn't seen in her before and didn't like the sight. He guessed carrying the weight of the pack and being a target changed a person. "You have a life."

Under the porch light with silence baring down on them, they stared at each other at the same time the tension from the group ate the air and nipped at Jordyn. She met Rutger's mahogany gaze and watched the flakes of gold dissolve under the weight of his thoughts. Jordyn knew without feeling their bond or reading his mind they shared the same thought. It wasn't going to end. There was going to be other sentinels, soldiers, shadows, and pack members following the baron's orders to spy on them. The witches and Flint had nothing on the three attacks in three days and Prime's challenge. If they were going to have any kind of a life with one another they were going to have to carve it out of the chaos their lives had become.

"I know. I do," Jordyn whispered. She hadn't meant it like that. Jordyn was slowly fading and the Cascade's soothsayer was moving in like a storm.

"Do you want to go in or go home?" Rutger asked. They needed to go home.

"Please, come in," Claudia insisted. "You're right. We are friends."

"I want to go home, but we have to go inside." Jordyn covered his hand with her own. *They are our normal.*

"I know."

"Perfect. I have wine for the lady and bourbon for the director," Claudia said with a smile.

Rutger's hand slipped from her arm as she entered the house. Across the threshold, she stopped and faced the sentinels. "Both of you, inside."

"We have to stand our post," Charles countered.

"There are no threats. And Jason is right, no one needs to see a newly inhabited house with guards out front after midnight. I'm not worried about the enforcer's patrol. I'm worried about human law enforcement."

"I'm not overstepping Jo's authority when I say, she's right and the both of you need to be inside." Rutger started. "We don't need law enforcement taking notice."

"Ma'am. Sir." Passing Tracy, Charles cleared the stairs and entering the house took his position on the left side of the double doors.

"Mistress," Tracy replied as she closed the door behind her. Taking her place on the right side of the door, she stared forward. "Wait."

"Yes," Jordyn replied, and met the questions in her gaze.

"How do you know there isn't a threat? You didn't sense the elf?" Tracy questioned.

"Are you challenging me?" Jordyn asked. Why did this have to be so damn difficult. Why couldn't she sit down, have wine, relax after having been attack? Instead, she was burning energy she didn't have. "Are you?"

"No, Mistress, my apologies. It wasn't my intent. I need to know what to expect. We're here to guard you, and if you're able to sense a threat, you can give us a warning," Tracy explained quickly.

Jordyn's insides fell into a pit of embarrassment with her overreaction. Her emotions were getting the best of her. "I overreacted." She held Tracy's stare while she searched her territory with her senses. Like a fog flowing over the land, she felt the contours, smelled the varied scents the soil held, and the wind as she travelled. Jordyn drew a breath and was back in the house. "There's nothing except animals." How hadn't she sensed the elf? The baron informed her he was going to sacrifice Rutger for a power position and to prove a point. "I can give you a warning."

"Affirmative, Mistress," Tracy replied.

Her gaze lingered on Jordyn as her power, like a gentle breeze, circled her. Her black eyes slowly bled to copper and the breeze faded.

"You get weirder by the day," Claudia said.

"You have no idea," Jordyn replied. She left the sentinels by the door and followed Claudia through the foyer to the living room where Jason and Rutger waited.

Soft lighting sent a honey hue over the pale pine walls, stone flooring, and dark gray area rug. A large, cream-colored leather sectional took the center of the spacious room, its chasse end sitting in front of the fireplace. There were no decorations on the walls while opened boxes, large and small were scattered about.

"How long have you been here?" Rutger asked.

"A week. It's taken us awhile, we were trying to be stealthy," Jason answered. "Have a seat, I'll get drinks."

Jordyn sat on the chasse next to the fire, Rutger sat beside her with his arm behind her, and Claudia took a seat across from them. "This is nice. I always wondered what it looked like inside."

"I want to say sorry again. I know I should have told you," Claudia started.

"The baron gave the order. Neither one of us would go against him," Jordyn pointed out.

"You would. You do," Claudia countered. "It's said the baron ordered you not to challenge Prime and you did."

Jordyn laughed a sad sound. "I did, and for the record, it's not my best move. His Numen, that's code for creature thing, stabbed me in the back, I had to do something to prove my power."

"No shit," Jason mocked as he handed her a glass of red wine. "Because healing and walking away wasn't enough."

"Thanks." Jordyn meet his blue gaze and the humor in his eyes, his boyish charm, and saw respect. *Maybe.* She released the hold on her anxiety, letting the day slough from her like dead skin. She was becoming someone new, and wanted ... no, needed to enjoy their company even if it was for a minute. It felt good to laugh and they weren't looking at her like she was a stranger or a monster.

"Did the elf really cut your face?" Claudia asked.

Jordyn touched her cheek, felt the blade in her skin, heard her fingers break, and stopped herself from shuddering. "He did. With White 47 blades then I broke my hand on his face."

"Jordyn, I'm so sorry," Claudia began. "You don't have a mark on you."

"A side effect," Jordyn mumbled. *Do not get lost in your thoughts.*

Rutger took the tumbler of bourbon from Jason and tried thinking of something to change the subject. "Jason, you aren't working as the baron's sentinel, what are you doing?" Rutger should have known, it was his job, the report and change of position was in the stack of papers on his desk. But he had been distracted with Jo and lost track. He wasn't completely sure what day it was.

Jason sat beside Claudia, his eyes losing their easy-going gleam and turned serious. "I've been promoted to Executioner of the Slayers," he explained. His voice hardened, making the words stone cold.

Jordyn looked at Claudia to watch her cast her emerald eyes to her wine, her knuckles turning white from her grip on the glass. Lando Bryzon had been the Executioner for three decades and commanded the elite team of assassins with precision. Jordyn understood his emotionless view and single-minded focus when the baron threatened to send the slayers after her when she left Trinity to face Louis. Something was happening if the baron replaced him and Jordyn didn't know what it was. Kinda like she didn't know Jason and Claudia moved into a house a mile away from them. "Why? What happened to Bryzon?"

"The baron felt he was ready to be replaced. Lando is training the shadows. Firearm tactics and sniper training." It was Jason's turn to look at his glass and the tawny liquid staring back at him. He inhaled, exhaled, and met Rutger's narrowed gaze. "After Prime's attack, and then the elf's, the baron is coming down hard on everyone. An alert went out to all branches and those in charge. Each branch is required to have two teams on standby at all times."

"What's the alert?" Rutger asked. He felt he abandoned his job, responsibilities, and felt incompetent for having to ask. He understood why the baron hadn't confided in him, he had to be there for Jo and was emotionally involved, but it didn't make being left out of the loop less painful. It didn't have to be business all the time, his dad could have told him.

"There have been three attacks on Jordyn's life in three days. One from a doctor associated with Patriot Angels and an anti-paranormal group. Which she is a witness, a victim, and has filed charges against both men, both humans, with human law enforcement. It makes her a target and it means her life is in danger. The pack can't lose its soothsayer, let alone the Second to the Alpha and his mate," Jason explained.

Her status and presence put the entire pack in danger. She was responsible for their lives. "You should know, the sheriff's department handed the case over to the Organized Paranormal Investigations unit and I'm a consultant for the OPI under Detective Watt's authorization," Jordyn said like it was a confession. "He's my handler and knows I can read minds."

"How?" Jason gripped his tumbler and leaned forward.

This was a breach in security. Jordyn's insides caved as she explained how she had contacted Rutger while held prisoner, and then how she described the doctor's warehouse to the sheriff's department. Like she needed defending, Rutger stressed, Jordyn hadn't volunteered the information.

Jason listened to them in silence, his face giving nothing away, while Claudia stared at Jordyn. The Executioner of Slayers was sitting across from her. Would Jason be as detached and driven to obey the baron as Bryzon? *Yes.* Like she was driven to obey him. She didn't see the detachment in his eyes, yet, and didn't have to when his cold determination sent a chill down her spine. Any boyish charm Jason exuded was a lie.

"The baron is aware of the situation," Rutger assured. "He considers Detective Watt's relationship with the pack an advantage."

Of course he does, he doesn't have to answer to Detective Watt. Jordyn didn't need her senses, or the ability to read minds to understand what was happening. "I'm sure the baron gave you a complete file on me, the detective, and our relationship." She assumed Jason's razor edge was because of the change in leadership and maybe he felt bad for Bryzon. She was fooling herself. "It's not news to you." She easily ignored Claudia's reaction.

Jason lowered his glass. "I'm understanding there's no point to try to keep anything from you. You sensed we were here."

"You could try," Jordyn challenged. "I wouldn't advise it though." She sounded harder, colder, and as soon as she said the words, delivered as a threat, she wished she could take them back. Threatening her friends wasn't what she wanted. Her heart ached with the understanding she would never have friends loyal to her. Still, she would never betray someone's trust by invading their mind without their consent. She didn't need to read Jason's mind to know he was uneasy and didn't trust her, it radiated from him. Jordyn hated seeing doubt in their eyes, and sadly there was nothing she was going to do about it. If they didn't tell her the truth, she would treat herself to a trip through their thoughts. It was self-defense.

Claudia was staring at her, and Jordyn knew her eyes were onyx and the copper usually swirling in them was gone. She wasn't trying, and still she was projecting the soothsayer. Jordyn wanted them to understand she would protect herself and Rutger from them, the pack, and the baron. Because she wouldn't be able to help herself.

"Hard pass. We've been given intel about you, the case, and the detective. Anytime you do something, like command an attacking elf to stop, we're updated. We have your medical records, the video feed from the attempted kidnapping, the elf's attack, and the med room. I've watched it at least a dozen times. We were given the video feed to study you and better understand how to protect you," Jason explained. "I'll report what you did tonight. Sensing us and using your senses to search the area."

Jordyn ceased to be a person. She was a thing. "At least I know where I stand." She was losing everyone in her life.

"We both know," Rutger growled. He felt like he was losing his friends and authority to the baron's orders. Rutger needed to get back to the office to have a presence, and he needed to talk to the baron about setting boundaries.

"Jordyn, you have to understand. What you did for the Olivers was in the report. You eased their grief by giving them their son. You possess our history and our lives. You healed from an attack that would have killed anyone else. You aren't a photographer living in bug valley, you've gained a greater purpose," Claudia tried. "With your abilities comes consequences. We're here to protect what is ours."

Protects what is ours? Jordyn was going to run on about unfairness and how she wanted her life back, then stopped ... she had been playing the 'feel sorry for me' card for months. It didn't make accepting what she was turning into any easier. Claudia and Jason were staring at her when her cell phone sang making her jump. "Sorry." Exactly what she needed was a phone call. Not. Taking it from her pocket, she looked at the screen, groaned, and answered the call. "Detective Watt."

Rutger faced her, and she shrugged her shoulders. She had no idea why he was calling. Staring at Rutger, she listened to Detective Watt tell her a sheriff's deputy reported he watched Rutger, with another vehicle following, stop his truck in the street, watched her jump out, head to the house where she banged on the door, then threatened the occupants. Jordyn couldn't stop herself from cringing as he described a crazy person.

"I know what time it is, it's not unusual. ... Yes, Rutger stopped the truck. ... Yes, I got out and went to the house. And banged on the door. They let me in." Jordyn stared down at the rug as heat crept up her throat to her cheeks. "I know them, Detective. I'm sitting and having wine with them as we speak. ... Yes, the people in the second vehicle are with us. ... We all know what time it is. Fine." Jordyn handed the cell to Claudia, figuring she would be easier to talk to than Jason. "He wants to talk to an owner."

"Can I help you?" Claudia asked.

Jordyn took a drink of her wine and wished she had the bottle. "Detective Watt thinks the stress from Louis and Dr. Holmes' near kidnapping and upcoming hearing is causing a breakdown. He fears I'm a threat to myself and now others. He believes I'm losing my mind. He brought up my mental health."

"Yet he blackmails you in order to have you work for him." Rutger was going to explain a couple of things to the detective.

"He wants to talk to you," Claudia said as she handed the cell back to Jordyn.

"What did he say?" Rutger asked. He heard Claudia's side and some of the detective's both made his imagination spin out of control.

"Wanted to make sure we didn't feel threatened and she was doing all right. Louis has been transferred to a secured hospital for psychiatric help, making the detective worry Jordyn might feel guilty. The doctor remains in jail and his bail has been denied after they found the warehouse and evidence." Claudia inhaled and exhaled. "I assured him Jordyn is fine and your visit tonight was friends and pack getting together. And we're shapeshifters, time is different for us."

"Why did he tell you when he could have told Jo?" Rutger asked.

"I don't know," Claudia mumbled.

Jordyn ended the call, shoved her cell in her pocket, then picked up her glass. "He was too busy accusing me of losing my mind." She stood and walked to the fire. "I get it. After acting the way, I did. Anyone who lived through Butte Springs would have. My only worry concerning Louis is he won't go to jail and Dr. Holmes will continue his experiments. Prime and the challenge outweigh both humans. He has no clue, and I have no defense."

"Mea, this is why it's hard for us to work with humans. He's investigating a crime and has no idea what you're dealing with. Humans will never understand." Rutger set his bourbon on the table and closed the distance between them. "You will have to protect our way of life by keeping it a secret."

Lying. "I understand." Jordyn was exhausted and Detective Watt's call served as a reminder she was living in two worlds. She was a werewolf soothsayer responsible for her pack's safety, and a woman with special magical gifts the OPI wanted to exploit.

"We need to go home," Rutger urged.

He was right. She needed silence and sleep. Jordyn nodded, agreeing with Rutger, and let him turn her towards the doors and her sentinels.

"Have a goodnight," Claudia said from behind them.

Jordyn twisted enough to meet her gaze. Was that pity? "You too."

CHAPTER TWENTY-NINE

Jordyn deliberately slid out of bed, doing her best not to bother Rutger. When he continued to sleep undisturbed, she pulled on a pair of lounge pants, a zip-up hoodie, and headed downstairs. Walking through the silent house, she enjoyed the minutes of solitude, and making her way to the kitchen turned on the coffee maker.

With a mug of hot coffee in hand, she opened the French door and walked out to the railing of the deck. A sweep of brisk October air nipped at her, sending a chill racing over her skin. Everything was normal, the water lapped at the shore, varied birds chirped and cooed, and chipmunks and squirrels were scurrying along the forest floor. Perfectly normal like she wasn't a soothsayer, a power, and wasn't about to face Prime. Crisp yellow started to rise above the mountain's ridge, casting a warm sheen over treetops, and inching down its edges reached toward the lake.

Jordyn inhaled as her territory began waking and the day unfolded before her and embraced her. As if called by the sun, magic rose up from the land, its threads wrapping around her ankles, calves, legs, and moving up sparked her power. The energy fueled her ancestors, giving her the feel of dragons as if they were beside her. Their presence taking her worries, and easing the anxiety coursing in her muscles.

The magic brought them at the same time it was fighting for its place in a world that had cast it out. It was part of her, and Jordyn was going to help it gain strength and it would be tangible, like she could touch it with her hands.

"What payment was magic going to demand?" she mumbled to the lake. And just like that the morning stopped being normal.

Like she hadn't been paying for it since she had taken her place as soothsayer. Jordyn shut down her thoughts-she didn't need that kind of negativity-and held onto the dragons and their security. Despite the back and forth of her mood, Jordyn smiled when Rutger's essence feathered her senses, and like satin ribbons caressed her wolf. Rutger was awake and trying to find her.

For a minute, Rutger stood in the door she left open. His first instinct was to lecture her on the dangers, but then he stopped. He watched Jo soak up the morning's sun and the energy from the woods. Her face was lifted, her raven hair up in a messy bun caught the gold rays of sunshine, and she looked relaxed. He held her throughout the night, claiming her warmth and not wanting to let her go. He im-agined them using the darkness of night to run away from the challenge, the pack, and the baron. For a heartbeat, while he drifted between sleep and awareness, he was sure his plan would work, then reality hit him like a hammer. They had responsibilities to the pack, klatch, magic-born, and the Highguard. His thoughts chased one another, and every time ended in the same place. He knew what he had to do. Knowing she knew he was there he wasn't going to linger. Rutger left the door, and crossing the deck set his cup on the table.

"Mea, what are thinking about?" He wrapped his arms around her middle, his lips by her ear.

Magic is getting stronger and it wants us. "It's a beautiful morning."

"You're lying, but I'll take it." Rutger straightened. His nerves were going to tie themselves in knots at the same time his heart burst through his sternum. Inhaling, he drew in her vanilla and spice while feeling her essence in their link. It was now or never. "Do you see that spot right there?" Rutger pointed to the shore, nowhere specific.

"Right where?" Jordyn leaned forward, following Rutger's hand.

"There," he said at her ear. "There, the big rock."

There were several big rocks. "Sure. The big rock. Why?"

With his lips touching her ear, he whispered, "I kissed a girl there once."

Jordyn turned in his hold to face him. "You did?"

"Mmmm ... she likes being by the lake and being kissed."

"You know a lot about this girl." Jordyn let her power free to surround them and Rutger's eyes rolled gold.

"There's something I need her to know."

"Then you should tell her." Jordyn didn't know why they were talking in third person and was having trouble reading his face. She felt the link between them and sensed apprehension and let a sliver of fear work inside her. The shard slid through the intimacy Rutger initiated with his closeness.

"Jo." Rutger rested his forehead on hers for a moment, then met her gaze. He needed to look at her. "I love you, Jo." Rutger couldn't stop a grin from curving his lips and the feeling a weight had been lifted from his shoulders. "I love you."

The words tumbled through her, their meaning gripping her heart. Jordyn never would have guessed him saying those three words would affect her so deeply. She had been wanting to tell him how much she loved him and out of fear and what she was becoming put it off. She didn't have to wait any longer. The three little words carried weight and gave meaning to their life, the sacrifices they were making, and gave them a future.

"I love you, Wolf," Jordyn whispered. "I love you."

"You had me worried, you were silent there for a minute." Rutger's apprehension released its hold on him and he plowed forward. "Jo. Jordyn Langston, would you marry me?"

They were bound by One-Flesh the Scared Writ etched in the history of the pack, and were fated mates. Marriage and a wedding, as much as she wanted both, seemed out of her reach and with the uncertainty irrelevant. "You mean it?" Jordyn asked holding his gaze. "I was attacked by an elf."

"You kicked his ass. Yes, I do. I want you to be Jo Kanin. Mistress Kanin. I want you to carry my name. Is it barbaric and old fashioned?" Rutger asked.

Not to me. Jordyn's heartbeat pounded as her love and need for Rutger overpowered every emotion. When his eyebrows furrowed and a mask covered his face, she realized she had been staring at him and hadn't given him an answer. "I said yes before and it never changed. I loved you then and I love you now. I will marry you, Rutger Kanin."

"Dear god, woman." Ruger picked Jo up, her legs went around his waist, and setting her on the railing he kissed her with an urgency coming from deep inside him. It rup-tured the well of need and pain he had been carefully guarding.

Jordyn tightened her hold on his middle, bringing him closer to her, their bodies touching, but it wasn't enough. She pulled his T-shirt up to touch his warm skin, and her hands roamed over his chest to feel his muscles tense un-der her palms.

"While this could be considered awkward, it will help."

Jordyn froze. She heard the voice and it sounded inside her head while Rutger tightened his hold on her and growled. Meeting Rutger's heated gaze, she whispered, "You took the words out of my mouth."

Rutger let go of Jo and she hopped off the railing. They both faced Prime and found him staring at them. Sur-rounding the house, he sensed several beings and easily assumed they were Prime's Numina. "Prime."

"Director. Soothsayer. Beautiful morning, isn't it?" Prime took a step forward, his black shined shoes a contrast against the rough wood planks. His honey hued hair fell loose over his shoulders and gleamed in the sunlight while his narrowed azar eyes held a hint of time. "I think it is."

Jordyn saw Prime, the demon. His violet eyes ringed with white gleamed in the cool light of the early morning. Highlights of sapphire glittered in his thick, silver hair and his exposed black skin reflected the sun. Dressed in a pew-ter gray suit, and a black, button-up shirt, his sophisticated looks didn't match his relaxed stance. Jordyn didn't believe the show. He wanted something. She stared at him won-dering if he was allowing her to see his true form.

"What can we do for you?" Rutger knew why he was there. Prime could have waited and let them have the mo-ment. Rutger wanted to enjoy being with Jo before they had to go to Foxwood and face the chancellor, the baron, and obviously Prime.

"I'll get to that. I forget what the mountains are like on this side of the world." Prime took another step closer to the soothsayer. "Practically primitive."

Jordyn stepped around Rutger, this was her fight, her problem, and Prime wasn't going to push Rutger to lose control. He had held onto his control over the last couple days and nothing was going to push him over the edge. "The challenge isn't until tomorrow night. Unless you're here to start it early." Jordyn watched his gaze waiver between violet ringed with white and azar as if the colors were fighting one another. His entire being fought to show itself, his body moving like heated waves off asphalt. Was it her imagination or was Prime messing with her head? She didn't know.

"I'm not. After going over the evidence regarding yesterday's attack, I have decided to hand it over to the Highguard's exploratory team. They will investigate and ensure its recorded. It means the meeting with Chancellor Roarke is cancelled. Soothsayer, the reports of your ability to heal weren't exaggerated. Your skin is flawless," Prime said with an edge of admiration.

Rutger looked down at Jo and back at Prime who was staring at her. He didn't like the possession he saw in Prime's eyes. "Is that why you're here?" He placed his hands on Jo's shoulders, squeezed, and felt her tension.

"Yes and no. I wanted to see the soothsayer and assure her she is safe, and her safety is top priority. But I'm here for you as well. Second to the Alpha, it's time for you to mark your mate."

"No," Jordyn mumbled.

They knew it was coming, it hung over their heads like an ax about to fall and she should have expected it with Prime's arrival. She wanted to ask if he was going to demand silver like he threatened in his letter? Dear god, she prayed not. She didn't want Rutger half shifted, his wolf demanding control, biting into her, and then silver poured into the wound. Jordyn envisioned the molten scar smearing the skin of her neck, arm, shoulder, down her back, and when it hardened, she wouldn't be marked, she would be labeled. Like an animal. She heard Louis' voice call their traditions animalistic. Jordyn fought the memory, her thoughts, and latched onto Rutger and what would happen if his wolf gave up to the beast.

"Is this some kind of punishment?" Jordyn asked. Rutger. Bestial.

"No, Soothsayer, there will be enough punishment in your future I don't have to invent it." Prime waited, and when Second didn't protest, he continued. "By your lack of a response, you don't object, Second. I imagine you've been conflicted by the instinct and the shame for needing to mark her for months."

True. Rutger's teeth ached to sink into Jo's skin, the sensation tempting his wolf's instincts. Prime called him out of control, what was he expecting Rutger to do? Tear Jo apart? Damn, he was going to mark her and prove his control over his wolf and his place as her mate and Second to the Alpha. He wasn't going to hurt Jo and he wasn't going to bring disgrace to the Cascade pack.

"You warned us and we expected this," Rutger replied.

"Of course, you did. We should go inside, you never know who is listening and the others are waiting," Prime stated.

"Others?" Jordyn mumbled. Punishment in her future. She couldn't let it bother her. They were going to get through this like they had everything else. She hoped.

"In the house?" Rutger growled. Prime bypassed the security systems at Foxwood, why wouldn't he be able to do the same to Rutger's. Who the hell was in his house?

With a stride impowering his authority, Prime walked to the entrance, stood by the door, and waved Jordyn inside. "Ladies first."

"How nice." Jordyn walked into the house and stopped. Their home had been invaded.

Standing as if at attention was the baron, baroness, Lady Sloan, Lord Ervin, and two strangers. An old man and an equally old woman, both with silver hair, wrinkled skin, wearing loose gray cotton pants and purple tunics, stared at her with twin emerald green eyes. Their gazes held youth as if their younger selves were trapped in their aging bodies. Jordyn's senses warned her of danger as magic drifted from the old couple. She hadn't felt anything like them before.

"Daughter," Sloan greeted.

Jordyn looked in Lady Sloan's direction, but didn't respond. What was she supposed to say? Good morning, Mom. I'm about to have sex with all of you in my living room and Rutger is going to mark me?

Instead she met the baron's narrowed gaze.

Her anxiety added weight to the air as Rutger stood behind her and watched the group in their living room. He saw the baron's narrowed gaze on Jo, his helplessness to stop Prime adding weight to his eyes. They had to have been summoned to serve as witnesses to the Second to the Alpha and director marking his mate and the pack's soothsayer. Everyone knew the ritual, banned for more than four hundred years was being resurrected, and Prime would force Rutger to mark Jo.

Rutger's thoughts zeroed in on the banned ritual and the lust it created, then his mind shifted gears. The rite would make them an example of the old ways and the epitome of Prime's authority over all magic-born. Prime was potentially causing a divide between the Cascade pack and the population of magic-born, which would put their lives in danger. If Rutger refused and they disobeyed his order, Prime would imprison him and take Jo to Mountain Fortress. Rutger gave the old couple a sideways glance as the weight from fear and passion tangled inside of him.

"Baron and baroness, Lord Ervin and Lady Sloan please have a seat." Prime held Jo's arm and pulled her to his side. "Abel and Abela meet the Cascade pack's soothsayer."

"Does she have a name?" Abela asked. Her deep whisper carried a hard edge that didn't match her frail looks.

"Answer her, Soothsayer," Prime demanded.

He squeezed her arm, his thin fingers sinking into her flesh. "Jordyn."

"Your full name." Prime increased the pressure on her, pushing her fear and the small flame of anger.

"Jordyn Lily Langston," Jordyn replied through clenched teeth. She wasn't going to give Prime the satisfaction of her asking him to let her go.

"Jordyn Lily Langston," Abel slowly repeated. The words floated from him like the air held them.

"Who are they and what are they doing?" Rutger asked. He watched the old couple, his instincts telling him they weren't what they appeared.

Prime hesitated to answer when Soothsayer's essence sank into him, its familiar thread weaving between them.

His signature remained behind as he knew it would, except his magic remained as well. *Impossible.* It had been two full nights since she used his power to heal her wounds and any residual effects of her drawing from him should have been gone.

Jordyn felt Prime searching her, his touch like a feather on her, and she tried to disguise her power when he jerked her toward him.

"I have a question for the soothsayer," Prime growled.

Jordyn nearly stumbled when he twisted her, the motion making pain wrap around her arm where his fingers continued to dig in. "What?" As if being in her own home with the creepy twins and knowing Rutger was going to mark her wasn't enough.

Prime ignored her. Taking her, he turned her, then dragged her to the doors. The right side opened without him touching it, and he pushed her through, and following it slammed closed. "Explain."

Jordyn stepped back, held her upper arm, and pretended to struggle to understand what he was talking about. "Explain what?"

"I allowed you to drink from me to help you and to evaluate your strength. Whatever power you received you should have used and it would have been extinguished. Especially after healing from the wounds inflicted by the Fae. It's there, I feel it inside of you," Prime explained.

Soothsayer stared at him, part of her fearing him, part of her wanting to argue with him. He watched her and knew she wasn't seeing his human façade but his true form. "What form do you see?" he demanded.

"Y-You. Your violet eyes ringed with white, r-rows of sharp teeth, black skin, and silver hair. I s-see you," Jordyn stammered. She wanted to look at the doors to see if Rutger was watching. Fear for him and the truth stopped her from looking away.

"As a decedent of Ceuthonymus, daemon of the underworld, I am death. It is a part of me." Prime took a step toward her. "I sense it's a part of you. As a shapeshifter, I should sense life and your wolf, not death."

Jordyn forced herself to hold his gaze and not back down.

Prime leaned in, leaving a sliver between them, and whispered, "Tell. Me."

"I died." Jordyn gave up and with her shoulders caved in broke eye contact and looked at the lake.

"The witch murdered you?" Prime straightened and took a step back giving her room. His face hardened and promised, if the witch hadn't died, he would have made sure he suffered.

"No and yes. I could have saved myself and shifted but the witches would have escaped," Jordyn explained. She felt her heart stop in her chest and her last exhale. Saying it didn't make her feel guilty, it made her free. It was a confession and she needed to confess.

"You gave your life to protect the pack?" Prime asked.

She felt her eyes change, not to copper or onyx, but glassy with the memory. "Yes. I will always protect the pack," Jordyn answered and met his narrowed violet eyes.

"There are consequences for the baron's actions. He isn't god and doesn't have the right to abuse his power and that of the pack to bring back the dead," Prime began. "He's taken the sanctity of death from you. It's a painful loss."

Death among the immortal magic-born has always been considered a scared event. The loss effecting generations and depending on their position and the hierarchy of their faction. Burial rituals and traditional committal clothing symbolize the effect death had on those left behind. Jordyn fought the weight of guilt for choosing death over life. She hadn't considered the sanctity taken from her. Jordyn melded the denied death with her powers and the Collective when she accepted her place in the pack. If she were to die it would have to be instant in order to kill her lifeforce and magic. If she were left to linger the fight between her wolf and death would tear her apart from the inside out. She would lose the Collective to the ether and then follow them.

Prime walked to the rail, placed his hands on the wood, gazed out at the lake, and inhaled the fresh air coming from the water. "As my power should have dissipated with time, so should have the denied death. It didn't. I believe you know why, Soothsayer."

Yes, she did. Jordyn watched his muscled shoulders tense under his suit jacket.

"I'm waiting." Prime turned and faced the soothsayer.

"Death gave my ancestors life."

Rutger stood at the door watching Jo and Prime talking and couldn't hear a damn thing. When he upgraded the house's security, along with the doors and windows, it made the house soundproof. He started regretting the changes when Jo called it her prison, and now, he hated them because it put him on the inside and Jo on the outside. He could push the button on the control panel engaging audio except it would allow all of them to listen to the conversation. He wouldn't do that to her.

"Son, how are you doing?" Healey asked.

"Living the dream," Rutger growled.

"Have you and Jordyn talked about this?" Healey asked.

"Yes, we've discussed it. Unlike the changes you have made, and then moving Jason and Claudia down the street." Rutger turned from the window to meet the baron's stare. "What else have you done?"

"The world is changing. The elf's attack and the Krijgers are proof there are magic-born against the rise of magic, this Emanation. It's my responsibility to protect the pack, klatch, and you, son. I will do everything in my power to keep my kin from harm. If it means placing guards all over my territory I will," Healey promised. His voice carried a low growl with his frustration from the situation and the threats surrounding them.

The baron was right, leaving Rutger with little argument and his focus was on Jo not Jason, the baron, or where the guards were going to be stationed. "You could have told me. Not only as your son, but as the director," Rutger countered needing to argue. "If I have to ask someone it makes me look incompetent. You don't trust me." He didn't wait for the baron to reply before turning back to the window to watch the pantomime on the other side.

"I understand. The updates are on your desk, in the stacks of reports. You've been preoccupied," Healey responded.

"What could Prime have to talk to her about?" Sloan asked. Rutger didn't turn around, he had nothing to say. The room sank into silence as time stretched on. "Anyone?"

"Death," Abela answered.

"What does that mean?" Sloan demanded.

"They have it in common, your Ladyship," Abel answered. "With it she communes with her ancestors."

"The soothsayer has imbibed of Prime. Never has he allowed a being to possess a globule of his power and live," Abela stated plainly, her accent chipping every word.

"His Numen stabbed her through the back, nearly killing her. Jordyn sought power to strengthen her and help her but she can't keep it. Power isn't a physical thing you can keep," Healey explained.

"A soothsayer can," Abel countered.

"They are vessels. It is natural for them to collect." Abela met her ladyship's gaze. "They are capable of containing anything."

"Not all soothsayers possess the ability. If they do, it's strictly forbidden to take from anyone and use or keep what they have stolen," Sloan explained. "Three hundred years ago Jordyn would have been put to death."

"It isn't stolen if it's given freely. Prime knew what she was doing and allowed her to use him," Healey argued. He didn't know why Prime allowed her to use him and didn't know how his power was going to influence Jordyn.

"All of that is beside the point." Sloan waved her hands as if it would help clear the conversation from the room. "Prime's power is unmatched, and Jordyn is untrained and weak. It should have killed her. There are twelve soothsayers holding the Collective of the Highguard and they're powerful and skillfully trained. There aren't a thousand soothsayers skilled enough to retain Prime's life and essence. His years and powers being too vast to contain."

"Explains why he is talking to her in private," Ervin said. "If she does in fact have a globule of his power, he'll want to know how she has kept it and not died."

It was true, she drew power from Prime. Maybe it helped her heal from the elf's attack. He should have asked her. *When*? Rutger twisted at his waist to see the old pair and the weight from knowledge crease their faces while Lady Sloan's rigid body warned him, she was losing control. What was driving her toward the edge he didn't know and didn't care, it wasn't his problem. He was ordered by Prime to mark Jo as the baron and baroness waited, and after he made love to her, then tore into her, the alchemists were going to make sure she wore a scar. He was going to be responsible for hurting Jo and making her wear her pain for the world to see. With his thoughts growing darker, Rutger turned from the group and watched Jo and Prime.

"Baron, you did this to her. You brought her back when she should have died," Sloan accused. "My daughter should have died."

"No. If she was meant to die, she would have. Know this, Sloan, if faced with the situation again, I would do the same damn thing. Jordyn is kin and a clansman." Healey gathered himself forcing his anger back. "While I take responsibility for my actions, you have to take responsibility for yours. You left your daughter with no guidance. She didn't know what she was and hated herself for it."

"She should have never accepted her powers and never should have been made soothsayer," Sloan protested.

"There was no accepting. It's who she is, you said it yourself, without it she would die, yesterday was proof. There is no stopping the magic inside of her," Healey argued. "By enshrining her as the pack's soothsayer I protected her. She has sentinels, Rutger, everyone in the pack is aware of her importance. Would you rather I hadn't and she be left alone to go insane?"

"Jordyn can't be the first in your family able of holding onto death and able to use it to resurrect her ancestors. The dragons, Balaur, didn't materialize out of thin air or her imagination for that matter. I'll add, she might not have gotten into this mess if we were more educated and her mother had been here to help her," Laurel added. Yes, she blatantly took her husband's side against Sloan. "Magic is subtly invading our carefully crafted world, making us all weary of what we'll become and fearful of the future. I ask you this, how long before it takes a foothold and breaks the dam to pour in? Do you have an answer? Because I don't. We have to focus on this right now and we need to help Jordyn. She needs our support and our strength, they both do. More importantly, we need to remember why we're here." Laurel saw Rutger's shoulders tense under his T-shirt with her words, and fear for her son gripped her heart.

Healey held his wife's tawny brown eyes and saw the sadness in them. "Well said."

"We're here to obey Prime's order and witness Rutger marking my daughter in a barbaric ritual. By experimenting with the old ways, you've forced Jordyn to pay the price for your selfish wants," Sloan continued.

"The Second to the Alpha will mark his mate, the pack's soothsayer, and she will take her place among the powers," Abel nearly sang the words. His pink lips rounding as if he was going to start cooing.

"Once she is stripped down, we will see her life-spark. The infusion will draw out her power and will summon her true self to reveal the magic within," Abela followed.

"Her ladyship is incorrect," Abel sang. He raised his hands, palms facing up, whispered words, then lowering them folded his fingers together.

Taken back by the insult, Sloan looked at Abel's gleam-ing eyes and the endless fathoms they held. "I'm incorrect?"

"Fate demanded Jordyn Lily Langston cease to be a single entity. The baron obeyed and turned the Pureblood into a soothsayer. He bestowed the pack's Collective to her. His reward for submitting is the responsibility of protecting the soothsayer. Fate is pleased." Abel's eyes closed and his face went slack.

"Without him an outsider would have taken her," Abela explained. "Used her. The soothsayer's magic is great. She needs a protector. She needs a warrior."

"Jordyn isn't a great power, she's a mess," Sloan argued.

Abela's green eyes narrowed on her. "Her ladyship is mistaken. There are those who wish to possess her, they seek her out."

"Our faith in fate will never wavier," Abel promised.

They were going to drive him insane. "You're talking about my mate. The woman I love. A person. Jo isn't a thing or a dog you feel is a threat and you're thinking about putting down." Rutger kept his back to them, not wanting to look at any of them because if he did the fury building inside of him would explode. He stared at Jo, her strength, and the woman he didn't want to lose. "Unless you have something constructive to contribute, I suggest you keep your mouths shut. All of you."

CHAPTER THIRTY

"You're a keeper of the ancients." Leaning back against the rail, Prime crossed his arms over his chest. His sliver hair drifted on the breeze, its ends feathering the sides of his suit. "Soothsayer, I have been in power for a long time. I've been alive for a long time. I've seen the world embrace magic, and I have witnessed the world reject its existence. That's why this development pains me." His voice dropped, adding to his distress as if his words weren't enough.

"I don't understand." Jordyn searched Prime's face, amazed at the way his onyx skin seemed to soak up the sun's light while it made his violet eyes gleam like crystals. That was all she saw. No anger. Happiness. Sadness. There was nothing giving away his thoughts.

"You're selfish. Immature. Untrained. Weak. Undisciplined. Inexperienced in the use of magic, and until the second the baron pressed the Collective on you, forcing you to stay, you were part of the world rejecting magic," Prime explained.

That hurts. "You're saying I'm not good enough. My magic and traits are wasted on me." She respected his honesty, but his criticism stung more than she wanted to admit. Having stood up to him, healing her wound, and surviving another attack, she thought she might gain some of his respect. *Selfish.* Jordyn reminded herself of the conversation she had with Jason and Claudia, and it reaffirmed her promise to not let any harm come to the pack. It was her responsibility. She couldn't fail. "Then why are you here? Why did you attack me at Foxwood, push a challenge, demand an audience with the pack and klatch, and why the hell are you forcing Rutger to mark me, if I'm not worthy?"

Prime tilted his head to the right, shifted his weight, and inhaled a deep breath. He caught the soothsayer's anger drifting on the air as if its scent came from a newly bloomed flower. "I didn't say you weren't worthy. I said this pained me and I told *you* what *your* current state is. There is a reason why your ancestors have chosen you and you have attracted the attention of the Highguard and others who are in power. Soothsayer, you have the ability to become strong, disciplined, trained, and you could gain experience to use the abilities you've been given with confidence. If you chose to overcome your weaknesses, an expert hand would mold you and cast you into a deadly *xiphos*."

His accent twisted the last word. Not knowing what it meant and trying to wrap her mind around what he was saying, Jordyn lowered her head without replying. Silence was safe.

"It's a short, double-edged, one-handed sword once carried by Greek warriors. If they lost their spears, or were fighting in close combat, they relied on their xiphos. The kind of fighting where they looked one another in the eyes knowing they could die at the same time were in control of a man's death. It is an intimate affair," Prime began explaining. "A xiphos was cast from bronze rather than forged from iron."

Swords? What did they have to do with her? "You think I'm a weapon?" Jordyn asked, meeting his gaze. An undisciplined threat to her pack's safety.

"The attack is proof the world sees you as such. They believe you've been forged from pain and hate and are a threat that will never change but will eventually rust, becoming damaged and dangerous. They do not believe you could be cast from discipline and knowledge. Ever evolving."

Forged, unyielding. Cast, yielding. She felt like she was being forged from pain and hate and it was going to change her to cold and detached. She felt herself losing the fight. The elf was proof. Jordyn wanted to kill him. She saw herself beating him until his heart stopped.

"I sense the war waging inside of you."

Like he sensed death and his power inside of her. Jordyn needed to make sure he wasn't going to punish her for holding onto his power. "What are you going to do about your power?"

"I gave freely and you used it to heal yourself, and somehow, without my essence infecting you and driving you mad, have been able to contain it within your own death. Can you manipulate it?" Prime asked.

With his question, weakened threads of his power reached up from inside of her as if detaching themselves from her and seeking their master. After the elf's attack, she used the Collective to heal but hadn't felt Prime's power. Because there had been another who helped her focus on the Collective. Blue eyes bled silver. The image faded and she saw Christian. Did she create him? With a continual fight with her emotions, her instincts, and multiple changes happening within her, she doubted her own mind. "No. I feel it weakening."

"There's your answer, Soothsayer."

Jordyn met his violet gaze and doubted he believed it was taking its course, like she doubted he was going to let her go. There would be a punishment sometime. She made a metal note and added it to her list of worries. Right then she wondered if Prime was manipulating her for a second time? Jordyn turned from him, giving him her back as her thoughts trudged down the beaten path of wanting to go back to change the past. Her mind clung to the idea like a waking dream she was fighting to make real and Jordyn desperately wanted to believe in it. *Weak.* She saw Rutger standing at the door watching them, his T-shirt pulled tight across his chest, his hands on his hips, and his fingers playing with the waist of his cotton pants, while his eyes blazed gold. She loved him. She was going to marry him. Whatever happened, she wasn't going to lose him. She wasn't going to lose herself in the pain, hate, and responsibility of protecting her pack, or the fear of threats. Jordyn was going to remain Jordyn.

I am going to hate myself. She quenched the thoughts of changing the past, turned toward the door, and held Rutger's gold gaze. Without facing Prime, she asked, "How do I become a *xiphos*?"

Jordyn felt Prime's eyes on her as if they were going to drill into her back. "You will observe the ritual, sacrifice your blood, making you blood bound to the Second to the Alpha and kin to the baron. It will prove your loyalty to him and your clansmen. You will need their faith."

Rutger tried reading Jo's face and watched her lips curve around silent words in an attempt to understand what they were talking about. He thought he caught the words, *how do I*, but wasn't sure. How does she do what? When Jo closed her eyes and nodded, his heart sank. What was happening? He sensed their link and felt caution at the same moment she looked at him. Behind her, Prime didn't stop talking. They stared at each other, him on the inside, her on the outside, a divide between them. He hated it.

When Jo reached for the handle, Rutger took several steps backward giving her room to open the door. She entered the house with Prime close behind her.

Rutger grabbed Jo, and holding her upper arm pulled her close and asked, "What was that about?"

"Later," Jordyn whispered. She wasn't going to start a conversation about her ancestors, Prime's power, and she wasn't going to tell the baron, baroness, Lady Sloan, Lord Ervin, or the creepy alchemists she had made a deal with the devil. Literally. Mostly she wasn't going to tell Rutger. She would keep it a secret for as long as she could.

"You know why you've been brought here," Prime started. "Second to the Alpha, Director of Enforcers, fated mate to the soothsayer, is going mark his mate. The soothsayer will prove her allegiance to her kith and kin with blood."

"And the alchemists?" Healey asked, eyeing Prime and Jordyn.

"We have explained our purpose, Baron," the couple answered in unison.

A little too creepy. Jordyn's nerves jumped under her skin, threatening to burst through. She needed to calm down and keep her stress under control.

"Mistress, Lord Ethan and Lady Mia are here," Tracy announced.

"This just keeps getting better," Jordyn mumbled, and gave Rutger a sideways glance.

The door swung wider, letting Ethan march in with Mia trailing behind him. He stopped at the edge of the living room. "What the hell is going on here?"

An alert should have been sent to his cell. Where was his cell? Rutger looked up at the double doors to their bedroom. *Doesn't do any good if it's not in your hand.* "What are you doing here?" he asked.

"I heard *my* daughter had been attacked by someone from the Seelie court," Ethan stated for the entire room. His attention focused on Sloan when he noticed her, and his anger and jealousy spiked. "I came to make sure she was all right."

"Lord Ethan Langston," Prime greeted before anyone replied. Silence flooded the room and everyone's attention went to Prime.

"Prime, my apologies. Wh-When I asked about J-Jordyn, I was told she was s-sick from silver," he stammered over his words as his stare jumped from Sloan to Jordyn.

"Obviously details of the attack were greatly exaggerated in order to worry you," Mia taunted. "She doesn't have a mark on her."

"I assure you, they were not," Healey protested.

I have video feed, if you have popcorn. She was losing it. "Dad, I'm fine. It's all right," Jordyn assured with a smile. Her lips barley curved and whatever truth was in her words didn't reach her eyes.

"No, it's not, *all right*, why didn't you tell me?" Ethan saw her blank look, then turned his attention to Healey. "Attacked. Why didn't you tell me? I'm her father."

"It was imperative to keep the details from the public until the proper authorities had been notified and the proper action taken," Healey explained.

"Proper authorities? What kind of attack was it?" Ethan demanded.

"An assassination attempt," Rutger answered. If they wanted to know, he would tell them.

"Enough. No one is divulging details at this time. I have instructed the Highguard's exploratory team to oversee the investigation," Prime stated. "Unless you think them incompetent and this is a matter for humans?"

Fear slid down Ethan's spine. "Of course not, Prime." He directed his attention to Healey. "Sloan is here. Was she with Jordyn yesterday?" Ethan growled his dissatisfaction with the situation and his jealousy of Sloan. "No one could call her father?"

"No," Jordyn answered. "Foxwood was on lockdown, and I was locked in the med room. Lady Sloan knew because she is a guest of the baron and baroness, not because anyone told her. I didn't see her and I didn't talk to her. I'm sorry, I should have told you, Dad." *How do you like it? Maybe you shouldn't have let me live a lie and then lied about what I was.* Damn. Was this where she was at? Punishing her dad because he made a mistake and didn't tell her the truth? How long was she going to blame him? *Forever.*

Forged.

Cast.

Jordyn wasn't going to cling to anger and let it change her. "Dad, I should have told you. Next time, I'll make sure you're notified."

"Next time? No, there won't be a next time," Ethan assured her.

"You're killing him, you know. Every time you turn your back on your father it destroys another piece of him," Mia accused. "Because of the trouble you create, our relationship suffers."

Fury erupted through Jordyn as her head screamed, she hadn't been on vacation and forgot to tell them. She looked at her hands, stretched her fingers, then felt her cheek. "You are responsible for your relationship problems, not me."

"Lady Mia, remember who you are speaking to and the soothsayer's status versus your own," Prime warned. "You do not rate an explanation."

Stunned, Mia targeted Jordyn with an icy glare before shifting her gaze to the floor, showing the appropriate submission to Prime. "My apologies, Prime. I worry for my husband's life."

Prime ignored Lady Mia and concentrated his attention on Lord Ethan. "You are correct, you should have been notified of the attack on your daughter. As you can see, she is doing well. However, after your wife's reaction it's easy to assume this would have been too much of a strain for either of you to handle." Prime's voice dropped and held an edge of a condescending tone.

"I assure you, Prime, my wife is overreacting. I don't understand what is happening." Ethan's instincts warned him he wasn't going to like what Prime was going to say. How much more pain was his daughter going to have to endure?

"Then I owe you another apology. As her father and an elder in the pack you should be present when the Second to the Alpha, Director of Enforcers, and the soothsayer's fated mate, marks her," Prime replied.

Ethan took a good look around the room, and for the first time noticed the old couple. "No. It's a barbaric, outlawed tradition."

"Your dispute has been noted. Soothsayer, Second to the Alpha, the time has come." Prime's violet eyes met Jordyn's.

"Wait, who are they?" Ethan asked.

"Alchemists," Prime answered.

"Marked and scarred. The soothsayer is well deserving," Mia cooed.

"Lady Mia, Soothsayer is not an animal to be bitten and branded. She is a power to be strengthened, sharpened, and when she has been blood bound to the Second, the alchemists will infuse her life-spark and her true self will manifest," Prime calmly clarified as if he were speaking to children. "She will reach υπέρβαση." He slanted his head, knowing no one understood him. "Transcendence."

No pressure. Jordyn almost believed it wasn't going to be some weird ceremony making both her and Rutger look like barbaric asses when it was over. Sex. Biting. Alchemists and their infusion. It was a bad paranormal porn with an edge of horror thrown in for kicks. Her imagination gave her images, making her cringe. The entire pack would have another reason to stare at her like she was a freak.

"Second, Soothsayer, you're dismissed," Prime ordered.

Rutger's heart seized in his chest as he looked at Jo, not believing Prime gave him permission and it was going to happen. He was going to mark his mate and the thought made his teeth ache and his wolf howl in his ears. His entire body throbbed with anticipation and anxiety. He kept a death grip on his control as everyone's stares bared down on them like they were a sideshow. Rutger's instincts overrode his excitement and demanded he get Jo out from under their judgements. Grabbing Jo's upper arm, he pulled her toward the stairs. Once in their room and behind closed doors, he could talk to her.

When Rutger tugged her arm, Jordyn half stumbled, caught herself, and trailed after him. Behind them, Mia mumbled about brutal rituals, how uncivilized blood binding was, and the end of the world as they knew it. *'The soothsayer brought this on us.'* Jordyn half expected to hear Prime defend her, but he didn't. No one did. Figures.

Rutger shoved her in front of him, keeping his hand at the center of her back and shadowing her steps as they climbed the stairs. His power drummed inside him like a physical thing and was fighting him for its release. Each of his touches felt like he was sizzling Jo's skin with his wolf's urgency. He tried to keep it a low roar and knew he was failing. It was burning the link between them carrying his heated desire.

Rutger wanted this. Needed this.

There was nothing she could do to stop it from happening. Jordyn left the last stair as the alchemists began chanting, their words rising above the other's grumbling. She stopped to look down at the pair as their voices melted into one strained tone. Their melody made chills skate over her skin and down her spine.

"Mea," Rutger whispered, a rough growl, and nudged her forward. He wanted his mate safe from their judgements and he needed to protect her. *Protect her. Mark her. Make her mine.*

The exigence whipped out at her, its edges like razors slicing across their link. With her nerves feeding her anxiety,

Jordyn couldn't stop herself from flinching, the reaction a sad reminder of days in the past. She wanted to apologize, felt she needed to explain, but words failed her. Instead, she left the rail, the singing pair, the multiple sets of eyes holding their worry, and walked down the hall to their bedroom. Jordyn worked to kept the fear, anxiety, and her hesitation where Rutger was concerned as deep as she could bury it to protect him from her doubt. And to protect herself from provoking a werewolf demanding to mark his mate.

Jo's emotions drained from her, leaving a blank canvas behind and telling him she was hiding her feelings. She didn't want him to feel whatever she was thinking. *She's hiding out of fear. She thinks I'm going to hurt her.* The thoughts blasted his confidence, making him growl a deep rumble from his chest. As Jo flinched, his guilt spiked like she stabbed him, then he felt her muscles tense when he rested his hand on the soft skin between her shoulder and neck. His best efforts to control himself didn't stop his heart from beating fast ... one, two, three times. He would mark her there, his teeth sinking into her yielding flesh making, her his.

Jo's steps picked up speed as she approached the set of double doors, but he stopped her before she touched the wrought iron handle and opened it for her. The door swung wide, creating a breeze carrying the air from inside the room. Rutger inhaled their combined scents and relished the vanilla, spice, their wolves, and the undertones of smoke from the fireplace. It was like walking into their own private world where no one else was allowed and they could escape.

Sunshine and warmth met Jordyn's face, releasing a sliver of tension from her neck and shoulders. She crossed the threshold, took a deep breath of air, and felt a smooth calmness erase a pinch of fear. Behind her, Rutger lingered by the door for a second, then she heard it click closed, the lock engaged, and his footsteps grew closer. If anyone wanted inside, they could break the handle, lock, or the door ... or Prime would open it without having to touch it. She figured locking it was a warning not to bother to them, because everyone had to have heard it click. Maybe. The odd couple's concert was getting louder and their verses longer. Jordyn focused on the bed and making her legs obey. When she reached it without crumbling to the floor, she sat down on the edge and faced Rutger.

"I feel stupid," she whispered. Scooting back, she folded her legs and tried for relaxed, comfortable, not riddled with anxiety.

No doubt their audience downstairs was waiting for them to talk, argue, or for them to get on with it. She couldn't think about what they were going to do or what the audience thought they were going to do or what they thought about the situation. It would make her insane. She didn't want to know how the pack was going to react after they found out. The stares, talk, gossip, and impact following were going to add to their freak status. Jordyn was making herself stressed out and nervous. She was going be with her mate. Her fiancé. With the presence of Prime, their families, and the singing duo, she nearly forgot he asked her to marry him. She said yes, just as she had three years earlier.

"What did you talk to Prime about?" Rutger asked. He was fighting his wolf's instincts, and his burning need. He waited long enough. *Slow down*. Rutger saw himself grabbing Jo and pushing her backward onto the bed, the floor, or taking her and pinning her against the wall. It consumed him.

"I'm guessing the conversation inside wasn't good. What did they say?" Jordyn wasn't going to divulge information.

The baron should have let you die. "You cheated death bringing your ancestors to life, then used Prime's power to help you heal. The strange duo said you were able to contain any power if you chose, and if it was a hundred years ago or something you have been put to death. And his power should have killed you. This isn't about me marking you. They said your true self will reveal itself. What does it mean? And why do I think Prime already knows?" Rutger kept his voice low as he hit the hot topics. There wasn't time to go over the entire conversation and she was right when she guessed it hadn't been good.

One thing at a time. "It's true, Prime allowed me to use his power to heal. No, I can't keep it, it's fading quickly," she replied. It was the truth. "I don't know why it didn't kill me. Maybe because I have death, or it could be I have my ancestor's power. Prime doesn't know either. Or he does and it's his little secret." Recognizing the determined look on Rutger's face, she knew the questioning wasn't going to end. The Director of Enforcers had his interrogation glare going. She waited for the next question.

"What is your true self?" he repeated.

"I don't know. It could have something to do with my ancestors and the dragons, or it doesn't. After accepting the Collective, the fractures are gone and I feel complete. Could be I'll turn into a princess from a fairy tale." Jordyn smiled as the image of a blue grown and a pumpkin filled her head. Rutger did not smile.

"Did Prime say anything to you about what it might be?"

"No. He didn't say anything." The fairly tale crashed and burned.

"What did you ask him?" Rutger pushed onward.

"What? What do you mean?" Guilt had her mind racing. There was no way he heard what she said. The doors, windows, the entire damn house was a sound-proof vault. *Unless he turned the speaker on ...*

No, if he did, he would have heard her and Prime. There would have been more questions. His focus had been on her and watching her; he read her lips. Sneaky wolf.

"You said, 'How do I', I didn't catch the rest. I saw him smile, Jo. Prime smiled and answered you." Rutger took a step closer to her and his wolf rose inside him. Confident, azar eyes mocked Rutger and his failing possession of his mate.

Would it be worth lying? No. There was a dark resolve in his glare, in the way he clenched his jaw, and in every muscle of his body. She would risk skirting the truth. "After telling me I was untrained and undisciplined, he advised me to learn to control my magic. I asked him how." *Cast by my hand and honed into a sharpened blade.*

"What did he say?" Jealousy burned through him, forcing him to fight the instinct to leave Jo, jump from the loft, and tear Prime apart for going near his mate. Prime would kill him before he hit the floor, instant death, but at least Jo wouldn't have to worry about him.

"As Prime, he can't personally train me, a conflict of interest, or something. He said he would find someone the pack could trust," Jordyn answered. It was true and it wasn't.

With his emotions raging, his body craving Jo's touch, and his wolf demanding he mark her, he couldn't differentiate between the chaos and sense if she was lying to him. Did he think she was lying? No, not lying to him. Shielding him from the truth and her real feelings because she was protecting Prime. He couldn't stop his mind from replaying the way Prime watched her, or from jealousy coloring his imagination. Rutger tried telling himself to stop his suspicions and interrogating her, they would have time to talk afterwards. When he wasn't being torn into a million pieces and was rational. Then none of it would matter.

One more question. "He allowed you to take from him and didn't reprimand you when he found out you held his power. He wanted you to have his power, it's proof he favors you. That's what they're all thinking. As I stand here as your mate, they think Prime favors you," Rutger growled through clenched teeth.

Easy Wolf. "Prime favors power and sees me as an untapped opportunity. More than any of us, he feels the rising magic infecting the world, and in the magic-born. He is using this and the challenge as tests. Prime has his own agenda," Jordyn explained. Whispering didn't make it sound as persuasive as she needed. She was going to convince herself she believed what she was saying. Deep down, she needed to prove to Prime she wasn't undisciplined, untrained, and weak, and it made her feel like she was somehow betraying Rutger. Without dwelling on her thoughts, she plowed forward. "He'll collect those of us with increased gifts and we'll be used as tools. I'm nothing."

Then why are you hiding your feelings? "It doesn't look like it," Rutger argued. "He challenged me in my own damn home." He wanted to continue to argue, to let everything plaguing him have its way, but Jo's explanation started weakening his anger. With the slice of clarity, he let his frustration drain from him and his desire for Jo gained strength.

"Prime flaunted the fact he could go anywhere he wanted any time he wanted in our territory, it's what he does. He's been doing it for centuries. Then he comes to *our* home in person and accompanied by his creepy couple to order us to go through a ritual that's been outlawed for hundreds of years. Why? To make an example out of us. Magic is increasing. Magic-born are becoming more powerful. Does doing this change the pack's standing with the Highguard? I'm not sure, but I do know it doesn't mean he favors me. If he did, why would he blood bind me to you and the pack?"

"I don't know." Jo was right.

"Without any of this, Prime could have easily separated us and ordered me to serve at Mountain Fortress," Jordyn whispered and ran her fingers through her hair. She was tired of thinking about the baron's threat to sacrifice Rutger, and tired of Prime, the challenge, the ritual, and didn't want to continue the conversation. Her anxiety eased when the sharpest of Rutger's jealousy pulled back like claws retracking from her skin. *That's right my wolf, believe whatever I'm saying. Someone has to.*

"I know. He's a threat, every instinct is telling me to keep him from you." His instincts were screaming, his wolf was howling, and the control he held with a death grip over the months was crumbling before his eyes. He lived with the feeling of helplessness, displaying enough authority and power to remind himself he was a man. Rutger stared at Jo, felt helpless, and wished he could see what she was thinking.

For the first time since Butte Springs, she believed she didn't have to depend on others and could take care of herself. Jordyn needed to protect her pack. "Wolf, we'll protect each other."

"Mea," he breathed. His eyes bled gold, his muscles twitched, and his fisted hands began shaking. He wasn't going to hurt her. He wasn't going to make her hate him. If he did, Jo would turn her back on him. *She would run to Prime,* his mind taunted him. "I need you."

His hands unclenched and clenched in fists when a force of energy gripped Rutger's entire body as he struggled for control. She watched him and felt the threads of his hesitation. "I love you. We're going to do this like they aren't downstairs and there is no pressure. We are going to make this about us. Just us. No one else. They don't deserve anymore of our lives." Jordyn held his gold gaze with her copper one and hoped he was listening to her and she was getting through to him. She wasn't going to fear him. She was going to give him what he needed and be there for her mate. Then if she somehow survived the challenge in one piece, she was going to find out why this was happening.

Rutger was listening and wasn't listening. Jo sat on the bed with her legs crossed and her eyes holding him, and there wasn't fear in her gaze. He forced himself to move, nodded, and took an uneasy step, his muscles feeling as if they were made from rebar, and the pressure from his wolf threatening to burst through his skin. When he made it to the bed and sat down, relief flooded him.

"Wolf." He sank into the thick comforter, making her lean into him. With their conversation, Prime's attention looming over her, and the audience the last thing she expected was responding to his passion. Her body warmed all over as her wolf sought him through their link.

He felt her reaching for him and slowly raised his hand to Jo's face, fearing she might flinch, and when she didn't, he cupped her cheek. *This isn't real.* With her warmth against his, he convinced himself she wanted him and she trusted him. Her eyes closed, her black lashes resting on her cheeks, and she leaned into his hold.

My girl. "I love you," Rutger whispered.

Every time she heard him say those words, it sent shards of hope their relationship and love was going to last, and was it real, tangible, through her. She could hold onto it and believe in them. Right then she needed the unfaithful bitch of hope to get through the day. Jordyn tilted her head and saw his set jaw, the lines fanning out from his eyes, and the morning's shadow of dark hair on his chin and cheeks. They weren't superbeings ... right then they were as normal as they were ever going to be. She met Rutger's gaze and knew either they conformed to their new life, or every time something weird happened it was going to act as a stumbling block and set them back.

This wasn't going to set them back, she couldn't let it, it was going to move them forward. Jordyn knew what she had to do. She straightened, her feet landed on the plush carpet, and she tested the strength in her legs. Finding she wasn't going to crash to the floor, she gingerly stepped around Rutger's knee to stand between his thighs.

"Mea?" Rutger's rough whisper gave away the fight raging inside him.

In silence, Jordyn leaned forward, putting her face close to his. He lightly kissed her as she inhaled his spice and wolf, and tugged the hem of his T-shirt loose. Rutger obeyed her unspoken request and raised his arms, allowing her to free him of the cotton. Dropping the shirt to the floor, she stared at the black ink starting at his right shoulder covering the muscle with knot-work, then curving under his collarbone and to the center of his chest where it stopped at the Kanin family crest of a wolf's head.

Every Pureblood werewolf family within the Cascade pack wore a crest. It proved their Pureblood linage, separated them from the Illuminate and the Wights, and gave them status. Each one was their personal rendering of a wolf's head. For a split second, she heard Louis' voice condemn her for her tattoos and the barbaric ways of the pack. She took pride in the Langston family crest, inked between her shoulder blades. A wolf's head, its nose pointed to the sky as if staring at the full moon, it wore seven onyx stones linked by a silver chain, representing her ancestors, in its ear. Now, she would have to add a dragon to pay respect to her ancestors.

Jordyn traced the right side of the wolf's head, doing a lazy circle around its gold eye, dark fur, then feathered his skin to touch the naked skull and the silver bands linked together in its left socket. Jordyn lost herself in touching him, the way his chest rose with his inhales, his muscles flexing under her fingers, and the way he responded to her.

"You're thinking," Rutger whispered. He couldn't wait to talk normal. Out loud. Direct. He hated feeling like they were hiding.

"I'm looking at you," Jordyn replied. "Memorizing this, your heavy breathes when I touch you, the way your skin feels under my palm." She trailed her fingers to the dark hair starting in the center of his stomach, his skin a soft bronze next to hers. He sucked in a breath as she leisurely followed it to the waist of his pants.

"You make me crazy." Rutger grabbed her wrist and held her while he drew a calm breath, then raised it to his lips to kiss the inside. With his lips on her skin, Jo's need raced the link, setting it on fire and making it burn between them. Its heat intensified, becoming physical flames that licked at him and burned openings in his flesh. The cavities widened, eating more of his skin for the heated flares to enter his body and scorch the shreds of his control. Rutger met Jo's gaze and imagined the reds and golds of the blaze swallowing him mirrored in her onyx gaze. "What are you doing to me?" He didn't recognize the need in his rough voice.

She didn't know. She did know. When she touched him, something inside her broke through the worry, stress, fear, and forced her to obey her instincts.

"Wolf," Jordyn mouthed, her lips curling around the soundless word. *Need you.* The dragons burst from her dark depths, and joining her wolf they bathed in the inferno of passion and power taking over her body.

Rutger let go of her wrist to hold Jo's hips, his splayed fingers digging into her. He closed his eyes, bowed his head, and prayed he didn't hurt her. *Mine.* Holding his face,

Jo urged him to raise his head. "I don't want to hurt you." Rutger looked at his mate and watched copper and onyx swirl in her heated gaze.

"I believe in you." Her power was simmering inside of her, waiting for Rutger to mark her, of this she was sure. It would complete something that was out of her reach. *Her true self will emerge.* And apart from not loving her and leaving her alone to fight by herself, there was nothing he could do to hurt her. Her body healed to fight another day.

"You trust me?" Rutger pulled her toward him, and lifting her she straddled him. Through her clothing he could feel the power in her heat.

"I trust you," Jordyn promised.

He stared at her as his hands slid up her thighs to her zip-up hoodie, and drawing the zipper down, he peeled the material off her. "Now?"

"Yes," Jordyn whispered.

With her bare in front of him, he wrapped her in his arms and clamped her to his chest. He didn't want to let go of her, his wolf, his control, none of it for fear he would lose them all at once. The heat between them increased, turning his need to mark her into desperation his wolf willingly chased at the same time its shadow veiled him. *Don't lose control.* "Now?"

"Yes." Jordyn straightened. She met the weight in his eyes as they held his unrestrained passion, need, and his wolf. With the beast shadowing him and his raw emotion turning his gold gaze into bright yellow like the sun, guilt threaded through her. The wolf wanting its freedom to fully shift into the beast stared at her as if it knew her intentions. *That's right, my wolf, you won't be a sacrifice.* Jordyn understood and didn't understand and it left her questioning her power and the dragons. She was untrained, she didn't know the extent of her powers, and was playing with fire and Rutger's life was on the line. And if she forced Rutger to shift without his consent and things went to hell, he would hate her. For an eternity. Only if there was a part of him left that remembered her.

Leaning forward, Jo lightly kissed his lips. She teased the top with her tongue, then the bottom as if tasting him. Her closeness made the soft skin of her breasts graze his chest, bringing a male growl to his lips. Jo bit his bottom lip, sucked it between her own. He groaned in appreciation, then she scooted back, and trailed kisses down his throat and nuzzled the underside. It sent a shudder down his spine, making his body shake, his muscles tense, and his grip on Jo tightened. With his desire building, he turned them onto the bed and Jo lay on her back under him.

"Trust me?" he nearly growled.

Jordyn arched her back and their bodies touched. "Always."

Rutger slid his right hand down her side to the waist of her pants and underwear, and shoved them down her hips then her legs. He paused to stare at her naked body, the curves of her hips, her waist, and breasts framed by the thick crimson comforter behind her. "Trust me?"

"With my life," Jordyn replied with a breathy whisper. He was taking his time, openly admiring her, showing her what she meant to him, leaving light touches on her skin, and it fed her need.

Rutger's eyes fell to the supple curve of her shoulder and neck where he could imagine his teeth sinking in, marking her, and the world would know she was his. She was the Cascade pack. She was their soothsayer. The gravity of who and what she was and her status made his heart hurt and his wolf howl in his ears. *'She will take her place among the powers.'* Transcendence. For now, she was with him, yielding her body to him and giving a piece of herself to him. Only him.

"You're thinking," Jordyn teased. She raised her head and kissed the skin above Rutger's heart.

"Mmmm." Rutger took Jo's mouth with a kiss, meaning to brand her at the same time he covered her entire body with his own.

With his weight restraining her, and his senses opened to inhale her vanilla scent, her breathes, her skin, her hooded copper gaze, he relished the way her skin tasted on his tongue. The intensity surged from his core, filling his head with flashes of himself and Jo. He saw her face down on the comforter, a scarlet veil staining her shoulder, her tattoos peeking from under the glittering sheen. Rutger stepped away and looking at his hands panic gripped him. They weren't hands but a combination of wolf and man. Was he seeing the future? Or his worst fear? It was his nightmare. It wasn't real and he wouldn't let it dictate his life. Rutger broke the kiss, and leaning on his elbow breathed deep and met Jo's copper eyes clouded with her lust. Her reddened lips were swollen and slightly parted. A wave of love tangled with possession swept him up and overwhelmed him.

They had been together for years. They had been apart for years. This moment would make them something else entirely. Not pack. Not fated mates. Not husband and wife. Not lovers. They would be bound by blood. He would draw the blood of the soothsayer, take it into himself as he gave her his wolf. The Pureblood lycanthrope virus would seep from his teeth and into Jo, and after her body absorbed it into itself, it would change the virus she carries. They would be linked by her blood and his venom, and Jo would become his to lose. He cursed Prime and the challenge.

Jordyn felt Rutger pull back from her, making the fire between them even out and smolder as the silent minutes ticked into the past. Rutger stared at her, his narrowed golden gaze feeling like he was seeing inside her while his hand moved up and down her side. She thought it might be their audience, time was passing, the alchemists were waiting, and the next day would bring the challenge. She was wrong. Without needing to read his mind, she knew Rutger was stalling because he was scared. Had he sensed her intentions through their link? Not possible. His fear glided over her like a cold caress and she understood he realized the significance of the situation. It had sat in her head, on her shoulders, and defined her actions for months. This was going to change them. She would lose more of herself, and the Jordyn everyone once knew would become the soothsayer. They wouldn't have Jordyn their friend. They would have their soothsayer, carrier of the dead, weapon for the pack. With her emotions spinning out of control, she wanted to cry over the loss.

"Wolf," Jordyn whispered, not wanting to let her unshed tears play in the word. She needed him, his touch, and his wolf to remind her he was there with Jo, not the soothsayer. She raised enough to draw her tongue along his jaw line. The salt and spice of his skin sat in her mouth making him hers. In response, he growled a low rumble. "Make love to me."

Curling his fingers around the back of her neck, Rutger held her, felt the beat of her heart, and keeping her gaze, leaned in and kissed her. He was going to make love to her. He was going please her, and after giving her what she desired, he would mark her. Jo kissed him back, and her tongue tasted him as her nails dug into his arms and her leg draped over his urged him closer.

He had kissed her before, but this was different ... like his needs were taking over, its flavor was on his lips, and she felt his possession of her. *Yes, wolf.* She could do nothing but cave to his claiming kiss and his wolf's hunger. Its heat ignited the coals and the blaze spread over her skin in a sweet veil of lust. He left barely there kisses on her chin, neck, and shoulder, then dipped his head and feathered the Balaur on her thigh. Jordyn pictured it glowing silver, glittering in the sunlight filtering through the windows. 'Her true self.' Rutger drew his hand over the shimmering rune then slowly inched up to her hip and held her.

"What we're doing will change us," he whispered.

"It is changing us."

Rutger cupped her breast, teased the peak with his tongue, paused, drew back to stare at the wetness covering her, and with gold eyes licked the flesh. Jo arched her back off the bed, pushing herself closer to his mouth, a husky moan leaving her lips in a breath.

In long, sweet strokes his tongue left hot, wet trails while his hands roamed her body. He paused only to squeeze her hip and thigh, his thumb brushing the Balaur sending pulses of lust through her. His fingers feathered the inside of her thigh, and moving up to the center of her heat, he slowly stroked her desire. His touches seared raw need into her, making the hunger to have it quenched desperate. "Wolf." The word sounded breathy, rough, eager. She didn't care.

Releasing Jo, his muscles tightening as he leaned on his left elbow, and with frantic shoves got his pants down his legs and off the bed. Free from the material, he covered Jo with his bare body creating heat between them. With his right hand he nudged her legs wider, situated himself in the triangle of her body, and slowly slid himself inside of her. Slick, wet heat met him and guided him deeper. He growled a low sound, his arms flexed, his pelvis touching Jo as he rocked his hips.

Rutger's weight against her epitomized his male sexuality and called her wolf's desire for her mate. As she met Rutger's rhythm, creating a sensual tempo, their bodies beaded with sweat and the scent of their combined arousal drifted between them. Rising up from the downstairs, the creepy couple's voices deepened into inhuman sounds, the words from another language flowed on the air, charging it with power and creating pressure. Outside of their room, the enchanted hymn sat against the door waiting for them.

Jordyn felt its weight in her head as the power drummed in her body. "Rutger," she whispered.

"Mea." His low growl drawing the word out. He increased the rhythm and met Jo's onyx gaze. The ink swallowed her eyes and he knew if stared at them for too long, he would drown in their fathoms.

"Now. Mark me now," she breathed, and met Rutger's gaze and saw his wolf's form wavering between animal and beast as it shadowed him. Like ribbons wrapping around her, pleasure caressed her insides, sending her closer to the edge.

"No." Rutger bowed his head. *Coward.* He wasn't going to look at her. His right hand slid under her hip to her lower back and lower he held her backside and lifting her sank deeper inside of her. His control turned to ash, there was nothing left. If he marked her, he was going to hurt her.

"Now. Wolf." Jordyn slowed the tempo. "Do you trust me?"

Rutger inhaled and exhaled, held her against him, and keeping himself seated deep continued to rock his hips. "Yes," he ground out. The damn song-no it was an intoning-ate the air while it pressed on his wolf and changing it, the beast swam under his skin. "I can't."

"You can. You have to." With Rutger holding her bottom off the bed, her shoulders sank into the comforter. She lowered her left arm and rested it beside her, then turned her head to the right. "Wolf, mark your mate."

CHAPTER THIRTY-TWO

Mark her. Mine. Rutger didn't answer, his desperation pushing the fight between the beast and marking Jo. His hips rocked, the strokes increasing in speed as if making Jo writhe from the pleasure he gave her was going to ease the battle.

With each thrust Jordyn's body hummed, pleasure pooled, and her inhales came in ragged pulls. Above her, Rutger's beast veiled him in a sliver sheen, his human features blurred under the beast. "Let go."

He tightened his fingers on her sweat-slick skin, her voice and demand drowning in his need to pleasure her at the same time deny himself.

"Let go," she demanded. His thrusts slowed, her middle ached, unsated, and she met his dark gold, like the black of his irises leaked into his gaze. "Let go."

"Mea." Rutger knew she didn't mean she wanted him to let her go. She wanted him to let go of his beast. "I'll hurt you," he whispered as he rocked his hips.

"Trust me." Rutger hesitated, then lowered her to the bed and continued to slide in and out of her, slowly, letting her feel him.

"You want me to shift. I see it in your eyes. It's in my head like you're there."

"Yes." She sucked in a breath as a blast of pleasure rippled through her. "Please." Jordyn wanted more, needed more of him.

Heat spread out from her middle as she clamped around him, and arching her back, he felt her pulses stroking him. Leaning down, he licked the peak of her breast, rocked his hips, her slickness caressing him. Rutger wouldn't deny her. With Jo's breathless moans in his ears, his beast slipped over him, his canines elongated, and his muscles bunched. His eyes changed and he saw her power, a luminous silver dragon. As they shared their bodies, they were sharing they're beasts. The alchemists' descant amplified, its density escalating, and weaving its power through the door and into the room it found them. Its presence carrying their essences.

Jordyn held the back of Rutger's neck as she met his thrusts, and keeping his gaze, watched his eyes turn from black gold to warm amber like bourbon. His canines touched his lower lip and sharpened to points as his muscles undulated under his skin. He licked his lips to taste her while he thickened inside of her, his trusts harder and his weight pinning her in place. Jordyn rolled her hips, lowered her arm to the comforter, and turned her head to the right, exposing her shoulder and neck.

"Mine," the word rolled over his low growl.

Rutger drew back, gazing at Jo's perfect skin as need and instinct surged through him, his protests and fears forgotten. He tilted his head back, felt his canines against his lip, his heart beating against his sternum, roared, then plunged his teeth into her flesh. He felt her magic hit his mouth at the same time her blood flowed from her, giving him her tangle of spice and wolf as its warmth coated his throat. With his teeth and body restraining her petite figure, he rocked his hips, driving into her and building his arousal.

Jordyn cried out from the pain and pleasure spreading like fire from Rutger's bite. Her moans filled her ears, and for a second, he crushed the world with his fierce need. Her vision returned, she heard the alchemists, Rutger's primal growls, and her thigh burned as if kissed by a torch. Holding her wrists to the bed, his lips on the curve of her neck, his teeth embedded inside of her, he seduced her with his hard thrusts. Each rock of his hips sending strokes of fiery threads through her.

The beast took more of him as raw lust clawed its way from his middle to explode inside of him. His climax rolled over him in heated waves, forcing him to retrack his teeth from her flesh, and leaning back, he howled a deep sound of possession. Jo was his. *Mine*.

Rutger released her, letting air invade the punctures at the same time the resonance of his howl echoed in the room. Jordyn matched his lazy thrusts as sweat trailed down the sides of her thighs and ecstasy from pleasure and pain erupted and lathered her in its heat.

He heard Jo's cry, felt her tense beneath him, and when the haze of his passion cleared, reality hit him in the stomach. Rutger rose to his elbows to see her eyes were closed, her head turned, her lips parted, and heard her rough inhales. Scarlet stained her throat, its smears reaching over her shoulder and down to her left breast. More blood welled up from dark wounds surrounded by frayed skin.

God what did he do to her? He hurt her.

"Mea." He did exactly what he said he wasn't going to do. What he promised he wouldn't do. She trusted him and he failed her.

With half opened eyes, Jordyn faced Rutger, his blood-stained mouth, cheeks, and neck, and met his worried gaze. "Wolf. This isn't over."

"What?" Lost in his instincts, he hurt her, she was bleeding, and wore crimson and purple bruises on her wrists. The pleasure and passion from moments before died under his guilt and shame.

"Shift into your beast form," she whispered through a rough breath. Jordyn called her power and wolf and fed both with her magic.

"No. No." Rutger tried backing away from her when she grabbed his arms and her magic buzzed between them. "I won't. I won't put you in danger."

"Trust me." Jordyn gathered more magic, making her eyes turn completely onyx. She needed him to shift. She needed to make him part of the Balaur. She needed her warrior.

Jo's magic reached out from her and clutching Rutger with claws, he was helpless to stop his beast from responding. "Why?" he growled.

"You're my warrior." She arched her back as if the increasing magic was holding her. "This is fate." Her voice sounded foreign and distant and had taken on age, like someone was speaking through her. "You are part of the Balaur."

This wasn't Jo. It wasn't her voice. She was wrong. Rutger stared at her, the woman he loved, the woman he hurt, and knew she was under a lot of pressure ... did it finally break her. Did he do this to her? Blame for everything that happened between them weighed on his shoulders while his shame for being weak and hurting Jo made it impossible for him to say no. Deep down, he knew it was an excuse to let go of the control he clung to morning, noon, and night. Rutger kissed her lips, left a scarlet smear and crawled backwards, leaving Jo naked, marked, and her body marred with wounds and bruises on the bed. When he stood, his skin heated, his hair felt heavy, and his muscles became pliable as his body started altering.

"I'm going to lose myself." Fear grabbed him, telling him he didn't believe her and he didn't believe in himself. His arms hung at his sides as his eyes turned black gold then rolled amber, his black irises a stark contrast, and his power flooded the room.

His voice sounded dead, regretful, and carried sadness while his shoulders slumped in defeat, and his entire presence turned dim. It wasn't going to stop her. Jordyn cast her magic to Rutger as his beast's veil blazed for a second, then sank inside of him and thrust out.

The beast devoured his wolf, sending Rutger into himself. He bent at the waist, his hands on his knees as the beast grabbed him and the transformation exploded in blinding pain. Hair punched through the skin on his arms, legs, chest, as his hands shifted to claws, his nails grew out and turned black. His chest widened, his muscles lengthening and molding to new bones, his spine pressing against taut flesh. Rutger straightened, targeted his dark stare on Jo, and surrendered to the beast.

She watched his face contort with the pain of the shift and his regret. He didn't make a sound. Not one whisper. His skin stretched, his muscles reformed, his back bowed, and she wanted it to stop. Wanted to end whatever she forced him to do. She needed to stop the look of betrayal on his face and the pain warping his body. Jordyn didn't. This was the way things had to be. It was fate. It was the force behind the Balaur and the ancients. Jordyn surrounded him with more magic, trying to lessen the pain and fear. Feeling her strength draining from her, she watched the mutating beast gain its hold over Rutger as it engulfed her magic.

Lit by a single yellow bulb, a cell with a concrete floor reinforced with White 47, no windows, and bars of silver loomed in front of him, promising containment and death. They were going to find him going Bestial and cage him. Take him from Jo. Take him from life. Jo was going to watch him fail. Who would take care of her when they dragged him to his cage? The demon waiting downstairs. Prime ordered him to mark Jo, knowing he would lose control, knowing Rutger wanted to lose control. And when Rutger turned feral, Prime would take Jo from the Cascade pack. The progression of the shift fractured his mind, he inhaled a ragged breath through his forming muzzle, and felt himself drowning in the chaos of the beast's mind.

"Stay with me, Wolf," Jordyn pleaded. She sat up, forced herself to keep from healing Rutger's mark, and concentrated her power on him.

"Losing," Rutger mumbled from his muzzle.

"No." Jordyn entered his mind as gently as possible, the threads of her power seeking his wolf.

His feel bordered on primitive and she prayed she didn't lose him to the beast. It would be her fault. She would have to tell the baron and baroness, the pack, the factions she forced Rutger's beast from him and turned him savage. They would put him out of the pack's misery, and a piece of her would die.

Stay with me. Diving deeper into his thoughts, they hit her one after another like someone was shooting them at her. He hurt her. Prime would take her from the pack. He loved her. He failed her. She deserved a warrior not a coward. *My Wolf.* Tears slipped down her cheeks, dropped to her skin to leave trails in the drying crimson. Jordyn thought about leaving his mind to tell him she needed him and he wasn't a coward, when the torrent of consciousness slowed and clearing, she found him. Out of the chaos confident gold eyes of his wolf held her. It warned her not to cross the threshold of Rutger's secrets. She backed away, leaving Rutger's secrets his own. She wouldn't break his defense and do to him what Lady Sloan had done to her. Jordyn found his root verve, sent her magic into its pureness, and when she was confident it weaved itself into his magic, she left him. Rutger might have his fears but he wasn't a coward, and he knew at his core he was her warrior.

After minutes, that felt like hours, Rutger stood straight and flexed his newly formed arms, back, and legs. His body became a deadly mixture of wolf and man. His power awakened from deep inside of him, as if it had been chained and waited a lifetime to be free. He opened his mouth, working his jaw, tasted the air, felt his teeth, fangs, and the sharp tips.

When he looked at her through amber eyes, like glistening stones of his bestial form, it reminded her of his bourbon. Warm caramel. If you drank until you were sated, he turned dangerous. "My beautiful beast." Jordyn gazed at the eight foot tall, mass of hard muscles Rutger had become. His long muzzle ended in a black nose, the points of his white teeth peeked out, his thick corded neck lead to rounded shoulders. Rippling with muscles, his enormous arms ended in hands with long black nails. His dark fur sat close to his body, his amber eyes narrowed while his chest rose and fell with easy inhales and exhales.

It was over.

The threat of Rutger going Bestial and caged until his death, was no more. She beat them. They beat them. There would be no sacrifice.

Rutger kept his eyes on his mate, her scent in his head, as he took a step closer, the pads of his feet sinking into the carpet. Textures, smells, the feel of the air on his fur, and the other's magic hit his senses, trying to scramble his thoughts. He focused as he approached the bed and the glow of copper set in a passive face. *Mate. Mark her. Mine.* The words punched his mind, demanding he obey, their echo bouncing off his skull. Her magic wrapped around him, calling him, making him stronger, his thoughts clearer. When his knees touched the supple fabric, he wrapped his long claws around her thin ankle, his nails grating against each other, pulled her down the bed, bunching the comforter under her, then flipped her.

The air rushed from her lungs when she landed on her stomach, her hands out to her sides, and her wounds open and bleeding freely. Jordyn remained silent, obedient, in tuned to Rutger's emotions in the link, and listening to him breathe.

"Mine," Rutger growled.

That's right, my Wolf. She sucked in a breath when he grabbed her by the throat, his nails at the front of her neck, and lifted her off the bed as if she were a doll. Suspended, pain shot through her shoulder to reach into its core while fresh blood slid down her chest and back. Jordyn held her cries inside and didn't fight his hold. Without denying him, she slowly slipped her knees on the comforter to lean on them and ease some of the strain. Jordyn held her breath, struggling to remain clam, and told herself Rutger wouldn't hurt her, he was in there somewhere, she had made sure of it. He lowered her, and she sat back while he moved his hand from the back of her neck to the side where his nails grazed fresh blood. With a lazy movement he raised his free hand, extended his fingers, pointed, and the nail grew another inch. Staring at the sharpened edge, he moved his hand from her vision. One second. Two seconds. The tip cut skin as he dipped it into a puncture. Swallowing a scream, fire erupted and burned a path down her arm. His rough throaty growl rumbled and faded as he lapped the blood from his nail.

The power and strength coursing through him after months of feeling helpless and riddled with fear made him drunk. It didn't touch the intoxication he felt when his mate's blood sat on his tongue. From it he could taste her arousal, her magic, and it sizzled in his mouth with her de-votion, and the fire of the dragons. Rutger's mind splintered, going in different directions, his new senses giv-ing him information faster than he could process it. *Balaur.* His mate earned the crest. He earned his warrior form. They were fated mates. With pride weaving into his loyalty and love for his mate, Rutger growled a low rumble, put his arm around her, pulled her close, and cupped her left breast in his palm, his nail flicking her tight nipple. Next to her small body, his hand, nails, and forearm looked four times her size. If he put his hands on her waist his nails would touch one another. *Mistress Balaur.* He loomed over her as her weight, like a light touch from a feather, rested against him. He was her warrior. She needed his protection. His instincts rode him, telling him part of the protection was giving her his mark. No one would take her from him. They would be bound by blood and magic.

Jordyn waited while Rutger held her, his soft fur like velvet on the bare skin of her back, his strength sinking into her, and his power matching her own. They were complete. *Mark your mate, Wolf.*

Rutger hesitated as he gazed at the punctures on her shoulder and the blood creating streams down her bronze-tinted skin. Smears marred her neck, and strands of hair crusted with dried blood stuck to her. Her strong heartbeat drummed in his head, giving him comfort and assurance. Leaning down, his muzzle next to her face, a silver from her cheek, he inhaled her delicious scent. As he drew back, he released her breast. Rutger slid his arm to her waist, his left hand gripping her neck, and turning her head to the right, he clamped his teeth into her shoulder. The points sank in, hit bones, and she whimpered a strangled cry.

Jordyn clutched his muscled forearm, and digging her nails into fur and skin, she squeezed her eyes closed. She gritted her teeth, and forced herself to fight through the sting from his virus. Rutger nudged her head to the right and back until it rested on him. She tried swallowing, her throat seized, and the sensation of choking grabbed her and wouldn't let go. When she thought she was going to pass out from the violent pain racking her body, his magic flared. Its caress surrounded her, called her wolf, and together their magic intertwined. The dragons roared, her wolf howled, and the rune on her thigh burned.

"Second. Soothsayer."

Prime's voice sounded in her head before she heard him. Jordyn forced her eyes open and angled her head to see him. He stood in their room, smiling, and she tried to imagine what the scene looked like.

As if answering her, Jordyn saw herself through Prime's eyes. She would have gasped if she could. She was a naked bloody mess with a beast at her throat. Sitting on her hunches with her left arm limp at her side, her right gripping Rutger's, and her wrists stained with purple, yellow, and green bruises. Scarlet and crimson marred her shoulder, chest, and back. The sight was archaic, primitive, and echoed the dark ages. This was her life. Their life. Rutger's massive body stood behind her, his corded arm covered in dark fur around her waist, and his thick hand at her neck holding her in place. His head heaved as he drank in her blood from the punctures he made with his beast's teeth.

"I'm going to assume this was your idea." It wasn't a question. Prime's violet eyes drained, letting the white blaze from his coal-painted face.

She closed her eyes. *"Yes."*

"Second, release her," Prime ordered.

Rutger didn't respond.

"Second, enough. Release her," Prime repeated his order. His voice dropped to a low brutal growl as it travelled across the room to hit them with his power and authority.

Rutger straightened, roared at the man and the old couple in his bedroom, his territory, and tightened his hold on his mate.

"You've been warned. Next time I will drain you of your power," Prime threatened. He took a step closer, the creepy couple following him.

"Wolf, let me go." Jordyn patted his arm. His hold weakened, letting her create distance between them, at the same time she drew her power in, taking it from the room. When Rutger released her, she swayed, nearly falling to her side. It had to be blood loss, exhaustion, and she burned through her magic, but it was nothing compared to his absence. It left her skin cold.

"Mea," Rutger mumbled through his jaws.

He looked at Prime as if seeing him for the first time then at Jo. Ravaged holes tore the skin on her back and front, and blood slid down her curves and dropped. What did he do? Guilt swam through him. He drew his power back into himself, and his Bestial form melted into his human form. He dropped to the carpet in a half crouch, exhaustion pulling on his muscles, and the taste of Jo's blood coating his mouth like thick oil. He looked down at his hands shocked to see dried crimson flaking from his skin while more darkened the underneath of his fingernails.

"Second, get dressed and take a seat. Soothsayer, get comfortable," Prime ordered.

Jordyn covered herself with the comforter, leaned against the pillows, and met Prime's violet gaze.

He approached the bed and sat down next to her. "You did this?"

"Yes."

"You risked his life."

"You risked mine." she countered. Barely able to keep her eyes open, Jordyn struggled to focus on Prime.

"I'm in the room," Rutger pointed out. He tugged a pair basketball shorts on and collapsed in the overstuffed chair by the fireplace. A nagging voice reminded him he needed to add wood so it wouldn't go out. He ignored it. His mind played thoughts from the beast and images of what he had done. He held Jo by her throat.

"You've done enough damage today, Second. Sit and stay." Prime turned his attention back to her. "How did you know he wouldn't lose his mind?"

"How did you know your power wouldn't kill me?" Jordyn whispered.

"I researched your family's history and consulted the foremost historians in the world. I've watched your mother use her magic and I've consulted her. I've tested the effects my magic would have on her, which I observed varied results. I had evidence backing my decision. And I'm Prime. I was born in the dark ages and witnessed the sharing of magic. I was alive when the light bringers summoned the first animal spirits."

Damn. She wanted to laugh. So much magic and he did research. Jordyn held his violet gaze as best she could and knew there was more to his answer and what it meant to her. With her mind racing and her body weakening, she let it go. "I followed the ancients demands and they guided my instincts. As a soothsayer, I needed a warrior." He merely stared at her, then she felt him in her head. She was telling him the truth.

"I witnessed Second to the Alpha in Bestial form. I could have him sent to a cage and a quick death," Prime threatened.

Jordyn smiled and couldn't stop from laughing. It sounded tired and insane. "If you were there with the light bringers ... you witnessed the creation of warriors in their Bestial forms."

"I may have," he replied as he bowed his head.

"We are bound by blood and magic. His wolf. His Bestial form. To take him would be taking a part of me. I would die. You know that," she said through a yawn.

"Your ancestors serve you well. You're in sync with them. Abel and Abela, she waits." He rested his hand on her thigh, pressing against the Balaur, and sent a familiar splinter of power into her. "I'll see you on the other side, Soothsayer."

She didn't know what he did or what they were going to do and was too tired to care. Despite her willpower, her eyes fluttered. *Don't go to sleep. However,* closing them, she blocked Prime out. Jordyn felt the absence of his weight when he stood and the creepy couple's presence closed in on her. Through half closed eyes, Jordyn saw Abela on her right and Abel on her left, their twin emerald gazes staring at nothing while directing their attention to her. As they hummed, they raised their hands in front of them, their magic weaving between them and over her. The humming faded, the intonation sharpened, and they began singing. Her eyelids felt like they weighed tons, and unable to fight it, she closed her eyes.

"The warrior has drawn her essence, drank in her blood, stripped her of her innocence and exposed her life-spark. The magic of her wolf and the ichor of the gods," Abel sang the words drawing them out. His voice light and airy as if it would float away.

"We call the elements of earth, wind, water, and fire." Abela's voice lowered its tone sweet. "We beseech you to find your vessel."

Rutger lifted his head, opened his eyes, and watched the alchemists. They each held a stone over Jo's chest and the bleeding wounds on her shoulder. He felt the link and sensed a void. She hadn't blocked him. It was like she wasn't there. Jo was in front of him and he couldn't sense her.

"What did they do to her?" he mumbled.

"She is in the ether," Prime replied.

Abel placed his stone beside Jo and took a ceramic flask with symbols, runes, and images hand painted on its sides from the inside of his tunic. He lifted the flask over Jo, removed the leather stopper, and sprinkled the contents over the wounds of his mark. Shiny dust fell with the weight of stones to land on Jo. A crackling like a spark catching dry tinder sounded, and fingers of smoke reached into the air, giving off the scents of earth, water, fire, and wind and they drifted in the room.

"Soothsayer, keeper of the ancients, ewer of the Collective, descendant from Dacia accept the infusion into yourself," Abel sang.

Jo's back arched off the blanket, making the comforter fall from her chest. She whimpered, the sound embodying her pain, and sank back into the bed. Rutger tried to stand, his knees gave out and he fell back to the chair. His body screamed with exhaustion from using magic, shifting into the Bestial form, and back to his human form. He wanted to sleep, but wasn't going to leave Jo alone with the creepy duo and Prime. Especially Prime. As if mocking him and feeding his jealousy, Prime leaned down, took the edge of the comforter, held it for several seconds as he studied Jo, then covered her. When he was done, he looked at Rutger with an azar glare.

Rutger was a fool. Prime planned the entire thing. They had been his playing pieces. If he wasn't fighting sleep, his body, and his wolf-which had gone silent as if it had retreated-he would have faced Prime and interrogated him. There was nothing he could do but watch from the chair and listen to Jo's suffering as the alchemists weaved their magic.

Jordyn sank deeper into the void as her magic flowed, her wolf howled, the dragons roared, and the Collective waited in silence. She saw the wounds from Rutger's mark, the blood as it slid down her skin, then heard her rapid pulse as she reacted to alchemist's hallowed song. Their power bore down on her, inside her, like they had started a war.

"Can you hear me, Soothsayer," Prime asked.

His voice slid through her mind leaving a wake cleared of life as if lava had scorched the land. *"Yes."*

"Are you in pain?"

"Yes. They're tearing me apart." Jordyn's middle felt like it was being shredded as each element tried taking root inside of her. *"Please, make them stop."*

"I cannot."

"Why can't I wake up?"

"You're in a trance, Soothsayer. It's safer. Let your magic guide you. Let the combination of what you are chose your verve."

No. She was going to fight whatever was causing the pain.

"Let your true self manifest."

What does that mean? Her entire body went rigid when fire licked her insides, water flooded her middle, and the wind worked to steal her breath from her, then earth plowed through them all. It was like watching waters from the world, the winds from storms, the blazes of the past that scarred the land, and the earth which bound them all, battle each other. She was in the middle catching their rage and their raw need to be alive. The wind whipped around her, water soaked her skin, and fire swept through scorching the air and drying the water.

"Fire," Abel sang.

"Water," Abela countered, her voice low.

"Wind," Abel sang louder.

"Earth," Abela yelled.

Earth.

A sense of peace teased her. Jordyn saw herself standing in the woods with the magic rising from the earth, her territory, and it called her, embraced her. She smelled the scent of fresh rain on dirt, saw pine needles shielding the forest floor, and heard the wind rustling through the treetops. *Earth.* Gold, black, red, and green dragons roared as they flew through the chaos of elements. Entering the center of the tornado, they hurtled into one another. Jordyn screamed, bodies disintegrated in the fire, wings, claws, and legs burst into flames, and the ashes shot out when the wind caught them and sucked them back into the storm. From the center of her chest flames stretched outwards to her arms, sides, and down her legs. The heat touched every part of her, stopping when it found the Balaur. It intensified and pulled the rune, twisted it, warped its feel, and fed the dragon's magic into it. No. She needed them. She didn't want to lose her ancestors. The storm stalled, shifted, and like a hungry beast followed the magic to the Balaur where it thrust its force into the rune.

The flames retreated, the water ebbed, the wind waned, leaving Jordyn alone in the ether. Where was the Collective? Zachery? Christian? Where was her pack? They abandoned her. With her dread she felt the ether closing in on her and reality drifting further away from her.

"Can you hear me?" Prime asked, his voice sounding far away.

Yes. No. She was drifting, leaving the world of the living. The alchemists were killing her. Jordyn swore he was trying to talk to her. She couldn't form words and strained to hear him as numbness overtook her and the darkness swallowed her.

CHAPTER THIRTY-THREE

Rutger heard Jo's screams, their despair running him through to his core, and he jerked awake. Pushing the gray fog and splintered memories from his mind, and with his wolf howling in his ears, he struggled to dislodge himself from the chair. After a sloppy struggle, he stood on weak legs and using the arm of the chair to steady himself, he watched the room spin, making the alchemists and Prime's form dark blurs. Rutger bowed his head, inhaled, exhaled, and waited for the worse to pass, and gained his balance.

Prime stood beside the bed, staring down at Jo, with Abela next to him. The alchemist's arms stretched out over Jo, her hands cradling a glowing, blue stone. Across from her, Abel mirrored her and held a white crystal. Its prisms reflected the azar and cerulean from Abela's stone, and the colors danced on Jo's chest. Her chest. The comforter had been removed. Rutger growled a low rumble, nausea rose carrying the taste of Jo's blood. Swallowing it down, he focused on his anger and marched over to the bed.

"What are you doing?" Gold and blue powder dusted her chest, breasts, her neck up to her chin, and the ragged openings of the puncture wounds.

"Be quiet." Prime refused to face him.

Rutger opened his mouth to protest when Jo's back arched off the bed and she inhaled as if she had burst through water and come up for air. After several seconds, she relaxed, her body going limp, and her face held a hint of peace. How was that possible? What was happening to her? The powder dissolved in the blood and Rutger winced when the puncture wounds seeped scarlet. The violence. The damage. He betrayed her trust.

"Soothsayer of the Cascade pack, the earth is your verve center, the Collective is your heart, the dragons are your mind. Your blood sacrifice is your fetter to your mate, your kith and kin. You are blood bound to your warrior," Abela chanted. "Give yourself to your ancestors. Bring forth your dragon."

"Jordyn Lily Langston is no more. Soothsayer for the Cascade pack, take your place among the powers," Able sang.

Listening to them tell him Jo wasn't herself anymore broke his heart. He saw the look of sorrow on her face when Claudia and Jason explained she was their soothsayer and their job was to protect pack property. Like a thin haze, Jo's power drifted over her, catching the blue and gold from the powder glittering on her skin. Rutger watched torn flesh weave to knit the puncture wounds closed at the same time the bruises faded and disappeared. Relief flooded him as her wounds healed and yet sadness and confusion took him. He didn't understand why his marks were gone as if they were never there. When Prime ordered he mark her and then use silver, the threat hung over their heads like an ax about to fall. It haunted them. When they talked, they avoided the topic like it was the plague, and now it was over and done with. Finished. With nothing left to indicate he marked her.

"What's going on?" Rutger demanded. "You threaten us. The Highguard threatens us." He almost blurted out the threats coming from Shadow Lord but stopped himself. "What's the point?"

"I doubted her and her power. There were too many conflicting stories," Prime whispered to himself. *"O drákos zei."*

What the hell was that? He didn't care. "Is this another test? What are the alchemists doing?" Rutger continued. He didn't know what he looked like besides half mad. His hands rested on his hips, his fingers digging into his skin. If he didn't burn the nervous energy consuming him, he was going to take it out on Prime. And that wouldn't help any-one.

Prime gathered himself, tore his attention from Sooth-sayer, and answered, "It was a test. They have concentrated her magic on her verve. Soothsayer has chosen earth, un-derstandable when you think about her territory. The pack has chosen her as their soothsayer and they have become her heart. Zachery is proof of the purity of love she has for them. It is time for her to reveal her true self. It means she will call her ancestors, merge with the dragons, the same way she merged with the Collective."

Prime knew every move she made … but the dragons. "How? How do you know about the dragons?" Rutger's mind went straight back to the conversation Jo and Prime had out on the deck. And to them being Prime's playing pieces.

"They represent her ancestors and the root of her magic. And she told me." Prime faced Second, his eyes ze-roing in on the dried blood on his chin and cheeks as it cracked then fell off. Prime met his glare and replied, "It's her destiny."

Destiny. He was starting to hate the word. Rutger thought the possessive look in Prime's azar eyes was for Jo. The photographer, the woman who laughed easily at his jokes, who drank wine and giggled, and liked to sit in the sun until sweat beaded on her skin. It made him crazy with jealousy until he saw red while it made his wolf furious and desperate for possession. What did he have compared to Prime, with his power, influence, and status? Rutger had nothing. It was good and bad that he was wrong. Prime looked at Jo and saw a thing to possess, to put on a shelf and show others how powerful he was.

'I'm powerful enough to contain the Cascade pack's soothsayer whose ancestors were blessed by Balaur a gold dragon god. Ladies and gentlemen, watch as she pulls beasts from men, performs tricks on demand, and then reads your minds.'

Prime saw the dark ages awakening *with* her.

Rutger looked back at Jo, her stillness, her lashes resting on her cheeks, her lips partly open, and her raven hair against the scarlet comforter. He saw the woman he loved, who cried when frustrated, and cursed when sad. Then he saw the pack's soothsayer, her strength, and her determination. She made him her warrior. She needed him to protect her from Prime, the Highguard, and Shadow Lord. Rutger was going to master shifting into his Bestial form and he was going to get stronger, better. *Beautiful beast.* Her voice feathered his thoughts as the memory climbed out from the chaos in his head. Jo's power built, then flared like a blast, its force filling the air around them, then it was gone. She drew it back inside of herself and the room returned to normal.

"It is absolute," Abel sang as he sank to the floor.

"There are no boundaries," Abela confirmed as she sank to the floor. Their radiant gems sat beside Jo's legs, glowed for a heartbeat, then dimmed and looked like stones once more.

"What happened? What's absolute?" Rutger asked. It can't be over. He expected her life to be threatened, her heart to stop, and when it did, he would beg her to come back to him. It would be his turn to want to give up believing they weren't strong enough for whatever waited for them. Nothing happened.

"You have a wolf spirit, separate from your human spirit. She is no longer separated. Her wolf, the dragons, the Collective, and her magic are intertwined and move through her as freely as her blood. When she shapeshifts, it'll be seamless, as if her entire body is liquid to form and reform." He paused. Prime closed his eyes, his right hand over Soothsayer, and whispered, "What has been done cannot be undone."

Magic carried and there was an underlying tone in his voice when he said the last line. Rutger didn't like it. It made his instincts roar, and his suspicions rage out of control. No. It was too easy. That's what was happening. Too easy. She was alive, unhurt, mostly, and resting in their bed.

"This is true." Abela slowly stood and faced Prime, her emerald eyes dimming to pale green. "Her form is endless."

"Ilario, descendant of Ceuthonymus, Prime to the magic-born," Abel stated as he stood. "It cannot be undone."

Rutger saw her shapeshifting as she entered the house and then when she jumped from the stairs. He couldn't imagine Jo's body forming and reforming or what she would be able to do with her wolf form. Would she be able to transform her hands, one part of her body at will, or shift into her Bestial form? He didn't know.

Prime put his hand on Abela's shoulder. "Infinite. Second, move the covering from her thigh."

Rutger gave Prime a questioning glare, held his azar gaze, then with a shaking hand gently pulled the comforter from around her leg. He dropped the edge and stared where the Balaur had been. Replacing the X with the box in its center, was a silver dragon, its wings, tail, and scales highlighted by an iridescent blue bordering on cobalt. Kneeling beside the bed, Rutger ran his hand over the smooth skin making the colors shimmer under his palm. The tail started above her knee, its back legs tucked under it as if it was flying through the air, while its elongated body with scales covered most of her thigh. Thick wings expanded to wrap around her leg, the right front leg of the dragon stopped at her hip with its claws extended. The left leg stopped at the back of her hip, its claws digging into her flesh. The dragon's head was turned to face him, its onyx eyes streaked with ribbons of copper. As if it was alive, they held the same fathoms as Jo's.

"What the hell is that?" Rutger asked. He swept his hand over the image again and again it shimmered.

"The crest of Balaur's inner circle. She is a direct descendant of his chosen," Abela answered. She moved like exhaustion held her body and she was fighting to remain standing. Taking the stone from the bed, she slipped it behind her tunic. "The first in centuries."

"I thought the rune was Balaur's crest?" Rutger reluctantly took his hand back from Jo's thigh and stood. "Lady Sloan described it as such."

"Yes, I've heard her telling, and it was or so it was believed. There is another tale describing the end of magic when the world began moving on. It was believed humans understanding magic was fading and leaving the magic-born weak, raided the fortress of Balaur and his Dacia priests, and murdered his chosen warriors, priests, and soothsayers. There were no survivors of the massacre," Prime explained.

"Go on," Rutger urged. If he was going to be there for Jo, he needed to know everything, whatever it was. The elf's attack, and the group he belonged to was the beginning. Then there was the pack, the klatch, and the challenge.

"Every story needs a hero, heroine, a martyr to believe in, and for the story to hold its power through the ages. There isn't one. No one fought back, no telling of a great battle, they were gone. According to statements taken at the time and reports years later, the followers of Balaur died in the Carpathian Mountains. When asked for proof of their deaths, it's said the temple had been destroyed along with their remains. Obliviously, that is untrue, like the massacre. Through the years the rune, like the one Soothsayer wore, started to manifest. From years of assimilating with humans and their beliefs, it destroyed the weaker magics leaving very few runes to identify soothsayers. Lord Ethan and Lady Sloan are from different backgrounds, yet they share the same rune. That alone made it unlikely it was Balaur's. Meaning the others wearing the rune weren't from the correct linage."

"You wanted a descendant of the chosen. When the baron petitioned the Highguard about Jo, he had to prove she wore a symbol." Rutger's mind chased trails of information that over the last couple of months and days he ignored deciding to wallow in self-pity. The changes in alphas whose territories border Cascade wasn't a coincidence. "You knew about the rune from the beginning, and thought if she wore it, there was a chance it was real. Then you put your people in place around Cascade to spy on her, gather intel, and when they reported it looked like she was the real deal, you planned this elaborate charade in order to pull the dragon from her," Rutger accused. "You used me to get to her. It was never about me marking her."

"Specific people are in charge, it's not a secret. The request of protection came from Lady Sloan after witches kidnapped her daughter. The Highguard agreed Soothsayer needed protection and chose the appropriate people."

"This has been going on for months," Rutger mumbled.

"Yes. It goes much deeper than the Cascade pack. Second, you are no different than she. It's been centuries since a shapeshifter had the instinct to mark its mate and fate influenced the magic-born and drew mates together, yet here you are. As a soothsayer with a fated mate, she needed to be marked in order for the alchemists to perform the ritual. A soothsayer with the amount of magic she possesses, needs an anchor. She doesn't live in one world; her mind is in the world of the Collective and the past, while her body is in this reality. She could lose herself there and never wake, never leave, deciding to make her place in the ether. You have the power to keep her among the living, and if she does plunge into her mind, you have the power to bring her back. You're her warrior. She marked you as such." Prime turned from Rutger to look at the dragon.

"I don't feel her mark," Rutger mumbled.

"You will when you call your magic to shapeshift, to either form," Prime answered. "This is her dark awakening."

"She isn't dark," Rutger quickly protested. He heard Lady Mia and Lady Sloan arguing over dark magic and the end of times.

Prime laughed, its edges mocking. "Soothsayer is not dark. The chosen magic-born with enhanced powers are the Dark Awakening. We know magic from the dark ages is making a resurgence and need to be ready. Like your Bestial form, Second, it's from the past. A forbidden past."

Fear skated down Rutger's spine with the implications. "What happens now?" His mind was racing, his muscles were screaming from being strained and exhausted, and he wanted to tell everyone to get the hell out of his house.

"You *shall* not tell anyone about Soothsayer's changes or yours. No one is to know what happened here. By the power used and your roaring, the witnesses understand you marked your mate. A ritual was preformed and the outcome was satisfactory. Whatever they assume will be their truth until the challenge. It will serve as an unveiling of sorts."

Shall. They will serve as a display of power, proving Prime's authority over the magic-born. Prime glared at him, and while his eyes held his authority and otherworldly magic, Rutger saw a glint of humor in them. It scared him worse than understanding they were heading toward a magic apocalypse. "You still expect her to go through with the challenge?"

"Yes." Prime faced the alchemists who were standing beside one another, their strength fading. "It's time for us to leave."

"Warrior of Balaur," they said in unison and bowed. When they straightened, they both looked at Jo as if she were a sleeping queen, bowed, then turned and walked out of the room with Prime following.

Rutger waited as Prime's hard voice ordered everyone to leave the house. The baron and Lord Ethan protesting and demanding to know what happened. They all wanted to know if Jo and Rutger were all right. Prime didn't respond, and after several minutes Rutger's senses told him they left and the house was empty. He was alone. Rutger walked over to Jo, sat beside her, and gazed at the woman who now wore a dragon on her thigh. They had become the poster children for the dark ages. What was going to happen to them?

"Do you know, Soothsayer?" Rutger asked. "Are you dreaming about the future and what will happen to us?"

Jo slept. The dragon glittered silver.

"Jo, do you know what will happen to us?"

Unfazed by his voice and question, she slept.

Rutger closed his eyes, inhaled, smelled iron from blood and cringed. He needed to clean the alchemist's dust and blood off of her. Rutger went to the bathroom, grabbed a washcloth, wet it with warm water, and looked in the mirror. Crimson tainted his cheeks, chin, neck, and more dried blood stained his chest. He resembled a mad man. After placing the washcloth on the counter, Rutger turned the shower on, and stripped out of his shorts. Stepping under the warm spray, he let his worries go down the drain with the rose-tinted water.

Jordyn rolled to her side, grabbed the blanket, and cuddled into its thickness. Reaching out, she felt for Rutger, and when she grazed his side, she scooted closer. He moaned a half sleep, half awake sound, and moving the mass of fabric away drew her to him.

"What time is it?" Jordyn asked. She kept her eyes closed and her body close to Rutger's warmth.

"Six in the evening. You slept all day."

"I had the strangest dream."

"Tell me," he whispered. Rutger prepared himself to hear about dragons, priests, wolves, the Highguard, Prime, the Collective, her magic, and the horrors they brought. He waited to hear about the coming war with humans, the rise in magic, and how the dark ages were going to sweep over the land, spreading its cloak to trap them underneath. A magic apocalypse.

"We were hiking." Simple. Safe. In the mountains. Her territory.

His mind jarred. *What?* Rutger waited for her to continue, and when she didn't, he asked, "That's it?"

"Mmmm. Nothing else. Just us hiking. In the woods." She scooted back and, on her side, raised and leaned on her elbow to look at Rutger. His mahogany eyes held an amber hue. "Your eyes have changed colors, my warrior."

"I noticed. How do you feel?" Rutger drew his fingers up and down her spine.

He washed the blood off of her as best he could, then got a clean blanket, but didn't bother trying to get a T-shirt over her head or underwear on her. After his shower, he sat on the bed, intending on watching her, and waiting for her to wake up. Instead he fell asleep and slept like the dead.

"Different. Complete. What happened?" The memories were splintered, images came and went with the alchemist's voices.

"You mean after we had sex and I shifted into my Bestial form?" His eyes narrowed on her.

Jordyn smiled then frowned. What she did hadn't been fair. "Yes, my beautiful beast. I'm sorry."

Rutger inhaled. "You could have warned me."

"I wasn't sure if I was going to go through with it. Then it changed, everything felt right, and my instincts told me I needed you. It was natural," she tried explaining. With sleep closing in on her, she didn't think she was doing a good job.

"I didn't doubt you. I doubted myself. If I had gone Bestial you could have been hurt. We've spent a lifetime being told it was wrong. Some will continue to think it is." Letting what he said linger between them, he watched her eyes darken. There was a vastness in their depths, a world he didn't know anything about contained in copper and onyx. "Letting go made me feel powerful and terrified." He kissed her forehead, and she met his gaze from under her lashes. He couldn't lose her. "The creepy twins dusted you with some kind of powder that smoked, then they chanted, your power filled the room, the marks healed, and it was over," he answered. An over simplified answer. How did he tell her what actually happened?

"That's all?"

"You don't remember anything?" he asked, his voice low.

"No. Bits and pieces, but I don't know if it's real or I dreamt it." Jordyn laid back down and scooted closer to him.

He draped his arm over her side. "Maybe it'll come to you later. Right now, let's enjoy this."

Sounded good to her. "Why am I still naked?"

"I like you naked. Any other questions?" His voice was rough with sleep and male appreciation.

She could picture his wolf's grin. "No." Jordyn felt secure, happy, and loved. They faced the worse of their fears, taking the weight off her shoulders and stress from between them. Even with the challenge in their future, no matter how fleeting the feeling, she felt as if she could take on the world and win. Jordyn snuggled closer to Rutger, skin to skin, and heard him growl. Warm, cozy, and with Rutger beside her, she yawned and let sleep take her to her dreams where her territory opened before her.

Jordyn- 1.

Prime- 0.

CHAPTER THIRTY-FOUR

Jordyn pushed the images of trees, mountains, and the sound of rushing water over rocks from the haze of sleep and opened her eyes. The rising sun broke through the windows, casting its golden hue over the bed, making the morning softer and less intrusive. Sitting up, she gazed at the reflection of snowcapped-mountains on the glassy lake as her dream filtered through her. With her movement the blanket fell, pooling at her waist, and crisp air touched bare skin. She shivered, looked at the darkened fireplace, and considered starting a fire when Rutger's hand grabbed her waist and pulled her back to the bed.

"We have to get up," she said through a laugh.

"No, we don't," Rutger protested with a growl running through his words. He wrapped his arms around her and held her to him.

Jordyn untangled herself and turned to him, and they lay together face-to-face. His amber touched eyes heavy with sleep, his lips slightly curved with a grin, and his dark hair sticking up from his head. She raised her hand and combed through its thickness with her fingers, letting them trail to the curls at his neck. "I want to stay this way forever, but you know we can't. You have to tell me what happened yesterday. What happened to me. I have to understand, the challenge is tonight."

"Is it selfish I don't want to do this right now?" Rutger asked as he rolled to his back. It felt like the first time they were able to relax without interruption from the pack, Prime, assassins, and kidnappers.

"If you're hesitant to tell me then it has to be bad." *It's always bad.* She was starting to let the entire event gather weight and it added to the challenge ahead of her. *Stop.* She couldn't think about it all at once. Jordyn worked to compartmentalize each incident by storing completed tasks, like being marked, to one side and uncompleted tasks, like the challenge, to the other. This was an uncompleted task. "I can't remember anything beyond Prime telling me I was in a trance. It's all dark and somewhere I can't reach." Jordyn searched Rutger's face looking for any sign of what happened and why he didn't want to tell her.

"He told you, you were in a trance?" While Jo was unconscious, Rutger didn't remember him saying anything.

"Yes. Why?"

"Nothing. It's not bad. Not really." He covered his face in the bend of his elbow and inhaled and exhaled.

"I'm supposed to believe you when you're acting the way you are?" Jordyn sat up and stared at him. The blanket sat at his hips, the line of dark hair disappearing underneath the thick fabric. "Wolf, please."

"You're a direct descendant from Balaur's chosen." Rutger lowered his arm, sat up in a fluid motion, and his gaze nailed her with a cautious stare. "Direct. I guess the dragon god had his own soothsayers, warriors, and priests. Look at your thigh."

Jordyn held his stare with her own and felt her eyes change like they were going to drill through him to find the truth. He wasn't lying to her, she sensed that much. Her eyes remained on Rutger as she deliberately tugged the blanket, making it slip over her legs. When the chill rested on her skin, she looked at her thigh. It was going to come alive and attack. Jordyn scrambled backwards to the edge of bed where she nearly fell off. She stared at the dragon as it appeared to move with her, and her feet hit the carpet and she stumbled backwards until she landed hard in a chair.

"You can't get away from it, it's on your leg," Rutger mocked with a laugh.

"Laugh it up." Jordyn tore her eyes from the dragon to Rutger. "What the hell?"

"Your crest. Proof you're from the ancient linage and gifted by Balaur. The dragon god marked you." Rutger stopped and tried to remember what Prime told him. *She is no longer separated. Her wolf, the dragons, the Collective, and her magic are intertwined and move through her as freely as her blood. When she shapeshifts, it'll be seamless as if her entire body is molten and able to form and reform.* In a monotone voice, Rutger explained it exactly the way Prime had explained it to him. Word for word.

Jordyn dissected what Rutger said as she brushed her palm over the dragon's head as if petting it, and watched it glitter silver and cobalt. *Interesting.* She thought about her magic and it glowed silver almost white, then she brought her wolf, and the dragon's eyes bleed copper. *No way.* When she jumped from the stairs, she called her wolf from her magic. Now it slid through her, flowing under her skin, waiting to burst through in an instant or trickle up like water from a spring teasing her with its feel. Jordyn looked at Rutger to see him sitting on the edge of the bed, the sides of his feet hidden by the plush carpet, and his head bowed.

"You're thinking," Jordyn whispered. "Look at me. Tell me how you feel about this."

Rutger lifted his head, surprise gripped his face as he stared at her.

"What?"

"Move your hair from your shoulder," Rutger ordered. He knew his voice sounded rough, like his wolf was talking through him.

With his eyes glowing gold and the urgency in his voice, Jordyn pulled her hair away from her shoulders, grabbed the hair band off the side table, and put the tangled mess in a bun. It wasn't his marks, she healed those. "What is it?" *What is it now?*

"It's there," he whispered. His wolf howled in his ears as he stared at eight gold punctures, the details of the violence evident as they highlighted Jo's shoulder. Rutger couldn't believe it. When she marked him as her warrior, he felt weak, and weaker when his markings, vicious as they had been, healed. Selfishly he wanted to see a physical mark, proof she was his and he marked his mate. "My mark. Gold, the color of the Kanin linage marks you."

Jordyn sat still wrapping her mind around what he said. First the dragon and now gold markings. That's what she needed to make her stand out in crowd. She stood, and passing Rutger and his dazed look, walked to the bathroom and stopped in front of the mirror. There they were. Eight gold punctures, resembling unhealed wounds, their frayed edges wavering on her skin like ghosts. She groaned, not from the marks, from the streaks of crimson smeared over her shoulder, chest, and neck, and the ends of her hair sitting on her head in clumps. She was a mess and needed a shower.

Rutger was behind her, his hands on her hips, his lips next to her ear. "How do you feel about it?"

Her fingers hovered over the healed skin here gold glowed. "It's beautiful and sad at the same time."

"Sad. How?" Rutger straightened and looked at Jo's reflection. Was she upset he marked her? Please no. She ordered him to do it despite his fear he would hurt her. "Tell me, Jo."

"Sad, because it's another reason for people to stare at me." She turned around and faced him, his eyes holding his worry. "Beautiful, because I'm yours and the world will know it."

"Mea, I love you." Rutger took her lips in a kiss of possession, lifted her, and set her on the counter. Breaking the kiss, he rested his forehead against hers. "The only people who will see it are magic-born. It's invisible to humans."

"I know. It's something else that separates us from everyone else. Along with the dragon, they make quite the statement. I've lost all touch with who *I am.*"

"You are Jo to me. The woman I love, the woman who can't remember the name of her favorite wine, and insists on leaving the doors open." Rutger met her cocoa gaze and saw Jo. Not a soothsayer from an ancient line of Purebloods.

"You'll never let me live that down, will you?" Her hands sat on his hips, the muscles of his back tensing when he moved.

"Not a chance. It's all I have." Rutger backed away, Jo's fingers trailing over his skin. He looked at the marks, the dragon, and back to her. "The pack will see their soothsayer, as will all magic-born, and they'll understand your mate marked you and you have significance to Prime, meaning the Highguard has added you to their list of important people." Pausing, he debated whether to continue the conversation or let it die. He had to tell her his worries. "After the alchemists were finished, Prime said, 'What has been done cannot be undone.' I don't like it and I don't trust him. Jo there have been changes with the other packs and the Highguard is responsible. Your mother, Lady Sloan, requested the Highguard protect you after Butte Springs, and in a strategic move, they moved their people into place."

Of course, she did. "Prime could have been talking about the dragon crest, it isn't going anywhere. Or about us. No one can change, doubt, or refute what we are." Jordyn didn't believe what she said. Prime's intentions for them could be endless. Inhaling, she tasted aged iron from dried blood and cringed. She hopped off the counter, walked to the shower, and started the water. "What kind of changes?"

"The territories circling Cascade have new alphas, they were handpicked by the Highguard," he answered. Rutger watched her test the water then disappeared into the shower. He waited a couple of seconds, and when she didn't say anything he went into the bedroom and grabbed a pair of cotton pants. He returned to the bathroom, turned on the faucet, and began his morning routine. His normal routine.

Their world was getting smaller. "At least we know they have our backs," Jordyn said as she stood under the warm spray. *Right?* "We've overcome the hardest obstacles; I've been marked, you've shifted into your Bestial form without going insane, and I've survived the alchemists pulling my true self from me. If Prime wants to threaten us, he has to change his tactics. He can't take you from me and he can't take me from you. Neither of us are leaving Cascade."

Rutger put his toothbrush back and grabbed the shaving cream. "You think they'll back the pack up?" Rutger didn't trust them. It could be his director side, but his instincts told him they had their own agenda.

"I don't know. They have to do whatever the Highguard orders them to. I'm a descendant from the chosen, they'll have to stand by me." Jordyn was joking and not joking ... she had to or she was going to go insane. Suds from the shampoo circled the drain, and she grabbed the conditioner.

"My apologies, oh great soothsayer," Rutger teased as he turned toward the shower with shaving cream covering his face. A direct descendant and if they had children of their own? The thought squeezed Rutger's heart ... what the hell was he thinking?

Jordyn peeked from around the steam fogged glass. She was kinda sad he was shaving; she liked the shadow of his beard and mustache darkening his face. "You're forgiven, White Beard."

"Milady." Rutger bowed, then faced the mirror.

Jordyn checked her appearance in the mirror. Her makeup was black and chocolate to highlight the copper in her eyes, and she chose to leave her raven hair straight. She wasn't wearing jewelry because she might have to shapeshift. Her form fitting black V-neck top covered the marks, and she wore jeans, and running shoes. She wasn't going to do anything special for the challenge. They were going to see Jordyn as a person, not a "dressed up in pretty clothes" soothsayer. She'd never been a fashionista, and wasn't going to be one, ever. Jordyn grabbed the blankets from the bed, checked the sheets for alchemist dust and blood, and finding none, headed downstairs. At the bottom stair she saw Tracy by the front door and met a wall of tension.

"Good morning," Jordyn greeted, her voice light, relaxed, and lacking tension.

"Good morning, Mistress," Tracy replied. Her brown eyes narrowing on the blankets and everywhere else but Jordyn.

"Do you have any questions?" She shifted the blankets in her arms, making sure the ends were off the floor.

"No, Mistress."

"If you do, don't hesitate to ask. This is only going to get weirder." She gave the sentinel a tight smile and continued to the laundry room.

Both Tracy and Charles were there when Prime and his entourage arrived at the house, watched the alchemists, then heard Rutger roar as he shifted into his Bestial form. Jordyn had wanted to cry out from the pain when his teeth sank into her and grated against her shoulder blade. She didn't, and was glad she kept herself under control. It would have added to the tension between her and her sentinels. There had to be questions. Jordyn wasn't going to push either of them; if they wanted to know they could ask. She couldn't stop the smile when she knew the twenty-four hours they spent in their bedroom hadn't helped the situation. Jordyn shoved the blankets into the washer, dumped detergent in, and started the machine.

Rutger stood at the railing of the deck, coffee cup in hand, and gazed out at the lake. It had been a peaceful night, a relaxing morning, and it worried him. When was the ax going to drop? When were the problems going to start? And who or what was going to be the reason behind it? Prime and his damn challenge? Shadow Lord and his threats?

Shadow Lord had to know about Prime, the attack on Jo, and the gathering at the Summit. It was an open invitation. What he wouldn't know about was his mark on Jo, and the dragon. The damn dragon. It was sexy as hell and just as scary. A descendant of the chosen. He didn't know what it meant for her, for them, or the pack. The thought of children came back and he shoved it away. Far away.

Jo was right when she said the new alphas and their packs would obey the Highguard and protect her. Prime made her part of his chosen, Dark Awakening. Rutger couldn't stop from remembering the look in Prime's eyes as he stared at Jo while her power flowed from her. He shut down his worries and half turned when Jo's essence feathered his senses with her approach.

Wearing a chocolate brown, long-sleeved Henley, the hem on the right side caught in the waist of his dark denim jeans that hugged his hips and thighs, he leaned against the rail. Rutger raised the mug, he took a drink of coffee making the muscles of his arm and shoulder flex. He knew she was there staring, the feel of his self-assurance thickened in their link.

"You left the door open, Director," Jordyn accused as she walked across the deck.

Rutger laughed. "I'm trying to understand why it's so fascinating to you." He faced her and met her black-lined eyes, her humor and the sliver of challenge gleaming in the cocoa. She took his breath away with her confidence. "What about it would make you risk security protocol."

"Security protocol? Director, that's harsh." Jordyn joined him by the railing and faced the lake. "It's a beautiful morning."

"Agreed." Rutger looked out over the water and the mountains across the lake.

"Are you wondering when it will end?" Jordyn sipped her coffee. "The peace we have right now?"

"As a matter of fact … I know the challenge is tonight, and it's up to you to succeed. I don't know what my place is or how I can help you. I'm back to feeling helpless. I'm responsible for the pack's security and I have no idea where to begin."

"Would it make you feel better if you went to the office?"

"No, I'm not leaving you. Ansel can take care of it, and if he needs help, he'll call," Rutger answered.

Relief flooded her. She didn't want to be by herself. "We're going to have to tell the baron and baroness about us." Jordyn was going to keep the mood light but time was ticking by and they needed to talk.

"My Bestial form? Your marks and dragon? Or our engagement?" Rutger asked. They were really going to get married. Like a normal couple. Their wedding meant more than them getting married. It would override the mark, them being fated mates, and would make them Rutger and Jo Kanin.

"Pick one," Jordyn replied. They had a lot going on. "I think we should tell them about our engagement. The rest might be resolved tonight whether we want it to or not."

"True. After the challenge, we'll make plans to meet with them. I want it to be low key, family only. You can make the choice to tell your dad, Mia, Lady Sloan, and Lord Ervin. They have to be sworn to secrecy." Rutger set his cup on the railing and faced Jo. "No one else needs to know until we're settled and Prime and the Highguard aren't in our lives."

"Yes, Director," Jordyn replied. She was going to continue with some witty banter when her senses warned her, they were going to have company. "Incoming," she said as she turned toward the open door.

Rutger watched for her eyes to change, when they didn't, he relaxed. "Who?" He barely finished saying the word when four cell phones alerted them of their visitor. "You're good, but my security system is quicker." Rutger winked at her and grabbed his phone. "Mandy apologizes for not notifying us sooner. It's a delivery truck sent by the baron and baroness."

"One male and one female, magic-born, pack. I don't need a security system." Jordyn gave Rutger a smug look, held her coffee cup in both hands, sipped then walked into the house. Her cell phone sat on a table beeping with the same alert as Rutger's. She hit ignore and kept walking. After the incident with Louis, she had her number added to the list. Anytime someone drove to the house an alert would be sent to her as well Tracy and Charles.

"Show off." Rutger followed her inside, closed the door behind him, and they made their way to the front door to meet their visitors.

Charles stood in the opening, allowing two people to enter, both carrying stainless steel trays with the smell of bacon, sausage, muffins, and eggs drifting out from them. Food.

"Craig and Nicole Burns, they own Mountain Ridge Catering," Tracy explained.

"Thank you," Rutger replied.

"What is this?" Jordyn asked. They were pack, their essences flowed from them to her.

"Breakfast. The baron and baroness didn't want you to worry about anything this morning, Soothsayer. We would have been here sooner but we didn't want to be too early." Craig replied with an easy smile. "We brought coffee and champagne. They said you had something to celebrate."

Jordyn looked at Rutger, his brows drawn, and shrugged. "Thank you."

"We'll set everything in the kitchen, if that's okay?" Nicole asked. Her hazel eyes, holding more green than brown, narrowed on Jordyn.

"By all means." Rutger watched both of them stare at Jo, who despite their attention stood tall.

Nicole placed her tray on the concrete counter, left the kitchen, headed back to the van, and returned with a carafe of coffee, its smoky aroma escaping, and a bottle of champagne.

"Everything is set. If you need anything at all don't hesitate to call." Craig gave each of them another easy smile and started toward the door. He stopped at the entrance and faced them. "Soothsayer, we'll be there tonight. You have our confidence."

His truth and the emotion behind it buzzed like electricity. They would stand before the pack and would give their lives for her. What the hell was happening? How could she demand the happy couple with a catering company defend her? "Thank you, I appreciate the support." Jordyn gave them a smile of assurance and the feeling of being a fraud inched closer.

Nicole matched her husband's smile with her own as if it meant she whole heartily agreed with him, then walked out of the house. Charles stood at the bottom stair and watched as they backed the van up, turned around, and left. Jordyn waited and stared out the open door at the driveway, her SUV, Rutger's work truck, and the sentinel's SUV. *You have our confidence.*

"They're rallying behind you. The pack chose you and they can't go against their natural instincts," Rutger offered. Jo's eyes darkened to onyx, the air thinned, and the feel of her wolf weaved around her to protect her.

"I'm responsible for their safety. If they stand too tall someone might use them and make an example out of them." She thought about Zachery. She couldn't handle another death and the haunted eyes of the family. "If anything happens to them, the husband and wife caterers, it's my fault."

"We don't know what will happen. Worrying about it will only make you miserable," Rutger warned. "There's another car coming." Two seconds and their cells all beeped with the alert.

Calming her frustration and worry, Jordyn pulled her power back in. "Who is it?"

Rutger read the message. "Prime's car."

"I'm not in the mood," Jordyn mumbled.

"What do you want us to do?" Tracy asked.

They weren't going to tell him no. "Look official and threatening." Jordyn walked out to the porch and stood at the first step; Charles remained at the bottom, his body rigid. Rutger's warmth was suddenly behind her, his hands on her shoulders. She wanted to lean into him and soak up the comfort he was offering.

The sleek, black luxury car with dark-tinted windows rolled toward the house, its purring engine a pinch louder than the tires crunching rocks and leaves. It stopped behind Rutger's truck, and without turning the engine off the passenger door opened. A tall woman stepped out, her green high heels clicking as she approached them. Her strawberry-blonde hair touched her shoulders, its soft curls bouncing with her walk. She tucked her white silk blouse into a green pencil skirt. The shoes and skirt matched. Jordyn's jeans matched her running shoes. She almost laughed out loud. The woman's emerald green eyes narrowed on Jordyn as her power sparked. She was magic-born ... witch, no, Jordyn concentrated on the woman's power. Mage. She was letting Jordyn know the extent of her magic and not hiding what she was.

"Soothsayer. I'm Ava, messenger for Prime, this is for you. It's your invitation and it states the canons for this evening." She took one step toward Charles and handed him a black envelope with purple undertones that looked like it could have been made from silk. It drank in the sunlight filtering through the tree limbs as if it was its lifeforce. Charles held the envelope, turned it over, and facing Jordyn stepped up and passed it to her.

She was convinced it was silk, had no idea how they managed it, and knew it represented Prime's true form. "Thank you." Ava nodded but didn't leave. Jordyn could take a hint. She carefully opened the flap and took out a crisp white card with black lettering. She read it once, then again, and again. "Tell Prime, I understand."

"Very well." Ava gave them a calculated smile that didn't reach her eyes, then turning clicked her way back to the car. When it was heading away from the house Jordyn released the breath she had been holding.

"What does it say?" Rutger asked.

"Read it yourself," Jordyn replied, and handed it to him.

She hadn't thought about the elves assuming the investigation would take time, and there was the morning Prime ordered Rutger to mark her. When Prime said he had taken care of the situation, he absolved the pack of the responsibility and it freed them of being accused of acting out based on emotion. The Highguard would conduct an investigation forcing the Seelie court to obey. It was all very professional and no one could blame the other. Plus, there was feed from the surveillance cameras. Jordyn hadn't thought about how much she wanted it until Prime stated it in his note. She was getting exactly what she wanted and she couldn't wait to see it happen.

"He's publicly executing Arvid for his assassination attempt on your life, and dispensing punishment to Agnar, Bendik, and Erling at the Summit. The baron can't be happy about this," Rutger said. "It will make us vulnerable to human law enforcement."

"He might not be happy, but you know he isn't against it. Two things are happening; the public execution, like we're living in the *dark ages*, outside of human influence, and the challenge. There's a chance Prime will use this to expose us. I'm marked by the Second to the Alpha, and wear the crest of Balaur. This will be witnessed by the pack, klatch, and with the open invitation, anyone who attends."

"You have to overcome whatever Prime has planned for you. This will either solidify Cascade's place with the Highguard and raise its power value or kill it. They'll use your failure against us," Rutger added.

The pack is too important to destroy and the baron's authority over the klatch was to vital. "I have the confidence of the pack. Prime can't change that, and to replace the baron would be like taking a trusted general from his army. This whole thing doesn't make sense. Like I said, his threats are useless, he has to change his tactics. I have the Collective, and I'm blood bound to you. What the hell does he have planned?" Jordyn groaned. She just thought herself into a circle.

"I don't know," Rutger mumbled. "If there's a high attendance at the meeting, it could attract attention. If law enforcement investigates and finds out there was an execution, the OPI won't hesitate to investigate you. The murder investigation into the witches' deaths will be reopened and I'll be their number one suspect. Prime is putting the pack at risk, and every single person attending."

"My presence will bring unnecessary attention to the meeting. It's like the sheriff's department is watching me," Jordyn added.

"Luckily, we have the full moon as an excuse. Our runs are common knowledge and the pack gathering isn't uncommon. If they are watching you, they might be trying to decide whether or not they can trust you."

"Maybe. At least the elf is going to die. I like how Prime kept their Scandinavian names. That's going to send a message to the other Krijgers, and their entire group."

"Soothsayer is being savage," Rutger mocked.

Jordyn gave him a sideways glance, her eyes gleaming copper. "He tried to kill me, and then the Esme from the Lapis Lazuli had to help me. She saved my life and now I owe her."

"The coven gave willingly. The Esme would never make the pack's soothsayer responsible for repaying a favor," Rutger assured. He knew because he had the Esme sign a contract stating she wouldn't. It hadn't been completely necessary-Dr. Baines the Esme's son was employed with the pack-but it was better to be safe than sorry. "I promise, my savage mate."

"Very well. Would the Director like some champagne, in celebration of our first public execution?" Jordyn asked as her eyes bleed onyx.

"Savage and dark."

CHAPTER THIRTY-FIVE

Jordyn sat back in the passenger seat of Rutger's work truck and watched the mountains and woods pass in a blur beside her. The truck swallowing the broken yellow lines as it ate the miles. Between them, the computer console beeped, dinged, and chimed with messages, alerts, and who knew what else. Behind them, Charles drove the SUV with Tracy sitting in the passenger seat monitoring the same alerts and messages.

After sleeping in, then the baron and baroness having breakfast delivered, they spent the afternoon relaxing on the deck, drinking champagne and then coffee. They did celebrate. They toasted to their engagement, future wedding, Rutger's gold marks, and the hours of peace they had been given. The road opened to the valley and Jordyn's nerves jumped under her skin, her anxiety racing through her, and she wanted to stop the truck and run back home and hide.

"What are the beeps saying?" she asked, trying to make conversation.

"Ansel is finalizing the security details for the Summit, Foxwood, and our place. He is mobilizing soldiers to monitor the Summit, making sure no one is there before they're supposed to be," Rutger explained. "We're going to prove to Prime, the elite guests, and the Seelie court the pack is united and strong. As much as we need a good show of force there has to be ample security. I can't have anyone arrested for murder." Damn, he wanted to be the person in charge making sure it was done properly.

"I can feel you. I appreciate you staying with me," Jordyn whispered.

"I'm sorry. The only reason I want to be there is to make sure you're safe." Rutger gave Jo a sideways glance. Stress held her face and darkened her features. "It's useless to try and assure you everything will be all right."

"Basically," she mumbled. It was getting real. The challenge. She was going to face the pack, klatch, the alphas from other factions, and watch an execution all before dealing with Prime and his challenge. She couldn't fuck it up.

The invitation stated the rules, crystal clear, for the evening. She was to arrive at the Summit alone, her escort would be Prime's messenger, Ava. To arrive in his car was like saying she was royalty or it was her last ride before her death sentence. Either way, it was too much to think about.

"Are you going to be all right?" Rutger asked. "And before you start telling me how bad you hate the question, just answer it."

"I'll have a stroke before I get to the Summit." Jordyn's pulse raced in her veins, its rushing sounding in her ears, and she was sure her heart was going to explode. She wanted to be home with catered food pretending none of it was real.

"You can't have a stroke." Rutger drove through the gates of Foxwood and down the drive.

"Nervous breakdown?"

"No."

"How about you ask me if I want to go home," Jordyn tried.

"No. I know your talking out of nervousness and I think it's adorable. You're going to be fine." Stopping the truck in his parking spot, Rutger killed the engine. The baron's silver SUV-able to seat eight, fitted with armor, ballistic glass, and the same system as in his truck-waited in front of the house, while behind it, Prime's sleek car waited for Jo.

"This is it," Jordyn whispered.

"You can do this, Jo. You were born to do this. Just ask the dragon."

"No, I think it might answer." She turned in the seat to face him, his wolf, his beast, his gold gaze, and focused on him. She needed to feel him. "I love you."

"Mea, I love you." Her essence glided through their link like warm silk, and carrying her uninhibited love wrapped around him. Rutger was in their bedroom, his hips touching her sweat-slick skin as he thrust inside of her. He wanted to take her in his arms, run as far as they could go, and hide. He inhaled and exhaled. "That's cruel. We aren't leaving."

"Fine." Jordyn grinned, her lips curving. "I feel better."

"I feel used," Rutger's rough voice carried a growl. He cleared his throat, pushed the images of Jo's naked body and the sounds of her breathing down, and focused. "Your sentinels are coming for you."

"Ready or not." Jordyn zipped up her hoodie and opened the door. She almost grabbed a cropped jacket that hugged her slim waist but decided against it. It might get ruined. She mentally prioritized her clothing and didn't care if the hoodie ended up destroyed or covered in blood. A sad reminder of the night.

"Jo," Rutger said before he got out of the truck.

"What?"

"How did you do that?" His eyes held onto gold like his body held onto to her feel.

"The blood binding strengthened our link. When this is over, I'll show you," she answered.

Rutger lips curved into a barely there smirk. "I'm going to hold you to that."

Jordyn laughed, closed the door, and walked with her sentinels to the house.

Rutger watched her shoulders straighten as she raised her head and walked as if she owned the place. Tracy and Charles flanked her, displaying the same pride while enforcers and soldiers paused to stare then went back to work. He got out of his truck, closed the door, and headed to the office where he would be alone for a few precious minutes.

"The perimeter of the Summit is secure, as well as the Conclave. I've coordinated with Jason and there will be slayers perched in the tree houses. They sit above the lights, giving them concealment and they'll have eyes on the gate, parking lot, Conclave, and the rostrum where the baron, baroness, Jordyn, you, and Prime will be sitting. There will be four others tracking movement to the east and west sides. I have three teams roaming the parking lot to monitor attendees, another ready to escort the faction leaders, Prime, and the baron and baroness. The Highguard dispatched a team and they will escort the elves. The Seelie court didn't want Cascade involved, and the baron didn't want the chancellor's people involved."

"Figures. We have to do something about the road. If traffic gets backed up because everyone is being checked, someone will report it. I don't want the sheriff's department or the OPI, and I definitely don't want Detective Watt calling and questioning Jo or us. There will a public execution and we don't need to be brought up on murder charges," Rutger stated.

"I'll have two spotters moving traffic. To change the subject, Gavin called this afternoon stating after news spread of Jordyn's meeting with Prime, his meeting became a success and they'll be back in two days. That's another eight hundred shapeshifters and magic-born and the confidence of the Lassen Range. Whatever happens tonight will determine Cascade's ability to keep its territory and its reach," Ansel reported. He handed Rutger the outline of the four thousand square foot partial of land, the security measures, and team leaders. "If the pack appears weak, the extended confidences will pull back, the klatch could rally together, and if the doubters in the pack join them, they could overthrow the baron. Half the pack will scatter because they're citizens and not prepared to fight. The klatch who aren't aligned will scatter as well."

Rutger thought about what Jo said concerning the caterers. "Tonight isn't about unseating the baron or proving his weaknesses. It's about verifying Jo's power. No one is going to challenge the baron or the Cascade's soothsayer," Rutger replied. He studied the map, the team leaders, the teams, and memorized where everyone would be stationed if it did go to shit.

"How is she?" Ansel asked cautiously as he sat back in his chair.

"Nervous. She doesn't know what Prime has planned and it's a defining moment for her." Rutger set the paper down and sat back. Time was slipping through his fingers.

"No, I mean how is she after you marked her?" Ansel met Rutger's gaze.

"How do you know?" Rutger straightened, his elbows on the desk, and readied a half ass speech to defend himself.

"Calm down. I'm the only person who was near Lady Sloan and I haven't told anyone. She didn't know I was there," Ansel explained.

"What was she doing?" He sat forward as tension weaved in his shoulders and waited.

"They were in the back and she was talking to Lord Ervin. I was checking quadrant two's cameras. A bird nested on top of it."

"What did she say?"

"You sounded like an animal and Jordyn didn't make a sound. She feared you hurt her," Ansel replied.

Groaning, Rutger sat back, and Prime's order not to tell anyone drifted over his thoughts. "I did hurt her."

"And?" Ansel waited. "Can't say?"

"No. Direct order from Prime ... he used the word shall. I have a feeling you'll see the truth tonight." He drew his fingers through his hair, then rubbed his neck where tension was starting to pool.

"Are you all right?" Ansel asked.

He understood why Jo hated the question. "I'm good."

There was a knock on the door, silencing both of them, then Mandy peered inside. "Director, Prime's security is waiting for you. You'll ride with Lady Sloan, Lord Ervin, the baron and baroness. And the sentinels will be taking a separate vehicle."

"Understood." Rutger stood, not liking the change, and walked around his desk. He grabbed Ansel's upper arm, making him stay. "Mandy, I'll be there in a minute."

"Yes, sir." Her eyes held her worry and maybe stress, and she closed the door behind her.

"There is another threat ... Shadow Lord. He will either confront us head-on or have his people in the crowd. I think he'll try to take Jo," Rutger explained. He was almost whispering, as if saying his fears out loud was going to make them real.

"Why Shadow Lord?" Ansel asked automatically. "Damn, the witches. He's after Jordyn?"

"Yes. I received a letter saying I couldn't protect her. She'll be in the open tonight with a crowd he could use to distract us. Three thousand people could be chaos. If he knows Prime is here, a group tried to assassinate Jo, and about the execution, he might back off. Keep it precautionary. He doesn't know Jo is bound to me, making it impossible for him to take her anywhere." Damn, he said to much.

"Blood bound." Ansel's eyes glowed with his wolf. It made him think about fated mates, Dr. Hyde, and her research into what had been a myth.

"Affirmative." Rutger let go of his arm. "I want an elite team, selected in absolute secrecy. They have to take orders from you and I ... their pack or faction is secondary. They have to be magic-born, have the ability to adapt, have tactical training, the stronger the better, and I don't care where they come from."

"What will be their purpose?"

"To work independently from their packs or factions. They won't report anything they do to their leaders. When we have more time, I'll go into greater detail," Rutger answered.

"Do we get a tacticool code name?" Ansel asked. "I have to entice the recruits with something."

Rutger smiled despite himself. "Affirmative." He started toward the door.

"Rutger, we'll keep her safe. I'll have background information and a roster for you to overlook by next week," Ansel assured.

"Excellent." Opening the door, Ruger left Ansel, his captain and friend in the office.

Jordyn sat in the greeting room, alone and in silence, where after Prime's Numen attacked her, Lady Sloan exposed her secrets. Guarding them the way she had felt like a moot point since Rutger marked her and she wore a dragon. Standing at the window, she watched soldiers and enforcers organize their troops and ready their vehicles. Rutger wasn't among them, meaning he was in his office overseeing the plans with Captain Wolt. She hoped he was confident with the security measures and it allowed him to focus on the evening. On watching her back.

Lost in thought, Jordyn stared, not really concentrating, when a plain white van pulled into the parking lot, stopped, and the driver talked to an enforcer. Aydian talked into a mic, and a second later the van maneuvered and backed up to the side door of the office.

What was the van for? Jordyn eased her magic across the yard, searching for the driver. Her senses felt a magic-born who was armed with mental walls. While he guarded himself, they weren't solid. She eased up to the walls as she spread her power out and searched for breaches. An echo of his thoughts wafted through its cracks, like a sieve, and against her power.

'Going to transfer the prisoners to the Summit, by order of Lord Conway with the Prosecution Administration, of the Highguard.'

Jordyn drew her power back, releasing the man's mind, and left his mental walls in place and untouched. Prime was in Trinity, Lady Sloan, Lord Ervin, leaders of the surrounding factions, and now the Prosecution Administration. She couldn't help but feel guilty for bringing the Highguard to their doorstep. She thought about Craig and Nicole and their catering business. A couple who had been living a normal life. With her nerves and anxiety coiling inside of her, guilt tainted the bile rising to her throat with the thought. By the end of the night, the happy couple-along with the others-would become accessories to a murder.

What the hell was Prime thinking by ordering a public execution? Yes, Jordyn wanted to see the elf dead. Yeah, he tried to kill her, slowly, in front of Rutger, and her pack. *Damn, did it need to be public*? She understood magic was changing and it was changing the magic-born. But did they have to dive headfirst into the dark ages? What happened to baby steps?

Orders rang out, and soldiers and enforcers hurried to their assigned vehicles and loaded up. With the commotion coming to an end, she decided she was going to sit down when Rutger existed the office and started toward the house. His shoulders filled out his shirt, his jeans snug enough to let you know there was muscle there but loose enough to look relaxed, and he wore new boots not his broken in and three shades lighter pair.

His face held his concentration and worry until a woman wearing a black pant suit intercepted him, then he looked ticked off. He shook his head with his reply, and looking at Jordyn saw her and held her stare from across the yard.

Feeling his frustration through their link, she figured the Highguard and Prime were both changing the plans he had made.

"Soothsayer."

Jordyn felt the feather of the mage's magic and the familiar thread reaching out to her. She didn't know what it was or why, and at the moment didn't give it much thought. Half turning, she greeted Prime's messenger. "Ava."

"We'll be leaving shortly," she reported. "Is there anything I can get you?"

"I need to speak with Director Kanin." Jordyn had the feeling she was going to be denied, like she had the feeling Prime wanted them separated.

"Sorry, Soothsayer. You won't be allowed to speak to each other until the challenge is completed," Ava replied, with her strawberry-blonde curls sitting next to her cheeks. The messenger wore a wine-colored pant suit, black heels, and a black blouse, making Jordyn wonder if the pant suit was their uniform.

"Jordyn," Lady Sloan said from the hallway. "I need to speak to my daughter."

"Lady Sloan, you know the rules. It isn't permitted," a short man wearing a tailored gray suit replied. His auburn hair was cut close to his head, as if he was prior military, and his blue eyes looked almost like metal. Magic-born. A Wight. Half human and half shapeshifter.

The baron, baroness, Lord Ervin, and Lady Sloan stood in the hall staring at her. She felt like she had been put on display with a sign telling them not to touch her. The baron wore dark denim jeans, dress shoes, and a button-up shirt he left open at the collar, and a fitted jacket. The baroness, always classy, wore dark plum slacks, a silver cashmere V-neck sweater, and light jacket. Lady Sloan's copper turtleneck matched her gaze; both were sharp and warned you of her authority. Lord Ervin's black suit and matching copper button-up shirt added to the lines of worry on his face. Jordyn wanted to ask him what was he worried about.

"Daughter, are you all right?" Lady Sloan asked.

"I'm fine." Jordyn couldn't say anything else with the lump in her throat.

"Despite their games," Healey started and glared at their escort, "you are not alone. Do you understand?"

"Yes." Jordyn should have given a better answer and maybe ease their worry but she didn't have it in her. Everything-not being able to talk to Rutger, or have contact with the baron and baroness-jump-started her anxiety.

"This way, Baron Kanin," the man ordered.

Jordyn watched them disappear down the hall, heard the door open, Rutger's voice carrying his frustration, and the door closed, leaving her in silence. She turned to the window to see them approach the large SUV, their escort taking the driver's seat, and the woman in black taking the passenger seat. The baron and baroness' sentinels were waiting in the standard SUV with the Cascade pack's crest on its doors. The white van was gone, as well as the soldiers and enforcers and their vehicles. The parking lot was empty save for Rutger's work truck, another truck, and two other cars. Foxwood was down to a skeleton crew. Two enforcers in communications, two in the reception area on standby, and two taking their positions at the corners of the building.

Rutger stood beside the SUV while he waited for the baron and baroness to take their seats, then he climbed inside.

"Look at me, Wolf," Jordyn whispered.

As if hearing her, he leaned forward, met her gaze with gold, and mouthed, 'I love you.' It made her heart hurt and she could have cried. She had no idea what was going to happen to them. This could be a ridiculous plan to kill them all for all she knew.

Jordyn replied, 'I love you,' saw him smile, then he closed the door and was gone behind dark-tinted windows.

What was she supposed to be? A fighter? A soothsayer? A defender of the Cascade pack? A puppet? She felt like a fool. She hadn't trained for anything, scarcely understood her magic and its extent. Was this a chance for Prime to prove she was untrained, undisciplined, and unworthy of their confidence? Sure it was. Like Rutger was taking a part of her with him, Jordyn watched the SUV pull away from the house without her. Time had finally run out.

"It's time for us to leave, Soothsayer," Ava announced. "Did they leave him here on purpose?"

Jordyn turned back to the window and saw Aydian walking from the house, where the SUV had been parked, to the office. "Not sure." Like she was going to explain anything to Prime's spy.

Then she watched Ava's gaze follow Aydian as he climbed behind the wheel of Rutger's truck, sat for a minute, then backed up, turned around, caught them staring at him, and drove away. A portion of her stress eased knowing Rutger would have his truck. It meant they had a means of escape.

"Be careful, you keep staring and I might think you like him," Jordyn teased. It was probably uncalled for and inappropriate, but she didn't care.

"He is handsome," Ava responded casually, then caught herself. Jordyn wanted to laugh from the horrified expression on her face and how it made her appear human. "My apologies, Soothsayer."

"Don't worry about it. He'll be at the Summit." As an enforcer he would be part of security, but what his position was she had no idea.

Ava gathered her professional demeanor and plastered a neutral mask on her face. "Soothsayer, this way."

"Is Jordyn all right?" Lady Sloan asked, breaking the silence.

Rutger wanted out of the SUV. "Yes, she is fine under the circumstances."

"What happened yesterday?" Lady Sloan leaned forward, getting closer to Rutger's seat. "What did you do to my daughter?" she accused.

"I'm not at liberty to say," Rutger replied as he stared out the window. The baroness rested her hand on his thigh, he faced her, and she gave him a soft smile.

"This conversation isn't helping anyone," Healey advised.

"She isn't your daughter. What did the alchemists do?" Lady Sloan demanded.

"I'm not at liberty to say." *And wouldn't even if I could.*

"I have been more of a parent to Jordyn than you have ever been." Healey turned in his seat and nailed Sloan with his glare.

"He can't tell me. Can he can tell you?" Lady Sloan asked Healey. "Furthermore, I'm with the Highguard."

"With all due respect, Lady Sloan, you don't out rank Prime," Rutger advised, his voice monotone.

"She's my daughter, I have a right to know."

"Ask Prime."

Giving up, Lady Sloan exhaled and sat back in her seat. Lord Ervin patted her thigh, gave her a slight smile, and looked forward.

Silence sat thick between them while tension weaved throughout the SUV. Rutger went back to staring out the window, listening to the tires on asphalt, and watching the sun set on his evening.

CHAPTER THIRTY-SIX

"Are you well?" Ava asked.

She was on her way to face her pack, the factions from the surrounding territories, the klatch ... meaning there was a good chance she was going to make a fool of herself. Was she supposed to be *well?* Jordyn sat back in the chocolate leather seat and felt its softness hug her body at the same time warmth penetrated the leather and through her clothing. The seats were heated. Was this a chariot taking the condemned to their death? Had Prime planned on two public executions? Jordyn wished she knew.

They had been raised as humans including school, college, jobs, family, and relationships whose only troubles were petty squabbles. No one talked about magic, their power, wolves, or what it was like living as a shapeshifter. They dealt with the humans' judgements, being labeled non-human, and the differences between their species. It was their normal. That life burned to ash when the baron ignited her powers, gave her his life and the life and past of the pack and she became a soothsayer. The process had been slow and grueling, but Jordyn accepted what she was. A thing. A weapon. A soothsayer with the attention of Prime and the Highguard.

"Soothsayer, are you well?" Ava repeated the question. Jordyn listened to her voice, the way she said different words, and the way she didn't. Ava wasn't from the United States.

"I'm fine. Where are you from?" Jordyn asked trying to take her mind off the drive.

"Europe."

Broad answer. She guessed she wasn't expecting a heart-to-heart. "Have you ever been to the mountains before?" Jordyn could hear Rutger while wearing a grin, tell her she was talking because she was nervous. Yes, and she was about to start rambling.

"Not in the United States. I have visited Mount Olympus in Greece." The words rolled from her tongue.

Prime's home country. "I see." Jordyn looked out the window while her nervous energy continued building. "What kind of mage are you?"

"How do you know I'm a mage?" Ava's gaze narrowed. "My apologies, for the question. Prime warned me about you."

"What did he say?" Jordyn turned slightly in her seat.

"You recognize magic-born and to tell you whatever you wanted to know. I'm a Caster," she replied, staring forward.

"Like a witch casting spells?" Jordyn kept her voice neutral, striving to conceal her hate of all things witch and the urge to sink into the black hole of her memories.

Outside, the landscape slipped from ranch lands to city scape and a four-lane highway busy with traffic. Gold hues highlighted with wine and cobalt smeared the sky, its colors reflecting off windows and the hoods of cars. In seconds, the city morphed into rural countryside that gave way to a two-lane road and the woods as if they were taking back what had once been theirs. Jordyn felt their pull like they were calling her home. *Soon.* The plump moon sat at the horizon, waiting to take the sky with the night. The car moved over the road like it sat on a cloud and there was no noise from the engine or from outside. The exact opposite of the Jeep. Lost in thought, Jordyn forgot she asked Ava a question.

"No. Witches have an innate magic they use to power spells they don't cast them. As a whole, mages are more powerful than witches," she explained.

"What is a Caster?" Jordyn asked. This conversation had the potential to kill time and distract her from the night ahead.

"My magic creates the spell or circle rune. My specific trait is circle runes." She turned slightly in her seat to face Jordyn, and her bright emerald eyes landed on her. "This car is protected by a circle rune. When it's active, as it is now, no one can use magic to harm us. If we were to use our magic, no one outside the car would sense it. Your werewolf senses wouldn't detect the power or those inside of the car. Depending on the type of rune circle, I would absorb whatever magic was used and it would filter through me. Doing so would take the energy from it, making it harmless."

"Impressive." Explained how Prime could have drove into Foxwood without anyone sensing them. Maybe the mage wasn't as bad as she thought. Jordyn would have to research circle runes and their uses. "With your power, could you take the Esme of Lapis Lazuli coven?"

"Easily," Ava replied with arrogance, then caught herself. "But I would never. I'm not saying I would. I'm never going to," she stammered.

"Stop." Ava stopped. "I never said you would, it was a question. I'm a werewolf, we gauge people by brute strength. You're still impressive."

"Thank you. While it might be impressive, I'm not a master. By mage standards, I'm weak," Ava explained.

If she was weak, Jordyn would hate to be on the bad side of a master. The tension and worry creased her face and her eyes darkened. Ava was a terrible liar. She wore whatever she was thinking or feeling on her face like a neon light.

"If you're weak, then why are you with Prime? Since this whole thing started, I assumed he surrounded himself with those he considered powerful magic-born." Untrained. Undisciplined. *Cast by my hand.* Her imagination was getting the best of her.

"He does. You're proof of the power he amasses." Ava inhaled, mumbled something in a language Jordyn didn't understand and exhaled. "Where I'm from, when a child shows traits of magic they are taken to the Conservatory. There they learn about their magic and are trained to manipulate their powers. In some instances, it's strengthens their magic."

"Did you go to the Conservatory?" She wasn't given the chance to learn about her powers ... rather they let her believe she was a monster of some kind. A dark monster.

"Yes, and graduated." Her pride carried in her words. It had been an accomplishment.

Jordyn knew it wasn't the complete story and she didn't know if she cared or not. She felt like Rutger when he interrogated people. She saw where they were in the drive and a shot of anxiety ripped through her. "What happened?"

"I thought I was in love," Ava mumbled.

"Nothing good comes from that," Jordyn offered.

Ava smiled. "It gets worse. When I was ten years old my parents arranged a marriage between myself and Thomas. With the stipulation the wedding wouldn't take place until after my twenty-first birthday."

"That was nice of them," Jordyn said to say something. The pressure from the baron and baroness and the pack for her and Rutger to be the perfect couple nearly crippled them while it tried destroying any shred of friendship they had between them. They had known each other their entire lives, no learning about weird quirks, dated like normal people, were fated mates, and it hadn't been enough for them to put their doubts aside. Jordyn saw Rutger looking at her from the yard, his gold eyes holding her, his wolf in their link, and shuddered at the thought she almost lost him. No, she couldn't imagine an arranged marriage with a stranger.

"My parents didn't want my education interrupted." Another inhale followed by intangible words. Jordyn waited. "Thomas graduated two years earlier, worked for a local company doing surveys. He's an earth mage. He can scan an area of land and tell you where to dig for ore, precious metals, or gems. It was a good job, comfortable, it gave him a level of prestige, a home, and a secure future to share with his family. After I graduated from the Conservatory, we started our courtship, and the infatuation of a child turned into a mature love. I did love him. Over the months we spent together I realized he was jealous of my abilities. I didn't understand then and I don't understand now."

"Did he breakup up with you?" Jordyn asked. The outside world sat forgotten as their conversation changed from Prime's spy to two women talking. Jordyn hadn't realized how much she missed simply talking to someone.

"I wish he had. I was hired by a recovery firm to create circle runes that would allow them to blast through several meters of ground. The spell would react to dirt and rocks, while keeping whatever was buried intact." Ava paused, stared at Jordyn, and when she didn't say anything continued. "The firm required these circle runes to be used multiple times."

"You put it on something they could carry with them?" Jordyn asked.

"Yes. The circle runes were etched on two pieces of plexiglass. Light. Mobile. And afterwards the blood could be washed off," Ava explained.

"Blood?" Jordyn's eyes widened in surprise. "Like a sacrifice?"

"Not quite that exaggerated. The circle rune is powered by the user's blood. Magic is concentrated in your blood and it's a sacrifice for using the spell. Nothing to dramatic ... a drop smeared across the lines. The more magic the user has the more power is fed into the rune." Ava sat back, crossed her legs, and smoothed an invisible wrinkle. Jordyn knew the end of the story was coming and felt bad for having dragged Ava down the trail of her past. "The recovery firm had found some artifacts from the twelfth century. They were said to be worth millions."

"If this is too painful, you don't have to tell me," Jordyn said softly.

"No, it's the perfect way to kill time." Ava smiled at Jordyn who nodded in agreement. "Thomas was in financial trouble, saw the opportunity, and stole one of the boards. He tried combining his root verve with the circle rune. It failed. He leveled part of the town we lived in, killing six people. I know it could have been worse, but six people

were gone because of my magic and someone's selfishness."

"It wasn't your fault. He did it on his own," Jordyn tried
assuring her.

"He used our relationship to get details about the
boards. All he did was ask and I told him where they were.
After a short investigation, the Highguard found him guilty
and sentenced him to death. A public execution, like tonight." Ava met Jordyn's gaze. "For my part in the tragedy, I
was stripped of my magic. It's the reason why I'll never be a
master."

"It could have killed you." Jordyn tried to purge the Collective with her magic and it almost killed her. Then it hit
her … the Highguard possessed the ability to take your
magic from you.

"They left me with enough to continue to work. I'm
serving my years of punishment with Prime. I'm not one of
his chosen, the Dark Awakening, I'm not professionally
trained, and I continually make mistakes." Ava looked down
at her hands. "It's time served."

Jordyn figured the story had a point, besides filling the
time it took to drive to the Summit, what it was she didn't
know. Or she was overthinking the conversation to take her
attention from the challenge. "We all make mistakes. I'm
not trained, as matter of fact I've been called undisciplined
and selfish."

"You are not selfish, Soothsayer." Ava stilled when the
car began slowing.

The car eased over the gate's rails, and slowly continued. Jordyn's anxiety coursed through her, and suddenly
she had pterodactyls fluttering in her stomach. The car
made several turns then stopped. Jordyn could picture

them parked at the sidewalk of the Conclave. She didn't want to get out and she didn't want to face the pack.

"Soothsayer, thank you," Ava offered from her side of the car.

"Thank you. For a while there I wasn't thinking about myself or about what is going to happen tonight."

"You didn't ask me if I knew Prime's plans. Why not?" Ava asked. "You could have read my mind and I wouldn't have known."

"I'm not going to betray your trust by taking a trip through your head, nor was I going to put you in that situation," Jordyn explained. "It would have been unfair."

Her door opened, letting the evening breeze inside, the scents of the woods, and light chatter from the Conclave. The chauffeur stepped to the side as Aydian approached. Jordyn smiled, didn't know what to say, and got out of the car.

"Mistress, we'll escort you," Aydian reported.

Aydian. Jordyn leaned down. "Ava." Jordyn moved her eyes to indicate Aydian.

Ava smiled, looked behind Jordyn then back at her. "No. Yes. No. Yes. Maybe. I'm serving a sentence."

"No matter. That's a yes." Jordyn winked at her, straitened, stepped back from the car, and the chauffeur closed the door cutting off Ava's laugh. At least someone was laughing.

"Mistress, this way," Aydian advised. His sandy blond hair was cropped close to his skull, making his face look leaner and cut from stone. It was his glacier blue eyes drilling into her that would warn anyone he would do whatever was necessary to get the job done.

Jordyn tilted her head to look at him and smiled. "Lead the way Aydian."

For a split second, he looked taken off guard, a softness held his eyes, then his enforcer appearance with his glare cut through her and his shoulders curled with tension as if he was waiting for someone to put the weight of the world on them. Did she look like that?

"This way," Aydian said.

Jordyn stared at the monstrosity in front of her as the realization of what she was going to face swallowed her. Aydian had taken three steps, and the three enforcers had taken two when they figured out, she wasn't following them. They all stopped, and Aydian turned to face her.

"Mistress?" His hand rested on the butt of his gun, easy, held by muscle memory, and she knew he wore it more often than not.

"It's over you know." Jordyn stared at the Conclave that no longer blended into the woods surrounding it but resembled a sports stadium. She had no idea who worked on it or how they managed to change it in a matter of days. "I have lived with this hanging over my head for months. It will end tonight, but I don't know what the hell *it* is." The words rushed from her like the flood gates had been opened. "Then what? What am I supposed to do afterwards? If I live. What the fuck does a soothsayer do anyway? Do I wait for magic to take over the world? Do I sit and wait and if that's it what am I waiting for? Do I wait for someone to attack me? Do I wait for someone to attack one of you? What if someone attacks one of the pack? There's going to be a public execution tonight." The worries she had been accumulating crammed themselves into questions and sounded like gibberish. "I'll say this, don't ever challenge Prime, it's not worth it."

She was an idiot for rambling nonsense to Aydian and the enforcers when they would make a report, give it to the team leaders to read, analyze, and after briefing the enforcers, soldiers, and slayers of her meltdown, the report would be added to her file. She lost her friendship with Claudia and Jason when they turned into spies who reported her actions to the baron. Did she care? Yes. No. If they wanted to judge her for having a minor breakdown before facing the masses and a challenge, let them. *Selfish. Untrained.* She wanted to cringe from her own weakness.

From the Conclave, murmurs from the crowd carried in every direction while their combined powers rode the air and vibrated on her skin. The Conclave was alive with every magic-born in the county and the outer territories. Behind her, the parking lot sat packed with their cars, SUVs, and trucks. The full moon was rising higher and casting its silver glow on the them as twilight darkened to bled into night. She was a hundred yards from proving herself or failing her pack.

"Soothsayer, no one is going to attack us or you. They can try but they will not succeed. I'm giving you my word as one of your pack and as an enforcer," Aydian began, his voice low and carrying a hint of a growl. "I have your back. *We* have your back."

He hadn't tried to feed her a line about how everything was going to be all right and he didn't answer any of her questions. He didn't have to. She felt better having expelled some of her nervous energy and spike of panic. When he said he had her back it jarred her self-centeredness forcing her to see the bigger picture. They had her back and that was good enough for her.

"Thank you. When you write your report about this, don't make me sound like a broken mess of a woman," Jordyn requested.

"I'm not writing a report about this, Soothsayer." Aydian's eyes gleamed sapphire with a hint of violet. "This way."

Jordyn held his serious gaze for a breath, inhaled and exhaled, and started walking. The enforcers moved into position around her, and together they entered the arena.

Industrial lights flooded the rostrum where Rutger, the baron, baroness, Lord Ervin, Lady Sloan, and Lord Conway of the Highguard's Prosecution Administration were sitting. Lord Conway's job was to enumerate the charges against the elf, proclaim his guilt, and then order the execution. The elf, Randy, deserved the punishment coming to him, but it didn't stop tension from weaving through Rutger's muscles with the thought. Did he want the elf dead? Yes. Because he attacked Jo, put the pack in danger, and planned to do the same thing to others. Was it worth making everyone present an accessory? No.

Above the crowd, who were staring at them, a soft glow from lighting gave the atmosphere a comfortable ambiance. It was strange and necessary. Rutger caught the Esme of the Lapis Lazuli coven and her son Dr. Williams talking while the members of the coven sat silent. Chancellor Roarke of the Seelie court, his entourage, and the court wore neutral masks. Factions sat behind them clustered with their own as did the Cascade pack, klatch, and the other territories. The Conclave had undergone a drastic renovation in order to accommodate seating for several thousand guests. Teeming with people, he didn't think it was going to be enough.

A tall man dressed in a black suit, with white hair, and pale green eyes walked up the stairs, made eye contact with each of them, then faced the crowd. "Ladies and Gentlemen, please stand for Prime." His voice carried over the conversations and reaching out toward the back of the Conclave, seeming to absorb any hint of noise as it traveled. If someone were to drop a pin, it would have sounded like a shotgun had gone off.

As one, they stood, the sound of feet and clothing the only noise. Prime strode down the aisle; his human features looked sharper, he wore his honey brown hair back, the ends at his waist. His silver jacket and trousers and violet shirt made the varied colors pale as it cut through the dullness. The tailored suit accentuated his athletic build and exuded his authority. Rutger's jealousy squirmed inside him like a snake.

"Second," Prime greeted with a slight accent. Their gazes met for a second before he sat down.

"Prime," Rutger greeted in return. He sat to Rutger's left, beside him another chair sat empty.

"You may be seated," the man ordered. As one, they obeyed and sat down. "The Cascade pack's soothsayer, Jordyn Lily Langston."

Rutger's heart felt it was going to seize in his chest at the same time his lungs stopped and he held his breath. Aydian came into view followed by Kia, Luke, and Quinn. Jo was in the center, her height making it difficult for him to see her. When they approached the rostrum, the enforcers split, and his gaze met her copper eyes and she gave him a reassuring smile. He released the breath he had been holding, his wolf howled, and their link came alive with their feel. He loved her with everything he had.

"Soothsayer, please," Prime insisted, and motioned to the empty chair beside him.

"Yes, Prime," Jordyn replied as she cleared the steps and sat down. She looked right to see Rutger, and the tension marching across her shoulders eased a bit.

"Bring the prisoners," Prime ordered.

"Sir," the man replied. "Bring forth the prisoners."

From the back of the Conclave, ten guards wearing black slacks and red button-up shirts escorted the four elves down the aisle. They wore Cobalt 27 restraints and their black skintight ninja outfits. Arvid/Randy caught sight of her, surprise gripped his face, then as if his hate pushed through his skin, he glared at her. It had been three days since the attack, and where he wore his bruises, cuts, and his right arm was in a sling, there wasn't a mark on her. *That's right.*

The guards took their positions behind the four elves, leaving them standing in front of the rostrum facing the line of seats. The day came back in a slow reel. The baron had told her he was going to use Rutger as a sacrifice to find out if Bestial form was possible, she exposed Gavin's childhood weakness to Lady Sloan, and then she tried to purge the Collective and almost killed herself. All Jordyn wanted to do was see Rutger and feel his strength, so she headed to the office. She hadn't made it across the lot when Randy attacked. The first cuts scored her arms, neck, hands, and cheeks, cutting them open, and then he cut her waist and thighs. He used poisoned White 47 blades. The pain, the secrets, the overwhelming feel of drowning mutated into pure rage and broke her. Jordyn had come close to killing him.

"Lord Conway." The man bowed, stepped down the stairs, and took his seat.

"Prime, Baron, Baroness, Second to the Alpha, and Soothsayer, I greet you." He bowed, sending strands of white hair falling forward, held Jordyn's gaze, then gave them his back to face the crowd. "Ladies and Gentlemen, I am Lord Conway Tabolt acting Justice for the Highguard's Prosecution Administration. Randy Kadison, of the White Water Seelie court, kneel."

Lord Conway's death reached out to her as if recognizing something in her. A vampire. After merging her death with her magic, the dragons, and the Collective, it had become a part of her like her wolf. The magic-born were going to sense her as a werewolf and feel her death. Jordyn felt his cold, yellow eyes boring holes in her as Randy knelt in front of them. The crowd's energy intensified, and like a wave it rolled from the back of the Conclave to the front and over her. Jordyn fought the urge to suck in a breath and exhale as it continued to bring her their emotions. The pack's feel was like a hum in her head while the emotions coming from the others were like a million tiny needles on her skin.

"You are charged with trespassing on Cascade territory, Baron Kanin's personal estate of Foxwood with the intent to harm a magic-born. You are charged with the attempted assassination of the Cascade pack's soothsayer, Jordyn Lily Langston. Kin to Baron and Baroness Kanin. Fated mate to Second to the Alpha, Rutger Kanin. Scion and sole heir of Pureblood Lady Sloan Casellati, Soothsayer of the Diablo pack, One of Twelve of the Highguard."

The Conclave took a collective gasp, their wide eyes landing on Jordyn, Lady Sloan, her dad, Mia, and back to her. Jordyn sat straighter, squared her shoulders, and refused to think about what could be going through their minds. Besides the secret being exposed, she was losing herself to titles. He attempted to kill her, Jordyn, daughter to her father and mate to Rutger. Lord Conway gently folded his hands and held them at chest level as he waited for the murmurs to die down. When the Conclave grew silent and the crowd was waiting to hear what was next, he continued.

"Eldest daughter to Lord Ethan Langston, Pureblood elder within the Cascade pack. Pureblood soothsayer Jordyn Lily Langston. Pureblood Jordyn Lily Langston. Randy Kadsion, you are charged with illegal possession of a lethal substance with the intent to harm a magic-born. You are charged with illegal possession of weapons with the intent to harm a magic-born. You are charged with treason and conspiracy to commit treason against the magic-born. The punishment is death. The punishment for the attempted assassination is death. The punishment for disobeying the Highguard's canons is death. The punishment for disobeying the Seelie court's canons is death. The punishment for being a member of a secret sec whose purpose is to spread fear, overthrow a faction, terrorize through force is death. Randy Kadison, the Highguard finds you guilty of the mentioned charges. The Highguard exercises its authority to proceed with the harshest punishment in order for justice to be served. The convicted is sentenced to death."

Silence took the Conclave for several heartbeats as Lord Conway explained to the crowd their responsibility of viewing a public execution. The other three elves were staring at Randy, then their gazes jumped to Jo, Prime, and back to Randy. Rutger's attention was on Jo and the way she had gone still, her hard eyes blazing copper, and her face set as if in stone. If she blinked the copper would crack and the dragon living inside of her would fly through the shards and take its revenge. He knew this.

Jordyn held Randy's cold gaze as Lord Conway reminded the crowd of their oaths, and to obey the canons of the Highguard and their factions. The world she lived in a year ago no longer existed. Her new world consisted of attacks on her, threats to her pack, secret secs targeting those they disagreed with, security systems, and public executions. Everyone present was having their foundation crumble beneath them as they came face-to-face with the new world order.

"The Highguard received the petition, deliberated, and upon accepting the terms has relinquished its obligation for carrying out Randy Kadison's punishment. It will be handed to his victim, Pureblood Jordyn Lily Langston, fated mate to Second to the Alpha, and soothsayer to the Cascade pack," Lord Conway announced.

Jordyn didn't register the crowd's outburst and murmurs as she slowly turned her head to meet the pale hazel of Lord Conway's narrowed but humored gaze. This was a setup. They were going to watch her kill someone. She saw herself shooting Randy only to miss and hit someone behind him. It was a disaster. Her mind reeled as the crowd's murmurs rose to outbursts of agreeing and disagreeing. This was putting faction against faction and it was going to turn into a fight. Prime created this. Randy created this. She had to calm down and think. Jordyn's eyes skated over the faces tight with worry and fear. Was Prime going to force her to kill Randy with thousands of witnesses? The crowd's weight bared down on her, their doubt in the baron blatant. This was a chance for Jordyn to prove the baron was telling them the truth and she would do anything to protect her pack.

"Stand, Soothsayer," Prime ordered. He stood and offered her his arm.

With her heart beating too fast and her lungs feeling like they were wrapped in steel, Jordyn looked at him knowing the two simple words, one identifying her, and didn't want to obey. The fight was draining from her and she wanted to hide. Maybe she wasn't ready.

"Stand," he repeated. His violet eyes ringed with white gleamed, his coal-painted skin swallowed the light, while the sliver of his suit emphasized his height and build. He was a beautiful tragedy.

Jordyn stood, placed her hand in the crook of his left elbow-the material feeling like silk under her palm-his muscle tensed as she held him, and she let him guide her. Passing Rutger, she felt a tug on her senses from his power and a tinge of fear in the link between them. Prime stopped them when she stood in front of Randy.

"Soothsayer Langston's root verve is the ability to hold the Cascade pack's Collective. When you attempted to assassinate her, you attempted to destroy the Cascade's Collective and send them to the ether, where they would have been lost." Prime took his violet glare from Randy and pinned it on his audience. Power flowed from him like it was flames reaching out of an inferno, and Jordyn wanted to step back. "Soothsayer's secondary magic is mind manipulation," Prime announced.

Could have kept it a secret. Thousands of eyes were on her, drilling into her, and she felt a slight push on her mind. Someone was trying to get into her head. Who? Out of a couple thousand people from several factions she had no idea. Being a soothsayer wasn't unheard of, especially when the Highguard had twelve of their own and the Diablo pack had Lady Sloan. But being able to manipulate minds put her in a different category.

"Soothsayer Langston will demonstrate her power," Prime stated, addressing the crowd. To her he said, "I expect you to make an example of out of him." Violet eyes ringed in white, burned, then dimmed.

"An example?" Jordyn repeated, trying for time. Mind manipulation. Is that what she was capable of doing?

"Yes." Prime pointed to the elf. "He's part of a secret sec determined to destroy Potents, like you, because they decided you needed to be eliminated. They will continue to kill innocent magic-born if you don't make an example out of him. Prove to the others you're strong enough to protect your pack and stand for all magic-born," Prime whispered as he leaned closer. The words sat heavy in her mind as if he was speaking only to her. His closeness drew her in until they were the only people there. "He invaded your territory, your alpha's home, and aimed to assassinate you. Do you feel the blade cutting your flesh, your throat, your beautiful face, your sides? Do you feel your mate's fear as he watched you suffer?"

Prime was handling her, molding her, and guiding her emotions and she wasn't going to stop him. "Yes." She could feel the sting from the blade in her skin and the poison in her veins. Rutger's fear of losing her stained their link.

"Give him the punishment he deserves, Soothsayer." Prime straightened and took a step back. "Let this be a warning to anyone who defies the canons." Prime's voice carried his power, authority, and silence sat thick in the crowd.

Jordyn met Randy's sharp yellow gaze, and for the first time saw fear in their depths. If they weren't changing, if magic wasn't increasing, the attack would have been reported to human law enforcement and an investigation would have taken place. He would have had a trial, and if he had been found guilty, he would have been sentenced to prison. Randy wouldn't have faced a death sentence, let alone a public execution. As he knelt in front of her, she weaved her magic, and the certainty he was going to go through the human court system drained from him. Reaching out to him, her magic met the mental walls protecting his thoughts and mind.

"No." An elven woman rushed down the aisle towards the rostrum with bloodshot eyes and tears leaving wet trails down her cheeks.

Rutger watched four enforcers-Kia, Quinn, Luke, and Aydian-come from the back and sides to meet her before she reached Jo and Prime. Prime raised his hand, stopping them from intervening, and the enforcers took their positions.

"Go back to your seat," Prime ordered.

"This is barbaric. You can't do this. Where's law enforcement?" she demanded, clipping every word. Anger and terror played in her voice as she worked herself up.

Dark circles sat under her bloodshot eyes that darted between Prime and Jordyn. The distraught woman risked looking over her shoulder as Chancellor Roarke closed the distance between them, his guards, dressed in white and black uniforms, close behind. Unlike Randy, her ears were more rounded, giving away her weaker blood line. If she hadn't known the woman was from the Seelie court, Jordyn would have assumed she was human. Prime watched the elven woman as if she was nothing more than light entertainment and wasn't trying to stop the execution. Jordyn remained silent as she threaded her power through the elf's mind and as if it had barbs slid them into his brain and reaching further, wrapped it around his spinal cord. While she weaved a web inside Randy's head, he gave her a smirk as if expecting the woman and the chancellor were going to save him.

"Chancellor Roarke, please have your kindred take her seat before she regrets her actions and joins her mate," Prime warned. His low voice held the flames of his power.

"Prime." Chancellor Roarke nodded, placed his hands on the woman's shoulders, and leaned close to her. "Kate, you were given guidance and warned about this evening. This is the way of our people. We are magic-born." His soothing voice felt heavy and sat in the air like it was a physical thing. "He harmed one of our own and planned to do so to others."

"No. He tried to kill her," Kate argued as she pointed at Jordyn. "She isn't one of us."

"She is magic-born, a Pureblood, and has standing with the Highguard. You've insulted her," Chancellor Roarke warned.

Kate didn't shrug off the chancellor's hold, she did glare at Prime, Jordyn, then turned her pale brown eyes to Randy. "May I say something to my husband?"

"Of course. Let this be a lesson," Prime warned.

Jordyn didn't take it as an insult. She stopped being one of them when reports of her powers became reading material for the pack's section leaders. She held onto Randy's brain and spinal cord as Kate knelt beside him and began whispering. It was an attempt. Jordyn heard every word and felt them as Randy's emotions reacted to what his wife was saying to him. She wanted to fight for him, she felt it was her fault, and she would love him for the rest of her life. Her last words were lower, mumbled, and laced with her tears. She vowed to get revenge on the people who betrayed him.

Was it their court? The pack? The Krijgers? Jordyn?

Jordyn didn't know who Kate was blaming. She did know, if she heard Kate's vow it meant Prime did as well and she didn't have to tell him. Jordyn had been so caught up in Ava, her story, Prime, and facing the factions she didn't think about the Highguard's investigation. Questions rose about the charges against the elves, and how the Highguard referred to the Krijgers as a secret sec. Human law enforcement would have charged him with one count of attempted murder, criminal possession of weapons, reckless endangerment, assault with deadly weapons, and possession of an illegal substance regardless of her titles and family. Jordyn forced the thoughts of what could have been back; she didn't need her doubts clouding her actions.

Jo's power touched Rutger's senses as she intensified its strength. When he felt for the link between them it turned cold, dark, like death, and filled with an energy working to block him. For a heartbeat he saw a shadow slithering toward him, its silhouette fading as a dragon emerged. He no longer recognized Jo's essence. She was becoming someone, something else. There was something happening to her and he was helpless to stop it and Prime. He sat in silence, his nerves acting like they were being actively electrocuted, while anxiety tightened his muscles, and a pounding started at the base of his skull.

"It's time, Kate," Chancellor Roarke advised. He leaned down, took her by her arms, and pulled her backwards without a fight. "Prime, there will be no more interruptions."

"Thank you, Chancellor Roarke. Soothsayer." Prime met her gaze, held it, then stepped back, giving her the stage.

Onyx swallowed her copper eyes. She inhaled, exhaled, fed her threads of power, turning them into thick strands of pure energy. Jordyn reached further, deeper, as she gathered more of her power. She held onto it with a firm grip, trying to ease it over his mind, under his skull, and around blood vessels. With her power building, her wolf flowing through her, and the dragons embracing her, she felt powerful and complete. Invincible.

Losing his composer, Randy protested, "You're an abomination. All Potents are abominations. They are a threat to our survival. They will destroy the peace we have worked for." His sun yellow eyes met Jordyn's onyx gaze. "You have failed. Your power is nothing."

Murmurs from the crowd told her they believed Randy and doubted her magic. She smiled; it felt hard, and didn't reach her eyes ... it wouldn't. Her eyes were coal stones set in her face.

"You will destroy your pack." He choked on the last word, his eyes widened, and he struggled in the restraints as he tried to free himself.

Jordyn saw her power's web like silver strings threaded over and under his brain as she squeezed the thickening strand. Tightening them, the barbs sliced through matter and blood vessels. Scarlet bubbled from connective tissue and spread out and over opaque ridges. Randy met her stare as blood began seeping from his yellow eyes, nose, and when she fed the barbs more power, scarlet leaked from his ears. He opened his mouth to cry, and failed. The inhuman sound gurgled from him as blood coated his lips and chin. Jordyn continued to nourish the bands of energy with her power and felt them pulse and saw the silver shimmer with her strength. Randy's head dropped, his chin rested on his chest, blood poured from his ears, and she squeezed the noose around his spinal cord. The bands of power constricted like a dozen snakes working to crush their prey.

The world went silent. She felt cold, calm, letting her feelings fall from her and focusing her power on the threads. They sliced, the barbs took chunks of matter, and his spinal cord crumpled under her pressure. "No one will raise a hand against me." She didn't recognize her voice or the amount of power it carried.

Jordyn dove into his thoughts. His screams of pain vibrated inside his mind like they were trapped by his skull, and he fought the darkness taking him apart piece by piece. Jordyn would remember the guttural cries and the vision of his of brain being shredded as long as she lived. A spike of guilt burned through her, telling her she had gone too far and needed to end his suffering.

Cast.

Forged.

She wasn't going to become one of them. Her mood twisted ... she was one of them, an abomination, it was the reason Prime ordered her to make him an example. She would end his suffering, but before she granted him peace, she played his wife's last words and told him Kate was going to be next. Jordyn gave him an image of his wife with scarlet veiling her pale skin while her eyes stared blankly at him. Randy's panic pierced her and what he could process sounded like a weak child begging. With a quick jerk her power ripped from him and frayed what was left of his mind. He fell to the left, landed hard on his shoulder, his head bouncing off the flagstone, his arms flopped in front of him.

Jordyn pulled her power back, letting it swirl around her before snuffing its feel. Chancellor Roarke, the Seelie court, the pack, and the others in the Conclave sat in silence. Her breath caught in her lungs, her heart hammered in her chest, as she registered their gazes. Fear drenched in disgust rolled from them like a title wave toward her and over her.

They were staring at a monster.

They were staring at her. She was the horror in their nightmares.

Jordyn looked down at Randy's body, his blood-streaked face, his open mouth, and his limp arms and legs. She might as well have opened his skull with a can opener and shredded his brain with a mixer. What the hell happened to her?

"Soothsayer," Prime said from behind her. "Stand with me."

She tore her eyes from Randy, her methodical violence, and the dragons receded as she turned and faced Prime. The look in his violet gaze was the opposite of the horror scarring the audiences' faces. There was pride and another that scared her. He looked at her as if he had been stared at and judged the same way and he respected her. What did he have to do to become Prime and what did he have to do to keep his throne? Ice shards skated down her spine, forcing her to physically stop herself from shuddering. Following orders, Jordyn crested the last step, met Rutger's concerned gaze, and stood beside Prime.

"Lord Conway, please continue," Prime ordered.

"Sir. Bruce Labowski, Rich Dabiri, Dean Saddler you are charged with being active members of a secret sec of terrorists. You are charged with violating the canons of the Seelie court and the Highguard. Conspiring against the magic-born and putting the population of magic-born at risk."

Lord Conway hadn't looked twice at Randy's body as he continued to state the charges against the remaining elves. What the hell did they do at the Mountain Fortress? Jordyn listened and wasn't listening, some of the charges were repeated, Soothsayer Jordyn Lily Langston, on and on they went. She stared forward trying to ignore the sets of eyes on her, Prime, Lord Conway and tried harder to ignore Rutger's feel and his apprehension.

"The Highguard finds you guilty. Your punishment is five years exile at Хрустальный дворец, Crystal Palace in Northern Siberia. Protectors of the Highguard, take the prisoners into custody," Lord Conway ordered.

More murmurs spread out from the crowd as four guards, the same ones who had escorted the elves in, marched up the aisle. The three elves stood, Cobalt 27 re-straints at their wrists, another set at their ankles, a deep blue glittering under the lights. At the same time, they turned slightly to see the crowd, probably looking for the women, and a child, that had started crying. Rutger won-dered if they thought trying to assassinate Jo and the other Potents was worth putting their family's lives in danger. Five years at Crystal Palace didn't seem like a long time. However, Crystal Palace, besides being born of someone's sick sense of humor, was also called The Ice Pit of Death. If you were sent there, you died there. It was exile and a death sentence wrapped in one. The palace was set in the middle of a tundra where winter temperatures dipped to twenty-eight below. Rumors said under the massive con-crete prison was another prison a mile underground where the most dangerous magic-born, some mystical creatures, were kept locked up without sunlight. The elves were being sent to their deaths.

His director instincts kicked in and he wanted to know if the Highguard knew the names of the other members of the secret sec? What had Jo said they called themselves? Krijgers, meaning warriors. She also reported they were preparing to hunt and kill Potents from around the world. The group had to have a leader, someone with money to fund them, and supply them with weapons and poisons. It was organized if they were recruiting members, gathering intel, and training them in military tactics in order to assas-sinate their targets. Who was the leader? And where was their headquarters? He would ask the Highguard, maybe Lord Ervin, and if he didn't get the answers he wanted, Rut-ger was going to find out for himself. His wolf longed for a hunt and thirsted for blood. It would be different from the witches. Rutger felt his wolf rise and the tease of his Bestial form.

"Justice has been served and the Highguard is pleased," Lord Conway announced. "As acting Justice for the Prosecution Administration, I deem this indictment closed." He faced Prime and bowed deep making white strands fall freely to feather the sides of his narrow face. When he straightened, he gave Jordyn a slight smile, revealing the points of his fangs that barely touched his lower lip.

"Excellent Lord Conway, have a nice evening," Prime responded. "Soothsayer, are you ready for the challenge?" Prime asked.

What? Killing Randy wasn't enough? Jordyn's strength crumbled under the realization she could still fail. She looked at Randy and back to Prime and saw the baron stand. This was her fight and hers alone and there was no way she was going to let Prime trick the baron like he manipulated her. Especially in front of the factions, the pack, and the klatch.

"Yes."

"Jordyn-" Healey started.

She nailed the baron with a copper glare and asked Prime, "What is the damn challenge?"

With her question, the baron went back to his seat and when he was sitting, the baroness placed her hand on his thigh. Their eyes met for a moment, and it was enough. The baroness wasn't looking at Jordyn, she was looking at a stranger who had turned into a monster.

Prime's face wore its mask of indifference as he faced the audience, and waited. Jordyn stood beside him, searching the crowd, the faces of her pack, and the aisle. She stopped searching and froze when four Numina escorted a man, tall and slender, his bronze skin a stark contrast to the woman's. He wore his long, black hair pulled back and his almond-shaped eyes targeted Jordyn. The woman at his side with bloodshot eyes, stifled a cry with her right hand, then wiped tears from her cheeks. Her auburn hair was up, her open jacket revealed a white blouse, and she wore jeans and boots. Dear God, no. She didn't know what it meant but knew it wasn't good.

"Thank you for joining us," Prime greeted. "Soothsayer, who are our guests?"

Her pack. Jordyn's magic reached out, touched each of them, and sank inside of her where the Collective lived. From the depths their essences gave her their happiness, sadness, and desperation. They were parents of a baby girl. Her insides caved. "Boone and Lori Ann Milan, of the Cascade pack. Parents to six month old Joyli Chenoa Milan."

The arena erupted in chatter, their deep voices holding their collective anger and revulsion. Energy from their fury swept through the air, making it thick with tension.

"Where is little Joyli?" Prime asked. He said her name with a delicate twist within the lit of his accent.

The sound infuriated Jordyn. She was going to kill him. Jordyn searched the Summit and found nothing. Pushing power into her search, she scanned again. The baby wasn't there. Jordyn met Lori Ann's wounded eyes, holding hope Jordyn was going to be able to save their daughter. She drew from the Collective, and repeated the process. Nothing. There was nothing.

"I don't know?"

Lori Ann's knees weakened as her cries turned to sobs. Boone held her, helped her stand, then wrapped his arms around her. Hate and rage gripped his face and his eyes promised if Jordyn didn't find their daughter, he would make her responsible and kill her in retaliation. This was going to make or break her. If she failed, what would happen to the baby? How was she supposed to find the baby? If the factions, pack, and klatch watched her fail would they turn their back on the baron, baroness, and the Kanin family?

"Take your seats," Prime ordered. His Numina guided the couple to a set of chairs to the right side of the rostrum and a couple of feet from the baroness. When they were seated, and the Numina shifted their clawed paws into razor sharp spears and pointed them at the couple. Prime faced the audience like he was the host of a show. "Ladies and gentlemen, you're here to witness what happens when you challenge your Prime."

Jordyn wanted to crawl in a hole and die. The crowd gasped as if she had committed genocide. The very thing she feared was happening. Prime was using her pack against her. If she failed the crowd would turn into a mob and put what was left of her in a hole.

"The Cascade pack's soothsayer formally challenged me. Your Prime. In retribution for this act of disrespect for authority and her disobedience, she will prove herself as your soothsayer. May the factions be witness to the strength or weakness of the Cascade pack, their baron, and their soothsayer."

Shit. Shit. Shit. Jordyn turned to Rutger, she needed to see confidence in his eyes and he believed in her. Right then she didn't believe in herself. Jordyn searched, didn't see the confidence she needed and gave him her back.

"Soothsayer, you have to find their daughter, Joyli. If you aren't able to locate the child, the girl and her parents will die. I believe you remember what my Numina are capable of."

His violet eyes pierced through her, giving her a glimpse of the evil living inside of him and the truth he would kill them. Jordyn wouldn't forget the spear sticking out from her chest, its tip slicing through her shirt. As a soothsayer and vessel for the Collective, if the three of them died at once it would cripple her. She would fall to the floor, curl into the fetal position, and her entire body would ache as she grieved their deaths. Zachery's absence hadn't weakened … no, it felt like an open wound.

"I understand." She didn't and didn't know how she was going to find the baby when she couldn't sense her and searching for her essence hadn't helped.

"You do not understand. You have to search the grounds, defeat her captures, and bring her back in twenty minutes. Every five minutes a chime will alert you. When there is one minute remaining, the chime will ring twice. Joyli's life and the lives of her parents are depending on you. You must be in human form when you return. Don't let the past and the helplessness you embraced deter you from your task. Don't let the mistake you made with Zachery haunt you. The feel of his loss. His parents' pain. The shame your pack felt as you hid from them." His low words slithered to her where they dug into her guilt. "Do you still understand?" he asked. He wore superiority and triumph like a second skin.

Jordyn looked over at the baron and baroness with sorrow in her eyes. Twenty minutes. She was going to fail them, Boone, Lori Ann, and baby Joyli. Just like Zachery. With guilt spiraling out of control she met his violet eyes and replied, "Yes."

"Go find your clansman, Soothsayer."

CHAPTER THIRTY-EIGHT

Look at me, Mea. He knew he hadn't given her the assurance she asked for when she searched him out. Her desperation made him freeze under its weight and her silent begging almost killed him. *Please, Mea.* Jo paused halfway down the aisle with stares and judgements baring down on her. She took a slow step, another, then stopped and turned slightly. Their gazes met, gold and copper. They stared at each other as if no one else was there, and he gave her the assurance and the promise he would be waiting. Then the sounds and feel of a couple thousand magic-born broke the connection. Jo smiled with haunted eyes, turned, and ran out of the arena.

"Tell me you have eyes on her," Rutger demanded into the mic clipped to his collar.

"Negative. The target is black," Sawyer, a slayer, reported from his perch in a tree house.

His muffled answer sounded in the Rutger's ear piece. *Damn.*

"Incoming," Riley, a solider reported. She had requested a transfer from the soldiers to enforcers. Rutger was sure the paperwork was on his desk, somewhere.

"ID?" Rutger met the questioning gazes of the baron and baroness while the Conclave sat waiting for the next installment of Prime's entertainment.

"Director, Shadow Lord is requesting entrance," Riley's hard tone answered.

Fuck. The assurance he willfully showed Jo turned to ash and blew away in the wind. At least Shadow Lord wasn't going to use the mass of people as a distraction to kidnap her. It left Rutger wondering what his intentions were. He stood getting the attention of Prime. "Shadow Lord is requesting entrance."

"This is your territory, making him your guest," Prime replied. "It's your decision."

Right. "Did you know he would be here?" Rutger asked, keeping his voice neutral. He didn't need to make anything harder for Jo.

"I would think having your mate running around searching for a baby in order to save her parents, your clansmen, while my Numina hunt her would be your focus," Prime charged.

"Jo can handle whatever you've planned." In Rutger's ear, Riley repeated the request. "Did you know he was coming here?"

"His presence is necessary," Prime answered, and leaving the steps took his seat and ended the conversation.

Right. Saying no would be a mistake. Saying yes was going to be a mistake. "Permission granted," Rutger growled. He took the seat beside the baron and leaned in his father's direction. "Shadow Lord is here."

"For Jordyn?" Healey asked. He sat forward and started scanning the crowd and the aisle. "He should have requested permission to enter my territory."

"An open invitation was offered to all magic-born. I don't know what he's here for. If it is Jo, it doesn't matter when we're fated mates, she is bound to the pack, and enshrined as the soothsayer, and I marked her. Shadow Lord isn't above the Highguard's canons," Rutger explained.

"What is done cannot be undone. His presence is necessary." He heard Prime's voice in his head. "He can't take her even if he wanted to." He needed to believe what he was saying. Rutger looked at the night beyond the arena setting and hated having Jo searching the Summit alone, with Prime's Numina.

"He doesn't know you've marked her. No one does." Healey's eyes gleamed burnt gold. "No one knows what happened between you. Will you explain it to me?"

"I can't." Gold met gold as they stared at each other. "Understand I would if I could. I'm under orders and I'm not prepared to disobey as long as Jo and the baby are somewhere out there. I don't have eyes on her and had no idea the Numina were out there. No one can see them or sense them. We're blind." It reminded him of the witch's spell.

"Son." Healey sat straighter, his mind trying to put the pieces together. "This is a demonstration of power. And whatever happened between you and Jordyn is the reason. Prime came here with an agenda and we're all his game pieces."

"That's an understatement. We're being played."

The background noises of murmurs, conversations, whispers, and people shifting in their seats stopped, and for the third time in the evening, the Conclave sat in silence. The crowds' attention turned to the aisle as a man dressed in black slacks, royal blue button-up shirt, black jacket, and black dress shoes made his way to the front. Following him were four people-two men and two women-their clothing mirroring his, their appearance sharp and controlled. Rutger wanted to order him to get the hell out of the Summit and out his territory as the threads of death mixed with power and magic drifted in the air.

Vampires.

Tonight, was going to be a night of reckoning.

He stopped at the end of the aisle and the first step. "Good evening," he greeted, his accent decorating the words, as he bowed.

"Shadow Lord," Prime greeted. "Good evening."

"Second, Baron, Baroness, terrified couple." His hazel eyes narrowed on Randy's limp body, the restraints at his wrists and ankles, the dried crimson on his face, and his dull yellow eyes staring at nothing. "I see I've missed some of the festivities. At least I'm in time for the climax."

"Please, have a seat," Prime offered. In a sweeping motion, he indicated the seat next to Rutger.

"Thank you." Shadow Lord took the steps with the elegance of a nocturnal predator while his guards took their positions behind him. "Second, a pleasure to meet you in person."

"Shadow Lord. How many others are with you?" Rutger asked.

"With your extensive security system, I assumed you would know." He smiled. The tips of his fangs indented his bottom lip, and his hazel eyes, amber and green, bled emerald.

Rutger wasn't going to acknowledge the dig on his security system, and faced the audience that was staring at them all. Among the magic-born they had become a freak show.

Jordyn stood in a clearing with October's breeze rustling tree tops, pine needles, and freed the last of burnt gold and amber leaves clinging to limbs. The chill caressed her face, she inhaled, calmed her nerves, and focused her thoughts. Clinging to the thread of Joyli's essence she drew from the Collective, she used it to search the area. Nothing. Her frustration boiled into anger and repeating the process, she failed. Jordyn was wasting time and felt the seconds and minutes as if they were being torn from her body.

Think. Think. The full moon glared down with its sliver beam, demanding she protect one of her own. She needed time. As if reading her thoughts, the first chime sounded, its echo carrying the high-pitched resonance. Five minutes gone.

She twisted around to face two Numina, their hands molded into spears, the edges razor sharp, their yellow eyes glowing in the dark. All right. Was she supposed to fight them? Hand to spear? She would lose. Was she going to shapeshift? No. She wasn't taking a chance of forfeiting the challenge. Jordyn darted to the left, going deeper into the woods, and heard their footsteps behind her. She ran with the speed of her wolf, heading deeper and toward the back of the Summit and her territory opened for her. If she could lead them away ...

Away from what? She didn't know where they were keeping Joyli.

Jordyn stopped, spun around, and faced the Numina. It had to work. "Take me to the baby," she demanded as she poured herself into their minds.

Ignoring her, they stalked closer, their arms and spears raised and ready to strike. Their faces were devoid of emotion as their elongated bodies moved with a fluid motion and their clawed feet stepped effortlessly over and around limbs, shrubs, rocks, and saplings. Watching them close in on her, Jordyn felt the spear in her chest and the fear of bleeding to death and losing Rutger. The difference between then and now, she would lose the Collective, Boone, Lori Ann, and Joyli would lose their lives, and the pack would blame her. With her death, they would shift their blame to someone alive, the baron.

How long before a revolt would take place in the name of disregarding the increasing magic so they could keep their manufactured lives? Cars. Houses. Money. Their ignorance and selfishness wouldn't end. It would when magic flooded the world and forced them to fight for their lives. The Crimson years would be repeated. The bigger picture grew then expanded, its weight crashing down on her. Jordyn's senses felt a magic-born approaching. She spun around, when with superhuman speed, the first Numen circled her, its spear slicing her arm and side. She twisted as fire seared from the lacerations.

Cursing, Jordyn swore the first thing she was going to do was train with Leo. She had to learn how to fight and defend herself. The second Numen stepped in; its long, gray arm reached out and the spear stabbed her thigh. Their height and reach made it easy for them to get close, strike, and back up. It reminded her of Leo and she hated it. The next strike made her falter and putting her weight on her left leg, she took a step backward. They didn't take chase. Blood soaked her shirt and zip up hoodie, and she felt warmth slipping down her leg. She healed the wounds on her side and arm, and worked on the stab wound in her thigh.

Protect herself. Find Joyli. That was all she had to do.

The elf's accusation came roaring back, accompanied by Boone's hatred of her. It was her fault his baby daughter was in the woods somewhere with a Numen. Jordyn couldn't continue with guilt and fear riding her. She wasn't an abomination. Wasn't going to become an abomination. She was going to be part of the magic-born serving as protectors. It was up to her to protect the pack, the factions, and train and learn. She had a purpose. A stick broke, jerking her attention back to the Numen but not before its spear cut her right side. It struck at her, and side stepping, it missed her arm and caught the edge of her hoodie.

She would dissect, analyze, and scrutinize everything when she had time. "Stop," Jordyn ordered. The word carried a growl and thundered in the silence. They stopped. Letting the breath she had been holding go, she straightened. "Take me to Joyli."

They stood unmoving in front of her, their glowing eyes holding her, while inside their minds she fought for control through the chaos. Prime's orders were imbedded in them to hunt her, and fight her, but there wasn't a kill order. They were there to fight her, maybe slow her down, to test her. Jordyn sifted through the orders and didn't understand. *Doesn't matter.*

"Take. Me. To. The. Baby. Now," she demanded. From the Conclave the second chime sounded. She burned through ten minutes and was facing the last ten.

The first Numen sluggishly turned, piling up pine needles and leaves with his clawed foot, and when she had a clear view of the bones protruding from its spine, it stopped. Pouring more of herself into their minds, she found Prime's link and easily followed his tracks. Jordyn pushed more of her magic into the connection, lightly changing the feel from Prime to herself, and felt the burn at the back of her head. Two at a time was going to be tough. She couldn't risk one of them separating and attacking her. The strain forced her to use more magic, more energy. After focusing to create the elaborate web weaved into Randy's mind, then using a substantial amount of power to manipulate each stand and barb, controlling two Numina at the same time was going to be a challenge.

Ten minutes remained. "Lead the way," she urged and took a hesitant step. Feeling them inside her head, she was positive she controlled them. Still, it didn't mean Prime couldn't highjack them since he was their master.

The second Numen followed the first, their gray bodies disappearing as they crossed into the moon's light and re-appearing in the shadows as they started back towards the Conclave. Her irritation ate at her, making her want to yell at them to hurry, time was wasting, but knew it wouldn't do any good. She was using too much power and influence to hold them and make them follow orders. There was a baby girl waiting for Jordyn to save her and take her back to her parents. The problem was Jordyn didn't know what else was waiting. They walked for another couple of minutes, zig zagging through the woods like they were on a lazy stroll. Her anxiety spiked with every step as she anticipated the third chime.

"Are we there yet?" she asked.

Neither acknowledged her as they continued stalking through the forest. Jordyn stepped over a fallen tree, counted the seconds, felt her heart beating the inside of her chest and heard her pulse in her ears. When she thought she had wasted her time, the Numina stopped and stared forward at something in a cluster of trees. Jordyn's hope rushed through her as she stepped around them and stared into night's heavy curtain. She couldn't see anything, couldn't sense anything, and her hopes sank knowing they lead her around like she was a lost dog.

Jordyn felt time slipping from her and her failure sitting in Prime's eyes and those of her pack. Using her senses, she searched the area. Neither of the Numina moved, hadn't turned away from the thicket. It was a dead zone. Dead. Nothing there.

Jordyn didn't need to ask her what Prime was going to do when Ava's story was the key. Jordyn approached the thicket, walked around trees to the other side where soft white moonlight veiled a Numen. *Oh Ava.* It sat cross-legged on the ground with a pink blanket draped over its sinuous gray legs. From its lap a light cooing sounded. Joyli. Jordyn rushed to the Numen, and when she was within arm's reach, she hit a barrier that threw her, and she landed on her back.

The hit knocked her breath from her and she sucked in air while healing cuts and scrapes from the limbs, rocks, and bramble. Jordyn didn't feel the pain, she was numb with happiness, she found little Joyli-and annoyance, how the hell was she going to get past the barrier. Sitting up, she got to her feet and walked, her hands out in front of her. Jordyn reached out, found it, and placed her palms flat against the magic wall. It vibrated on her skin. The pulses of power sank into her hands, wrists, and travelled to her shoulders. It felt familiar.

Jordyn sank to her knees. There was no doubt the Numen was sitting on a circle rune, and someone had made a blood sacrifice to give it power. Magic was in the blood. She knew exactly who was responsible. This wasn't a challenge. He knew she didn't have to fight them. He knew she could control the Numina. He knew she would order them to lead her to the baby. Jordyn was convinced he instructed Ava to tell her the story. It would explain her hesitation. Most of all, Prime knew she wouldn't risk the life of a child and he wanted to show her what he had done, who her master was, and he wanted her blood bound to the land.

It was entrapment.

Jordyn looked at the pink blanket as a tiny hand reached out at the same time two feet kicked from underneath the material. If she did this, she would know the full extent of her mistake. What was done cannot be undone. "Damn him."

The cooing turned to a frustrated cry and the kicking increased. An innocent wasn't going to pay for her mistakes. Lifting her right hand, palm facing up, the Numen approached and with its spear sliced across her flesh. A sting bit into her and she raised her left hand, palm facing up. The Numen sliced her flesh. With both hands bleeding, she placed them against the barrier. It pulsated. A purple light started at the base, weaved into the intricate circles and runes, creating a violet column encompassing the Numen and Joyli.

Jordyn pushed magic into the wall, kept her hold on the Numina, and felt it drain her. "Come on, break." She gathered a surge and shoved it into the violet light. It flashed bright for several seconds, lines of cracks appeared, and were gone. She fell forward her hands flat on the ground. Pine needles stuck in the cuts, rocks crunched her fingers, and the smell of fresh dirt drifted. Magic rose up from within her territory, and holding her in place demanded its due. It pulled blood from her, its rush coursing into her hands and into the ground as her lifeforce left her body.

Jordyn bowed her head, heard Joyli's faint cry, and the chimes warning her she had five minutes.

"You are blood bound to this land." He stood in front of her, his ghostly body wavering above the ground.

"Christian." Jordyn raised her head and met blue eyes whirling with silver. "How?"

"The soil of your territory has accepted the blood offering from you, Soothsayer. The land is sharing its magic," Christian explained. *"You have saved your kith."*

Energy shot into her hands, gripped her wrists, and made her arms feel numb as it saturated her body. Gritting her teeth, she prayed the pain ended. The world flashed white then went black, and she blinked her eyes. *Don't pass out.*

It snapped back into focus. She was staring at the Numen and the pink blanket. Christian was gone, and the power of the barrier was dead. With her knees in the soft dirt, she sat back on her calves, inhaled and exhaled, and gazed up at the night sky and the million stars staring down on her. *Why?* Two chimes resonated over the curves of the land to find her.

One minute. She didn't have enough time to make it back to the Conclave. Jordyn recited the rules Prime stated as she stood and started taking her clothes off. "Stand." The Numen holding Joyli stood. The baby with its blanket wrapped around her small body looked out of place in its arms. "You recognize who I am. Carry her. The rest of you guard them." Jordyn wasn't completely sure they would continue to obey her after she shifted. She looked at them as failure inched closer. Damn, it was a risk she was going to have to take.

The wind whipped around her, its cold edges cutting through Jordyn's bare skin and striking her bones. She shivered from the cold, took a step, her wolf embraced her, her magic surged, her dragon intertwined within her, and she stood in wolf form. There wasn't a pause between worlds as her wolf and human body shifted shape, one relinquishing its power to the other. It slipped over her as if she were both at the same time.

Joyli's cries made Jordyn pause. Turning back to the Numen and the baby, knowing seconds were ticking by and confirming her failure, the Numen bent down. Jordyn rubbed the baby's cheek with her nose, and heard the wolf within Joyli's small body howl inside Jordyn's head.

"Your soothsayer has failed," Shadow Lord mocked as he smoothed his slacks then crossed his legs.

"There's still time," Rutger growled.

"Seconds. She has to make it back here in human form while carrying a baby." Shadow Lord inhaled as if he was bored, then watched the Purifiers work where Randy's body had been. "Maybe I overestimated her power."

After Shadow Lord's threats hung over him for months and lying to Jo about them, he wanted nothing more than to rip the vampire limb from limb. "She'll make it." She had to, or three innocent people were going to lose their lives and the baron was going to have to fight for his position and for the pack. This night.

A rich howl resonated through the air, carrying Jo's emotions and power as if she proved herself to the full moon. Rutger stood and walked to the edge of the rostrum, his heart in his throat, his pulse energizing his nerves, and watched the aisle for his mate. One second. Two. Three.

"Ten. Nine. Eight," Shadow Lord started. "When she fails and the great Cascade pack crumbles, I'm petitioning the Highguard for possession of the soothsayer."

"She isn't a possession," Rutger growled out. *Damn, Jo, where the hell are you?* In answer to his question, a shadow entered the Conclave followed by a wolf with dark chocolate coat and tawny red fur feathering her sides. Copper glowed from her eyes as she raced down the aisle toward them.

"She broke a rule. This is void," Shadow Lord insisted. He was standing in front of his chair watching, his hazel eyes turning completely black.

"She needs to stand on the rostrum in human form," Rutger pointed out.

"There isn't time," Shadow Lord declared.

Jordyn saw the rostrum as the countdown played in her head. She pushed harder, and at the last moment leaped into the air, shifted, and landed in a low crouch, one knee on the stone, and her hands out in front of her. Exhilaration cascaded through her body and quickly joined relief, she made it. Behind her the crowd erupted in cheers and gasps of awe. Before she had time to stand, Rutger was kneeling in front her, his hands on her shoulders and his face next to hers.

"Where's the baby?" he whispered.

"It's good to see you, too," Jordyn said with a grin. It was sheer victory and she couldn't stop herself. She had to wipe the smile off her face before she faced Prime.

"Mea." Rutger stood with Jo, his gold marks on her collarbone and on the back of her shoulder, and her dragon shimmering silver. "I could stand beside you and feel your power forever."

"You're going to." Jordyn gave him a sly smile, cut it from her face and met Prime's narrowed violet gaze. He gave her a once over from her feet to the dragon, to her chest, the marks, and then her face.

"The factions, your pack, and the klatch, have witnessed your true self. A descendant of Balaur's chosen. Marked by your mate. Soothsayer to the Cascade pack. Member of the Coterie of the Highguard's court. You are part of the Dark Awakening. Show them, Soothsayer," Prime demanded.

Jordyn swallowed, hard, inhaled and exhaled, then hesitantly turned around to face the crowd. Her skin crawled over her as they first stared at her naked body, then the marks glowing gold and moving on, stared at the dragon with its silver scales and iridescent wings. Her face heated as embarrassment spread from her chest to her throat, and finally setting her cheeks on fire.

"Impressive, Soothsayer. You're forgetting one thing, where is the child?" a man asked with a touch of an accent. Irish? Scottish? Norwegian? She didn't know.

Thankful for the diversion, she was going to show them exactly where Joyli was, she turned to face the unknown man, giving the audience her back. Wearing a mask of detachment, his hazel eyes flickered, amber, emerald, as they considered her. He had tucked his black hair with auburn highlights behind his ears, the ends sat, with a slight curl, at his shoulders. His face held a chiseled look as if ocean water and wind had carved his cheek bones and jaw line, and battle had trained his features. Jordyn met his emerald gaze with copper when he leaned forward, studied the marks, and his power surrounded them. She inhaled as his death and magic feathered her like it was searching for something, and he purposely grinned revealing sharp fangs. The relief she felt melted and she tried backing away from the vampire. Shadow Lord.

"Easy, Soothsayer." His intimate tone stopped her. He shrugged out of his black suit jacket, and with a dramatic twist held it over her shoulders. "You've proven yourself to them."

On auto, she pushed her arms through, the material feeling like satin on her bare skin. The hem stopped barley below her rear, but it covered her, and that's all she needed. Jordyn wondered what in the hell he wanted?

"There. Where is the child?" Shadow Lord repeated as he straightened. "If you were unable to procure her, you will have failed."

Jordyn lost her ability to concentrate. She fought to gather herself, and clutching the front of the jacket closed, she turned to the aisle. "Bring her here," she whispered.

Five Numina merged from the dark and marched toward them. Two in front, one in the middle holding Joyli, and two at the back. Like soldiers, they marched, and when they stopped, the front two parted, and the one carrying Joyli approached Jordyn. She reached out, and taking the baby and blanket, held the tiny bundle in her arms. Dark brown eyes caught Jordyn, and she heard Joyli's wolf howl as if the girl recognized her as pack. Jordyn left the stairs, past the baron and baroness, giving them a reassuring smile, and stopped when she stood in front of Boone and Lori Ann.

"Here's your little girl," Jordyn said as she leaned down. "Accept my apologies."

"No, accept ours. Thank you," Boone mumbled, his voice thick with emotion.

"Thank you, Soothsayer," Lori Ann nearly cried. She wrapped her arms around Joyli and clasped the tiny girl to her chest.

As the Numina lowered their spears, they shifted to their natural claws, then they took two steps from the family. Leaving them, she walked to where Rutger, Prime, and Shadow Lord waited. The commotion and conversations reaching a new level. She wanted out of there and she wanted to go home. Passing Rutger, she stood beside Prime, who looked like he was getting ready to address their audience.

"This was a charade," Jordyn accused, a slight growl in her words.

Prime turned toward her, his left side shielding her body from the crowd, and bent his six foot three inch frame. "Yes, Soothsayer. As necessary as it was for you to enter a realm of our world, it was necessary he be taught a lesson in humility," Prime answered.

"And the rest?" With their closeness, his magic drifted over her, as if caressing her, one of its own.

"You're bound to the territory by blood. You wanted to stay here without fearing someone would take you from your pack, your mate, and now they can't," Prime answered. "Everything has a price."

"Am I going to serve you the same way Ava does?"

He didn't answer her. "You controlled my Numina?"

"You knew I would." A sliver separated their faces. "They recognized your presence."

"There's your answer."

"And if I fail you, will you take my magic?"

"You won't fail."

Prime's tone dismissed her and he put distance between them. Jordyn walked down the steps and took her clothes from the Numen, then released them from her control. Which was simply pulling back as Prime's magic seamlessly replaced hers. Jordyn held the bundle in her arms, took the stairs and stood at Rutger's side. There they all waited for Prime to end the evening.

"Ladies and gentlemen of the magic-born, we stand united. This day marks the moment we reclaimed our past, our birthrights as magic-born, as we cast off our chains tethering us to the shadows. This day will be honored as the day we achieved our rebirth. Every year we shall celebrate the strength, power, magic, and the unity of all magic-born around the world. As one, we will defend our Dark Awakening."

Rutger put his arm around Jordyn, and she soaked in his warmth. The conclave erupted in cheers, whistles, howls, and roars, while some of them stood. They took the word of their Prime, their leader, their king, and would follow him. The baron was safe, the pack was safe, and she was never leaving.

"This night you witnessed the immense power of the Cascade pack's soothsayer and her sacrifice as your territory accepted her and blood bound her to the land. You've seen the proof she is a descendant from Balaur's chosen and Second to the Alpha's fated mate as she wears the mark of his bloodline. As such with magic-born displaying these traits, Soothsayer Jordyn Lily Langston has been inducted as a member of the Coterie of the Highguard's court," Prime announced. He began clapping his hands and the entire arena followed.

Lady Sloan stood, her eyes a liquid copper, and they stared at each other mother and daughter, both owned by

Prime and entrenched in the Highguard. Lady Sloan nodded and sat down, and Lord Ervin put his arm around her.

Blood bound to the territory. Rutger squeezed Jo as her unease drummed in their link. It increased as Prime announced her status with the Highguard and the noise inside the Conclave became deafening. He needed to get them out of there. "Ready to leave?"

"More than anything," Jordyn replied.

Rutger held her arm as he walked them over to the baron and baroness. "We're leaving."

"I'll make the necessary apologies," Healey assured with a smile. "I'm proud of you, Jordyn."

"We all are," Laurel added.

"The keys are in it, and don't worry about work, I'll have Ansel take charge," Healey offered.

"Thank you," Rutger replied.

"What keys?" Jordyn asked.

Healey smiled at her and replied, "You better hurry."

"Primary escape, red quadrant," Rutger reported.

"Affirmative. Clear," Jace, a soldier responded.

"Con initiative," Rutger ordered.

"What about my sentinels?" Jordyn asked. Did she care? No.

"It'll take them at least an hour to get out of the mass of cars and another hour or so in the traffic. I planned this for our escape," Rutger explained.

When they left the lights, rostrum, Conclave, and the crowd behind them, Jo stopped to put her underwear and running shoes on. Rutger wasn't going to risk being caught in the flood of people as they searched for them, then poured from the Conclave trying to leave. He absolutely wasn't taking the chance of being seen and then stopped by anyone wanting to talk to them. Who knows what they saw when they looked at Jo? They headed deeper into the woods and when the sounds faded and they were walking with the moon their only light, Rutger's nerves eased.

"What is con initiative?" Jordyn asked. She bunched her clothes and held them in right hand, keeping her left hand free.

"Enforcers will drive my truck pretending to be us."

"No shit." Jordyn laughed. *Sneaky wolf.*

"I thought it was pretty good." Rutger enjoyed the sound of her laughter, light, easy going, natural. It made him hesitate to ask her what happened. "What did you have to do?"

Jordyn heard the reluctance in his voice, like he didn't want to ask and wasn't sure he wanted to know. He did ask because that's what the Director of Enforcers did. He had his questions. "I had to break a circle rune."

"You did it?" He helped her over a fallen tree and they continued.

"Ava told me how on the drive here."

"You asked her and she told you?" No way it was that easy.

"I didn't ask. She explained what kind of mage she was and included a story. Prime ordered her to tell me because this wasn't about the challenge. I'm blood bound to the territory, your marked mate, and the question of my connection to the Collective can't be questioned. I'm not leaving Cascade. I'm with the Coterie which means I have status." Jordyn stopped them. "Prime said he did this for me, in return he used me to get Shadow Lord here, he needed a lesson in humility."

He definitely needed the lesson. Which meant there was no reason to continue the lie and he needed to be honest with Jo. "After Butte Springs, when the Highguard's messengers delivered the letter, Shadow Lord threatened to take you from me. He planted the bodies at the tree and planned to blackmail me. I received another letter a couple days ago stating I couldn't protect you." Rutger pushed his fingers through his hair. "I know I lied to you. I'm sorry. I should have been honest knowing you can take care of yourself."

Jordyn stared at him as he stood in the moonlight, his eyes flickering gold when he turned his head. His body was a mass of muscle and tension. "There's nothing to be sorry about. I wouldn't have told you." Rutger's head jerked up and he met her gaze. "We do stupid things thinking we're protecting each other." She was doing it right then. "Prime said we're in a new realm of our world and I'm part of his Dark Awakening. We move on from here and we protect each other."

"I love you, Jo," Rutger growled. He leaned down and kissed her. "Come on, the Jeep is over here."

CHAPTER THIRTY-NINE

Jordyn stood at the railing of the deck, coffee in hand as snow flurries swirled in the wind and gradually landing blanketed the ground in white. Drops of water peppered her skin where snowflakes melted while whips of steam from her coffee disappeared in winter's breath. She inhaled fresh air, infused with the sweet scent of pine, oak, and manzanita, and a hint of the French roast she was drinking. Usually she hated winter-it was cold, dark, and the snow covered forest made her feel isolated from her territory. Things change.

Over the month since Rutger marked her, the dragon of Balaur exposed her as one his chosen, and Prime proved with the challenge he marked her with his magic, they hadn't been attacked, questioned, and the pack stood united. The population of magic-born stood united. If this was going to be their winter, she would deal with the cold and the snow. Rutger's essence drifted in the link between them, and a thread of heat caressed her, reminding her there was one more thing they had to do before they were free. Mostly free. Jordyn cringed with the lies she was keeping. When Rutger confessed to keeping Shadow Lord's threats from her, she hadn't gotten mad, or accused him of lying ... no, she couldn't. She had lies of her own which she knew would surface eventually, but not in the immediate future, she was sure.

If her lies were exposed, it meant all hell had broken lose and her misguided betrayal would amount to nothing. Jordyn took one last look at the mountains disappearing in the thickening storm clouds, falling snow, the lake, and after enjoying the muted quiet turned from the serene scene and went back inside. The fire crackled and popped, its flames reaching up the chimney, its warmth and amber glow making the living room cozy and safe. She didn't want to leave.

"Are you ready?" Rutger asked as he left the last stair. He wore a black T-shirt, under a chocolate brown sweater, a dark pair of jeans that hugged his hips and thighs, and his pair of old, broken in boots. They did not match the rest of him. He had shaved and combed his dark brown hair back away from his face, letting all attention focus on his eyes. Mahogany with amber.

"I am. Are you ready?" Jordyn met his gaze and the deadly feel of pure happiness filled her. She tried to quench it; she didn't want to embrace it and have it show on her face. She would look like a love-struck teenager. And it would give away her feelings that could be used against her. She had to work on controlling her facial reactions.

"I love you, too, Mea," Rutger whispered his voice thick. Her raven hair hung straight, her cocoa eyes were lined with black and smokey browns. She wore a fitted long-sleeved red shirt, jeans that molded to her curves, and running shoes. Of course, she wasn't wearing snow boots. They made it, were making it and survived.

"That obvious." She met him and put her arms around him and he squeezed her to him. Muscle, warmth, and his wolf wrapped around her. "Are you ready? This will be our first step."

"Yes. With the rune Ava drew and your blood, I've practiced this hundreds of times. It's as natural as shapeshifting into my wolf form. Are you nervous?" he asked. Rutger rested his chin on her head and held her.

"Not sure what your parents are going to think. Gavin's jealousy might break him," Jordyn answered.

They discussed this day for an entire month and decided the best way to demonstrate Rutger's ability to shift into his Bestial form was to show them, and prove to them he could control himself and the beast. By them, it had to be the entire family. Only family. With the exception of Tanner and Bailey. Jordyn loved her sister. However, she didn't trust Bailey not to say anything to Mia, who had finally accepted, to an extent, the changes in magic, and the pack. No reason to throw Bestial form at them ... yet.

"If we keep him in the circle of information it will make him feel included. He's not the weak link he was when he was young. Gavin is a strong wolf, a stronger man, and needs to realize it. He helped secure the confidence of the Lassen Range." Rutger stepped back from Jo. "We have to trust him."

"I know." Jordyn walked to the entry where her coat and scarf hung on a railroad nail and stared at Shadow Lord's suit jacket. She figured if he wanted it back, he would have sent someone to get it. "We're heading to Foxwood," she reported to Tracy and Charles. They had started all three vehicles and were waiting outside.

"Affirmative, Mistress," Charles responded.

She didn't like having sentinels, basically babysitters, but it made the baron feel better, and since he felt better, he allowed her to send them home at night.

"Your chariot awaits, mate," Rutger said with a wave of his hand.

"Why are we here again?" Gavin asked, as he shifted his feet. His eyes held a bored glare, and landing on Jo, the baron, baroness, and lastly Rutger. He needed to ditch the chip on his shoulder.

They were alone at the back of the Enforcer's office, standing in the gym with equipment one side of them and the mat on the other. It took an hour of explaining the procedure, another hour of questions, and another hour to get the soldiers and enforcers to leave their posts for the drill. That's what Rutger told them it was and the baron happily backed him up. At that moment, Foxwood stood abandoned.

"There needs to be full disclosure among the leaders," Jordyn explained.

"You've spent too much time with Leo and Torin," Gavin mocked.

"You have no idea," Rutger replied with an easy grin. "She kicks my ass, then gives me orders."

"Language, son," Laurel chided with a smile.

Jordyn laughed. "The reason we're here."

"Pardon me, you said full discloser. Where is Tanner and Bailey?" Laurel interrupted. "Tanner is Fourth to the Alpha, he needs to be here."

"No." Jordyn knew it sounded harsh, and by the baroness' shocked response it was. "Not yet."

"Are you afraid what Baily will say to Mia?" Healey asked.

"Yes. At least for now," Jordyn replied.

"Does this have something to do with Potents?" Healey looked at Jordyn then Rutger, while his imagination chased trails. They've had a month to relax and settle into a routine and their relationship. He didn't want anyone, anything, interfering with them.

"No." Jordyn gave Rutger a sideways glance. "Not entirely." Did she want to start the conversation? She wasn't there to talk about her or the changes in her magic.

"Tell them." Rutger could wait.

"I can feel the other Potents," Jordyn explained.

"That's not creepy or anything," Gavin mumbled.

"Right. It's the strength of their magic making them stand out from the other magic-born. Their magic has a bigger presence." Gavin's eyes held his doubt. All right.

"Is that all?" Healey asked.

"I believe, they can feel me. It might be the wakening letting me feel them but they're there." Jordyn senses picked up the slightest magic, analyzed it, and she knew what kind of magic-born they were.

"Any trouble with Shadow Lord?" Healey could hear the vampire tell them if she failed the challenge and the Cascade pack was dismantled, he wanted possession of Jordyn.

"No. Thankfully." And she meant it.

"Are you still working with Sloan?" Healey asked.

Interrogation. Like father, like son. "Yes. She has given me the name of another soothsayer who's willing to help."

"That's good, Jordyn." Laurel gave her a smile.

"Enough about me. Rutger, you're up." Jordyn watched his body tense; a tinge of anxiety hit their link, then it was gone.

"I'll get ready." He left them, and crossing the room took a bulletin board covered in posters of different workout positions, examples of weight lifting, and instructions on how to use the equipment, and placed it on the floor.

"What is that?" Healey asked. Hidden behind the board and painted in black on the wall was a mass of circles, runes, and glyphs. "Is that magic?"

"Yes, it's a circle rune. Once activated any use of magic inside the Enforcer's building will remain in the building," Jordyn explained.

"If you took this precaution why make everyone leave? Foxwood is unguarded," Healey pointed out.

"We're here. It's not unguarded," Rutger replied as he faced them.

"Your soothsayer is here and your Director of Enforcers is here," Gavin teased. He tried teasing. No one missed the sarcasm edging his voice. "If it's trapped in here, what happens to the magic?" He looked around the room at the walls, windows, and ceiling.

"In this case it will filter through me," Jordyn answered.

"Is it safe?" Laurel asked.

"Yes." Jordyn tried giving them a reassuring smile, wanting them to believe her without her explaining she had been practicing for weeks.

"Who did the drawing?" Healey eyed her with his alpha's brunt gold gaze. "Who taught you how to power it?"

"Ava. She was the woman traveling with Prime. She's a mage," Jordyn explained.

"I'm officially weirded out," Gavin mumbled.

"What does Rutger have to get ready for?" Laurel asked.

"A demonstration." Jordyn walked over to the wall, and when she stood in front of the drawing, she took a small knife from her pocket and sliced across two fingertips. When she asked Ava to create the circle rune, to protect them from being sensed by others, Ava advised Jordyn to use power words. The words Jordyn chose would become an invocation and needed to have meaning to Jordyn and she needed to say them in Greek, due to Prime's essence intertwined with her magic. She chose her words and practiced them until she said every syllable correctly. Every time it reminded her of her lie and her link to Prime. Link. It was like a damn leash.

"Προστατέψτε το σπίτι μου," Jordyn whispered as she smeared scarlet across two joining circles and the rune of protection. It translated to 'shield my house' was short, easy to remember, and she needed with all her heart for her house to be protected.

"Blood. This can't be good," Gavin argued. "Since when was it all right to use blood magic?"

Jordyn's blood, the power words, and magic created an invocation and linked her power to the rune. She inhaled as a rush of energy, from the magic infusing the circle rune, reached out, its threads following the corners and encased the building. The black lines glowed deep violet, pulsed, and dimmed to a pale purple. Another reminder of Prime. With the surge, the baron sucked in a breath, the baroness rubbed her arms, and Gavin searched the walls and ceiling like they were going to come alive and grab him.

"Is this blood magic?" Healey asked.

"Yes and no." How to explain it. "The circle rune needs magic to work. The first step, the mage creates the drawing from runes, glyphs, whatever is required. The second step, the mage ensconces the spell into the rune and gives the user the rune. Since blood is required, and Ava gave me this circle rune, I own it. Lastly, the user's blood connects them to the circle rune. My magic powers the circle rune, not my blood. It's the connection."

"Ava taught you this?" Healey asked.

She understood his hesitation where Ava was concerned. She had explained to Jordyn how to break the circle rune protecting Prime's Numen. No one, except Rutger, knew Ava had told Jordyn the story. But with Ava being Prime's property it was enough not to trust her.

"I don't owe her, and the pack isn't indebted to her. We traded information." This was going to be funny. So funny. Jordyn was having a hard time keeping a straight face.

"What kind of information would a mage and servant of Prime need from you?" Healey demanded. His shoulders straightened, his demeanor turning baron and alpha ready to protect his pack, than father-in-law.

"Well ..." Jordyn dragged it out letting silence and their imagination get the better of them. When burnt gold ate the brown of the baron's eyes and she couldn't keep from smiling, she confessed, "I gave her Aydian's cell number. She thinks he's hot."

The baron opened his mouth, stopped, and shook his head as the baroness laughed. Jordyn couldn't help but enjoy the stunned reaction from the baron and the sweet sound of an easy laugh from the baroness. It was another testament to their victory. They survived, they were living their lives, and no one could take that from them. Jordyn was laughing when the locker room door opened and they watched Rutger walk out wearing nothing but a towel around his waist. A soft bronze from summer held his skin as the muscles in his chest constricted with his gait.

"We get it, Rutger, you workout," Gavin said.

"We're in the gym, you could start," Rutger shot back as he flexed.

"I like," Jordyn teased.

"Yeah, baby." Rutger stood beside her and grabbed her by her waist.

"Remember why we're here. Please, son, remember your mother and I are here," Healey advised. It was good to feel relaxed and see his boys interacting.

"All right." Jordyn's heart was suddenly in her throat. "We requested your presence because Rutger has something to show you."

"No," Healey blurted out. "You can't do this. Why would you do this?"

"Do what?" Laurel asked, concern taking the softness from her face.

"He's naked. He's going to shift," Gavin answered.

"Why would shifting be a big deal?" She met Rutger's gaze. "No, son. You're not doing this. The Highguard and Prime have left us alone. Don't bring them back."

"What are you talking about?" Gavin asked. His eyes skated over them in confusion.

"Rutger, think about what your mother said. What this would do the pack," Healey urged. "And if you lose yourself."

"That's why I have the circle rune and there is no one else here," Jordyn explained. "No one will find out."

Healey turned in a circle, then faced her. "You plan on lying to the Highguard?"

"Yes."

"You're comfortable with this?" Healey stared at Rutger. Yes, he planned on Rutger shifting, but not now, not like this.

"Yes. Let him show you," Jordyn insisted.

"Get it over with."

"Wait, is this safe? I don't want you to, you know …" Laurel stumbled over her words, her worry out for everyone to hear.

"Oh my god. Are you insane, you can't do this," Gavin breathed as he took a step backwards. "It's wrong."

"It's safe." A growl mixed with a tinge of pain laced Rutger's answer.

His wolf shadowed his body, and pushing the shift his arms and legs lengthened, his muscles stretched and coiled under his skin. Hair sprouted from his flesh sheathing his ears, muzzle, and chest in black, then it faded out to dark walnut and blending with charcoal ran down his sides and belly. He let the towel fall to the gym floor when his hips thickened, exposing the taught muscles of his thighs. A surge of power whipped in the gym, forcing Rutger to bend at the waist. His heartbeat shifted to his Bestial form, and his pulse raced in his ears as the shift overtook his human body.

Jordyn saw the baron and baroness take several steps backwards. They didn't go as far as Gavin, who stared with wide eyes. The magic and power echoed off the spell and into her, its vibration filtering through her body and then her magic.

Rutger straightened, stretched into his newly formed arms, and standing before them in his Bestial form, shook his head. His canines touched his lower lip and sharpened to points as his muscles undulated under his skin.

"My beautiful beast," Jordyn whispered. Rutger's magic slid through her like water over rocks while it traveled their link.

Rutger faced her, reached out with a clawed hand, and feathered her cheek with black nails. "Mea," he growled.

"I can't believe this," Healey said in awe. "When did this happen?"

"When I marked Jo," Rutger replied. The words came out rough, slightly off, and carried by a growl. "I'm not as impressive as Jo. Who shapeshifts as she leaps through the air."

"I'm good that's all." Jordyn shrugged her shoulders, displaying zero humility.

"This is weird shit." Gavin pushed his fingers through his hair and took another step backwards. "Wrong. Weird. Shit."

"I had no idea it was possible after all these years living in fear of Bestial. Then what happened to the ones we thought went Bestial?" Laurel asked. She ignored Gavin's bad language and approached Rutger, staring at him as if he was an oddity.

"They did lose themselves to the beast, making the threat real. Rutger was already strong, self-disciplined, and forced control over his wolf. Add in my magic and it was a controlled shift. We aren't saying anyone can shapeshift," Jordyn replied.

"Is it hard to speak?" Healey asked.

"Yes," Rutger answered. "I've gotten better."

"What about telepathy?" Healey looked at Jordyn.

"First this, and telepathy?" Gavin walked over to Rutger, and side stepping him stood by Jordyn. "I leave as an ambassador and come back to this. You're telepathic?"

"Yes, and yes I can speak to Rutger or you."

"Say something," Gavin dared her.

"You're sure?"

"Yes. Let's add to the weirdness of the day."

"Boo."

"Shit," Gavin said as he jumped. "All right, don't do that again."

"Language, son," Laurel half heartily chided.

"This is incredible. Who else knows?" Healey asked.

"Prime. He saw him," Jordyn answered. "Rutger is marked by one of the descendants of Balaur, me. I shared my magic with him and made him my warrior. Prime understands this." Because he planned it that way.

"He announced your inclusion into the Coterie of the Highguard and allowed Rutger to shift into his Bestial form without consequence. If you're ever called to court, Rutger will go with you as your guardian." Healey's mind was reeling.

"Exactly," Rutger growled.

"Is it hard to shift back to human?" Laurel asked. "Please shift back to human."

"Yes, Mother," Rutger replied.

His wolf howled in his ears, as it always did when he called his magic. His muscles reformed, his bones reshaped anticipating his human body, and his face lost its Bestial muzzle. In a weaker fusion of magic Rutger melted back into his human form. Jo picked the towel off the floor, held it to cover him as he stretched his skin and muscles.

Taking it from her, he wrapped it around his waist, then met their gazes. He wasn't sure what to say and didn't see anything except worry in their eyes. "That's it."

"I wouldn't say that," Healey started. "What does it feel like?"

"A power rush. It's like two worlds are combining when the wolf and human give over to the beast," Rutger answered.

"I'm glad you're safe, son." Laurel gave him a smile of relief but wasn't going to hug him.

"We've witnessed Rutger's Bestial form, Jordyn's inclusion into the Coterie, the factions are united, and the pack, whether they like it or not, understand magic is changing. We'll take this time of peace to let the pack resume their normal lives."

"Normal?" An ache was starting at the base of her skull. Jordyn could pretend their lives were back to normal, whatever that was for them, but knew Prime was waiting. Cast. Forged. He said he was going to send someone to train her. *Honed by my hand.*

"Well ... as much as possible. They witnessed your power, Jordyn," Healey started. "If anyone doubted you as their soothsayer, they don't now. And with Prime publicly supporting you, whatever enemies come from the Krijgers, they know there will be zero tolerance if they attack another Potent."

"It's back to business," Laurel groaned.

Rutger kissed Jo, held his towel, and started toward the locker rooms. "You got this?" he asked as he pointed to the circle rune.

"Yes." Jordyn walked across the gym to the wall with the baron, baroness, and Gavin behind her.

"How do you disarm it?" Healey asked.

A weight rack sat to the side, and sitting on its top was a container of sanitizer wipes. She grabbed one and began scrubbing the dried crimson from the rune. The pastel purple lines of the circles, runes, and glyphs faded to white, and then black. It looked like a someone had painted on the wall, nothing more, completely harmless. "All done."

"Well that was easy," Laurel said.

"I expressed my need for it to be easy to Ava. No reason to make it harder than it has to be." Jordyn stepped back from the wall, grabbed the board, and hung it on the hooks concealing the circle rune. Several minutes later, the locker room door opened and Rutger entered the gym wearing his enforcer's uniform.

"Everything good?" he asked. Rutger stood relaxed, his hand on the butt of his gun, and radiating authority.

"Yes, Director." The baron and baroness laughed, Gavin groaned, and she felt Rutger's essence in their link. She was enjoying their time together. Jordyn's humor came to halt when her cell phone rang. It was her turn to groan as she pulled it free from her pocket and looked at the name and number. "Hello, Detective Watt." She met Rutger's questioning gaze and shrugged her shoulders. Jordyn took the cell from her ear, the screen lit up, and she hit speaker.

"I'm not going to bother with small talk. Is there a reason there are multiple vehicles parked outside Foxwood's gates? And the gates are closed?" Detective Watt asked.

Jordyn looked at the baron, then to Rutger. Neither said anything. "They're doing a drill. Prepared readiness."

"Are you currently at Foxwood?"

"Yes, sir."

"As a solider?" Even through the phone his voice had taken on a serious tone.

"No. I'm the damsel in distress," she answered and smiled. She thought it was funny.

He coughed like he had choked on something. "That is grossly inadequate. Does the *drill* have anything to do with the large gathering at the Summit a month ago?" His emphasis on drill didn't go unnoticed. He didn't believe them.

Jordyn laughed and heard Detective Watt's low rumble. "No."

"What was the reason behind the gathering?" Back to the interrogation.

"It was the full moon run. And Rutger and I are officially engaged." She squinted one eye, in an uh-oh look, met Rutger's narrowed gaze, and whispered, "It slipped." The baron and baroness glared at them while Gavin covered his face in his hands.

"Congratulations." He didn't believe her. "When you left the pack three years ago, did you give Baron Kanin your resignation?"

"No," she answered hesitantly.

"Right now, you're considered active?" He sounded like he was reading from a list.

Jordyn looked at the baron who looked at Rutger, who nodded yes. "Yes." *That's too bad.*

"Excellent. Is there a statement of proof?"

Again, she looked at the baron who looked at Rutger, who nodded yes. "Yes." No way they kept her records.

"Excellent." He was definitely reading from a list. "As a solider for the Cascade pack, you completed tactical training including firearm training, a physical fitness boot camp, fulfilled patrolling hours, and passed a criminal justice class, in addition to a Paranormal History class. Is this accurate?"

Jordyn closed her eyes. "Yes."

"You were a partner at the gallery where your work was displayed. I've seen your photography, why did you become a soldier?" he asked. There was rustling of shuffling papers in the background.

What the hell did he want? "Every member of the pack has to serve two years as a soldier. It gives them a better understanding of pack politics and the diversity of the pack." And educates them about human law enforcement.

"Smart. Do you have certificates?"

No, she hoped not. She wasn't going to check with the baron and decided Rutger knew the answer. He was busy typing something into his cell. When he finished, he nodded yes. "Yes."

"Your favorite color?" Rutger whispered.

Detective Watt was interrogating her and he wanted to know her favorite color. She had no idea. He mouthed the question again. "Red."

"What?" Detective Watt asked.

"Nothing. What were you saying?"

"You trained under Leo Greene a California state certified combatant instructor?"

"Yes." Jordyn was officially confused.

"You have those certs as well? And any kind of progress reports stating your qualifications?"

Rutger was grinning as he nodded yes. *Damn.* "Yes."

"Could I get copies of everything I listed?" More paper shuffling, he scribbled something on a piece of paper, then drank something. If he remembered they were werewolves and could hear everything he did, he didn't act like he cared.

Rutger's attention was back on his cell, as he nodded yes. "Of course."

There was a ding, a second ding. "Thank you that was fast."

"Rutger is right here," Jordyn mumbled. If she wasn't blatantly denying what was going on it would make accepting Rutger and the baron's lack of objecting easier.

"Good Afternoon, Rutger. Now, Miss Langston, as your handler I've turned in your recruitment packet. This will be a lateral move from the Cascade pack's solider unit to the Paradise County sheriff's department. Since you have already completed extensive training, you'll attend the last six weeks of the sheriff's academy. After you graduate, you'll transition to a four-week evaluation period. During that time, I'll be your FTO, Field Training Officer. Upon completion of the four weeks you will be promoted to detective and transferred to the Organized Paranormal Investigations task force. We'll be partners."

Jordyn's heart was pounding in her chest. There was no way they would let her do this. She looked at Rutger, the baron, then the baroness. No help. "Detective Watt, I'm not deputy material. As you know, I'm a photographer. Landscapes. Sunsets. Trees. Waterfalls. Law enforcement has never been an interest."

"I understand what your passion is, Jordyn, but this is a necessity. Two women connected to the non-human group of Fae, have gone missing. The report states they were kidnapped. There are no witnesses, no one is talking, and there were traces of a non-human at the scene. I need someone they will talk to, that's you. In order to retain you for the duration of the case and future cases, I have to go through the state's committee in charge of task forces and get approval. This is exponentially quicker."

Jordyn's heart seized in her chest as she met Rutger's gold gaze and shook her head. Sure she could help find out who kidnapped the women, but if the women committed a crime? She would be working both sides. It was a conflict of interest. "This is wrong," she whispered.

"You have to go through with it," Healey urged. "What if it's the Krijgers?"

Everything Prime did at the challenge, her inclusion into the Coterie, the lower court of the Highguard, announcing she was a descendant of Balaur made her into something she wasn't and responsible for the Seelie court's safety. The Seelie court bordered Cascade's territory and were part of the klatch who had pledged their loyalty at the challenge and in front of Prime. Chancellor Roarke sent her a card congratulating her for the inclusion into the Coterie. She couldn't turn her back on them. And the OPI would give her the resources she needed.

"Hello?" The rustling papers stopped and silence sat thick.

"I'm here. I understand," Jordyn replied.

"Excellent. I do want to extend my apologies over my conduct, Jordyn. I needed to make sure you were doing all right. I didn't know how to go about it."

"It's in the past, Detective." Jordyn squeezed the bridge of her nose.

"So it is. I'll email you the appropriate paperwork, you'll need to sign the forms and return them to me. Understand, Recruit?" He chuckled. "It'll have all the information you'll need to know, dates, equipment, and so on."

"Yes, sir," Jordyn replied. *Recruit.* She was an idiot.

"It's settled. I will see you tomorrow to go over the case, I would like your input, and I want you to visit the scene. Rutger it was good talking to you as usual. Recruit, I'll call you." Detective Watt paused, like he was debating something, and she could hear him breathing. "Jordyn, I'm glad you're all right. For the record, you have never been or will ever be a damsel in distress." Without waiting for her to reply, he ended the call.

She hit the end button to make sure and closed the screen closed. "What the hell am I supposed to do?" Jordyn asked.

"Language, daughter," Laurel chided. She smiled as her brown eyes glittered with humor.

"Get ready, Recruit. I think you'll look hot in a uniform," Rutger growled.

"You are zero help." She shoved him away from her when he closed the distance.

"It seems the detective has a soft spot for you." Healey chuckled, his deep voice making it almost a growl. "Seriously, this is a great opportunity. You'll have access to the OPI's computers and their cases," Healey tried convincing her. "You made a good solider. You have a natural instinct for it, or Detective Watt wouldn't have put his reputation on the line for you."

"True." She guessed. Jordyn wanted to go home where wine and a fire would block out the outside world.

"It really is a good opportunity," Rutger agreed, trying to be serious. "Since the sentinels can't go with you, your truck will arrive next week. It'll be out fitted the same as mine. Armor platting, bullet resistant glass, computer system, the works. And it'll be red."

Jordyn gave him a flat stare. "How nice. What's wrong with my SUV?"

"It's a security breach," Rutger stated. "My mate and soothsayer for the pack isn't going to go to the sheriff's academy without protection, you're part of Cascade pack, and the coterie."

"Yes, Director Kanin," she mocked.

"Wait one minute. You said the two of you were officially engaged. Is this true?" Healey asked. Laurel stood beside him, her hand on his arm.

"Yes, is this true? And you didn't tell us?" Laurel added.

Rutger laughed and drew Jo to his side. "Yes. I asked, and she said yes."

"Great, another wedding." Gavin shook his head.

"Wonderful." Laurel let go of Healey and hugged Rutger and Jordyn. "Just wonderful."

"We weren't going to plan anything until next year. Now it won't be until after my four-week probation period. Maybe I can invite my detective buddies," Jordyn mocked. She had to put an end to any plans her future in-laws were making.

"Yes." Laurel smiled again and stepped back. "Of course."

Jordyn knew she was going to lose the battle. "I'll let you get back to business and let the troops back in. I'm heading home. How long are you staying?" Jordyn turned to Rutger.

"A couple of hours and I'll be on my way."

"Enjoy your afternoon Jordyn," Healey said.

His arm was around Laurel and they were staring at her. She could practically see the wheels turning and their wedding becoming an event. She had to tell her parents before someone else did. "Thanks, I will. Have a good afternoon, Gavin, future bother in-law."

He mumbled something in response, making Jordyn laugh as she headed out to her security breach of a car.

CHAPTER FORTY

After the moon run, turned challenge, Jordyn feared Prime would show up, Shadow Lord would show up, attacks were imminent, and the pack would revolt. Nothing happened. Day after day she held her breath and waited. Still nothing. Jordyn had to accept worrying about it wasn't going to make it stop from happening nor was it going to force it to happen. Instead of being alert and ready, she was wasting precious time. It was time to relax and start living, and it was time for her and Rutger to be a couple. Fated mates. Engaged. Officially.

They took advantage of the days by talking, sitting in comfortable silence, running, training, and Rutger practiced shifting into his Bestial form and she practiced powering the circle rune. Then, when a snow storm moved in they locked themselves in the house by the fire, the only material between them a thick blanket. They made love, they had sex, they ate, they drank, and they slept in each other's arms. It felt too good to be true. The storm lasted four days, dropped twenty inches of snow, threatened them with hurricane-strength winds, then vanished as quickly as it came. With clear roads and good weather, the excuses for avoiding the storage unit had dwindled to nothing. She had to face her stuff.

Lined against the studio's crème walls were a dozen moving boxes, some with their flaps open, some tapped closed, and some she rummaged through then closed. Going through her life at Butterfly Valley hurt enough she didn't want to look at it too long. With Louis' and Detective Watt's words about the house ringing in her head, she attempted to make the house *theirs* not *his.* She started by hanging several prints, then took knick-knacks and different decorations and peppered the house with them, and stocked the kitchen with her utensils and tableware. It was coming along. She was relieved to find Rutger had broken down boxes and cleaned up packing paper and the only boxes left were the ones she occasionally glanced at over the top of her laptop.

Jordyn sat at her desk, secluded in the studio with her sentinels in the living room, staring at the screen, her digital signature, the contracts, release forms, and waiver for a psychological evaluation. If they pulled her records from Celestial, they might deny her. *Here's hoping.* Detective Watt knew Dr. Carrion diagnosed Jordyn with PTSD, he mentioned it when she landed on Claudia's doorstep in the middle of the night. He also knew Jordyn had been held for observation for three weeks, at which point Jordyn was forced to shift into her human form, and start rehabilitation and counseling. After they released Rutger, they were both ordered to attend counseling, together. Her medical record read like a rap sheet for the emotionally troubled and mentally deranged. An image of Randy's bleeding eyes sat in her head, and she heard his screams as she showed him his wife being tortured. She murdered someone and was going to attend the Paradise County sheriff's academy. What the hell was going on in her life? A deputy. A detective with the OPI.

Her cell rang, its high-pitched ring making her jump and her heart beat a hundred times in a matter of a second. She took it from the desk, read the unknown number, not good, and answered. "Hello."

"Miss Jordyn Langston?"

"Yes." Jordyn sat straighter with her full name.

"Cynthia Lark. My office, Seaworthy Acquisitions, is in Crescent City."

Jordyn rolled her eyes, then looked at the screen and the forms. "What can I do for you, Miss Lark."

"Mrs. And please call me Cynthia. I understand you once showed your photography at the gallery, Epic Sights, in Butterfly Valley?"

"Yes." Maybe the woman called to tell her, her prints had been burned in protest because she was a werewolf. Lycan.

"I understand you're a lycan?" Cynthia hesitated for breath. "A Pureblood?"

"Yes." One word answers, nice. Jordyn listened to the woman talk, her voice turning sugary as she sweet talked her way to what she wanted. Jordyn's thoughts wondered, she looked at the manilla folder sitting beside her laptop with Sloan's delicate handwriting on the front. *I'm not collecting personal information on the lords of the Highguard.* No, it's mother-daughter, correspondence. Like the stack of aged books. Light reading.

"I have a client who has an *interest* in non-humans, specifically lycans. He saw your print." She paused and shuffled papers. "Butte Springs."

Jordyn's attention jerked back to Cynthia when her heart stopped, she forgot how to breathe, and had to force herself to talk. The news exploded with her kidnapping, criminalizing her for being a lycan, then victimizing her for having been tortured and nearly murdered. In the aftermath of learning she lied to them for years, and the ugly breakup with Louis, the gallery took her prints down and shoved them in their storage room. They didn't want to be associated with a lycan and were quick to send her documents stating she wasn't allowed to set foot inside the gallery. Ever. The baron offered his horde of lawyers to force the gallery's board of directors to release the prints, but Jordyn refused, not wanting to fight anyone. Anyway, she figured the prints would be safe at the gallery.

"How did this person see Butte Springs?" Jordyn asked, her suspicions about Cynthia escalating.

"You have an eye and it shows in your work." Cynthia paused again. "I'll admit, June was an incredible setback for you as a photographer. It doesn't mean your work stopped being noticed or there wasn't a demand. The gallery has been giving private showings."

Setback. Sure, if being kidnapped then ordered to stay away was a setback. *Private showings.* "Then you know I'm not in possession of Butte Springs."

"Yes, I talked to them. They are willing to release the print with your consent."

What the hell? "Who is this man?" *Interested in non-human and lycans?* The Fae women drifted through her thoughts.

"He would like to remain anonymous. He has given me the authority to pay you well above what the print is worth."

Jordyn couldn't lie to herself or deny the excitement of selling a print and knowing she was good at what she did. That part of her life was over. A photographer wasn't going to help keep the pack safe. She needed the OPI. Jordyn nearly laughed out loud when she pictured herself working as a detective and moonlighting as a photographer, then when there was an attack, she would don her soothsayer cape and fight crime. She squeezed the bridge of her nose.

"I'm willing to sell the piece." Jordyn had priced it at five hundred dollars, but would have taken two hundred and fifty in the off season.

"I'm offering two thousand dollars."

For a dusty print of a twisted tree. "I don't understand."

"He wants the print. He understands the significance of Butte Springs and wants a print taken by the Pureblood Jordyn Langston of the Cascade pack and wants you, Miss Langston, properly compensated. This amount guarantees his purchase and your compensation. Since your self-induced exile from the public, your work has gained an eccentric following."

A chill made from glass shards slid down her spine at the same time her instincts raged. Self-induced exile. Eccentric. It wasn't about her ability to capture a scene. It was about having been kidnapped and being a werewolf and the publicity making her a spectacle. The attention she was getting was a security breach and she needed to talk to Rutger. But nothing could take away from the calculating undertone in Cynthia's voice that made her instincts scream. The woman sounded like she was prepared to hunt Jordyn down to get what she wanted.

Did she want to hold onto the print? No. Was she prepared to tell Cynthia to go pound sand? No. She didn't want to be harassed. Anyway, it was picture not a secret window into her soul. "The price is acceptable. You can mail the payment to the enforcer's office and direct it to Director of Enforcers, Rutger Kanin. Is this your cell number?"

Jordyn asked. She kept her voice stern, business-like; she wasn't impressed by the money or the attention. Jordyn made a note of Cynthia's name, company, and city to give to Rutger.

"Yes, it is." Her voice sounded drenched in syrup.

Yeah, you got what you wanted. "I'll text you the address, then I'll contact the gallery and have them release the print to you."

"He is grateful, Miss Langston." The phone went dead.

Jordyn hit the end button to be sure, set the phone on the desk, and went back to the forms and stared at her name. She hated giving up photography. With a pained grumble, she needed to call the gallery. New dread filled her middle. Would Lizzie talk to her? Did Lizzie still work there? Only one way to find out. Jordyn grabbed her phone, went through her contacts, and finding Epic Sights, hit dial. Every ring added fear and uncertainty to her anxiety.

"Epic Sights, Lizzie speaking."

"Lizzie, it's Jordyn. Jordyn Langston." Silence stretched out and she thought Lizzie might hang up on her.

"You have some nerve calling here," Lizzie hissed into the phone.

Damn, not what she wanted, but it was expected.

"You get kidnapped and not one damn word. I thought you were dead."

What? "I'm sorry. And I'm sorry, sorry isn't good enough." Jordyn placed her elbow on the desk and covered her face with her free hand. Relief flowed through her.

"It's all right. I do understand. I would love to chitchat with my lycan friend who never calls, but I know you called for a reason."

"Yes. What do you know about Cynthia Lark?"

"She's a shark." Lizzie laughed. "Seaworthy Acquisitions. She deals with the rich and famous of the non-human world. Shapeshifters, the Fae, witches, warlocks, it doesn't matter. If it's rare, expensive, an antique, and they want it, they call her."

"Then you know she called me about the print Butte Springs. She said her client knew its significance and wanted something by Jordyn Langston." Just saying it made Jordyn cringe.

"Yes. She requested a viewing of all your work, spent an hour going over them, then chose Butte Springs. And before you ask, no I have no idea who her client is. What do you want to do?" Lizzie asked.

"Give it to her. I'm not sure I ever want to look at it," Jordyn mumbled.

"I understand. I'll send you an email with the release forms. Your work is getting renewed attention, Jordyn. I would love to have fresh prints," Lizzie said.

"Thank you. I'll think about it. It was good to talk to you." Jordyn waited as Lizzie said her good-byes and ended the call. It was all too weird. It made her think of the two missing Fae women. No one would kidnap people to have them. A photograph, sure. People, no. Right?

Jordyn sat back, checked the time, saw it was five in the evening-Rutger was getting ready to come home-and closed her laptop on the forms. They could wait. Leaving everything where it was, she left the studio and started through the dark kitchen when she stopped in front of the window. Gold and scarlet hues of the setting sun sank behind the ridges of the mountains. The snow-covered peaks glistened like beds of diamonds for several seconds before the clouds' shadows stole over them.

A vibration touched her skin at the same time her senses told her someone was coming. A second later, her cell chimed with an alert. She left the kitchen and met Tracy at the front door. They decided between the two of them, when Jordyn was alone, and one of them needed to go outside, Tracy would be inside, and Charles outside. Neither wanted to upset the Director. When they explained this to her, she wanted to laugh, but she didn't and wouldn't disrespect them. The last thing Rutger was worried about was Charles.

"Mistress, Mandy hasn't sent an ID. Do you know who it is?" Tracy asked. The delay meant Mandy was having a hard time with the license plate.

Death. Cold. Blood. "Shadow Lord. Please let him in and then escort him to the bar," Jordyn ordered.

Tracy nodded her acknowledgement, took her place at her post beside the door, and wore her sentinel face. Jordyn left her, intending on looking casual, she headed to the bar. When she was sitting in a leather chair, she messaged Rutger, telling him who arrived, she was fine, not to worry, and if there was a problem she would be in contact. Hopefully he stayed at the office and let whatever conversation was going to happen, happen. It was important to know why Shadow Lord was at her house.

With her mind racing, she analyzed the bar. Over the month, and several visits to storage and the local home store later, the bar had gone from bachelor pad to a lodge-inspired sitting area. If they decided to entertain guests, the baron and baroness, Jordyn's parents, sister and brother-in-law, it would be a comfortable place to relax. Hung on the pine walls were her photographs of the Trinity area, wild life, Shasta mountain, and the Cascade Range. Scented candles sat on the dark walnut side tables, while thick throws were draped over the arms or backs of the cream chenille couch and chairs. The fire in the living room warmed the room enough it didn't get hot and she could hear it crackle and pop. The feeling in the bar remained masculine with enough fabric to soften the edges.

Jordyn heard Charles' austere voice as he asked Shadow Lord questions-more like an interrogation-and after a couple of seconds she heard the lightly accented responses from the vampire. She smiled knowing Charles would stall Shadow Lord to test the boundaries of the vampire's control over his tempter. She poured a glass of wine, sat back, crossed her legs, and waited. Jordyn realized she was curious, not worried. They had overcome several threats to their relationship and their status with the Highguard. Rutger mastered shifting into his Bestial form, the baron knew about it, and she was bound to her territory, and Prime made it impossible for her to leave her pack. What could Shadow Lord possibly want?

The door opened with a whisper, letting in clean chilled air of winter, and Shadow Lord's presence filled the entrance, his authority and power weaving throughout the house. Jordyn felt it on her skin and her wolf howled in warning.

"This way, sir," Tracy advised.

Jordyn half turned in her seat when they stood at the entrance.

"Mistress, Shadow Lord is here to see you. Director Kanin has been advised and will be en route shortly," Tracy reported.

Shadow Lord waited with his hands clasped behind his back. His black hair with auburn highlights hung loose, and his amber and emerald eyes glittered in the light. He wore a long, black, wool coat over a royal blue button-up shirt that was tucked into jeans ending with boots. Snow clung to the sides of the dark brown leather, turning it darker as it melted. Jordyn's irritation burned through her. She told Rutger to wait to hear from her meaning Tracy went behind her back. "Dully noted. You may wait outside."

Tracy's face pinched into a scowl but she didn't argue. The sentinel turned on her heel and marched off. Jordyn waited to hear the door open and close before meeting Shadow Lord's hazel stare.

Shadow Lord watched the sentinel go with a grin tugging on his lips. Facing the soothsayer, he greeted, "Good evening, Jordyn."

Outside the clouds darkened the sky, promising a storm, as the sun sank behind the mountains casting the house in an early night. It gave a solemn feel to the evening and his visit. "To what do I owe the visit, Edmond."

His eyes bled emerald as his grin exposed sharp fangs. "I should have known Sloan's scion would do an inquiry." He shrugged his arms out of his coat and laid it over the back of the closest chair as if he owned the place. She was sure he acted like he owned whatever and wherever he found himself.

"Edmond Ironside, from clan Ironside. I didn't know Scotland was home to vampires," Jordyn replied. She did her homework and Sloan had been all too happy to help. Jordyn learned her mother was cunning, cutthroat, and powerful in the world of the Highguard and the Diablo pack. She also realized Sloan would do anything to protect her daughter from Shadow Lord.

"The wars brought many people to my land. May I," Shadow Lord asked.

"Please." Jordyn waved her hand at the chair across from her. "I have your jacket. I never had the chance to say thank you. Thank you."

Shadow Lord walked past the chair to the bar and stood behind it. "You're welcome. I was impressed you didn't engage in a hand-to-hand fight. You are a werewolf, brutality is in your DNA. You knew it would have wasted time and you could have been injured. You used information and your magic to safely rescue the child." He bent down and stood with a bottle of scotch in his hand. "You've amassed quite a collection." He read the label, then poured two fingers into a crystal cut glass.

His actions were human ... forced human. "I didn't know vampires drank scotch. Or you could go out in daylight." She hadn't known anything about vampires or Greek demons which was why she requested the books.

"I'm old and powerful, it allows me to do as I wish," he answered dismissively and took a sip. "Nice."

"Thank you. Why are you here?" she asked. Jordyn held her glass and sipped. It was almost empty. Sad.

"The wine with the bear on the label." Shadow Lord raised the bottle; she set her glass down, and he poured.

"You've done an inquiry, if you know that." She wasn't going to allow fear or anxiety to take control. He would sense it and believe he had the upper hand. What in the world did he want?

"Business," he said ignoring her. His accent became more pronounced, natural as if he wasn't trying to hide it from anyone. She watched him as he sipped his scotch and took the seat across from her. "You are alive and hold death inside of you. I am dead and hold life of inside me. It is a burning flame and a reminder of the weak being I once was."

"I thought vampires had to die before crossing over." Sure they could have a conversation over drinks. If Rutger barged in on them she was going to be mad. She had to know what this was about.

"In some instances. In others, when they crossover their lifeforce is changed, their bodies morphing to accommodate their new physiology. The lifeforce holds onto the soul until true death. At true death we become what we once were," he explained. "Everyone is judged for their actions." He brought the glass to his lips as if lost in thought. "Myths are myths not truths. As much as you and I are opposites we are the same."

Edmond Ironside, Shadow Lord, died in the Scottish Highlands during a battle, roughly around the fifteenth century. The report states scavengers scoured the battlefield and found Edmond's body. Jordyn pictured hunched over, dirty, cloak wearing vagrants searching for money or clothing, but was corrected when Sloan told her they weren't scavengers, they were an army of vampires who were highly trained soldiers led by the ruthless General Emric. He gave Edmond his crossover and had become, for a lack of a better term, Edmond's father. After Edmond's crossover from human to vampire, he left General Emric and returned to his clan only to have them try to kill him and then banish him for being a devil.

With nowhere else to go, Edmond returned to General Emric and the vampire army. He gained the rank of Captain of the Blood Horde, and they continued to terminate their enemies. Like the decline of shapeshifters, humans learned the vampires' weaknesses and fought back. With the vampires overtaking the humans and their campaigns bringing sanguinary to the lands, other magic-born joined the fight, and together, magic-born and human, abolished the army and a good portion of the vampire population.

Edmond's records ended with a battle where he disappeared. Decades passed when General Emric's descendant, Lady Yosaris, and her team seized a castle where they found him in its bowels. His arms had been chained above his head, and his ankles shackled shoulder width apart. His emaciated body was bloody, dirty, and covered in wounds, while his eyes were onyx from starvation. He lost his voice, the ability to speak, and growled for over year during his rehabilitation. Jordyn was convinced they should have put him down like a rabid dog. It's said, not written in the Scared Writ, Lady Yosaris and Edmond became lovers until he left to find his own territory. The next report stated Edmond Ironside no longer existed, he would be known as Shadow Lord of the Regulus, Latin for King of Serpents, of his homeland in the Scottish Highlands. He rules his coven with the same iron will of the Captain of the Blood Horde, and solidified his mysterious presence through fear.

Jordyn openly stared at him. What Latin and snakes had to do with Scotland and vampires, she had no idea. "We aren't anything alike."

"We are. I've been dead and have harbored life for centuries. You've been alive and have harbored death a short time."

He left the chair, his shirt pulled around his shoulders, his jeans snug around his thighs. He was a solider from old whose eyes had witnessed death, blood, and torture. "Did you come here to tell me that?"

"Yes. There is a war coming, Silver Dragon, you can't deny it when you feel magic rising." Shadow Lord narrowed his emerald eyes on her and she saw the captain's blood thirst. "Magic is going to change us and this world. We need to be ready."

Silver Dragon. "If you're trying to recruit me it won't work. I'm blood bound to my mate, my territory, and wear the mark of Balaur." Her mind went to Prime. She shook it off, held his stare as the man, Edmond, disappeared and Shadow Lord's coldness targeted her.

"The territory is only as strong as its pack. When the Cascade pack's kingdom collapses, and it will under the stress of having to keep a human façade, the territory will give up its hold. It will release you to save itself. You will be adrift while your anchor, your mate, tries to hold you." Jordyn didn't know if it was true but was going to find out. Shadow Lord walked around the bar, taking in the photographs, then faced her. "I know Prime possesses you. He must have been planning this for some time to get you to accept his magic, challenge him, and then orders your mate to mark you while he embeds himself into your magic. What is done cannot be undone. Am I correct?"

"You know the answer." Jordyn felt embarrassed for having been manipulated and then belittled by Shadow Lord. There was nothing she could do about it, it was over. Both Prime and Shadow Lord researched the Balaur, her connection to the descendants, having Rutger mark her, and what she would turn into. Silver Dragon.

"Yes, I do. You broke the circle rune with your blood and his magic, just as you controlled his Numina as he would have."

Dammit. She was glad Rutger was nowhere in sight and the sentinels were outside.

"The look on your face and elevated heart rate tells me you didn't volunteer, and no one else knows. First your mate lies to you about me, then you lie to him about Prime. A relationship based on honesty. What will he say about this conversation?"

Jordyn looked away from him and shook her head. "Is that what this is about? You spent hours, days, maybe a week researching what I might be, and when you had confirmation, Prime beat you to it." She saw Randy writhing on the ground and bleeding out and felt power. The pack had stared at her like she was a thing. A weapon.

"I admit I lost." He bowed as if conceding. "I underestimated him. Prime has been apathetic to the magic-born over the years, decades. I didn't think he cared about the Emanation and the rising fear from factions from around the world. Then you were kidnapped, died, was brought back, and weeks later while kneeling in mud, you twisted the witch's thoughts and he killed himself. A soothsayer hasn't had that kind of magic, power, to manipulate a mind in centuries. Reading thoughts, yes, understanding the Collective, yes, making a person commit a physical act that goes against their belief system, no."

Jordyn remained silent.

"The Emanation, the rise in magic means we need a leader, a commander willing to fight for his people. Despite his disinterest, Prime is powerful, it's the reason no one has usurped his authority. He out maneuvered me. It doesn't change the fact there is a war coming and I'll have my army. Prime is no different," Shadow Lord stated. "He isn't your mentor or your hero. If you can't fight and become insignificant, you'll be cast aside."

War. Cast. Forged. "It will be magic-born against the humans. But you're not worried about the humans. Are you going to use your army to fight Prime and the Highguard?" Jordyn looked at him.

"If need be."

Right. Civil war. She didn't want to imagine the future. "In the end, you will do the same. Cast me aside, like yesterday's trash. You aren't my mentor and you don't care about my life."

"I never said I was. I want a power. You are power. Your life is important or Prime would not have risked possessing you. His magic kills, and it goes against the canons of the Highguard. You have an alpha, a fated mate, the Collective, and a territory. He invaded your lands and rooted himself there. Silver Dragon, you are from the Balaur, royalty among the magic-born. Prime's promise of protection, the display of power and authority at the challenge was proof." Shadow Lord gave her his back and stared at a photograph of the Cascade Range.

Jordyn wondered what he was thinking as he stared at the print. Maybe he had prints in his house. She doubted it. He purposely took his homeland back and gave it a Latin name as if getting revenge on his family that had cast him out. She saw him as more of a tapestry, banner with his crest and colors, this is my castle, kind of vampire.

"You have a wildness living inside of you. You hate feeling trapped as your freedom gives you control. Others believe trapped means secure, safety in the comfort zone. Freedom means the unknown. You're comfortable with chaos," he mumbled. "In the beginning we'll be brothers in arms and we'll fight the humans, together. When they fall under our forces it'll be faction against faction to prove who among us is the strongest. Prime's reign will come to an end, leaving the door open for a new order to rise from the blood and ash. You'll have to pick a side, Silver Dragon, defender of Cascade."

She thought about those in the pack and the klatch who doubted the increasing magic and its effects. The Emanation. If they didn't standup and fight, the chance they would relive the Crimson years was a real threat. United Force, an agency specifically designed to deal with non-humans, implemented laws, sanctions, and restrictions to their rights would also rise from the ash. Was she going to let Joyli grow up in an encampment? No. If they were in an encampment, would they wait for the next generation to decide they were manageable? No. Would the magic-born slink off into untamed lands and hide their existence? No.

A chill raced down her spine as her wolf howled in her ears. She was going to fight for her pack. She would be their protector. Humans be damned. Jordyn couldn't stop thinking about Detective Watt. She was trapped and she didn't like the suffocating feel. "I'm not burning bridges, nor am I standing down. When the time comes, I'll make the decision." Jordyn didn't have anything else to say, and if she tried Shadow Lord would catch the tremble in her voice.

"The elf and his attempted assassination are proof those like you, Potents, are a threat to the world the Standards covet," he continued. Shadow Lord faced her with amber and emerald eddying around black. "I understand Prime has placed you under his watch. Still, you need protection, and I'm offering you that. Think about what I've said and what I'm offering."

Jordyn was silent. Would she think about it or forget about him? "How did you know?"

"As I said, I'm old and powerful." He placed his empty glass on the bar. "No need to worry, Silver Dragon." Leaving her, he took his coat from the chair.

Jordyn set her glass down, and leaving her chair walked to the coat rack. Taking the black jacket from the hook, she handed it to Shadow Lord. "Thank you, again."

He held her hands around the jacket. "The pack doesn't merit seeing your bare body or the mark of Balaur unless they're paying their respects to their soothsayer." He let go of her and held the jacket to his nose, inhaled, then lowered his hand. "Your dark awakening has a scent, the territory, and its power make you primal. Wild and enticing."

"Goodnight, Edmond." Jordyn was thankful her voice held.

"Goodnight, Jordyn." He waited as she opened the door, then stepped out into winter's night and the storm's flurries. Turning around, he stood with the lights at his back, the night shadowing him, and stark white flakes landing on his black hair. His hazel eyes bleed to charcoal and his face sharpened. He was giving her a view of the monster living inside of him. "Live well Silver Dragon, the next time we meet it may be on the battlefield." His accent drenched every word.

"Shadow Lord." Jordyn's eyes rolled onyx. Her magic surrounded her like her private wind storm, and reaching out, his life and her death met. Charles and Tracy took a step backward, their wolves' warning echoing in Jordyn's head. She and Shadow Lord were opposite. And they were alike.

Shadow Lord bowed and retreated down the stairs and to the sleek black car waiting for him. Jordyn inhaled and watched it as it left her property and hopefully her territory.

Having the feel of his essence, she would do a quick search in the morning to be sure.

"That's enough excitement for one night. The director is on his way, the both of you can go home. Plus, there's a storm, no reason for you to be here." Jordyn stared at the night.

"Are you sure Mistress?" Charles asked.

"Yes. Everyone has had their fun." She took her cell and messaged Rutger.

"Yes, Mistress," Tracy replied.

"Yes, Mistress," Charles replied. "Could I have a word?"

Jordyn faced Charles. "Yes. Let's go inside. Tracy, have a good evening."

Charles followed her inside, and she went to the bar, grabbed her glass, and crossing the room sank into an overstuffed chair. "What can I do for you?"

"Are you all right?"

She hated that question. "Yes. Politics." Jordyn watched him hesitate.

"I shouldn't be telling you this." Charles looked like was going to change his mind, then straightened his shoulders. "If you need assistance this evening, don't call Tracy, call me first."

"Why? What difference does it make?" Jordyn wanted to cut to the chase, read his mind, and get the info.

"She lives across town. I don't." He met her gaze and waited.

Jordyn smiled. "I got it. How close are you?"

"Shouting distance," Charles confessed. "I didn't want to keep it from you."

"Charles, it's greatly appreciated and not your fault. We all have our orders," Jordyn replied. She was Jordyn by name only, the woman she had been died somewhere be-tween becoming a soothsayer and her dark awakening. Like Prime, she lost herself to a title. Not like Shadow Lord who had given himself a title. When they talked about her, they wouldn't say Jordyn loved her pack, they would say the soothsayer protected her pack. The conversation with Claudia drifted through her thoughts as she turned the stem of her glass with her fingers. The deep ruby clung to the sides of the bowl releasing a tangle of rich chocolate, spice, and vanilla notes, then slowly slid down into itself.

"Have a goodnight, Mistress," Charles said.

"Thank you, have a goodnight." Jordyn wanted to laugh. The sentinels guarded her like she was delicate and would break. Not like glass or a rare flower but an unstable explo-sive they stored in a locked box. Neither of her sentinels knew Shadow Lord had threatened to neutralize the pack's power, start a civil war with Prime, then in the same breath offered her a partnership. She definitely needed to talk to Sloan. Rutger. Baron. "Charles."

"Mistress." He turned to meet your gaze.

"Would you turn off the lights, please?" Jordyn asked.

"Yes, Mistress," Charles replied. He hit the paddle, cast-ing the bar in darkness.

Rutger pulled into the driveway of the construction site of the house next door, parked, and killed the engine and headlights. A couple of seconds later, he watched Charles stop at the end of his driveway, wait, then turn right onto Mill Creek road. His truck with its black paint frosted with snow, and the Cascade pack's crest glittering. Rutger shook his head and chuckled to himself. Mill Creek road was a dead end, at its end were two houses. The baron placed Charles in of them, and if he did that, there was another pack member in the other house. He would have to ask Jo to do a search and find out who it was.

When he read Jo's message saying Shadow Lord was there, his heart did a flip in his chest, then he read Tracy's and wondered what was going on. He waited for Jo to respond and when she didn't it was clear Tracy had taken matters into her own hands and sent the message without consulting Jo. Why? Did the sentinel doubt Jo? If so, Jo needed a new sentinel.

Charles' truck's headlights cut through the night and snow as he headed home. It meant Jo dismissed Tracy, and Shadow Lord's visit hadn't been a threat.

Tracy. She was becoming more and more demanding, as if she was letting the job get to her. He would have to ask what Jo thought about the sentinel, because he didn't like it. He sat back in the seat, the cab's temperature lowering with winter's cold. He exhaled to see ribbons of his breath take form then fade. A muted silence only winter could create sat around him and for a moment he soaked it in. Then his thoughts bombarded him. As if sensing his anticipation, Rutger's cell rang, the screen lighting up the cab with Ansel's name and number.

"What do you have for me?"

"Twenty files." There was a pause. "One of the applicants is a female witch," Ansel reported.

Rutger's instant reaction was to veto the witch, he didn't care she was a she. He hesitated. Ansel chose her for a reason, and he would listen to his recommendation. "A witch? Explain to me why I should give her a chance."

"You need to read her file."

"I want to hear your reasons for choosing her," Rutger demanded. They were going to have to be good. The more he thought about the witch the more he didn't like it.

Ansel inhaled like he was preparing for a speech. "Served in the military, was recruited to special ops for counterintelligence. When her contract was up, she left the military to become a merc for a company specializing in seizing persons of interest. She's a weapons expert with a mastery in blades and poisons. Silent death, she called it. Her military and counterintelligence career are riddled with awards and she has a spotless record. No disciplinary problems."

"Witchcraft?"

"Affirmative. She's powerful, like the Esme knows about her."

She had Rutger's attention. "If she is on the Esme's radar, why would she want to work with us? It doesn't compare, and the money is going to be slim."

"She was at the Summit. She believes magic is changing and wants in on whatever is going to happen," Ansel answered. "She doesn't care about the money."

"I'll read her file. We'll meet up tomorrow at the black house to go over them and discuss the applicants. There we'll have access to a computer the pack doesn't have a connection with, and we'll draw up contracts. If we could keep all twenty, I'm for it, if not, I'll need to fill those slots. Once we have our people, we'll set up interviews in a different location," Rutger explained.

"Copy."

"If one of them tries to expose what we're doing they will be eliminated. I can't have Jo's future with the sheriff's department compromised." Rutger started his truck and turned the heater on high.

"Copy. Have you given this group of soldiers a tacticool name?" Ansel asked.

"Dark Rouges. They need to remember what they are and what their objective is."

"Understood. They'll like the name. I'll see you tomorrow."

Rutger ended the call, set his cell in the center console, and thought about what he was doing. Dark Rouges. He was creating his own group of mercenaries. If the baron found out he would lose his birthright, status, and Jo. He didn't have to worry about Prime, Shadow Lord, or the Highguard trying to get between them, when by his own actions he was putting their relationship at risk. Jo's safety.

Rutger put the truck in gear, and crept out of the driveway, while the truck's windshield wipers glided over the bulletproof glass taking a thin layer of white and pushed it off the side. At the entrance of his driveway he inhaled, exhaled, and calmed his nerves knowing Jo would sense him. Rutger parked the truck, killed the engine, and gathering his gear stepped out into the building storm. He walked down the stone walkway, noticed the sets of prints, took the stairs, and at the door placed his palm on the screen, then entered the code. The locking mechanisms sounded, and he opened the door to a rush of warm air laced with Jo, her wine, vampire, and scotch. *He drank the good stuff.*

Rutger hung his coat on the rack, noticed the missing suit jacket, took his tactical belt off and set it aside with his gun. Shadow Lord's presence hung in the house like a dense fog, and Rutger wanted it gone. He brought his wolf to the surface, his power weaving through the air, and it found Jo. His wolf reached out to her, making the link between them buzz, and he gave her the feel of his hands on her, his skin on hers, their lips touching, and desire erupting between them.

"I should never have showed you how to do that," she whispered. Jordyn closed her eyes letting him fill her head with his fantasies.

Kneeling in front of the chair, Rutger placed his hands on her thighs. "You don't have to admit liking it, Mea."

She giggled softly and covered his hands with hers. "Wolf."

"Come here," he whispered.

"Don't you want to know what Shadow Lord said?" Jordyn wanted to follow him anywhere. "I also got a phone call today about the prints at Epic Sights."

"It can wait." He gathered Jo in arms and lifted her out of the chair. He needed her and needed her touch. "I trust you."

Jordyn exhaled. He was right, it could wait. She didn't want to think about Prime or Shadow Lord and their conversation. Jordyn wrapped her arms around Rutger's neck, felt his muscles tense, and breathed in his scent of the woods and spice of his wolf. Right then, that moment, all was right in their world.

    Jordyn – 1
    Life – 0

The End

Upcoming releases: 2021

Crimson Moon
Cascade Wolves (Book One)

Werewolf and Cascade pack member, Clio Hyde, is an emergency room doctor at Celestial, a magic-born specific hospital. Clio works in an environment mirroring a human hospital, save for her patients who are witches, fairies, elves, therians and werewolves of the magic-born. Helping those in need and making Celestial a sanctuary, Clio takes pride in her work.

Ansel Wolt once a rogue on the run, has spent the last ten years with the Cascade pack. Despite the fear the enemies of his past might find him, he rose through ranks to become Captain of Enforcers. Cascade's elite police force and made Trinity his home. If heading the team wasn't keeping him busy enough, the new construction, security upgrades, and restructuring of the pack's hierarchy has his attention going in a hundred different directions. The distraction isn't enough to stop the plaguing feeling he's being watched.

When a member of the Fae is shot by an unknown assailant and rushed to Celestial's ER, Clio calls the Cascade pack's enforcers to investigate. Meeting with Dr. Hyde, Ansel can't stop himself from being drawn to her, but when she hands him a piece of evidence, his instincts warn him the past is coming for him.

If he doesn't find the shooter, it puts the safety of pack at risk. If he finds the shooter, it's proof of his lies. Ansel faces betraying his pack family and losing them...

Wolf Within
Moonlight Territory (Book One)

Detective Macy Gray, with the Bureau of Paranormal Investigations, ignores an order to kill a charging therianthrope headed at her team. In the aftermath, she fears she is going to lose her job, and doesn't think it can get any worse-until tests prove the shapeshifter's DNA was altered-and there may be others. Left with no other options, Macy works to prove her loyalty to her superiors, she isn't siding with the shapeshifters, and vows to solve the case. Those plans are derailed when the Department of Justice's shapeshifter team, Blood Rain arrives in town to take control of the investigation. With her tainted past, can Macy clear her name before they make her the spy?

When DOJ Agent Kayne Sinclair, team leader of Blood Rain, is ordered to the Southern California city of Desert Rock to investigate the BPI, he intends to use his werewolf senses to find the spy and let the BPI search for the person behind the altered shapeshifters. As alpha of his pack, Kayne needs to solve the case and get back to hunting the ghosts of his past. His instincts are telling him there's more to the detectives than the threat of a spy, forcing him to dig deeper. With his personal plans on hold, the investigation takes an unexpected turn and focuses on one detective. Kayne wants to know why Detective Gray is lying, who she is protecting, and why a human detective has ties to the hidden world of the paranormal.

Kayne's new mission is to find out why Detective Gray has been thrown into the middle of the investigation. Is she the spy? And is she the connection to the altered shapeshifters?

With a spy in the ranks, a lack of trust among the

detectives, increasing threats from the shapeshifter population ... and pressure from the DOJ and Agent Sinclair closing in on Macy, she struggles to keep up with the investigation. The threats around them increase, and she fears the altered shapeshifters will destroy the fragile relationship between paranormals and humans.

M.A. Kastle resides in sunny California with her family and two German Shepherds. She is the author of Bone Chimes, the first book in the Cascade Saga, and the soon to be released Wolf Within, the first book in the Moonlight Territory. For news about upcoming books, news, and a picture or two of her dogs, visit her at Facebook, Instagram, and Twitter.

Facebook @Makastle
Instagram @Makastleauthor
Twitter @Makastle